Praise for the Merchant Princes series

"Great fun!"   —Paul Krugman, Nobel Prize–winning economist

"Stross brings to fantasy the same kind of sly humor and clear-eyed extrapolation that he previously brought to space opera and horror . . . presented with great wit and high suspense."

—*San Francisco Chronicle*

"Inventive, irreverent, and delightful . . . an alternate world where business is simultaneously low and high tech, and where romance, murder, marriage, and business are hopelessly intertwined—and deadly."   —L. E. Modesitt, Jr., author of the Saga of Recluce

"Fantasies with this much invention, wit, and gusto don't come along every day."   —*SFX*

"Fans of the author's previous work will recognize his trademark skill at world building—you can almost see the filth on the streets of New England, feel the closeted oppression of the Clan hierarchy, and experience Miriam's terror at the horrifying circumstances she finds herself in."   —*SciFiNow*

"Fast-moving action with a number of interesting characters . . . Stross's ability to combine interesting ideas with solid plotting is one of his great strengths."   —*Asimov's Science Fiction*

"One of the defining phenomena of twenty-first-century SF is Charles Stross, for the quality of his work at its best."   —*Time Out*

"For sheer inventiveness and energy, this cliffhanger-riddled serial remains difficult to top."   —*Publishers Weekly*

D1516167

THE BLOODLINE FEUD

THE

BLOODLINE FEUD

Originally published separately as

THE FAMILY TRADE and THE HIDDEN FAMILY

Charles Stross

A TOM DOHERTY ASSOCIATES BOOK
NEW YORK

THE BLOODLINE FEUD

A Tor Book
Published by Tom Doherty Associates, LLC
175 Fifth Avenue
New York, NY 10010

www.tor-forge.com

Tor® is a registered trademark of Tom Doherty Associates, LLC.

ISBN 978-0-7653-7866-8 (trade paperback)
ISBN 978-1-4668-6393-4 (e-book)

Tor books may be purchased for educational, business, or promotional use. For information on bulk purchases, please contact Macmillan Corporate and Premium Sales Department at 1-800-221-7945, extension 5442, or write specialmarkets@macmillan.com.

Originally published in the United States in somewhat different form, in two separate volumes, as *The Family Trade* in 2004 and *The Hidden Family* in 2005.

This revised and updated edition was originally published in Great Britain by Tor, an imprint of Pan Macmillan, a division of Macmillan Publishers Limited.

First U.S. Edition: September 2014

Printed in the United States of America

0 9 8 7 6 5 4 3 2 1

For Steve and Jenny Glover

Acknowledgments

No novelist works in a creative vacuum. Whatever we do, we owe a debt to the giants upon whose shoulders we stand. This book might not have happened if I hadn't read the works of H. Beam Piper and Roger Zelazny.

Nor would this book have been written without the intervention of several other people. My agent, Caitlin Blaisdell, nudged me to make a radical change of direction from my previous novels. David Hartwell of Tor encouraged me further, and my wife, Feòrag, lent me her own inimitable support while I worked on it.

Finally, I'd like to thank all those (too numerous to name) who helped by test-reading and typo-spotting at various times in the history of this book.

PART ONE

PINK SLIP

WEATHERMAN

Ten and a half hours before a mounted knight with a machine gun tried to kill her, tech journalist Miriam Beckstein lost her job. Before the day was out, her pink slip would set in train a chain of events that would topple governments, trigger civil wars, and kill thousands. It would be the biggest scoop in her career, in any journalist's career – bigger than Watergate, bigger than 9/11 – and it would be Miriam's story. But as of seven o'clock in the morning, the story lay in her future: All she knew was that it was a rainy Monday morning in October, she had a job to do and copy to write, and there was an editorial meeting scheduled for ten.

*

The sky was the color of a dead laptop display, silver-gray and full of rain. Miriam yawned and came awake to the Monday morning babble of the anchorman on her alarm radio.

'– Bombing continues in Afghanistan. Meanwhile, in business news, the markets are down forty-seven points on the word that Cisco is laying off another three thousand employees,' announced the anchor. 'Ever since 9/11, coming on top of the collapse of the dot-com sector, their biggest customers are hunkering down. Tom, how does it look from where you're sitting – '

'Shut up,' she mumbled and killed the volume. 'I don't want to hear this.' It was late 2002 and most of the tech sector was taking a beating. Which in turn meant that *The Industry Weatherman*'s readers – venture capitalists and high-tech entrepreneurs, along with the wannabe day traders – would be taking a beating. Her own beat, the biotech firms, were solid, but the collapsing internet sector was making waves. If something didn't happen to relieve the plummeting circulation figures soon, there would be trouble.

Trouble. Monday. 'I'll give you trouble,' she muttered, face forming a grin that might have frightened some of those readers, had they been able to see it. 'Trouble is my middle name.' And trouble was good news, for a senior reporter on *The Industry Weatherman*.

She slid into her bathrobe, shivering at the cold fabric, then shuffled along stripped pine boards to the bathroom for morning ablutions and two minutes with the electric toothbrush. Standing before the bathroom mirror under the merciless glare of the spotlights, she shivered at what she saw in it: every minute of her thirty-two years, in unforgiving detail. 'Abolish Monday mornings and Friday afternoons,' she muttered grimly as she tried to brush some life into her shoulder-length hair, which was stubbornly black and locked in a vicious rear-guard action against the ochre highlights she bombarded it with on a weekly basis. Giving up after a couple of minutes, she fled downstairs to the kitchen.

The kitchen was a bright shade of yellow, cozy and immune to the gloom of autumn mornings. Relieved, Miriam switched on the coffee percolator and made herself a bowl of granola – what Ben had always called her rabbit-food breakfast.

Back upstairs, fortified by an unfeasibly large mug of coffee, she had to work out what to wear. She dived into her closet and found herself using her teeth to tear the plastic bag off one of the three suits she'd dry-cleaned on Friday – only to discover it was her black formal interview affair, not at all the right thing for a rainy Monday pounding the streets – or at least doing telephone interviews from a cubicle in the office. She started again and finally managed to put together an outfit. Black boots, pants, jacket, turtleneck, and trench coat: as black as her Monday morning mood. *I look like a gangster*, she thought and chuckled to herself. 'Gangsters!' That was what she had to do today. One glance at her watch told her that she didn't have time for makeup. It wasn't as if she had to impress anyone at the office anyway: They knew damned well who she was.

She slid behind the wheel of her four-year-old Saturn, and thankfully it started first time. But traffic was backed up, one of her wiper blades needed replacing, the radio had taken to crackling erratically, and she couldn't stop yawning. Normally she'd catch the T, but she expected to have to head out of town to an interview in the afternoon, so today she got to battle rush-hour traffic in Cambridge. *Mondays*, she thought. *My favorite day! Not.* At least she had a parking space waiting for her – one of the handful reserved for senior journalists who had to go places and interview thrusting new economy executives. Or money-laundering gangsters, the *nouveau riche* of the pharmaceutical world.

Twenty minutes later she pulled into a crowded lot behind an anonymous office building in Cambridge, just off Kendall Square, with satellite dishes on the roof and fat cables snaking down into the basement. Headquarters of *The Industry Weatherman*, journal of the tech VC community and Miriam's employer for the past three years. She swiped her pass-card, hit the elevator up to the third floor, and stepped out into cubicle farm chaos. Desks with PCs and drifts of paper overflowed onto the floor: A couple of harried Latina cleaners emptied garbage cans into a trolley laden with bags, to a background of phones ringing and anchors gabbling on CNN, Bloomberg, Fox. Black space-age Aeron chairs everywhere, all wire and plastic, electric chairs for a fully wired future.

''Yo, Emily,' she nodded, passing the departmental secretary.

'Hi! With you in a sec.' Emily lifted her finger from the 'mute' button, went back to glassy-eyed attention. 'Yes, I'll send them up as soon as – '

Miriam's desk was clean: The stack of press releases was orderly, the computer monitor was polished, and there were no dead coffee cups lying around. By tech journalist standards, this made her a neat freak. She'd always been that way about her work, even when she was a toddler. Liked all her crayons lined up in a row. Occasionally she wished she could manage the housework the same way, but for some reason the skill set didn't seem to be transferable. But this was work, and work was always under control. *I wonder where Paulie's gotten to*?

'Hi, babe!' As if on cue, Paulette poked her head around the side of the partition. Short, dark-haired, and bubbly, not even a rainy Monday morning could dent her enthusiasm. 'How's it going? You ready to teach these wiseguys a lesson?'

'Wiseguys?' Miriam raised an eyebrow. Paulette took the cue, slid sideways into her cubicle, and dropped into the spare chair, forcing Miriam to shuffle sideways to make room. Paulie was obviously enjoying herself: It was one of the few benefits of being a research gofer. Miriam waited.

'Wiseguys,' Paulette said with relish. 'You want a coffee? This is gonna take a while.'

'Coffee.' Miriam considered. 'That would be good.'

'Yeah, well.' Paulette stood up. 'Read this, it'll save us both some time.' She pointed out a two-inch-thick sheaf of printouts and photocopies to Miriam, then made a beeline for the departmental coffeepot.

Miriam sighed and rubbed her eyes as she read the first page. Paulie had done her job with terrifying efficiency yet again: Miriam had only worked with her on a couple of investigations before – mostly Miriam's workload didn't require the data mining Paulette specialized in – but every single time she'd come away feeling a little dizzy.

Automobile emissions tests in California? Miriam squinted and turned the page. Failed autos, a chain of repair shops buying them for cash and shipping them south to Mexico and Brazil for stripping or resale. 'What's this got to do with – ' she stopped. 'Aha!'

'Nondairy creamer, one sweetener,' said Paulie, planting a coffee mug at her left hand.

'This is great stuff,' Miriam muttered, flipping more pages. Company accounts. A chain of repair shops that – 'I was hoping you'd find something in the small shareholders. How much are these guys in for?'

'They're buying about ten, eleven million in shares each year.' Paulette shrugged, then blew across her coffee and pulled a face. 'Which is crazy, because their business only turns over about fifteen mil. What kind of business puts eighty percent of its gross into a pension fund? One that bought two hundred and seventy-four autos last year for fifty bucks a shot, shipped them south of the border, and made an average of forty thousand bucks for each one they sold. And the couple of listed owners I phoned didn't want to talk.'

Miriam looked up suddenly. 'You phoned them?' she demanded.

'Yes, I – oh. Relax, I told them I was a dealership in Vegas and I was just doing a background check.'

'"Background check."' Miriam snorted. 'What if they've got caller-ID?'

'You think they're going to follow it up?' Paulette asked, looking worried.

'Paulie, you've got eleven million in cash being laundered through this car dealership and you think they're not going to sit up and listen if someone starts asking questions about where those beaters are coming from and how come they're fetching more than a new Lexus south of the border?'

'Oh. Oh shit.'

'Yes. "Oh shit" indeed. How'd you get into the used car trail anyway?'

Paulette shrugged and looked slightly embarrassed. 'You asked me to follow up the shareholders for Proteome Dynamics and Biphase Technologies. Pacific Auto Services looked kind of odd to me – why would a car dealership have a pension fund sticking eight digits into cutting-edge proteome research? And there's another ten like them, too. Small mom-and-pop businesses doing a lot of export down south with seven- or eight-digit stakeholdings. I traced another – flip to the next?'

'Okay. Dallas Used Semiconductors. Buying used IBM mainframe kit? That's not our – and selling it to – oh shit.'

'Yeah.' Paulie frowned. 'I looked up the book value. Whoever's buying those five-year-old computers down in Argentina is paying ninety percent of the price for new kit in cash greenbacks – they're the next thing to legal currency down there. But up here, a five-year-old mainframe goes for about two cents on the dollar.'

'And you're sure all this is going into Proteome and Biphase?' Miriam shook the thick sheaf of paper into shape. 'I can't believe this!'

'Believe it.' Paulette drained her coffee cup and shoved a stray lock of hair back into position.

Miriam whistled tunelessly. 'What's the bottom line?'

'"The bottom line?"' Paulette looked uncomfortable. 'I haven't counted it, but – '

'Make a guess.'

'I'd say someone is laundering between fifty and a hundred million dollars a year here. Turning dirty cash into clean shares in Proteome Dynamics and Biphase Technologies. More than enough to show up in their SEC filings. So your hunch was right.'

'And nobody in Executive Country has asked any questions,' Miriam concluded. 'If I was paranoid, I'd say it's like a conspiracy of silence. Hmm.' She put her mug down. 'Paulie. You worked for a law firm. Would you call this . . . circumstantial?'

'"Circumstantial?"' Paulette's expression was almost pitying. 'Who's paying you, the defense? This is enough to get the FBI and the DA muttering about RICO.'

'Yeah, but . . .' Miriam nodded to herself. 'Look, this is heavy. Heavier than usual anyway. I can guarantee you that if we spring this story we'll get three responses. One will be flowers in our hair, and the other will be a bunch of cease-and-desist letters from attorneys. Freedom of the press is all very well, but a good reputation and improved circulation figures won't buy us defense lawyers, which is why I want to double-check everything in here before I go upstairs and tell Sandy we want the cover. Because the third response is going to be oh-shit-I-don't-want-to-believe-this, because our great leader and teacher thinks the sun shines out of Biphase and I think he's into Proteome too.'

'Who do you take me for?' Paulette pointed at the pile. 'That's primary, Miriam, the wellspring. SEC filings, public accounts, the whole lot. Smoking gun. The summary sheet – ' she tugged at a Post-it note gummed to a page a third of the way down the stack – 'says it all. I was in here all day yesterday and half the evening – '

'I'm sorry!' Miriam raised her hand. 'Hey, really. I had no idea.'

'I kind of lost track of time,' Paulette admitted. She smiled. 'It's not often I get something interesting to dig into. Anyway, if the boss is into these two, I'd think he'd be glad of the warning. Gives him time to pull out his stake before we run the story.'

'Yeah, well.' Miriam stood up. 'I think we want to bypass Sandy. This goes to the top.'

'But Sandy needs to know. It'll mess with his page plan – '

'Yeah, but someone has to call Legal before we run with this. It's the biggest scoop we've had all year. Want to come with me? I think you earned at least half the credit . . .'

*

They shared the elevator up to executive row in silence. It was walled in mirrors, reflecting their contrasts: Paulette, short and dark-haired with disorderly curls and a bright red blouse, and Miriam, a slim five-foot-eight, dressed entirely in black. The business research wonk and the journalist, on their way to see the editorial director. Some Mondays are better than others, thought Miriam. She smiled tightly at Paulette in the mirror and Paulie grinned back: a worried expression, slightly apprehensive.

The Industry Weatherman was mostly owned by a tech venture capital firm who operated out of the top floors of the building, their offices intermingled with those of the magazine's directors. Two floors up, the corridors featured a better grade of carpet and the walls were genuine partitions covered in oak veneer, rather than fabric-padded cubicles. That was the only difference she could see – that and the fact that some of the occupants were assholes like the people she wrote glowing profiles of for a living. *I've never met a tech VC who a shark would bite*, Miriam thought grumpily. Professional courtesy among killers. The current incumbent of the revolving door office labeled editorial director – officially a vice president – was an often-absent executive by the name of Joe Dixon. Miriam led Paulette to the office and paused for a moment, then knocked on the door, half-hoping to find he wasn't there.

'Come in.' The door opened in her face, and it was Joe himself, not his secretary. He was over six feet, with expensively waved black hair, wearing his suit jacket over an open-necked dress shirt. He oozed corporate polish: If he'd been ten years older, he could have made a credible movie career as a captain of industry. As it was, Miriam always found herself wondering how he'd climbed into the boardroom so young. He was in his mid-thirties, not much older than she was. 'Hi.' He took in Miriam and Paulette standing just behind her and smiled. 'What can I do for you?'

9

Miriam smiled back. 'May we have a moment?' she asked.

'Sure, come in.' Joe retreated behind his desk. 'Have a chair, both of you.' He nodded at Paulette. 'Miriam, we haven't been introduced.'

'Oh, yes. Joe Dixon, Paulette Milan. Paulie is one of our heavy hitters in industrial research. She's been working with me on a story and I figured we'd better bring it to you first before taking it to the weekly production meeting. It's a bit, uh, sensitive.'

'"Sensitive."' Joe leaned back in his chair and looked straight at her. 'Is it big?'

'Could be,' Miriam said noncommittally. *Big? It's the biggest I've ever worked on!* A big story in her line of work might make or break a career; this one might send people to jail. 'It has complexities to it that made me think you'd want advance warning before it breaks.'

'Tell me about it,' said Joe.

'Okay. Paulie, you want to start with your end?' She passed Paulette the file.

'Yeah.' Paulie grimaced as she opened the file and launched into her explanation. 'In a nutshell, they're laundries for dirty money. There's enough of a pattern to it that if I was a DA in California I'd be picking up the phone to the local FBI office.'

'That's why I figured you'd want to know,' Miriam explained. 'This is a big deal, Joe. I think we've got enough to pin a money-laundering rap on a couple of really big corporations and make it stick. But last November you were talking to some folks at Proteome, and I figured you might want to refer this to Legal and make sure you're firewalled before this hits the fan.'

'Well. That's very interesting.' Joe smiled back at her. 'Is that your file on this story?'

'Yeah,' said Paulette.

'Would you mind leaving it with me?' he asked. He cleared his throat. 'I'm kind of embarrassed,' he said, shrugging a small-boy shrug. The defensive set of his shoulders backed his words. 'Look, I'm going to have to read this myself. Obviously, the scope for mistakes is – ' he shrugged.

Suddenly Miriam had a sinking feeling: *It's going to be bad.* She racked her brains for clues. *Is he going to try to bury us?*

Joe shook his head. 'Look, I'd like to start by saying that this isn't about anything you've done,' he added hurriedly. 'It's just that we've got an investment to protect and I need to work out how to do so.'

'Before we break the story.' Miriam forced another, broader, smile. 'It was all in the public record,' she added. 'If we don't break it, one of our competitors will.'

'Oh, I don't know,' Joe said smoothly. 'Listen, I'll get back to you in an hour or so. If you leave this with me for now, I just need to go and talk to someone in Legal so we can sort out how to respond. Then I'll let you know how we're going to handle it.'

'Oh, okay then,' said Paulette acceptingly.

Miriam let her expression freeze in a fixed grin. *Oh shit*, she thought as she stood up. 'Thanks for giving us your time,' she said.

'Let yourselves out,' Joe said tersely, already turning the first page.

Out in the corridor, Paulette turned to Miriam. 'Didn't that go well?' she insisted.

Miriam took a deep breath. 'Paulie.'

'Yeah?'

Her knees felt weak. 'Something's wrong.'

'What?' Paulette looked concerned.

'Elevator.' She hit the 'call' button and waited in silence, trying to still the butterflies in her stomach. It arrived, and she waited for the doors to close behind them before she continued. 'I may just have made a bad mistake.'

'"Mistake?"' Paulette looked puzzled. 'You don't think – '

'He didn't say anything about publishing,' Miriam said slowly. 'Not one word. What were the other names on that list of small investors? The ones you didn't check?'

'The list? He's got – ' Paulette frowned.

'Was Somerville Investments one of them?'

'Somerville? Could be. Why? Who are they?'

'Because that's – ' Miriam pointed a finger at the roof and circled. She watched Paulette's eyes grow round.

'I'm thinking about magazine returns from the newsstand side of the business, Paulie. Don't you know we've got low returns by industry standards? And people buy magazines for cash.'

11

'Oh.'

'I'm sorry, Paulie.'

When they got back to Miriam's cubicle, a uniformed security guard and a suit from Human Resources were already waiting for them.

'Paulette Milan? Miriam Beckstein?' said the man from HR. He checked a notepad carefully.

'Yes?' Miriam asked cautiously. 'What's up?'

'Would you please follow me? Both of you?'

He turned and headed for the stairwell down to the main entrance. Miriam glanced around and saw the security guard pull a brief expression of discomfort. 'Go on, ma'am.'

'Go on,' echoed Paulette from her left shoulder, her face white.

This can't be happening, Miriam thought woodenly. She felt her feet carrying her toward the staircase and down, toward the glass doors at the front.

'Cards, please,' said the man from Human Resources. He held out his hand impatiently. Miriam passed him her card reluctantly: Paulette followed suit.

He cleared his throat and looked them over superciliously. 'I've been told to tell you that *The Industry Weatherman* won't be pressing charges,' he said. 'We'll clear your cubicles and forward your personal items and your final paycheck to your addresses of record. But you're no longer allowed on the premises.' The security guard took up a position behind him, blocking the staircase. 'Please leave.'

'What's going on?' Paulette demanded, her voice rising toward a squeak.

'You're both being terminated,' the HR man said impassively. 'Misappropriation of company resources; specifically, sending personal e-mail on company time and looking at pornographic websites.'

'"Pornographic – "' Miriam felt herself going faint with fury. She took half a step toward the HR man and barely noticed Paulette grabbing her sleeve.

'It's not worth it, Miriam,' Paulie warned her. 'We both know it isn't true.' She glared at the HR man. 'You work for Somerville Investments, don't you?'

He nodded incuriously. 'Please leave. Now.'

Miriam forced herself to smile. 'Better brush up your résumé,' she said shakily and turned toward the exit.

*

Two-thirds of her life ago, when she was eleven, Miriam had been stung by a hornet. It had been a bad one: Her arm had swollen up like a balloon, red and sore and painful to touch, and the sting itself had hurt like crazy. But the worst thing of all was the sense of moral indignation and outrage. Miriam-aged-eleven had been minding her own business, playing in the park with her skateboard – she'd been a tomboy back then, and some would say she still was – and she hadn't done anything to provoke the angry yellow-and-black insect. It just flew at her, wings whining angrily, landed, and before she could shake it off, it stung her.

She'd howled.

This time she was older and much more self-sufficient – college, pre-med, and her failed marriage to Ben had given her a grounding in self-sufficiency – so she managed to say good-bye to an equally shocked Paulie and make it into her car before she broke down. And the tears came silently – this time. It was raining in the car park, but she couldn't tell whether there was more water inside or outside. They weren't tears of pain: They were tears of anger. *That bastard –*

For a moment, Miriam fantasized about storming back in through the fire door at the side of the building, going up to Joe Dixon's office, and pushing him out of the big picture window. It made her feel better to think about that, but after a few minutes she reluctantly concluded that it wouldn't solve anything. Joe had the file. He had her computer – and Paulie's – and a moment's thought told her that those machines were being wiped *right now*. Doubtless, server logs showing her peeking at porn on the job were being fabricated too. She'd spoken to some geeks at a dot-com startup once who explained just how easy it was if you wanted to get someone dismissed. 'Shit,' she mumbled to herself and sniffed. 'I'll have to get another job. Shouldn't be too hard, even without a reference.'

Still, she was badly shaken. Journalists didn't get fired for exposing money-laundering scams; that was in the rules somewhere, wasn't it? In fact, it was completely crazy. She blinked away the remaining angry tears. *I need to go see Mom,* she decided. Tomorrow would be soon enough to start looking for a new job. Or to figure out a way to break the story herself, if she was going to try and do it freelance. Today she needed a shoulder to cry on – and a sanity check. And if there was one person who could provide both, it was her adoptive mother.

*

Iris Beckstein lived alone in her old house in mid-Cambridge. Miriam felt obscurely guilty about visiting her during daytime working hours. Iris never tried to mother her, being content to wander around and see to her own quiet hobbies most of the time since Morris had died. But Miriam also felt guilty about not visiting Iris more often. Iris was convalescent, and the possibility of losing her mother so soon after her father had died filled her with dread. Another anchor was threatening to break free, leaving her adrift in the world.

She parked the car on the street, then made a dash for the front door – the rain was descending in a cold spray, threatening to turn to penetrating sheets – and rang the doorbell, then unlocked the door and went in as the two-tone chime echoed inside.

'Ma?'

'Through here,' Iris called. Miriam entered, closing the front door. The hallway smelled faintly floral, she noticed as she shed her raincoat and hung it up: The visiting home help must be responsible. 'I'm in the back room.'

Doors and memories lay ajar before Miriam as she hurried toward the living room. She'd grown up in this house, the one Morris and Iris had bought back when she was a baby. The way the third step on the staircase creaked when you put your weight on it, the eccentricities of the downstairs toilet, the way the living room felt cramped from all the bookshelves – the way it felt too big, without Dad. 'Ma?' She pushed open the living room door hesitantly.

Iris smiled at her from her wheelchair. 'So nice of you to visit! Come in! To what do I owe the pleasure?'

The room was furnished with big armchairs and a threadbare sofa deep enough to drown in. There was no television – neither Iris nor Morris had time for it – but there were bookcases on each wall and a tottering tower of paper next to Iris's chair. Miriam crossed the room, leaned over, and kissed Iris on top of her head, then stood back. 'You're looking well,' she said anxiously, hoping it was true. She wanted to hug her mother, but she looked increasingly frail. She was only in her mid–fifties, but her hair was increasingly gray, and the skin on the backs of her hands seemed to be more wrinkled every time Miriam visited.

'I won't break – at least, I don't think so. Not if you only hug me.' Iris grimaced. 'It's been bad for the past week, but I think I'm on the mend again.' The chair she sat in was newer than the rest of the furniture, surrounded by the impedimenta of invalidity: a little side trolley with her crochet and an insulated flask full of herbal tea, her medicines, and a floor-standing lamp with a switch high up its stem. 'Marge just left. She'll be back later, before supper.'

'That's good. I hope she's been taking care of you well.'

'She does her best.' Iris nodded, slightly dismissively. 'I've got physiotherapy tomorrow. Then another session with my new neurologist, Dr. Burke – he's working with a clinical trial on a new drug that's looking promising and we're going to discuss that. It's supposed to stop the progressive demyelination process, but I don't understand half the jargon in the report. Could you translate it for me?'

'Mother! You know I don't do that stuff any more – I'm not current; I might miss something. Anyway, if you go telling your osteopath about me, he'll panic. I'm not a bone doctor.'

'Well, if you say so.' Iris looked irritated. 'All that time in medical school wasn't wasted, was it?'

'No, Mom, I use it every day. I couldn't do my job without it. I just don't know enough about modern multiple sclerosis drug treatments to risk second-guessing your specialist, all right? I might get it wrong, and then who'd you sue?'

'If you say so.' Iris snorted. 'You didn't come here just to talk about that, did you?'

Damn, thought Miriam. It had always been very difficult to pull one over on her mother. 'I lost my job,' she confessed.

'I wondered.' Iris nodded thoughtfully. 'All those dot-coms of yours, it was bound to be infectious. Is that what happened?'

'It wasn't like that.' Miriam shook her head. 'I stumbled across something and mishandled it badly. They fired me. And Paulie . . . Remember I told you about her?'

Iris closed her eyes. 'Bastards. The bosses are bastards.'

'Mother!' Miriam wasn't shocked at the language – Iris's odd background jumped out to bite her at the strangest moments – but it was the risk of misunderstanding. 'It's not that simple; I screwed up.'

'So you screwed up. Are you going to tell me you deserved to be fired?' asked Iris.

'No. But I should have dug deeper before I tried to run the story,' Miriam said carefully. 'I was too eager, got sloppy. There were connections. It's deep and it's big and it's messy; the people who own *The Weatherman* didn't want to be involved in exposing it.'

'So that excuses them, does it?' asked Iris, her eyes narrowing.

'No, it – ' Miriam stopped.

'Stop making excuses for them and I'll stop chasing you.' Iris sounded almost amused. 'They took your job to protect their own involvement in some dirty double-dealing, is that what you're telling me?'

'Yeah. I guess.'

'Well.' Iris's eyes flashed. 'When are you going to hang them? And how high? I want a ringside seat!'

'Ma.' Miriam looked at her mother with mingled affection and exasperation. 'It's not that easy. I think *The Weatherman*'s owners are deeply involved in something illegal. Money laundering. Dirty money. Insider trading too, probably. I'd like to nail them, but they're going to play dirty if I try. It took them about five minutes to come up with cause for dismissal, and they said they wouldn't press charges if I kept my mouth shut.'

'What kind of charges?' Iris demanded.

'They say they've got logfiles to prove I was net-surfing pornography at work. They . . . they – ' Miriam found she was unable to go on speaking.

'So were you?' Iris asked quietly.

'No!' Miriam startled herself with her vehemence. She caught Iris's sly glance and felt sheepish. 'Sorry. No, I wasn't. It's a setup. But it's so easy to claim – and virtually impossible to disprove.'

'Are you going to be able to get another job?' Iris prodded.

'Yes.' Miriam fell silent.

'Then it's all right. I really couldn't do with my daughter expecting me to wash her underwear after all these years.'

'Mother!' Then Miriam spotted the sardonic grin.

'Tell me about it. I mean, everything. Warm a mother's heart, spill the beans on the assholes who took her daughter's job away.'

Miriam flopped down on the big overstuffed sofa. 'It's either a very long story or a very short one,' she confessed. 'I got interested in a couple of biotech companies that looked just a little bit odd. Did some digging, got Paulette involved – she digs like a prairie dog – and we came up with some dirt. A couple of big companies are being used as targets for money laundering.

'Turns out that *The Weatherman*'s parent company is into them, deep. They decided it would be easier to fire us and threaten us than to run the story and take their losses. I'm probably going to get home and find a SLAPP lawsuit sitting in my mailbox.'

'So. What are you going to do about it?'

Miriam met her mother's penetrating stare. 'Ma, I spent three years there. And they fired me cold, without even trying to get me to shut up, at the first inconvenience. Do you really think I'm going to let them get away with that if I can help it?'

'What about loyalty?' Iris asked, raising an eyebrow.

'I gave them mine.' Miriam shrugged. 'That's part of why this hurts. You earn loyalty by giving it.'

'You'd have made a good feudal noble. They were big on loyalty, too. And blind obedience, in return.'

'Wrong century, wrong side of the Atlantic, in case you hadn't noticed.'

Now Iris grinned. 'Oh, I noticed that much,' she conceded. 'No foreign titles of nobility. That's one of the reasons why I stayed here – that, and your father.' Her smile slipped. 'Never could under-stand what the people here see in kings and queens, either the old hereditary kind or the modern presidential type. All those paparazzi, drooling after monarchs. I like your line of work. It's more honest.'

'Harder to keep your job when you're writing about the real world,' Miriam brooded gloomily. She struggled to sit a little straighter. 'Anyway, I didn't come around here to mope at you. I figure I can leave job-hunting until tomorrow morning.'

'Are you sure you're going to be all right?' Iris asked pointedly. 'You mentioned lawsuits – or worse.'

'In the short term – ' Miriam shrugged, then took a deep breath. 'Yes,' she admitted. 'I guess I'll be okay as long as I leave them alone.'

'Hmm.' Iris looked at Miriam sidelong. 'How much money are we talking about here? If they're pulling fake lawsuits to shut you up, that's not business as usual.'

'There's – ' Miriam did some mental arithmetic – 'about fifty to a hundred million a year flowing through this channel.'

Iris swore.

'Ma!'

'Don't you "Ma" me!' Iris snorted.

'But – '

'Listen to your old ma. You came here for advice, I'm going to give it, all right? You're telling me you just happened to stumble across a money-laundering operation that's handling more money in a week than most people earn in their life. And you think they're going to settle for firing you and hoping you stay quiet?'

Miriam snorted. 'It can't possibly be that bad, Ma, this isn't wiseguys territory, and anyway, they've got that faked evidence.'

Iris shook her head stubbornly. 'When you've got criminal activities and millions of dollars in cash together, there are no limits to what people can do.' For the first time, Miriam realized with a sinking feeling, Iris looked worried. 'But maybe I'm being too pessimistic – you've just lost your job and whatever else, that's going to be a problem. How are your savings?'

Miriam glanced at the rain-streaked window. *What's turned Ma so paranoid?* she wondered, unsettled. 'I'm not doing badly. I've been saving for the past ten years.'

'There's my girl,' Iris said approvingly.

'I put my money into tech-sector shares.'

'No, you didn't!' Iris looked shocked.

Miriam nodded. 'But no dot-coms.'

'Really?'

'Most people think that all tech stocks are down. But biotech stocks actually crashed out in ninety-seven and have been recovering ever since. The bubble didn't even touch them. People need new medicines more than they need flashy websites that sell toys, don't they? I was planning on paying off my mortgage year after next. Now I guess it'll have to wait a bit longer – but I'm not in trouble unless I stay unemployed over a year.'

'Well, at least you found a use for all that time in med school.' Iris looked relieved. 'So you're not hard up.'

'Not in the short term,' Miriam corrected instinctively. 'Ask me again in six months. Anyway, is there anything I can get you while I'm here?'

'A good stiff drink.' Iris clucked to herself. 'Listen, I'm going to be all right. The disease, it comes and it goes – another few weeks and I'll be walking more easily again.' She gestured at the aluminum walking frame next to her chair. 'I've been getting plenty of rest and with Marge around twice a day I can just about cope, apart from the boredom. I've even been doing a bit of filing and cleaning, you know, turning out the dusty old corners?'

'Oh, right. Turned anything up?'

'Lots of dustballs. Anyway,' she continued after a moment. 'There's some stuff I've been meaning to hand over to you.'

'"Stuff."' For a moment, Miriam couldn't focus on the problem at hand. It was too much to deal with. She'd lost her job and then, the very same day, her mother wanted to talk about selling her home. 'I'm sorry, I'm not very focused today.'

'Not very – ' Iris snorted. 'You're like a microscope, girl! Most other people would be walking around in a daze. It's not very considerate of me, I know, it's just that I've been thinking about things and there's some stuff you really should have right now. Partly because you're grown up and partly because it belongs to you – you might have some use for it. Stuff that might get overlooked.'

Miriam must have looked baffled because Iris smiled at her encouragingly. 'Yes. You know, "stuff." Photograph albums, useless things like Morris's folks' birth certificates, my old passport, my parents' death certificates, your adoption papers. Some stuff relating to your birth-mother, too.'

Miriam shook her head. 'My adoption papers – why would I want them? That's old stuff, and you're the only mother I've ever had. You're not allowed to push me away!'

'Well! And who said I was? I just figured you wouldn't want to lose the opportunity. If you ever felt like trying to trace your roots. It belongs to you, and I think now is definitely past time for you to have it. I kept the newspaper pages too, you know. It caused quite a stir.' Miriam made a face. 'I know you're not interested,' Iris said apologetically. 'Humor me. There's a box.'

'A box.'

'A pink and green shoebox. Sitting on the second shelf of your father's bureau in the attic. Do me a favor and fetch it down, will you?'

'Just for you.'

Miriam found the box easily enough. It rattled when she picked it up and carried it, smelling of mothballs, down to the living room. Iris had picked up her crochet again and was pulling knots with an expression of fierce concentration. 'Dr. Hare told me to work on it,' she said without looking up. 'It helps preserve hand-eye coordination.'

'I see.' Miriam put the box down on the sofa. 'What's this one?'

'A Klein-bottle cozy.' Iris looked up defensively at Miriam's snort. 'You should laugh! In this crazy inside-out world, we must take our comforts from crazy inside-out places.'

'You and Dad.' Miriam waved it off. 'Both crazy inside-out sorts of people.'

'Bleeding hearts, you mean,' Iris echoed ominously. 'People who refuse to bottle it all up, who live life on the outside, who – ' she glanced around – 'end up growing old disgracefully.' She sniffed. 'Stop me before I reminisce again. Open the box!'

Miriam obeyed. It was half-full of yellowing, carefully folded newsprint and elderly photocopies of newspaper stories. Then there was a paper bag and some certificates and pieces of formal paper-work made up the rest of its contents. 'The bag contained stuff that was found with your birth-mother by the police,' Iris explained. 'Personal effects. They had to keep the clothing as evidence, but nobody ever came forward and after a while they passed the effects on to Morris for safekeeping. There's a locket of your mother's in there – I think you ought to keep it in a safe place for now; I think it's probably quite valuable. The papers – it was a terrible thing. Terrible.'

Miriam unfolded the uppermost sheet; it crackled slightly with age as she read it. Unknown woman found stabbed, baby taken into custody. It gave her a most peculiar feeling. She'd known about it for many years, of course, but this was like seeing it for the first time in a history book, written down in black and white. 'They still don't know who she was?' Miriam asked.

'Why should they?' Iris looked at her oddly. 'Sometimes they can reopen the case when new evidence comes to light, or do DNA testing, but after thirty-two years most of the witnesses will have moved away or died. The police officers who first looked into it will have retired. Probably nothing happens unless a new lead comes up. Say, they find another body or someone confesses years later. It's just one of those terrible things that sometimes happen to people. The only unusual thing about it was you.' She looked at Miriam fondly.

'Why they let two radicals, one of them a resident alien and both of them into antiwar protests and stuff like that, adopt a baby – ' Miriam shook her head. Then she grinned. 'Did they think I would slow you down or something?'

'Possibly, possibly. But I don't remember being asked any questions about our politics when we went to the adoption agency – it was much easier to adopt in those days. They didn't ask much about our background except whether we were married. We didn't save the newspapers at the time, by the way. Morris bought them as morgue copies later.'

'Well.' Miriam replaced the news clipping, put the lid back on the box, and contemplated it. 'Ancient history.'

'You know, if you wanted to investigate it – ' Iris was using that look on her, the penetrating diamond-tipped stare of inquisition, the one Miriam tried to think herself into when interviewing difficult customers – 'I bet a journalist of your experience would do better than some doughnut-stuffed policeman on a routine job. Don't you think?'

'I think I really ought to help my real mother figure out what she's going to do about not going stir-crazy while she gets better,' Miriam replied lightly. 'There are more immediate things to investigate, like whether your tea is cold and if there are any cookies in the kitchen. Why don't we leave digging up the dead past for some other time?'

PINK SLIPPERS

Miriam drove away slowly, distractedly, nodding in time to the beat of the windshield wipers. Traffic was as bad as usual, but nothing untoward penetrated her thoughts.

She parked, then hunched her shoulders against the weather and scurried to her front door. As usual, her keys got muddled up. *Why does this always happen when I'm in a hurry?* she wondered. Inside, she shook her way out of her raincoat and jacket like a newborn moth emerging from its sodden cocoon, hung them on the coat rail, then dumped her shoulder bag and the now-damp cardboard box on the old telephone table and bent to unzip her boots. Free of the constraints of leather, her feet flexed luxuriously as she slid them into a pair of battered pink slippers. Then she spotted the answering machine's blinking light. 'You have new messages,' she sang to herself, slightly manic with relief at being home. 'Fuck 'em.' She headed for the kitchen to switch on the coffeepot, then poured a mug and carried it into her den.

The den had once been the dining room of this suburban home, a rectangular space linked to the living room by an archway and to the kitchen by a serving hatch. Now it was a cramped office, two walls jammed with bookcases and a third occupied by a huge battered desk. The remaining wall was occupied by a set of French windows opening onto the rear deck. Rain left twisting slug trails down the windows, kicking up splashes from the half-submerged ceramic pots outside. Miriam planted the coffee mug in the middle of the pile of stuff that accumulated on her desk and frowned at the effect. 'It's a mess,' she said aloud, bemused. 'How the hell did it get this untidy?'

'This is bad,' she said, standing in front of her desk. 'You hear me?' The stubborn paperwork and scattering of gadgets stubbornly refused to obey, so she attacked them, sorting the letters into piles, opening unopened mail and discarding the junk, hunting receipts and filing bills. The desk turned out to be almost nine months deep in trivia, and cleaning it up was a welcome distraction from having to think about her experience at work. When the desk actually showed a clear surface – and she'd applied the kitchen cleaner to the coffee rings – she started on the e-mail. That took longer, and by the time she'd checked off everything in her inbox, the rain battering on the windows was falling out of a darkening sky as night fell.

When everything was looking shipshape, another thought struck her. 'Paperwork. Hmm.' She went through into the hall and fetched the pink and green shoebox. Making a face, she upended it onto the desk. Papers mushroomed out, and something clattered and skittered onto the floor. 'Huh?'

It was a paper bag. Something in it, a hard, cold nucleus, had spilled over the edge of the desk. She hunted around for a few seconds, then stooped and triumphantly deposited bag and contents next to the pile of yellowing clippings, rancid photocopies, and creamy documents. One of which, now that she examined it, looked like a birth certificate – no, one of those forms that gets filled in in place of a birth certificate when the full details are unknown. Baby Jane Doe, age approximately six weeks, weight blah, eye color green, sex female, parents unknown . . . for a moment Miriam felt as if she was staring at it down a dark tunnel from a long way away.

Ignoring the thing-that-rattled, Miriam went through the papers and sorted these, too, into two stacks. Press clippings and bureaucracy. The clippings were mostly photocopies: They told a simple – if mysterious – tale that had been familiar to her since the age of four. A stabbing in the park. A young woman – apparently a hippie or maybe a Gypsy, judging by her strange clothes – found dead on the edge of a wooded area. The cause of death was recorded as massive blood loss caused by a deep wound across her back and left shoulder, inflicted by some kind of edged weapon, maybe a machete. That was unusual enough. What made it even more unusual was the presence of the six-week-old baby shrieking her little heart out nearby. An elderly man walking his dog had called the police. It was a seven-day wonder.

Miriam knew the end to that story lay somewhere in Morris and Iris Beckstein's comforting arms. She'd done her best to edit this other dangling bloody end to the story out of her life. She didn't want to be someone else's child: She had two perfectly good parents of her own, and the common assumption that blood ties must be thicker than upbringing rankled. Iris's history taught better – the only child of Holocaust refugees settled in an unfriendly English town after the war, she'd emigrated at twenty and never looked back after meeting and marrying Morris.

Miriam shook out the contents of the paper bag over the not-quite birth certificate. It was a lens-shaped silver locket on a fine chain. Tarnished and dull with age, its surface was engraved with some sort of crest of arms: a shield and animals. It looked distinctly cheap. 'Hmm.' She picked it up and peered at it closely. This must be what Ma told me about, she thought. Valuable? There was some sort of catch under the chain's loop. 'I wonder . . .'

She opened it.

Instead of the lover's photographs she'd half-expected, the back of the shell contained a knotwork design, enamel painted in rich colors. Curves of rich ocher looped and interpenetrated, weaving above and beneath a branch of turquoise. The design was picked out in silver – it was far brighter than the exposed outer case had suggested.

Miriam sighed and leaned back in her sprung office chair. 'Well, there goes *that* possibility,' she told the press clippings gloomily. No photographs of her mother or long-lost father. Just some kind of tacky *cloissoné* knotwork design.

She looked at it closer. Knotwork. Vaguely Celtic knotwork. The left-hand cell appeared to be a duplicate of the right-hand one. If she traced that arc from the top left and followed it under the blue arc –

Why had her birth-mother carried this thing? What did it mean to her? (The blue arc connected through two interlinked green whorls.) What had she seen when she stared into it? Was it some kind of meditation aid? Or just a pretty picture? It certainly wasn't any kind of coat of arms.

Miriam leaned back further. Lifting the locket, she dangled it in front of her eyes, letting the light from the bookcase behind her catch the silver highlights. Beads of dazzling blue-white heat seemed to trace their way around the knot's heart. She squinted, feeling her scalp crawl. The sound of her heart beating in her ears became unbearably loud: There was a smell of burning toast, the sight of an impossible knot twisting in front of her eyes like some kind of stereoisogram forming in midair, trying to turn her head inside out –

Three things happened simultaneously. An abrupt sense of nausea washed over her, the lightbulb went out, and her chair fell over backward.

'Ouch! Dammit!' Something thumped into Miriam's side, doubling her over as she hit the ground and rolled over, pulling her arms in to protect her face. A racking spasm caught her by the gut, leaving her feeling desperately sick, and the arm of the chair came around and whacked her in the small of her back. Her knees were wet, and the lights were out. 'Hell!' Her head was splitting, the heartbeat throb pounding like a jackhammer inside her skull, and her stomach was twisting. A sudden flash of fear: *This can't be a migraine. The onset is way too fast. Malignant hypertension?* The urge to vomit was strong, but after a moment it began to ebb. Miriam lay still for a minute, waiting for her stomach to come under control and the lights to come back on. *Am I having an aneurism?* She gripped the locket so tightly that it threatened to dig a hole in her right fist. Carefully she tried to move her arms and legs: Everything seemed to be working and she managed a shallow sigh of relief. Finally, when she was sure her guts were going to be all right, she pushed herself up onto her knees and saw –

Trees.

Trees *everywhere*.

Trees inside her den.

Where did the walls go?

Afterward, she could never remember that next terrible minute. It was dark, of course, but not totally dark: She was in twilight on a forested slope, with beech and elm and other familiar trees looming ominously out of the twilight. The ground was dry, and her chair lay incongruously in a thicket of shrubbery not far from the base of a big maple tree. When she looked around, she could see no sign of her house, or the neighboring apartments, or of the lights along the highway. *Is there a total blackout?* she wondered, confused. *Did I sleepwalk or something?*

She stumbled to her feet, her slippers treacherous on leaf mulch and dry grass stems. She shivered. It was cold – not quite winter-cold, but too chilly to be wandering around in pants, a turtleneck, and bedroom slippers. And –

'Where the hell am I?' she asked the empty sky. 'What the hell?'

Then the irony of her situation kicked in and she began to giggle, frightened and edgy and afraid she wouldn't be able to stop. She did a twirl, in place, trying to see whatever there was to see. Sylvan idyll at nightfall, still-life with deranged dot-com refugee and brown office furniture. A gust of wind rattled the branches overhead, dislodging a chilly shower of fat drops: A couple landed on Miriam's arms and face, making her shudder.

The air was fresh – too fresh. And there was none of the subliminal background hum of a big city, the noise that never completely died. It didn't get this quiet even out in the country – and indeed, when she paused to listen, it wasn't quiet; she could hear distant birdsong in the deepening twilight.

She took a deep breath, then another. Forced herself to thrust the hand with the locket into her hip pocket and let go of the thing. She patted it obsessively for a minute, whimpering slightly at the pain in her head. *No holes,* she thought vaguely. She'd once worn pants like this where her spare change had worn a hole in the pocket lining and eventually spilled on the ground, causing no end of a mess.

For some reason, the idea of losing possession of the locket filled her with stomach-churning dread.

She looked up. The first stars of evening were coming out, and the sky was almost clear of cloud. It was going to be a cold night.

'Item,' she muttered. 'You are not at home. *Ouch.* You have a splitting headache and you don't think you fell asleep in the chair, even though you were in it when you arrived here.' She looked around in wild surmise. She'd never been one for the novels Ben occasionally read, but she'd seen enough trashy TV series to pick up the idea. *Twilight Zone, Time Squad,* programs like that. 'Item: I don't know where or when I am, but this ain't home. Do I stay put and hope I automagically snap back into my own kitchen or . . .'what? It was the locket, no two ways about it. Do I look at it again to go back?'

She fumbled into her pocket nervously. Her fingers wrapped around warm metal. She breathed more easily. 'Right. Right.'

Just nerves, she thought. Alone in a forest at night – what lived here? Bears? Cougars? There could be anything here, anything at all. Be a fine joke if she went exploring and stepped on a rattler, wouldn't it? Although in this weather . . . 'I'd better go home,' she murmured to herself and was about to pull the locket out when she saw a flicker of light in the distance.

She was disoriented, tired, had just had a really bad day, and some cosmic trickster-god had dumped a magic amulet on her to see what she'd do with it. That was the only explanation, she reasoned afterward. A sane Miriam would have sat down and analyzed her options, then assembled a plan of action. But it wasn't a sane Miriam who saw those flickers of orange light and went crashing through the trees downhill toward them.

Lights. A jingle, as of chains. Thudding and hollow clonking noises – and low voices. She stumbled out into the sudden expanse of a trail – not a wide one, more of a hiking trail, the surface torn up and muddy. *Lights!* She stared at them, at the men on horseback coming down the trail toward her, the lantern held on a pole by the one in the lead. Dim light glinted off reflecting metal, helmet, and breastplate like something out of a museum. Someone called out something that sounded like: 'Curl!' *Look. He's riding toward me,* she thought dazedly. *What's that he's –*

Her guts liquid with absolute fright, she turned and ran. The flat crack of rifle fire sounded behind her, repeated short bursts firing into the night. Invisible fingers ripped at the branches overhead as Miriam heard voices raised in hue and cry behind her. Low branches scratched at her face as she ran, gasping and crying, uphill away from the path. More bangs, more gunshots – astonishingly few of them, but any at all was too many. She ran straight into a tree, fell back winded, brains rattling around inside her head like dried peas in a pod, then she pushed herself to her feet again faster than she'd have believed possible and stumbled on into the night, gasping for breath, praying for rescue.

Eventually she stopped. Somewhere along the way she'd lost her slippers. Her face and ribs felt bruised, her head was pounding, and she could barely breathe. But she couldn't hear any sounds of pursuit. Her skin felt oddly tight, and everything was far too cold. As soon as she was no longer running, she doubled over and succumbed to a fit of racking coughs, prolonged by her desperate attempts to muffle them. Her chest was on fire. *Oh god, any god. Whoever put me here. I just want you to know that I hate you!*

She stood up. Somewhere high overhead the wind sighed. Her skin itched with the fear of pursuit. *I've got to get home,* she realized. Now her skin crawled with another fear – fear that she might be wrong, that it wasn't the locket at all, that it was something else she didn't understand that had brought her here, that there was no way back and she'd be stranded –

When she flicked it open, the right-hand half of the locket crawled with light. Tiny specks of brilliance, not the phosphorescence of a watch dial or the bioluminescence of those plastic disposable flashlights that had become popular for a year or two, but an intense, bleached blue-white glare like a miniature star. Miriam panted, trying to let her mind drift into it, but after a minute she realized all she was achieving was giving herself a headache. 'What did I do to make it work?' she mumbled, puzzled and frustrated and increasingly afraid. 'If she could make it – '

Ah. That was what she'd been doing. Just relaxing, meditating. Wondering what her birth-mother had seen in it. Miriam gritted her teeth. How was she going to re-create that sense of detached curiosity? Here in a wild forest at night, with strangers shooting at her in the dark? How – she narrowed her eyes. *The headache. If I can see my way past it, I could –*

The dots of light blazed up for a moment in glorious conflagration. Miriam jackknifed forward, saw the orange washout of streetlights shining down on a well-mowed lawn. Then her stomach rebelled and this time she couldn't keep it down. It was all she could do to catch her breath between heaves. Somehow her guts had been replaced by a writhing snake, and the racking spasms kept pulsing through her until she began to worry about tearing her esophagus.

She heard the sound of a car slowing – then speeding up again as the driver saw her vomiting. A yell from the window, inarticulate, something like 'Drunk fucking bums!' Something clattered into the road. Miriam didn't care. Dampness and cold clenched their icy fingers around her, but she didn't care: She was back in civilization, away from the threatening trees and her pursuers. She stumbled off the front lawn of somebody's house and sensed harsh asphalt beneath her bare feet, stones digging into her soles. A street sign said it was somewhere she knew. One of the other side roads off Grafton Street. She was less than two miles from home.

Drip. She looked up. *Drip.* The rain began to fall again, sluicing down her aching face. Her clothes were stained and filthy with mud and vomit. Her legs were scratched and felt bruised. *Home.* It was a primal imperative. Put one foot in front of another, she told herself through the deafening hammering in her skull. Her head hurt, and the world was spinning around her.

An indefinite time – perhaps thirty minutes, perhaps an hour – later, she saw a familiar sight through the downpour. Soaked to the skin and shivering, she nevertheless felt like a furnace. Her house seemed to shimmer like a mirage in the desert when she looked at it. And now she discovered another problem – she'd come out without her keys! *Silly me, what was I thinking?* she wondered vaguely. *Nothing but this locket,* she thought, weaving its chain around her right index finger.

The shed, whispered a vestige of cool control in the back of her head.

Oh, yes, the shed, she answered herself.

She stumbled around the side of her house, past the cramped green rug that passed for a yard, to the shed in back. It was padlocked, but the small side window wasn't actually fastened and if you pulled *just so* it would open outward. It took her three tries and half a fingernail – the rain had warped the wood somewhat – but once open she could thrust an arm inside and fumble around for the hook with the key dangling from it on a loop. She fetched the key, opened the padlock – dropping it casually on the lawn – and found, taped to the underside of the workbench, the spare key to the French doors.

She was home.

WALK ON THE WILD SIDE

Somehow Miriam found her way upstairs. She worked this out the next morning when she awakened sprawled on her bed, feet freezing and hot shivers chasing across her skin while a platoon of miners with pickaxes worked her head over. It was her bladder that finally forced her up and led her, still half-asleep, to the bathroom, where she turned on all the lights, shot the deadbolt on the door, used the toilet, and rummaged around for an Advil to help with the hangover symptoms. 'What you need is a good shower,' she told herself grimly, trying to ignore the pile of foul and stinking clothes on the floor that mingled with the towels she'd spilled everywhere the night before. Naked in a brightly lit pink and chromed bathroom, she spun the taps, sat on the edge of the bathtub, and tried to think her way past the haze of depression and pain.

'You're a big girl,' she told the scalding hot waterfall as it gushed into the tub. 'Big girls don't get bent out of shape by little things,' she told herself. Like losing her job. 'Big girls deal with divorces. Big girls deal with getting pregnant while they're at school, putting the baby up for adoption, finishing med school, and retraining for another career when they don't like the shitty options they get dealt. Big girls cope with marrying their boyfriends, then finding he's been sleeping with their best friends. Big girls make CEOs shit themselves when they come calling with a list of questions. They don't go crazy and think they're wandering around a rainy forest being shot at by armored knights with assault rifles.' She sniffed, on the edge of tears.

A first rational thought intruded: *I'm getting depressed and that's no good.* Followed rapidly by a second one: *Where's the bubble bath?* Bubble bath was fun. Bubble bath was a good thought. Miriam didn't like wallowing in self-pity, although right now it was almost as tempting as a nice warm shower. She went and searched for the bubble

32

bath, finally found the bottle in the trashcan – almost, but not entirely, empty. She held it under the tap and let the water rinse the last of the gel out, foaming and swirling around her feet.

Depression would be a perfectly reasonable response to losing my job, she told herself, *if it was actually my fault. Which it wasn't.* Lying back in the scented water and inhaling steam. *But am I going nuts? I don't think so.* She'd been through bad times. First the unplanned pregnancy with Ben, in her third year at college, too young and too early. She still couldn't fully articulate her reasons for not having an abortion; maybe if that woman from the student counseling service hadn't simply assumed . . . but she'd never been one for doing what everyone expected her to do, and she'd been confident – maybe too confident – in her relationship with Ben. Hence the adoption. And then, a couple of years later when they got married, that hadn't been the smartest thing she'd ever done either. With twenty-twenty hindsight it had been a response to a relationship already on the rocks, the kind that could only end in tears. But she'd weathered it all without going crazy or even having a small breakdown. *Iron control, that's me.* But this new thing, the stumbling around the woods being shot at, seeing a knight, a guy in armor, with an M16 or something – that was scary. Time to face the music. 'Am I sane?' she asked the Toilet Duck.

Well, whatever this is, it ain't in the DSM-IV. Miriam racked her memory for decade-old clinical lectures. No way was this schizophrenia. The symptoms were all wrong, and she wasn't hearing voices or feeling weird about people. It was just a single sharp incident, very vivid, realistic as –

She stared at her stained pants and turtleneck. 'The chair,' she muttered. 'If the chair's missing, it was real. Or at least something happened.'

Paradoxically, the thought of the missing chair gave her something concrete to hang on to. Dripping wet, she stumbled downstairs. Her den was as she'd left it, except that the chair was missing and there were muddy footprints by the French doors. She knelt to examine the floor behind her desk. She found a couple of books, dislodged from the shelf behind her chair when she fell, but otherwise no sign of anything unexpected. 'So it was real!'

A sudden thought struck her and she whirled then ran upstairs to the bathroom, wincing. *The locket!*

It was in the pocket of her pants. Pulling a face, she carefully placed it on the shelf above the sink where she could see it, then got into the bathtub. *I'm not going nuts,* she thought, relaxing in the hot water. *It's real.*

An hour later she emerged, feeling much improved. Hair washed and conditioned, nails carefully trimmed and stripped of the residue of yesterday's polish, legs itching with mild razor burn, and skin rosy from an exfoliating scrub, she felt clean: as if she'd succeeded in stripping away all the layers of dirt and paranoia that had stuck to her the day before. It was still only lunchtime, so she dressed again: an old T-shirt, jeans that had seen better days, and an old pair of sneakers.

The headache and chills subsided slowly, as did the lethargy. She headed downstairs slowly and dumped her dirty clothing in the washing machine. Then she poured herself a glass of orange juice and managed to force down one of the granola bars she kept for emergencies. This brought more thoughts to mind, and as soon as she'd finished eating she headed downstairs to poke around in the gloom of the basement.

The basement was a great big rectangular space under the floor of the house. The furnace, bolted to one wall, roared eerily at her; Ben had left lots of stuff with her, her parents had passed on a lot of their stuff too, and now one wall was faced in industrial shelving units.

Here was a box stuffed with old clothing that she kept meaning to schlep to a charity shop: not her wedding dress – which had gone during the angry month she filed for divorce – but ordinary stuff, too unimportant to repudiate. There was an old bag full of golf clubs, their chromed heads dull and speckled with rust. Ben had toyed with the idea of doing golf, thinking of it as a way up the corporate ladder. There was a dead lawn mower, an ancient computer of Ben's – probably a museum piece by now – and a workbench with vice, saws, drill, and other woodworking equipment, and maybe the odd bloodstain from his failed attempts to be the man about the house. There on that high shelf was a shotgun and a box of shells. It had belonged to Morris, her father. She eyed it dubiously. Probably nobody had used it since Dad bought it decades ago, when he'd lived out west for a few years, and what she knew about shotguns could be written on one side of a postage stamp in very large letters, even though Morris had insisted on dragging her to a range in New Hampshire to teach her how to use a handgun. Some wise words from the heavyweight course on industrial espionage techniques the *Weatherman* HR folks had paid for her to take two years ago came back: You're a journalist, and these other folks are investigators. You're none of you cops, none of you are doing anything worth risking your lives over, so you should avoid escalating confrontations. Guns turn any confrontation into a potentially lethal one. So keep them the hell out of your professional life! 'Shotgun, no,' she mused. 'But. Hmm. Handgun.' *Must stop talking to myself,* she resolved.

'Do I really expect them to follow me here?' she asked the broken chest freezer, which gaped uncomprehendingly at her. 'Did I just dream it all?'

Back upstairs, she swiped her leather-bound planner from the desk and poured another glass of orange juice. *Time to worry about the real world,* she told herself. She went back to the hall and hit the 'play' button on the answering machine. It was backed up with messages from the day before.

'Miriam? Andy here. Listen, a little bird told me about what happened yesterday and I think it sucks. They didn't have any details, but I want you to know if you need some freelance commissions you should give me a call. Talk later? Bye.'

Andy was a junior editor on a rival tech-trade sheet. He sounded stiff and stilted when he talked to the telephone robot, not like a real person at all. But it still gave her a shiver of happiness, almost a feeling of pure joy, to hear from him. Someone cared, someone who didn't buy the vicious lie Joe Dixon had put out. *That bastard really got to me,* Miriam wondered, relief replaced by a flash of anger at the way she'd been treated.

Another message, from Paulette. Miriam tensed. 'Miriam, honey, let's talk. I don't want to rake over dead shit, but there's some stuff I need to get straight in my head. Can I come around?'

She hit the 'pause' button. Paulette sounded severely messed up.

It was like a bucket of ice water down her spine. *I did this. I got us both fired,* she began thinking, and her knees tried to turn to jelly. Then she thought, *Hold on. I didn't fire anybody!* That switched on the anger again, but left her feeling distinctly shaky. Sooner or later she'd have to talk to Paulie. Sooner or –

She hit the 'next message' button again.

Heavy breathing, then: 'Bitch. We know where you live. Heard about you from our mutual friend Joe. Keep your nose out of our business or you'll be fucking sorry' – click.

Wide-eyed, she turned and looked over her shoulder. But the yard was empty and the front door was locked. 'Bastards,' she spat. But there was no caller ID on the message and probably not enough to get the police interested in it. Especially not if Joe's minions at *The Weatherman* started mud slinging with forged firewall logs: They could make her look like the next Unabomber if they wanted to. For a moment, outrage blurred her vision. She forced herself to stop panting and sit down again, next to the treacherous, venomous answering machine. 'Threaten me in my own home, will you?'

The gravity of her situation was only just sinking in. 'Better keep a gun under my pillow,' she muttered under her breath. 'Bastards.' The opposite wall seemed to be pulsing slightly, a reaction to her fury. She felt her fingers clenching involuntarily. 'Bastards.' Kicking her out of her job and smearing her reputation wasn't enough for them, was it? She'd show them –

– *Something.*

After a minute she calmed down enough to face the remaining message on the answering machine. She had difficulty forcing herself to press the button. But the next message wasn't another threat – quite the opposite. 'Miriam, this is Steve from *The Herald*. I heard the news. Get in touch.'

For that, she hit the 'pause' button yet again, and this time frowned and scribbled a note to herself. Steve wasn't a chatty editor, like Andy; Steve treated words like dollar bills. And he wouldn't be getting in touch if it didn't involve work, even freelance work. A year ago he'd tried to headhunt her, offering a big pay raise and a higher position. Taking stock of her options – and when they were due to mature – she'd turned him down. Now she had reason to regret it.

That was the end of her mailbox, and she hit the 'erase' button hard enough to hurt her finger. Two editors talking about work, a former office mate wanting to chew over the corpse – and what sounded like a death threat. *This isn't going to go away*, she realized. *I'm in it up to my neck now.* A stab of guilt: *So is Paulie. I'll have to talk to her.* A ray of hope: *For someone who's unemployed, I sure get a lot of business calls.* A conclusion: *Just as long as I stay sane, I should be all right.*

The living room was more hospitable right now than the chairless den, its huge french doors streaked with rain falling from a leaden sky. Miriam went through, considered building a fire in the hearth, and collapsed into the sofa instead. The combination of fear, anger, and tension had drained most of her energy. Opening her planner, she turned to a blank page and began writing:

I NEED WORK
Call Andy and Steve. Pass 'Go'. Collect freelance commissions.
Collect two hundred dollars. Keep up the mortgage payments.
I AM GOING CRAZY
Well, no. This isn't schizophrenia. I'm not hearing voices, the walls
aren't going soft, and nobody is beaming orbital mind control lasers
at me. Everything's fine except I had a weird fugue moment, and the
office chair is missing.
DID SOMEONE SLIP ME SOMETHING?
Don't be silly: Who? Iris? Maybe she and Morris tripped when they
were younger, but she just wouldn't do that to me. Joe Dixon is a
sleazebag with criminal connections, but he didn't offer me a drink.
And who else have I seen in the past day? Anyway, that's not how
hallucinogens work.
MAGIC
That's silly, too, but at least it's testable.

Miriam's eyes narrowed and she chewed the cap of her pen. This was going to take planning, but at least it was beginning to sound like she had her ducks lined up in a row. She began jotting down tasks:

1. Call Andy at *The Globe*. Try to sell him a feature or three.
2. Make appointment to see Steve at *The Herald*. See what he wants.
3. See Paulie. Check how she's doing. See if we can reconstruct the investigation without drawing attention. See if we can pitch it at Andy or Steve. Cover the angles. If we do this, they will turn nasty. Call FBI?
4. See if whatever I did last night is repeatable. Get evidence, then a witness. If it's me, seek help. If it's not me . . .
5. Get the story.

*

The next day Miriam went shopping. It was, she figured, retail therapy. Never mind the job-hunting, there'd be time for that when she knew for sure whether or not she was going insane in some obscurely nonstandard manner. It was October, a pretty time of year to go hiking, but fall had set in and things could turn nasty at the drop of a North Atlantic depression. Extensive preparations were therefore in order. She eventually staggered home under the weight of a load of camping equipment: tent, jacket, new boots, portable stove. Getting it all home on the T was a pain, but at least it told her that she could walk under the weight.

A couple of hours later she was ready. She checked her watch for the fourth time. She'd taken two ibuprofen tablets an hour ago and it should be doing its job by now.

She tightened the waist strap of her pack and stretched nervously. The garden shed was cramped and dark and there didn't seem to be room to turn around with her hiking gear and backpack on. *Did I put the spare key back?* she asked herself. A quick check proved that she had. Irrelevant thoughts were better than *Am I nuts?* – as long as they weren't an excuse for prevarication.

Okay, here goes nothing.

The locket. She held it in her left hand. With her right she patted her right hip pocket. The pistol was illegal – but as Ben had pointed out, he'd rather deal with an unlicensed firearms charge than his own funeral. The rattling memory of a voice snarling at her answering machine, the echo of rifle fire in the darkness, made her pause for a moment. 'Do I really want to do this?' she asked herself. Life was complicated enough as it was.

Hell yes! Because either I'm mad, and it doesn't matter, or my birth-mother was involved in something huge. Something much bigger than a billion-dollar money-laundering scam through Proteome and Biphase. And if they killed her because of it – A sense of lingering injustice prodded her conscience. 'Okay,' she told herself. 'Let's do it. I'm right behind myself.' She chuckled grimly and flicked the locket open, half-expecting to see a photograph of a woman, or a painting, or something else to tell her she needed help –

The knot tried to turn her eyes inside out, and then the hut wasn't there any more.

Miriam gasped. The air was cold, and her head throbbed – but not as badly as last time.

'Wow.' She carefully pushed the locket into her left pocket, then pulled out her pocket dictaphone. 'Memo begins: Wednesday, October 16, 8 p.m. It's dark and the temperature's about ten degrees colder . . . here. Wherever the hell "here" is.' She turned around slowly. Trees, skeletal, stretched off in all directions. She was standing on a slope, not steep but steep enough to explain why she'd skidded. 'No sign of people. I can either go look for the chair or not. Hmm. I think not.'

She looked up. Wind-blown clouds scudded overhead, beneath a crescent moon. She didn't turn her flashlight on. No call for attracting attention, she reminded herself. Just look around, then go home . . .

'I'm an astronaut,' she murmured into the dictaphone. She took a step forward, feeling her pack sway on her back, toward a big elm tree. Turning around, she paused, then knelt and carefully placed an old potsherd from the shed on the leafy humus where she'd been standing. 'Neil and Buzz only spent eight hours on the moon on that first trip. Only about four hours on the surface, in two excursions. This is going to be my moonwalk.' *As long as I don't get my damn fool self shot,* she reminded herself. Or stuck. She'd brought her sleeping bag and tent, and a first-aid kit, and Morris's pistol (just in case, and she felt wicked because of it). But this didn't feel like home. This felt like the wild woods – and Miriam wasn't at home in the woods. Especially when there were guys with guns who shot at her like it was hunting season and Jewish divorcées weren't on the protected list.

Miriam took ten paces up the hill, then stopped and held her breath, listening. The air was chilly and damp, as if a fog was coming in off the river. There was nothing to hear – no traffic noise, no distant rumble of trains or jets. A distant avian hooting might signify an owl hunting, but that was it. 'It's really quiet,' Miriam whispered into her mike. 'I've never heard it so silent before.'

She shivered and looked around. Then she took her small flashlight out and slashed a puddle of light across the trees, casting long sharp shadows. 'There!' she exclaimed. Another five paces and she found her brown swivel chair lying on a pile of leaf mold. It was wet and thoroughly the worse for wear, and she hugged it like a long-lost lover as she lifted it upright and carefully put it down. 'Yes!'

Her temples throbbed, but she was overjoyed. 'I found it,' she confided in her dictaphone. 'I found the chair. So this is the same place.' But the chair was pretty messed up. Almost ruined, in fact – it had been a secondhand retread to begin with, and a night out in the rainy woods hadn't helped any.

'It's real,' she said quietly, with profound satisfaction. 'I'm not going mad. Or if I'm confabulating, I'm doing it so damn consistently – ' She shook her head. 'My birth-mother came here. Or from here. Or something. And she was stabbed, and nobody knows why, or who did it.' That brought her back to reality. It raised echoes of her own situation, hints of anonymous threatening phone calls, and other unfinished business. She sighed, then retraced her steps to the potsherd. Massaging her scalp, she sat down on the spot, with her back to the nearby elm tree.

She stopped talking abruptly, thrust the dictaphone into her hip pocket, pulled out the locket, and held her breath.

The crunch of a breaking branch carried a long way in the night. Spooked, she flicked the locket open, focused on its depths, and steeled herself to face the coming hangover: She really didn't want to be out in the woods at night – at least, not without a lot more preparation.

*

The next morning – after phoning Andy at *The Globe* and securing a commission for a business supplement feature on VC houses, good for half a month's income, with the promise of a regular weekly slot if her features were good enough – Miriam bit the bullet and phoned Paulette. She was nerving herself for an answering machine on the fifth ring when Paulette answered.

'Hello?' She sounded hesitant – unusual for Paulie.

'Hi, Paulie! It's me. Sorry I didn't get back to you yesterday, I had a migraine and a lot of, uh, issues to deal with. I'm just about getting my head back together. How are you doing? Are you okay?'

A brief silence. 'About as well as you'd expect,' Paulette said guardedly.

'Have you had any, uh, odd phone calls?'

'Sort of,' Paulette replied.

Miriam tensed. *What's she concealing?*

'They sent me a re-employment offer,' Paulie continued, guardedly.

'They did, did they?' asked Miriam. She waited a beat. 'Are you going to take it?'

'Am I, like hell!' Paulette sounded furious. Miriam hadn't expected Paulie to roll over, but it was good to get this confirmation.

'That bad, huh? Want to talk about it? You free?'

'My days are pretty open right now – listen, are you busy? How about I come over to your place?'

'Great,' Miriam said briskly. 'I was worried about you, Paulie. After I got past being worried about me, I guess.'

'Well. Should I bring a pizza?'

'Phew . . .' Miriam took stock. *Just a bitch session together? Or something more going on?* 'Yeah, let's do that. I'll lay on the coffee right away.'

'That'd be wonderful,' Paulette said gratefully.

After she'd put the phone down, Miriam pondered her motives. She and Paulette had worked together for three years and had occasionally hung out together in their off-hours. Some people you met at work, socialized with, then lost contact after moving on; but a few turned into friends for life. Miriam wasn't sure which Paulie was going to turn out to be. *Why did she turn the re-employment offer down?* Miriam wondered. Despite being shell-shocked from the crazy business with the locket, she kept circling back to the Monday morning disaster with a rankling sense of injustice. The sooner they blew the lid off it in public, the sooner she could go back to living a normal life. But then the locket kept coming back up. *I need a sanity check,* Miriam decided. *Why not Paulie?* Better to have her think she'd gone nuts than someone whose friendship went back a long way and who knew Iris. Or was it?

An hour later the doorbell rang. Miriam stood up and went to answer it, trying to suppress her worries about why Paulette might be coming. She was waiting on the doorstep, impatiently tapping one heel, with a large shopping bag in hand. 'Miriam!' Paulette beamed.

'Come in, come in.' Miriam retreated. 'Hey, what's that? Have you been all right?'

'I've been worse.' Paulie bounced inside and shut the door behind her, then glanced around curiously. 'Hey, neat. I was worried about you, after I got home. You didn't look real happy, you know?'

'Yeah. Well, I wasn't.' Miriam relieved her of her coat and led her into the living room. 'I'm really glad you're taking it so calmly. For me, I put in three years and nothing to show for it but hard work and junk bonds – then some asshole phoned me and warned me off. How about you? Have you had any trouble?'

Paulette peered at her curiously. 'What kind of warning?'

'Oh, he kind of intimated that he was a friend of Joe's, and I'd regret it if I stuck my nose in any deeper. Playing at wiseguys, okay? I'd been worrying about you . . . What's this about a job offer?'

'I, uh – ' Paulette paused. 'They offered me my job back with strings attached,' she said guardedly. 'Assholes. I was going to accept till they faxed through the contract.'

'So why didn't you sign?' Miriam asked, pouring a mug of coffee while Paulette opened the pizza boxes.

'I've seen nondisclosure agreements, Miriam. I used to be a paralegal till I got sick of lawyers, remember? This wasn't a nondisclosure agreement; it was a straitjacket. If I'd signed it, I wouldn't even own the contents of my own head – before and after working for them. Guess they figured you were the ringleader, right?'

'Hah.' There was a bitter taste in Miriam's mouth, and it wasn't from the coffee. 'So. Found any work?'

'Got no offers yet.' Paulette took a bite of pizza to cover her disquiet. 'Emphasis on the yet. You?'

'I landed a freelance feature already. It's not going to cover the salary, but it goes a hell of a way. I was wondering – '

'You want to carry on working the investigation.'

It wasn't a question. Miriam nodded. 'Yeah. I want to get the sons of bitches, now more than ever. But something tells me moving too fast is going to be a seriously bad idea. I mean, there's a lot of money involved. If we can redo the investigative steps we've got so far, I figure this time we ought to go to the FBI first – and then pick a paper. I think I could probably auction the story, but I'd rather wait until the feds are ready to start arresting people. And I'd like to disappear for a bit while they're doing that.' A sudden bolt of realization struck Miriam, so that she almost missed Paulette's reply: *The locket! That's one place they won't be able to follow me! If –*

'Sounds possible.' Paulie looked dubious. 'It's not going to be easy duplicating the research – especially now that they know we stumbled across them. Do you really think it's that dangerous?'

'If it's drugs money, you can get somebody shot for a couple of thousand bucks. This is way bigger than that, and thanks to our friend Joe, they now know where we live. I don't want to screw up again. You with me?'

After a moment, Paulette nodded. 'I want them too.' A flash of anger. 'They don't think I matter enough to worry about.'

'But first there's something I need to find out. I need to vanish for a weekend,' Miriam said slowly, a fully formed plan moving into focus in her mind – one that would hopefully answer several questions. Like whether someone else could see her vanish and reappear, and whether she'd have somewhere to hole up if the anonymous threats turned real – and maybe even a chance to learn more about her enigmatic birth-mother than Iris could tell her.

'Oh?' Paulette perked up. 'Going to think things over? Or is there a male person in play?' Male persons in play were guaranteed to get Paulie's notice: Like Miriam, she was a member of the early thirties divorcée club.

'Neither.' Miriam considered her next words carefully. 'I ran across something odd on Monday night. Probably nothing to do with our story, but I'm planning on investigating it and I'll be away for a couple of days. Out of town.'

'Tell me more!'

'I, um, can't. Yet.' Miriam had worked it through. The whole story was just too weird to lay on Paulie without some kind of proof to get her attention. 'However, you can do me a big favor, okay? I need to get to a rest area just off a road near Amesbury with some hiking gear. Yeah, I know that sounds weird, but it's the best way to make sure nobody's following me. If you could ride out with me and drive my car home, then put it back there two days later, that would be really good.'

'That's . . . odd.' Paulette looked puzzled. 'What's with the magical mystery tour?'

Miriam improvised fast. 'I could tell you, but then I'd have to get you to sign a nondisclosure agreement that would make anything *The Weatherman* offered you look liberal. And the whole thing is super-secret; my source might spike the whole deal if I let someone in on it without prior permission. I'll be able to tell you when you pick me up afterward, though.' If things went right, she'd be able to tell a more-than-somewhat-freaked Paulie why she'd vanished right in front of her eyes and then reappeared in front of them. 'And I want you to promise to tell nobody about it until you pick me up again, okay?'

'Well, okay. It's not as if I don't have time on my hands.' Paulette frowned. 'When are you planning on doing your disappearing act? And when do you want picking up?'

'I was – they're picking me up tomorrow at 2 p.m. precisely,' said Miriam. 'And I'll be showing up exactly forty-eight hours later.' She grinned. 'If you lie in wait – pretend to be eating your lunch or something – you can watch them pick me up.'

*

Friday morning dawned cold but clear, and Miriam showered then packed her camping equipment again. The doorbell rang just after noon. It was Paulette, wearing a formal black suit. 'Hey, Paulie, who died?'

'I had a job interview this morning.' Paulette pulled a face. 'I got sick of sitting at home thinking about those bastards shafting us and decided to do something for number one in the meantime.'

'Well, good for you.' Miriam picked up her backpack and led Paulie out the front door, then locked up behind her. She opened her car, put the pack in, then opened the front doors. 'Did it go well?' she asked, pulling her seat belt on.

'It went like – ' Paulette pulled another face. 'Listen, I'm a business researcher, right? Just because I used to be a paralegal doesn't mean that I want to go back there.'

'Lawyers,' Miriam said as she started the engine. 'Lots of work in that field, I guarantee you.'

'Oh yeah,' Paulette agreed. She pulled the sun visor down and looked at herself in the mirror. 'Fuck, do I really look like that? I'm turning into my first ex-boss.'

'Yes indeed, you look just like – naah.' Miriam thought better of it and rephrased: 'Congresswoman Paulette Milan, from Cambridge. You have the floor, ma'am.'

'The first ex-boss is in politics now,' Paulie observed gloomily. 'A real dragon.'

'Bitch.'

'You didn't know her.'

They drove on in amiable silence for the best part of an hour, out into the wilds of Massachusetts. Up the coast, past Salem, out toward Amesbury, off the Interstate and on to a four-lane highway, then finally a side road. Miriam had been here before, years ago, with Ben, when things had been going okay. There was a rest area up on a low hill overlooking Browns Point, capped by a powder of trees, gaunt skeletons hazed in red and auburn foliage at this time of year. Miriam pulled up at the side of the road just next to the rest area and parked. 'Okay, this is it,' she said. There were butterflies in her stomach again: *I'm going to go through with it*, she realized to her surprise.

'This?' Paulette looked around, surprised. 'But this is nowhere!'

'Yeah, that's right. Best place to do this.' Miriam opened the glove locker. 'Look, I brought my old camcorder. No time for explanations. I'm going to get out of the car, grab my pack, and walk over there. I want you to film me. In ten minutes either I'll tell you why I asked you to do this and you can call me rude names – or you'll know to take the car home and come back the day after tomorrow to pick me up. Okay?'

'Miriam, this is nuts – '

She got out in a hurry and collected her pack from the trunk. Then, without waiting to see what Paulette did, she walked over to the middle of the parking lot. Breathing deeply, she hiked the pack up onto her back and fastened the chest strap – then pulled the locket out of the outer pocket where she'd stashed it.

Feeling acutely self-conscious, she flicked it open and turned her back on the parked car. Raised it to her face and stared into the enameled knot painted inside it. *This is stupid,* a little voice told her. *And you're going to have your work cut out convincing Paulie you don't need to see a shrink.*

Someone was calling her name sharply. She screened it out. Something seemed to move inside the knot –

HIDE-AND-SEEK

This time it was raining gently.

Miriam winced at the sudden stabbing in her head and pocketed the locket. Then she did what she'd planned all along: a three-sixty-degree scan that took in nothing but autumn trees and deadfall. Next, she planted her pack, transferred the pistol to her right hip pocket, retrieved her camera and the recorder, and started taking snapshots as she dictated a running commentary.

'The time by my watch is fourteen twelve hours. Precipitation is light and intermittent, cloud cover is about six-sevenths, wind out of the northwest and chilly, breeze of around five miles per hour. I think.'

Snap, snap, snap: The camera had room for a thousand or so shots before she'd have to change hard disks. She slung it around her neck and shouldered the pack again. With the Swiss army knife Ben had given her on their second wedding anniversary – an odd present from a clueless, cheating husband with no sense of the difference between jewelry and real life – she shaved a patch of bark above eye level on the four nearest trees, then fished around for some stones to pile precisely where she'd come through. (It wouldn't do to go back only to come out in the middle of her own car. If that was possible, of course.)

As she worked, she had the most peculiar sensation: *I'm on my second moon mission,* she thought. Did any of the Apollo astronauts go to the moon more than once? Here she was, not going crazy, recording notes and taking photographs to document her exploration of this extraordinary place that simply wasn't like home. Whatever 'home' meant, now that gangsters had her number.

'I still don't know why I'm here,' she recorded, 'but I've got the same alarming prefrontal headache, mild hot and cold chills, probable elevated blood pressure as last time. Memo: Next time bring a sphygmomanometer; I want to monitor for malignant hypertension. And urine sample bottles.' The headache, she realized, was curiously similar to a hangover, itself caused by dehydration that triggered inflammation of the meninges. Miriam continued: 'Query physiological responses to . . . whatever it is that I do. When I focus on the knot. Memo: Scan the locket, use Photoshop to rescale it and print it on paper, then see if the pattern works as a focus when I look at it on a clipboard. More work for next time.'

They won't be able to catch me here, she thought fiercely as she scanned around, this time looking for somewhere suitable to pitch her tent and go to ground. *I'll be able to nail them and they won't even be able to find me to lay a finger on me!* But there was more to it than that, she finally admitted to herself as she hunted for a flat spot. The locket had belonged to her birth-mother, and receiving it had raised an unquiet ghost. Somebody had stabbed her, somebody who had never been found. Miriam wouldn't be able to lay that realization to rest again until she learned what this place had meant to her mother – and why it hadn't saved her.

With four hours to go before sunset, Miriam was acutely aware that she didn't have any time to waste. The temperature would dip toward frost at night and she planned to be well dug-in first. Planting her backpack at the foot of the big horse chestnut tree, she gathered armfuls of dry leaves and twigs and scattered them across it – nothing that would fool a real woodsman, but enough to render it inconspicuous at a distance. Then she walked back and forth through a hundred-yard radius, pacing out the forest, looking for its edge. That there was an edge came as no surprise: The steep escarpment was in the same place here as on the hiking map of her own world that she'd brought along. Where the ground fell away, there was a breathtaking view of autumnal forest marching down toward a valley floor. The ocean was probably eight to ten miles due east, out of sight beyond hills and dunes, but she had a sense of its presence all the same.

Looking southwest, she saw a thin coil of smoke rising – a settlement of some kind, but small. No roads or telegraph poles marred the valley, which seemed to contain nothing but trees and bushes and the odd clearing. She was alone in the woods, as alone as she'd ever been. She looked up. Thin cirrus clouds stained the blue sky, but there were no jet contrails.

'The area appears to be thinly populated,' she muttered into her dictaphone. 'They're burning something – coal or wood – at the nearest settlement. There are no telegraph poles, roads, or aircraft. The air doesn't smell of civilization. No noise to speak of, just birds and wind and trees.'

She went back to her clearing to orient herself, then headed on in the opposite direction, down the gentle slope away from her pack. 'Note: Keep an eye open for big wildlife. Bears and stuff.' She patted her right hip pocket nervously. Would the pistol do much more than annoy a bear? She hadn't expected the place to be quite this desolate. There were no bears, but she ran across a small stream – nearly fell into it, in fact.

There was no sign of an edge to the woods, in whichever direction she went. Nor were there signs of habitation other than the curl of smoke she'd seen. It was four o'clock now. She returned to her clearing, confident that nobody was around, and unstrapped her tent from the backpack. It took half an hour to get the dome tent erected, and another half-hour with the netting and leaves to turn it into something that could be mistaken for a shapeless deadfall. She spent another fifteen minutes returning to the stream to fill her ten-liter water carrier. Another half-hour went on digging a hole nearby, then she took ten minutes to run a rope over a bough and hoist her bag of food out of reach of the ground. As darkness fell, it found her lighting her portable gas stove to boil water for her supper. *I did it*, she thought triumphantly. *I didn't forget anything important!* Now all she had to do was make it through tomorrow and the morning of the next day without detection.

The night grew very cold without a fire, but her sleeping bag was almost oppressively hot with the tent zipped shut. Miriam slept lightly, starting awake at the slightest noise – worried at the possibility of bears or other big animals wandering through her makeshift camp, spooked by the sigh of wind and the patter of a light predawn rainfall. Once she dreamed of wolves howling in the distance. But dawn arrived without misadventure and dragged her bleary-eyed from the tent to squat over the trench she'd remembered to dig the day before. 'The Girl Scout training pays off at last,' she dictated with a sardonic drawl.

A tin of sausages and beans washed down with strong black coffee made a passable breakfast. 'Now what?' she asked herself. 'Do I wait it out with the camp or go exploring?'

For a moment, Miriam quailed. The enormity of the wilderness around her was beginning to grind on her nerves, as was the significance of the situation she'd thrown herself into. 'I could break a leg here and nobody would ever find me. Or – ' Gunfire in the night. 'Someone stabbed my mother, and she didn't come here to escape. There must be a reason why, mustn't there?'

Something about the isolation made her want to chatter, to fill up the oppressive silence. But the words that tumbled out didn't tell her much, except that she was – *Let's face it. I'm scared. This wasn't the sensible thing to do, was it? But I haven't been doing sensible properly since I got myself fired on Monday.*

Unzipping the day pack from her backpack, she filled it with necessities, then set out for the escarpment.

It was a clear, cold morning, and the wisp of smoke she'd seen yesterday had disappeared. But she knew roughly where she'd seen it, and a careful scan of the horizon with binoculars brought it into focus once more – a pause in the treeline, punctuated by nearly invisible roofs. At a guess, it was about three miles away. She glanced at the sky and chewed on her lower lip: *Doable,* she decided, still half-unsure that it was the right thing to do. *But I'll go out of my skull if I wait here two days, and Paulie won't be back until tomorrow.* Bearing and range went into her notepad and onto the map, and she blazed a row of slashes on every fifth tree along the ridgeline to help her on the way back. The scarp was too steep to risk on her own, but if she went along the crest of the ridge, she could take the easy route down into the valley.

Taking the easy route was not, as it happened, entirely safe. About half a mile farther on – half a mile of plodding through leaf mounds, carefully bypassing deadfalls, and keeping a cautious eye open – an unexpected sound made Miriam freeze, her heart in her mouth and ice in her veins. *Metal,* she thought. *That was a metallic noise! Who's there?* She dropped to a squat with her back against a tree as a horse or mule snorted nearby.

The sound of hooves was now audible, along with a creaking of leather and the occasional clatter or jingle of metalwork. Miriam crouched against the tree, very still, sweat freezing in the small of her back, trying not to breathe. She couldn't be sure, but it sounded like a single set of hooves. With her camouflage-patterned jacket, knitted black face mask, and a snub-nosed pistol clutched in her right hand, she was a sight to terrify innocent eyes – but she was frightened half out of her own wits.

She held perfectly still as a peculiarly dressed man led a mule past, not ten yards away from her. The animal was heavily over-loaded, bulging wicker baskets towering over its swaying back. Its owner wore leggings of some kind, but was swathed from head to knees in what looked like an ancient and moth-eaten blanket. He didn't look furtive; he just looked dirt-poor, his face lined and tanned from exposure to the weather.

The mule paused. Almost absently, its owner reached out and whacked it across the hindquarters with his rod. He grunted some-thing in what sounded like German, only softer, less sibilant.

Miriam watched, fear melting into fascination. That was a knife at his belt, under the blanket – a great big pigsticker of a knife, almost a short sword. The mule made an odd sort of complaining noise and began moving again. *What's in the baskets?* she wondered. *And where's he taking it?*

There were clearly people living in these woods. *Better be careful,* she told herself, taking deep breaths to calm down as she waited for him to pass out of sight. She pondered again whether or not she shouldn't go straight back to her campsite. In the end curiosity won out – but it was curiosity tempered by edgy caution.

An hour later, Miriam found a path wandering among the trees. It wasn't a paved road by any stretch of the imagination, but the shrub-bery to either side had been trampled down and the path itself was muddy and flat: Fresh road apples told her which way the man with the mule had gone. She slashed a marker on the tree where her path intersected the road, crudely scratching in a bearing and distance as digits. If her growing suspicion was true, these people wouldn't be able to make anything of it. She picked her way through the trees along one side of the path, keeping it just in sight. Within another half-mile the trees ended in a profusion of deadfalls and stumps, some of which sprouted amazing growths of honey fungus. Miriam picked her way farther away from the path, then hunkered down, brought out binoculars and dictaphone, and gave voice to her fascination.

'This is incredible! It's like a museum diorama of a medieval village in England, only – Eww, I sure wouldn't drink from that stream. The stockade is about two hundred yards away and they've cleared the woods all around it. There are low stone walls, with no cement, around the field. It's weird, all these rows running across it like a patchwork quilt made from pinstripe fabric.'

She paused, focusing her binoculars in on a couple of figures walking in the near distance. They were close enough to see her if they looked at the treeline, so she instinctively hunched lower, but they weren't paying attention to the forest. One of them was leading a cow – a swaybacked beast like something from a documentary about India. The buildings were grayish, the walls made of stacked bundles of something or other, and the roofs were thatched – not the picturesque golden color of the rural English tourist trap she'd once stayed in outside Oxford, but the real thing, gray and sagging. 'There are about twelve buildings; none of them have windows. The road is unpaved, a mud track. There are chickens or some kind of fowl there, pecking in the dirt. It looks sleazy and tumbledown.'

She tracked after the human figures, focused on the stockade. 'There's a gate in the stockade and a platform or tower behind it. There's something big in there, behind the wall, but I can't see it from here. A long house? No, this doesn't look . . . wrong period. These aren't Vikings, there's, uh – '

Around the curve of the stockade an ox came into view, dragging some kind of appliance – a wooden plow, perhaps. The man walking behind it looked as tired as the animal. 'They're all wearing those blankets. Women too. That was a woman feeding the chickens. With a headscarf wrapped around her face like a Muslim veil. But the men wear pretty much the same, too. This place looks so poor. Neglected. That guy with the mule – it must be the equivalent of a BMW in this place!'

Miriam felt distinctly uneasy. History book scenes were outside her experience – she was a creature of the city, raised with the bustle and noise of urban life, and the sordid poverty of the village made her feel unaccountably uneasy. But it left questions unanswered. 'This could be the past; we know the Vikings reached New England around the eleventh century. Or it could be somewhere else. How can I tell if I can't get in and see what's inside the stockade? I think I need an archaeologist.'

Miriam crouched down and began to snap off photographs. Here three hens pecked aimlessly at the dirt by an open doorway, the door itself a slab of wood leaning drunkenly against the wall of the hut. There a woman (or a man, the shapeless robe made it impossible to be sure) bent over a wooden trough, emptying a bucket of water into it and then lifting and pounding something from within. Miriam focused closer –

'Wer find thee?' Someone piped at her.

Miriam jolted around and stared: The someone stared right back, frozen, eyes wide. He looked to be about fourteen or fifteen years old, dressed in rags and barefoot: He was shorter than she was. Pipecleaner arms, legs like wire, big brown eyes, and a mess of badly trimmed hair in a pudding-bowl cut. Time slowed to a crawl. *That's a skin infection*, she realized, her guts turning to ice as she focused on a red weal on the side of his neck. He was skinny, not as thin as a famine victim but by no means well-fed. He had a stick, clenched nervously in his hands, which he was bringing up –

Miriam glared at him and straightened up. Her right hand went to her hip pocket, and she fumbled for the treacherous opening. 'You'll be sorry,' she snapped, surprised at herself. It was the first thing that entered her head. Her hand closed on the butt of the pistol, but she couldn't quite draw it – it was snagged on something.

She yanked at her pocket desperately, keeping her eyes on his face, despite knees that felt like jelly and a churning cold in her gut. She had a strong flashback to the one time she was mugged, a desperate sense of helplessness as she tried to disentangle the gun from her pocket lining and bring it out before the villager hit her with his stick.

But he didn't. Instead, his eyes widened. He opened his mouth and shouted, 'An solda'des Koen!' He turned, dropping the stick, and darted away before Miriam could react. A moment later she heard him wailing, 'An solda!'

'Shit.' The gun was in her hand, all but forgotten. Terror lent her feet wings. She clutched her camera and ran like hell, back toward the forest, heedless of any noise she might make. *He nearly had me! He'll be back with help! I've got to get out of here!* Breathless fear drove her until branches scratched at her face and she was panting. Then the low apple trees gave way to taller, older trees and a different quality of light. She staggered along, drunkenly, as behind her a weird hooting noise unlike any horn she'd heard before split the quiet.

Ten minutes later she stopped and listened, wheezing for breath as she tried to get her heart under control. She had run parallel to the path, off to one side. Every instinct was screaming at her to run but she was nearly winded, so she listened instead. Apart from the horn blasts, there were no sounds of pursuit. *Why aren't they following me?* She wondered, feeling ill with uncertainty. *What's wrong?* After a moment she remembered her camera: She'd lost the lens cap in her mad rush. 'Damn, I could have broken my ankle,' she muttered. 'They'd have caught me for – ' she stopped.

'That look in his eye.' Very carefully, she unslung the camera and slid it into a big outer hip pocket. She glanced around the clearing sharply, then spent a moment untangling the revolver from her other pocket. Now that she had all the time in the world, it was easy. 'He was scared,' she told herself, wondering. 'He was terrified of me! What was that he was shouting? Was he warning the others off?'

She began to walk again, wrapped in a thoughtful silence. There were no sounds of pursuit. Behind her the village hid in the gloom, like a terrified rabbit whose path had just crossed a fox on the prowl. 'Who are you hiding from?' she asked her memory of the boy with the stick. 'And who did you mistake me for?'

*

It was raining again, and the first thing she noticed once she crossed over – through the blinding headache – was that Paulette was bouncing up and down like an angry squirrel, chattering with indignation behind the camcorder's viewfinder. 'Idiot! What the hell do you think you were doing?' she demanded as Miriam opened the passenger door and dumped her pack on the backseat. 'I almost had a heart attack! That's the second time you've nearly given me one this week!'

'I said it would be a surprise, right?' Miriam collapsed into the passenger seat. 'God, I reek. Get me home and once I've had a shower I'll explain everything. I promise.'

Paulette drove in tight-lipped silence. Finally, during a moment when they were stationary at a traffic light, she said: 'Why me?'

Miriam considered for a moment. 'You don't know my mother.'

'That's – oh. I see, I think. Anything else?'

'Yeah. I trusted you to keep your mouth shut and not to panic.'

'Uh-huh. So what have you gotten yourself into this time?'

'I'm not sure. Could be the story of the century – the second one this week. Or it could be a very good reason indeed for burying something and walking away fast. I've got some ideas – more, since I spent a whole day and a half over there – but I'm still not sure.'

'Where's over there? I mean, where did you go?' The car moved forward.

'Good question. The straight answer is: I'm not sure – the geography is the same, the constellations are the same, but the landscape's different in places and there's an honest-to-god medieval village in a forest. And they don't speak English. Listen, after I've had my shower, how about I buy supper? I figure I owe you for dropping this on your lap.'

'You sure do,' Paulette said vehemently. 'After you vanished, I went home and watched the tape six times before I believed what I'd seen with my own two eyes.' Her hands were white on the steering wheel. 'Only you could fall into something this weird!'

'Remember Hunter S. Thompson's First Law of Gonzo Journalism: "When the going gets tough, the tough get weird"?' Miriam chuckled, but there was an edge to it. Everywhere she looked there were buildings and neon lights and traffic. 'God, I feel like I spent the weekend in the Third World. Kabul.' The car smelled of plastic and deodorant, and it was heavenly – the stink of civilization. 'Listen, I haven't had anything decent to eat for days. When we get home I'm ordering take out. How does Chinese sound?'

'I can cope with that.' Paulette made a lazy right turn and slid into the slow-moving stream of traffic. 'Don't feel like cooking?'

'I've got to have a shower,' said Miriam. 'Then I've got a weekend of stuff to put in the washing machine, several hundred pictures to download and index, memos to load into the computer, and an explanation. If you figure I can do all that and a pot roast too, then you don't know me as well as I think you do.'

'That,' Paulette remarked as she pulled over into the parking space next to Miriam's house, 'was a very mixed metaphor.'

'Don't listen to what I say; listen to what I mean, okay?'

'I get the picture. Dinner's on you.'

After half an hour in the bathroom, Miriam felt human, if not entirely dry. She stopped in her bedroom for long enough to find some clean clothes, then headed downstairs in her bare feet.

Paulette had parked herself in the living room with a couple of mugs of coffee and an elegant-looking handbag. She raised an eyebrow at Miriam: 'You look like you've been dry-cleaned. Was it that bad?'

'Yeah.' Miriam settled down on the sofa, then curled her legs up beneath her. She picked up one of the mugs and inhaled deeply. 'Ah, that's better.'

'Ready to tell me what the hell is going on?'

'In a moment.' Miriam closed her eyes, then gathered up the strands of still-damp hair sticking to her neck and wound them up, outside her collar. 'That's better. It happened right after they screwed us over, Paulie. I figured you'd think I'd gone off the deep end if I just told you about it, which is why I didn't call you back the same day. Why I asked you to drive. Sorry about the surprise.'

'You should be: I spent an hour in the woods looking for you. I nearly called the police twice, but you'd said precisely when you'd be back and I thought they'd think I was the one who was nuts. 'Sides, you've got a habit of dredging up weird shit and leaving me to pick up the pieces. Promise me there are no gangsters in this one?'

'I promise.' Miriam nodded. 'Well, what do you think?'

'I think I'd like some lemon chicken. Sorry.' Paulette grinned impishly at Miriam's frown. 'Okay, I believe you've discovered something very weird indeed. I actually videoed you vanishing into thin air in front of the camera! And when you appeared again – no, I didn't get it on tape, but I saw you out of the corner of my eye. Either we're both crazy or this is for real.'

'Madness doesn't come in this shape and size,' Miriam said soberly. She winced. 'I need a painkiller.' She rubbed her feet, which were cold. 'You know I'm adopted, right? My mother didn't quite tell me everything until Monday. I went to see her after we were fired . . .'

For the next hour Miriam filled Paulette in on the events of the past week, leaving out nothing except her phone call to Andy. Paulette listened closely and asked about the right questions. Miriam was satisfied that her friend didn't think she was mad, wasn't humoring her. 'Anyway, I've now got tape of my vanishing, a shitload of photographs of this village, and dictated notes. See? It's beginning to mount up.'

'Evidence,' said Paulette. 'That would be useful if you want to go public.' Suddenly she looked thoughtful. 'Big *if* there.'

'Hmm?' Miriam drank down what was left of her coffee.

'Well, this place you go to – it's either in the past or the future, or somewhere else, right? I think we can probably rule out the past or future options. If it was the past, you wouldn't have run across a village the way you described it; and as for the future, there'd still be some sign of Boston, wouldn't there?'

'Depends how far in the future you go.' Miriam frowned. 'Yeah, I guess you're right. It's funny; when I was a little girl I always figured the land of make-believe would be bright and colorful. Princesses in castles and princes to go around kissing them so they turned into frogs – and dragons to keep the royalty population under control. But in the middle ages there were about a thousand peasants living in sordid poverty for every lord of the manor, who actually had a sword, a horse, and a house with a separate bedroom to sleep in. A hundred peasants for every member of the nobility – the lords and their families – and the same for every member of the merchant or professional classes.'

'Sounds grimly real to me, babe. Forget Hollywood. Your map was accurate, wasn't it?'

'What are you getting at? You're thinking about . . . What was that show called: *Sliders*? Right?'

'Alternate earths. Like on TV.' Paulette nodded. 'I only watched a couple of episodes, but . . . well. Suppose you are going sideways, to some other earth where there's nobody but some medieval peasants. What if you, like, crossed over next door to a bank, walked into exactly where the vault would be in our world, waited for the headache to go away, then crossed back again?'

'I'd be inside the bank vault, wouldn't I? Oh.'

'That, as they say, is the sixty-four-thousand-dollar question,' Paulette commented dryly. 'Listen, this is going to be a long session. I figure you haven't thought all the angles through. What were you planning on doing with it?'

'I – I'm.' Miriam stopped. 'I told you about the phone call.'

Paulette looked at her bleakly. 'Yeah. Did I tell you – '

'You too?'

She nodded. 'The evening after I told them to go fuck themselves. Don't know who it was: I hung up on him and called the phone company, told them it was a nuisance call, but they couldn't tell me anything.'

'Bastards.'

'Yes. Listen. When I was growing up in Providence, there were these guys . . . it wasn't a rich neighborhood, but they always had sharp suits. Momma told me never to cross them – or, even talk to them. Trouble is, when they talk to you – I think I need a drink. What do you say?'

'I say there're a couple of bottles in the cabinet,' said Miriam, massaging her forehead. 'Don't mind if I join you.'

Coffee gave way to a couple of modest glasses of Southern Comfort. 'It's a mess,' said Paulette. 'You, uh – we didn't talk about Monday. Did we?'

'No,' Miriam admitted. 'If you want to just drop it and forget the whole business, I'm not going to twist your arm.' She swallowed. She felt acutely uneasy, as if the whole comfortable middle-class professional existence she'd carved out for herself was under threat. Like the months when she'd subliminally sensed her marriage decaying, never quite able to figure out exactly what was wrong until . . .

'"Drop it?"' Paulette's eyes flashed, a momentary spark of anger. 'Are you crazy? These hard men, they're really easy to understand. If you back down, they own you. It's simple as that. That's something I learned when I was a kid.'

'What happened – ' Miriam stopped.

Paulie tensed, then breathed out, a long sigh. 'My parents weren't rich,' she said quietly. 'Correction: They were poor as pigshit. Gramps was a Sicilian immigrant, and he hit the bottle. Dad stayed on the wagon but never figured out how to get out of debt. He held it together for Mom and us kids, but it wasn't easy. Took me seven years to get through college, and I wanted a law degree so bad I could taste it. Because lawyers make lots of money, that's numero uno. And for seconds, I'd be able to tell the guys Dad owed where to get off.'

Miriam leaned forward to top off her glass.

'My brother Joe didn't listen to what Momma told us,' Paulette said slowly. 'He got into gambling, maybe a bit of smack. It wasn't the drugs, but one time he tried to argue with the bankers. They held him down and used a cordless drill on both his kneecaps.'

'Uh.' Miriam felt a little sick. 'What happened?'

'I got as far as being a paralegal before I figured out there's no point getting into a job where you hate the guts of everybody you have to work with, so I switched track and got a research gig. No journalism degree, see, so I figured I'd work my way up. Oh, you meant to Joe? He OD'd on heroin. It wasn't an accident – it was the day after they told him he'd never walk again.' She said it with the callous disregard of long-dead news, but Miriam noticed her knuckles tighten on her glass. 'That's why I figure you don't want to ever let those guys notice you. But if they do, you don't ever back off.'

'That's – I'm really sorry. I had no idea.'

'Don't blame yourself.' Paulette managed an ironic smile. 'I, uh, took a liberty with the files before I printed them.' She reached inside her handbag and flipped a CD-ROM at Miriam.

'Hey, what's this?' Miriam peered at the greenish silver surface.

'It's the investigation. I got everything before you decided to jump Sandy's desk and get Joe to take an unhealthy interest in us.'

'But that's stealing!' Miriam ended on a squeak.

'And what do you call what they did to your job?' Paulette asked dryly. 'I call this insurance.'

'Oh.'

'Yes, oh. I don't think they know about it – otherwise we'd be in way deeper shit already. Still, you should find somewhere to hide it until we need it.'

Miriam looked at the disk as if it had turned into a snake. 'Yeah, I can do that.' She drained her glass, then picked up the disk and carried it over to the stereo. 'Gotcha.' She pulled a multidisk CD case from the shelf, opened it, and slid the extra disk inside. '*The Beggar's Opera*. Think you can remember that?'

'Oh! Why didn't I think of doing that?'

'Because. Why didn't I think of burning that disk in the first place?'

'We each need a spare brain.' Paulette stared at her. 'Listen, that's problem number one. What about problem number two? This crazy shit from another world. What were you messing around with it for?'

Miriam shrugged. 'I had some idea that I could hide from the money laundry over there,' she said slowly. 'Also, to tell the truth, I wanted someone else to tell me I wasn't going crazy. But going totally medieval isn't going to answer my problem, is it?'

'I wouldn't say so.' Paulette put her glass down, half-empty. 'Where were we? Oh yeah. You cross over to the other side, wherever that is, and you wander over to where your bank's basement is, then you cross back again. What do you think happens?'

'I come out in a bank vault.' Miriam pondered. 'They're wired inside, aren't they? After my first trip I was a total casualty, babe. I mean, projectile vomiting – ' she paused, embarrassed. 'A fine bank robber I'd make!'

'There is that,' said Paulette. 'But you're not thinking it through. What happens when the alarm goes off?'

'Well. Either I go back out again too fast and risk an aneurism or . . .' Miriam trailed off. 'The cops show and arrest me.'

'And what happens after they arrest you?'

'Well, assuming they don't shoot first and ask questions later, they cuff me, read me my rights, and haul me off to the station. Then book me in and stick me in a cell.'

'And then?' Paulette rolled her eyes at Miriam's slow uptake.

'Why, I call my lawyer – ' Miriam stopped, eyes unfocused. 'No, they'd take my locket,' she said slowly.

'Sure. Now, tell me. Is it your locket or is it the pattern in your locket? Have you tested it? If it's the design, what if you've had it tattooed on the back of your arm in the meantime?' Paulette asked.

'That's – ' Miriam shook her head. 'Tell me there's a flaw in the logic.'

'I'm not going to do that.' Paulette picked up the bottle and waved it over Miriam's glass in alcoholic benediction. 'I think you're going to have to test it tomorrow to find out. And I'm going to have to test it, to see if it works for me – if that's okay by you,' she added hastily. 'If it's the design, you just got your very own "Get Out of Jail Free" card. Doesn't matter if you can't use it to rob bank vaults, there's any number of other scams you can run if you can get out of the fix instantaneously. Say, uh, you walk into a bank and pull a holdup. No need for a gun, just pass over a note saying you've got a bomb and they should give you all the money. Then, instead of running away, you head for the staff rest room and just vanish into thin air.'

'You have got a larcenous mind, Paulie.' Miriam shook her head in awe. 'You're wasted in publishing.'

'No, I'm not.' Paulette frowned seriously. 'Y'see, you haven't thought this through. S'pose you've got this super power. Suppose nobody else can use it – we can try me out tomorrow, huh? Do the experiment with the photocopy of the locket on you, then try me. See if I can do it. I figure it's going to be you, and not me, because if just anybody could do it it would be common knowledge, huh? Or your mother would have done it. For some reason somebody stabbed your mother and she didn't do it. So there must be some kind of gotcha. But anyway. What do you think the cops would make of it if instead of robbing banks or photographing peasant villagers you, uh, donated your powers to the forces of law and order?'

'Law and order consists of bureaucracies,' Miriam said with a brisk shake of her head. 'You've seen all those tedious FBI press conferences I sat in on when they were lobbying for crypto export controls, huh?' A vision unfolded behind her eyes, the poisonous fire blossom of an airliner striking an undefended skyscraper. 'Jesus, Paulie, imagine if al Qaeda could do this!'

'They don't need it: They've got suicide volunteers. But yeah, there are other bad guys who . . . if you can see it, so can the feds. Remember that feature about nuclear terrorism that Zeb ran last year? How the NIRT units and FEMA were able to track bombs as they come in across the border if there's an alert on?'

'I don't want to go there.' The thought made Miriam feel physically ill. 'There is no way in hell I'd smuggle a nuclear weapon across the border.'

'No.' Paulette leaned forward, her eyes serious: 'But if you have this ability, who else might have it? And what could they do with it? There are some very scary, dangerous national security implications here, and if you go public the feds will bury you so deep – '

'I said I don't want to go there,' Miriam repeated. 'Listen, this is getting deeply unfunny. You're frightening me, Paulie, more than those assholes with their phone calls and their handle on the pharmaceutical industry. I'm wondering if maybe I should sleep with a gun under my pillow.'

'Get frightened fast, babe; it's your ass we're talking about. I've had two days to think about your vanishing trick and our wiseguy problem, and I tell you, you're still thinking like an honest journalist, not a paranoid. Listen, if you want to clean up, how about the crack trade? Or heroin? Go down to Florida, get the right connections, you could bring a small dinghy over and stash it on the other side, no problems – it'd just take you a while, a few trips maybe. Then you could carry fifty, a hundred kilos of coke. Sail it up the coast, then up the Charles. Bring it back over right in the middle of Cambridge, out of nowhere without the DEA or the cops noticing. They say one in four big shipments gets intercepted – that's bullshit – but maybe one in five, one in eight . . . you could smuggle the stuff right under their noses in the middle of a terrorist scare. And I don't know whether you'd do that or not – my guess is not, you've got capital-P principles – but that is the first thing the cops will think of.'

'Hell.' Miriam stared into the bottom of her glass, privately aghast. 'What do you suggest?'

Paulette put her own glass down. 'Speaking as your legal adviser, I advise you to buy guns and move fast. Mail the disk to another newspaper and the local FBI office, then go on a long cruise while the storm breaks. That – and take a hammer to the locket and smash it up past recognition.'

Miriam shook her head, then winced. 'Oh, my aching head. I demand a second opinion. Where is my recount, dammit?'

'Well.' Paulette paused. 'You've made a good start on the documentation. We can see if it's just you, run the experiments, right? I figure the clincher is if you can carry a second person through. If you can do that, then not only do you have documents, you've got witnesses. If you go public, you want to do so with a splash – so widespread that they can't put the arm on you. They've got secret courts and tame judges to try national security cases, but if the evidence is out in the open they can't shut you up, especially if it's international. I'd say Canada would be best.' She paused again, a bleak look in her eye. 'Yeah, that might work.'

'You missed something.' Miriam stabbed a finger in Paulette's direction. 'You. What do you get?'

'Me?' Paulette covered her heart with one hand, pulled a disbelieving face. 'Since when did I get a vote?'

'Since, hell, since I got you into this mess. I figure I owe you. Noblesse oblige. You're a friend, and I don't drop friends in it, even by omission.'

'Friendship and fifty cents will buy you a coffee.' Paulie paused for a moment, then grinned. 'But I'm glad, all the same.' Her smile faded. 'I didn't get the law job.'

'I'm sorry.'

'Will you stop doing that? Every chance you get to beat yourself up for getting me fired, you're down on your knees asking for forgiveness!'

'Oh, sorry. I didn't realize it was getting on your nerves,' Miriam said contritely.

'Fuck off!' Paulette giggled. 'Pardon my French. Anyway. Think about what I said. Tomorrow you can mail that disk to the FBI if you want, then go on a long vacation. Or stick around and we'll work on writing a story that'll get you the Pulitzer. You can catch all the bullets from the hitmen while I'll be your loyal little gofer, get myself a star-spangled reference and a few points of the gross. Like, fifty percent. Deal?'

'Deal. I think my head hurts.' Miriam shuffled around and stood up. She felt a little shaky: Maybe it was the alcohol hitting her head on an empty stomach. 'Where's that takeout?'

Paulette looked blank. 'You ordered it?'

'No.' Miriam snapped her fingers in frustration. 'I'll go do that right now. I think we have some forward planning to do.' She paused unevenly in the doorway, looking at Paulette.

'What?'

'Are you in?' she asked.

'Am I in? Are you nuts? I wouldn't miss this for anything!'

PART TWO

MEET THE FAMILY

HOTEL MAFIOSI

They came for her in the early hours, long after Paulette had called a taxi and Miriam had slunk into bed with a stomach full of lemon chicken and a head full of schemes. They came with stealth, black vans, and H&K MP5s: They didn't know or care about her plans. They were soldiers. They had their orders; this was the house the damp brown chair was collocated with, and so this was the target. That was all they needed.

Miriam slept through the breaking of the French window in her den because the two men on entry detail crowbarred the screens open, then rolled transparent sticky polyurethane film across the glass before they struck it with rubber mallets, then peeled the starred sheets right out of the frame. The phone line had been cut minutes before; there was a cell-phone jammer in the back garden.

The two break-and-enter men took point, rolling into the den and taking up positions at either side of the room. The light shed by the LEDs on her stereo and computer glinted dimly off their night-vision goggles and the optics of their guns as they waited tensely, listening for any sign of activity.

Hand signals relayed the news from outside, that Control hadn't seen any signs of motion through the bedroom curtains. His short-wavelength radar imager let him see what the snatch crew's night-vision gear missed: It could pinpoint the telltale pulse of warm blood right through a dry wall siding. Two more soldiers in goggles, helmets, and flak jackets darted through the opening and into the hall, cautiously extending small mirrors on telescoping arms past open doorways to see if anyone was inside. Within thirty seconds they had the entire ground floor swept clean. Now they moved the thermal imager inside: Control swept each ceiling carefully before pausing in the living room and circling his index finger under the light fitting for the others to see. One body, sleeping, right overhead.

Four figures in black body armor ghosted up the staircase, two with guns, and two behind them with specialist equipment. The master bedroom opened off the small landing at the top of the stairs – the plan was to charge straight through and neutralize the occupant directly.

However, they hadn't counted on Miriam's domestic untidiness. Living alone and working a sixty-hour week, she had precious little time for homemaking: All her neat-freakery got left behind at work each evening. The landing was crowded, an overflowing basket of dirty clothing waiting for a trip down to the basement beside a couple of bookcases that narrowed the upstairs hall so that they had to go in single-file. But there were worse obstacles to come. Miriam's house was full of books. Right now, a dog-eared copy of *The Cluetrain Manifesto* lay facedown at one side of the step immediately below the landing. It was precisely as cold as the carpet it lay on, so to the night-vision goggles it was almost invisible. The first three intruders stepped over it without noticing, but the fourth placed his right boot on it, and the effect was as dramatic as if it had been a banana skin.

Miriam jolted awake in terror, hearing a horrible clattering noise on the landing. Her mind was a blank, the word *intruder* running through it in neon letters the size of headlines – she sat bolt upright and fumbled on the dressing table for the pistol, which she'd placed there when she found she could feel it through the pillow. The noise of the bedroom door being shoved open was infinitely frightening and as she brought the gun around, trying to get it untangled from the pillowcase –

Brilliant light lanced through her eyelids, a flashlight: 'Drop it, lady!'

Miriam fumbled her finger into the trigger guard –

'Drop it!' The light came closer, right in her face. 'Now!'

Something like a freight locomotive came out of the darkness and slammed into the side of her right arm.

Someone said 'Shee-it' with heartfelt feeling, and a huge weight landed on her belly. Miriam gathered breath to scream, but she couldn't feel her right arm and something was pressing on her face. She was choking: The air was acrid and sweet-smelling and thick, a cloying flowery laboratory stink. She kicked out hard, legs tangled in the comforter, gasping and screaming deep in her throat, but they were muffling her with the stench and everything was fuzzy at the edges.

She couldn't move. 'Not funny,' someone a long way away at the end of a black tunnel tried to say. The lights were on now, but everything was dark. Figures moved around her and her arm hurt – distantly. She couldn't move. *Tired.* There was something in her mouth. *Is this an ambulance?* she wondered. *Lights out.*

The dogpile on the bed slowly shifted, standing up. Specialist A worked on the subject with tongue depressor and tubes, readying her for assisted ventilation.

The chloroform pad sitting on the pillow was an acrid nuisance: For the journey ahead, something safer and more reliable was necessary. Specialist B worked on her at the same time, sliding the collapsible gurney under her and strapping her to it at legs, hips, wrists, and shoulders.

'That was a fucking mess,' snarled Control, picking up the little snub-nosed revolver in one black-gloved hand. 'Double action: she could have shot someone. Who screwed up on the landing?'

'Sir.' It was Point B. 'There was a book. On the stairs.'

'Bitchin'. Okay, get little Miss Lethal here loaded and ready to move. Bravo, start the cleanup. I want her personal files, wherever she keeps them. And her computer, and all the disks. Whoever the hell was with her this evening, I want to know who they are too. And everything else. Charlie, pack her bags like she's going on vacation – a long vacation. Clothing, bathroom stuff. Don't make a mess of it. I want to be ready to evacuate in twenty minutes.'

'Sir. Yes, sir.' Control nodded. Point B was going to pull a shitwork detail when they got home, but you didn't discipline people in the field unless they'd fucked up bad enough to pull a nine-millimeter discharge. And Point B hadn't. A month cleaning the latrines would give him time to think on how close he'd come to getting plugged by a sleepy woman with a thirty-eight revolver.

Spec A was nearly done; he and Spec B grunted as they lifted the coffin-shaped framework off the bed. Miriam was unconscious and trussed like a turkey inside it. 'Is she going to be okay?' Control asked idly.

'I think so,' said Spec A. 'Bad bruising on her right arm, and probably concussed, but I don't expect anything major. Worst risk is she pukes in her sleep and aspirates her own vomit, and we can deal with that.' He spoke confidently. He'd done paramedic training and Van Two was equipped like an ambulance.

'Then take her away. We'll be along in half an hour when we're through sanitizing.'

'Yes, my lord. We'll get her home.'

Control looked at the dressing table, strewn with underwear, month-old magazines, and half-used toiletries. His expression turned to disgust at the thought of searching through piles of dirty clothing. 'Sky Father, what a mess.'

*

There was an office not far from Miriam's cell. The office was quiet, and its dark oak paneling and rich Persian carpets gave it something of the ambiance of a very exclusive Victorian gentlemen's club. A wide walnut desk occupied the floor next to the window bay. The top of the desk was inlaid with a Moroccan leather blotter, upon which lay a banker's box full of papers and other evidence.

The occupant of the office sat at the desk, reading the mess of photocopies and memos from the file box. He was in his early fifties, thickset with the stomach of middle age, but tall enough to carry it well. His suit was conservative: He might have been a retired general or a corporate chairman. Neither guess would be wrong, but neither would be the full truth, either. Right now he looked as if he had a headache; his expression was sour as he read a yellowing newspaper clipping. 'What a mess,' he murmured. 'What a blessed mess . . .'

A buzzer sounded above the left-hand door.

The officeholder glanced at the door with wintry gray eyes. 'Enter,' he called sharply. Then he looked back at the papers.

Footsteps, the sound of male dress shoes – leather-soled – on parquet, were abruptly silenced as the visitor reached the carpeted inner sanctum.

'You summoned me, uncle? Is there any movement on my proposal? If anyone wants me to – '

Angbard Lofstrom looked up again and fixed his nephew with a long icy stare. His nephew shuffled, discomfited: a tall, blond fellow whose suit would not have been out of place in an advertising agency's offices. 'Patience,' he said in English.

'But I – '

'I said patience.' Angbard laid the newspaper clipping flat on his blotter and stared at his nephew. 'This is not the time to discuss your proposal. About which there is no news, by the way. Don't expect anything to happen soon; you need to learn timing if you want to make progress, and the changes you are suggesting we make are politically difficult.'

'How much longer?' The young man sounded tense.

'As long as I deem necessary.' Angbard's stare hardened. 'Remember why you are here.'

'I – yes, my lord. If it pleases you to accept my apologies . . .'

'How is the prisoner?' Angbard asked abruptly.

'Oh. Last time I checked – fifteen minutes ago – she was unconscious but sleeping normally. She is in one of the doppelgänger cells. I removed the mnemonic she was wearing on her person and had one of the maids search her for tattoos. Her cell has no mirror, no shaving apparatus. I left instructions that I am to be called when she awakens.'

'Hmm.' Angbard chewed on his upper lip with an expression of deep disapproval.

'What does the doctor say?'

'The doctor says that he might have to splint her arm, later – there is bruising – but she sustained no serious harm in the course of the pickup.'

'Well.' Angbard waved one hand in the direction of the chairs positioned before his desk. 'Sit down.' His nephew sat with alacrity, his back stiff. 'Do we have any known loose ends, Earl Roland?'

'Yes, sir, but nothing critical. We have retrieved the documents, camera, recorder, personal computer, and all the other effects that we could find. Her house was untidy, but we are fairly sure we were able to locate everything – her office was well-organized. The windows have been repaired, and the neighbors informed indirectly that she is on assignment away from home. She is unmarried and has few attachments.' Roland looked faintly disapproving. 'There is reference to an elderly mother who lives alone. The only possible problem is referred to in the contractor's report. Evidently on her last excursion a woman, identity unknown, arrived, collected her car, then her person, and drove her home. Presumably a friend. The problem is that she left the stakeout by taxi without any notice – I assume she summoned it by means of a portable telephone – and our contractor team was too short-staffed to dispatch a tail. I have therefore instructed them to continue surveillance and reinstate the line tap, in the hope that the friend reappears. Once she does so – '

Roland shrugged.

'See that you do – I want them in custody as soon as possible.' Angbard harrumphed. 'As to the prisoner's disposition . . .' He paused, head cocked slightly to one side.

'Sir?' Roland was a picture of polite attentiveness.

'The prisoner is to be treated with all the courtesy due to one of your own station, indeed, as a senior Clan member, I say. As a respected guest, detained for her own protection.'

'Sir!' Roland couldn't contain his shock.

Angbard stared at him. 'You have something to say, my earl?' he asked coldly.

Roland swallowed. 'I hear and . . . and will of course obey,' he said. 'Just, please permit me to say, this is a surprise – '

'Your surprise is noted,' Angbard stated coldly. 'Nevertheless, I will keep my reasons to myself for the time being. All you need to know at present is that the prisoner must be treated with kidskin gloves.' He stared at the young officer intently, but he showed no sign of defiance: and after a moment Angbard relented slightly. 'This – ' he gestured at the box before him – 'raises some most disturbing possibilities.' He tapped one finger on the topmost sheet. 'Or had you noticed any strangers out with the Clan who are gifted with the family talent?'

'Mm, no, sir, I had not.' Roland looked suddenly thoughtful. 'What are you thinking?'

'Later. Just see she's transferred to a comfortable – but securely doppelgängered – suite. Be polite and hospitable, win her trust, and treat her person with the utmost respect. And notify me when she is ready to answer my questions.'

'I hear and obey,' Roland acknowledged, less puzzled, but clearly thoughtful.

'See that you do,' Angbard rumbled. 'You are dismissed.'

His nephew rose, straightened his suit jacket, and strode toward the door, a rapier banging at his side. Angbard stared at the door in silence for a minute after he had gone, then turned his eye back to the items in the file box. Which included a locket that he had seen before – almost a third of a century ago.

'Patricia,' he whispered under his breath, 'what has become of you?'

*

Daylight. That was the first thing that Miriam noticed. That – and she had the mother of all hangovers. Her head felt as if it was wrapped in cotton wool, her right arm hurt like hell, and everything around her was somehow wrong. She blinked experimentally. Her head *was* wrapped in cotton wool – or bandages. And she was wearing something unfamiliar. She'd gone to bed in her usual T-shirt, but now she was wearing a nightgown – but she didn't own one! *What's going on?*

Daylight. She felt muzzy and stupid and her head was pounding. She was thirsty, too. She rolled over and blinked at where the nightstand should have been. There was a whitewashed wall six inches from her nose. The bed she was lying in was jammed up against a rough cinder-block wall that had been painted white. It was as weird as that confused nightmare about the light and the chemical stink –

Nightmare?

She rolled the other way, her legs tangling up in the nightgown. She nearly fell out of the bed, which was far too narrow. It wasn't her own bed, and for a moment of panic she wondered what could possibly have happened. Then it all clicked into place. 'Gangsters or feds? Must be the feds,' she mumbled to herself. *They must have followed me. Or Paulie. Or something.*

A vast, hollow terror seemed to have replaced her stomach. *They'll bury you so deep,* she remembered. *So deep that –*

Her throat felt sore, as if she'd spent the entire night screaming. Odd, that.

Maybe it was anticipation.

Somehow she swung her legs over the side of the strange bed. They touched the floor much too soon, and she sat up, pushing the thin comforter aside. The far wall was too close, and the window was set high up; in fact, the whole room was about the size of a closet. There was no other furniture except for a small stainless-steel sink bolted to the wall opposite the door. The door itself was a featureless slab of wood with a peephole implanted in it at eye level. She noted with a dull sense of recognition that the door was perfectly smooth, with no handle or lock mechanism to mar its surface: It was probably wood veneer over metal.

Her hand went to her throat. The locket was gone.

Miriam stood, then abruptly found that she had to lean against the wall to keep upright. Her head throbbed and her right arm was extremely sore. She turned and looked up at the window, but it was above the top of her head, even if she had the energy to stand on the bed. High and small and without curtains, it looked horribly like the skylight of a jail cell. *Am I in jail?* she wondered.

With that thought, Miriam lost what calm she had. She leaned against the door and pounded it with her left hand, setting up a hollow racket, but stopped when her hand began to throb and the fear swept back in a suffocating wave, driving a storm surge of rage before it. She sat down and buried her face in her hands and began to sob quietly. She was still in this position a few minutes later when the door frame gave a quiet click and opened outward.

Miriam looked up suddenly as the door opened. 'Who are you?' she demanded.

The man standing in the doorway was perfectly turned out, from his black loafers to the ends of his artfully styled blond hair: He was young (late twenties or early thirties), formally dressed in a fashionable suit, clean-shaven, and his face was set in neutral lines. He could have been a Mormon missionary or an FBI agent. 'Miss Beckstein, if you'd be so good as to come with me, please?'

'Who are you?' She repeated. 'Aren't you guys supposed to read me my rights or something?' There was something odd about him, but she couldn't quite get her head around it.

Past his shoulder she could see a corridor, blurry right now – then she realized what it was that she was having trouble with. *He's wearing a sword,* she told herself, hardly believing her eyes.

'You seem to be laboring under a misapprehension.' He smiled, not unpleasantly.

'We don't have to read you your rights. However, if you'll come with me, we can go somewhere more comfortable to discuss the situation. Unless you're entirely happy with the sanitary facilities here?'

Miriam glanced behind her, suddenly acutely aware that her bladder was full and her stomach was queasy. 'Who are you?' she asked uncertainly.

'If you come with me, you'll get your answers,' he said soothingly. He took a step back and something made Miriam suspect there was an implicit *or else* left dangling at the end of his last sentence. She lurched to her feet unsteadily and he reached out for her elbow. She shuffled backward instinctively to avoid contact, but lost her balance against the edge of the bed: She sat down hard and went over backward, cracking her head against the wall.

'Oh dear,' he said. She stared up at him through a haze of pain. 'I'll bring a wheelchair for you. Please don't try to move.'

The ceiling pancaked lazily above her head. Miriam felt sick and a little bit drowsy. Her head was splitting. *Migraine or anesthesia hangover?* she wondered.

The well-dressed man with the sword sticking incongruously out from under his suit coat was back, with a wheelchair and another man wearing a green medical smock. Together they picked her up and planted her in the chair, loose as a sack of potatoes. 'Oww,' she moaned softly.

'That was a nasty bash,' said her visitor. He walked beside the chair. Lighting strips rolled by overhead, closed doorways to either side. 'How do you feel?'

'Lousy,' she managed. Her right arm had come out in sympathy with her skull. 'Who're you?'

'You don't give up, do you?' he observed. The chair turned a corner: More corridor stretched ahead. 'I'm Roland, Earl Lofstrom. Your welfare is my responsibility for now.' The chair stopped in front of burnished stainless-steel panels – an elevator. Mechanisms grumbled behind the door. 'You shouldn't have awakened in that isolation cell. You were only there due to an administrative error. The individual responsible has been disciplined.'

A cold chill washed down Miriam's spine, cutting through the haze of pain.

'Don't want your name,' she muttered. 'Want to know who you people *are*. My rights, dammit.'

The elevator doors opened and the attendant pushed her inside. Roland stepped in beside her, then waved the attendant away. Then he pushed a button out of sight behind her head. The doors closed and the elevator began to rise, but stopped only a few seconds later. 'You appear to be under a misapprehension,' he repeated. 'You're asking for your rights. The, uh, Miranda declaration, yes?'

She tried to look up at him. 'Huh?'

'That doesn't apply here. Different jurisdiction, you know.' His accompanying smile left Miriam deeply unnerved.

The elevator doors opened and he wheeled her into a silent, carpeted corridor with no windows – just widely spaced doors to either side, like an expensive hotel. He stopped at the third door along on the left and pushed it open, then turned her chair and rolled it forward into the room within. 'There. Isn't this an improvement over the other room?'

Miriam pushed down on the wheelchair arms with both hands, wincing at a stab of pain in her right forearm. 'Damn.' She looked around. 'This isn't federal.'

'If you don't mind.' He took her elbow, and this time she couldn't dodge. His grip was firm but not painful. 'This is the main reception room of your suite. You'll note the windows don't actually open, and they're made of toughened glass for your safety. The bathroom is through that door, and the bedroom is over there.' He pointed. 'If you want anything, lift the white courtesy phone. If you need a doctor, there is one on call. I suggest you take an hour to recover, then freshen up and get dressed. There will be an interview in due course.'

'What is this place? Who are you people?'

Finally Roland frowned at her. 'You can stop pretending you don't know,' he said. 'You aren't going to convince anyone.' Pausing in the doorway, he added, 'The war's over, you know. We won twenty years ago.' The door closed behind him with a solid-sounding click, and Miriam was unsurprised to discover that the door handle flopped limply in her hand when she tried it. She was locked in.

*

Miriam shuffled into the white-tiled bathroom, blinked in the lights, then sat down heavily on the toilet. 'Wow,' she mumbled in disbelief. It was like an expensive hotel – a fiendishly expensive one, aimed at sheikhs and diplomats and billionaires. The floor was smooth, a very high grade of Italian marble if she was any judge of stonework. The sink was a molded slab of thick green glass and the taps glowed with a deep luster that went deeper than mere gilding could reach. The bath was a huge scalloped shell sunk into the floor, white and polished, with blue and green lights set into it amid the chromed water jets. An acre of fluffy white towels and a matching bathrobe awaited her, hanging above a basket of toiletries. She knew some of those brand names; she'd even tried their samplers when she was feeling extravagant. The shampoo alone was a hundred dollars a bottle.

This definitely isn't anything to do with the government, she realized. *I know people who'd pay good money to be locked up in here!*

She sat down on the edge of the bathtub, slid into one of the seats around its rim, and spent a couple of minutes puzzling out the control panel. Eventually she managed to coax half a dozen jets of aerated water into life. *This is a prison,* she kept reminding herself. Roland's words haunted her: 'Different jurisdiction, you know.' Where was she? They'd taken the locket. That implied that they knew about it – and about her. But there was absolutely no way to square this experience with what she'd seen in the forest: the pristine wilderness, the peasant village.

The bedroom was as over the top as the bathroom, dominated by a huge oak sleigh-bed in a traditional Scandinavian style, with masses of down comforters and pillows. Rather than fitted furniture there were a pair of huge oak wardrobes and a chest of drawers and other, smaller items – a dressing table with mirror, an armchair, something that looked like an old linen press. Every piece of furniture in the bedroom looked to be an antique. The combined effect was overwhelming, like being expected to sleep in an auction house's display room.

'Oh wow.' She looked around and spotted the windows, then walked over to them. A balcony outside blocked the view of whatever was immediately below. Beyond it she had a breathtaking view of a sweep of forested land dropping away toward a shallow valley with a rocky crag, standing proud and bald on the other side. It was as untainted by civilization as the site of her camping expedition. She turned away, disquieted. Something about this whole picture screamed *Wrong!* at her, but she couldn't quite put her finger on it.

The chest of drawers held an unpleasant surprise. She pulled the top drawer open, half-expecting it to be empty. Instead, it contained underwear. Her underwear. She recognized the holes in one or two socks that she hadn't gotten around to throwing away.

'Bastards.' She focused on the clothing, mind spinning furiously. *They're thorough, whoever they are.* She looked closer at the furniture. The writing desk appeared to be an original Georgian piece, or even older, a monstrously valuable antique. And the chairs, Louis XV or a good replica – disturbingly expensive. A hotel would be content with reproductions, she reasoned. The emphasis would be on utility and comfort, not authenticity. If there were originals anywhere, they'd be on display in the foyer. It reminded her of something that she'd seen somewhere, something that nagged at the back of her mind but stubbornly refused to come to the foreground.

She stood up and confirmed her suspicion that the wardrobes held her entire range of clothing. More words came back to haunt her: 'There will be an interview in due course.'

'I'm not in a cell,' she told herself, 'but I could be. They showed me that much. So they're playing head games. They want to play the stick-and-carrot game. That means I've got some kind of leverage, doesn't it?' *Find out what they want, then get out of here fast,* she decided.

Half an hour later she was ready. She'd chosen a blouse the color of fresh blood, her black interview suit, lip gloss to match, and heels. Miriam didn't normally hold with makeup, but this time she went the whole hog. She didn't normally hold with power dressing either, but something about Roland and this setup suggested that his people were much more obsessed with appearances than the dot-com entre-preneurs and Kendall Square startup monkeys she usually dealt with. Any edge she could get . . .

A bell chimed discreetly. She straightened up and turned to look at the door as it opened. *Here it comes,* she thought nervously.

It was Roland, who'd brought her up here from the cell. Now that she saw him in the daylight from the windows with a clear head, her confusion deepened. He looks like a secret service agent, she thought. Something about that indefinably military posture and the short hair suggested he'd been ordered into that suit in place of combat fatigues.

'Ah. You've found the facilities.' He nodded. 'How are you feeling?'

'Better,' she said. 'I see you ransacked my house.'

'You will find that everything has been accounted for,' he said, slightly defensively. 'Would you rather we'd given you a prison uni-form? No?' He sized her up with a glance. 'Well, there's someone I have to take you to see now.'

'Oh, goody.' It slipped out before she could clamp down on the sarcasm. 'The chief of secret police, I assume?'

His eyes widened slightly. 'Don't joke about it,' he muttered.

'Oh.' Miriam dry-swallowed. 'Right, well, we wouldn't want to keep him waiting, would we?'

'Absolutely not,' Roland said seriously. He held the door open, then paused for a moment. 'By the way, I really wouldn't want you to embarrass yourself trying to escape. This is a secure facility.'

'I see,' said Miriam, who didn't – but had made her mind up already that it would be a mistake to simply cut and run. These people had snatched her from her own bed. That suggested a fright-ening level of competence.

She approached the door warily, keeping as far away from Roland as she could.

'Which way?'

'Along the passage.'

He headed off at a brisk march and she followed him, heels sinking into the sound-deadening carpet. She had to hurry to keep up.

'Wait one moment, please.'

She found herself fetched up behind Roland's broad back, before a pair of double doors that were exquisitely paneled and polished. *Odd*, she wondered. *Where is everybody?* She glanced over her shoulder, and spotted a discreet video camera watching her back. They'd come around two corners, as if the corridor followed a rectangle: They'd passed a broad staircase leading down, and the elevator – there ought to be more people about, surely?

'Who am I – '

Roland turned around. 'Look, just wait,' he said. 'Security calls.' She noticed for the first time that he had the inside of his wrist pressed against an unobtrusive box in the wall.

'Security?'

'Biometrics, I think it's called,' he said. There was a click from the door and he opened it slowly. 'Matthias? Ish hafe gefauft des'usher des Angbard.'

Miriam blinked – she didn't recognize the language. It sounded a bit like German, but not enough to make anything out; and her high school German was rusty, anyway.

'Innen gekomm', denn.'

The door opened and Roland caught her right arm, tugged her into the room after him, and let the door close. She pulled her arm back and rubbed the sore spot as she glanced around.

'Nice place you've got here,' she said. Thick draped curtains surrounded the window. The walls were paneled richly in dark wood: The main piece of furniture was a desk beside an inner office door. A broad-shouldered man in a black suit, white shirt, and red tie waited behind the desk. The only thing to distinguish the scene from a high-class legal practice was the submachine gun resting by his right hand.

'Spresh'she de Hoh'sprashe?'

'No,' said Roland. 'Use English, please.'

'Okay,' said the man with the gun. He looked at Miriam, and she had the disquieting sense that he was photographing her, storing her face in his memory.

He had frizzy black hair, swept back from high temples, combined with a nose like a hatchet and a glare like a caged hawk. 'I am Matthias. I am the Boss's secretary, which is, his keeper of secrets. That is his office door. You go in there without permission over my dead body. This is not an, um, how would you say it?' He glanced at Roland.

'Metaphor,' Roland offered.

'Metaphor.' Matthias looked at her again. He wasn't smiling. 'The Boss is expecting you. You may enter now.'

Miriam looked sidelong at him as Roland marched over to the door and opened it, then waved her forward. Matthias kept his eyes on her – and one hand close to the gun. She found herself involuntarily giving him a wide berth, as she would a rattlesnake. Not that he looked particularly venomous – a polite, clean-shaven man in a pinstriped suit – but there was something about his manner . . . she'd seen it before, in a young DEA agent she had dated for a couple of months before learning better. Mike Fleming had been quietly, calmly, crazy, in a way that made her cut and run before she got dragged too far in with him. He'd been quite prepared to give his life for the cause he believed in – or to make any other sacrifice for that matter: He was utterly unable to see the walls of the box he'd locked himself in. The kind of guy who'd arrest a cripple with multiple sclerosis for smoking a joint to deaden the pain. She suppressed a shudder as she entered the inner office.

The inner office was as excessive as the suite they'd given her, the Mafia special with the locked door and the auction house's ransom in antiques. The floor was tiled in hand-polished hardwood, partially covered by a carpet that was probably worth as much as her house. The walls were paneled in wood blackened with age. There were a couple of discreet oil paintings of big red-faced men in medieval-looking armor or classical robes posed before a castle, and a pair of swords rested on pegs in the wall above the desk. There was a huge walnut desk positioned beside the window bay and two chairs were drawn up before it, positioned so that the owner of the office would be all but invisible from the window.

Roland stopped before the desk, drew himself up to attention, and saluted. 'My lord, I have the pleasure of presenting to you . . . Miriam Beckstein.'

The presence in the chair inclined his head in acknowledgment. 'That is not her real name, but her presence is sufficient. You may be at ease.' Miriam squinted, trying to make out his features against the glare. He must have taken her expression for hostility, for he waved a hand: 'Please be seated, the both of you. I have no argument with you, ah, Miriam, if that is the name you wish to be known by.'

Roland surprised her by pulling a chair out and offering it to her. She startled herself in turn by sitting down, albeit nervously, knees clenched together and back stiffly erect 'Who are you people?' she whispered.

Her eyes were becoming accustomed to the light: She could see the man in the high-backed chair smile faintly. He was in late middle age, possibly as old as Morris Beckstein would have been, had he lived. His suit was sober – these people dressed like a company of undertakers – but so well cut that it had to be hand-tailored. His hair was graying, and his face was undistinguished, except for a long scar running up his left cheek.

'I might ask the same question,' he murmured. 'Roland, be seated, I say!' His tone of voice said he was used to being obeyed. 'I am the High Duke Angbard of House Lofstrom, third of that name, trustee of the crown of guilds, defender of the king's honor, freeman of the city of Niejwein, head of security of the Clan Reunified, prince of merchant-princes, owner of this demesne, and holder of many more titles than that – but those are the principal ones.' His eyes were the color of lead, a blue so pale she found them hard to see, even when they were focused directly on her. 'Also, if I am not very much mistaken, I am your uncle.'

Miriam recoiled in shock. 'What?' Another voice echoed her. She glanced sideways to see Roland staring at her in astonishment. His cool exterior began to crack.

'My father would never – ' Roland began.

'Shut up,' said Angbard, cold steel in his voice. 'I was not referring to your father, young man, but to your aunt once removed: Patricia.'

'Would you mind explaining just what you're talking about?' Miriam demanded, anger finally getting the better of her. She leaned forward. 'Your people have abducted me, ransacked my house, and kidnapped me, just because you think I'm some kind of long-lost relative?'

Angbard nodded thoughtfully. 'No. We are *absolutely certain* you're a long-lost relative.' He glanced at his nephew. 'There is solid evidence.'

Roland leaned back in his chair, whistled tunelessly, all military pretense fled. He stared at her out of wide eyes, as if he was seeing a ghost.

'What have you got to whistle about?' she demanded.

'You asked for an explanation,' Angbard reminded her. 'The arrival of an unknown world-walker is always grounds for concern. Since the civil war . . . suffice to say, your appearance would have been treated drastically in those days. When you stumbled across the old coast trail a week ago, and the patrol shot at you, they had no way of knowing who you were. That became evident only later – I believe you left a pair of pink house-shoes behind? – and triggered an extensive manhunt. However, you are clearly not connected to a traitorous faction, and closer research revealed some interesting facts about you. I believe you were adopted?'

'That's right.' Miriam's heart was fluttering in her ribs, shock and unpleasant realization merging. 'Are you saying you're my long-lost relatives?'

'Yes.' Angbard waited a moment, then slid open one of the drawers in his desk. 'This is yours, I believe.'

Miriam reached out and picked up the locket. Tarnished with age, slightly battered – an island of familiarity. 'Yes.'

'But not this.' Angbard palmed something else, then pushed it across the desk toward her.

'Oh my.' Miriam was lost for words. It was the identical twin to her locket, only brightly shining and lacking some scratches. She took it and sprang the catch –

'Ouch!' She glared at Roland, who had knocked it out of her hand. But he was bending down, and after a moment she realized that he was picking it up, very carefully, keeping the open halves facedown until it was upon the duke's blotter.

'We will have to teach you how to handle these things safely,' Angbard said mildly. 'In the meantime, my sister's is yours to keep.'

'Your sister's,' she echoed stupidly, wrapping her fingers around the locket.

'My sister went missing thirty-two years ago,' Angbard said with careful lack of emphasis. 'Her caravan was attacked, her husband slain, and her guard massacred, but her body was never found. Nor was that of her six-week-old daughter. She was on her way to pay attendance to the court of the high king, taking her turn as one of her family's hostages. The wilds around Chesapeake Bay, as it is called on your side, are not heavily populated in this world. We searched for months, but obviously to little effect.'

'You found the box of documents,' Miriam said. The effort of speaking was vast: She could hear her heart pounding in her ears.

'Yes. They provide impressive supporting evidence – circumstantial but significant. While you were unconscious, blood samples were taken for, ah, DNA profiling. The results will be back tomorrow, but I am in no doubt. You have the family face and the family talent – or did you think world-walking was commonplace? – and your age and the documentary evidence fits perfectly. You are the daughter Helge, born to my elder sister, Patricia Thorold Hjorth, by her husband the western magistrate-prince, Alfredo Wu, and word of your survival is going to set the fox among the Clan chickens when it emerges.'

He smiled thinly. 'Which is why I took the precaution of sending away the junior members of the distaff side, and almost all the servants, before bidding you welcome. It would not have done for the younger members of the Clan to find out about your existence before I looked to your safety. Some of them will be feeling quite anxious about the disruption of the braid succession, your highness.'

'Highness? What are you talking about?' Miriam could hear her voice rising, out of control. 'What are you on about? Look, I'm a business journalist covering the pharmaceutical sector in Massachusetts, not some kind of Disney princess! I don't know about any of this stuff!' She was on her feet in front of the desk. 'What's world-walking, and what does it have to do – '

'Your highness,' Angbard said firmly, 'you *were* a business journalist, on the other side of the wall of worlds. But world-walking is how you came here. It is the defining talent of our Clan, of the families who constitute the Clan. It is in the blood, and you are one of us, whether you will it or no. Over here, you are the eldest heir to a countess and a magistrate-prince of the outer kingdom, both senior members of their families, and however much you might wish to walk away from that fact, it will follow you around. Even if you go back over *there.*'

He turned to Roland, ignoring her stunned silence. 'Earl Roland, you will please escort your first cousin to her chambers. I charge you with her safety and protection until further notice. Your highness, we will dine in my chambers this evening, with one or two trustworthy guests, and I will have more words for you then. Roland will assign servants to see to your comfort and wardrobe. I expect him to deal with your questions. In the meantime, you are both dismissed.'

Miriam glared at him, speechless. 'I have only your best interests at heart,' the duke said mildly. 'Roland.'

'Sir.' Roland took her arm.

'Proceed.'

Roland turned and marched from the office, and Miriam hurried to keep up, angry and embarrassed and trying not to show it. You bastard! she thought. Out in the corridor: 'You're hurting me,' she hissed, trying not to trip. 'Slow down.'

Roland slowed and – mercy of mercies – let go of her arm. He glanced behind, and an invisible tension left his shoulders. 'I'm sorry,' he said.

'You're sorry?' she replied, disbelievingly. 'You nearly twisted my arm out of its socket!' She rubbed her elbow and winced.

'I said I'm sorry. Angbard isn't used to being disobeyed. I've never seen anyone take such liberties with him and escape punishment!'

'Punishment – ' she stopped. 'You weren't kidding about him being the head of secret police, were you?'

'He's got many more titles than he told you about. He's responsible for the security of the entire Clan. If you like, think of him as the head of the FBI here. There was a civil war before you or I were born. He's probably ordered more hangings than you or I have had hot dinners.'

Miriam stumbled. 'Ow, shit!' She leaned against the wall. 'That'll teach me to keep my eye on where I'm going.' She glanced at him. 'So you're telling me I wasn't paying enough attention?'

'You'll be all right,' Roland said slowly, 'if you can adapt to it. I imagine it must be a great shock, coming into your inheritance so suddenly.'

'Is that so?' She looked him up and down carefully, unsure how to interpret the raised eyebrow – *Is he trying to tell me something or just having a joke at my expense?* – then a second thought struck her. 'I think I'm missing something here,' she said, deliberately casually.

'Nothing around here is what it seems,' Roland said with a little shrug. His expression was guarded. 'But if the duke is right, if you really are Patricia's long-lost heir – '

Miriam recognized the expression in his eyes: It was belief. *He really believes I'm some kind of fairy-tale princess,* she realized with dawning horror. *What have I got myself into?*

'You'll have to tell me all about it. In my chambers.'

CINDERELLA 2.0

Roland led her back to her suite and followed her into the huge reception room at its heart. He wandered over to the windows and stood there with his hands clasped behind his back. Miriam kicked her heels off and sat down in the huge, enveloping leather sofa opposite the window.

'When did you discover the locket?' he asked.

She watched him curiously. 'Less than a week ago.'

'And until then you'd grown up in ignorance of your family,' he said. 'Amazing!'

He turned around. His face was set in a faintly wistful expression.

'Are you going to just stand there?' she asked.

'It would be impertinent to sit down without an invitation,' he replied. 'I know it's the case on the other side, but here, the elders tend to stand on points of etiquette.'

'Well – ' her eyes narrowed. 'Sit down if you want to. You're making me nervous. You look as if you're afraid I'll bite.'

'Um.' He sat down uneasily on the arm of the big chair opposite her. 'Well, it's irregular, to say the least, to be here. You being unwed, that is.'

'What's that got to do with it?' she snapped. 'I'm divorced. Is that another of the things you people are touchy about?'

'Divorced?' He stared at her hand, as if looking for a ring. 'I don't know.'

Suddenly he looked thoughtful. 'Customs here are distinctly different from the other side. This is not a Christ-worshiping land.' Another thought struck him. 'Are you, uh . . . ?'

'Does Miriam Beckstein sound Christian to you?'

'It's sometimes hard to tell with people from the other side. Christ worship isn't a religion here,' he said seriously. 'But you are divorced.

And a world-walker.' He leaned forward. 'What that means is you are automatically a Clan shareholder of the first rank, eligible, unwed, and liable to displace a dozen minor distant relatives from their Clan shares, which they thought safe. Your children will displace theirs, too. Do you know, you are probably a great-aunt already?'

To Miriam this was insupportable. 'I don't want a huge bunch of feuding cousins and ancestors and children! I'm quite happy on my own.'

'It's not as simple as that.' A momentary flash of irritation surfaced: 'Our personal happiness has nothing to do with the Clan's view of our position in life. *I* don't like it either, but you've got to understand that there are people out there whose plans will be disrupted by the mere knowledge of your existence, and other people who will make plans for you, regardless of your wishes!'

'I – ' she stopped. 'Look, I don't think we've got this straight. I may be related to your family by genetics, but I'm not one of you. I don't know how the hell you think or what your etiquette is like, and I don't care about being the orphan of a countess. It doesn't mean anything to me.' She sighed. 'There's been some huge mistake. The sooner we get it over with and I can go back to being a journalist, the better.'

'If you want it that way.' For almost a minute he brooded, staring at the floor in front of her. Miriam hooked one foot over the other and tried to relax enough to force her shoulders back into the sofa. 'You might last six weeks,' he said finally.

'Huh?'

He frowned at a parquet tile. 'You can ignore your relatives, but they can't ignore you. To them you're an unknown quantity. All Clan inner family members have the ability to walk the worlds, to cross over and follow you. Over here they're rich and powerful – but your current situation makes them insecure because you're unpredictable. If you do what's expected of you, you merely disrupt several inheritances worth a baron's estate. The heirs will hate you for it, but that's their problem and theirs alone. However, if you try to leave, they will think you are trying to form a new schismatic family, maybe even lure away family splinters to set up your own Clan to rival ours. That's a much more serious threat, and how do you think the rich and powerful deal with threats to their existence?' He looked grave. 'I'd rather not measure you for a coffin so soon after discovering you. It's not every day I find a new relative, especially one who's as educated and intelligent as you seem to be. There's a shortage of good conversation here, you know.'

'Oh.' Miriam deflated. *What happens to business life when there's no limit to liability and the only people you can work with are your blood relatives?* She changed the subject. 'What did your uncle mean about tonight? And servants, I mean, servants!'

'Ah, that.' Roland slipped down into the seat at last, relaxing a little. 'We are invited to dine with the head of one of the families in private. The most powerful family in the Clan, at that. It's a formal affair. I suppose he'll be interested in seeing how you present yourself, to get an idea of your likely impact at court. As for the servants, you're entitled to half a dozen or so ladies-in-waiting, your own guard of honor, and various others. My uncle the duke sent the minor family members away, but in the meantime there are maids from below stairs who will see to you.

'Really I would have sent them earlier, when I brought you up here, but he stressed the urgent need for secrecy and I thought – ' he paused. 'You really did grow up over there, didn't you? In the middle classes.'

She nodded, unsure just how to deal with his sudden attack of snobbery. Some of the time he seemed open and friendly, then she hit a blind spot and he was Sir Medieval Aristocrat writ large and charmless. 'I don't do upper class,' she said. 'Well, business class, maybe.'

'Well, you aren't in America any more. You'll have to get used to the way we do things here eventually.' He paused. 'Did I say something wrong?'

He had, but she didn't know how to explain. Which was why a couple of hours later she was sitting naked in the bathroom, talking to her dictaphone, trying to make sense of the insanity outside – without succumbing to hysteria – by treating it as a work assignment and reporting on it.

'Now I know how Alice felt in looking-glass land,' she muttered, holding her dictaphone close to her lips. 'They're mad. I don't mean schizophrenic or psychotic or anything like that. They're just not in the same universe as anyone else I know.' The same universe was a slip: She could feel the hysterical laughter bubbling up inside her. She bit her lower lip, painfully hard. 'They're nuts. And they insist I join in and play their game by their rules.'

There was some bumping and thumping going on in the main room of the suite. That would be the maidservants moving stuff around. Miriam paused the tape for a moment, considering her next words. 'Dear Diary, forty-eight hours ago I was hanging out in the forest, happy as a clam with my photographs of a peasant village that looked like something out of the middle ages. I was exploring, discovering something new, and it was great, I had this puzzle-box reality to crack open, a whole new story. Now I discover that I own that village, and a hundred more like it, and I literally have the power of life and death over its inhabitants. I can order soldiers to go in and kill every last one of them, on a whim. Once the Clans recognize me officially, at an annual session, that is. And assuming – as Roland says – nobody assassinates me. Princess Beckstein, signing off for *The Weatherman*, or maybe *Business 2.0*. Jesus, who'd have thought I'd end up starring in some kind of twisted remake of *Cinderella*? Or that it would turn out so weird?'

And I called Craig Venter and Larry Ellison robber barons in print, she thought mordantly, keying the 'pause' button again.

'Put that way it sounds funny, but it isn't. First I thought it was the feds who broke in and grabbed me, and that's pretty damn scary to begin with. FEMA, secret security courts with hearings held *in camera*. Then, it could have been the mob, if the mob looked like FBI agents. But this could actually be worse.

'These guys wear business suits, but it's only skin-deep. They're like sheikhs from one of the rich Gulf Emirates. They don't dress up medieval, they think medieval and buy their clothes from Saks or Savile Row in England.'

A thought occurred to her. *I hope Paulette's keeping the video camera safe. And her head down.* She had an ugly, frightened feeling that Duke Angbard had seen right through her. He scared her: She'd met his type before, and they played hardball – hard enough to make a Mafia don's eyes water. She was half-terrified she'd wake up tomorrow and see Paulie's head impaled on a pike outside her bedroom window. *If only Ma hadn't given me the damned locket –*

A tentative knock on the door. 'Mistress? Are you ready to come out?'

'Ten minutes,' Miriam called. She clutched her recorder and shook her head. Four servants had shown up an hour ago, and she'd retreated into the bathroom. One of them, called something like Iona, had tried to follow her. Apparently countesses weren't allowed to use a bathroom without servants in attendance. That was when Miriam had locked the door and braced the linen chest against it.

'Damn,' she muttered and took a deep breath. Then she surrendered to the inevitable.

They were waiting for her when she came out. Four women in severe black dresses and white aprons, their hair covered by blue scarves. They curtseyed before her as she looked around, confused. 'I'm Meg, if it please you, your highness. We is to dress you,' the oldest of them said in a soft, vaguely Germanic accent: Middle-aged and motherly, she looked as if she would be more at home in an Amish farm kitchen than a castle.

'Uh, it's only four o'clock,' Miriam pointed out.

Meg looked slightly shocked. 'But you are to be received at seven!' She pointed out. 'How're we to dress you in time?'

'Well.' Miriam looked at the other three: All of them stood with downcast eyes. *I don't like this*, she thought. 'How about I take something from my wardrobe – yes, they kindly brought all my clothes along – and put it on?'

'M-ma'am,' the second oldest ventured: 'I've seen your clothes. Begging your pardon, but them's not court clothes. Them's not suitable.'

Court clothes? More crazy formal shit. 'What would you suggest, then?' Miriam asked exasperatedly.

'Old Ma'am Rosein can fit you up with something to measure,' said the old one, 'should I but give her your sizes.' She held up a very modern-looking tape measure. 'Your highness?'

'This had better be good,' Miriam said, raising her arms. *Why do I never get this kind of service at Gap?* she wondered.

Three hours later Miriam was readied for dinner, and knew exactly why she never got this kind of service in any chain store – and why Angbard had so many servants. She was hungry, and if the bodice they'd squeezed her into allowed her to eat when she got there, she might consider forgiving Angbard for his invitation.

The youngest maidservant was still fussing over her hair – and the feathers and string of pearls she had woven into it, while lamenting its shortness – when the door opened. It was, of course, Roland, accompanied now by a younger fellow, and Miriam began to get an inkling of what a formal dinner involved.

'Dear cousin!' Roland saluted her. Miriam carefully met his eyes and inclined her head as far as she could. 'May I present you with your nephew twice removed: Vincenze?' The younger man bowed deeply, his red embroidered jacket tightening across broad shoulders. 'You look splendid, my dear.'

'Do I?' Miriam shook her head. 'I feel like an ornamental flower arrangement,' she said with some feeling.

'Charmed, ma'am,' said Vincenze with the beginning of a stutter.

'If you would like to accompany me?' Roland offered her his arm, and she took it with alacrity.

'Keep the speed down,' she hissed, glancing past him at his younger relative, who appeared to be too young to need to shave regularly.

'By all means, keep the speed down.' Roland nodded.

Miriam stepped forward experimentally. Her maidservants had taken over an hour to install her in this outfit: it was like something out of a medieval costume drama, she thought. Roland's high linen collar and pantaloons didn't look too comfortable, either, come to think of it. 'What sort of occasion is this outfit customary for?' she asked.

'Oh, any formal event where one of our class might be seen,' Roland observed, 'except that in public you would have a head covering and an escort. You would normally have much more jewelry, but your inheritance – ' he essayed a shrug. 'Is mostly in the treasury in

Niejwein.' Miriam fingered the pearl choker around her neck uncomfortably.

'You wore, um, American clothing today,' she reminded him.

'Oh, but so is this, isn't it? But of another period. It reminds us whence our wealth comes.'

'Right.' She nodded minutely. Business suits as informal dress for medieval aristocrats, and formal dress that was like something that belonged in a movie about the Renaissance. *Everything goes into the exterior*, she added to her mental file of notes on family manners.

Roland escorted her up the wide stairs, then at the tall doors at the top a pair of guards in dark suits and dark glasses announced them and ushered them in.

A long oak table awaited them in a surprisingly small dining room that opened off the duke's reception room. Antique glass globes rising from brass stems in the wall cast a pale light over a table glistening with silver and crystal. A servant in black waited behind each chair. Duke Angbard was already waiting for them, in similarly archaic costume: Miriam recognized a sword hanging at his belt. *Do swords go with male formal dress here?* she wondered. 'My dear niece,' he intoned, 'you look marvelous! Welcome to my table.' He waved her to a seat at the right of the head, black wood with a high back and an amazingly intricate design carved into it.

'The pleasure's mine,' Miriam forced herself to smile, trying to strike the right note. *These goons can kill you as soon as look at you*, she reminded herself. Medieval squalor waited at the gate, and police cells down in the basement: Maybe this wasn't so unusual outside the western world, but it was new to her. She picked up her skirts and sat down gingerly as a servant slid a chair in behind her. The delicacy of its carving said nothing about its comfort – the seat was flat and extremely hard.

'Roland, and young Vincenze! You next, by the Sky Father.'

'P-pleased to accept,' Vincenze quavered.

The outer door opened again, sparing him further risk of embarrassment, and a footman called out in a low voice: 'The Lady Margit, Châtelaine of Praha, and Her Excellency the Baroness Olga Thorold.'

Six women came in, and now Miriam realized that she was

probably underdressed, for the two high-born each wore the most voluminous gowns she'd ever seen, with trains that required two maids to carry them and hair so entangled in knots of gold and rubies that they resembled birds' nests. They looked like divas from a Wagner opera: the fat lady and the slim virgin. Margit of Praha was perhaps forty, her hair beginning to turn white and her cheeks sagging slightly. She looked as if she might be merry under other circumstances, but now her expression was grimly set. Olga Thorold, in contrast, was barely out of adolescence, a coltish young girl with a gown of gold and crimson and a neck swathed in gemstones that sparked fire whenever she moved. Olga looked half-amused by Miriam's cool assessing glance.

'Please be seated,' said Angbard. Olga smiled demurely and bowed her neck to him. Margit, her chaperone, merely nodded and took a seat. 'I believe you have heard tell of the arrival of our return-ing prodigal,' he commented. 'Pitr, fetch wine if you please. The Medoc.'

'I have heard quite a few strangenesses today,' Margit commented in English that bore a strangely clipped accent. 'This songbird in your left hand, she is the daughter of your sister, long-lost. Is this true?'

'It is so,' Angbard confirmed. A servant placed a cut-crystal glass of wine in front of Miriam. She began to reach toward it, then stopped, noticing that none of the others made such a gesture. 'She has proven her heritage – the family trait – and the blood tests received barely an hour ago affirm her. She is of our bloodstock, and we have information substantiating, sadly, the death of her dam, Patricia Thorold Hjorth. I present to you Helge, also known as Miriam, of Thorold Hjorth, eldest heir surviving.'

'So charmed!' Olga simpered at Miriam, who managed a wordless nod in reply.

Plates garnished with a starter materialized in front of everybody – roasted fowl of some kind, tiny enough to fit in Miriam's gloved hand. Nobody moved, but Angbard raised his hands. 'In the name of the Sky Father – '

Miriam froze, so utterly startled that she missed the murmured continuation of his prayer, the flick of wine from glass across the tabletop, the answering murmur from Roland and Olga and Margit, and the stuttered response from Vincenze.

He said this wasn't a Christian country, she reminded herself, in time to move her lips as if saying something – anything, any response – just to fit in.

Completing his brief prayer, Angbard raised his glass. 'Eat, drink, and be safe under my roof,' he told them, then took a mouthful of wine. After which it appeared to be open season.

Miriam's stomach grumbled. She picked up knife and fork and attacked her plate discreetly.

'One hears the strangest stories, dear.' Miriam froze and glanced across the table: Margit was smiling at her sympathetically. 'You were lost for so long, it must have been terrible!'

'Probably.' Miriam nodded absentmindedly and put her fork down. 'And then again, maybe not.' She thought for a moment. 'What have you heard?'

'Lots,' Olga began breathlessly. 'You were orphaned by savages and raised in a workhouse as a scrub, isn't that so, nana? Forced to sleep in the fireplace ashes at night! Then Cousin Roland found you and – '

'That's enough, dear,' Margit said indulgently, raising a gloved hand. 'It's her story, to tell in her own way.' She raised an eyebrow at Miriam. Miriam blinked in return, more in surprise at the girl's art-lessness than her chaperone's bluntness.

'I would not mind hearing for myself how your upbringing pro-ceeded,' Angbard rumbled.

'Oh. Indeed.' Miriam glanced down, realizing that her appetizer had been replaced by a bowl of soup – some kind of broth, anyway – while they spoke. 'Well. I wouldn't want to disappoint you – ' she nodded at Olga – 'but I had a perfectly normal upbringing. You know my birth-mother disappeared? When she was found in, uh, on the other side, I was taken to a hospital and subsequently adopted by a young childless couple.' Of student radicals who grew up to be aca-demics, she didn't say. Olga was hanging on her every word, as if she was describing some kind of adventure with pirates and exploits in far-off lands. Either the girl was an idiot or she was so sheltered that all of this sounded exotic to her. Probably the latter.

'A university professor and his wife, a critic and reviewer. I think there was some issue with my – with Patricia's murder, so the adoption agency gave my adoptive parents her personal effects to pass on, but blocked inquiries about me from anywhere else, it being a matter for the police: unsolved murder, unidentified victim, and so on.'

'There's only so much you can do to prevent a suicide bomber,' Angbard said with deceptive mildness. 'But we're not at immediate risk here,' he added, smiling at Miriam, an expression clearly intended to reassure her. 'I've taken special measures to ensure our safety.'

'Your schooling,' Olga said. 'Did you have a personal tutor?'

Miriam frowned, wondering just what she meant. 'No, I went to college, like everybody else,' she said. 'Premed and history of economics, then med school. Then, well, instead of continuing with med school, I went back to college again to study something else. Medicine didn't get on with me.'

'You double-majored?' Roland interrupted.

'Yes, sort of.' Miriam put her spoon down. She couldn't eat any more, her stomach felt too full and her back ached. She leaned her shoulders against the chair but couldn't relax. 'I switched to journalism. Did an MA in it.' Her gloved hands felt hot and damp. They reminded her of a long shift on a geriatric ward, a different type of glove she'd ended up wearing for hours on end, cleaning up blockages. 'I began on the biotech sector beat but found the IT industry shysters more interesting.' She paused. Olga's expression was one of polite incomprehension, as if she'd suddenly begun speaking fluent Japanese.

'Yourself?'

'Oh, *I* had a personal tutor!' Olga enthused. 'But Daddy didn't want to send me away to school on the other side. We were having a spot of bother and he thought I'd need too many bodyguards.'

Angbard smiled again, in a manner that Miriam found disquietingly avuncular.

'There has been a threat of rebellion in Hel these past two years,' he explained with a nod in Miriam's direction. 'Your father needed the troops. Perhaps next year we can send you to Switzer-Land?'

'Oh, yes!' Olga clapped her hands together discreetly. 'I'd like that.'

'What would you like to study?' Miriam asked politely.

'Oh, everything! Deportment, and etiquette, and management of domestic events – balls and banquets. It's so important to get the little things right, and how are you to supervise everything if you don't know what your steward is doing?'

She gave a little squeal. 'I do hope they'll let me continue with the violin, though.'

Miriam forced herself to keep a straight face. 'I guess you're going to make a very good marriage,' she said, voice neutral. It made a horribly consistent picture: the older woman as chaperone, the total eagerness for the description of her own upbringing and education, the wistfulness for a place at an expensive finishing school. *This could be a problem,* she thought tiredly. *If they expect me to behave like this, someone is going to be very disappointed. And it won't be me . . .*

'I'm sure she'll marry well,' said Margit, venturing an opinion for the first time. Vincenze whispered something to Roland, who forced a knowing chuckle.

'She's of the right age.' Margit looked at Miriam dubiously. 'I expect you'll – ' she trailed off.

'Discussions of Countess Helge's eventual disposition are premature,' Angbard said coolly. 'Doubtless she will want to make a strong alliance to protect herself. I'm sure she has a solid head on her shoulders, and will want to keep it there.' He smiled: a thin, humourless expression.

Miriam swallowed. *You old bastard! You're threatening me!* Servants removed her plate and refilled her wine glass. Growing anger threatened to overwhelm her. She took an overhasty mouthful to conceal her expression, leaving a bleeding ring of lip gloss on the crystal. Her heart was pounding and she couldn't seem to get enough air.

'To set your mind at ease, my dear, you are quite safe for the time being,' said Angbard. 'This is a doppelgängered house, with a secured installation on the other side, as strongly defended there as here – but if you were to venture outside of it, you would be in danger. I am concerned about your other relatives, such as the family Hjorth, and your late father's heirs of family Wu, in the far west. A strong alliance would go a long way toward protecting you.'

'An alliance,' she said thickly. It seemed to be hot in the dining room. She finished her glass, to buy some time. 'Y'know, it seems to me that you're taking a lot for granted. That I'll fit in and adapt to your ways.'

'Isn't that how it always works?' asked Olga, sounding confused. A dessert appeared, individual plates of chocolate truffles drizzled in syrup, but Miriam had no room for food. Her meal sat heavily on the top of her stomach.

'Not always, no,' Miriam said tightly. She picked up her full wineglass, then frowned, remembering two – three? – refills before it, and put it down again, a little harder than she'd intended. Roland smiled at her indulgently. They all seemed to be smiling at her too much this evening, she noticed. As if they expected her to break down in tears and thank them for rescuing her from a life of drudgery. She forced herself to straighten her shoulders, sipped sparingly from her glass, and tried to ignore the growing pains in the small of her back. If she could just get through the remainder of the meal she'd be all right. 'But we'll worry about that when we get to it, won't we?' She mustered a pained smile and everyone pretended she hadn't said anything. *The strange cousin's faux pas*, she thought, as Vincenze asked Roland something about cavalry maneuvers.

A few minutes later, Angbard rapped a silver dessert spoon on his glass. 'If you have finished eating, by all means let the after-dinner entertainment commence,' he said.

Servants wheeled a tall trolley in and Miriam blinked in surprise. A huge thirty-inch Sony flat-panel television faced them, glassy-eyed, blocking the doorway. A black video recorder sat on a shelf below it, trailing cables. A white-gloved footman handed the remote to the duke on a silver plate. He bowed himself out as Angbard picked it up and pointed it at the set.

It was all Miriam could do to keep her jaw from dropping when a familiar signature tune came welling out of concealed speakers around the dining chamber. A helicopter descended onto a rooftop pad outside a penthouse suite: The famous Stetson-wearing villain stepped out into a sea of family intrigue. Miriam gulped down her wine without choking and reached for the inevitable – invisible – refill, barely tasting it. Her nose was going numb, a warning sign that she normally ignored at her peril, but this was just too bizarre to take while remaining sober. *Dallas!* she thought, making it a curse.

As a choice of after-dinner videos, it fitted the evening perfectly. But she'd been wrong about the ordeal being nearly over: The meal was only the beginning.

*

Roland tried to say something as they left Angbard's rooms. 'Hush,' she said, leaning on his arm as they descended the grand staircase. She was wobbling on her heels. 'Just get me back to my room.'

'I think we need to talk,' he said urgently.

'Later.' She winced as they reached the corridor. *Take lots of little steps,* she thought. The ache in her back was worst in the region of her kidneys. She felt drunk. 'Tomorrow.'

He held the door open for her. 'Please – '

She looked into his eyes. They were wide and appealing: He was a transparently gallant, well-meaning young man – *Young? He's only a couple of years younger than I am* – with a great ass, and she instinctively distrusted that. 'Tomorrow,' she said firmly, then winced. 'I'm tired. Maybe after breakfast?'

'By all means.' He stepped back and Miriam turned to close the door, only to find the head maidservant, Meg, standing ahead of her.

'Ah. Meg.' Miriam smiled experimentally. Glanced at the bathroom. 'I've had a long day and I'm going to bed shortly. Would you mind leaving?'

'But how is you to undress?' Meg asked, confused. 'What if you want something in the night?'

'What's the usual arrangement?' Miriam asked.

'Why, we sleep inside the door here, against your needs.' She dipped her head.

'Oh my.' Miriam sighed, and would have slumped but for her dress, which seemed to be holding her upright. 'Oh God.' She took a stride toward the bathroom, then caught herself on the door frame with one arm. 'Well, you can start by undressing me.' It took the combined efforts of two maids ten minutes to strip Miriam down to her underwear. Eventually something gave way and her ribs could move again. 'Oh. Oh!' Miriam took a breath, then gulped. ''Scuse me.' She fled dizzily into the bathroom, skidding on the tiled floor, and locked the door.

'Oy . . .' she planted herself firmly on the toilet.

After a moment, she breathed a sigh of relief. Her gaze fell on the dictaphone and she picked it up. 'Memo to self,' she muttered. 'At a formal banquet, the pain in the small of your back might be the chair, but on the other hand, it might be your kidneys backing up.' Four, no five, glasses of wine. She shook her head, still wobbly, and took another deep breath. 'And the breathing trouble. Fuck 'em, next time – if they want formal, they can put up with whatever I can buy off the rack in Boston. I'm not turning myself into an orthopedic basket case in the name of local fashion.'

Miriam took another deep breath. 'Right. More notes. Margit of Praha, middle-aged, looks to be a chaperone for Olga Thorold, who seems to be senior to her. Olga is a ditz. Thinks a Swiss finishing school is higher education. Main ambition is to make a good marriage. I think Angbard may have been showing her to me as a role model – maybe that's what high-born women do around here. I think Vincenze is just horribly shy. May be some sort of all-male schooling for menfolk here. Their English is better than the women's. I wonder if that means they get out more.'

She hit the 'pause' button, then finished with the toilet. Standing up, she stripped off, then luxuriated in the sensation of having nothing at all in contact with her skin.

A thought struck her. 'I'm going to have a bath,' she called through the door. 'Don't wait up for me. I don't need any help.'

It was Miriam's third bath of the day, but it didn't strike her as excessive.

Her skin itched. She poured expensive bath salts and perfumed oil into the water without remorse, then slid down into the sea of foam. 'Memo: The bath obviously came over from the other side, and they've got hot and cold water on tap. That means they must have some way of moving heavy items, plumbing equipment. I need to find out how. If some asshole cousin is going to try killing me because of my name, I'd like to know whether they're likely to use a pistol or a B-52.' A thought struck her. 'It looks like they're stuck in a development trap, like the Gulf Emirates. The upper class is fabulously rich and can import luxury items to their heart's content, and send their kids for education overseas, but they can't import enough, uh – stuff – to develop their population base. Start an industrial revolution. Whatever.' She leaned back, feeling her spine unkink. 'I wish I knew more about developing world economics. Because if that's what this all boils down to, I'll have to change things.'

She put the recorder down for a couple of minutes while she soaped herself all over, trying to scrub away the sweat and stress.

'Personal File: Roland. He's too damn smooth.' She paused, biting her upper lip. 'Reminds me of the college jocks, same kind of clean-cut hunky outdoors thing, except he's painfully polite and doesn't smell of beer or cigarettes. And he's trying to hide something. First cousin, which means, um. I have no idea what that means in the context of this extended Clan-family structure thing, except he treats me like I'm made of eggshells and soap bubbles. Great class, behaves like a real gentleman, then again, he's probably a gold-plated bastard under the smooth exterior. That, or Uncle Angbard is trying to throw us together for some reason. And he is a tough cookie. Right out of *The Godfather*. Trust him as far as you can throw him.'

She leaned back farther. 'Next Memo: sexual politics. These people are basically medievals in suits. And tonight they were just medievals. Olga is the giveaway, but the rest of it is pretty hard to miss. Better not talk about Ben or the divorce, or the kid, they might get weird. Maybe I can qualify as an aged spinster aunt who's too important to mess with, and they'll leave me alone. But if they expect me to lie back and act like a – a countess, someone's going to be in trouble.' *And it could be me*, she admitted. *Stuck in a strange land with weird and stifling customs, under guard the whole time –*

'Memo: The locket is not unique. Duke Angbard owns its twin. He gave it back to me to keep and talked about a doppelgängered house.

And the family trait. Which means they know all about it – and about how it works and how you use them. Hmm. Find out what they know before you start messing.'

There was a lot to think about. 'Most kids sometimes play make-believe, that they're actually the long-lost prince or princess of a magical kingdom. Not Ruritania with poison-tasters, armed guards, and *Dallas* reruns as the height of sophisticated after-dinner entertainment.' She hummed tunelessly. 'I wonder where they get the money to pay for the toys?' Something Paulette had said was trying to surface, but she couldn't quite remember what.

The bathtub drained and Miriam caught herself yawning as she toweled herself dry. 'Maybe it'll all go away in the morning,' she told herself.

ECONOMICS LESSON

Miriam jolted awake with her eyes open and a strong sense of panic. Incoherent but unpleasant dreams dogged her: goggled soldiers looming over her bed, limbs moving through molasses, too slow, too slow . . .

The bed was too big, much too big. She groped for the side of it, floundering across cold white sheets like an arctic explorer.

'Aagh.' She reached open air, found herself looking down at the floor from an unaccustomed height. Her arm hurt, her mouth tasted horrible – something had obviously died in it the night before, and she ached everywhere but especially in a tight band across her forehead. 'Mornings!' The air was distinctly cold.

Shivering, she threw the comforter off and sat up, then jumped.

'What are you doing in here!' she squeaked, grabbing the covers.

'Excuse, ma'am – we required to attend?' The maid's accent was thick and hard to make out: English clearly wasn't her first language, and she looked shocked, though whether it was at Miriam's nakedness or her reaction to her presence wasn't clear.

'Well.' Miriam held her breath for a moment, trying to get her heart under control. 'You can just wait outside the door. I'll be up in a minute.'

'But how is you to be dress?' asked the woman, a rising note of unhappiness in her voice.

'I'll take care of that myself.' Miriam sat up again, this time holding the bedding around her. 'Out. I mean, right out of my chambers, all of you, completely out! You can come back in half an hour. And shut the door.'

She stood up as the door clicked shut, her heart still pounding. 'How the hell do they manage?' she wondered aloud. 'Jesus, royalty!' It came out as a curse.

It had never occurred to her to sympathize with the Queen of England before, but the idea of being surrounded by flunkies monitoring her every breath gave her a sinking feeling in her stomach. *I've got to get away from this for a while*, she realized. *Even if I can't avoid them in the long term, they'll drive me mad if I don't get some privacy.*

Domestic servants were something that had passed out of the American middle-class lifestyle generations ago. Just the idea of having to deal with them made Miriam feel as if she was about to break out in hives.

Right. I've got to get away for a bit. How? Where? Miriam glanced at the bedside table and saw temporary escape sitting there, next to her dictaphone. Ah. A plan! She approached the huge chest of drawers and rummaged through it, hunting clothes. Ten minutes later she was dressed in urban casual – jeans, sneakers, sweater, leather jacket. Someone had helpfully installed some of her bags in the bottom of a cavernous wardrobe, and her small reporter's briefcase was among them, preloaded with a yellow pad, pens, and some spare tapes and batteries.

She poked her nose around the bedroom door cautiously. No, there was nobody lurking in ambush. *It worked!* She told herself. Five minutes in the bathroom and she was ready to activate her plan. Ready, apart from a hollow feeling in the pit of her stomach, anyway.

'Damn. I'll need money.' She ransacked the reception room in haste, hunting for her personal effects, and found them in a closed bureau of exquisite workmanship – her wallet, driving license, credit cards, and house keys. Either the servants didn't dare tamper with the private possessions of a relative of the duke – or they didn't know what they were. She found some other items in the bureau that shook her – her snub-nosed pistol and a box of ammunition that she didn't remember buying. 'What is this?' she asked herself before putting the gun in her jacket pocket. She kept her hand around it. If what she was planning didn't work . . . well, she'd jump that hurdle when she reached it.

They're treating me as family, she realized. Adult, mature, sensible family, not like Olga the ditz. Servants and assassins crawling out of the woodwork, it was a whole different world.

Carefully not thinking too hard about the likely consequences of her actions, Miriam walked to the center of the reception room between sofa and fireplace, snapped open her locket with her left hand, and focused on the design inside.

'Owww!' She stumbled slightly and cradled her forehead. Vision blurred, and everything throbbed. 'Hell!' She blinked furiously through the pounding of her abruptly upgraded headache. The room was still there: bureau, chairs, fireplace –

'I wondered how long you'd take,' Roland said from behind her.

She whirled, bringing her gun to bear, then stopped. 'Jesus, don't do that!'

Roland watched her from the sofa, one hand holding a pocket watch, the other stretched out along the cushioned back. He was wearing a sports jacket and chinos with an open-necked shirt, like a stockbroker on casual Friday.

The sofa was identical to the unoccupied one in the suite she'd just left – or so close as to be its twin. But Roland wasn't the only different feature of the room. The quality of light coming in through the window was subtly altered, and some items had appeared on the side table, and the bedroom door was shut. 'This isn't the same apartment,' she said slowly, past the fog of headache. 'It's a doppelgänger, right? And we're on the other side. My side.'

Roland nodded. 'Are you going to shoot me or not?' he asked. 'Because if you aren't, you ought to put that away.'

'Sorry.' She lowered the pistol carefully and pointed it at the floor. 'You startled me.'

Roland relaxed visibly. 'I think it's safe to say that you startled me, too. Do you always carry a gun when you explore your house?'

'I hope you'll excuse me,' she said carefully, 'but after waking up in bed with a stranger leaning over me for the second time in as many days, I tend to overreact a little. And I wasn't sure how the duke would respond to me going walkabout.'

'Really?' He raised an eyebrow.

'No shit.' She glanced around. The bathroom door was closed – she needed some Tylenol or some other painkiller bad. 'Do you keep hot and cold running servants on this side, too?'

'Not many; there's a cook and some occasional cleaning staff, but mostly this is reserved for Covert Operations, and we pay much more attention to secrecy. Over here it's a . . . a safe house, I guess you'd call it, not a palace. I take it you haven't eaten – can I invite you to join me downstairs for breakfast?'

'As long as I don't have to dress for it,' she said, checking then pocketing her gun. She picked up her briefcase. 'I dug the lecture about not being able to hide, I don't want you to misunderstand me. But there are some things I really need to do around town today. Assuming I'm not under house arrest?'

Roland shrugged. 'I don't see why not,' he said. 'I can answer for your security, in any case. Will you be able to do your stuff if I come along?'

Miriam looked out of the window and took a deep breath. 'Well.' She looked at him again. 'I guess so.' *Damn, there goes my chance to warn Paulie.* 'Is it really that risky?'

'Breakfast first.' He was already heading for the door. He added, over his shoulder, 'By now news of your arrival will have leaked out and junior members of at least two of the other families will be desperate, absolutely desperate. But they don't know what you look like so you probably don't need a permanent bodyguard yet. And once your position is secure, they won't be able to touch you.'

'"Breakfast,"' she said, '"first."'

*

There was a kitchen on the ground floor, and there was nothing medieval about it. With its stainless-steel surfaces, huge chest freezer, microwave ovens, and gas range, it could have been the back of a restaurant. The dining room attached to it didn't look anything like Angbard's private apartment, either. It reminded Miriam more of a staff room at an upmarket consultant's office. A couple of guys in dark suits nodded at Roland from a table, but they were finishing up cups of coffee and they cleared out as soon as he offered her a seat.

'Tell me, what did you think of, uh, Olga?'

While she tried to puzzle out what he meant by that question, a waitress appeared, notepad poised. 'What's on the menu this morning?' Miriam asked.

'Oh, anything you'd like.' She smiled breezily. 'Coffee, we have a whole range of different types at present. Eggs, bacon, sausages, granola, breakfast cereal, juice – whatever.'

'Double espresso for me,' said Roland. 'Rye sourdough toast, extra-mature thick-peel marmalade, unsalted butter. Two fried eggs, sunny-side up.'

'Hmm. A large cappuccino for me, I think,' said Miriam. 'Can you manage a Spanish omelet?'

'Sure!' Miss Breezy grinned at her. 'With you in five minutes.'

Miriam blinked at her receding back. 'Now that is what I call service.'

'We take it seriously around here,' Roland said dryly.

'You run this household like a company.' Miriam frowned. 'In fact, this is a family business, isn't it? That's what you're in.' She paused. 'Interuniversal import/export. Right?'

'Right.' He nodded.

'And you've been doing it for hundreds of years.'

'Right you are,' he said encouragingly. 'You're figuring it out for yourself.'

'It's not that hard.' The distinctive noise of a coffee percolator made her raise her head. 'How do you think last night went?'

'I think – ' he watched her examining him. 'Do you know you've got a very disquieting stare?'

'Yes.' She grinned at him. 'I practice in the mirror before I go in to an interview. Sometimes it makes my victims give away more than they intended to. And sometimes it just gives them bad dreams afterward.'

'Eeh. I can see you'd be a bad enemy, Miss Beckstein.'

'Miz, to you.' She paused. The waitress was back, bearing a tray laden with coffee, milk, and a sugar bowl.

'Call if you need anything more,' she reassured them, then disappeared again.

Roland's eyes narrowed as he looked at her. 'You remind me of when I was at college,' he said.

'You were at college?' she asked. 'Over here, I mean?'

'Oh, yes.' He picked up his espresso and spooned a small quantity of brown sugar crystals into it.

'The girls don't seem to get that treatment,' she pointed out sharply.

'Oh, but some of them do,' he replied, blowing on his coffee. 'At least, these days, this generation. Olga is a throwback – or, rather, her father is. I'm not sure quite what the duke was trying to prove, inviting you to dine with us, but he said something about culture shock earlier. He's a perceptive old coot, gets hold of some very unexpected ideas and refuses to let them go. He was testing you. Seeing how you comport yourself in a formal setting. Also seeing if you'd break under stress or how you'd hold up in public by using an audience he could silence if the need arose.'

'A-ha.' She took a first sip of her coffee. 'So what did you study?'

'As an undergrad, economics and history. Before Harvard, my parents sent me to Dartmouth,' he said quietly. 'I think I went a bit crazy in my first couple of years there. It's very different over here. Most of the older generation don't trust the way everything has changed since 1910 or so. Before then, they could kid themselves that the other side, this America, was just different, not better. Like the way things were when our first ancestor accidentally stumbled upon a way to visit a town in New England in 1720 or so. But now they're afraid that if we grew up here or spent too much time we'd never want to come home.'

'Sort of like defecting diplomats and athletes from the old Communist Bloc,' Miriam prodded.

'Exactly.' He nodded. 'The Clan's strength is based on manpower. When we go back, you and me, we'll have to carry some bags. Every time we cross over, we carry stuff to and fro. It's the law, and you need a good reason to flout it. There's a post room: You're welcome to come and go at will as long as you visit it each time to carry post bags back and forth.'

'A post room,' she echoed.

'Yes, it's in the basement. I'll show you it after – ah, food.'

For a few minutes they were both too busy to talk. Miriam had to admit that the omelet she'd ordered was exceptionally good. As she was draining her coffee, Roland took up the conversation again. 'I'm over here to run some business errands for the Boss today. I hope you don't mind if I take a few minutes out while you're doing whatever it is you were planning to do?'

'No, I mean, be my guest – ' Miriam was nonplussed. 'I'm not sure,' she added after a moment. 'There are a few things I needed to do, starting with, well, just seeing that I'm allowed out and about, know what I mean?'

'Did you have any concrete plans?' Roland looked interested.

'Well,' she leaned back and thought. 'I have – had, before all this landed on me – a commission to write a feature for a magazine. Nothing hard, but I'll need my iMac to write it on. And I must write it, if I don't want to vanish off the face of the earth, career wise.' She tried a smile. 'Got to keep my options open. I'm a working girl.'

Roland nodded. 'I understand. And after that?'

'Well. I was thinking about going home. Check my answering machine, make sure everything's okay, reassure the neighbors that I'm all right, that kind of thing.' *Make sure they haven't found Paulie's CD-ROM. Try to get a message to her to keep her head down.* 'I don't have to stay for long,' she added hastily. 'I'm not thinking about running away, if that's what you're worried about.'

Roland frowned thoughtfully. 'Is it just your mail and phone that you need? Because if so, it would be a lot safer just to divert everything. We've got a telephone switch in the subbasement and we can slam your domestic subscriber lines right over. But it would be a good thing if you avoided your home for the next few days. I can send someone around if there's anything you need, but – ' he shrugged.

'Why?' she asked.

'Because.' He put his butter knife down. 'We, uh, when there's a succession crisis or a war within the Clan, things can get very messy, very fast.' He paused for a moment, then rushed on: 'I wouldn't want to risk anyone getting a clean shot at you.'

Miriam sat very still, blood pounding in her ears. 'Does that mean what I think it means?' she asked.

'Yes – your house is a target. We have it under surveillance, but accidents can always happen, someone can miss something, and you might be walking into a booby trap. Tripwires inside the front door. It won't be secure until we've doppelgängered it, which might take some time because it's way out in the sticks on this side, and we'd need to fortify the area to stop anyone crossing over inside your living room. It took days for us to find you, even with the office chair in the forest as a marker. But you might not be so lucky next time.'

'Oh.' Miriam nodded to herself, absorbing this new and unwelcome fact. *So you found me by the chair?* 'What about my mother?'

Roland looked puzzled. 'But your mother's – '

'No, I mean my adoptive mother.' Miriam gritted her teeth. 'You know, the woman who raised me from a baby as her own? Who is now all alone and wheelchair-bound? Is she at risk? Because if so – ' she realized that her voice was rising.

'I'll see to it at once,' Roland said decisively and pulled out his cell phone. It obviously hadn't occurred to him that Iris was of any importance.

'Do so,' Miriam said tersely. 'Or I'll never speak to you again.'

'That's uncalled for.' Roland looked disapproving. 'Is there anyone else I should know about?' he asked after a moment.

Miriam took a deep breath. *Here goes,* she thought. 'My ex-husband is remarried and has a wife and child,' she said. 'Is he at risk?'

Roland mulled it over for a minute. 'He's a commoner,' he said finally. 'There were no children and you're divorced. So I guess he's out of the frame.'

No children. Miriam shook her head. 'You'll have to tell me about your inheritance laws,' she said carefully. *Oh, what complications!* Somewhere out there in America was a twelve-year-old girl – Miriam didn't know where, she only knew general details about her adoptive family – who might have inherited Miriam's current problem. *She's too young,* Miriam thought instinctively. *And she has no locket. But the adoption records were sealed, and nobody but Ben and Iris knew about the pregnancy. If the family hadn't found her, then –*

'Oh, they're simple enough,' said Roland, a slightly bitter note in his voice. 'The, um, family talent? It only breeds true among the

110

pure-blooded line. They found that out pretty early. It's what the biologists call a recessive trait. On the other side, um, marriage customs are different – cousin marriages are allowed, for one thing – and for another, children who don't have the talent aren't part of the Clan. But they're kept in the families. They form the outer, nonshareholding part of the Clan, but if two of them marry some of their children may inherit the talent.'

Good news mixed with bad news. On the one hand, her daughter – who she hadn't seen since two days after her birth – was safe from the attentions of the family, safe to lead a normal life unless Miriam drew attention to her. As long as the family dug no deeper than they had so far. On the other hand – 'You're telling me that my parents were cousins.'

'Second cousins once removed, I think,' Roland replied. 'Yes. By family law and custom marrying out is forbidden. You might want to bear that in mind, by the way, it's the one big taboo.' He glanced aside nervously. 'But you're probably safe because you did it over here and divorced him before anyone knew.' He was staring at the wall, she realized, staring at something that wasn't there in an attempt to avoid her gaze. Unpleasant memories? 'Otherwise there would be repercussions. Bad ones.'

'You're telling me.' She noticed her fingers turning white around the rim of her coffee cup. 'So presumably Uncle Angbard will make life hard for me if I try to take off and he wants me to marry someone who's a not-too-close family member.'

'That's an understatement.' Roland's cheek twitched. 'It's not as if the council would give him any other options.'

'What else?' Miriam asked as the silence grew uncomfortable.

'Well!' Roland shook himself and sat up. He began ticking off points on his fingers, his movements precise and economical and tense. 'We are expected to abide by the rules. First, when you come over here, you stop by the post room in each direction and carry whatever's waiting there. You got a free pass this time, but not in the future. Second, you check with Security before you go anywhere. They'll probably want you to carry a cell phone or a pager, or a bodyguard if the security condition is anything but blue – blue for cold.

Oh, and third – ' he reached into an inner pocket – 'the duke antici-pated that you might want to go shopping, so he asked me to give you this.' He passed her an envelope, the hint of a smile tugging at his lips.

'Hmm.' Miriam opened it. There was an unsigned silvery-coloured Visa card inside with her name on it. 'Hey, what's this?'

'Sign it.' He offered her a pen, looking pleased with himself, then watched while she scribbled on the back. 'Your estate is in escrow for now, but you should consider this an advance against your assets, which are reasonably large.' His smile widened. 'There may be problems with the family, but spending money isn't one of them.'

'Oh.' She slid it into her purse. 'Any other messages from the duke?'

'Yes. He said, "Tell her she's got a two-million-dollar credit limit and to try not to spend it all at once."'

Miriam swore in a distinctly unladylike manner.

He laughed briefly. 'It's your money, Miriam – Countess Helge. The import/export trade your ancestors pioneered is lucrative, and you can certainly earn your keep through it. Now, shall we visit the post room so I can attend to business, and then maybe you can do whatever it is that you need to do?'

*

The post room was a concrete-lined subbasement, with pigeonholes sized to accommodate the big wheeled aluminum suitcases that the family used for 'mail'.

Roland picked a clipboard from the wall and read through it. 'Hmm. Just two cases to FedEx today and that's it.'

'Suitcases.' She looked at them dubiously, imagining all sorts of illegal contraband.

'Yes. Help me. Take that one. Yes, the handle locks into place as the wheels come out.'

Struggling slightly, Miriam tugged the big suitcase out of the post room and into the stark cargo elevator next to it. Roland hit the button for the basement, and they lurched downward.

'What's in these things?' she asked. Then, after a moment: 'Tell me if it's none of my business.' *I'm not sure I want to know*, she thought, unable to avoid a flashback to the meeting in Joe's office, the threats on her phone.

'Oh, it's perfectly legal,' Roland assured her. 'No drugs, if that's what you were worrying about. This is all stuff that is cheap enough in Gruinmarkt and Soffmarkt or the other kingdoms of the coast and wants shipping to the Outer Kingdom – that would be California and Oregon – on this side. On the other side, there are no railroads or airports and cargo has to go by mule train across the Great Plains and the Rocky Mountains. Which are full of nomad tribes, so it takes months and is pretty risky. We bring our goods across to this side, heavily padded, and ship them by FedEx. The most valuable items in here are the sealed letters sent by the family post – we charge several times their weight in gold in return for a postal service that crosses the continent in a week. We also move intelligence. Our western Clan members – the Wu family, formerly known as Arnesen, and braided with the eastern families – exchange information with us. By coordinating our efforts, we can protect our traditional shipping on the other side from large bandit tribes. It also helps us exert political leverage beyond our numbers. For example, if the Emperor of the West dies and there is a succession struggle, we can loan the Wu family funds with which to ensure a favorable outcome and do so long before news would otherwise reach us across the continental divide.'

Miriam's eyes were nearly bulging as she tried to make sense of this. 'You mean there's no telegraph?' she asked.

'We *are* the telegraph,' he told her. 'As for the rest of what's in these suitcases, it's mostly stuff that only comes from the east and is expensive in the west. Like, for example, diamonds from India. They're expensive enough in the Gruinmarkt and almost impossible to get in the Outer Kingdom – it's much cheaper to ship them across the Boreal Ocean by barque than the western ocean by junk, especially since the Mongols refuse to trade with the east. Or penicillin. The ability to guarantee that a prince's wife will not die of childbed fever is worth more than any amount of precious stones.'

'And going the other way . . .'

'More messages. More diplomatic intelligence. Spices and garnets and rubies and gold from the Outer Kingdom's mines.'

Miriam nodded. The elevator doors opened onto the underground garage, and she followed him out into the concrete maze.

Several vehicles were parked there, including a long black Mercedes limousine – and her own slightly battered Saturn. Roland headed for the Merc. 'Once we've fitted your car with some extras, you can use it – if you want,' he said. 'But you can use any of the other cars here, too.'

Miriam shook her head, taking in a sleek Jaguar coupe parked behind a concrete column. 'I'm not sure about that,' she murmured. *What would it do for my independence?* she wondered, watching as Roland opened the Mercedes's trunk and lifted the suitcases into it. The two-million-dollar card in her purse was much more intoxicating than the wine last night, but didn't feel as real. *I'll have to try it,* she realized. *But what if I get addicted?*

*

The Mercedes was huge, black, and carried almost a ton of armor built into its smoothly gleaming bodywork. Miriam only realized this when she tried to open the passenger side door – it was heavy, and as it swung open she saw that the window was almost two inches thick and had a faint greenish tint. She sat down, pulled her seatbelt on, and tugged the door shut. It thudded into position as solidly as a bank vault.

'You're serious about being attacked,' she said soberly.

'I don't want to alarm you,' said Roland, 'but the contents of those two suitcases are worth the equivalent of twenty million dollars each on the other side. And there are several hundred active family members that we know of – and possibly ones we don't in hidden cells established by their family elders to gain a competitive edge over their rivals in the Clan. You're unusual in that you're a hidden one who was never intended to be hidden. The families *in camera* could raid us, and unless we took precautions, we'd be sitting ducks. A young man like Vincenze – ' he shrugged – 'maybe a bit more mature. Waiting on a street corner. Can set off a bomb or walk up behind someone and shoot him, then just vanish into thin air. Unless there's a doppelgänger on the other side or maybe a hill where over here there's a cleared area, there's no way of stopping that.'

'Twenty million.'

'At a very approximate exchange rate,' Roland offered, starting the engine.

Bright daylight appeared from an electrically operated door at the top of the exit ramp. He put the Mercedes in gear and gently slid forward. 'We're fairly safe, though. This car has been customized by the same people that made Eduard Shevardnadze's car. The President of the Republic of Georgia.'

'Should that mean something?' asked Miriam.

'Two RPG-7s, an antitank mine, and eighty rounds from a heavy machine gun. The passengers survived.'

'I hope we're not going to encounter that sort of treatment,' she said with feeling, reaching sideways to squeeze his fingers.

'We aren't.' He squeezed back briefly, then accelerated up the ramp. 'But there's no harm in taking precautions.'

They came up out of the ground near Belmont, and Roland chauffeured them smoothly onto the Concord turnpike and then the inner ring road and the tunnel. Roland took a circuitous root, spending as much time in tunnels or on fast highways as possible. They exited the highway near Logan International, and Roland drove toward the freight terminal. Miriam relaxed against the black leather. It smelled like a very expensive private club, redolent of the stink of money. She'd been in rooms with billionaires before and any number of sharkish venture capitalists, but somehow this was different.

Most of the billionaires she had met were manipulative jerks or workaholics, obsessive and insecure about something or other. Roland, in contrast, was 'old money' – old and unselfconscious, mature as a vintage wine. So old that he'd never known what it was like to be poor – or even upper-middle class. For a moment, she felt a flash of green-eyed envy – then remembered the two-million-dollar ballast in her purse.

'Roland, how rich am I?' she asked nervously.

'Oh, very,' he said casually. He swung the Mercedes into the entrance to a parking lot, where an automatic barrier lifted – also automatically – and then brought them to a halt in front of an anonymous-looking office with a FedEx sign above it. 'I don't know for sure,' he added, 'but I think your share may run to almost one percent of the Clan's net worth. Certainly many millions.'

'Oh, how marvelous,' she said sarcastically. Then more thought-fully, 'I could pay all Iris's medical bills out of the petty cash. Couldn't I?'

'Yes. Help me with the suitcases?'

'If you help me sort out Iris's medical bills. Seriously.'

'Seriously? Yes, I'll do that.' She stood up and stretched, then waited while Roland lifted the heavy cases out of the trunk. She took one and followed him as he rolled the other up to the door, swiped a magnetic card, and entered under the watchful eye of a security camera.

They came to a small office where a middle-aged man in a white shirt and black tie was waiting. 'Today's consignment,' said Roland. 'I'd like to introduce you to Miriam. She might be making runs on her own in future – if things work out. Miriam, this is Jack. He handles dispatch and customs at this end.'

'Thank you, sir,' said Jack, handing Roland a board with a three-part form ready to sign. 'This is just a formality to confirm I've received everything,' he added for her benefit. Balding, overweight, and red-faced, Jack was about as homely as anyone she'd seen since she'd been pitched headfirst into this nightmare of aristocracy. Miriam smiled at him.

'There, that's it, then,' he said, taking the papers back from Roland. 'Have a nice day, now!'

'My best to your wife,' Roland replied. 'Come on, Miriam. Time to go.'

'Okay.' She followed him back to the car. He started the engine and eased them back out into the local traffic around the light in-dustrial area. 'Where next?'

'Oh, we pick up the cases for the return leg, then we're at liberty,' he said. 'I thought you wanted to do some shopping? And some other things to see to? How about a couple of hours at Copley Place and messing around Back Bay, then lunch?'

'Sounds good,' she agreed.

'Okay.' He pulled over, into another parking lot. 'Give me a hand again?'

'Sure.'

They got out and Miriam followed him into yet another office. The procedure was the same in reverse: Roland signed a couple of forms and this time collected two identical, ribbed aluminum suitcases, each so heavy that Miriam could barely carry hers. 'Right, now into town,' he said after he lifted them both into the car's trunk. 'It's almost ten o'clock. Think you've got time to hit the shops and be back by five?'

'I'm sure I have.' She smiled at him. 'There's some stuff I could do with your help for, actually. Want to hang around?'

'Delighted to oblige.'

*

The Copley Place shops weren't exactly ideal, but it was totally covered and had enough stuff in it to keep Miriam occupied for a couple of hours. The platinum card didn't catch fire – it didn't even show signs of overheating when she hit Niemann Marcus and some less obvious shops for a couple of evening outfits and an expensive piece of rolling luggage.

After the first half hour, Roland did what many polite men did: zoned out and smiled or nodded whenever she asked him for an opinion. Which was exactly what Miriam was hoping for, because her real goal wasn't to fill her wardrobe with evening dresses and expensive lingerie (although that was an acceptable side effect), but to pull out a bundle of cash and use some of it to buy certain accessories. Such as a prepaid cell phone and a very small Sony laptop with a bundle of software ('If I can't go back home, I'll need something to write my articles on,' she pointed out to Roland, hoping he wouldn't figure out how big a loss-leader that would make it). She finished her spree in a sports shop, buying some outdoor tools, a pocket GPS unit, and a really neat folding solar panel, guaranteed to charge her laptop up – which she picked up while he was poking around a display of expensive hunting tackle.

She wasn't totally sure what she was going to do with this stuff, but she had some ideas. In particular, the CD-ROMs full of detailed maps of the continental United States and the other bits of software she'd slipped in under his nose ought to come in handy. Even if they didn't, she figured that if Angbard expected her to shop like a dizzy teenager, then she ought to get him used to her shopping like a dizzy teenager. *That way he'll have one less handle on me when I stop,* she thought.

Twelve thousand dollars went really fast when she was buying Sony notebooks, and even faster when she switched to Hermès and Escada and less well-known couture.

But it felt unreal, like play money. Some of the clothes would have to be altered to fit, and delivered: She took them anyway. 'I figure it can be altered on the other side,' she murmured to Roland by way of explanation. He nodded enthusiastically and she managed to park him for a few minutes in a bookshop next door to her real target, a secondhand theatrical clothing shop for an old-fashioned long skirt and shirtwaist that could pass for one of the servants' outfits.

Theatrical supplier, my ass, she thought. *The escape committee supply store is more like it!*

Around two o'clock she took mercy on Roland, who by this time was flagging, checking his watch every ten minutes and following her around like a slightly dejected dog. 'It's okay,' she said, 'I'm about done. How about we catch that lunch you were talking about, then head back to the house? I've got to get some of these clothes altered, which means looking up Ma'am Rosein, and then I need to spend a couple of hours on the computer.'

'That's great,' Roland said with unconcealed sincerity. 'How about Legal Seafood for lunch?'

Miriam really didn't go for clam chowder, but if it kept him happy that was fine by her. 'Okay,' she said, towing along her designer escape kit. 'Let's go eat!'

They ate. Over lunch she watched Roland carefully. He was about twenty-eight, she noted. Dartmouth. Harvard. Real Ivy League territory and then some. Classic profile. She sized him up carefully. Shaves well. Looks great. No visible bad habits, painfully good manners. *If there wasn't clearly something going on, I'd be drooling. Wouldn't I?* She thought. In fact, maybe there's something in that?

Maybe that's why Angbard is shoving us together. Or not. I need to find out more about the skeletons in the Clan closet and the strange fruit rotting on the family tree. And there were worse ways of doing that than chatting with Roland over lunch.

'Why is your uncle putting you on my case?' she finally asked over dessert, an exquisite crème brûlée. 'I mean, what's your background? You said he was thinking one step ahead. Why you?'

'Hmm.' Roland stirred sugar into his coffee, then looked at her with frank blue eyes. 'I think your guess is as good as mine.'

'You're unmarried.' She kicked herself immediately afterward. *Very perceptive, Ms. Holmes.*

'As if that matters.' He smiled humorlessly. 'I have an attitude problem.'

'Oh?' She leaned forward.

'Let's just say, Angbard wants me where he can keep an eye on me. They sent me to college when I was eighteen,' he said morosely. 'It was – well, it was an eye-opener. I stayed for four years, then applied to Harvard immediately. Economics and history. I thought I might be able to change things back home. Then I decided I didn't want to go back. After my first year or so, I'd figured out that I couldn't stay over here just on the basis of my name – I'd have to work. So I did. I wasn't much of one for the girls during that first degree – ' he caught her speculative look – 'or the boys.'

'So?' *Personal Memo: Find out what they think of sex, as opposed to marriage. The two are not always interchangeable.* 'What next?'

'Well.' He shrugged uncomfortably. 'I wanted to stay over here. I got into a graduate research program, studying the history of economic development in the Netherlands. Met a girl named Janice along the way. One thing led to another.'

'You wanted to marry her?' asked Miriam.

'Sky Father, no!' He looked shocked. 'The Clan council would never have stood for it! Even if it was just over here. But I could buy us both a house over here, make believe that – ' He stopped, took a sip of coffee, then put his cup down again. All through the process, he avoided Miriam's gaze.

'You didn't want to go back,' she stated.

'You can cross over twice in a day, in an hour, if you take beta-blockers,' he said quietly. 'Speaking of which.' He extracted a blister pack of pills from his inner pocket and passed it across to her. 'They do something about the headaches. You can discharge your duty to Clan and family that way, keep the post moving, and live nine-tenths of your life free of . . . of . . . of . . .'

Miriam waited for him to sort his tongue out.

'Jan and I had two years together,' he finally said quietly. 'Then they broke us up.'

'The Clan.' She turned the pack of pills over and over, reading the label. 'Did they – '

'Indirectly.' He interrupted her deliberately, then finished his coffee cup. 'Look, she kept asking questions. Questions that I couldn't answer. Wasn't allowed to answer. I'd have been required to go home and marry someone of high rank within the Clan sooner or later, just to continue the bloodline. I'm a man: I'm allowed to spend some time settling down. But eventually . . . if we marry out, we go extinct in two, maybe three generations. And the money goes down faster, because our power base is built on positive market externalities – have you – '

'Yes,' she said, mouth dry despite the coffee she'd just swallowed without tasting. 'The more of you there are, the more nodes you've got to trade between and the more effectively you can run your import/export system, right?'

'Right. We're in a population trap, and it takes special dispensation to marry out. Our position is especially tenuous because of the traditional nobility; a lot of them see us as vile upstarts, illegitimate and crude, because we can't trace our ancestry back to one of the hetmen of the Norge fleet that conquered the Gruinmarkt away from the Auslaand tribes about four, five hundred years ago.

'We find favor with the Crown, because we're rich – but even there we are in a cleft stick: It does not do well to become so powerful that the crown itself is threatened. If you get the chance to marry into the royal family – of Gruinmarkt or of one of our neighbors – that's about the only way you could marry out without the council coming down on you.'

'Huh. Other kingdoms? Where did they come from, anyway? It's, I'd have said medieval – '

'Nearly.' Roland nodded. 'I did some digging into it. You are aware that in your world the feudal order of western Europe emerged from the wreckage of the Roman Empire, imposed largely by Norse – Viking – settlers who had assimilated many of the local ways? I am not sure, but I believe much the same origin explains our situation here. On this coast, there are several kingdoms up and down the seaboard. Successive waves of emigration from the old countries of the Holy Empire conquered earlier kingdoms up and down the coast, forced into a militarized hierarchy to defend themselves against the indigenous tribes. Vikings, but Vikings who had assimilated the Roman Church – the worship of the divine company of gods – and such learning as the broken wreckage of Europe had to offer. We sent agents across the Atlantic to explore the Rome of this world thirty years or so ago: It lies unquiet beneath the spurs of the Great Khan, but the churches still make burned offerings before the gods. Maybe when there are more of us we will open up trade routes in Europe . . . but not yet.'

'Um. Okay.' Miriam nodded, reduced to silence by a sudden sense of cultural indigestion. *This is so alien!* 'So what about you? The Clan, I mean. Where do you – we – fit into the picture?'

'The Clan families are mostly based in Gruinmarkt, which is roughly where Massachusetts and New York and Maine are over here. But we, the Clan families, were ennobled only in the past six generations or so – the old landholders won't ever let us forget it. The Clan council voted to make children of any royal union full members – that way, the third generation will be royalty, or at least nobility, and have the talent. But nobody's done that yet – either in the Gruinmarkt, or north or south for that matter.

'In the Outer Kingdom, to the west, things are different again – there are civil service exams. Again, we've got an edge there. We have schools over here and ways to cheat. But I was talking about the population trap, wasn't I? The council has a long arm. They won't let you go free, and it'll take more than just one person on the inside, pushing, to make them change. I've tried. I got a whole huge reform program mapped out that'd break their dependency, begin developing the Gruinmarkt – but the council tore it up and threw it out without even reading it. Only Duke Angbard kept them from going further and declaring me a traitor.'

'Let me get this straight,' Miriam said, leaning forward. 'You lived with Janice until she couldn't put up with you not telling her what you were doing for two hours a day, couldn't put up with not knowing about your background, and until your elders began leaning on you to get married. Right?'

'Wrong,' he said. 'I told Uncle Angbard where he could shove his ultimatum.' He hunched over. 'But she moved out, anyway. She'd managed to convince herself that I was some kind of gangster, drug smuggler, whatever, up to my ears in no good. I was trying, trying, to get permission to go over for good, to try to make it up to her, to make everything all right. But then she was killed by a car. A hit-and-run accident, the police said.'

He fell silent, story run down.

Well, she thought. Words failed her for a minute. 'Were the two things connected? Causally, that is?'

'You mean, did the council have her killed?' he asked harshly. 'I don't know. I've refused to investigate the possibility. Thousands of pedestrians are killed by hit-and-run drivers every year. She'd walked out on me, and we might never have got back together. And if I did discover that one of my relatives was responsible, I'd have to kill them, wouldn't I? You didn't live through the war. Trust me, you don't want to go there, to having assassins stepping out of thin air behind people and garroting them. Far better to let it lie.'

'That doesn't sound like the same man speaking,' she speculated.

'Oh, but it does.' He smiled lopsidedly. 'The half of me that is a cold-blooded import/export consultant, not the half of me that's a misguided romantic reformer who thinks the Gruinmarkt could industrialize and develop in less than half a century if the Clan threw its weight behind the project. I'm hoping the duke is listening . . .'

'Well, he has you where he can keep an eye on you.' Miriam paused. 'For your own good, to his way of thinking.'

'Politics!' Roland swore. 'I don't care about who gets the credit as long as the job gets done!' He shook his head. 'That's the problem. Too many vested interests, too many frightened little people who think any progress that breaks the pattern of Clan business activities is a personal attack on them. And that's before we even get started talking about the old aristocracy, the ones who aren't part of us.'

'He's keeping you under his thumb until he can figure out a way to get a hold on you,' Miriam suggested. 'Some way of tying you down, maybe?'

'That's what I'm afraid of.' He looked around, trying to catch the waiter's eye. 'I figured you'd understand,' he said.

'Yes, I guess I do,' she agreed. *And if that's what he's got in mind for you, what about me?*

*

They drove back to the house in the suburbs in thoughtful silence. From the outside, the doppelgängered mansion looked like a sedate business unit, possibly a software company or an accounting firm. As they rolled onto the down ramp, Roland cued the door remote, and the barrier rolled up into the ceiling. For the first time Miriam realized how thick it was. 'That's bombproof, isn't it?'

'Yes.' He drove down the ramp without stopping and the shutters were already descending behind them. 'We don't have the luxury of a beaten fire zone on this side.'

'Oh.' She felt a chill. 'The threats. It's all real.'

'What were you expecting, lies?' He slid them nose-first into a parking spot next to the Jaguar, killed the engine, then systematically looked around before opening the door.

'I don't know.' She got out and stretched, looking around. 'The garage door. That's what brought it home.'

'The only home for the likes of us is a fortress,' he said. 'Remember the Lindbergh baby? We've got it a hundred times worse. Never forget. Never relax. Never be normal.'

'I don't – ' she took a deep breath. 'I don't think I can learn to live like that.'

'Helge – Miriam – ' he stopped and looked at her closely, concerned. 'It's not as bad as it sounds.'

She shook her head wordlessly.

'Really.' He walked around the car to her. 'Because you're not alone. You're not the only one going through this.'

'It's – ' She paused. 'Claustrophobic.' He was standing close to her. She stepped close to him, and he opened his arms and embraced her stiffly.

'I'll help, any way I can,' he murmured. 'Any way you want. Just ask, whatever you need.' She could feel his back muscles tense.

She hugged him. Wordless thoughts bubbled and seethed in her mind, seeking expression. 'Thank you,' she whispered, 'I needed that.' *Letting go.*

Roland stepped back promptly and turned to the car's trunk as if nothing had happened. 'It'll all work out; we'll make sure of it.' He opened the car's trunk. 'Meanwhile, can you help me with these? My, you've been busy.'

'I assume we can get it all back?'

'Whatever you can carry,' he said. 'Even if it's just for a minute.'

'Whatever,' she said, bending to take the strain of another of the ubiquitous silvery aluminum wheeled suitcases and her own big case stuffed with shopping.

'Downstairs and across?' he asked.

'Hmm.' She shrugged. 'Does the duke expect us to dine with him tonight?'

'Not that I've heard.'

'Then we don't need to go back immediately.'

He opened the lift gates. 'I'm afraid we do; we've got to keep the post moving, you see. Two trips a day, five days on and five days off. It's the rules.' He waved her into the lift and they stood together as it began to descend.

'Oh, well.' She nodded. 'I suppose . . .'

'Would you mind very much if I invited you to dine with me?' he asked in a sudden rush. 'Not a formal affair, not at all. If you want someone else around, I'm sure Vincenze is at a loose end . . .'

She smiled at him uncertainly, surprised at her own reaction. She bit her lip, not wanting to seem overeager. 'I'd love to dine with you,' she said. 'But tonight I'm working. Tomorrow?'

'Okay. If you say so.'

At the bottom of the shaft he led her into the post room. 'What's here?' she asked.

'Well.' He pointed to a yellow square marked on the floor, about three feet by three feet. 'Stand there, facing that wall.'

'Okay. What now?' she asked.

'Pick up the two cases – yes, I know they're heavy, you only need to hold them clear of the floor for a minute. Do you think you can do that? And focus on that cupboard on the wall. I'll look away and hit this button, and you do what comes natural, then step out of the square – fast. I'll be through in a couple of minutes; got an errand to run first.'

'And – oh.'

She saw the motorized screen roll up; behind it was a backlit knot-like symbol that made her eyes swim. It was just like the locket. In fact, it was the same as the locket, and she felt as if she was falling into it. Then her head began to ache, viciously, and she slumped under the weight of the suitcases. Remembering Roland's instructions, she rolled them forward, noting that the post room looked superficially the same, but the screened cupboard on this side was closed and there were some scrapes on the wall.

'Hmm.' She glanced around. No Roland, as yet. *Well, well, well*, she thought.

She glanced down at the case she'd carried over, blinked thoughtfully, then walked over to the wall with the pigeonholes, where another case was waiting.

One that hadn't been prepared for her. She bent down and sprang the catch on it, laid it flat on its side and lifted the lid. Her breath caught in her throat.

She wasn't sure what she'd been expecting. She'd been hoping for gold, jewels, scrolls, or maybe antibiotics and computers. This was what she'd been afraid of.

She shut the case and stood it upright again, then walked back to the ones she'd brought over and concentrated on quieting her racing heartbeat and smoothing her face into a welcoming, slightly coy smile before Roland the brilliant reformer, Roland the sympathetic friend, Roland the lying bastard, could bring his own suitcase through.

Who did you think you were kidding? she wondered bitterly. *You knew it was too good to be true.* And indeed it had been clear from the start that there had to be a catch somewhere.

The nature of the catch was obvious and ironic with twenty-twenty hindsight, and when she thought about it, she realized that Roland hadn't actually lied to her. She just hadn't asked the right questions.

What supplied the family's vast wealth on her own, the other, the *American* side of the border? It sure wasn't a fast postal service, not when it took six weeks to cross an untamed wilderness on pack mules beset by savage tribes. No, it was a different type of service – one intended for commodities of high value, low weight, and likely to be interrupted in transit through urban America. Something that the family could ship reliably through their own kingdoms and move back and forth to American soil at their leisure. In America they made their money by shipping goods across the Gruinmarkt fast; in the Gruinmarkt they made their money by moving goods across America slowly but reliably. The suitcase contained almost twenty kilograms of sealed polythene bags, and it didn't take a genius with degrees in journalism and medicine to figure out that they'd be full of Bolivian nose candy.

She thought about the investigation she'd been running with Paulie, and she didn't know whether to laugh or cry. Instead she began whistling a song by Brecht and Eisler – 'Supply & Demand (The Trader's Song)' – as she picked up her own suitcase and headed for the elevator to her suite.

My long-lost medievalist world-walking family are drug import/ export barons, she realized. *What the hell does that make me?*

IN THE FAMILY WAY

Alone in her apartment with the door locked, Miriam began to unpack her suitcase full of purchases. She'd arrived to find the maids in a state of near panic: 'Mistress, the duke, he wants to see you tomorrow lunchtime!' In the end she'd dismissed them all except for Meg, the oldest, who she sat down with for a quiet talk.

'I'm not used to having you around all the time,' she said bluntly. 'I know you're not going to go away, but I want you to make yourselves scarce. Ask one of the electricians to put a bell in, so I can call you when I need you. I don't mind people coming in to tidy up when I'm out of my rooms, but I don't want to be surrounded all the time. Can you do that?' Meg nodded, but looked puzzled. 'Any questions?' Miriam asked. 'No, ma'am,' Meg replied. But her expression said that she thought Miriam's behavior was distinctly strange.

Miriam sighed and pointed at the door. *Maybe if I act like they're hotel staff* . . . 'I'll want someone to come up in about three hours with some food – a tray of cold stuff will do – and a pot of tea. Apart from that, I don't expect to see anyone tonight and I don't want to be disturbed. Is that okay?'

'Yes'm.' Meg ducked her head and fled. 'Okay, so that works,' Miriam said thoughtfully. Which was good because now she had some space to work in, unobserved.

Fifteen minutes later the luggage was stowed where Miriam wanted it. Her new laptop was sitting on the dresser, plugged in to charge next to a stack of unopened software boxes. Her new wardrobe was hung up, awaiting the attentions of a seamstress whenever Miriam had time for a fitting. And the escape kit, as she was already thinking of it, was stashed in the suitcase at the back of the wardrobe.

'Memo.' She picked up her dictaphone and strolled through into the bathroom. It was the place she found it easiest to think. Cool white tiles, fine marble, nothing to aggravate the pounding headache she'd been plagued by for so much of the past week. Plus, it had a shower – which she turned on, just for the noise.

'Need to look for a bug-sweeping kit next time I get a chance on the other side. Must try the beta-blockers too, once I've looked up their side effects. Wonder if they've got a trained doctor over here? Or a clinic of some kind? Anyway.'

She swallowed. 'New memo. Must get some dictation software installed on the laptop, so I can transcribe this diary. Um. Roland and the family business bear some thought.' *That's the understatement of the century*, she told herself.

'They're . . . oh hell. They're not the Medelin cartel, but they probably ship a good quantity of their produce. It's a family business, or rather a whole bunch of families who intermarry because of the hereditary factor, with the Clan as a business arrangement that organizes everything. I suppose they probably smuggled jewels or gold or something before the drugs thing. The whole nine yards about not marrying out – whether the ability is a recessive gene or not doesn't matter – they've got *omertà*, the law of silence, as a side effect of their social setup. In this world, they're upwardly mobile nobles, merchant princes trying to marry into the royal family. In my world, they're gangsters. Mafia families without the Sicilian in-laws.'

She hit the 'pause' button for a moment.

'So I'm a Mafia princess. Talk about not getting involved with wiseguys! What do I make of it?'

She paused again, and noticed that she was pacing back and forth distractedly.

'It's blood money. Or is it? If these people are the government here, and they say it's legal to smuggle cocaine or heroin, does that make it okay? This is one huge can of worms. Even if you leave ethics out of the question, even if you think the whole war on drugs is a bad idea like prohibition in the twenties, it's still a huge headache.' She massaged her throbbing forehead. 'I really need to talk to Iris. She'd set me straight.'

She leaned her forehead against the cool tiles beside the mirror over the sink. 'Problem is, I can't walk away from them. I can't just leave, walk out, and go back to life in Cambridge. It's not just the government who'd want to bury me so deep the sun would never find me. The Clan can't risk me talking. Now that I think about it, it's weird that they let Roland get as far as he did. Only, if he's telling the truth, Angbard is keeping him on a short leash these days. What does that suggest they've got in mind for me? A short leash *and* a choke collar?'

She could see it in her mind's eye, the chain of events that would unfold if she were to walk into an FBI office and prove what she could do – maybe with the aid of a sack of cocaine, maybe not. Maybe with Paulie's CD full of research, too, she realized, sitting up. 'Damn.' A dawning supposition: Drug-smuggling rings needed to sanitize their revenue stream, didn't they? And the business with Biphase and Proteome was in the right part of the world, and the Clan was certainly sophisticated enough . . . if her hunch was right, then it was, in fact, her long-lost family's investments that Paulie was holding the key to.

In the FBI office, first there'd be disbelief. Then the growing realization that a journalist was handing them the drugs case of the century. Followed by the hasty escalation, the witness protection program offers – then their reaction to her demonstrated ability to walk through walls. The secondary scenarios as the FBI realize that they can't protect her, can't even protect themselves against assassins from another world. Then blind panic and bad decisions.

'If the families decided to attack the United States at home, they could make al-Qaeda look like amateurs,' she muttered into her dictaphone, stricken. 'They have the resources of a government at their disposal, because over here they're running things. Does that make them a government? Or so close it makes no difference? They're rich and powerful on the other side, too. Another generation and they'll probably be getting their fingers into the pie in D.C. I wonder. They make their money from smuggling, and they're personally immune to attempts to imprison them. The only thing that could hurt them would be if Congress decriminalized all drugs, so the price crashed and they could be shipped legally. Maybe the families are actually pushing the war on drugs? Paying politicians to call for tougher sanctions, border patrols against ordinary smugglers? Breaking the competition and driving the price up because of the law of supply and demand. *Damn.*'

She flicked the 'stop' button on her dictaphone and put it down, shuddering. It made a frightening amount of sense. *I am sitting on a news story that makes the attack on the World Trade Center look like a five-minute wonder*, she realized with a sinking feeling. *No, I am sitting* in the middle *of the story. What am I going to do?*

At that exact moment the telephone out in her reception room rang.

Old habits died hard, and Miriam was out of the bathroom in seconds with the finely honed reflexes of a journalist with an editor on the line. She picked the phone up before she realized there were no buttons, nothing to indicate it could dial an outside line. 'Yes?'

'Miriam?'

She froze, heart sinking. 'Roland,' she said.

'You locked your door and sent your maids away. I wanted to make sure you're all right.'

'All right?' She considered her next words carefully. 'I'm not all right, Roland. I looked in the suitcase. The other one, the one waiting in the post room.' Her chest felt tight. He'd lied to her, but on the other hand, she'd been holding more than a little back herself –

A pause. 'I know. It was a test. The only question was which one you'd open. I don't know if it makes any difference, but I was ordered to give you the opportunity. To figure it all out for yourself. "Give her enough rope" were his exact words. So now you know.'

'Know what?' she said flatly. 'That he's an extremely devious conspirator or about the family's dirty little secret?'

'Both.' Roland waited for her to reply.

'I feel used,' she said calmly. 'I am also extremely pissed off. In fact, I'm still working out how I feel about everything. It's not the drugs, exactly: I don't think I've got any illusions about that side of things. I studied enough pharmacology to know the difference between propaganda and reality, and I saw enough in med school, from ODs and drunk drivers and people coughing up lung cancers, to know you get the same results whether the drug's illegal or not. But the manipulative side of it – there's a movie on the other side called *The Godfather*. Have you ever seen it?'

'Yes. That's it, exactly.' He paused. 'By the way, Don Corleone asked me to tell you that he expects to see you in his office tomorrow at ten o'clock sharp.' His voice changed, abruptly serious. 'Please don't shout at him. I think it's another test, but I'm not sure what kind – it could be very dangerous for you if you anger him. I don't want to see you get hurt, Miriam. Or Helge, as he'll call you. But you're Miriam to me. Listen, for your own good, whatever he says, don't refuse a direct order. He is much more dangerous than he looks, and if he thinks you'll bite him, he may put family loyalty aside, because his real loyalty is to the Clan as a whole. You're a close family member, but the Clan, by the law of families, comes first. Just sit tight and remember that you've got more leverage than you realize. He will want you to make a secure alliance, both to keep you safe – for the memory of his stepsister – and to shore up his own position. Failing that, he'll be able to pretend to ignore you as long as you don't disobey a direct order. Do you hear what I'm saying?'

'Yes.' Her heart pounded. 'So it's going to happen.'

'What?'

'Fucking Cinderella. Never mind. Roland, I am not stupid. I need some time to myself to think, that's all. I'm angry with you in the abstract, not the particular. I don't like being made to jump through hoops. I hear what you're saying. Do you hear me?'

'Yes.' A pause. 'I think I do. I'm angry too.'

'Oh, really?' she asked, half-sarcastically.

'Yes.' This time, a longer pause. 'I like your sense of humor, but it's going to get you into deep trouble if you don't keep it under control. There are people here who will respond to sarcasm with a garrote. Trying to change the way the Clan works from the inside is hard.'

'Goodbye.' She hung up hastily and stood next to the phone for a long minute, heart thudding at her ribs, head throbbing in time to it. The smell of leather car seats was strong in her nose, the memory of his smile over lunch fixed in her mind's eye. *Duke's orders*, she thought. *Well, he would say that, wouldn't he?*

She managed to pull herself away from the telephone and walked back into her bedroom, to the dresser with the tiny PictureBook computer perched next to the stack of disks and the external DVD-ROM drive. She had software to install. She riffled through disks containing relief maps of North America, an electronic pharmacopoeia, and a multimedia history of the Medici families. She put them down next to the encyclopedia of medieval history and other textbooks that had seemed relevant.

Once she'd made her first notes for the article Andy had commissioned, she'd start installing the software. Then she had a long night of cramming ahead, reading up on the great medieval merchant princes and their dynasties. The sooner she got a handle on this situation, the better . . .

*

Another morning dawned – a Sunday, bright and cold. Miriam blinked tiredly and threw back her bed clothes to let the cold air in. *I may be getting used to this*, she thought blearily. *Oh dear*. She looked at her watch and saw that the ten o'clock interview with Duke Angbard was worryingly close. 'Damn,' she said aloud, but was gratified to note that the word brought no maidservants scurrying out of the woodwork. Even better, the outer suite was empty except for a steaming jug of strong coffee and a tray piled with croissants, just as she'd requested. 'I could get used to this level of room service,' she muttered to herself

She laid out a conservative suit for the meeting with the duke. 'Think medieval,' she told herself. 'Think demure, feminine, unprovocative.' For a touch of color, she tied a bright silk scarf round her throat. 'Think camouflage.' And remember what Roland said about not defying the old bastard openly. At least, not yet. How and where to get the leverage was the sixty-four-thousand-dollar question, to be followed by the bonus question of when and how to use it, but she doubted she'd find such tools conveniently lying around while she lived as a guest – or valued prisoner – in his house. And being beholden to a powerful man left a nasty taste in her mouth.

However, there was one thing she could carry to even up the

odds – a very potent equalizer. To complete her ensemble, Miriam chose a small black makeup bag, clearly too small to hold a gun or anything threatening. She didn't load it down with much: just a tube of lipstick, some tissues, and a running dictaphone.

The door to her suite was cooperating today, she noted as she pushed into the corridor outside. She remembered the way to the duke's suite and made her way quietly past a pair of diligent maidservants who were busy polishing the brass-work on one of the doors and a footman who appeared to be replacing the flowers on one of the ornamental side tables. They bowed out of her way and she nodded, passing them hastily. The whole palace appeared to be coming awake, as if occupants who had been sleeping were coming out of the woodwork to resume their life.

She reached the duke's outer office door and paused. Big double doors, closed, with a room on the other side. She took a deep breath and pushed the button set beside the door.

'Wer ish?' His voice crackled tinnily: a loose wire somewhere.

'It's Miriam – Helge. I believe the duke wanted to talk to me,' she replied to the speaker.

'Enter.' The lock clicked discreetly and Miriam pushed the door inward. It was astonishingly heavy, as if lined with steel, and it drifted shut behind her.

Matthias, the frightening secretary, was waiting behind the big desk in shirtsleeves, his jacket slung over the back of his chair. This time she noted the pile of papers in front of him. Some of them looked like FedEx waybills, and some of them looked like letters.

'Helge. Miriam.' Matthias nodded to her, almost friendly.

'Yes.' *Why does he make me so nervous?* She wondered. Was it just the shoulder holster he wore so conspicuously? Or the way he avoided eye contact but scanned across and around her all the while?

'You have an appointment,' he said. 'But you should call first, before setting out. So that we can send an escort for you.'

'An escort?' She asked. 'Why would I want an escort?'

He raised an eyebrow. 'Why wouldn't you? You are a lady of status, you deserve an escort. To be seen without one is a slight to your honor. Besides, someone might seek to take advantage.'

'Uh-huh. I'll think about it.' She nodded at the inner door. 'Is he ready?'

'One moment.' Matthias stood, then knocked on the door. A muttered exchange followed. Matthias pulled the door ajar, then held it for her. 'You may enter,' he said, his expression unreadable. As she passed his desk, he moved to place his body in front of the papers there.

Miriam pretended not to notice as she entered the lion's den. As before, Duke Angbard was seated at his writing desk, back to the window, so that she had to squint into the light to see him. But this time there was nobody else present, and he rose to welcome her into his study.

'Ah, Miriam, my dear niece. Please come in.'

He was trying for the kindly uncle role, she decided, so she smiled warmly in return as she approached the desk. 'Uncle. Uh, I'm unfamiliar with the proper form of address. I hope you don't mind if I call you Angbard?'

'Not in private.' He smiled benevolently down at her. 'In public, it would be best to call me "Your Excellency" or "Uncle", depending on context – official or familial. Please have a seat.'

'Thanks.' She sat down opposite him, and he sat down in turn. He was wearing another exquisitely tailored suit of conservative cut with, she couldn't help noticing, a sword. It was curved: a saber, perhaps, but she couldn't be sure – the blades with which she was most familiar were scalpels. 'Is there anything in particular you wanted to talk to me about?'

'Oh, many things.' His broad wave took in half the world. 'It isn't customary here to introduce conversations with business, but I gather you are accustomed to a life conducted at a brisker pace.' He leaned back in his chair, face shadowed. 'Roland tells me you opened the second case,' he said briskly. 'What have you to say for yourself?'

The moment of truth. Miriam leaned back, consciously mirroring his posture.

'Well, I'd have to say that only an idiot lets themselves be sucked into any business arrangement without a full awareness of what it involves,' she said slowly. 'And nobody had ordered me not to peek.

You should also note that I'm here to discuss it with you, and the only other person who knows about it is Roland. What do you think?'

'I think that shows the necessary level of discretion,' he replied after a moment. 'Now. What is your opinion of the business? And of your own relationship to it?'

'It makes a lot of sense for a group of families in the position that ours so clearly occupies,' she said, carefully trying to avoid giving the wrong impression. 'I can see why you might want to test a new, ah, family member. As businesses go it is neatly orchestrated and appears to be efficiently run.' She shrugged, biting back the urge to add: *For an eighteenth-century family concern. As business organizations go, it's still in the dark ages* . . . 'And it's hardly appropriate for me to comment on where that platinum credit card came from, is it?'

'Indeed not,' he said. 'But you seem to be clear on your position.' A slight tightening of the skin around his eyes alerted her, a moment before his next question: 'Are you a drug user?'

'Me?' She laughed, mentally crossing her fingers. 'No! Never.' *At least, not heroin or crack. Please don't let him ask about anything else.* Like many students, she'd acquired a passing familiarity with marijuana, but had mostly given it up some time ago. And she didn't think he was the type to count coffee, cigars, or whiskey as drugs.

'That's good,' he said seriously. 'Most users are indiscreet. Can't keep secrets. Bad for business.'

'Sobriety is next to godliness,' she agreed, nodding enthusiastically, then wondered if she'd overdone it when he fixed her with a slightly jaundiced stare. Oops, five glasses of wine, she remembered – and shrugged self-deprecatingly. His glare slowly faded.

'You have your mother's sly tongue,' he commented. 'But I didn't call you here to ask you questions about your opinion of our business. I gather that Roland has been filling in a few of the gaps in your education – some of them, like a working knowledge of High Tongue, will take a long time to remedy – but I dare say he has not been forthcoming in full with the details of your position in the Clan. Is that the case?'

Miriam could feel her forehead wrinkle. 'He said I was rich and of very high position. But he didn't explain in detail, no. Why?'

'Well, then,' said the duke, 'perhaps I had better hasten to explain. You see, you are in a unique position – two unique positions.'

'Really? What kind?' she asked brightly.

'You know that there are five families in the Clan,' Angbard began. 'These are Lofstrom – the senior family – Thorold, Hjorth, Wu, Arnesen, and Hjalmar. Yes, I know that's six. The familial name does not necessarily correspond to a lineage. Our families are the descendants of the children of the founder, Angmar Lofstrom. He had many children, but the blood ran thin – only when their children married and the great-grandchildren showed the family trait were we able to come together to form the Clan.'

He cleared his throat. 'Wu is not the name of one of our original ancestors; it is a name that the second son of line Arnesen took upon emigrating to the Outer Kingdom, two thousand miles to the west, perhaps a hundred and twenty years ago.

'The idea was that family Wu would become our western arm, trading with us by way of the Union Pacific Railroad, to mutual benefit. That wasn't the first attempt, by the way. Angmar the elder's youngest son, Marc, tried to cross the wilderness far earlier, but the attempt came to nothing and Marc was lost. So, we have branches on both sides of the Continental Divide. And a history of other families. Once there were seven lineages – but I digress.'

'But how does it all work?' Miriam asked. 'How does the Clan come out of all this?'

'The Clan is not what you'd call a limited liability company – it is a partnership. A family firm, if you like. You see, we hold our lands and riches and titles in common trust for the Clan, which operates in concert and receives the profits from all our ventures. The Clan makes use of all who have the world-walking talent – the members of the inner families – and arranges or authorizes marriages that braid the families together across generations, avoiding both out-breeding and too many close-kin marriages. It also controls the outer family – those who lack the talent, but whose children might possess it if they marry like with like – and finds jobs for them over here. For example, Matthias cannot ever visit Boston on his own – but he has a talent for security, and makes a most excellent mailed fist. We number almost five hundred world-walkers now, and with two thousand in the outer families the pickings at the lower ranks are slim.'

He coughed. 'One iron rule is that family members are required to marry into another family lineage – otherwise the blood runs thin within a generation. The only exceptions are by prior dispensation of the council, to permit an alliance outside the Clan, such as adoption into the nobility. The second iron rule is that inheritance follows Clan shareholdings, not lineage or family. If you die, your children inherit whatever the Clan allocates to them – you hold your estates from the Clan, they don't belong to you because without the Clan you would be nothing. The system is supposed to encourage cooperation and it usually succeeds, but there are exceptions. Sixty years ago, a war broke out within the Clan, between families – Wu and Hjorth on one side, Thorold, Lofstrom, Arnesen, and Hjalmar on the other. Nobody is certain what started it – those who knew died early on – but my personal supposition is that the Wu family, in their ambition to climb into the Eternal Palace itself, exposed themselves to court intrigue and were turned into a weapon against us by the Palace of the Outer Kingdom, which considered the Wu lineage to be a threat. In any event, during the war years our numbers fell from perhaps a thousand of the true blood to fewer than two hundred. The war ended thirty-five years ago with a treaty, solemnized by the marriage of Patricia Lofstrom Thorold to Alfredo Wu. Patricia was my half-sister, and I inherited custody of the Lofstrom estates.'

He paused to clear his throat. 'Your mother's death is now confirmed, although neither her nor Alfredo's body was recovered. Since then, there has been no pretender to the estates of the Thorold–Hjorth shareholding, which were therefore administered as a trusteeship under the order of the High Crown.'

'The High Crown?'

'Yes, the royal family,' he said irritably. 'You don't have one, I know. We have to put up with them, and they can be a blithering nuisance!'

'Ah, I think I begin to see. So. There's a big shareholding in the Clan enterprise, under the control of an external party who knows who and what you are. Then I come along and offer you a lever to take it back under the family's control. Is that right?'

'Yes. As long as nobody kills you first,' he said.

'Now, wait a minute!' She leaned forward. 'Who would do that? And why?'

'Oh, several parties,' Angbard said with an unnerving tone of relish. 'The Crown, to maintain their grip on almost a tenth of our properties and revenues without forcing an outright war with their most powerful nobles. Whoever killed Patricia, for the same reason. Any of the younger generations of lineages Hjorth and Thorold, who must be hoping that the shares will escheat to them in due course should no pretender emerge and should those families recreate the braid of inheritance. And finally, the Drug Enforcement Agency.'

'What are *they* doing here?'

'They aren't, I merely name them as another party who would take an instant dislike to you were they to become aware of your existence.' He smiled humorlessly. 'Think of it as another test, if you like.'

'Ri-i-ight,' she drawled. *I already figured that much out for myself, thanks.* 'I believe I see where you're coming from, Uncle. One question?'

'Ask away, by all means.'

'Roland. Does *he* have a motive for killing me?'

Angbard startled her by laughing loudly. 'Roland the dreaming runaway?' He leaned back in his chair. 'Roland, who tried to convince us all to sign away our lands to the peasantry and set up a banking system to loan them money? Roland the rebel? He's squandered all the credibility he might have built by refusing to play the game over here. I think Roland Lofstrom will make a suitable husband for Olga Thorold. And she should make him an excellent wife – she'll slow him down and that's necessary, he has disruptive tendencies. Once he's yoked to the Clan, it might be time to revisit some of his ideas, but as things stand, the council can't afford to be seen taking him seriously – by rebelling in his youth he has automatically tainted any valid reformist ideas he may advocate. Which is a shame. Meanwhile, you are my direct niece. Patricia, your mother, was the daughter of my father's first wife. Roland, in contrast, is the son of my half-brother, by my father's third wife. He's not a blood relative of yours

138

– at least, not within four generations. Three wives, three children, three scandals! My father lent our affairs much complexity . . .

'Anyway, Roland will create another Thorold–Lofstrom braid, which will be of considerable use to my successor, whoever he is. But he's not important and he has no stake in your disarray. That is why it was safe for him to know of your existence so early.'

Miriam shook her head. The family intricacies confused her, and she was left with nothing but a vague impression of plaited families and arranged marriages. 'Have you asked Olga's opinion about this?' she asked.

'Why would I? She'll do as she's told for the good of the Clan. She's a sweet child.'

'Oh, that's all right then,' Miriam said, nodding slightly and biting her cheek to keep a straight face.

'Which brings me to you, again,' Angbard nodded. 'Obviously, you are *not* a sweet child. You're an experienced dowager, I would say, and sharp as a razor. I approve of that. But I hope I have made it clear to you that your future is inextricably tied to the Clan. You can't go back into obscurity on the other side – your enemies would seek you out, whether you will it or no. Nor can you afford not to take sides and find a protector.'

'I see,' she stated, biting the words out sharply.

'I think it would be best for you to see something of the other families before we discuss this further,' Angbard continued, ignoring her coolness. 'As it happens, Olga is summoned to pay attendance upon the person of the king for the next three months, who as it also happens is not one of us – it would be a good thing at this juncture for you to make your debut before the royal court and that part of the Clan that is in residence in the capital in her company. Your presence should lure certain lice out of the bedding in an, ah, controlled manner. Meanwhile you will not entirely be at a loose end, or without support, when you make the rounds of the eligible nobility before the annual grand meeting at Beltaigne, seven months hence. Olga can advise you on bloodlines and shareholdings and etiquette, and begin language lessons. I place no obligation upon you to make a hasty alliance, just so long as you understand your situation.'

'Right. So I'm to go looking for an alliance – a husband who meets with your approval – at court. When do you expect me to do this?' Miriam asked, summoning a forced brightness to conceal her slowly gathering anger. 'I assume you're planning on exhibiting me widely?'

'Olga departs tomorrow morning by stage,' Angbard announced. 'You shall travel with her, and on arrival at court in Niejwein she will help you select your ladies-in-waiting – of low but family rank, not base servants such as you have had here. Your maids are already packing your bags, by the way.' He fixed her with a coldly unamused smile. 'Think of it as another test, if you like. You do see this is for your own long-term good, don't you?' he asked.

'Oh, I see, all right,' Miriam said and smiled at him, as sweet as cyanide-laced marzipan. 'Yes, I see everything very clearly indeed.'

*

Miriam politely declined the duke's invitation to lunch and returned to her apartment in a state of barely controlled fury. Her temper was not made better by the discovery that her maids had packed most of her clothes in heavy wooden trunks.

'Shit!' She spat at the bathroom mirror. 'You will be good, won't you,' she muttered under her breath. 'Patronizing bastard, my dear.'

Murderous bastard, a still small voice reminded her from inside. Duke Angbard was quite capable of killing people, Roland had said. Paulie's words came back to haunt her: 'If you back down, they own you; it's as simple as that.' And what the hell was that crack about luring lice out of the bedding meant to mean? She sobered up fast. *I need advice*, she decided. And then a thought struck her – a thought simultaneously wicked and so delicious that it brought a smile to her lips. A perfect scheme, really, one that would gain her exactly what she needed, while simultaneously sending an unequivocal message to the duke, if she went all the way through with it.

She headed back into the suite, chased her maids out, shut the door, and picked up the phone. 'Put me through to Earl Roland,' she demanded in her most imperious voice.

'Yes, ma'am,' the operator confirmed. 'One moment.'

'Roland?' she said, suddenly much less confident. 'Roland the dreamer', his uncle called him. Roland the disruptive influence, who looked too good to be true. Did she go through with this? Just picking up the phone made her feel obscurely guilty. It also gave her a thrill of illicit anticipation.

'Miriam! What can I do for you?'

'Listen,' she said, licking her suddenly dry lower lip, 'about yesterday. You invited me to . . . dinner? Does that invitation still stand?'

'You've seen the old man?' he asked.

'Yes.' She waited.

'Oh. Well, yes, the invitation still stands. Would you like to come?'

'As long as it's just you and me. No servants, no company, no nothing.'

'Oh!' He sounded amused. 'Miriam, have you any idea how fast word of that would get around, now that the palace is fully staffed again? That sort of thing just doesn't happen you know. Not with servants.'

'It's not like that: I need confidential advice,' she said. Lowering her voice, 'They must know I've spent over thirty years on the other side. Can I catch a couple of hours with you, without anyone snooping?'

'Hmm.' He paused for a bit. 'Only if you can manage to become invisible. Listen, I am in the suite on the floor above you, second along. I'll have dinner laid out at six, then send the servants away. Still, it'll be best if nobody sees you. It would cause tongues to wag – and give your enemies words to throw back at you.'

'I'll think of a way,' she promised. 'Lay on the wine and dress for dinner. I'll be seeing you.'

PART THREE

HOTHOUSE FLOWERS

THE INVISIBLE WOMAN

The small town of Svarlberg squatted at the mouth of the Fall River on the coast, a day's ride south of Fort Lofstrom. Overlooked by a crumbling but huge stone fortress built on the Roman model, brought to the western lands by survivors of the Roman Gothic war against the Turkic occupiers of Constantinople and now used as a bulwark against threat of invasion by sea, Svarlberg was home to a thriving fishing community and a harbor much used by coast-hugging merchants.

Not that many merchants would put into this harbor so late in the year. A few late stragglers coming down the coast from the icy trapping settlements up north, and perhaps an overdue ship braving the North Atlantic winter to make the last leap from the Ice Isles to western civilization – but winter was beginning to bite, and only rich fools or the truly desperate would brave the boreal gales this late in the year.

When the horseman reined in his tired mount outside the portside inn, wearily slid out of the saddle, and banged on the door, it took a minute for the owner to open the hole and look out. 'What are you wanting?' he asked brusquely.

'Board, beer, and stable.' The rider held up a coin so the innkeeper could see it. 'Or are you already asleep for the winter, like a bear fattened on salmon since I was here last, Andru?'

'Ah, come you in.' Andru the innkeeper unbarred the heavy door and yelled over his shoulder: 'Markus! Markus! Where is the boy?' A freezing draft set him to shivering. 'It's perishing cold out. Will you be staying long this time, sir?'

A thin boy came rushing out of the kitchens. 'Ma said I was to – ' he began.

'Horse,' said Andru. 'Stable. Brash. Oats. You know what to do.'

'Yes, master.' The boy half-bowed cringingly, then waited while the rider unstrapped one saddle bag before leading the gelding around the side of the inn.

'Layabout would rather stay in the warmth,' Andru said, shaking his head and glancing along the street in the vain hope of some more passing trade, but it was twilight, and everyone with any sense was already abed. He stepped aside to let his customer in, then pulled the door shut. 'What'll it be first, sir?'

'Whatever you've got.' The rider bared his teeth in a smile half-concealed by a heavy scarf. 'I'm expecting a visitor tonight or tomorrow. If you've got a private room and a pipe, I'll take it.'

'Be at your ease sir, and I'll sort it out immediately.' The innkeeper hurried off, calling: 'Raya! Raya! Is the wake room fit for a king's man?'

The inn was half-empty, dead as a doornail by virtue of the time of day and the season of year. A drunken sailor lay in one corner, snoring quietly, and a public scribe sat at one end of a table, mumbling over a mug of mulled wine and a collection of fresh quills as he cut and tied them for the next week's business. It was definitely anything but a thriving scene. Which suited the horseman fine, because the fewer people who saw him here, the better.

A moment later, the innkeeper bustled up – 'This way, this way please, kind sir!' – and herded the rider through a side door. 'We've laid out the wake room for you, sir, and if you will sit for it a selection of cold cuts and a bottle of the southern wine: Will that be sufficient? It's late in the season, but we will be roasting a lamb tomorrow if you should be staying – '

'Yes, yes – ' The innkeeper hurried out again and the rider settled himself in the armchair beside the table and stretched out his legs, snarling quietly when the kitchen girl didn't hurry to remove his boots fast enough.

Two hours later he was nodding over his second cup of wine – the room was passably warm, and a couple of large chunks of sausage and pickled tongue had filled his belly comfortably – when there was a discreet tap on the door. He was on his feet instantly, gun at the ready. 'Who is it?' he asked quietly.

'When the dragon of the north wind blows – shit, is that you, Jacob?'

'Hello, Esau.' Jacob dragged the door open one-handed. The revolver vanished.

'It's freezing out there.' The man called Esau blew on his fingers, shook his head, then began to peel his gloves off.

Jacob kicked the door shut. 'You really need to observe proper security discipline,' he said.

'Yeah well, and how many times have we done this?' Esau shrugged. 'Stupid Christ-cultist names from the far-side, dumb pass-phrases and secret handshakes – '

'If I was ill and sent proxies, the dumb pass-phrases would be the only thing that could tell you who they were,' Jacob pointed out.

'If you were ill, you'd have radioed ahead to call off the meeting. Is that a bottle of the local emetic? I'll have a drop.'

'Here. Settle down.' Jacob poured. 'What have you got for me?'

Esau shrugged. 'This.' A leather purse appeared, as magically as Jacob's pistol. 'Pharmaceutical-grade, half a kilo.'

'That'll do.' Jacob transferred it to his belt pouch without expression.

'Anything else?'

'Well.' Esau settled down and picked up the full tankard. 'Certain feathers have been – ruffled, shall we say – by the news of those pink slippers. That account was supposed to have been settled a very long time ago. Do you have an update for me?'

'Yes.' Jacob nodded, then picked up his own mug. 'Nothing good. A couple more sightings and then a search and sweep found a very wet chair in the woods near Fort Lofstrom. It was from the other side. Need I say any more? It was too obvious to cover up, so the old man sent a snatch squad through and they pulled in a woman. Age thirty-two, professional journalist, and clearly a long-lost cousin.'

'A woman journalist? Things are passing strange over there.'

'You're telling me. Sometimes I get to visit on business. It's even weirder than those sheep-shagging slant-eyes on the west coast.' Jacob put the empty mug down – hard – on the table. 'Why does this shit always happen when I'm in charge?'

'Because you're good,' soothed Esau. 'Don't worry, we'll get it sorted out and I'm pretty sure the – control – will authorize a reward for this. It's exactly what we've been looking out for all these years.' He smiled at Jacob and raised his tankard. 'To your success.'

'Huh.' But Jacob raised his (empty) mug right back, then refilled both of them. 'Well. The old asshole put the runaway on her case, but she's turning out to be a bit hot. She's the grand dowager's granddaughter, you know? And a rebel. All too common in women from over there, you know. She's poking her nose into all sorts of corners. If the old bat recognizes her formally, seven shades of shit will hit the Clan council balance of power, but I have a plan that I think will cover the possibility. She could be very useful if I can coopt her.'

'What about her mother?' Esau leaned forward.

'Dead.' Jacob shrugged. 'The baby was adopted on the other side. That's why she was missing for so long. We've got the foster mother under surveillance, but . . .' he shook his head. 'It's a thirty-two-year-old trail. What do you expect?'

'I expect her to – ' Esau frowned. 'Look, I'm going to have to break cover on this and go get instructions from my superiors. There may be pre-existing orders in effect for just this situation, but if not, it would be as well for you to proceed as you see fit. Anything that keeps the Clan from asking awkward questions is all right by us, I think. And I don't want to risk using one of your magical radio thingies in case they've got a black chamber somewhere listening in. Are you going to be here overnight?'

'I will be.' Jacob nodded. 'I was planning to leave in the morning, though.'

'That's all right. I'll cross over and ask for directions. If anyone knows anything, I'll pass on your instructions before you leave.' He rubbed his forehead in anticipation, missing Jacob's flash of envy, which was in any case quickly masked. 'If I don't show, well, use your imagination. We don't need the Clan raking over the evidence . . .'

'Evidence that might point to your faction's existence.'

'Exactly.'

*

Servants were invisible, Miriam realized, as she hurried through the narrow rough-walled corridor below stairs. Take this particular servant, for example.

She was wearing the parlour maid outfit she'd bought from the theatrical supplier's, hurrying along beneath a tray with a pot of coffee on it. Nobody paid her a second glance. Maybe they should have, she decided, carefully putting one foot in front of another. The servant outfit was inauthentic, machine-woven, obviously wrong if anyone had looked closely, and bulked up from hiding something underneath. But the house was still in upheaval, individual servants were mostly beneath notice to the noble occupants, and the staff was large enough that she didn't expect to be noticed by the real maids. *This is going to be useful*, Miriam decided, balancing the tray carefully as she mounted the staircase.

The tight spiral steps were a trial, but she managed not to tread on her hem as she wound her way up to the floor above. Once she squeezed against the wall to let an equerry by: He glanced at her in mild disgust and continued on. *Score one to the invisible woman*, she told herself. She stalked along the corridor, edgy with anticipation. Planning this move in cold blood was all very well, but she wouldn't be able to go through with it if the idea of an illicit assignation with Roland didn't set her pulse racing. And now she came to the final passage, she found her blood wasn't cool at all.

She found the right door and entered without knocking. It was another private apartment, seemingly empty. She put the tray down on the sideboard beside the door, then looked around. One of the side doors opened: 'I didn't order – oh.'

'We meet again.' She grinned nervously at him, then dropped the latch on the door. 'Just in case,' she said.

Roland looked her up and down in mild disbelief. 'You're a mistress of disguise, too? It's a good thing I swept the room earlier. For bugs,' he added, catching her raised eyebrow.

'Well, that was prudent. You look great, too.' He'd dressed in a black tuxedo, she noted with relief. He'd taken her seriously; she'd been a little worried.

'Where's the bathroom?'

'Through there.' He looked doubtful.

'Back in a minute,' she said, ducking inside.

She closed the door, hastily untied her servant's apron, shook her hair out of the borrowed mob cap, then spent a minute fumbling with her waistband. She stripped off the servant's outerwear, then paused to look in a mirror. 'Go kill him, girl,' she told herself. She deftly rolled on a coat of lip gloss, installed earrings and a single string of pearls. Finally she pulled on her black evening gloves, did an experimental twirl that set two thousand dollars' worth of evening dress swirling, blew herself a kiss in the mirror, and stepped out.

Roland was waiting outside, holding a goblet of wine out toward her: He nearly dropped it when he saw her. 'You look absolutely spectacular,' he said, finally. 'How did you do it?'

'Oh, it wasn't hard.' She shrugged her shoulders, which were bare. 'You could conceal an arsenal under one of those maids' uniforms.' *I know. I did.* She took the glass from him, then took his hand, led him to the sofa. 'Sit.' She sat herself, then patted the leather seat next to her. 'We need to talk.'

'Sure.' He followed her, looking slightly dazzled.

She felt a stab of tenderness mixed with regret, unsettling and unexpected.

What am I really doing here? she half-wondered, then shoved the thought aside.

'Come on. Sit down.' He sat in the opposite corner of the huge leather sofa, one arm over the back, the other cradling his glass in front of him, almost hiding behind it. 'I had my chat with Angbard today.'

'Ah.' He looked defensive.

She took a sip from the glass and smiled at him. The wine was more than good, it was excellent, a rich, fruity vintage with a subtle aftertaste that reminded her of strawberries and freshly mowed lawns. She fired another smile at him, and he cracked, took a mouthful, and tried to smile back.

'Roland, I think the duke may be lying to us – separately. Or merely being economical with the truth.'

'Ah, "lying"?' He looked cautiously defensive.

'Lying.' She sighed, then looked at him sidelong. 'I'm going to tell you what he told me, then you can tell me if that's what he told you. Do you think you can do that? No need to reveal any secrets . . .'

'"Secrets",' he echoed. A shadow flickered across his face. 'Miriam, there are things I'm not allowed to tell you, and I don't like it, but it's possible that – well, some of them may be seeds.'

'Seeds?'

'False secrets, to detect loose lips by identifying the source of the leak.' He took a mouthful of the Cabernet. 'Stuff that, if I tell you, will probably make you do something predictable, so that he'll know I told you. Do you understand? I'm not considered trustworthy. I came back with ideas about, well, about trying to change the way things are done. Ideas that upset a lot of people. The duke seems to like me – or at least think some of my ideas could be useful – but he certainly doesn't trust me. That's why he keeps me so close at hand.'

'Yes.' She nodded thoughtfully. Her opinion of him rose yet again: He doesn't lie to himself. 'I guessed that. Which is why I'm going to tell you what he told me and you're just going to decide whether to confirm it if it's true.'

'Uh, okay.' He was intensely focused on her. Good, she thought, feeling a little thrill. She slid one leg over the other, let a calf encased in sheer black stocking peek out. *The game's afoot*, she thought to herself, then noticed his response and felt her breath catch in her throat. *Then again, maybe it's not all a game.*

'Okay, this is what he told me. He says I'm in an exposed position and liable to be attacked, maybe murdered, if I don't dig myself inextricably into the Clan power structure as soon as possible. He says I have some discretion, but I ought to marry within the families and do it soon. Which I think is bullshit, but I let him lead me on. So he's sending me to the royal court with Olga, for a formal presentation and coming-out. We leave tomorrow.' When she said tomorrow he frowned.

'There's more.' She paused to drink, then put her empty glass down. Her stomach felt warm, relaxed. She met his eyes. 'Is what he told me about expecting me to find a husband among the families what you heard?'

'Yes.' Roland nodded. 'I didn't know you were to leave tomorrow, though,' he said, sounding a little disappointed.

Miriam straightened up and leaned toward him. 'Yes, well, he also discussed you,' she said. 'He said he's going to marry you off to Olga.'

'Bastard – ' Roland raised his glass to hide his expression, then drank its contents straight down.

'What, no comment?' Miriam asked, her heart pounding. This was the critical moment –

'I'm sorry. Not your fault,' he said hoarsely. 'I'd guessed he was going to try something to tie me down, but not that crude.' He shook his head, frustrated. 'Stupid.' He took a deep breath, visibly struggling for control.

'I take it that's a no.'

He put his glass down on the low table beside the sofa. As he straightened up, Miriam laid one hand on his arm. 'What you told me the other day – he wants you nailed to a perch, just an obedient little branch on the family tree,' she said urgently. 'Angbard wants you to make an appropriate marriage and breed lots of little Thorold-Lofstroms to look after him in his old age. With Olga.'

'Yes.' Roland shook his head. He didn't seem to notice her hand on his arm. 'I thought he was at least still interested in – shit. Olga's loyal. It means he's been stringing me along with his warnings to shut up and play the political game – all along, all the time.' He stood up and paced across the room agitatedly. 'He's been keeping me here on ice to stop me making my case in public.' He reached the fireplace and paused, thumping the heel of his right hand into his left palm. 'Bastard.'

'So Uncle Angbard has been messing you around?'

'"Uncle" – ' he shook his head. 'He's much more your uncle than mine. You know how the family braids work? There are several deaths and remarriages in the tree.'

Miriam stood up. *Don't let him get distracted now*. This is the point of no return, she realized. *Do I want to go through with this?* Well, the answer that came to mind wasn't 'no'. She screwed up her courage and walked over to him.

'Olga would lock you in and throw away the key.'

'She'd – no, not deliberately. But the effect would be the same.' He didn't seem to notice her standing a few inches in front of him, close enough to feel her breath on his cheek. *Is he completely blind – or just too distracted to notice what his eyeballs are seeing?* Miriam wondered, half-turning to face him and pushing her chest up as far as she could without being blatant about it – which was difficult, given what she was wearing. 'He wants to tie me in with children, a family. I'd have to protect them.'

On second thoughts . . . he was looking her in the eyes, now, and he'd noticed her, all right. 'That's not the only option,' she murmured. 'You don't have to surrender to Angbard.'

'I don't – ' He trailed off.

She leaned forward and wrapped her arms around his waist. 'What you said earlier,' she tried to explain. 'You offered to help.' She looked up at him, still maintaining eye contact. 'How serious are you?' she asked, her voice a whisper.

He blinked slowly, his expression thoughtful, then she saw him focusing on her properly, and it did something odd to her. She felt suddenly embarrassed, as if she'd made some horrible faux pas in public. 'It wouldn't be sensible,' he said slowly. Then he embraced her, hugging her tightly. 'Are you sure it's what you want?'

And now she really felt something, and it wasn't what she'd expected when the idea of compromising Angbard's plans for Olga stole into her mind. 'The door's locked. Who's going to know? A serving girl goes in, a serving girl goes out, I'm in my bedroom working, it's all deniable.' She pressed her chin into his shoulder. 'I want you to pick me up, carry me into your bedroom, and take my clothes off – slowly,' she whispered into his ear.

'Okay,' he said.

She turned her head and laid her lips alongside his. He'd shaved. After a moment she felt his jaws loosen, exploration begin. Her whole weight fell against him and he lifted her, then put her down on her feet.

'Over here,' he said, arm dropping to her waist, half-leading her.

The bedroom furnishings were different. A big oak four-poster with a red- and gold-tapestried canopy dominated the room, and the secondary items were different. She pulled him toward the bed, then paused in front of it. 'Kiss me,' she said.

He leaned over her and she sank into him, reaching down to his trousers with one hand to fumble at unfamiliar catches. He groaned softly as she caressed him.

Then his jacket was on the floor, his bow tie dangling, his trousers loose. A shocking sense of urgency filled her.

*

Hours passed. They were both naked now: She lay with her back to Roland, his arms curled protectively around her. *This is unexpected*, she thought dizzily. A little tremor surged through her. *Wow*. Well, her plan had worked: pull him into bed and annoy the hell out of Angbard by being a loose cannon. Except that wasn't how it had turned out. She liked Roland too much. That wasn't in the script.

'This is so wrong,' he mumbled into her hair.

She tensed. 'What is?' she asked.

'Your uncle. He'll kill me if he suspects.'

'He'll – ' Her blood ran cold for a moment. 'You're sure?'

'You're immune,' he said in a tone of forced calm. 'You've got huge leverage, and he doesn't have specific plans for you. I'm meant to marry Olga, though, and that's an end to it. Open defiance is bad. He's probably been planning the marriage for years.'

'Surely I'm an, uh, acceptable substitute?' she asked, surprising herself. It hadn't been in the plan when she came upstairs, unless her subconscious had been working overtime on strategies for spiking Angbard's plans.

'That's not the point. It's not just about producing offspring with the ability, you know? You're about the most unsuitable replacement for Olga it's possible to imagine. Making me marry Olga would buy Angbard influence with her father's braid and tie me down with a family. But an alliance with you wouldn't do that – in fact, he'd risk losing influence over both of us, to no gain for himself.' He paused for breath. 'Aside from marrying out, one of the council's worst fears is fragmentation – world-walkers leaving and setting up as rivals. We're both classic fragmentation risks, disaffected rebellious adults with independent backgrounds. My plans . . . reform has to come from within or it's seen as a threat. That's why I was hoping he might still be listening to me. There's nothing personal about Clan alliances,

Miriam. Even if Angbard the kindly uncle wanted to let you and me stay together, Angbard the duke would be seen as weak by the council, which would open him up to challenge . . . he can't take that risk, he'd have to split us up.'

'I didn't know about the competition angle,' she murmured. 'What a mess.'

'This is a – it isn't a . . . a one-night stand?' he asked.

'I hope not.' She nuzzled back deeper into his arms. 'What about you? What do you want?'

'What I want seldom has anything to do with what I get,' he said bitterly. 'Although – ' he stroked her flank silently.

'We have a problem,' Miriam whispered. 'Tomorrow they're going to put me in a stagecoach with Olga and send us both to the royal court. Herself to pay respects to the king, me to be exhibited like some kind of prize cow. You're going to be staying here, under his eye. That right?'

She felt his nod: It sent a shiver through her spine. 'It's a test,' he murmured. 'He's testing you to see what you're made of – also to see if your presence lures disaffected elements into the open.'

'We can try for a different outcome. Olga can be taken out of the picture by, well, anything.'

He tensed. 'Do you mean what I think – '

'No.' She felt him relax. 'I'm not going to start murdering women in order to steal their husbands.' She stifled a laugh – if it came out, it would have been more than slightly hysterical. 'But we've got a couple of months, the whole of winter if I understand it, before anything happens. She doesn't need to know anything. I bought a prepaid phone, right under your nose. I'll leave you the number and try to arrange to talk to you when we're both on the other side. Hell, the horse might even learn to sing.'

'Huh?'

'There might be a plague of smallpox. Or the crown prince might fall truly, madly, deeply in love with a shallow eighteen-year-old ditz whose one redeeming feature is that she plays the violin, getting you off the hook.'

'Right.' He sounded more certain. 'I need that number.'

'Or my uncle might fall down a staircase,' she added.

'Right.' He paused.

'A thought?' she asked.

'Only this.' She felt lips touch the top of her spine. 'You'd better be sneaking back to your apartment soon, because it's three in the morning and we can't afford to be compromised – either of us. But I want you to know one thing. Something I kept meaning to tell Janice, but never got a chance to – and now it's too late.'

'What's that?' she asked sleepily.

'I know this is crazy and dangerous, but I think I'm falling in love with you.'

*

Somehow Miriam made it back to her rooms without attracting any notice – possibly the sight of disheveled and half-drunk maids stumbling out of an earl's rooms and through the corridors at night was not one to arouse undue interest. She undressed and folded her clothing carelessly, stuffing cheap theatrical maid's costume and designer gown alike into her suitcase. She freshened up in the bathroom, as much as she could without making the plumbing gurgle. Then she sat down in front of her laptop. Better check it before bed, she thought muzzily. Clicking on the photo utility, she spooled back through the day's footage, back to her own exit – neatly packaged in a gray suit – en route to her appointment with the duke.

She'd set the camera to grab one frame per second. She fast-forwarded through it at thirty FPS, two seconds to the minute, two minutes to the hour. After ninety seconds, she saw the door open. Pausing, she backed up then single-stepped through the footage. Someone, an indistinct blur, moved from the main door to her bedroom. Then a gray blur in front of the laptop itself, then nothing. She had a vague impression of a dark suit, a man's build. But it wasn't Roland, and she felt a moment of fear at the realization.

But she'd gone into the bedroom safely. Nobody had tampered with her suitcase, and her chests of clothing were already stashed in the main room. So before daring to go to bed, Miriam spent a fruitless half-hour searching her bedroom from top to bottom, peering under the bed and lifting mattresses, checking behind the curtains.

Nothing. Which left a couple of disturbing possibilities in mind. *Don't try world-walking in your bedroom,* she sternly warned herself, *and check the computer for back doors in the morning.* She packed the computer and its extras – and the gun – in her suitcase. Then she lay down and drifted into sleep disturbed by surprisingly explicit erotic phantoms that left her aching and sore for something she couldn't have.

She was awakened in the dim predawn light by a clattering of serving maids.

'What's going on?' she mumbled, lifting her head and wincing at her hangover. 'I thought I said – '

'Duke's orders, ma'am,' Meg apologized. 'We've to dress you for travel.'

'Oh hell.' Miriam groaned. 'He said that?'

He had. So Miriam did her waking up that morning with three other women fussing over her, haphazardly cramming her into a business suit – about the most inappropriate travel garb she could think of – and then from somewhere they produced a voluminous greatcoat that threatened her with heat stroke while she already felt like death warmed over.

'This,' she said through gritted teeth, 'is excessive.'

'It's cold outside, ma'am,' Meg said firmly. 'You'll need it before the day is out.' She held out a hat to Miriam. Miriam looked at it in disbelief, then tried to balance it on her head. 'It goes like this,' said Meg, and seconds later it did. With a scarf to hold it in place, Miriam felt cut off from the world almost completely. *Are they trying to hide me?* she wondered, anxious about what that could mean.

They led her downstairs, with a trail of grunting porters hefting her trunks – and incongruous metal suitcase – and then out through a pair of high double doors. Meg was right. Her breath hung steaming in the air before her face. In the past week, autumn had turned wintry with the first breath of air rushing down from the Arctic. A huge black wooden coach balanced on wheels taller than Miriam stood waiting, eight horses harnessed before it. A mounting block led up to the open door, and she was startled to see the duke standing beside it, wearing a quite incongruous Burberry overcoat.

'My dear!' he greeted her. 'A final word, if I may, before you depart.'

She nodded, then glanced up as the porters hoisted her trunks onto the roof and a small platform at the back of the carriage.

'You may think my sending you to court is premature,' he said quietly, 'but my agents have intercepted messages about an attempt on your life. You need to leave here, and I think it best that you be among your peers. You'll be staying at the Thorold Palace, which is maintained as a common residence in the capital by the heads of the families; it's doppelgängered and quite safe, I assure you. It will be possible for you to return later.'

'Well, that's a relief,' she said sarcastically.

'Indeed.' He looked at her oddly. 'Well, I must say you look fine. I do commend Olga to you; she is not as stupid as she appears and you will need to learn the High Speech sooner rather than later – English is only spoken among the aristocracy.'

'Well, uh, okay.' She shuffled nervously. 'I'll try not to trip over any assassins, and I may even meet an appropriate husband.' She glanced at the coach as one of the horses snorted and shook its harness. She felt even more peculiar when she realized that she was not entirely lying. If marrying Roland – even having another child with him – would get him into her bed on a regular basis, she was willing to at least contemplate the possibility. She needed an ally – and friend – here, and he had the potential to be more than that.

'Indeed.' He nodded at her, and for the first time she noticed that there was a certain translucency to his skin, as if he wasn't entirely well. 'Good hunting.'

And then he turned and strode away, leaving her to climb into the carriage and wait for departure.

COURT APPEARANCE

Miriam's unpleasant surprise – after finding that the Tylenol was all packed in her trunks and inaccessible – was that the carriage was unheated and the leather seats hard. Her second, as she shivered and tried to huddle into one corner under a thick blanket, came as Olga swept up the steps and into the seat opposite her. Olga's blonde hair was gathered up under a scarf and hat, and she wore a wool coat over an outfit that made her look like a brokerage house yuppie.

'Isn't this wonderful?' she cooed as plump Lady Margit, in twinset and pearls by day, huffed and puffed up and into the seat next to Miriam, expanding to flow over two-thirds of it.

'It's wonderful.' Miriam smiled weakly as the coachman cracked his whip overhead and released the hand brake. The noise and vibration of wooden wheels turning on cobblestones shuddered through her hangover as the coach creaked and swayed forward.

Olga leaned toward her. 'Oh dear, you look unwell!' she insisted, peering into Miriam's eyes at close range. 'What could it be?'

'Something I drank, I think,' Miriam mumbled, turning away. Her stomach was distinctly rough, her head pounded, and she felt too hot. 'How long will we be on the road?'

'Oh, not long!' Olga clapped her hands briskly and rubbed them together against the cold. 'We can use the duke's holdings to change teams regularly. If we make good time today and keep driving until dusk, we could be at Ode-markt tomorrow evening and Niejwein the next afternoon! All of two hundred miles in three days!' She glanced at Miriam slyly. 'I hear over on the other side you have magical carriages that can travel such a distance much faster?'

'Oh, Olga,' muttered Margit, a trifle peevishly.

'Um.' Miriam nodded, pained. *Two hundred miles in three days,* she thought. *Even Amtrak can do better than that!* 'Yes, but I don't think they'd work too well over here,' she whuffed out as a particularly bad rut in the road threw her against the padded side of the carriage.

'What a shame,' Olga replied brightly. 'That means we'll just have to take a little longer.' She pointed out of the carriage door's open window. 'Oh, look! A squirrel! On that elm!'

It was at this point that Miriam realized, with a sickly sinking feeling, that taking a carriage to the capital in this world might be how the aristocracy travelled – at least in autumn, when the threat of storms rendered the sea hazardous – but in comfort terms it was the equivalent of an economy-class airline ticket to New Zealand, in an ancient turboprop with malfunctioning air-conditioning. And she'd set off with a hangover and a chatterbox for a fellow traveller, without remembering to pack the usual hand luggage. 'Oh god,' she moaned faintly to herself.

'Oh, that reminds me!' Olga sat upright. 'I nearly forgot!' From some hidden pocket she pulled out a small, neatly wrapped paper parcel. She opened it and removed a pinch of some powdery substance, then cast it from the window. 'Im nama des'Hummelvat sen da' Blishkin un' da Geshes des'reeshes, dis expedition an' all, the mifim reesh'n,' she murmured.

Then Olga noticed Miriam looking at her blankly. 'Don't you pray?' she asked.

'Pray?' Miriam shook her head. 'I don't understand – '

'Prayers! Oh, yes, I forgot. Didn't dear Roland say that on the other side everybody is pagan? You all worship some dead god on a stick, impaled or something disgusting, and pray in English,' she said with relish.

'Olga,' Margit said warningly. 'You've never been there. Roland's probably telling fibs to confuse you.'

'It's all right,' Miriam replied. *Margit isn't a world-walker?* she wondered. Well, that would explain why she was stuck chaperoning Olga around. 'We don't speak, um, what is the language called again?'

'Hoh'sprashe?' said Olga.

'Yes, that's it. And the other side is similar to this side geographically, but the people and how they dress and act and talk are

160

different,' she said, trying to think of something it would be safe to talk about.

'I'd heard that,' said Olga. She leaned back against her bench, thoughtfully.

'You mean they don't know about the Sky Father?'

'Um.' Miriam's evident perplexity must have told its own story, because Olga beamed brightly at her.

'Oh, I see! I'll have to tell you all about the Sky Father and the Church!' Olga leaned forward. 'You don't believe, do you?' she said very quietly.

Miriam sat up. *Wha-a-at?* she thought, suddenly surprised. 'What do you mean?' she asked.

'Sky Father.' Olga glanced sideways at Margit, who appeared to be dozing. '*I* don't believe in him,' she said, quietly defiant. 'I figured that much out when I was twelve. But you mustn't ever – ever – act as if you don't. At least, in public.'

'Hmm.' Miriam tried to think straight, but her headache was militating against coherency. 'What's the problem? Where I come from, I was raised by unobservant Jews – Jews are, like, a minority religion – but I wasn't Jewish, either, I wasn't their child and it passes down by birth.' *Let's leave what I actually believe out of this or we'll be here all day.* 'Is there . . . what's the Church like? I haven't seen any sign of it at the duke's palace.'

'You didn't see the chapel because he told us you weren't ready,' Olga said quietly, pitching her voice just above the level of the road noise. 'But he told me you'd need to know before court. So you don't give your enemies anything to use against you.'

'Oh.' Miriam looked at Olga with something approaching respect. *The ditz is a self-made atheist? And the families are religious?* 'Yes, I think he was right,' she said evenly. 'Just how influential is the Church?' she asked, half-expecting bad news.

'Very!' Olga began with forced enthusiasm. 'Mass is held every day, to bring the blessing of Sky Father and Lightning Child down upon us. They both have their priests, as does Crone Wife, and the monastic orders, all organized under the Church of Rome by the Emperor-in-God, who rules the Church in the name of Sky Father and interprets Sky Father's wishes. Not that we hear much from Rome – it has been under the reign of the Great Khan these past decades, and the ocean crossing is perilous and difficult. Next month is Julf-mass, when we celebrate Lightning Child driving out the ice wolf of the north who eats the sun; there'll be big feasts and public entertainments, that's when betrothals and further knots in the braids are formally announced! It's so exciting. They're cemented at Beltaigne, as spring turns toward summer, right after the Clan meets – '

'Tell me about Julfmass,' Miriam suggested. 'What happens? What's it about? What do I need to know?'

*

Ten miles down the road they were joined by a mounted escort. Rough-looking men on horseback, they wore metal armor over leather. Most of them carried swords and lances, but two – Miriam peeped out at the leaders – had discreetly holstered AR-15s, identifying them beyond a shadow of a doubt as family troopers.

'Halle sum faggon,' the sergeant called out, and the coachman replied, 'Fallen she in'an seien Sie welcom, mif'nsh.'

Miriam shook her head. Riders ahead and riders behind. 'They're friendly?' she asked Olga over Margit's open-mouthed snores.

'Oh yes!' Olga simpered: Miriam waited for her to get over it. *She's been raised wholly apart from men, unless I am very much mistaken,* she reasoned. *No wonder she goes strange whenever anything that needs to shave passes through the area.* 'Your uncle's border guards,' she added. 'Aren't they handsome?'

'Mmmph.' Miriam blinked slowly. Handsome. She had a sudden hot flashback to the night before, Roland's hands gently teasing during a long-drawn-out game that ended with them both spent, damp, and woozy – then she took in Olga's innocent, happy face and felt abruptly dispirited, as if she'd stolen a child's toy. This wasn't part of the plan, she thought, downhearted. 'They're guards,' she said tiredly. 'Seen one set of guards, seen 'em all. I just wish I could get at my suitcase.' She'd stashed her pistol in it last night, along with her notebook computer and the rest of her escape kit.

'Why is that?' asked Olga.

'Well.' Miriam paused. How to put it diplomatically? 'What if they wanted to take advantage of us?' she asked, fumbling for an alternative to suggesting that Angbard's guards might not be effective.

'Oh, that's all right,' Olga said brightly. She fumbled with something under her blanket, then showed it to Miriam, who blinked again, several times. 'Be careful where you wave that,' she suggested.

'Oh, I'll be all right! I've been training with guns since I was this high,' she said, lowering the machine pistol. 'Don't you do it over there?'

'Ah.' Miriam looked at her faintly. 'No, but I suppose conditions are somewhat different.'

'Oh.' Olga looked slightly puzzled. 'Aren't you allowed to defend yourselves?'

'We've got this thing called a government,' Miriam said dryly. 'It does the defending for us. At least in theory.'

'Hah. There was nobody to do that for our grandmothers when the civil war began. Many of them died before . . . well, even Daddy said I needed to learn to shoot, and he's a terrible backwoodsman! There aren't enough of us with the talent, you know, we all have to muck in like commoners these days. I may even have to join the family trade after I marry, can you believe it?'

'The, ah, thought hadn't occurred to me.' Miriam tried to sound noncommittal; the idea of Olga running around Cambridge with a machine pistol, a platinum credit card, and a suitcase full of cocaine would have been funny if it hadn't been so frighteningly plausible.

'I really hope it happens,' Olga said, slightly more thoughtfully. 'I'd like to see . . . over there.' She sat up. 'But you asked about bandits! We are unlikely to meet any unless we travel in the spring thaw. They know too well what will happen if they try the Clan's post, but after a harsh winter some of them may no longer care.'

'I see.' Miriam tried not to show any outward sign of being disturbed, but for a moment she felt a chill of absolute fear at this naive, enthusiastic, emotional – but not stupid – child. She shuffled her legs together, trying to get her feet out of the draft. It would be a long day, without any distractions. 'Tell me more about the Church . . .'

*

Two extremely uncomfortable days passed in chilly boredom. They stopped at a coaching house the first night, and Miriam insisted on unloading a suitcase and trunk. The next day she scandalized Margit by wearing jeans, fleece, and hiking boots, and Olga by spending the afternoon engrossed in a book. 'You'd best not wear that tomorrow,' Margit said disapprovingly when they stopped that evening at another post house. 'It is for us to make a smart entrance, to pay our respects at court as soon as we arrive, do you see? Did you bring anything suitable?'

'Oh hell,' replied Miriam, confusing her somewhat (for Hel was a province administered by Olga's father). 'If you could help me choose something?'

Expensive western formal costume – Armani suits, Givenchy dresses, and their equivalents – appeared to be de rigueur among the Clan in private. But in public in the Gruinmarkt, they wore the finery of high nobility. Their peculiarities were kept behind closed doors.

The duke's resident seamstress had packed one of Miriam's trunks with gowns hastily fitted to her measurements, and at dawn on the third day Margit shoehorned her into one deemed suitable for a court debut. It was even more elaborate than the outfit they'd fitted her for dinner with the duke; it had underskirts, profusions of lace exploding at wrist and throat, slashed sleeves layered over tight inner layers. Miriam hated everything it said about the status of women in this society. But Olga wore something similar, with an exaggerated pink bustle behind that suggested to Miriam nothing so much as a female baboon in heat. Margit declared Miriam's presentation satisfactory. 'That's most fittingly elegant!' she pronounced. 'Let no time be lost, now, lest we be undone by our lateness.'

'Mmph,' said Miriam, holding her skirts out of the courtyard dampness and trying to avoid tripping over them on her way over to the coach. *Really*, she thought. *This is crazy! I should have just crossed over and caught the train*. But Angbard had insisted – and she could second-guess his reasoning. 'Avoid transport bottlenecks where somebody might intercept her – also, see if she breaks.' After three days on the road she was feeling ripe, long overdue for a shower. The last thing she needed was a new dress, let alone one as intricately excessive as this. Only a grim determination not to play her hand too early made her put up with it. She settled into her accustomed corner in a rustling heap of bottle-green velvet and tried to get comfortable, but her back was stiff, the dress vast and uncontrollable, and parts of her were sweating while other bits froze.

Plus, Olga was looking at her triumphantly.

'You look marvelous,' Olga assured her, leaning forward and resting a hand in the vicinity of Miriam's knee. 'I'm sure you'll make a great entry at court! You'll be surrounded by suitors before you've been there a moment – despite your age!'

'I'm sure,' Miriam said weakly. *Give me patience*, she prayed to the goddess of suffering and/or social conformity. *Otherwise I swear I'll strangle someone . . .*

Before they moved off, Margit insisted on dropping the blinds. It reduced the draft, but in the closeness of the carriage Miriam began to feel claustrophobic.

Olga insisted on painting Miriam's cheeks and eyebrows and lips, redoing the procedure while the carriage swayed and bumped along a stone-cobbled street. Other carriages and traffic rattled past. Presently they heard people calling greetings and warnings. 'The gates,' Olga said, breathlessly. 'The gates!'

Miriam sneaked a peek through the blinds before Margit noticed and scolded her. The gatehouse was made of stone, perhaps four stories high. She'd seen similar on a vacation in England many years ago. The walls themselves were of stone, but banked with masses of rammed earth in front and huge mounds of mud beyond the ditch. *Isn't that something to do with artillery?* she thought, puzzled by memories of an old History Channel documentary.

'Put that down at once, I say!' Margit insisted. 'Do you want everyone to see you?'

Miriam dropped the window blind. 'Shouldn't they?' she asked.

'Absolutely not!' Margit looked scandalized. 'Why, it would be the talk of society for months!'

'Ah,' Miriam said neutrally. Olga winked at her. *So this is how it works,* she realized. Enforcement through peer pressure. *If they get the idea that I'm not going to conform, I'm never going to hear the end of it*, she realized. Olga, far from being her biggest problem, was beginning to look more like a potential ally.

*

Their first call was at the Thorold Palace, a huge rambling stone pile at the end of the Avenue of Rome, a broad stone street fronted by mansions. The carriage drew right up to the front entrance, their escort of guards strung out behind it as servants emerged with a mounting box, which they shoved into place before holding the door open. Margit was the first to leave, followed by Olga, who squeezed through the door with a shake of her behind; Miriam emerged last, blinking in the daylight like a prisoner released from an oubliette.

A butler in some sort of intricate house uniform – a tunic over knee breeches and floppy boots – read from a letter in a loud voice before a gaggle of onlookers. 'His Excellency the High Duke Angbard of House Lofstrom is pleased to consign to your care the Lady Margit, Châtelaine of Praha, Her Excellency the Baroness Olga Thorold, and Her Excellency the Countess Helga Thorold Hjorth, daughter of Patricia of that braid.' He bowed deeply, then gave way to a man standing behind him. 'Your Excellency.'

'I bid you welcome to the house in my custody, and urge you to accept my hospitality,' said the man.

'Baron Oliver Hjorth,' Olga stage-whispered at Miriam. Miriam managed a fixed, glassy-eyed smile then followed Olga's lead by picking up her skirts and dipping. 'I thank you, my lord,' Olga replied loudly and clearly, 'and accept your protection.'

Miriam echoed him. English, it seemed, was still the general language of nobility here. Her Hoh'sprashe was still restricted to a couple of polite nothings.

'Delighted, my beaux,' said the earl, not cracking a smile. He was tall and thin, almost cadaverous, his most striking feature a pair of striking black-rimmed spectacles that he wore balanced on the tip of his bony nose; dusty black trousers and a flared red coat worn over a lace-throated shirt completed his outfit. There was something threadbare about him, and Miriam noticed that he didn't wear a sword. 'If you will allow Bortis to show you to your rooms, I believe you are expected at court in two hours.'

He turned and stalked away grimly, without further comment.

'Why, the effrontery!' Olga gripped Miriam's hand tightly.

'Huh?'

'He's snubbing you,' Olga hissed angrily, 'and me, to get at you! How peculiarly rude! Oh, come on, let the servant show us to our rooms – and yours. We still need to finish you for the royal court.'

*

An hour later Miriam had two ladies-in-waiting, an acute attack of dizziness, growing concerns about the amenities of this ghastly stone pile – which appeared to lack such essentials as running water and electricity – and a stiff neck from all the heavy metal they'd wrapped around her throat. The ladies-in-waiting were, like Margit, family members who lacked the fully expressed trait that allowed them to world-walk. The Misses Brilliana of Ost and Kara of Praha – one blonde, the other brunette – looked like meek young things waiting their turn for the marriage market, but after spending a couple of days with Olga, Miriam took that with a pinch of salt. 'Were you really raised on the other side?' Kara asked, wide-eyed.

'I was.' Miriam nodded. 'But I've never been presented at court before.'

'We'll see to that,' the other one, Brilliana, said confidently. 'You look splendid! I'm sure it will all go perfectly.'

'When do we need to leave?' asked Miriam.

'Oh, any time, I suppose,' Brilliana said carelessly.

The coach was even more claustrophobic with six overdressed women jammed into it. It jarred and bumped through the streets, and Brilliana and Kara made excited small talk with Olga's companions, Sfetlana and Aris. Olga, sandwiched between the two, caught Miriam's eye and winked. Miriam would have shrugged, but she was hemmed in so tightly that she could barely breathe, let alone move.

After what felt like an hour of juddering progress, the carriage turned into a long drive. As it drew to a halt, Miriam heard a tinkle of glassware, laughter, strains of string music from outside. Olga twitched. 'Hear, violins!' she said.

'Sounds like it to me.' The door opened and steps appeared, as did two footmen, their gold-encrusted livery as pompous and excessive as the women's dresses. They hovered anxiously as the occupants descended.

'Thank you,' Miriam commented, surprising the footman who'd offered her his hand. She looked around. They stood before the wide-flung doors of a gigantic palace, a flood of light spilling out through the glass windows onto the lawn.

Within, men in coats cut away over ballooning knee breeches mingled with women in elaborate gowns: The room was so huge that the orchestra played from a balcony, above the heads of the court.

Miriam went into a state of acute culture shock almost immediately, allowing the Misses Kara and Brilliana to steer her like a galleon under full sail. Someone bellowed out her name – or the parcel of strange titles by which she was known here. She shook herself for a moment when she saw heads turn to stare at her – some inquisitive, some surprised, others supercilious, and some hostile – the names meant nothing to her. All she could think of was trying not to trip over her aching toes and keeping her glassy eyes and shit-eating grin steady on her rouged and strained face. *This isn't me*, she thought vaguely, being presented to a whirl of titled pompous idiots and simpering women swathed in silk and furs. *This is a bad dream*, she repeated to herself. She shied away from the idea that these people were her family, that she might have to spend the rest of her life attending this sort of event.

Miriam had done formal dinners and award ceremonies before, dinner parties and cocktail evenings, but nothing that came close to this. Even though – from Olga's vague but enthusiastic description of the territories – Niejwein was a small kingdom, not much larger than Massachusetts and so dirt-poor that most of the population lived on subsistence farming, its ruling royalty lived in a casual splendor far beyond any ceremonial that the head of a democratic nation would expect. It was an imperial reception, the prototype that the high school prom or its upmarket cousin, the coming-out ball, aped. Someone clapped a glass into her gloved hand – it turned out to be a disgustingly sweet fruit wine – and she politely but firmly turned down so many invitations to dance that she began to lose track.

Please, make it all go away, she whimpered to herself, as Kara-Brilliana steered her into a queue running along a suspiciously red carpet toward a short guy swathed in a white fur cloak that looked preposterously hot.

'Her Excellency Helge Thorold Hjorth, daughter and heir of Patricia of Thorold, returned from exile to pay tribute at the court of His High Majesty, Alexis Nicholau III, ruler in the name of the Sky Father, blessed and awful be he, of all of the Gruinmarkt and territories!'

Miriam managed a deep curtsey without falling over, biting her lip to keep from saying anything inappropriate or incriminating.

'Charmed, charmed, I say!' said Alexis Nicholau III, ruler of the Gruinmarkt (by willing concession of the Clan). 'My dear, reports of your beauty do not do you justice at all! Such elegant deportment! A new face at court, I say, how charming. Remind me to introduce you to my sons later.' He swayed slightly on his raised platform, and Miriam spotted the empty glass in his hand.

He was a slightly built man with a straggly red beard fringing his chin who was going prematurely bald on top. He wore no crown, but a gold chain of office so intimidatingly heavy that it looked as if his spine would buckle at any moment. She felt a stab of sympathy for him as she recognized the symptoms of a fellow sufferer.

'I'm delighted to meet you,' she told the discreetly drunken monarch with surprising sincerity. Then she felt an equally discreet tug as Kara-Brilliana steered her aside with minute curtseys and simpering expressions of delight at the royal presence.

Miriam took a mouthful from her glass, forced herself to swallow it, then took another. *Perhaps the king had the right idea,* she thought. Kara-Brilliana drifted to a halt not far from the dais. 'Isn't he cute?' Kara squealed quietly.

'Who?' Miriam asked distractedly.

'Egon, of course!'

'Egon – ' Miriam fumbled for a diplomatic phrasing.

'Oh, that's right. You weren't raised here,' said Brilliana, practicality personified. Quietly, in Miriam's ear, she continued, 'See the two youngsters behind his majesty? The taller is Egon. He's the first prince, the likely successor should the council of electors renew the dynasty whenever his majesty, long may he live, goes to join his ancestors. The short one with the squint is Creon, the second son. Both are unmarried, and Creon will probably stay that way. If not, pity the maiden.'

'Why pity her, if it's not rude to ask?'

'He's addled,' Brilliana said matter-of-factly. 'Too stupid to – ' she noticed Miriam's empty glass and turned to fetch a replacement.

'Something a bit less sweet, please,' Miriam implored. The heat was getting to her. 'How long must we stay here?' she asked.

'Oh, as long as you want!' Kara said happily. 'The revelry continues from dusk till dawn.' Brilliana pressed a glass into Miriam's hand. 'Isn't it wonderful?' Kara added.

'I think my lady looks a little tired,' Brilliana said diplomatically. 'She's spent three days on the road, Kara.'

Miriam wobbled. Her back was beginning to seize up again, her kidneys were aching, and in addition her toes felt pinched and she was becoming breathless. 'I'm exhausted,' she whispered. 'Need to get some sleep. 'If you take me home, you can come back to enjoy yourselves. Promise. Just don't expect me to stay upright much longer.'

'Hmm.' Brilliana looked at her speculatively. 'Kara, if it pleases you, be so good as to ask someone to summon our coach. I'll help our lady here to make a dignified exit. My lady, there are a few names you must be presented to before taking your leave – to fail would be to give offence – but there'll be another reception the day after tomorrow; there is no need to converse at length with your peers tonight if you are tired. I'm sure we can spend the time between now and then getting to know our new mistress better.' She smiled at Miriam. 'A last glass of wine, my lady?'

WAIT TRAINING

Light.

Miriam blinked and twitched into vague wakefulness from a dream of painful desire and frustrated eroticism. Someone sighed and moved against her back, and she jerked away, suddenly remembering where she was with a fit of panic: Wearing a nightdress? In a huge cold bed? What is going on?

She rolled over and came up against heavy drapes. Turning around, she saw Kara asleep in the huge four-poster bed behind her, face a composed picture of tranquillity. Miriam cringed, racking her brain. *What did I get up to last night?* she wondered, aghast. Then she looked past Kara and saw another sleeping body – and an empty bottle of wine. Opening the curtain and looking on the floor, she saw three glasses and a second bottle, lying on its side, empty. She vaguely remembered talking in the cavernous stone aircraft hangar that passed for a countess's bedroom. It had been freezing cold in the drafty stone pile, and Kara had suggested they continue talking in the four-poster bed, which filled the room like a small pavilion. They'd fallen asleep, still mostly dressed.

A slumber party, she figured. She hadn't been in one of those since college.

Poor kids. I took them away from their disco and they just couldn't call it a night. Kara was only seventeen – and Brilliana an old maid of twenty-two. She felt relieved – and a bit sorry for them.

This would never do. She slipped out of the bed and shivered in the freezing cold air. *I'm adrift*, she thought. Turning, she looked back. The bed was as big as her entire room back home. *I need to get my perspective back.*

Acutely aware of her bare feet on the heat-sucking stone flags, she tiptoed across to the curtain that concealed the door to the toilet.

There were no modern conveniences here, just a pot full of dry leaves, and a latrine with a ten-foot drop over the curtain wall. What you saw was what you got. Without servants to substitute for domestic appliances, living conditions in the big city, even for nobility, were distinctly primitive.

After freezing her ass for the minute it took to get rid of last night's wine, Miriam re-entered her main chamber and began hunting through the chests that had been deposited there the afternoon before.

She dressed quickly and in silence, pulling on jeans and a sweater and fleece suited to the other side. There was no thought of waking the two ladies-in-waiting, for she couldn't begin to guess how they'd react and she wanted to move fast. Her shoulder bag was packed in the suitcase. It took her a moment to locate it, along with the Sony notebook, the phone, and the GPS compass. She spent a minute scanning the room with the notebook's built-in camera, then she pulled out a paper reporter's pad and wrote a quick note in ballpoint:

> My dear K & B,
> Gone over to the other side. Back before nightfall. Please see to storing my articles and arrange a dinner for the three of us when I get back, two hours after dark.
> Best, Miriam

She left it on the pillow next to Kara's head, pulled out her locket, and crossed over into the doppelgänger building on the other side.

Miriam's eyes blurred and her headache redoubled as she looked around. The space corresponding to her room in the palace or castle or whatever in Niejwein wasn't a palace in her own world. Two hundred miles southwest of Boston – *New York!* she thought with a jolt of excitement. It was dim in here, very dim, lit by emergency lights. There was a strong smell of sawdust, and it was bitingly cold. She stood on top of metal scaffolding, with yellow painted lines on the floor. *That'll be the layout of the castle back in the other world*, she realized. *I'd better get out of here before someone notices me.*

She switched on the GPS compass, waited for it to come up, then told it to store her location. Then she went down the metal stairs two at a time. She was on the ground floor of an elderly warehouse. Wooden crates stood between yellow alleyways – evidently blocking out the walls of the castle. She headed toward the grand staircase and the main entrance hall, found it open and a trailer sitting on some concrete blocks installed as a site office. The yellow light was coming from the trailer windows.

Miriam put her hand in her jacket pocket and took a grip on her pistol. Her head pounded, as cold air hit hangover-inflamed sinuses. *I need to dry out for a couple of days*, she thought abstractedly. Then she knocked on the door with her left hand.

'Who's there?'

The door swung open and an old man grimaced at her.

'I'm Miriam. From the Cambridge office,' she said. 'I'll be going in and out of here over the next few days. Inspecting things.'

'Marian something?' He blinked, looking annoyed.

'No, Miriam,' she said patiently. 'Do you have a list of people who're allowed in and out here?'

'Oh, yeah,' he said vacantly. He shuffled inside and surfaced with a dirty clipboard. The cabin smelled of stale smoke and boiled cabbage. 'Miriam Beckstein,' she said patiently and spelled her name. 'From Cambridge, Mass.'

'Your name isn't down here.' He looked puzzled.

'I work for Angbard Lofstrom,' she said curtly.

Evidently this was the right thing to say because he jolted upright. 'Yes, ma'am! That's fine, everything's fine. How do you spell your name?'

Miriam told him. 'Where are we on the street map, and what's the protocol for getting in and out of here?' she asked.

'Protocol?' He looked puzzled. 'Just come in and knock. This is just a lockup. Nothing important here. Nothing worth stealing, leastways.'

'Okay.' She nodded, turned, and walked toward the front door and freedom. As she did so, her phone beeped three times, acquiring coverage and notifying her that she had messages.

Once outside, she found herself in a dingy alleyway hemmed in by fire escapes. She walked to the end, then looked around. It was most peculiar. Security on the warehouse wasn't what she'd have expected, not at all. It was too easy to get in or out. Was she stuck in some kind of low-security zone? She came to a street with light traffic and shops on either side. Making a note of the street number, she waved down the first yellow cab to come past.

'Where to?' asked the driver, in an almost-comprehensible accent.

'Penn Station,' she said. He nodded a couple of times, then swung his car through a circle and flung it into the traffic.

Miriam lay back and watched the real world go by in a happy daze only slightly tempered by her throbbing head. *I'm really here!* she thought, feeling the bounce and lurch of pneumatic tires on asphalt and the warm breeze from the heater on her feet. *Isn't it great?* She wanted the cab ride to last forever, she realized with a warm glow of nostalgia. Lights and advertisements and people who didn't look like extras from an historical movie flowed past to either side of her heated cocoon. This was her world, an urban reality where real people wore comfortable clothes, made thoughtless use of conveniences like electricity and tap water, and didn't weave lethal dynastic games around the future lives of children she didn't intend to have.

Wait till I tell Ma, she thought. *Then Paulie.* Followed moments later by: *Damn, first I have to figure out what I can tell them.* Then: *Hey, at least I can talk to Roland . . .*

She picked up her phone and dialed her mailbox.

'Miriam?' His voice was distant and scratchy and her heart skipped a beat. 'I hope you get this message. Listen, I come across on a courier run every two days, between ten and four. I think your uncle may suspect something, he's put Matthias onto me as an escort. Last night he sent news that you'd arrived at the capital. How are you enjoying life there? Oh, by the way, don't trust anyone called Hjorth; they've got a lot to lose. And watch out for Prince Egon: He's been known to not take no for an answer. Call me when you get a chance.'

Her vision had misted at the sound of his voice. *Damn, I didn't plan this.* The taxi drifted in stop-and-go traffic, the driver thumping the steering column in time with the radio.

At the station Miriam's first act was to hunt down an ATM and try her card. It worked. She pulled out five hundred dollars in crisp green notes and stuffed them in her pocket. *That shouldn't tell them much beyond where I was*, she decided. Then she hit the ticket desk for a first-class return ticket to Boston on the next Acela. It took a wad, but once she found the train and settled into the seat, she was pleased with herself for spending it. It would take only three and a half hours, meaning she'd have maybe three hours in Boston before she'd have to go back again.

Miriam settled back in her seat, notebook computer opened on the table in front of her and phone beside it. *Do I have to go back there?* she asked herself. She'd just spent a week on the other side – and that week had been enough to last her a lifetime. She felt the stiff edges of the platinum credit card digging into her conscience. It was blood money, and their blood-is-thicker-than-water creed would drag her back – every time. *It didn't drag my birth-mother back,* she thought. *It killed her instead.* Which was even worse, and likelier than not what would happen to her if she ran now – because if she ran, they'd know she was untrustworthy. She wouldn't get another chance. Darker possibilities occurred to her. Even if they didn't want to kill her and reduce their precious gene pool, they could immobilize her permanently by blinding her. She doubted it was a common tactic – even given the Clan's ruthlessness, it would rapidly provoke fear and loathing, a catalyst for conflict – but they might use it as a special measure if they suspected treason, and the possibility filled her with horror.

On the other hand, the thought of voluntarily going back to the drafty castle and the insane family politics was depressing. So she picked up the phone and dialed Roland's number instead.

'Hello?' He answered on the first ring and she cheered up instantly.

'It's me,' she said quietly. 'Can you talk?'

'Yes.' A pause. 'He's not around right now, but he's never far away.'

'Are they still watching my house?' she asked.

'Yeah, I think so. Where are you?'

'On a train partway from New York to Boston.'

'Don't tell me you're running – '

'No,' she said hastily, 'but I've got unfinished business. Not just you – other stuff too. I want to see my mother, and I want to see some other people. Okay? Better not ask too many questions. I'm not going to do anything silly, but I have a feeling I don't want to draw any attention to people I know. Are you able to get away for a day? Say, to New York?'

'They've got you in that stone pile?' he asked.

'Yeah. Do you know what it's like?'

'You survived three days with Olga?' His tone was one of bemused disbelief.

'The facilities are, uh, open plan, and I get to sit cheek by jowl with two of Olga's less enlightened coworkers,' she said, eyes swiveling to track down the nearest passengers. She was clear – nobody in the two seats across the aisle from her. Quietly she added, 'The ladies-in-waiting are like jail guards, only prettier, if you follow me. They stick like glue. I woke up and they were in my goddamn bed with me. You'd think Angbard had set them on me as minders. Honestly, I'm at my wit's end. I'm going to go back this evening, but if you don't come and rescue me soon, I swear I'll kill someone. And I still haven't filed copy on that dot-com busted flush feature I'm supposed to be writing for Steve.'

'My poor journalist.' He laughed, a little sadly. 'You're not having a good time. Maybe we should form a club?'

'Culture shocked and brain damaged?'

'That's right.' A pause. 'Going back after six years away, that was the hardest thing, Miriam. You will go back to them?'

'Yes,' she said quietly. 'If I don't, I'll never see you again, will I?'

'Not today. I'll be over again the day after tomorrow,' he said. 'New York, is it?'

'Yes.' She thought for a moment. 'Rent a double room at the Marriott on Times Square. It's anonymous and bland, but I think you've got more travel time than I have. Leave voice mail with the room number and the name you're using, and I'll show up as early as possible.' She shivered at the thought, shuffling uncomfortably in her seat.

'I'll be there. Promise.'

'Bring a couple of new prepaid phones, bought with cash, as anonymous as you can. We'll need them. I miss you,' she added very quietly and hung up. Forty-eight hours to go. It had already been four days since she'd last seen him.

The conductor came around, and she glanced around again to confirm how much space she had. The carriage was half-empty: she'd missed the rush hour crush. Now she dialed another number, one she'd committed to memory because she was afraid to program it into the phone.

'Hi, you've reached the answering machine of Paulette Milan. I'm sorry I can't come to the phone right now, but – '

'Paulie, cut the crap and pick up the phone right now.'

The line clicked. 'Miriam! What the fuck are you playing at, sweetie?'

'Playing at? What do you mean?'

'Skipping out like that! Jesus, I've been so worried!'

'You think you've been worried? You haven't phoned my house, have you?' Miriam interrupted hastily.

'Oh yeah, but when you didn't answer I left a message about the bridge club. Something I made up on the spur of the moment. I've been so worried – '

'Paulie, you didn't mention the other stuff, did you? Or go around in person?'

'I'm not stupid,' Paulette said quietly, all ebullience gone.

'Good – uh, I'm sorry. Let me try again.' Miriam closed her eyes. 'Hi, I'm Miriam Beckstein, and I have just discovered the hard way that my long-lost family have got very long memories and longer arms, and they invited me to spend some time with them. It turns out that they're in the import/export trade, and they're so big that the story we were working on probably covers some of their turf. Hopefully they don't think you're anything other than a ditzy broad who plays bridge with me, because if they did you might not enjoy their company. Capisce?'

'Oh, oh shit! Miriam, I am so sorry! Listen, are you all right?'

'Yeah. Not only am I all right, I'm on a train that gets into South Station in – ' she checked her watch – 'about an hour and a half. I don't have long, this is a day trip, and I have to be on the four o'clock return train. I'm kind of on probation. But if you can meet me at the station, I'll drag you out to lunch and fill you in on everything, and I mean everything. Okay?'

'Okay.' Paulette sounded a little less upset. 'Miriam?'

'Yes?'

'What are they like? What are they doing to you?'

Miriam closed her eyes. 'Did you ever see the movie *Married to the Mob*?'

'No way! What about your locket? You mean they're – '

'Let's just say, it would be a bad idea for you to phone my house, visit it in person, talk to or visit my mother, or do anything that is in any way out of character for an out-of-work research geek who vaguely knows me from work and plays bridge once a week. At least, where they can see you. Which is why I'm phoning on a number you've never seen and probably won't ever see again. Meet me at one inside the station, near the south entrance?'

'Okay, I'll be there. Better have a good story!' Paulette hung up, and Miriam settled back to watch the countryside roll by.

*

Leaving the station, Miriam immediately hit the mall across the street. There was an ATM, and she pulled another two thousand in cash out of it. There seemed to be no end to the amount she could draw, as long as she didn't mind leaving an audit trail. This time she wanted to. Putting a timestamp on Boston would tell the Duke where she'd been. She planned on telling him anyway. Let him think she was being open and truthful about everything.

She headed back into the station in the same state she'd been in in the taxi. This was home, a place she'd been before, intimately familiar at the same time that it was anonymous and impersonal. She was shaken by how relieved she was to be back. Suddenly being jobless in a recession with her former employer threatening to blacken her name didn't seem so bad, all things considered. She almost walked right past Paulette, as unnoticed as any other commuter in a raincoat, but she swerved at the last moment, blinking the daze away.

'Paulie!'

'Miriam!' Paulette grabbed her in a hug, then held her at arm's length, inspecting her face anxiously. 'You look thinner. Was it bad, babe?'

'Was it bad?' Miriam shook her head, unsure where to begin. 'Jesus, it was weird, and bits of it were very bad and bits of it were, um, less bad. Not bad at all. But it's not over. Listen, let's go find something to eat – I haven't had any breakfast – and I'll tell you all about it.'

They found a booth in a not unbearable pizza joint in the mall, where the background noise loaned them a veneer of privacy, and Miriam wolfed down a weird Californian pizza with a topping of chicken tikka on a honeyed sourdough base. Between bites, she gave Paulette a brief run-down: 'They kidnapped me right out of my house after you left, a whole damn SWAT team. But then they put me up in this stately house, a palace really, and introduced me to a real honest-to-god duke. You know the medieval shit I came back with? It's real. What I didn't figure on was that my family, my real family, I mean, are, like, the aristocracy who run it.'

'They rule it.' Paulette's fork paused halfway to her mouth. 'You're not shitting me. I mean, they're kings and stuff?'

'No, they're just an extended trading Clan that happens to be an umbrella for about a third of the nobility that runs the eastern seaboard – the nouveau riche crowd. They're not long established, and deeply paranoid. Think like the Medicis. There are several countries over there, squabbling feudal kingdoms: the one hereabouts is called the Gruinmarkt, and they don't speak English – or rather, the ruling class do, the way the nobles in England spoke French during the middle ages. But anyway. The high king rules the Gruinmarkt, but the Clan – the Clan of the families who can walk between worlds – they own everything. I mean, the king wants to marry one of his sons into the Clan to tighten his grip on power.'

Miriam paused to finish her pizza, aware that Paulette was staring at her thoughtfully.

'Where do you fit in all this?' she asked.

'Oh.' Miriam put her fork down. 'I'm the long-lost daughter of a noblewoman whose coach was ambushed by bandits. Or assassins – there was a war on at the time, between branches of the Clan. She escaped, ran away to our world, but died before she could get help.' Miriam looked Paulette in the eye. 'When you were a kid, did you ever fantasize about maybe you were switched with another baby in the hospital, and your real parents were rich and powerful, or something?'

'Isn't that every little girl's daydream? Didn't Disney build a whole multinational brand on top of it?'

'Well, when you're thirty-two and divorced and have a life, and long-lost relatives from your newly discovered family show up and tell you that actually you're a countess, it might put a bit of a different spin on things, huh?'

Paulette looked slightly puzzled. 'How do you mean – '

'Like, they insist that you marry someone suitable, because they can't have independent women running around. You've got a choice between living in a drafty castle with no electricity and running water, oh, and having lots of children by the husband they've chosen for you, a choice between that and, well, there is no choice marked "B". Resistance is futile; you will be assimilated. Got it, already?'

'Oh sweet Jesus. No wonder you look fried!' Paulette shook her head slowly.

'Yeah, well, I was afraid I was going to go crazy if I didn't get away after the last week. What makes it really bad is that, well . . .' Miriam chewed her lower lip for a while before continuing. 'Your guesses about where they could make money were right on the nail. I don't know if they're into Proteome Dynamics and Biphase Technologies, but they're sure into everything else under the sun. They gave me a debit card and said, "Here's a two-million-dollar credit limit, try not to overload it." There is no way in hell that they will let me walk away from them. And the thing that frightens me most is that I'm not, like, one hundred percent sure I entirely want to.'

Paulie was studying her intently. 'Is there something else?' she asked.

'Oh yes, oh yes.' Miriam fell silent. 'But I don't want to talk about him just now.'

'Is he bad? Did he – '

'I said I didn't want to talk about it!' she snapped. A moment later, she added, 'I'm sorry. No, he isn't bad. You know, it's just you've never been able to resist ragging me about men, and I don't need that right now. It's messy, very messy, and things are bad enough without adding that kind of complication.'

'Lovely.' Paulette pulled a face. 'Okay, so I won't ask you about your mystery boyfriend. Let me see if I've got this straight? It turns out your family think you're a little lost heiress. They want to treat you like one, which is to say, not a hell of a lot like the way it works out in the fairy tales. You'd maybe tell them to screw off, but first they won't, and second they've got lots of money. Third, you've met a man who didn't want to strangle you after five minutes – sorry – and he's mixed up in all of it. Is that a fair summary?'

'Pretty much.' Miriam waved for the check. 'Which is why I had to get away from it all for the day. I'm not even a – a prisoner. I'm just considered valuable. Or something.' She frowned. 'It's absolutely crazy. Even their business operations! It's like something out of the middle ages. They're about three centuries overdue for modernization, and I'm not just talking about the cultural stuff. Pure zero-sum mercantilism, red in tooth and nail, in an environment where they have barely invented banking, never mind the limited liability company. Deeply primitive, not to say wasteful of resources, but they're set in their ways. I've seen companies like that before; sooner or later someone else comes along and eats their lunch. There ought to be something smarter they could be doing, if only I could think of it . . .'

'O-k-a-y. You do that, Miriam.'

The bill arrived and Miriam stuck down a fifty before Paulette could protest.

'Come on.' She stood up; Paulette hurried after.

'Did I just see that? Did I? Miriam Beckstein putting down a fifty percent tip?'

'I want out of this restaurant,' Miriam said flatly. Continuing on the hoof: 'Money doesn't mean anything any more, Paulie, didn't you catch that bit? I'm so rich I could buy *The Weatherman* if I wanted to – only it won't do me any good because my problems aren't money-related. There are factions among the families. One of them probably wants me dead. They had a nice little number going with my mother's shareholding in the Clan; now that I've shown up, I've disrupted a load of plans. Another faction wants me married off. The king, his number-two prince is a retard, Paulie, and you know what? I think my old goat of an uncle is going to try to marry me off to him.'

'Oh, you poor kid. Don't they have an equal rights amendment?'

'Oh, poor me, these guys don't even have a constitution,' Miriam said with feeling. 'It's a whole other world, and women like me get the . . . get the – hell, think about the Arabs. The Saudi royal family. They come over here in expensive suits and limousines and buy big properties and lots of toys, but they don't think like us, and when they go back home they go straight back to the middle ages. How would you feel if you woke up one morning and discovered you were a Saudi princess?'

'Not very likely,' Paulette pointed out, 'seeing as how I am half-Italian and half-Armenian and one hundred percent peasant stock, and damn happy to live here in the U.S. of A., where even peasants are middle class and get to be paralegals and managers and are allowed to vote. But yeah, I think I see where you're coming from.' Paulette looked at her pensively. 'You got problems,' she said. 'I'd worry about the bunch who want you out of the way before worrying about the risk of being married off to Prince Charming, though. At least they've got money.' She pulled a face. 'If *I* found I had a long-lost family, knowing my luck, the first thing they'd do is ask to borrow a hundred bucks until payday. Then they'd start with the death threats.'

'Well, you might want to think back to what you said about smuggling,' Miriam pointed out. 'I don't want to be involved in that shit. And I'm worried as hell about the string we were pulling on the other week. Have you had any other incidents?'

'Incidents?' Paulie looked angry. 'You could say that. Somebody burgled my apartment the day before yesterday.'

'Oh shit.' Miriam stopped dead. 'I'm so sorry. Was it bad?'

'It could have been. Only I was out at the time. The cops said it looked very professional. They cut the phone line and drilled the lock out on the landing, then went in and turned the whole place over.

Took my computer and every disk they could find. Ransacked the bookcases, went through my underwear – and left my spare credit card and emergency bankroll alone. They weren't after money, Miriam. What do *you* think?'

'What do I think?' Miriam stopped in the middle of the sidewalk. Paulette waited for her. 'Well, you're still alive,' she said slowly.

'Alive – ' Paulette stared at her.

'Paulie, these guys play hardball. They leave booby traps. You go into a place they've black-bagged and you open the door and it blows up in your face – or there's a guy waiting for you with a gun and he can leave the scene just by looking at a wrist tattoo. I figure either I'm wrong and the shit Joe Dixon's involved in isn't to do with the Clan, or they don't rate you as a threat – just sent some hired muscle to frighten you, rather than the real thing.'

'I am so relieved. Not.'

'*Do* be. I mean that seriously. If you're still alive, it means they don't think you're a threat. They didn't find the disk, so that's probably an end of it. If you want to get the hell out of this now, just say. I'll find the CD and burn it and you're out of the frame.'

Paulette began walking again. 'Don't tempt me,' she said tensely. Then she stopped and turned to face Miriam. 'What are you going to do?'

'I was hoping you could help me.' Miriam paused for a moment, then continued: 'Did you get the job?'

'As a paralegal?' Paulette shrugged. 'I didn't get that one, but I've got another interview this afternoon.'

'Well, how would you like another job? Starting today?'

'Doing what?' Paulette asked cautiously.

'Being my self-propelled totally legal insurance policy,' said Miriam. 'I need someone who can work for me on this side when I'm locked up being Princess Buttercup in a palace with toilets consisting of a drafty hole in the wall. You're clean, they didn't pin anything on you, and now that we know who the hell we're up against, we can make sure that you stay that way. What I've got in mind for the job will mostly involve handling non-stolen, non-illegal goods that I want to sell, keeping records, paying taxes, and making like a legitimate import/export business. But it'll also involve planting some records, very explicit records, in places where the families can't get their hands on them without getting caught.' Miriam stopped again, thinking. 'I can pay,' she added. 'I'm supposed to be very rich now.'

Paulette grinned. 'Would this be something to do with you bearing a grudge against the asshole who fired us both?'

'Could be.' Miriam thrust her hands deep in her pockets and tried to look innocent.

'When does it start and what does it pay?'

'It started fifteen minutes ago, and if you want to discuss pay and conditions, let's go find a Starbucks and talk over a coffee . . .'

*

Miriam became increasingly depressed on the train back to New York. It was late in the year, and darkness was already falling as the train raced through the bleak New England countryside. Soon the snow would be falling thick and deep, burying the bare branches beneath a layer of deadening numbness. She popped out one of the atenolol tablets that Roland had given her along with a couple of Tylenol, swallowing them with the aid of a Coke from the bar. She felt like autumn, too: The train was carrying her south toward a bleak world where she'd be enveloped in the snow of – well, maybe it was stretching the metaphor past breaking point.

Forty-four hours, and I'll be seeing Roland again, she thought. Forty-four hours? She brightened for a moment, then lapsed into even deeper gloom. Forty-four hours, forty of which would be spent in the company of . . . of . . .

She hailed a taxi from the station concourse, feeling slightly lightheaded and numb, as if she hadn't eaten. It took her to the block where she'd found the door. It looked a whole hell of a lot less welcoming after dark and closing time, and she hunched her shoulders as she stalked down the street, homing in on the alleyway by means of the green-lit display of her GPS compass.

When she reached the alley, she balked – it was black and threatening. But then, remembering who and what she was, she reached into her pocket and wrapped her right hand around the snub-nosed pistol she'd carried all day. *They can arrest you, but they can't hold you*, she reminded herself with a flicker of reckless glee. What must it be like to grow up with the talent on the other side, then to come over to this world and realize that you could do absolutely anything at all and melt away into the night undetected? She shivered.

As it happened, the alleyway was empty, a faint glow leaking from under the warehouse doorway. She opened it and walked past the cabin. Nobody hailed her. She followed the GPS compass until its directions hit zero and she saw the metal emergency staircase.

At the top of the steps she took a moment to look around. There was no sign of any burglar alarms, nothing to stop anyone coming in off the street. *I don't like the look of this*, she thought. Thirty feet farther on there was a sturdy brick wall. *I can't be sure, but it looks like most of the palace would be on the other side of that. Right?* It was weird, but she didn't have time to examine it right now. Putting her GPS compass away, she hauled out the locket from the chain around her neck that she wore under her sweater. She focused on the image and felt –

'Mistress! Oh my – ' she stumbled, black shadows pulling at the edges of her vision, and felt hands on her day pack, her shoulders, pulling her toward a richly cushioned ottoman – 'You startled us! What is that you're wearing? Oh, you're so cold!'

The black shadows began to fade, and she had a feeling like a headache starting a long way away. The huge fireplace in one side of the main room – a fireplace big enough to park her car in – was blazing with flames and light, pumping out heat. Kara helped her stand upright, a hand under one shoulder. 'You gave us such a fright!' she scolded.

'I'm back now. Is there anything to drink? Without alcohol in it?'

'I'll get it,' said Brilliana, the more practical of the two. 'Would my lady care for a pot of tea?'

'That would be fine.' Miriam felt herself closer to fainting than throwing up. *Yes, the beta-blockers seem to work*, she thought. 'Drop the "my lady" – just call me Miriam. You didn't tell anybody to search for me, did you?'

'No, my – Miriam.' This from Kara. 'I wanted to, but – '

'It's all right.' Miriam closed her eyes, then opened them again, to be confronted by a teenager with braided brown hair and a worried expression wearing a brown Dior suit and a blouse the color of old amber. 'Nothing to worry about,' she said, trying to exude confidence. 'I'll be fine when I've had some tea. This always happens. Did anything unusual happen while I was gone?'

'We've been busy making the servants unpack your wardrobe and travelling possessions!' Kara said enthusiastically. 'And Lady Olga sent you an invitation to walk with her in the orangery, tomorrow morning! Nobody is entertaining tonight, but there's another public reception in Prince Creon's name tomorrow and you have been invited!' Miriam nodded wearily, wishing Kara wouldn't end every sentence with an exclamation. She half-expected the girl to break out in squeals of excitement. 'And Sfetlana has been so excited!'

'About what?'

'She's had a proposal of marriage! Lady Olga bore it! Isn't that exciting?'

'What is that you're wearing?' asked Brilliana, returning from the fireplace with a silver teapot held carefully in her hands; for the first time Miriam noticed the spindly table beside the ottoman, the chairs positioned around it, the cups and saucers of expensive china. It appeared that ladies-in-waiting led a higher-maintenance lifestyle than regular servants.

'Something suited to the weather,' Miriam muttered. Brilliana was wearing a little black dress that would have passed unnoticed at any cocktail party from the 1960s through the 1990s. In a cold, sparsely furnished castle, there was something curiously surreal about it. 'Listen, that's a fire and a half. Is there any chance of using it to heat a lot of water? Like, enough for a bath? I want to get clean, then find something to eat.' She thought for a moment. 'Afterward you can choose something for me to wear tomorrow when I go to talk with Lady Olga. And for the reception in the evening as well, I guess. But right now, I'd kill for a chance to wash my hair.'

FIREWALL

There was a bathtub in her suite. The huge claw-footed cast-iron behemoth lived in a room she hadn't seen before, on the far side of the huge fireplace. There were even servants to fill it: three maids and a grumpy squint-eyed lad who seemed to have only half his wits about him. His job appeared to be to lurk in corners whenever anybody forgot to send him packing for another load of Pennsylvania coal.

Readying the bath involved a lot of running around and boiling coppers on the fireplace. While everybody else was occupied, Miriam pulled on her overcoat and went exploring, picking up Brilliana as a combination of tour guide and chaperone. She'd been half-asleep from exhaustion when she first arrived – and even more dead to the world after the reception at the palace. Only now was she able to take in her surroundings fully. She didn't much like what she was seeing. 'This palace,' she said, 'tell me about it.'

'This wing? This is the New Tower.' Brilliana followed a pace behind her. 'It's only two or three hundred years old.'

Miriam looked up at the roof of the reception room they'd walked into. The plasterwork formed a dizzyingly intricate layering of scalloped borders and sculpted bouquets of fruit and flowers, leaping over hidden beams and twisting playfully around the huge hook from which a giant chandelier hung. The doors and window casements were not built to a human scale, and the benches positioned against each wall looked lost and lonely.

'Who does it belong to?' asked Miriam.

'Why, the Clan.' Brilliana looked at her oddly. 'Oh, that's right.' She nodded. 'The families and the braids. You understand them?'

'Not entirely,' Miriam admitted.

'Hmm, I had thought as much.' Brilliana paced toward the far door, then paused. 'Have you seen the morning room yet?'

'No.' Miriam followed her.

'Our ancestor Angbard the Sly walked the worlds and accrued a huge fortune. His children lacked the ability, and there were five sons, sons who married and had families, and another six daughters. In that generation some kin married their cousins directly, as was done in those days to forestall dower loss, and the talent was rediscovered. Which was a good thing, because they had fallen upon hard times and were reduced to common merchants. Since then we have kept the bloodline alive by marrying first cousins across alternate generations: Three families are tied together in a braid, two in each generation, to ensure the alliances are kept close. The kin with the talent are shareholders in the Clan, to which all belong. Those who lack the talent but whose children or grandchildren might have it are outer family members, without the shares.' She waited at the door for Miriam, then lifted the heavy bolt with two hands and pulled it open.

'That's amazing,' Miriam said, peering into the vast gloomy recess.

'It is, isn't it?' replied Brilliana, squeezing through the half-open doorway as Miriam held it ajar for her. Miriam followed. 'These murals were painted by The Eye himself, it is said.' Miriam blinked at dusty splendor, a red wool carpet and walls forming scenes disturbingly similar to – and yet different from – the traditional devotional paintings of the great houses of Europe. (Here a one-eyed god hung from a tree, his hands outstretched to give the benefit of his wisdom to the kneeling child-kings of Rome. There a prophet posed before a cave mouth within which lurked something unspeakable.) 'This palace is held by the Clan in common trust. It is used by those family members who do not have houses in the capital. Each family owns one fifth of it – one tower – and Baron Oliver Hjorth occupies the High Tower, presiding over all, responsible for maintenance. I think he's angry because the High Tower was burned to a shell eight years ago, and the cost of rebuilding it has proven ruinous,' she added thoughtfully.

'Very interesting,' murmured Miriam, thinking: *Yes, it's about fifty feet long.* This part of the palace was clearly doppelgängered, if the wall she'd seen in the warehouse was where she thought it was. Which meant that her own corner was far less secure than Angbard had implied. 'Why was I accommodated here?'

'Why, because Baron Oliver refused you as a guest!' Brilliana said, a tight little smile on her face. Miriam puzzled for a moment, then recognized it as the nearest thing to anger she'd seen from the girl. 'It is unconscionable of him, vindictive!'

'I'm getting used to it.' Miriam looked around the huge, dusty audience chamber then shivered from the chill leaching through its stones. The shutters were closed and oil lamps burned dimly in the chandelier, but despite all that, it was as cold as a refrigerator. 'What does he have against me, again?'

'Your braid. Your mother married his elder brother. You should inherit the Thorold-Hjorth shares. You should, in fact, inherit the tower he has spent so long restoring. Duke Angbard has made it a personal project to bring Oliver to his knees for many years, and perhaps he thinks to use you to provoke the baron into an unforgivable display of disloyalty.'

'Oh shi – ' Miriam turned to face the younger woman. 'And you?' she demanded.

'Me?' Brilliana raised a slim hand to cover her mouth, as if concealing a laugh. 'I'm in disgrace, most recently for calling Padrig, Baron Oliver's youngest, a pimple-faced toad! My mother sent me away, first to the duke, then to the baron's table, thinking his would be a good household for a young maid to grow up in.' For a moment, a flicker of nearly revealed anger lit up her face like lightning. 'Hoping he'd take a horsewhip to me, more like.'

'Aha.' Miriam nodded. 'And so, when I arrived . . .'

'You're a countess,' Brilliana insisted. 'Travelling without companions! It's a joke, a position of contempt! Ser Hjorth sent me to dwell with you in this drafty decaying pile with a leaking roof – as a punishment to me and an insult to you. He thinks himself a most funny man, to lay the glove against a cheek that does not even understand the intent behind the insult.'

'Let's carry on.' Miriam surprised herself by reaching out and taking Brilliana's arm, but the younger woman merely smiled and walked by her side as she headed toward a small undecorated side door. 'What did you do to offend the baron?'

'I wanted to go across to the other side,' Brilliana said matter-of-factly. 'I've seen the education and polish, and the source of everything bright in the world. I know I have not the talent myself, but surely someone can take me there? Is that too much to ask? I've a mother who saw miracles in her youth: carriages that fly and ships that sail against the wind, roads as wide as the Royal Mile and as long as a country, cabinets that show you events from afar. Why should I not have this, but for an accident of birth?' The anger was running close to the surface, and Miriam could feel it through her arm.

She paused next to the small door and looked Brilliana in the eye. 'Believe me, if I could gift you with my talent I would, and thank you for taking it from me,' she said.

'Oh! But that's not what I meant – ' Brilliana's cheeks colored.

Miriam smiled crookedly. 'Did your mother by any chance send you away because you pestered her to take you over to the other side one time too often? And did Oliver banish you here for the same reason?'

'Yes,' Brilliana admitted. 'A lady is someone who never knowingly causes pain to others,' she said quietly. 'But what about causing pain to one's self?'

'I think – ' Miriam looked at her, as if for the first time: twenty-two years old, skin like milk, and blonde hair, blue eyes, a puzzled, slightly angry expression, a couple of small craterlike scars marring the line of her otherwise perfect jaw. Wearing a slim black dress and a scarf around her hair, a silver necklace set with pearls around her neck, she looked too tense to fit in here. Like a coiled spring. But give her a jacket and briefcase and nobody would look twice at her in a busy downtown rush hour. 'I think you have too low an opinion of yourself, Brill,' she said slowly. 'What's through this door, do you know?'

'It'll be the way up to the roof.' She frowned, puzzled. 'Locked, of course.'

'Of course.' This door had a more modern keyhole and lock. But when Miriam twisted the handle and tugged, it opened, admitting a frigid blast of damp air.

'I *think* you're right about it leading to the roof,' Miriam said, 'but I'd like to know just where the unlocked doors lead. Do you follow me?'

'Brr.' Brilliana shivered.

'Wait here,' Miriam instructed. She entered the doorway. Stone steps spiraled tightly up into blackness. She ascended, guided by touch as much as by vision. *This must be higher than the doppelgänger warehouse's roof,* she guessed. Cold wind smacked her in the face at the top. She turned and looked out across the steeply pitched roof, past machicolations, across gardens spread far below. And then the town, narrow streets and pitched roofs utterly unlike anything she'd see back home stretching away on all sides, dimly lit by lamplight. *What do they burn?* she wondered. Above the entire scene, riding high atop a tattered carpet of fast-moving white clouds, hung the gibbous moon. Someone had been up here recently, she realized. It was freezing cold, wet, and dark. Clambering about on the roof held no appeal, so she turned and carefully descended back into the relative warmth of the moth-eaten outer reception room.

Brilliana jumped as she emerged. 'Oh! By my soul, you gave me a fright, my lady. I was so worried for you!'

'I think I gave me a fright too.' She shut the door.

'We're going back to the heated quarters now,' she said. 'And we're going to bolt the door – on the inside. Come on. I wonder if that bath will be ready.'

*

The bath was indeed ready, although Miriam had to ransack her luggage for toiletries and chase two ladies-in-waiting and three servants out of the room before she could strip off and get in the tub. In any event, it grew cold too fast for her to soak in it for long. Baths hereabouts were a major chore, and if she didn't get across to the other side regularly, she'd have to get used to making it a weekly event. At least she didn't have to put up with the local excuse for soap, which was ghastly beyond belief.

Drying herself with her feet up against the back side of the fireplace – which for a miracle had warmed right through the stonework – she reflected on the progress she'd made. *Brilliana is going to be okay*, she mused. *Maybe I could give her to Paulie as a gofer?* If she survived the culture shock. *It's no joke*, she chided herself. She'd grown up with museums and films about the past – how much harder would she have it if she'd found herself catapulted into the equivalent of the twenty-sixth century, without any means of going home? She'd be helpless. Had Brilliana ever seen a light switch? Or a telephone? Perhaps – and then again, perhaps not.

She pulled on her jeans and sweater again, frowning – *Should have asked Kara to get something out for me* – then went back into the main room. The servants had pulled out a small dining table from somewhere, and it was set with silverware and a huge candelabra. 'Wonderful!' she said. Kara and Brill were standing beside it, Kara looking pleased with herself. 'Okay, sit down. Did anyone order any wine?'

Brill had, and the food, which she'd ordered up from the cavernous kitchens far below, was still edible. By the time they'd drained two bottles of a passable pinot noir, Miriam was feeling distinctly tired and even Kara had lost her tendency to squeal, bounce, and end every sentence with an exclamation point.

'Bedtime, I think,' she said, pointedly dismissing everyone from her chamber before pulling back the curtain on her bed, pulling out the warming pan, and burrowing inside.

The next morning Miriam awoke rapidly and – for a miracle – without any trace of a hangover. *I feel fine*, she realized, surprised. Pulling back the curtain, she sat up to find a maid sitting with down-turned face beside her bed. *Oh. I did feel fine*, she amended. 'You can send them in,' she said, trying to keep the tone of resignation out of her voice. 'I'm ready to dress now.'

Kara bounded in. 'It's your walk with Lady Olga today!' she enthused. 'Look what I found for you?'

Miriam looked – and stifled a groan. Kara had zeroed in on one of her work suits, along with a silvery top. 'No,' she said, levering herself off the bed. 'Bring me what I was wearing yesterday. I think it's clean enough to do. Then pass me my underwear and get out.'

'But! But – '

'I am thirty-two years old, and I have been putting on my own clothes for twenty-eight of those years,' Miriam explained, one gentle hand on Kara's back, propelling her gently toward the door. 'When I need help, I'll let you know.'

Miriam dressed quickly and efficiently, then exited her bedroom to find Kara and a couple of servants waiting by the dining table, on which was laid a single breakfast setting. She was about to protest when she took one look at Kara and bit her tongue. Instead, she sat down. 'Coffee or tea, whatever's available,' she said to the maid. 'Kara. Come here. Sit down with me. Cough it up.'

'I'm meant to dress you,' she said miserably. 'It's my job.'

'Fine, fine.' Miriam rolled her eyes. 'You do know I come from the other side?'

Kara nodded. 'If it makes you feel better, tell yourself I'm a crazy old bat who'll be sorry she ignored you later.' She grinned at Kara's expression of surprise. 'Listen, there's something you need to know about me: I don't play head games.'

'Games? With heads?'

Ye gods! 'If I think someone has made a mistake, I tell them. It doesn't mean I secretly hate them or that I've decided to make their life unpleasant. I don't do that because I've got other things to worry about, and screwing around like that – ' she saw Kara's eyes widen – *Don't tell me swearing isn't allowed?* – 'is a waste of time. Do you understand?'

Kara shook her head, mutely.

'Don't worry about it, then. I'm not angry with you. Drink your tea.' Miriam patted her hand. 'It's going to be all right. You said there's a reception this evening. You said we were invited. Do you want to go?'

Kara nodded, slowly, watching Miriam.

'Fine. You're coming, then. If you didn't want to go, I wouldn't make you. Do you understand? As long as you do your job properly when you're needed, as far as I'm concerned you're free to do whatever you like with the rest of your time. I am not your mother. Do you understand?'

Kara nodded again, but her entire posture was one of mute denial and her eyes were wide. *How do I get through to her?* Miriam asked herself. She sighed. 'Okay. Breakfast first.' The toast was getting cold. 'Is Brill going to the party?'

'Yes, mistress.' Kara seemed to have found her tongue again, but she sounded a bit shaky. *She's about seventeen,* Miriam reminded herself. *A teenager. Whatever happened to teenage rebellion here? Do they beat it out of them or something?*

'Good. Listen, when you've finished, go find her. I need someone to walk with me to Lady Olga's apartment. When Brill gets back, the two of you are to sort out whatever I'm wearing tonight. When I get back I'll need you both to dress me and tell me who everybody is, where the bodies are buried, and what topics of conversation to avoid. Plus a quick refresher in court etiquette to make sure I know how to greet someone without insulting them. Can you manage that?'

Kara nodded, a quick flick of the chin. 'Yes, I can do that.' She was about to say something else, but she swallowed it. 'By your leave.' She stood.

'Sure. Be off with you.'

Kara turned and scurried out of the room, her back stiff. 'I don't think I understand that girl,' Miriam muttered to herself. *Brill I think I've got a handle on, but Kara* – She shook her head, acutely aware of how much she didn't know and, by implication, of how much potential for damage this touchy teenager contained within her mood swings.

Brilliana turned up as Miriam finished her coffee, dressed for an outdoor hike.

Hey, have I started a fashion for trousers? Miriam rose. 'Good morning! Slept well after last night?'

'Oh.' Brilliana rubbed her forehead. 'You plied us with wine like a swain with his – well, I think it's all still there.' She waited for Miriam to stand up. 'Would you like to go straight to Lady Olga? Her Aris says she would receive you in the orangery, then take tea with you in her rooms.'

'I think, hmm.' Miriam raised an eyebrow, then nodded when she saw Brilliana's expression. *No newspapers, no telephones, no electri-*

city. Visiting each other is probably the nearest thing to entertainment they get around here when none of the big nobs are throwing parties. 'Whatever you think is the right thing to do,' she said. 'Where's my coat?'

Brilliana led her through the vast empty reception chamber of the night before, now illuminated with the clear white light of a snow-blanketed day. They turned down a broad stone-flagged corridor. It was empty save for darkened oil paintings of former inhabitants, and an elderly servant slowly polishing a suit of armor that looked strangely wrong to Miriam's untrained eye: The plates and joints not quite angled like anything she'd seen in a museum back home.

'Lady Aris said that Her Excellency is in a foul mood this morning,' Brilliana said quietly. 'She doesn't know why.'

'Hmmph.' Miriam had some thoughts on the subject. 'I spent a long time talking to Olga on the way here. She's . . . let's just say that being one of the inner Clan and fully possessed of the talent doesn't solve all problems.'

'Really?' Brilliana pointed Miriam down a wide staircase, carpeted in blue. Two footmen in crimson livery stood guard at the bottom, backs straight, never blinking at the two women as they passed. Their brightly polished swords looked less out of place to Miriam's eye than the submachine guns slung discreetly behind their shoulders. Any pitchfork-wielding mob who tried to storm the Clan's holding would get more than they bargained for.

They walked along another corridor. A small crocodile of maids and dubious-looking servants, cleaning staff, shuffled out of their way as they passed. This time Miriam felt eyes tracking them. 'Olga has issues,' she said quietly. 'Do you know Duke Lofstrom?'

'I've never been presented to him.' Brilliana's eyes widened. 'Isn't he your uncle?'

'He's trying to marry Olga off,' Miriam murmured. 'Funny thing is, now I think about it, not once during three days in a carriage with her did I hear Olga say anything positive about her husband-to-be.'

'My lady?'

They came to another staircase, this time leading down into a different wing of the preposterously huge mansion. They passed more guards, this time in the same colors as Oliver Hjorth's butler. Miriam didn't let herself blink, but she was aware of their stares, hostile and unwelcoming, drilling into her back.

'Is it my imagination or . . . ?' Miriam muttered as they turned down a final corridor.

'They may have been shown miniatures of you,' Brilliana said. She shivered, and glanced askance at Miriam. 'I wouldn't come this way without a companion, my lady. If I was mistrustful.'

'Why? How bad could it be?'

Brilliana looked unhappy. 'People with enemies have been known to find the staircases very slippery. Not recently, but it has happened within living memory.'

Miriam shuddered. 'Well, I take your point, then. Thank you for that charming thought.'

A huge pair of oak doors gaped ahead of them, a curtain blocking the vestibule. Chilly air sent fingers past it. Brilliana held it aside for Miriam, who found herself in a shielded cloister, walled on four sides. The middle was a sea of white snow as far as the frozen fountain. All sound was damped by winter's natural muffler. Miriam suddenly wished she'd brought her gloves.

'Whew! It's cold!' Brill was behind her. Miriam turned to catch her eye. 'Which way?' she asked.

'There.'

Miriam trudged across the snow, noting the tracks through it that were already beginning to fill in. Occasional huge flakes drifted out of a sky the color of cotton wool.

'Is that the orangery?' she asked, pausing at the door in the far wall.

'Yes.' Brilliana opened the door, held it for her. 'It's this way,' she offered, leading Miriam toward an indistinct gray wall looming from the snow.

There was a door at the foot of the hump. Brilliana opened it, and hot air steamed out. 'It's heated,' she said.

'Heated?' Miriam ducked in. 'Wow!'

On the other side of the wall, she found herself in a hothouse that must have been one of the miracles of the Gruinmarkt. Slender cast-iron pillars climbed toward a ceiling twenty feet overhead. It was roofed with a fortune in plate-glass sheets held between iron frames, very slightly greened by algae. It smelled of citrus, unsurprisingly, for on every side were planters from which sprouted trees. Brilliana ducked in out of the cold behind her and pulled the door to. 'This is amazing!' said Miriam.

'It is, isn't it?' said Brilliana. 'Baron Hjorth's grandfather built it. Every plate of glass had to be carried between the worlds – nobody has yet learned how to make it here in such large sheets.'

'Oh, yes, I can see that.' Miriam nodded. The effect was over-powering. At the far end of this aisle there was a drop of three feet or so to a lower corridor, and she saw a bench there. 'Where do you think Lady Olga will be?'

'She just said she'd be here,' said Brilliana, a frown wrinkling her brow. 'I wonder if she's near the boiler room? That's where things are warmest. Someone told me that the artisans have built a sauna hut there, but I wouldn't know about such things. I've never been here on my own before,' she added wistfully.

'Well.' Miriam walked toward the benches. 'If you want to wait here, or look around? I'll call you when we're ready to leave.'

When she reached the cast-iron bench, Miriam turned and stared back along the avenue of orange trees. Brill hadn't answered because she'd evidently found something to busy herself with. *Well, that makes things easier*, she thought lightly. Whitewashed brick steps led down through an open doorway to a lower level, past water tanks the size of crypts. The ceiling dipped, then continued – another green-lined aisle smelling of oranges and lemons, flakes of rust gently dripping from the pillars to the stone-flagged floor. Here and there Miriam caught a glimpse of the fat steam pipes, running along the inside of the walls. The trees almost closed branches overhead, form-ing a dark green tunnel.

At the end, there was another bench. Someone was seated there, contemplating something on the ground. Miriam walked forward lightly. 'Olga?' she called.

Olga sat up when she was about twenty feet away. She was wearing a black all-enveloping cloak. Her hair was untidy, her eyes reddened.

'Olga! What's wrong?' Miriam asked, alarmed.

Olga stood up. 'Don't come any closer,' she said. She sounded strained.

'What's the matter?' Miriam asked uncertainly.

Olga brought her hands out from beneath the cloak, and pointed a boxy machine pistol at Miriam's face. 'You are,' she said, her voice shaking with emotion. 'If you have any last lies to whisper before I kill you, say them now and be done with it, whore.'

PART FOUR

KILLER STORY

HOSTILE TAKEOVER

The interview room was painted pale green except for the floor, which was unvarnished wood. The single window, set high up in one wall, admitted a trickle of wan winter daylight that barely helped the glimmering of the electrical bulb dangling overhead. The single table had two chairs on either side of it. All three pieces of furniture were bolted to the floor, and the door was soundproofed and locked from the outside.

'Would you care for some more tea, Mr. Burgeson?' asked the inspector, holding his cup delicately between finger and thumb. He loomed across the table, overshadowing Burgeson's frail form: they were alone in the room, the inspector evidently not feeling the need for a stout sergeant to assist him as warm-up man.

'Don't mind if I do,' said Burgeson. He coughed damply into a wadded handkerchief. ''Scuse me . . .'

'No need for excuses,' the inspector said magnanimously. He smiled like a mantrap. 'The winters up in Nova Scotia are terrible, aren't they?'

'Character-building,' Burgeson managed, before breaking out in another wracking cough. Finally he managed to stop and sat up in his chair, leaning against the back with his face pointed at the window.

'That was how the minister of penal affairs described it in parliament, wasn't it?' The inspector nodded sympathetically. 'It would be a terrible shame to subject you to that kind of character-building experience again at your age, wouldn't it, Mr. Burgeson?'

Burgeson cocked his head on one side. So far the inspector had been polite. He hadn't used so much as a fist in the face, much less a knee in the bollocks, relying instead on tea and sympathy and veiled threats to woo Burgeson to his side. It was remarkably liberal for an HSB man, and Burgeson had been waiting for the other shoe to drop

– or to kick him between the legs – for the past ten minutes. 'What can I do for you, Inspector?' he asked, clutching at any faint hope of fending off the inevitable.

'I shall get to the point presently.' The inspector picked up the teapot and turned it around slowly between his huge callused hands. He didn't seem to feel the heat as he poured a stream of brown liquid into Burgeson's cup, then put the pot down and dribbled in a carefully measured quantity of milk. 'You're an old man, Mr. Burgeson, you've seen a lot of water flow under the bridge. You know what happens in rooms like this, and you don't want it to happen to you again. You're not a young hothead who's going to get hisself into trouble with the law anymore, are you? And you're not in the pay of the Frogs, either, else we'd have hanged you long ago. You're a careful man. I like that. You can do business with careful men.' He cradled the round teapot between his hands gently.

'And I much prefer doing business to breaking skulls.' He put the teapot down. It wobbled on its base like a decapitated head.

Burgeson swallowed. 'I haven't done anything to earn the attention of the Homeland Security Bureau,' he pointed out, a faint whine in his voice. 'I've been keeping my nose clean. I'll help you any way I can, but I'm not sure how I can be of use – '

'Drink your tea,' said the inspector.

Burgeson did as he was told.

''Bout six months ago a joe called Lester Brown sold you his dear old mother's dressing table, didn't he?' said the inspector.

Burgeson nodded cautiously. 'It was a bit battered – '

'And four weeks after that, a woman called Helen Blue came and bought it off you, didn't she?'

'Uh.' Burgeson's mouth went dry. 'I *think* so, but I'd have to check my books. Why ask me all this? It's in the books, you know. I keep records, as the law requires.'

The inspector smiled, as if Burgeson had just said something extremely funny. 'A Mr. Brown sells a dressing table to a Mrs. Blue by way of a pawnbroker who Mr. Green says is known as Dr. Red. In't that colorful, Mr. Burgeson? If we collected the other four, why, we could give the hangman a rainbow!'

Burgeson cringed. 'I don't know what you're talking about. What's all this nonsense about? Who are these Greens and Reds you're bringing up?'

'Seven years in one of His Majesty's penal colonies for sedition back in seventy-eight and you *still* don't have a fucking clue.' The inspector shook his head slowly. 'Levelers, Mr. Burgeson.' He leaned forward until his face was inches away from Burgeson's. 'That dressing table happened to have a hollow compartment above the top drawer and there were some most interesting papers folded up inside it. You wouldn't have been dealing in proscribed books again, would ye?'

'Huh?' The last question caught Burgeson off-guard, but he was saved by another tubercular spasm that wrinkled his face up into a painful knot before it could betray him.

The inspector waited for it to subside. 'I'll put it to you like this,' he said. 'You've got bad friends, Erasmus. They're no good for yer old age. A bit o' paper I can't put me finger on is one thing. But if I was to catch 'em, this Mrs. Blue or Mr. Brown, they'd sing for their supper sooner than put their necks in a noose, wouldn't they? And you'd be right back off to Camp Frederick before your feet touched the ground, on a one-way stretch. Which in your case would be approximately two weeks before the consumption carried you away for good an' all and Old Nick gets to toast you by the fires of hell.

'All their Godwinite shit and old-time Egalitarianism will get you is a stretched neck or a cold grave. And you are too old for the revolution. They could hold it tomorrow and it wouldn't do you a blind bit of good. What's that slogan – "Don't trust anyone who's over thirty or owns a slave"? Do you really think your young friends are going to help you?'

Burgeson met the inspector's gaze head-on. 'I have no Leveler friends,' he said evenly. 'I am not a republican revolutionary. I admit that in the past I made certain mistakes, but as you just said, I was punished for them. My tariff is spent. I cooperate fully with your office. I don't see what else I can do to prevent people who I don't know and have never heard of from using my shop as a laundry. Do we need to continue this conversation?'

'Probably not.' The inspector nodded thoughtfully. 'But if I was you, I'd stay in touch.' A business card appeared between his fingers. 'Take it.'

Burgeson reached out and reluctantly took the card.

'I've got my eyes on you,' said the inspector. 'You don't need to know how. If you see anything that might interest me passing through your shop, I'll trust you to let me know. Maybe it'll be news to me – and then again, I'll know about it before you do. If you turn a blind eye, well – ' he looked sad – 'you obviously won't be able to see all the titles of the books in your shop. And it'd be a crying shame to send a blind man back to the camps for owning seditious tracts, wouldn't it?'

*

Two women stood ten feet apart, one shaking with rage, the other frightened into immobility. Around them, orange trees cloistered in an unseasonable climate perfumed the warm air.

'I don't understand.' Miriam's face was blank as she stared down the barrel of Olga's gun. Her heart pounded. *Buy time!* 'What are you talking about?' she asked, faint with the certainty that her assignation with Roland had been overseen and someone had told Olga.

'You know very well what I'm talking about!' Olga snarled. 'I'm talking about my honor!' The gun muzzle didn't deviate from Miriam's face. 'It's not enough for you to poison Baron Hjorth against me or to mock me behind my back. I can ignore those slights – but the infamy! To do what you did! It's unforgivable.'

Miriam shook her head very slowly. 'I'm sorry,' she said. 'But I didn't know at the time it started between us. I mean, about your planned marriage.'

A faint look of uncertainty flickered across Olga's face. 'My betrothal has no bearing on the matter!' she snapped.

'Huh? You mean this isn't about Roland?' Miriam asked, feeling stupid and frightened.

'Roland – ' Olga stared at her. Suddenly the look of uncertainty was back. 'Roland can have nothing to do with this,' she claimed haughtily.

'Then I haven't got a clue what the "it" you're talking about is,'

Miriam said heavily. Fear would only stretch so far, and as she stared at Olga's eyes, all she felt was a deep wellspring of resignation at the sheer total stupidity of all the events that had brought her to this point.

'But you – ' Olga began to look puzzled, but still angry. 'What about Roland? What have you been up to?'

'Fucking,' Miriam said bluntly. 'We only had the one night together but, well, I really care about him. I'm fairly sure he feels the same way about me, too. And before you pull that trigger, I'd like you to ask yourself what will happen and who will be harmed if you shoot me.' She closed her eyes, terrified and amazed at what she'd just heard herself say. After a few seconds, she thought, *Funny, I'm still alive.*

'I don't believe it,' said Olga. Miriam opened her eyes.

The other woman looked stunned. However, her gun was no longer pointing directly at Miriam's face.

'I just told you, dammit!' Miriam insisted. 'Look, are you going to point that thing somewhere safe or – '

'You and Roland?' Olga asked incredulously.

A moment's pause. Miriam nodded. 'Yes,' she said, her mouth dry.

'You went to bed with that dried-up prematurely middle-aged sack of mannered stupidity? You care about him? I don't believe it!'

'Why are you pointing that gun at me, then?'

For a moment, they stood staring at each other; then Olga lowered the machine pistol and slid her finger out of the trigger guard.

'You don't know?' she asked plaintively.

'Know *what*?' Miriam staggered slightly, dizzy from the adrenaline rush of facing Olga's rage. 'What on earth are you talking about, woman? I've just admitted I'm having an affair with the man you're supposed to be marrying and that *isn't* why you're threatening to kill me over some matter of honor?'

'Oh, this is insupportable!' Olga stared at her. She looked very uncertain all of a sudden. 'But you sent your man last night.'

'*What* man?'

Their eyes met in mutual incomprehension.

'You mean you don't know? Really?'

'Know what?'

'A man broke into my bedroom last night,' Olga said calmly. 'He had a knife and he threatened me and ordered me to disrobe. So I shot him dead. He wasn't expecting that.'

'You. Shot. A. Rapist. Is that it?'

'Well, that and he had a letter of instruction bearing the seal of your braid.'

'I don't understand.' Miriam shook her head. 'What seal? What kind of instructions?'

'My maidenhead,' Olga said calmly. 'The instructions were very explicit. What is the law where you come from? About noble marriage?'

'About – what? Huh. You meet someone, one of you proposes, usually the man, and you arrange a wedding. End of story. Are things that different here?'

'But the ownership of title! The forfeiture. What of it?'

'What "forfeiture"?' Miriam must have looked puzzled because Olga frowned.

'If a man, unwed, lies with a maid, also unwed, then it is for him to marry her if he can afford to pay the maiden-price to her guardian. And all her property and titles escheat to him as her head. She has no say in the matter should he reach agreement with her guardian, who while I am in his care here would for me be Baron Hjorth. In my case, as a full-blood of the Clan, my Clan shares would be his. This commoner – ' she pronounced the word with venomous diction – 'invaded my chamber with rape in mind and a purse full of coin sufficient to pay his way out of the baron's noose.'

'And a letter,' Miriam said in tones of deep foreboding. 'A letter sealed with . . . what? Ink? Wax? Something like that, some kind of seal ring?'

'No, sealed with the stamps of Thorold and Hjorth. It is a disgusting trick.'

'I'll say.' Miriam whistled tunelessly. 'Would you believe me if I said that I don't have – and have never seen – any such stamp? I don't even know who my braid are, and I really ought to, because they're not going to be happy if I – ' she stopped. 'Oh, of course.'

'"Of course", what?'

'Listen, was there an open door to the roof in your apartment last night? After you killed him? I mean, a door he came in through?'

Olga's eyes narrowed. 'What if there was?'

'Yesterday I world-walked from my room to the other side,' said Miriam. 'This house is supposed to be doppelgängered, but there is no security on the other side of my quarters. Anyone who can world-walk could come in. Later, Brilliana and I found an open door leading to the roof.'

'Ah.' Olga glanced around, taking in whatever was behind Miriam. 'Let's walk,' she said. 'Perhaps I should apologize to you. You have further thoughts on the matter?'

'Yes.' Miriam followed Olga, knees weak with an adrenaline-rush of anger. 'My question is: Who profits? I don't have a braid seal, I didn't even know such a thing existed until you told me, but it seems clear that others in the – my – braid would benefit if you killed me. Or if that failed, if I was deprived of a friend in circumstances bound to create a scandal of monstrous proportions around me, it certainly wouldn't harm them. If you can think of someone who would also benefit if you were split apart from your impending alliance – ' She bit her tongue, but it was too late.

'About Roland,' Olga said quietly.

'Uh. Yes.'

'Do you really love him?' she asked.

'Um.' Tongue-tied, Miriam tried to muster her shredded integrity. 'I think so.'

'Well, then!' Olga smiled brightly. 'If the two of you would please conspire to convince your uncle to amend his plans for me, it would simplify my life considerably.' She shook her head. 'I'd rather marry a rock. Is he good in bed?'

Miriam coughed violently into her fist. 'What would you know about – '

'Do you think I'm *completely* stupid?' Olga shook her head. 'I know you are a dowager, you have no guardian, and you are competent in law. You have nothing to lose by such intrigues. It would be naive to expect you to abstain. But the situation is different for me. I have not my majority until marriage, and upon marriage I lose my independence.'

'I don't understand you people,' Miriam muttered, 'but I figure your inheritance and marriage law is seriously screwed. Rape as a tool of financial intrigue – it's disgusting!'

'So we agree on one thing.' Olga nodded. 'What do you think could be behind this?'

'Well. Someone who doesn't like me – obviously.' She began ticking off points on her fingers. 'Someone who holds you in contempt, too, or who actively wants you out of the way. By the way, what would have happened to you if you had shot me?'

'What?' Olga shrugged carelessly. 'Oh, they'd have hanged me, I suppose,' she said. 'Why?'

Miriam shuddered. 'Let's see. We have Item Two: someone who has it in for you as well as me. We all center around – ' something nagged at her for attention – 'No, it's not there yet. Well, Item Three is my unsecured apartment. That we can blame on Baron Oliver, huh? Someone took advantage of it to get their cat's-paw into place by way of the roof, I think that's clear enough. I got Brilliana to lock and bolt the inner apartment – which is doppelgängered – last night, when I realized the roof door was open onto areas that aren't secured on the other side. Maybe their first objective was to shoot me in my sleep, and they turned to you as a second target when that failed. By attacking you, they could either convince you that I was to blame – you shoot me, they win – or they could deprive me of an ally – you – and perhaps turn others against me. Do you think they believe Roland would think I'd do such a thing to you?'

Olga clutched her arm. 'That's it,' she said calmly. 'If they didn't know about you and Roland, they would believe him to be set on me as his prize. It would be a most normal reaction to be enraged at anyone who ordered his bride-to-be raped away by night. Out of such actions blood feuds are born.' Her fingers dug into Miriam's arm. 'You would swear to me you had no hand in it?'

'Olga. Do you really believe I'd pay some man to rape even my worst enemy? As opposed to simply shooting her and having done with the matter?'

Olga slowly untensed. 'If you were not raised over there, I might think so. But your ways are so charmingly informal that I find it hard to believe you would be so cruel. Or devious.'

'I don't know. The longer I spend here, the more paranoid I become. Is there any risk of some asshole trying to rape *me* for my presumed riches?'

'Not if you're a guest of someone who cares what happens on their estate, such as the duke. Even at other times, you are only at risk if your guards fail you, and your guardian is willing to accept maiden-price,' said Olga. 'As you are of age and able to act as your own guardian, I don't think that situation is likely to arise – an adventurer who took you against your will could expect to go to the gallows. But you do have guards, don't you, just in case?' She looked anxious. 'They're very discreet, wherever they're hiding!' A frown crossed her face. 'Assuming the baron hasn't managed to make sure the orders assigning a detachment to your household have been lost . . .'

'No shit,' Miriam said shakily as they climbed the steps toward the entrance, looking around at the same time for signs of Brilliana. 'I must congratulate them on their scarcity. When I find out who they are and where they live.'

*

The snow was falling thick and fast outside, from clouds the color of slate. The temperature was dropping, a blizzard in the making. 'You must come up to my receiving room for tea,' Olga insisted, and Miriam found herself unable to decline. Brilliana hurried alongside them as they re-entered the barely heated corridors of the palace, ascending through a bewildering maze of passages and stairs to reach Olga's private rooms.

Olga had left her guards behind. *She wanted no witnesses*, Miriam thought with a cold chill. Now she berated them as she entered her outer reception room, four strapping men in household livery worn with cuirasses, swords, and automatic weapons. 'Come in, be welcome, sit you down,' Olga insisted, gesturing toward a circle of sofas being moved hastily into place by a bevy of servants. Miriam accepted gratefully, placing Brilliana at her left, and presently Olga's own ladies-in-waiting shepherded in a small company of servants bearing side tables, a silver samovar, and sweetmeats on trays. With the blazing fireplace, it was almost possible to forget the gathering storm outside.

Now that Olga's fury at Miriam had been diverted toward a different target, she overcompensated, attempting to prove herself a charming hostess by heaping every consideration upon Miriam in a way that Miriam found more than a bit creepy after her earlier rage. Maybe it was just a guilt reaction, but it left Miriam feeling very relieved that Olga didn't share her interest in Roland. They were well into a second pot of tea, with Miriam eavesdropping on the Lady Aris's snide comments about the members of this or that social set at court, when there was a polite announcement at the door. 'Courier for Madame Thorold,' announced Olga's steward, poking his head in. 'Shall I admit him?'

'Certainly.' Olga sat up straight as the messenger – dripping wet and looking chilled to the bone – entered. 'My good man! What do you have for me?'

'Milady, I have been charged to deliver this into your hands,' he said, dropping to one knee and presenting a sealed envelope from a shoulder bag. Olga accepted it, slit the wrapping, and read. She frowned. 'Very well. You may tell your master I received word and passed it on to all present here. Feel free to leave immediately.'

The messenger backed out, bowing. Olga returned to her chaise longue, looking distracted. 'How unfortunate,' she said.

'Unfortunate?' Miriam raised an eyebrow.

'Tonight's reception is postponed, by virtue of the unusually foul weather. It shall in any event be held tomorrow, once arrangements have been made for additional shelter from the elements.' She glanced at the window. 'Well, I can't say I am surprised. This may be the season for storms, but this one appears to be setting in hard.' Wind howled against the shutters outside.

'Is this normal?' Miriam asked. 'To postpone events?'

'By your leave, it's not normal, my lady, but it's not unheralded.' Brilliana looked unhappy. 'They may need time to move the Life Guard Cavalry to other stables, to accommodate the coaches of the visitors. Or a roof may have caved in unexpectedly. This being the first real storm of winter, they may be hoping it will blow itself out overnight.'

'Hmm.' Miriam drained her teacup. 'So it'll be tomorrow night instead?'

'Almost certainly,' Olga said confidently. 'It's a shame to postpone once, twice is an embarrassment. Especially when the occasion is the return to court of his majesty's winter sessions. And his opening of the sessions and levy of taxes follows the next day, to be followed by a hanging-holiday.'

'Well, then.' Miriam nodded to herself. 'Is anything at all of consequence due to happen then?'

'Oh, a lot of drinking, and not a little eating and making merry,' Olga assured her. 'It's not a greatly important event for the likes of us. Our great sessions fall in six months, near upon Beltaigne, when alliances are discussed and braids rededicated, and the court of families-in-Clan hear grievances and settle treaties.'

'Hmm. Well, I suppose I'd better make sure I'm around for that, too,' said Miriam, waiting for a servant to refill her cup.

Olga winked at her. 'I expect you will be – if we find you some bodyguards first.'

*

Late in the afternoon, Miriam returned to her apartment – briefly. Dismissing the servants, she called Brilliana and Kara into her bedroom. 'I'm in trouble,' she said tersely.

'Trouble, my lady?' asked Kara, eyes glinting.

'Someone tried to force themselves upon Lady Olga last night. Someone with gold in their pocket and a commission bearing the seal of my braid. Which I have never seen, so I have to take Olga's word for it.' She sat down on a chest and waited for Kara's declarations of shock to die down. Brilliana just nodded thoughtfully.

'This room – and other parts of this suite – are not doppelgängered properly,' she continued. 'On the other side, security is virtually nonexistent – until you go fifty feet that way.' She gestured at the wall. 'I don't think that's an accident. Nor was that open door last night,' she added to Brilliana's questioning look.

'What are we going to do?' asked Kara, looking frightened.

'What *you* are going to do – both of you – is tell the servants we're going to have a quiet supper: cold cuts or a pie or something plain and simple. Then we're going to dismiss the servants and go to bed early so we are well rested for the morrow. After they bring our meal up and stoke the fireplace, they can leave.'

She stood up and paced. 'What's really going to happen, once the servants have left is that two of Lady Olga's guards – the guards Baron Hjorth hasn't assigned to me – are going to enter the near audience chamber through the side door.'

She grinned at Brilliana's surprise. 'You will put on your cloaks and go where they lead you, which will be straight to Lady Olga's rooms, where you will be able to sleep safe and warm until it's time to come back here, in the morning.'

'And you, my lady?' asked Kara, searching her face. 'You can't spend the night alone here!'

'She doesn't intend to,' Brill said. 'Do you?'

'Correct.' Miriam waited.

'You're going to go over there,' Brilliana added. 'How I'd like to follow you!'

'You can't, yet. Someone is conspiring against me. I am going to have to move fast and be inconspicuous. On the other side, there is a teeming city with many people and strange customs. I can't risk you attracting attention while I'm on the run.' She raised a finger to anticipate Brilliana's objection. 'I'll take you along later, I promise. But not this time. Do you understand?'

'Yes.' Brill muttered something under her breath. Miriam pretended not to notice.

'That's it, then. If someone comes calling in the night, all they'll find are beds stuffed with pillows: You'll be elsewhere. On the other side, the fewer people who know where I'm going, the safer I'll be. I'll meet you back here tomorrow afternoon, and we'll decide what to do then, depending on whether the opening of the court of winter sessions is going ahead or not. Any last questions?'

*

It was snowing in New York, too, but nothing like the blizzard that had dumped two feet of snow on Niejwein in a day. Miriam met nobody in the warehouse. At the top of the stairs she paused. *What was that trick?* she wondered, racking her brains. A flashback to the training course, years ago: It had been a giggle at the time, spy tradecraft stuff for journalists who were afraid of having their hotel rooms burgled in Kyrgystan or wherever. But now it came back to her.

Kneeling, she tied a piece of black cotton sewing thread from the wall to the handrail, secured with a needle. It was invisible in the twilight. If it was gone when she returned, that would tell her something.

On this trip, she wore her hiking gear and towed her suitcase. With street map in hand, she wanted to give the impression of being a lost tourist from out of state. Maybe that was why a taxi pulled up almost as soon as she emerged from the back street, while her phone was still chirping its voice mail alert.

'The Marriott Marquis, Times Square,' she told the driver. Head pounding, she hit the 'mail' button and clamped the phone to her ear.

'Marriott Marquis, room 2412, continuously booked for the whole week in the name of Mr. and Mrs. Roland Dorchester. Just ask at the front desk and they'll give you a key.'

Thank you, she thought, pocketing the phone and blinking back tears of relief.

The taxi took her straight to the main entrance and a bellboy was on hand to help her with her suitcase. She headed straight to the front desk.

'Mrs. Dorchester? Yes, ma'am, I have your card-key here, if you'd like to sign . . .'

Miriam did a little double-take, then scrawled something that she hoped she'd be able to replicate on demand. Then she took the key and headed for the elevator bank.

She was inside the glass-walled express elevator, and it was surging up from the third floor in a long glide toward the top, when a horrible thought occurred to her. *What if they've got to Roland?* she wondered. *After he booked the hotel. They could be waiting for me.*

It was a frightening realization, and Miriam instinctively reached toward her pocket. *How the hell do you do this?* Suddenly it occurred to her that the little revolver was as much of a threat as an asset in this kind of situation. If she went through the door and some bad guy was just inside, he could grab her before she had a chance to use it. Or grab the gun. And she was more than twenty stories up, high enough that – she looked out and down through the glass wall of the lift and took a deep breath of relief. 'Oh, that's okay,' she muttered, as the obvious explanation occurred to her just before the lift bell dinged for attention: Skyscrapers didn't need doppelgängering against attack from another world where concrete and structural steel were barely known.

Miriam stepped out into the thickly carpeted hallway and stopped. Pulling out her cell phone, she dialed Roland's number. It rang three times.

'Hello?'

'Roland, what happens if you're on the twenty-fourth floor of a tall building, say a hotel, and – ' quick glance in either direction – 'you try to world-walk?'

'You don't do that.' He chuckled dryly. 'That's why I chose it. I wasn't expecting you so soon. Come right on up?'

'Sure,' she said and rang off, abruptly dizzy with relief and anticipation.

I hope this works out, she thought, dry-swallowing as she walked down the corridor, hunting for room 2412. *Hell, we hardly know each other –*

She reached the door. All her other options had run out. She put the card in the slot and turned the handle.

*

Three hours later they came up for air. The bedding was a tangled mess, half the fluffy white towels were on the bathroom floor and the carpet was a wasteland of discarded clothing – but it had worked out.

'I have missed you so much,' she murmured in his ear, then leaned close to nibble at his lobe.

'That makes two of us.' He heaved up a little, bracing against the bed head, turning to look at her. 'You're beautiful.'

'I bet you say that to every naked woman you wake up in bed with,' she replied, laughing.

'No,' he said, in all seriousness, before he realized what he'd done. Then he turned bright red. 'I mean – '

He was too late. Miriam pounced. 'Got you,' she giggled, holding him down. Then she subsided on top of him. 'Like that?' she asked. 'Or this?'

'Oh.' He rolled his eyes. 'Please. A few minutes?'

'Frail male reed!'

'Guilty, I'm afraid.' He wrapped an arm around her. 'What's with the early appearance? I thought there was supposed to be a reception this evening?'

'There was, past tense.' Miriam explained about the cancellation.

'So you came over early, just in case I was here?'

'No.' She felt very sober, all of a sudden, even though they hadn't been drinking – and felt the need to remedy the condition, too.

'Why, then? I thought you were sticking with the program?'

'Not when people try to kill me twice in one day.'

'What?' His arms tensed and he began to sit up.

'No, no – lie down. Relax. They can't come through here and I took steps to throw off the trail.' She kissed him, again, tasted the sweat of their lovemaking.

'Wow. What did I do to deserve someone like you?'

'You were really, really wicked in a previous life?'

'Nonsense!'

'The killers.' She'd broken the magic, she realized with a sense of desolation.

'They won't follow us here, but there's a lot to tell,' she said. 'How about we dig a bottle out of the minibar and have a bath or something while I tell you?'

'I think we can do better than that,' he said with a glint in his eye. He reached for the bedside phone. 'Room service, please. Yes? It's room 2412. Can you send up the item I ordered earlier? Leave it outside.'

'Huh?' She raised her eyebrows.

'My surprise.' He looked smug.

'I thought *I* was your surprise.' He'd been surprised enough when she came through the door – but he'd kissed her, and one thing led to another, and they hadn't even made it as far as the bed the first time. Now she sat up on the rumpled sheets, brushing one hand up and down his thigh and watching his face.

'About your uncle's plans. What do you think Olga makes of them?'

Roland looked pained. 'She doesn't get a say in it. She's a naive little dutiful contessa who'll do as Angbard tells her parents to tell her.'

'If that's what you and Angbard think, you may be in for a nasty surprise.' Miriam watched him carefully. 'You don't know her very well, do you?'

'I've met her a time or two.'

'Well, I have just spent several days in her company and that little minx may be young and naive, but she isn't dumb. In fact, it's lucky for me she's smart and doesn't want to marry you any more than you want her – otherwise I wouldn't be here now.'

'What – '

'She nearly shot me.'

'Holy Crone Wife! What happened?'

'Let go! You're hurting – '

'Sorry.' He sat up and gently put an arm around her shoulders. 'I'm sorry. You caught me by surprise. Tell me all about it. Everything. Don't leave anything out. My gods – I am so glad you're here and safe now.' He hugged her. 'Tell me everything. In your own time.'

'Time is the one thing I don't think we've got.' She leaned against him.

'Someone sent Olga an unwelcome gift – a rape-o-gram. Luckily for me, but unluckily for the thug concerned, Olga's childlike enthusiasms include embroidery, violins, haute couture, and semiautomatic weapons. She found a commission in his back pocket, with my seal on it and a purse of coin sufficient to pay the kind of maiden-price Oliver might ask for someone he really didn't like much. Roland, I didn't even know I *had* a seal.'

'"A seal".' He looked away just as someone knocked on the door. Miriam jumped.

'I'll get it – '

'No! Wait!' Miriam scrabbled for her jacket, fumbled in its pockets. 'Okay, now you can open the door. When I'm out of sight.'

Roland glanced at her as he tied his bathrobe. 'It's only room service, isn't it?'

216

'I'm not taking any chances.' She crouched against the wall around the corner from the door, pistol cradled in both hands.

'Will you give that up? If it's the DEA, we have very expensive lawyers who'll have us both out on bail in about thirty microseconds.'

'It's not the DEA I'm worried about,' she said through gritted teeth. 'It's my long-lost family.'

'Well, if you put it that way . . .' Roland opened the door. Miriam tensed. 'Thank you,' she heard him tell someone. 'That's great, if you could leave it just here.' A moment later, she heard the door close, then a squeaking of wheels.

Roland appeared, pushing a trolley upon which sat an ice bucket with a bottle of something poking out of it.

'This is your surprise?' she asked, lowering the gun.

He nodded. 'You are on edge,' he observed. 'Listen, do you want me to chain the door and hang out a "Do Not Disturb" sign?'

'I think that would be a good start.' She was shivering. Worse, she had no idea where it had come from. 'I'm not used to people trying to shoot me, love. It's not the kind of thing that normally happens to a journalist, unless you're a war correspondent.'

She put the gun down on the bedside table.

'Listen, Taittinger Comtes de Champagne. Sound all right to you?' He raised the bottle.

'Sounds perfect. Open it now, dammit, I need a drink!'

He peered at her. 'You do, at that,' he said. 'One moment . . .' He popped the cork carefully, then slowly filled two fluted glasses, taking care not to spray the champagne everywhere. He passed her a glass, then raised his own. 'To your very good health.'

'To us – and the future.' She took a sip. 'Whatever the hell that means.'

'You were telling me about Olga.'

'Olga and I had a little conversation at cross-purposes. She was raised to never unintentionally cause offence, so she gave me time to confess before she shot me. Luckily, I confessed to the wrong crime. Did you know that you're an, uh, "dried-up prematurely middle-aged sack of mannered stupidity"? She doesn't want to marry you – trust me on this.'

217

'Well, it's mutual!' Roland sat in the chair opposite the end of the bed, looking disturbed. 'Have you any idea how the man got into her apartments?'

'Yup. Through my own, by way of the roof. Turns out that the rooms Baron Oliver assigned me aren't doppelgängered – or rather they are, but the location on this side is unprotected. And aren't I supposed to have bodyguards or something? Anyway, that's why I came here. I figured it was safer than spending the night in an apartment that has a neon sign on the door saying "*Assassins This Way*", with cousins next door who seem to have opened a betting pool on my life expectancy.'

'Someone tried to rape Olga?' Roland shook his head. 'That doesn't make sense to me.'

'It does if I was their first target and they meant to kill me, but couldn't get at me directly: it was a contingency plan, to set up a blood feud between us.' Briefly, she told him about the open stairwell, and her instructions to lock and bolt all the doors on the inside. 'I don't feel safe there, I really don't.'

'Hmm.' He took a mouthful of wine. 'I don't know.' He looked thoughtful rather than shocked. 'I can eliminate some suspects, but not everybody.' He glanced up at her, worry writ large across his face. 'First, it's not official. It's family, not Clan business. If it was the Clan, they'd have sent soldiers. You've seen what we've got over here.' She nodded. 'Our enforcement teams – you don't bother resisting. They're better armed, better trained, and better paid than the FBI's own specialist counterterrorism units.'

'Well, I guessed that much,' she said.

'Yes, but this isn't them. It's too damned blatant – and that's worrying. Whoever did it is out of control. Oliver Hjorth might dislike you and feel threatened, but he wouldn't try to kill you in his own house. Not offering you a guard of honor is another matter, but to be implicated – no.' He shook his head. 'As for Olga, that's very disturbing. It sounds as if someone set her up to kill you or cause a scandal that would isolate you – one or the other. And you are probably right about being the intruder's first target. That means it's an insider – and that's the frightening part. Someone who knows that you don't know the families well, that you can be cut apart from the pack and isolated, that you are unguarded. Someone like that, who is acting like they're out of control. A rogue, in other words.'

'Well, no shit, Sherlock.' She drained her glass and refilled it. 'Y'know something? One of these days we may eventually make an investigative journalist out of you.'

'In your dreams – I'm an economic historian.' He frowned at the floor in front of her feet, as if it concealed an answer. 'Let's start from where we are. You've told Olga about us. That means if we're lucky she doesn't tell Angbard. If she does, if Olga tells him about us, he could – do you have any idea what he could do?'

'What? Listen, Roland, I didn't grow up under the Clan's thumb. Thinking this way is alien to me. I don't really give a damn what Angbard thinks. If I behave the way they seem to expect me to, I will be dead before the week is out. And if I survive, things won't be much better for me. The Clan is way out of date and overdue for a dose of compulsory modernization, both at the business level and the personal. If the masked maniac doesn't succeed in murdering me, the Clan will expect me to go live like a medieval noble lady – fuck that! I'm not going to do it. I'll live with the consequences later.'

'You're – ' he swallowed. 'Miriam, you're strong, but you don't know what you're talking about. I've been trying to resist the pressure for years. It doesn't work. The Clan will get you to do what they want you to do in the end. I spent years trying to get them to do something – land reform on their estates, educating the peasants, laying the groundwork for industrialization. All I got was shit. There are deeply entrenched political groupings within the Clan who don't want to see any modernization, because it threatens their own source of power – access to imported goods. And outside the Clan, there are the traditional nobility, not to mention the Crown, who are just waiting for the Clan nobility to make a misstep. Jealousy is a strong motivating force, especially among the recently rich. If Angbard hadn't stood up for me, I'd have had my estate forfeited. I might even have been declared outlaw – don't you see?' There was anguish in his eyes.

'Frankly, no. What I see is a lot of frightened people, none of whom particularly like the way things work, but all of whom think they'll lose out if anyone else disrupts it. And you know something? They're wrong and I don't want to be part of that. You've been telling me that I can't escape the Clan, and I'm afraid you're right – you've convinced me – but that only means I've got to change things. To carve out a niche I can live with.' She stood up and walked toward him. 'I don't like the way the families live like royalty in a squalid mess that doesn't even have indoor plumbing. I don't like the way their law values people by how they can breed and treats women like chattels. I don't like the way the outer family feel the need to defend the status quo in order to keep from being kicked in the teeth by the inner families. I don't like the dehumanizing poverty the ordinary people have to live with, and I don't like the way the crazy fucked-up feudal inheritance laws turn an accident of birth into an excuse for rape and murder. But most of all, I don't like what they've done to you.'

She leaned down and pulled him up by the shoulders, forcing him to stand in front of her. 'Look at me,' she insisted. 'What do you see?'

Roland looked up at her sceptically. 'Do you really think you can take them all on?'

'On my own?' She snorted. 'I know I can,' she said fiercely. 'The whole country is ripe for modernization on a massive scale, and the Clan actually has the muscle to do that, if they'd just realize it. All it takes is a handful of people who believe that things can change to start the ball rolling. And that handful has to start somewhere! Now are you with me or against me?'

He hugged her right back, and she felt another response: He was stiffening against her, through his robe. 'You're the best thing that's happened to me in years. If ever. I don't want to lose you.'

'Me too, love.'

'But how do you think you're going to make it work?' he asked. 'And stop whoever's trying to kill you.'

'Oh, that.' She leaned into his arms, letting him pull her back in the direction of the bed. 'That's going to be easy. When you strip away the breeding program, the Clan is a business, right? Family-owned partnership, private shareholdings. Policy is set at annual meetings twice a year, next one at Beltaigne, that sort of thing.'

'So?' He looked distracted, so she stopped fumbling at his belt for a moment.

'Well.' She leaned her chin against the hollow of his neck, licked his pulse spot slowly. 'It may have escaped your attention, but I am an expert in one particular field – I've spent years studying it, and I think I probably know more about it than anyone else in the family. The Clan is an old-fashioned unlimited-liability partnership, with a dose of family politics thrown in. The business structure itself is a classic variation on import/export trade, but it's cash-rich enough to support a transition to some other model. All I need is a lever and an appropriate fulcrum, and then a direction to make them move in. Business restructuring, baby, that's where it's at. A whole new business model. The lever we need is one that will convince them that they have more to lose by not changing than by sticking with the status quo. Once we're in the driver's seat, nobody is going to tell us we can't shack up on this side and live the way we want to.'

He lifted her off her feet and lay down beside her. 'What leverage do you need?' he asked alertly. 'I spent years looking and didn't find anything that powerful . . .'

'It's going to be something convincing.' She smiled hungrily up at him. 'And they'll never know what hit them. We need to establish a power base by Beltaigne. A pilot project that demonstrates massive potential for making money in some way that relies on the Clan talent without falling into the classic mercantilist traps. It'll make me worth much more to them alive than dead, and it'll give us the beginning of a platform to recruit like-minded people and start building.' She looked pensive. 'A skunkworks within an established corporation, designed to introduce new ways of thinking and pioneer new business opportunities. I've written up enough stories about them – I just never thought I'd be setting one up myself.'

She stopped talking. There'd be time to work out the details later.

BUSINESS PLAN

Miriam dozed fitfully, unable to relax her grip on consciousness. She kept turning events over in her mind, wondering what she could have done differently. If there was anything in the past two weeks that she could have changed, what might have come of it? She might not have accepted the pink and green shoebox. She wouldn't be in this mess at all.

But she wouldn't have met Brill, or Roland, or Angbard, or Olga, or the rest of the menagerie of Clan connections who were so insistently cluttering up her hitherto-straightforward family life with politics and feuds and grudges and everything else that went with the Clan. *My life would be simpler, emptier, more predictable, and safer*, she thought sleepily. *With nobody trying to exploit me because of who I am.*

Who I am? She opened her eyes and stared at the ceiling in the dark. *Is it me they're after or someone else?* she wondered. *If only I could ask my mother.* Not the mother who'd loved her and raised her, not Iris – the other one, the faceless woman who'd died before she'd had a chance to remember her. The woman who'd borne her and been murdered, her only legacy a mess of –

She glanced sideways. Roland was asleep next to her, his face smooth and relaxed, free of worry. *I've gone from being completely independent to* this *in just two weeks.* Never mind Brill and Kara back in the palace, the weight of Angbard's expectations, the Clan's politics . . . Miriam wasn't used to having to think about other people when planning her moves, not since the divorce from Ben.

She glanced at the alarm clock. It was coming up to seven o'clock – too late to go back to sleep. She leaned over toward Roland's ear. 'Wake up, sleepyhead,' she whispered.

Roland mumbled something into the pillow. His eyelids twitched.

'Time to be getting up,' she repeated.

He opened his eyes, then yawned. 'I hate morning people,' he said, looking at her slyly.

'I'm not a morning person, I just do my best worrying when I should be asleep.' She took a deep breath. 'I'm going to have to go find that lever to move the Clan,' she told him. 'The one we were talking about last night. While that's going on, unless we can find out who's really got it in for me, we may not be able to meet up very often.'

'We can't talk about this publicly,' he said. 'Even if Olga keeps her mouth shut – '

'No.' She kissed him. 'Damn, I feel like they're all watching us from behind the bed!'

'What are you going to do today?' he asked diplomatically.

'Well.' She rolled up against him. 'First, we're going to order breakfast from room service. Then you're going to go and do whatever it is that Angbard expects of you this morning. If you come back here, I'll probably be gone, because I've got some research to do and some stuff to buy. There's someone I've hired – ' he raised an eyebrow – 'Yes, I've established a pattern of drawing out cash against that card, for as long as it'll hold out. I'm paying a friend who I trust implicitly to keep an eye out for me. I'm not going to tell you any more about it because the fewer people who know, the better. But when you come back to this room, even if I'm not here, you'll find a prepaid new cell phone. From time to time, I want you to check for voice mail. Only three people will know the number – you, me, and my employee. It's for emergencies only. There'll be a single number programmed into it, and that's for me – again, I'll only check for voice mail occasionally. I figure if I can't even hide a cell phone, there won't be anything you can do to help.'

'So you're going away,' he said. 'But are you going back to court or are you going underground?'

'I'm going back to face the music,' she replied. 'At least for this evening, I need to be seen. But I'm going to hole up on this side at night, at least until I can find a safely doppelgängered room or figure out who's after me. And then – ' she shrugged. 'Well, I'll have to play it by ear. For now, I'm thinking about setting up a new startup venture, in the import/export field.'

'That's not safe – they'll kill you if they find out! Clan business ventures are really tightly controlled. If you splinter off, they'll assume you're setting up as a rival.'

'Not if I do it right,' she said confidently. 'It's a matter of finding a new business model that hasn't occurred to any of them. Then get it going and deal the Clan shareholders in before they know what's happening. If I can finesse it, they'll have a vested interest in seeing me succeed.'

'But that's – ' Roland was at a loss for words. 'A new business? There *is* no scope for anything new! Nobody's come up with a new trade since the 1940s, when the drug thing began taking over from gold and hot goods. I was thinking you were going to try and do something like bootstrap reforms on your own estate, not – '

'That's because you're thinking about it all wrong.' She reached out and touched his nose. 'So are they. You did the postgraduate research thing,' she said.

'Economic history.'

'Right. What's that got to do with it?'

'Well. The family business structure is kind of primitive, isn't it? So you went looking for a way to modernize it, didn't you? Using historical models.'

'Yes. But I still don't see – '

'Historical models are the wrong kind. Look at me. They tried to train you up to improve things, but there's not a lot you can do when the management tree is defined by birth, is there?'

'Correct.' He looked frustrated. 'I did some work on this side, cutting overheads and reorganizing, but there's stuff I couldn't touch – I just wasn't allowed anywhere near it, in fact. There's no easy way to apply the European model in the Gruinmarkt. No investment banking infrastructure, no limited liability, all property rights ultimately devolve to the king – it's straight out of the late feudal period. There are lots of really competent, smart people who are never going anywhere because they can't world-walk, and lots of time-wasting prima donnas who are basically content to serve as couriers on a million-dollar salary.' He caught her eye and flushed.

'Whether I approve or not doesn't matter, does it?' she said tartly.

'The families are dependent on drug money and weaning them off it will be a huge job. But I'd like you to think on this. You said that their company structure is basically fifteenth- or sixteenth-century. They're still stuck in a mercantilist mode of thinking – "What can I take from these other guys and sell at a profit?" – rather than ways of generating added value directly. I am absolutely certain that there is a better way of running things – and one that doesn't run the risk of bringing the FBI and DEA and CIA down on everybody's heads – some way that lets us generate value directly by world-walking. It's just a matter of identifying it.'

'The legality of the Clan's current business isn't a problem, at least not from the commercial point of view; I think we spend a couple of hundred million a year on security because of it.' He shrugged. 'But what can we do? We're limited to high-value commodities because there's a limit to how much we can ship. Look, there are roughly three hundred active inner family members who can shuttle between the worlds, five days on and five days off. Each of us can carry an average of a hundred pounds each way. That means we can shift up to seven tons each way, each day. But maybe half of that is taken up by luxury items or stuff we need just to keep sane. An average of one in four trips is used to carry passengers piggyback. And there's the formal personal allowance. So we really only have a little over two tons per day – to fund an entire ruling class! The fixtures and fittings in Fort Lofstrom alone amount to a year's gross product for the family. That'd be, in U.S. dollar terms, several billion, wouldn't it?'

'So what? Isn't it a bit of a challenge to try and figure out a better way of using this scarce resource – our ability to ship stuff back and forth?'

'But two and a half tons a day – '

'Suppose you were shipping that into orbit, instead of to a world where the roads are dirt tracks and the plumbing doesn't flush. It doesn't sound very impressive, but that's about the payload-to-orbit capacity of Ariane or Lockheed.' Miriam crossed her arms. 'Who make billions a year on top of it. There are high-value, low-weight commodities other than drugs. Take saffron, for example, a spice that's worth three times its weight in gold. Or gold, for that matter.

You said they used to smuggle gold, back when bullion was a government monopoly. If you can barter your aristocratic credentials for military power, you can use modern geophysics-based prospecting techniques to locate and conquer gold-mining areas. A single courier can carry maybe a million dollars' worth of gold from the other side over here in a day, right?'

Roland shook his head. 'First, we have transport problems. The nearest really big gold fields are in California, the Outer Kingdom. Which is a couple of months away, as the mule train plods, assuming the natives don't murder you along the way. Remember, guns give our guards a quality edge, but quantity has a quality all of its own and ten guards – or even a hundred – aren't much use against an army. Other than that, there're the deposits in South Africa, the white man's graveyard. Do I need to say any more about that? It'd take us years to get that kind of pipeline running, before we had any kind of return on investment to show the families. It's very expensive. Plus, it'd be deflationary over here. As soon as we start pumping cheap gold onto the market, the price of bullion will fall. Or have you spotted something all of the rest of us have been missing for fifty years? When I was younger, I thought I might be able to change things. But it's not that simple.'

She shrugged. 'Sure it's hard, and in the long term it'd be deflationary, but in the long run we're all dead anyway. What I'm thinking is: We need to break the deadlock in the Clan's thinking wide open. Come up with a new business model, not one the existing Clan grandees have seen before. Doesn't matter if it isn't very lucrative at first, as long as it can fund textbooks – going the other way – and wheelbarrows. While we wean the families off their drug dependency problem, we need to develop the Gruinmarkt. Right now, the Clan could implode like that – ' she snapped her fingers – 'if Congress cancelled the war on drugs, for example. The price would fall by a factor of a hundred – overnight – and you'd be competing against pharmaceutical companies instead of bandits. And it's going to happen sooner or later. Look at the Europeans: Half of them have decriminalized marijuana already and some of them are even talking about legalizing heroin. Basing your business on a mercantilist approach to transhipping a single commodity is risky as hell.'

'That would be bad, I agree. In fact – ' his eyes unfocused, he stared into the middle distance – 'Sky Father, it would trigger a revolution! If the Clan suddenly lost its supply of luxury items – or antibiotics – we'd be screwed. It's amazing how much leverage you can buy by ensuring the heir to a duchy somewhere doesn't die of pneumonia or that some countess doesn't succumb to childbed fever.'

'Yeah.' Miriam began collecting her clothes. 'But it doesn't have to go that way. I figure with their social standing the Clan could push industrialization and development policies that would drag the whole Gruinmarkt into the nineteenth century within a couple of generations, and a little later it would be able to export stuff that people over here would actually want to buy. Land reform and tools to boost agricultural efficiency, set up schools, build steel mills, and start using the local oil reserves in Pennsylvania – it could work. The Gruinmarkt could bootstrap into the kind of maritime power the British Empire was, back in the Victorian period. As the only people able to travel back and forth freely, we'd be in an amazing position – a natural monopoly! The question is: How do we get there from here?'

Roland watched her pull her pants on. 'That's a lot to think about,' he said doubtfully. 'Not that I'm saying it can't be done, but it's . . . it's big.'

'Are you kidding?' She flashed him a smile. 'It's not just big, it's enormous! It's the biggest management problem anyone has ever seen. Drag an entire planet out of the middle ages in a single generation, get the families out of the drugs trade by giving them something productive and profitable to do instead, give ourselves so much leverage we can dictate terms to them from on high and make the likes of Angbard jump when we say "hop" – isn't that something you could really get your teeth into?'

'Yes.' He stood up and pulled open the wardrobe where he'd hung his suit the evening before. 'What you're talking about will take far more leverage than I ever thought . . .' Then he grinned boyishly. 'Let's do it.'

*

Miriam went on a shopping spree, strictly cash. She bought three pre-paid cell phones and programmed some numbers in. One of them she kept with Roland's and Paulette's numbers in it. Another she loaded with her number and Roland's and mailed to Paulie. The third – she thought long and hard on it, then loaded her own number in, but not Paulette's. Blood might be thicker than water, but she was responsible for Paulette's safety. A tiny worm of suspicion still ate at her; she was pretty certain that Roland was telling the truth, straight down the line, but if not, it wouldn't be the first time a man had lied to her, and – *What the hell is this? This is the guy you're thinking about spending the rest of your life with – and you're holding out on him because you don't trust him completely?* She confronted herself and answered: *Yeah. If Angbard told him my life depended on him giving Paulie away, how would I feel then?*

Next she collected essential supplies. She started by pulling more cash from an ATM. She stuffed three thousand dollars into an envelope, wrapped a handwritten note around it, and FedExed it to Paulette's home address. It was an eccentric way to pay an employee, but it wasn't as if she'd had time to set up a bank account yet. After posting the cash, Miriam hit on a couple of department stores, one for spare socks (there were no washing machines in history-land, she reminded herself) and another for some vital information. A CD-ROM containing the details of every patent filed before 1920 went in her pocket: She had difficulty suppressing a wild grin as she paid ten bucks for it.

With the right lever, I will move worlds, she promised herself.

She left the suitcase at the Marriott, but her new spoils went in a small backpack. It was late afternoon before she squeezed into a cab and gave directions back to the warehouse. *I hope I'm doing the right thing*, she thought, wistfully considering the possibility of spending another night with Roland. But he'd gone back to Cambridge, and she couldn't stay until he returned to New York.

Yet again there was nobody to challenge her in the warehouse office. It seemed even more deserted than usual, and a strange musty smell hung over the dusty crates. She went upstairs, then knelt and checked for the thread she'd left across the top step.

It was gone. 'Hmm.' Miriam glanced around. Nobody here now, she decided. She walked over to the spot that was doppelgängered with her bedroom chamber, took a deep breath, pulled out the locket, and stared at it. The knotwork, intricate and strange, seemed to ripple before her eyes, distorting and shimmering, forming a pattern that she could only half-remember when she didn't have it in front of her. Odd, it was a very simple knot –

The world twisted around Miriam and spat out a four-poster bed. Her head began to throb at the same time. She closed the locket and looked around.

'Mistress?' It was Kara, eyes wide open. She'd been bent over Miriam's bed, doing something.

'Yes, it's me.' Miriam put her backpack down. 'How did the assassination attempt go last night?'

'Assassination?' Kara looked as if she might explode. 'It was horrible! Horrible, mistress! I was so scared – '

'Tell me about it,' Miriam invited. She unzipped her jacket. 'Where's Brill?'

'Next door,' Kara fussed. 'The reception tonight! We don't have long! You'll have to listen – '

'Whoa!' Miriam raised her hands. 'Stop. We have what, three hours? I thought you were going to brief me on who else will be there.'

'Yes, my lady! But if we have to dress you as well – '

'Surely you can talk at the same time?' asked Miriam. 'I'm going to find Brilliana. I need to discuss things with her. While I'm doing that, you can get yourself ready.'

She found Brilliana in the reception room, directing a small platoon of maids and manservants around the place. She'd already changed into a court gown. 'Over there!' she called. 'No, I say, build it in front of the door, not beside it!'

She glanced at Miriam as she came in. 'Oh, hello there, my lady. It's hopeless, absolutely hopeless.'

'What is?' asked Miriam.

'The instructions,' said Brilliana. She sidestepped a pool of sawdust as she approached. Miriam glanced around as she added,

'They're no good at following them. Even when I tell them exactly what I want.'

'What have you been up to?' Miriam leaned against a tapestry-hung wall and watched the artisans at work.

'You were right about the door,' said Brilliana. 'So I summoned a locksmith to change the levers, and I am having this small vestibule added.' She smiled, baring teeth. 'A little trap.'

'I – ' Miriam snapped her fingers. 'Damn. I should have thought of that.'

'Yes.' Brilliana looked happy with herself. 'You approve?'

'Yes. Tell them to continue. I want a word with you in my room.' She retreated into the relative peace and quiet of her bedroom, followed by the lady-in-waiting. With the door shut, the noise of sawing outside was almost inaudible.

'What's the damage?'

'There were holes in your blankets – and scorch marks around them – when I checked this morning.' Despite her matter-of-fact tone, Brilliana looked slightly shaken. 'I had to send Kara away, the poor thing was so shocked.'

'Well, I had a good night's sleep.' Miriam glanced around the room bleakly. 'But I was right about the lack of a doppelgängered space on the other side. It's a huge security risk. This is serious. Did anyone tell Baron Hjorth?'

'No!' Brilliana looked uncertain. 'You said – '

'Good.' Miriam relaxed infinitesimally. 'All right. About tonight: In a while Kara's going to come back and sort me out for the reception. In the meantime, I need to know what I'm up against. I think I'm going to need to sleep in Lady Olga's apartment tonight. I want to vary my pattern a bit until we find whoever . . . whoever's behind this.' She sat down on the end of the bed. 'Talk to me.'

'About tonight?' Brilliana caught her eye and continued. 'Tonight is the formal ball to mark the opening of the winter session of his majesty's court tomorrow morning. There will be members of every noble family in the capital present. This is the session in which his majesty must assemble tribute to the emperor beyond the ocean, so it tends to be a little subdued – nobody wants to look too opulent

– but at the same time, it's essential to be seen. To be present in Niejwein at the beginning of winter used to mean one was snowed in, wintering here. Noble hostages at his majesty's pleasure. We don't do that these days, but still, it's a mark of good faith to be seen to offer obedience and at least one older family member. Your uncle sent word by way of his secretary that you be asked to bend the knee and pledge him obedience, by the way.'

'He did, did he?' muttered Miriam.

'Well!' Brill paced across the room in front of her. 'What this means is that it will be an assembly of some sixty families of note and their representatives and champions.' She spotted Miriam's surprised expression. 'Did you think we and ours were the sum and the end of the nobility? This is a small fraction of the whole, but thanes and earls from distant towns and estates cannot appear at court, and so many of them make supplication by proxy. We, the Clan families, are merely a small fraction – but the cream.'

'So there are going to be, what, several hundred people present?'

Brilliana nodded, looking very serious. 'At least that,' she said. 'But I'll be right behind you to remind you of anyone important.'

'Whew! Lucky me.' Miriam raised an eyebrow. 'How long does it go on for?'

'Hmm.' Brill tilted her head over to one side. 'It would be rude to leave before midnight. Are you going to be . . . ?'

'This time, I don't have a three-day coach journey behind me.' Miriam stood up. *And this time I'm going to do business*, she added mentally. 'So. What do I need to say when greeting people, by order of rank, so as not to offend them? And what have you and Kara decided I'm going to wear?'

*

This time it only took Kara and Brill an hour to dress Miriam in a midnight-blue gown. But then they insisted on taking another hour to paint her face, put up her hair, and hang a few kilograms of gold, silver, and precious stones off her. At the end of the process, Miriam walked in front of the mirror (a full two feet in diameter, clearly imported from the other side) and took a comic double-take. 'Is that me?' she asked.

'Should it not be?' Brilliana replied. Miriam glanced at her. Brilliana's outfit looked to Miriam to be both plainer and more elegant than her own, not to mention easier to move in. 'It is a work of art,' Brilliana explained, 'fit for a countess.'

'Hah. "A work of art"! And here I was, thinking I was a plain old journalist.'

Miriam nodded to herself. Medieval values. *It's all face*, she thought. *All the wealth goes on the outside to show how rich you are. That's how they think. If you don't display it, you ain't got it. Remember that.* This outfit seemed marginally less overblown than the last: Maybe she was getting used to local styles. 'Is there,' she asked doubtfully, 'anywhere that I can put a few small items?'

'I can assign a maid to carry them, if it pleases you – ' Brilliana caught her expression. 'Oh *that* kind of item,'

'Yes.' Miriam nodded, afraid that smiling would crack her makeup.

'She could use a muff, for her hands?' suggested Kara.

'A muff?' asked Miriam.

'This.' Kara produced a cylindrical fur hand-warmer from somewhere. 'Will it do?'

'I think so.' Miriam tried stuffing her hands in it. It had room to spare – and a small pocket. She smiled in spite of herself. 'Yes, this will do,' she said. She walked over to her day sack and fished around in it. 'Dammit, this is ridiculous – got it!' She stood up triumphantly clutching the bag and pulled out a number of small items that she proceeded to stuff into the muffler.

'Milady?' Kara looked puzzled.

'Never go out without a spare tampon,' Miriam told her. 'You know, tampons?' She blinked in surprise. 'Well, maybe you don't. And a few other things.' Like a strip of beta-blocker tablets, a small bottle of painkillers, a tarnished silver locket, a credit card wallet, and a mobile phone.

'Milady – ' Kara looked even more puzzled.

'Yes, yes,' Miriam said briskly. 'We can go now – or as soon as you're ready, right? Only,' she held up a finger, 'it occurs to me that it would be a good idea to keep our carriage ready to return at a moment's notice, against the possibility that my mystery admirer turns up again.'

'I'll see to it,' said Brilliana. She looked slightly worried.

'Do so. Shall we leave now?'

Travelling by carriage seemed to involve as much preparation as a flight in a light plane, and was even less comfortable. A twenty-minute slog in a freezing cold carriage, sandwiched between Kara and Brilliana, didn't do anything good to Miriam's mood. The subsequent hour of walking across the king's brilliantly polished parquet supporting a fixed, gracious grin and a straight back wouldn't normally have done anything to help, either – but Miriam had done trade shows before, and she found that if she treated this whole junket as a fancy-dress industry event, she actually felt at home in it. Normally she'd use a dictaphone to record her notes – a lady-in-waiting in a red gown would have been rather obtrusive at a trade show – but the principle was the same, she decided, getting into the spirit of things. 'Is that so?' she cooed, listening attentively to Lord Ragnr and Styl hold forth on the subject of the lobster fishermen under his aegis. 'And do they have many boats?' she asked. 'What kind do they prefer, and how many men crew them?'

'Many!' Lord Ragnr and Styl puffed up his chest until it almost overshadowed his belly, which was proud and taut beneath a layer of sashes and diadems. 'At last census, there were two hundred fishing crofts in my isles! And all of them but the most miserable with boats of their own.'

'Yes, but what type are they?' Miriam forced a smile.

'I'm sure they're perfectly adequate fishing boats; I shouldn't worry on their behalf, my lady. You should come and visit one summer. I am sure you would find the fresh sea air much to your favor after the summer vapors of the city, and besides – ' he huffed – 'didn't I hear you say you were interested in the whales?'

'Indeed.' Miriam dipped her head, chalking up another dead loss – yet another feudal drone who didn't know or wouldn't talk about the source of his own wealth, being more interested in breeding war horses and feuding with the king's neighbors. 'May I have the pleasure of your conversation later?' she asked. 'For I see an old friend passing, and it would be rude not to say hello – '

She ducked away from Ragnr and Styl, and headed toward the next nobleman and his son – she was beginning to learn how to spot such things – and wife. 'Ambergris, Brill, may be available from Ragnr and Styl. Make a note of that, please, I want to follow it up later. Who's this fellow, then?'

'This is Eorl Euan of Castlerock. His wife is Susan and the son is, um, I forget his name. Rural aristocracy, they farm and, uh, they're clients of the Lords Arran. How do you spell ambergris?'

Miriam advanced on Eorl Euan with a gracious smile. 'My lord!' She said. 'I am sorry, but I have not been gifted with the privilege of your acquaintance before. May I intrude upon your patience for a few minutes?'

It was, she had discovered, a surprisingly effective tactic. The manners were different, the glitz distracting, and the products and press releases took a radically dissimilar form – but the structure was the same. At a trade show she was used to stalking up to a stand where some bored men and women were waiting to fall upon visitors and tell them their business plans and their life stories. She'd had no idea what happened at a royal court event, but evidently a lot of provincial nobility turned up in hope of impressing all and sundry and carving out a niche as providers of this or that – and they were as much in search of an audience with a bright smile and a notepad as any marketing executive, did they but know it.

'What are you doing, mistress?' Brilliana asked during one gap in the proceedings.

'I'm learning, Brill. Observe and take notes!'

She was nodding periodically and looking serious, as Lord Something of This told her about Earl Other of That's infringement upon his historically recognized deer forest in pursuit of coal in the Netherwold Mountains down the coast, when she became aware of a growing silence around her. As Lord Something ran down, she turned her head and saw a posse advancing on her, led by a dowager of fearsomely haughty aspect, perhaps eighty years old but as dry as a mummy, with curiously drooping eyelids, two noble ladies to either side, and a train borne by no less than three pages astern.

'Ah,' said the dowager. 'And this is the Countess Thorold Hjorth I have heard so much about?' she asked the younger of her two companions, who nodded, avoiding Miriam's eyes. Miriam turned and smiled pleasantly. 'Whom do I have the honor of addressing?' she asked. *Where's Brill?* she wondered. *Dammit, why did she have to wander off right now?* The dowager was exuding the kind of chill Miriam associated with cryogenic refrigerants. Or maybe her venom glands were acting up. Miriam smiled wider, trying to look innocent and friendly.

'This is the Dowager Grand Duchess Hildegarde Thorold Hjorth, first of the Thorold line, last of the Thorold Hjorth braid,' announced the one who'd spoken to the dowager.

Oh. Miriam dipped as she'd been taught. 'I'm honored to meet you,' she said.

'So you should be.' Miriam nearly let her smile slip at that, the first words the duchess had spoken to her. 'Without my approval, you wouldn't be here.'

'Oh, really?' Her smile became fixed. 'Well, then I am duly grateful to you.' *Brilliana! Why now? Who is this dragon?*

'Of course.' The dowager's expression finally relaxed from intense disapproval into full-on contempt. 'I felt the need to inspect the pretender for myself.'

Pretender? 'Explain yourself,' Miriam demanded. There must have been something frightening about her expression: One of the ladies-in-waiting took a step backward and the other raised a hand to her mouth. 'Pretender to what?'

'Why, to the title you assume with so little preparation and polish, and manners utterly unfitted to the role. A mere commoner from the mummer's stand, jumped up and gussied up by Cousin Lofstrom to stake his claim.' The dowager's look of fierce indignation reminded Miriam of a captive eagle she'd once seen in a zoo. 'A pauper, dependent on the goodwill and support of others. If you were who you claim to be, you would be of substance.' Duchess Hildegarde Thorold Hjorth made a little flicking motion, consigning her to the vacuum of social obscurity. 'Come, my – '

'Now you wait right here!' Miriam took a step forward, right into the dowager's path. 'I am not an impostor,' she said, her voice pitched low and even. 'I am who I am, and if I am not here happily and of my own free will, I will not be spoken to with contempt.'

'Then how will you be spoken to?' asked the duchess, treating her to a little acid smile that showed how highly she rated Miriam in this company.

'With the respect due my station,' Miriam threw at her, 'or not at all.'

The dowager raised one hooded eyebrow. 'Your station is a matter of debate, child, but not for you – and it is a debate that will be settled at Beltaigne, when I shall take great pleasure in ensuring that it is brought before the Clan council and given the consideration it deserves. And you might wish to give some thought to the matter of your competence, even if your identity is upheld.' The little smile was back, dripping venom: 'If you joust with the elite, do not be surprised when you are unhorsed.' She turned and walked away, leaving Miriam gaping and angry.

She was just beginning to realize she'd been outmaneuvered when Brilliana appeared at her elbow. 'Why didn't you warn me?' she hissed. 'Who is that poisonous bitch?'

Brilliana looked astonished. 'But I thought you knew! That was your grandmother.'

'Oh. Oh.' Miriam clapped a hand to her mouth. 'I have a grandmother?'

'Yes and a – ' Brilliana stopped. 'You didn't know,' she said slowly.

'No,' Miriam said, looking at her sharply.

'Everyone says you've got the family temper,' Brill let slip, then looked shocked.

'You mean, like – that?' Miriam looked at her, aghast.

'Hmm.' Brill clammed up, her face as straight as a gambler with an inside flush.

'Oh look,' she said, glancing behind Miriam. 'Isn't that – '

Miriam glanced around, then turned, startled. 'I wasn't expecting to see you here,' she said, trying to pull herself together in the aftermath of the duchess's attack.

The duke's keeper of secrets nodded. 'Neither was I, until yesterday,' he said. He looked her up and down. 'You appear to be settling in here.'

'I am.' Miriam paused, unsure how to continue. Matthias looked just as intimidating in Niejwein court finery as he had in a business suit. It was like having a tank take a pointed interest in her. 'And yourself? Are you doing all right?'

'Well enough.' Matthias noticed Brilliana. 'You. Please leave us, we have important matters to discuss.'

'Humph.'

Brill turned and was about to leave. 'Do we?' Miriam asked, pointedly. 'I rather think we can talk in front of my lady-in-waiting.'

'No, we can't.' Matthias smiled thinly. 'Go away, I said.' He gestured toward the wall, where secluded window bays, curtain-lined against the cold, provided less risk of being overhead. 'Please come with me.'

Miriam followed him reluctantly. *If they ever make a movie about the Clan, they'll have to hire Schwarzenegger to play this guy*, she decided. *But Arnie has a sense of humor.* 'What is there to talk about?' she asked quietly.

'Your uncle charged me to deliver this to you.' Matthias held out a small wooden tube, like a miniature poster holder.

'For the king, a sworn affidavit testifying to your identity.' His expression was unreadable. 'I am to introduce you to his majesty on behalf of my master.'

'I, uh, see.' Miriam took the tube. 'Any other messages?'

'Security.' Matthias shook his head. 'It's not so good here. I gather that Baron Hjorth assigned you no guards? That's bad. I'll deal with it myself in the morning.' He leaned over her like a statue.

'Um.' Miriam looked up at him. 'Is that all?'

'No.' His cheek twitched. 'I have some questions for you.'

'Well, ask away.' Miriam glanced around, increasingly uncomfortable with the way Matthias had corralled her away from the crowd. 'What about?'

'Your upbringing. This is important because it may help me identify who is trying to kill you. You were adopted, I believe?'

'Yes.' Miriam shrugged. 'My parents – I was in care, the woman I was found with was dead, stabbed, a Jane Doe. So when Morris and Iris went looking for a child to adopt, I was around.'

'I see.' Matthias's tone was neutral. 'Was your home ever burgled when you were a child? Did anyone ever attack your parents?'

'My – no, no burglaries.' Miriam shook her head. 'No attacks. My father's death, that was a hit-and-run driver. But they caught him; he was just a drunk. Random chance.'

'Random chance?' Matthias sniffed. 'Do not underestimate random chance.'

'I don't,' she said tensely. 'Listen, why the third degree?'

'I take a personal interest in all threats to Clan security.'

'Bullshit. You're secretary to the duke. And a member of the outer families, I believe?' She looked up at him. 'That puts a glass ceiling right over your head, doesn't it? You sit in Fort Lofstrom like a spider, pulling strings, and you run things in Boston when the duke is elsewhere, but only by proxy. Don't you? So what's in it for you?'

'You are mistaken.' Matthias's eyes glinted by candlelight. 'To get here, I left the duke's side this morning.'

'Oh, I get it. Someone gave you a lift across and you caught the train.'

'Yes.' Matthias nodded. 'And there is something else you should understand, your ladyship. I am not of high birth. Or rather, but for an accident of heredity . . . but like many of my relatives I have reached an accommodation with the Clan.' He took her arm. 'I know a little about your history. Not everyone who lives here is entirely happy with the status quo, the way the Clan council is run. You have a history of digging – '

'Let go of my wrist,' Miriam said quietly.

'Certainly.' Matthias dropped his grip. 'Please accept my apologies. I did not intend to give offence.'

Miriam paused for a moment. 'Accepted.'

'Very well.' Matthias glanced away. 'Would you care to hear some advice, my lady?'

'It depends,' she said, trying to sound noncommittal, trying to stay in control. *First a hostile grandmother, now what . . . ?* She felt slightly dizzy, punch-drunk from too much information, much of it unwelcome. 'In what spirit is the advice offered?'

Matthias's face was as stiff and controlled as a mask. 'In a spirit of friendly solicitude and perfect altruism,' he murmured.

She shrugged uncomfortably. 'Well, then, I suppose I should take it in the manner in which it is intended.'

Matthias lowered his voice. 'The Clan has many secrets, as you have probably realized, and there are things here that you should avoid showing a conspicuous interest in. In particular, the alignment of inner members, those who vote within the council, could be vulnerable to disturbance if certain proxies were realigned. You should be careful of embarrassments; the private is public, and you never know what seeming accidents may be taken by your enemies as proof of your incompetence. I say this as a friend: You would do well to find a protector – or a faction to embrace – before you become a target for the fears of every conspirator.'

'Do you know who's threatening me? Are *you* threatening me?' she asked.

'No and no. I am simply attempting to educate you. There are more factions here than anyone will admit to.' He shook his head. 'I will visit you tomorrow and see to your guards – if that meets with your approval. I can provide you with a degree of protection if you choose to accept it. Do you?'

'Maybe. We'll see.' Miriam backed away from him, trying to cover her confusion. She retreated back into the flood of light shed by the enormous chandeliers overhead, back toward the torrent of faces babbling in their endless arrogant status games and power plays, just as Brilliana came hurrying up to her. 'You have a summons!' Brill said hastily. 'His royal highness would like you to present before him.'

'Present what, exactly? My hitherto-undiscovered family tree, a miracle of fratricidal squabbles and – '

'No, your credentials.' Brilliana frowned. 'He gave them to you?'

Miriam held up the small scroll and examined the seal. It was similar to the one Olga had shown her, but different in detail.

'Yes,' she said, finally.

'Was that all he wanted?' Brilliana asked.

'No.' Miriam shook her head. 'Time for that later. You'd better take me to his majesty.'

The royal party held their space in another window bay backed by curtains and shutters. All the cloth didn't completely block the chill that exuded from the stonework. Miriam approached the king as she'd been shown, Brilliana – and a Kara she'd found somewhere – in tow, and made the deepest curtsey she could manage.

'Rise,' said His High Majesty, Alexis Nicholau III. 'I believe we have met? Two nights ago?'

He smelled of stale wine and old sweat. 'Yes, your majesty.' She offered her scroll to him. 'This is for you.'

He cracked the seal with a shaky hand, unrolled it, then nodded to himself and handed it to a page. 'Well, if you're good enough for Angbard, you're good enough for me.'

'Um. Your majesty?'

He waved vaguely at the curtains. 'Angbard says you'll do, and what he says has a habit of sticking.' One of the two princes sidled up behind him, trailing a couple of attendants. 'So I've got m'self a new countess.'

'It would appear so, your majesty.'

'You're his heir,' said the king, relishing the last word.

Miriam's jaw dropped. 'M-majesty?'

'Well, he says so,' said King Alexis. 'Says so right there.' He stabbed a finger at the page who held the parchment. ''N' who d'you think really runs this place?'

'Excuse me, please? He hadn't told me.'

'Well, I'm telling you,' said the king. The prince – was it Creon or Egon? She couldn't tell them apart yet – leaned over his majesty's shoulder and stared at her frankly. 'Doesn't matter much.' The king sniffed. 'You won't fill that man's shoes, girl. The man you marry might, though. If you both live long enough.'

'I see,' she said. The prince was clearly in his twenties, had long dark hair, an embroidered gold blouse, and a knife at his belt that looked to be a solid mass of gemstones. He regarded her with an expression of slack-jawed vacancy. *What is this?* Miriam wondered with growing fear. *They're trying to set me up!*

'There's one way of seeing to that,' the king added. 'I believe you've not been introduced to my son Creon?'

'Delighted, absolutely delighted!' Miriam tried to smile at him. Creon nodded back at her happily.

'Creon is long past an age to marry,' the king said thoughtfully. 'Of course, whoever he took to wife would be a royal princess, you realize?' He looked down his nose at her. 'Anyone who would be pledged to a royal household would need a very special dowry – ' his glance was dark and full of veiled significance – 'but I believe Angbard's relatives might find the price affordable. And the prince would benefit from the intelligent self-interest of an understanding wife.'

'Uh-huh.' She looked past the king, at Prince Creon. The prince beamed at her, a delighted, friendly expression that was nevertheless undermined slightly by the way he drooled on his collar. 'I'd be delighted to meet with the prince later, under more appropriate circumstances,' she gushed. 'Delighted! Of course!' She beamed, desperately racking her brain for platitudes recovered from a thousand and one annual shareholders' meetings gone bad. 'I'd love to hear from you, really I would, but I am still being introduced to so many fascinating people and I owe you my full attention, it would be awful to devote less than my full energies and attention to your son! I quite appreciate your – '

'Yes, yes, that's enough.' The king beamed at her. 'There's no need for sycophancy. I have heard so much I am far beyond its reach, and he – ' he nodded at his son – 'will never be within it.'

Gulp. 'I see, your majesty.'

'Yes, he's an idiot,' King Alexis said genially. 'And you're too old.' Some instinct for self-preservation made Miriam swallow an automatic protest. 'But he's *my* idiot, and were he to marry his child would be third in line to the throne, at least until Egon's wife bears issue. I urge you to think on this, young lady: Should you meet anyone suitable, I would be most interested to hear of them. Now begone with you, to these vastly important strangers who fascinate you so conspicuously. I won't hold it against you.'

'Uh – thank you! Thank you most kindly!' Miriam fled in disarray, outmaneuvered for the third time this evening. *Just what is it with these people?* She wondered. The king's overture was undoubtedly well-meant; just alarming and demoralizing, for it highlighted the depths of her own inadequacy in trying to play power politics with these sharks. *The king wants to marry his son into the Clan, and he thinks I'm a useful person to talk to?* It was desperately confusing. And why had Angbard named her his heir? That was beyond astonishing.

Without an answer, nothing else seemed to make sense. What was he trying to achieve? Didn't it make her some kind of target?

Target.

She stopped, halfway from pillared bay to dancing floor, as if struck in the head by a two-by-four.

'Milady Miriam? What is it?' Brilliana was tugging at her sleeve.

'Shush. I'm thinking.'

Target. Thirty-two years ago someone had pursued and murdered her mother, while she was en route to this very court to pay attendance to the king – probably Alexis's father. During the civil war between the families, before the Clan peace was installed. Her mother's marriage had been the peace settlement that cemented one corner of the arrangement. And since she'd come here, someone had tried to kill her at least twice.

Miriam thought furiously. These people held long grudges. Were the incidents connected? If so, it could be more than Baron Hjorth's financial machinations. Or Matthias's mysterious factions. Or even the dowager grandmother, Duchess Hildegarde Thorold Hjorth.

Someone ignorant of her past. Of course! If they'd known about her before, or on the other side, she'd have been pushed under a subway train or run over by a car or shot in a random drive-by incident long before she'd discovered the way back.

How common is it to conceal an heir? She wondered.

'Mistress, you've got to come.'

'What is it?' Something about Brilliana's insistent nudging attracted Miriam's attention. *It's not me, it's something to do with who I am,* she realized vaguely, groping for the light. *I'm so important to these people that they can't conceive of me not joining in their game. It would be like the vice president refusing to talk to the Senate. Even if I don't do anything, tell them I want to be left alone, that would be seen as some kind of deep political game.* 'What's happening?' She asked distractedly.

'It's Kara,' Brill insisted. 'We've got a problem.'

242

'I'm here,' she said, shaking her head, dazed by her insight. *I've got to be a politician, whether I like it or not . . .* 'What is it now?'

As it happened, Kara was somewhat the worse for wear, not to say steaming drunk. A young Sir Nobody-in-Particular had been plying her with wine, evidently fortified by freezing – her speech was slurred and incoherent and her hair mussed – quite possibly with intent to climb into her clothing with her. He hadn't got far, perhaps because Kara was more enthusiastic than discreet, but it wasn't for want of trying. Though Kara protested her innocence, Miriam detected more than a minor note of concern on Brill's part. 'Look, I think there's a good reason for going home,' Miriam told the two of them. 'Can you get into the carriage?' she questioned Kara.

'Course I can,' Kara slurred. 'N'body does't better!'

'Right.' Miriam glanced at Brilliana. 'Let's get her home.'

'Do you want to stay, mistress?' Brilliana looked at her doubtfully.

'I want – ' Miriam stopped. 'What I want doesn't seem likely to make any difference here,' she said bleakly, feeling the weight of the world descend on her shoulders. *Angbard named me his heir because he wanted me to attract whatever faction tried to kill my mother,* she thought. *Hildegarde takes against me because I can't bring back, or be, her daughter, and now I've got these two ingénues to look out for. Not to mention Roland. Roland, who might be –*

'Got a message,' announced Kara as they were halfway to the door.

'A message? How nice,' Miriam said dryly.

'For th' mistress,' Kara added. Then she focused on Miriam. 'Oh!'

From between her breasts, she produced a thin scrap of paper. Miriam stuffed it in her hand-warmer and took Kara by the arm. 'Come on home, you,' she insisted.

The carriage was freezing. Icicles dangled from the steps as they climbed in, and the leather seats crackled as they sat down. 'Home,' Brilliana told the driver. With a shake of the reins, he set the horses to walking, their breath steaming in the frigid air. 'That was exciting!' she said. 'Shame you spoiled it,' she chided Kara. 'What were you arguing about with those gentles?' she asked Miriam timidly. 'I've never seen anything like it!'

'I was being put in my place by my grandmother, I think,' Miriam muttered. Hands in her warmer, she fumbled for the blister-pack of beta-blocker tablets. She briefly brought a hand out and dry-swallowed one, along with an ibuprofen. She had a feeling she'd be needing them soon. 'What do you know about the history of my family, Brill?' she asked.

'What, about your parents? Or your father? Families or braids?'

Miriam shut her eyes. 'The civil war,' she murmured. 'Who started it?'

'Why – ' Brilliana frowned. 'The civil war? 'Tis clear enough: Wu and Hjorth formed a compact of trade, east coast to west, at the expense of the Clan; Thorold, Lofstrom, Arnesen, and Hjalmar returned the compliment, sending Andru Arnesen west to represent them in Chang-Shi, and he was murdered on his arrival there by a man who vanished into thin air. Clearly it was an attempt to prevent the Clan of four from competing, so they took equivalent measures against the gang of two. What made it worse was that some hidden members of each braid seemed to want to keep the feud burning. Every time it looked as if the elders were going to settle things up, a new outrage would take place – Duchess Lofstrom abused and murdered, Count Thorold-Arnesen's steading raided and set alight.'

'That's – ' Miriam's eyes narrowed. 'You're a Hjalmar, right?'

'Yes?' Brilliana nodded. 'Why? What does it mean?'

'Just thinking,' Miriam said. Left-over grudges, a faction that didn't want the war to stop, to stop eating the Clan's guts out. She hit a brick wall. *It's as if someone from outside had stepped in, intervened to set cousins against each other* . . . She sat up.

'Weren't there originally seven sons of Angmar the Sly?'

'Um, yes?' Brill looked puzzled.

'But one was lost, in the early days?'

Brill nodded. 'That was Markus, or something. The first to head west to make his fortune.'

'Aha.' Miriam nodded.

'Why?'

'Just thinking.' *Hypothesis: There is another family, outside the*

Clan. The Clan don't know about them. They're not numerous, and they're in the same import/export trade. Won't they see the Clan as a threat? But why? Why couldn't they simply marry back into the braids? She shook her head. *I should have tried those experiments with the photograph of the locket.*

The carriage drew up at the door of the Thorold Palace, and Miriam and Brilliana managed to get Kara out without any untoward incidents. Then Kara responded to the cold air by stumbling to the side of the ornate portico, bending over as far as she could, and vomiting in an ornamental planter.

'Ugh,' said Brilliana. She glanced sidelong at Miriam. 'This should not have happened.'

'At least the plants were dead first,' Miriam reassured her. 'Come on. Let's get her inside.'

'No, that's not what I meant.' Brill took a deep breath. 'Euen of Arnesen plied her with fortified wine while she was out of my sight. I should have seen it, but was myself besieged when not following your lead.' She frowned. 'This was deliberate.'

'You expect me to be surprised?' Miriam shook her head. 'Come on. Let's get her up to our rooms and see she doesn't – ' a flashback to Matthias's warning – 'embarrass us further.'

Brill helped steer Kara upstairs, and Miriam ensured that she was sat upright on a chaise longue, awake and complaining with a cup of tea, before retreating to her bedroom. She started to remove her cloak then remembered the hand-warmer, and the message Kara had passed her. She unrolled it and read:

I have urgent news concerning the assassin who has been stalking you. Meet me in the orangery at midnight.

Your obedient servant, Earl Roland Lofstrom

'Shit,' she mumbled under her breath. 'Brill!'

'Yes, Miriam?'

'Help me undress, will you?'

'What, right now? Are you going to bed?'

'Not immediately,' Miriam said grimly. 'Our assassin seems to have gotten tired of trying to sneak up on me and is trying to reel me in like a fish. Only he's made a big mistake.' She turned to present her back. 'Unlace me. I've got places to go, and it'd be a shame to get blood on this gown.'

*

Black jeans, combat boots, turtleneck, and leather jacket: a gun in her pocket and a locket in her left hand. Miriam breathed deeply, feeling naked despite everything. She felt as if the only thing she was wearing was a target between her shoulder blades.

Across the room Brilliana looked worried. 'Are you sure this is the right thing to do?' she asked again. 'Do you want me to come? I am trained using a pistol – '

'I'll be fine. But I may have to world-walk in a hurry.' *I won't be fine*, Miriam corrected herself silently: *But if I don't deal with this trouble sooner or later, they'll kill me. Won't they?* And the one thing an assassin wouldn't be expecting would be for her – not one of the Clan-raised hotheads born with her hands on a pistol, but a reasonable, civilized journalist from a world where that sort of thing just didn't happen – to turn on them. She hoped.

Miriam hitched her day sack into place and checked her right pocket again, the one with the gun and a handful of spare cartridges. She didn't feel fine: There were butterflies in her stomach.

'If there's a problem, I'll stay the night on the other side, safely out of the way. But I need to know. I want you to wait half an hour, then take Kara around to Olga and sit things out with her there. With your gun, and Olga and her own guards in a properly doppelgängered area, you should be safe. But I don't want her tripping and falling downstairs before we learn who gave her that note. D'you understand? Matthias promised to sort me out some guards tomorrow, but I don't trust him. If he's in on this – or just being watched – there'll be an attempt on my life tonight. Except this time I think they got sloppy, expecting me to turn up for it like it's an appointment. So I'm going to avoid it entirely.'

'I understand.' Brill stood up. 'Good luck,' she said.

'Luck has nothing to do with it.' Miriam took two steps toward the door, then pulled out her locket.

Dizziness, mild nausea, a headache that clamped around her

head like a vice. She looked around. Nothing seemed to have changed in the warehouse attic, other than the dim light getting dimmer and the bad smell from somewhere nearby. It was getting worse, and it reminded her of something.

Miriam ducked behind a wall of wooden crates, her head pounding. She pulled the pistol out, slightly nervous at first. It was a double-action revolver, reliable and infinitely reassuring in the gloom. *Stay away from guns,* the training course had emphasized. But that was then, back where she was a journalist and the world made sense to rational people. *But if they're trying to kill you, you have to kill them first,* was another, older lesson from the firearms instructor her father had sent her to. And here and now, it seemed to make more sense.

Carefully, very slowly, she inched forward over the edge of the mezzanine floor and looked down. The ground floor of the warehouse was a maze of wooden cases and boxes. The mobile home that constituted the site office was blocked up in the middle of it. There was no sign of anybody about, none of the comforting noises of habitation.

Miriam rose to a crouch and scurried down the stairs as quietly as she could. She ducked below the stairs, then from shadow to shadow toward the door. There was a final open stretch between the site office and the exit. Instead of crossing it, Miriam tiptoed around the wall of the parked trailer, wrinkling her nose at a faint, foul smell.

The site office door was open and the light inside was on. Holding her gun behind her, she stood up rapidly and climbed the three steps to the door of the trailer. Then she looked inside.

'Damn!'

The stench was far worse in here, and the watchman seemed to be smiling at her.

Smiling? She turned away blindly, sticking her head out of the door, and took deep breaths, desperately trying to get her stomach back under control.

Cultivate your professional detachment, she told herself, echoing a half-forgotten professor's admonition from med school. Reflexes left over from anatomy classes kicked in. She turned back to the thing that had surprised her and began to make observations, rattled to her core but still able to function. She'd seen worse in emergency rooms, after all.

It was the old guy she'd met with the clipboard, and he was past any resuscitation attempt. Someone had used an extremely sharp knife to sever his carotid artery and trachea, and continued to slice halfway through his spine from behind. There was dried blood every-where, huge black puddles of it splashed over walls and floor and the paper-strewn desk, curdling in great thick viscous lumps – the source of only some of the smell, for he'd voided his bowels at the same time. He was still lying on top of his tumbled chair, his skin waxy and – she reached out to touch – cold. At least twelve hours, she thought, gin-gerly trying to lift an arm still locked in rigor mortis, but probably no longer. Would the intense cold retard the processes of decay? Yes, a little bit. That would put it before her last trip over here, but after she saw Paulette.

'Wiseguys,' she whispered under her breath: It came out as an angry curse.

Someone had entered the warehouse, casually murdered the old man, climbed the stairs – breaking the hair – and then, what? Brought the attacker who'd gone up on the roof and tried to attack Olga? Then he came back later, crossed over to the other side, and emptied a pistol into the dummy made of pillows lying in her bed? Gone away? *Correlation does not imply causality*, she reminded herself and gig-gled, shocked at herself and increasingly angry.

'What to do?' Well, the obvious thing was to use her most danger-ous weapon. So she pulled out her phone and speed-dialed Roland.

'Miriam?' He picked up at the fourth ring.

'Roland, there's a problem.' She realized that she was panting, breathing way too fast. 'Let me catch my breath.' She slowed down. 'I'm in the warehouse on the doppelgänger side of my rooms. The night watchman's had his throat cut. He's been dead for between twelve and thirty-six hours. And someone – did you send me a note by way of the reception on the other side, saying to meet you in the orangery at Palace Thorold?'

'No!' He sounded shocked. 'Where are you?' She gave him the

248

address. 'Right, I'll tell someone to get a team of cleaners around immediately. Listen, we're wrestling alligators over here tonight. It looks like the Department of Homeland Security has been running some traffic analysis on frequent fliers looking for terrorists and uncovered one of our – '

'I get the message,' she interrupted. 'Look, my headache is that I planted a hair across the top step when I came through last night, and it was broken when I went back over this morning. I'm fairly sure someone from the Clan came here, killed the watchman, headed up to the mezzanine that's on the other side of my suite – breaking the hair – and crossed over. There was another attempt to kill me in my suite last night, Roland. They want me dead, and there's something going down in the palace.'

'Wait there. I'll be around in person as soon as I can get unstuck from this mess.'

Miriam stared at the phone that had gone dead in her hand, paranoid fantasies playing through her head.

'Angbard set me up,' she muttered to herself. 'What if Roland's in on it?' It was bizarre. The only way to be sure would be to go to the rendezvous, surprise the assassin. Who had come over from this side. But if they could get into her apartment, why bother with the silly lure?

'What if there are two groups sending assassins?' she asked the night watchman. He grinned at her twice over. 'The obvious one who is clearly a Clan member, and, and the subtle one – '

She racked her brains for the precise number of paces from the stairs up to her room to the back door opening into the grounds of the palace. Then she remembered the crates laid out below. *The entrance will be next door,* she realized. She jumped out of the trailer with its reek of icy death and dashed across to the far wall of the warehouse – the one corresponding to the main entrance vestibule of the palace. It was solid brick, with no doors. 'Damn!' She slipped around to the front door and out into the alley, then paced out the fifty feet it would take. Then she carefully examined the next frontage.

It was a bonded warehouse. Iron bars fronted all the dust-smeared windows, and metal shutters hid everything within from view. The front door was padlocked heavily and looked as if nobody had opened it in years. 'This has got to be it,' she muttered, looking up at the forbidding facade. What better way to block off the entrance to a palace on the other side? Probably most of the rooms behind the windows were bricked off or even filled with concrete, corresponding to the positions of the secure spaces on the other side. But there had to be some kind of access to the public reception area, didn't there?

Miriam moved her locket to her left hand and pulled out her pistol. 'Does this work in real life as well as in the movies?' she asked herself as she probed around the chain. 'Hmm.' It was the work of a minute to return to the watchman's trailer and another minute – carefully ignoring the silent occupant – to locate a pry bar. The lock put up a fight, but eventually Miriam managed to put all her weight on the bar, breaking it. She yanked it away, opened the bolt, and pushed the door in.

An alarm began to jangle somewhere inside the building. She jumped, but there wasn't anything to be done about it. She found herself at one end of a dusty linoleum-floored corridor. A flick of a switch and the dim lights came on, illuminating a path into the gloom. It led past metal gates like jail cell doors, blocking access to rooms piled ceiling-high with large barrels. Miriam closed the door behind her and strode down the corridor as fast as she dared, hoping desperately that she was right about where it led. There was a reception room at the end, the cheap desks and chairs covered in dust sheets. At the far side there was a locked and bolted back door. It was about the right distance, she decided. Taking a deep breath, she raised her locket and focused on the symbol engraved inside it –

– And she was cold, and the lights were out, and her skull felt as if she'd run headfirst into a brick wall. Snowflakes fell on her as she doubled over, trying to prevent the intense nausea from turning into vomiting. *I did that too fast*, she thought vaguely between waves of pain. Even with the beta-blockers. The process of world-walking seemed to do horrible things to her blood pressure. *Good thing I'm not hypertensive*, she thought grimly. She forced herself to stand up and saw that she was just in the garden behind the palace – outdoors.

Anyone trying to invade the palace by way of the doppelgänger warehouse on the other side would find themselves under the guns of the tower above – if the defenses were manned. But it was snowing tonight, and someone obviously wanted as few witnesses around as possible . . .

An iron gate in the wall behind her was the mirror image of the door to the warehouse office. 'Orangery,' she muttered through gritted teeth. She slid along the wall like a shadow, letting her eyes grow accustomed to the darkness. The orangery was a familiar hump in the snow, but something about it was wrong: the door was ajar, letting the precious heat (and how many servants did it take to keep that boiler fed?) escape into the winter air.

'Well, isn't that just too cute,' she whispered, tightening her grip on her pistol. *Welcome to my parlor, said the spider to the fly,* she thought. *The style is all wrong. Assassin #1 breaks into my room and shoots up the bedding. Twice. Assassin #2 tries to bounce Olga into shooting me for him, then sends an RSVP on an engraved card. Assassin #3 shows me an open door. Which of these things is not like the other?* She shivered – and not from the cold: The hot rage she'd been holding back ever since she'd first been abducted was taking hold.

The wall at this end of the orangery was of brick, and the glassy arch of the ceiling was low, beginning only about ten feet up. Miriam gritted her teeth and fumbled for finger- and toeholds. Then she realized there was a cast-iron drain pipe, half-buried under the snow where the wall of the orangery met the corner of the inner garden wall. She put the pistol in her pocket and began to climb, this time with more confidence. On top of the wall she could look out across a corrugated sheet of whiteness – the snow was settling on the orangery faster than the heat from below could melt it.

Leaning forward, she used her sleeve to rub a clear swath in the glass.

Paraffin lamps shed a thin glow through the orangery, helping with the warmth and providing enough light to see by. To Miriam's night-adapted vision it was like a glimpse into a dim subterranean hell. She hunted around and saw, just behind the door, a hunched shadow. After a minute of watching – during which time her hands began to grow numb – she saw the shadow move, shifting in position just like a man shuffling his feet in the cold draft from outside.

'Right,' she whispered tensely, feeling an intense flash of hatred for the figure on the other side, just as the door opened further and someone else came in.

What happened then happened almost too fast to see – Miriam froze atop the window, unable to breathe in the cold air, her head throbbing until she wondered if she was coming down with a full-blown migraine. The shadow flowed forward behind the person who'd entered the orangery. There was a flurry of activity, then a body collapsed on the floor in a spreading pool of . . . of – *Holy shit,* thought Miriam, *he's killed him!*

Shocked out of her angry reverie, she slid back down the drain-pipe, scraping hands and cheek on the rough stonework, and landed in a snowdrift hard enough that it nearly knocked the breath out of her. Fumbling for her pistol, she skidded toward the door and yanked it open. She brought the gun up in time to see a man turning toward her. He was dressed all in black, his face covered by a ski mask or something similar: The long knife in his hand was red with blood as he straightened up from the body at his feet. 'Stop – ' Miriam called. He didn't stop, and time telescoped in on her. Two shots in the torso, two more – then the dry click of a hammer on a spent cartridge. The killer collapsed toward her and Miriam took a step back, wishing she hadn't heard the sound of bullets striking flesh.

Time caught up with her again. 'Hey!' She called out, heart lurching between her ribs like a frightened animal. A sense of gath-ering wrongness overcame her, as if what had just happened was impossible. Another old reflex caught up, and she stepped forward. 'Gurney – ' she bit her tongue. There were no gurneys here, no hemo-stats, no competent nurses to get the bleeding staunched and no defibrillators – and especially no packets of plasma and operating theaters in which to struggle for the victim's life.

She found herself an indefinite time later – probably only seconds had passed, although it felt like hours – staring down at a spreading pool of blood around her feet. Blood, and the body of a man, dressed from head to foot in black. A long curve-bladed knife lay beside him. Behind him – 'Margit!' It was Lady Margit, Olga's chaperone. The fat lady had sung her last: There was nothing to be done. She still twitched, and maybe a modern ER room could have done something for her – but not here, not with a massive exsanguinating chest wound that had already stopped pumping. *Probably severed the dorsal aorta or a ventricle*, she realized. *Oh hell. What was she doing here?* For a moment, Miriam wished she believed in something – someone – who'd look after Margit. But there wasn't time for that now.

She turned back to the assassin. He was alive – but no, that was just residual twitching, too. She'd actually nailed him through the heart with her first two shots, the second double-tap turning his chest into a bloody mess. There was already a stench of excrement in the air as his bowels relaxed. She pulled back his hood. The assassin was shaven-headed and flat-faced: *He looks Chinese*, she realized with a mixture of astonishment and regret. She'd just killed a man, but – there was a chain around his neck.

'What the hell?' she asked through the haze of her headache and anxiety, then she pulled out a round sealed locket, utterly unadorned and plain. 'Clan.' She put it in her pocket and glanced at Margit's cooling body. 'What on earth possessed you to come down here at midnight?' she asked aloud. 'Was it a message for – ' she trailed off.

They're after Olga, too, she realized, and with that realization came a sick fear. *I have to warn Olga!*

Miriam left the orangery and headed toward the palace, half-empty this evening as its noble residents enjoyed the king's hospitality. She wouldn't be able to world-walk from her own rooms any more, but if Brilliana was in, they'd have a little chat. *She knows more than she's saying*, Miriam realized.

The implication was just beginning to sink in. 'Wheels within wheels,' she muttered. Her hands were shaking violently and the small of her back was icy cold with sweat from the adrenaline surge when she'd shot the assassin. She paused, leaning against the cold outside wall of the orangery while she tried to gather her composure. 'He was here to kill me.' The chill from the wall was beginning to penetrate her jacket. She dug around in her pocket for spare cartridges, fumbling as she reloaded the revolver. *Got to find Olga. And Brill.*

And then she'd have to go undercover.

One way of looking at it was that there was a story to dig up, a story about her long-dead mother, blood feuds, and civil war, a tale of assassins who came in the night and drug-dealing aristocrats who would brook no rival. Just like any other undercover investigative exposé – not that Miriam was used to undercover jobs, but she'd be damned if she'd surrender to the editorial whims of family politics before she broke that story all over them – at the Clan gathering on Beltaigne night.

'Get moving, girl,' she told herself as she pushed off the wall and headed back toward the palace. 'There's no time to lose . . .'

PART FIVE

RUNAWAY

ENCOUNTER

The snow was falling thickly when Miriam reached the wall of the orangery, and she was shivering despite her leather jacket. It was dark, too, in a way that no modern city ever was – there were no streetlights to reflect off the clouds, she realized, as she fumbled with her pocket flashlight. The gate was shut, and she had to tug hard to open it. Beyond the gate, the vast width of the palace loomed out of the snow, row upon row of shuttered windows at ground level.

'Damn,' Miriam muttered in the wind. There were no guards. Wasn't this the east wing, under the Thorold tower, where Olga was living? She glanced up at the towering mass of stonework. The entrances were all round the front, but she'd attract unwelcome attention going in the main door. Instead she trudged over to the nearest window casement. 'Hey – '

It wasn't a shuttered window: It was a doorway, designed to blend in with the building's rear aspect. There was a handle and a discreet bell-pull beside it.

Cursing the architectural pretensions of whoever had designed this pile, Miriam tugged the rope. Something clanged distantly, behind the door. She stepped sideways and steeled herself, raising her pistol with a sick sense of anticipation in her stomach.

Rattling and creaking. A slot in the door, near eye level, squeaked as it moved aside. 'Wehr ish – ' quavered a hoarse voice.

'Unlock the door and step back now,' Miriam said, aiming through the slot.

'Sisch!'

'*Now.*' A click. Two terrified eyes stared at her for a moment, then dropped from view. Miriam kicked the door hard, feeling the impact jar through her foot.

For a miracle, the elderly caretaker had dropped the latch rather than shooting the bolt before he ran: Instead of falling flat on her ass with a sore ankle, Miriam found herself standing in a dark hallway facing a door opposite. *Did he understand me?* She wondered. No time for that now. She darted forward, pulling the door closed behind her as she headed for the other end of the short hall.

There she paused. There was a narrow staircase beside her, heading up into the recesses of the servants' side of the wing, but the old guy who'd let her in – gardener or caretaker? – had vanished through the door into the reception room off to one side. Which made her decision for her. Miriam took the stairs two at a time, rushed past the shut doors on the first landing as lightly as she could and only paused on the second landing.

'Where is everybody?' she whispered aloud. There should be guards, bells ringing, whatever – she'd just barged in and instead of security all she'd encountered was a frightened groundskeeper. The butterflies in her stomach hadn't gone away: if anything they were stronger. Either her imagination was working overtime or something was very wrong.

There were doors up here, doors onto cramped rooms used by the servants, but also a side door onto the main staircase that crawled around the walls of the tower's core, linking the suites of the noble residents. It was chilly, and the solitary oil lamp mounted in a wall bracket hardly lightened the shadows, but it was enough to show Miriam which way to go. She pushed the side door open and stepped out onto the staircase to get her bearings. It was no brighter in the main hall: the great chandelier was unlit and the lamps on each landing had been turned right down. Still, she was just one flight of stairs below the door to Olga's chambers. She was halfway to the landing before she noticed something wrong with the shadows outside the entrance. The door was open. Which meant, if Brill had gotten through in time –

Miriam crept forward. The door was ajar, and something bulky lay motionless in the shadows behind it. The reception room it opened onto was completely dark, but instinct told her it wasn't empty. She paused beside the entrance, her heart hammering as she waited for her eyes to adjust. *If it's another hit, that would explain the lack of guards,* she thought. Memories of a stupid corporate junket – a 'team building' paintball tournament in a deserted office building that someone in HR thought sounded like fun – welled up, threatening her with a sense of déjà vu. Very slowly, she looked round the edge of the door frame.

Something or someone clad in light-absorbing clothes was kneeling in front of the door at the far end of the room. Another figure stood to one side, the unmistakable outline of some kind of submachine gun raised to cover the door.

They had their backs to her. *Sloppy, very sloppy,* she thought. Unless they knew there was nobody else in this wing because they'd all been sent away.

The inner door creaked and the kneeling figure stood up and flowed to one side.

Now there was another gun. *This is so not good,* Miriam realized queasily. She was going to have to do something. Visions of the assassin in the orangery raising his knife and moving toward her – the two before her were completely focused on the door, preparing to make their move.

Then one of them looked round.

Afterward, Miriam wasn't completely sure what had happened. Certainly she remembered squeezing the trigger repeatedly. The evil sewing-machine chatter of automatic fire wasn't hers, as it stitched a neat line of holes across the ceiling. She'd flinched, dazzled and deafened by the sudden noise, and there'd been more hammering and she'd fallen over, rolling aside as fast as she could, then what sounded like a different gun. And silence, once she discounted the ringing in her ears.

'Miriam?' called Olga. 'Is that you?'

I'm still alive, she realized. Taking stock: If she was still alive, that meant the intruders weren't. 'Yes,' she called faintly. 'I'm out here. Where are you?'

'Get in here. *Quickly.*'

She took no second warning. Brill crouched beside the splintered wreckage of the door, a brilliant electric lamp held in one hand, while Olga stood to the other side. Her face cast sharp shadows that flickered across the walls as she scanned the room, gun raised. 'I am going to have harsh words with the baron,' she said calmly as Miriam scurried toward them. 'The guards he assigned me appear to have taken their leave for the evening. Perhaps if I flog a few until the ivory shows, it will convince him of my displeasure.'

'They're not to blame,' Miriam said hoarsely, feeling her stomach rise. The smell of burned cordite and blood hung in the air. 'Brill?'

'I brought Kara hither, my lady. I did as you told me.'

'She did.' Olga nodded. 'To be truthful, we did not need your help with such as these.' She jerked a thumb at the darkened corner of the room. 'There's an alarm that Oliver does not know of, the duke insisted I bring it.' The red eye of an infrared motion sensor winked at Miriam. 'But I am grateful for the warning,' she added graciously.

'I – ' Miriam shuddered. 'In the orangery. An assassin.'

'What?' Olga looked at her sharply. 'Who – '

'They killed Margit. Sent a note to lure me there, but I was expecting trouble.'

'That's terrible!' Brill looked appalled: The light swayed. 'What are we going to – '

'Inside,' Olga commanded. Brill retreated, and after a moment Miriam followed her. 'Close the door!' Olga called, and after a moment a timid serving maid scurried forward and began to yank on it. 'When it's shut, bar it Then get that chest braced across it,' Olga added, pointing to a wardrobe that looked to Miriam's eyes to be built from most of an oak tree. She stopped and turned to Miriam. 'This was aimed at you, not me,' she said calmly, lowering her machine pistol to point at the floor. 'They're getting overconfident. Margit – ' she shook her head – 'Brilliana told me of the note, you are lucky to have escaped.'

'What am I going to do?' Miriam asked. She felt dizzy and sick, the room spinning around her head. There was a stool near the fireplace: She stumbled toward it tiredly and sat down. 'Who sent them?'

'I don't know,' Olga said thoughtfully.

A door in the opposite wall opened and Kara rushed in. 'My lady! You're hurt?'

'Not yet,' Miriam said, waving her away tiredly. 'The killer in the orangery was of the Clan, he had a locket,' she said.

'That could tell us which braid he came from,' Olga said. 'Have you got it?'

'I think – yes.' Miriam pulled it out and opened it. 'Oh.'

'What is it?' asked Olga, leaning close. 'Oh my.'

Miriam stared at the locket. Inside it was a design like the knot-work pattern she was learning to loathe – but this one was subtly wrong. Different. A couplet with a different rhyme. One that she knew, instinctively, at a gut level, would take her somewhere else if she stared at it too long and hard. Not to mention making her blood pressure spike so high it would give her an aneurysm if she tried it in the next few hours.

She snapped it shut again and looked up at Olga. 'Do you know what this means?' she asked.

Olga nodded very seriously. 'It means you and Brilliana will have to disappear,' she said. 'These two – ' a sniff and a nod at the barricaded doorway – 'are of no account, but this – ' a glance at the locket – 'might be the gravest threat to the Clan in living memory.' She frowned uncertainly. 'I had not imagined that such a thing might exist. But if it does – '

' – They must stop at nothing to kill anyone who knows they exist,' said Brill, completing the thought for her. She looked at Miriam with bright eyes. 'Will you take me with you wherever you go, mistress? You'll need someone to guard your back . . .'

*

Two hours later.

Painkillers and beta-blockers are wonderful things, Miriam reflected as she glanced over her shoulder at Brill. She'd managed to relax slightly as Olga organized a cleanup, marshaling a barricade inside the doorway and chivvying Kara and the servants into making themselves useful. Then Olga had pointed out in words of one syllable what this meant: that two factions, at least one of them hitherto unknown, were after her, and it would be a good idea to make herself scarce. Finally, still feeling fragile but now accommodating herself to the idea, Miriam had crossed over. With her passenger. Who wore a smart business suit and an expression of mild bemusement. 'Where are we?' asked Brill.

'The doppelgänger warehouse.' Miriam frowned as she transferred her locket to her left hip pocket 'Other side from my own chambers. Someone should have cleaned up by now.'

Fidgeting in her pocket, she pulled out some cartridges. She shuffled quietly closer to the edge of the mezzanine and looked over the side as she reloaded her pistol.

'This wasn't what I expected,' the younger woman said in hushed tones, staring up at the dim warehouse lights.

'Stay quiet until I've checked it out.' She let a sharp note creep into her voice. 'We may not be alone here.'

'Oh.'

Miriam crept to the edge of the platform and looked down. There was no sign of movement below, and the front door of the warehouse – past the dismounted trailer that served as a site office – was shut. 'Wait here. I'll call you down when it's safe,' she said.

'Yes, Miriam.'

She took a deep breath, then darted down the stairs lightly, her gun raised.

Nobody shot at her from concealment. She reached the bottom step and paused for a couple of seconds before stepping off the metal staircase onto dusty wooden floorboards, then duck-walked over to the side of the site office, out of sight from its windows and the door. Creeping again, she sidled around the wall of the trailer and crouched next to the short flight of steps leading into it. She spent about a minute staring at the threshold, then stood up slowly, lowered her gun, and carefully returned it to her jacket pocket. She rubbed her forehead, then turned. 'You can come down now, as long as you come right over here. Don't touch anything with your hands.'

Brilliana stood up and dusted herself off, lips wrinkling in distaste as she tried to shake the warehouse cobwebs from the sleeve of her jacket. Then she walked down the stairs slowly, not touching the guard rail. Her back was straight, as if she was making a grand entrance rather than a low-life departure.

Miriam pointed at the steps to the trailer. 'Don't, whatever you do, even think about going in there,' she warned. Her expression was drawn. Brill sniffed, conspicuously, then pulled a face in disgust.

'What happened there?'

'Someone was killed,' Miriam said quietly. Then she bent down and pointed to something in the threshold. 'Look. See that wire? It's hair-thin. Don't touch it!'

'What wire – oh.'

A fine wire was stretched across the threshold, twelve inches above the floor.

'That wasn't here when I came this way three hours ago,' said Miriam. 'And nobody's been to clear up what's inside. Going from what Roland was telling me, that means that first, this is a trap, and second, it's not the kind where someone's going to jump out and start shooting at us, and third, if you touch that wire, we probably both die. Wait here and don't move or touch anything. I'm going to see if they're belt-and-braces people.'

Miriam shuffled gingerly over toward the big wooden doors of the warehouse – there was a smaller access door set in the side of one of them – with her eyes focused on the ground in front of her, every step of the way. Brill stayed where she was obediently, but when Miriam glanced at her, she was staring up at the lights, an odd expression on her face. 'I'm over here,' she said. 'I'm really on the other side!'

Miriam reached the inner door, bent low, looked up, and made a hissing noise through her teeth. 'Damn!'

'What is it?' called Brill, shaking herself.

'Another one,' Miriam replied. Her face was ghost-white. 'You can come over here and look. This is the way out.'

'Oh.' Brill walked over to the door, stopping short at Miriam's warning hand gesture. She followed Miriam's pointing finger, up at something in the shadows above the door. 'What's that?' she asked.

'At a guess, it's a bomb,' said Miriam. 'Probably a . . . what do you call them? A Claymore mine.' The green package was securely fastened to two nails driven into the huge main warehouse door directly above the access door cut in it. Miriam's compact flashlight cut through the twilight, tracing a fine wire as it looped around three or four nails. It came back to anchor to the access door at foot level, in such a way that any attempt to open the door would tug on it. Miriam whistled tunelessly. 'Careless, very careless.'

Brill stared at the booby trap in horror. 'Are you just going to leave it?' she asked.

Miriam glanced at her. 'What do you expect me to do?' she asked. 'I'm not a bomb disposal expert, I'm a journalist! I just learned a bit about this stuff doing a feature on Northern Ireland a couple of years ago.' For a moment, she felt a wave of helplessness and anger: she forced it back down. 'We've got to get out of here,' she said. 'I know somewhere safe, but "safe" is relative. We need to hole up where nobody is going to ask questions you can't answer, assassins can't find us, and I can do some thinking.' She glanced at the Claymore mine. 'Once I figure out a way to open this door without killing us both.'

'That was another, in the office?' asked Brill.

'Yes. I figure the idea was to kill anyone who comes sniffing. But the only people who know what's in there are me and whoever . . . whoever murdered the night watchman.'

'What about Roland?'

'Oh, yes. I told Roland. And he could have told – Damn, this means I can't trust anyone who works for Angbard, can I?'

She glanced obliquely at Brill.

'I don't work for Angbard,' Brill said slowly. 'Not that way. I work for you.'

'Well, that's nice to know.' Miriam gave her a lopsided grin. 'I hope it doesn't get you into trouble. Worse trouble,' she corrected.

'What are we going to do?' asked Brill, frowning as only a twenty-something confronted by fate can frown.

'Hmm. Well, I'm going to open this door.' Miriam gestured. 'Somehow or other. Then . . . there's a lot you don't know, isn't there? The door opens on an alley in a place called New York. It's a big city and it's after dark. I'm going to call a car service, and you're going to do what I do – get in after me, ride with me to where we're going, wait while I pay the driver, and go inside. I'll do all the talking. You should concentrate on taking in whatever you can without looking like a yokel. Once we're in private, you can talk all you want. All right? Think you can do that?'

Brill nodded seriously. 'It'll be for me like when you first arrived? On the other side?' she asked.

'Good analogy.' Miriam nodded. 'No, it'll be worse, much worse.' She grinned again. 'I had an introduction; the whole world didn't all get thrown at me all at once. Just try not to get yourself killed crossing the road, okay?' Then she glanced around. 'Look, over there below the mezzanine, see those crates? I want you to go and sit down on the other side of them. Shield your head with your arms, yes, like they're about to fall on you. And keep your mouth open. I'm going to try and get this door open without blowing us to pieces. I figure it should be possible because they were expecting people to come in from outside, not to materialize right inside the warehouse.'

'We're already supposed to be dead, aren't we?'

Miriam nodded. 'Go,' she said.

Brill headed off toward the stack of tea chests. Miriam bent down and followed the near-invisible wire off to one side. *I really don't like the look of this*, she thought, her heart hammering at her ribs. She glanced up at the green casing, ominous as a hornet's nest suspended overhead. 'Let's see,' she mumbled. 'The door opens inward, pulls on the wire . . . or the warehouse door opens inward, also pulls on the wire. But if it's spring-loaded, releasing it could also set the thing off. Hmm.'

She examined the wire as it ran around a rusting nail pounded into the wall beside the door. 'Right.' She stood up and walked back across to the trailer with its own booby trap and its cargo of death. Climbing the steps, she paused for a moment, took a deep breath, and stepped over the wire.

Nothing happened. *I'm still here*, she told herself. She took another deep breath, this time to avoid having to breathe in too close to the thing sprawled across the fallen office chair at the far side of the office. She'd called Roland, told him to send cleaners – instead, these booby traps had materialized.

When the Clan wants you dead, you die, she realized bleakly. *If indeed it is the Clan . . .*

There, on a rusting tool chest propped against the other wall, was exactly what she was looking for. She picked up the heavy-duty staple gun and checked that it was loaded. 'Yup.' She hefted it one-handed, then mustered up a smile and picked up a pair of rusty pliers and stepped back out of the trailer.

Two minutes later, she had the door open. The wire, firmly stapled to the door frame, was severed: The mine was still armed, but the trigger wire led nowhere.

'Come on,' she called to Brilliana. 'It's safe now! We can leave!' Brill hurried over. As she did so, Miriam glanced up once more. *What if they'd heard of infrared motion detectors?* It wouldn't do to assume the next booby trap would work the same way.

*

It was snowing lightly, and Miriam flagged down a taxi when they reached the street. Brill kept quiet, but her eyes grew wide as she took in the cars that rumbled past in the gloom. She glanced from side to side like a caged cat in a strange, threatening environment. 'I didn't know it would be like this!' she whispered to Miriam. Then she shivered. 'It's really cold.'

'It's winter, kid. Get used to it.' Miriam grinned, slightly manic from her success with the bomb.

'It's colder on the other side, isn't it?'

A cab pulled alongside, its light illuminated. Miriam walked over. She held open the rear door: 'Get in and slide across,' she told Brill. Then she gave directions and got inside, shutting the door.

The cab moved off. Brill looked around in fascination, then reached down toward her ankles. 'It's heated,' she said quietly.

'Of course it's heated,' said the driver in a Pakistani accent. 'You think I let my passengers freeze to death before they pay me?'

'Excuse my friend,' Miriam told him, casting a warning glance at Brill. 'She's from Russia. Just arrived.'

'Oh,' said the driver, as if that explained everything. 'Yes, very good, that.'

Brill kept her eyes wide but her mouth closed the rest of the way to the Marriott Marquis, but watched carefully as Miriam paid off the cabbie using pieces of green paper she pulled from a billfold. 'Come on, follow me,' said Miriam. Miriam felt Brill tense as the glass doors opened automatically ahead of them, but she kept up with her as she headed for the express elevator. 'One moment,' Miriam muttered to her, pushing the button. 'This is an elevator. It's a room, suspended on wires, in a vertical shaft. We use it instead of the stairs.'

'Why?' Brill looked puzzled.

'Have you ever tried to climb forty flights of steps?' Miriam shut up as another elevator arrived, disgorging a couple of septuagenarians. Then the express doors opened, and she waved Brill inside. 'This is easier,' she said, hitting the second from top button. The younger woman lurched against the wall as the elevator began to rise. 'We'll be there in no time.'

The glass-walled elevator car began to track up the outer wall of the tower.

'That's – oh my!' Brill leaned back against the far wall from the window. 'I'd rather walk, I think,' she said shakily.

A thought struck Miriam at the top. 'We'd better be careful going in,' she commented before the doors opened. 'I want you to wait behind me.'

'Why?' Brill followed her out of the lift into an empty landing. She looked slightly green, and Miriam realized she hadn't said anything on the way up.

'Because we're safely doppelgängered here. But Roland knows which room I'm using.' *He won't have told anybody*, she reasoned. *Even if he has, they can't have booby-trapped it from the inside, like the warehouse. Not on the twenty-second floor. I hope.*

'All right.' Brill swallowed. 'Which way?' she asked, looking bewildered.

'Follow me.' Miriam pushed through the fire doors, strolled along a hotel corridor, trying to imagine what it might look like to someone who'd never seen a hotel – or an elevator – before. 'Wait here.'

She swiped her card-key through the lock, then stood aside, right hand thrust in her jacket pocket as she pushed the door open to reveal an empty suite, freshly prepared beds, an open bathroom door. 'Quick.' She waved Brill inside then followed her, shut and locked the door, and sagged against it in relief.

'Oh shit, oh shit . . .' Her hands felt cold and shook until she clasped them together. *Delayed shock*, the analytical observer in her brain commented. *Tonight you killed an assassin in self-defense, defused a bomb, discovered a murder and a conspiracy, and rescued Brill and Olga. Isn't it about time you collapsed in a gibbering heap?*

267

'Where is – ' Brilliana was looking around, eyes narrowed. 'It's so small! But it's hot. The fireplace – '

'You don't have fireplaces in tall buildings,' Miriam said automatically. 'We're twenty-two floors up. We've got air-conditioning – that box, under the curtains, it warms the air, keeps it at a comfortable temperature all year around.' She rubbed her forehead: The pounding headache was threatening to make a comeback. 'Have a seat.'

Brill picked a chair in front of the television set. 'What now?' she asked, yawning.

Miriam glanced at the bedside clock: It was about one o'clock in the morning. 'It's late,' she said. 'Tonight we sleep. In the morning I'm going to take you on a journey to another city, to meet someone I trust. A friend. Then – ' she instinctively fingered the pocket with the two lockets in it, her own and the one she'd taken from the assassin – 'we'll work out what to do next.'

*

They spent a nervous night in the anonymous hotel room, high above any threat from world-walking pursuers. In the morning Miriam pointed Brill at the shower – she had to explain the controls – while she called room service, then went to check the wardrobe.

A big anonymous-looking suitcase nearly filled the luggage niche, right where she'd left it. While breakfast was on its way up, Miriam opened it and pulled out some fresh clothing. *Have to take time to buy some more*, she thought, looking at what was left. Most of the suitcase was occupied by items that wouldn't exactly render her inconspicuous on this side. *Later*, she resolved. Her wallet itched, reproaching her. Inside it was the platinum card Duke Angbard had sent her. Two million dollars of other people's blood money. Either it was her 'Get Out of Jail Free' card, or a death trap, depending on whether whoever had sent the first bunch of assassins – her enemy within the Clan, rather than without – was able to follow its audit trail. Probably they wouldn't be able to, at least not fast enough to catch up with her if she kept moving. If they were, Miriam wasn't the only family member who was at risk. *It's probably safe as long as it keeps working and I keep moving*, she reasoned. *If somebody puts a stop on it, I'm in trouble.* And better not go buying any air tickets. Not that she was planning on doing that – the idea of introducing airline passenger etiquette to Brill left her shaking her head.

There was a discreet knock at the door. Miriam picked up her pistol and, hiding it in her pocket, approached. The peephole showed her a bored bellhop pushing a trolley. She opened the door. 'Thanks,' she said, passing him a tip. 'We'll keep the trolley.'

Back inside the suite, Brill emerged from the bathroom looking pink and freshly scrubbed – and somewhat confused. 'Where does all the water come from?' she asked, almost complaining. 'It never stopped!'

'Welcome to New York, baby,' Miriam drawled, lifting the cover off a plate laden with a full-cooked breakfast. 'Land of plenty, home of – sorry,' she finished lamely and waved Brill toward a chair. 'Come on, there's enough food for both of us.' *Damn*, she thought. *I don't want to go rubbing her nose in it. Not like that.*

'Thank you,' Brill said, primly picking up a knife and fork and going to work.

'Hmm. It tastes slightly . . . odd.'

'Yeah.' Miriam chewed thoughtfully, then poured a couple of cups of coffee from the thermal jug. 'The eggs aren't as good. Are they?'

'It's all a little different.' Brill frowned, inspecting her plate minutely. 'They're all the same, aren't they? Like identical twins?'

'It's how we make things here.' Miriam shrugged. 'You'll see lots of things that are identical. But not people.' She began working on her toast before she noticed Brill surreptitiously following her example with the small wrapped parcels of butter. 'First, I'm going to call my friend. If she's all right, we're going to go on a journey to another city and I'm going to leave you with her for a few days. The way we tell it to anyone who asks is: You're a relative from out of state who's coming to stay. Your parents are weird backwoods types, which is why there's a lot of stuff you haven't seen. My friend will know the truth. Also, she's got a contact number for Roland. If I – ' she cleared her throat – 'she'll get you back in touch, so you can go home. To the other side, I mean, when you need to.'

'When I need to?' Brill echoed doubtfully. She glanced around the room. 'What's that?'

'That?' Miriam looked. 'It's a television set.'

'Oh. Like Ser Villem's after-dinner entertainments. I remember that! The cat and the mouse, and the talking rabbit, Bugs.' Brill smiled. 'They are everywhere, here?'

'That's one way of putting it.' *Kid, I prescribe a week as a dedicated couch potato before we let you go outdoors on your own*, she resolved. 'I've got a call to make,' she said, reaching for her mobile.

The first thing Miriam did was switch her phone off, open the back, and replace the SIM chip with one she took from her billfold. Then she reassembled it. The phone beeped as it came up with a new identity, but there was no voice mail waiting for her. Steeling herself for disappointment, she dialed a number – one belonging to another cell phone she'd sent via FedEx a couple of days before.

'Hello?' The voice at the end of the line sounded positively chirpy.

'Paulie! Are you okay?'

'Miriam! How's it going, babe?'

'It's going messy,' she admitted. 'Look, remember the other day? Are you still home?'

'Yes. What's come up?'

'I'm going to come pay you a visit,' said Miriam. 'First, I've got a lot of things to discuss, stuff to get in order – and a down payment. Second, I've got a lodger. How's your spare room?'

'You know it's been empty since I kicked that bum Walter out! What's up, you wanting him to stay with me?'

Miriam glanced at Brill. 'It's a she, and I think you'll probably like her,' she said guardedly. 'It's part of that deal I've made. I need you to put her up for a few weeks, on the company – I mean, I'm paying. Trouble is, she's from, uh, out of state, if you follow me. She doesn't know her way around *at all*.'

'Does she, like, speak English?' Paulette sounded interested rather than perturbed, for which Miriam was immensely grateful. Brilliana was toying with her coffee and pretending not to realize Miriam was discussing her, on an intimate basis, with a talking box.

'Yeah, that's not a problem. But this morning was the first time she'd ever met an electric shower, and that is a problem for me, because I've got a lot of traveling to do in the next few weeks and I need to put her where someone can keep an eye on her as she gets used to the way things are done over here. Can you do that?'

'Probably,' Paulette said briskly. 'Depends if she hates my guts on first sight – or vice versa. I can't promise more than that, can I?'

'Well – ' Miriam took a deep breath. 'Okay, we're coming up today on the train. You going to be home in the afternoon?'

'For you, any day! You've got a lot to tell me about?'

'Everything,' Miriam said fervently. 'It's been crazy.'

'Bye, then.'

Miriam put the phone down and rubbed her eyes. Brill was watching her oddly.

'Who was that?' she asked.

'Who – oh, on the phone?' Miriam glanced at it. So Brill had figured out that much? *Bright girl.* 'A friend of mine. My, uh, business agent. On this side. For the past few days, anyway. We're going to see her this afternoon.'

'Her?' Brill raised an eyebrow. 'All the hot water you want, no need to feed the fire, and women running businesses? No wonder my mother didn't want me coming here – she was afraid I'd never come back!'

'That seems to go with the territory,' Miriam agreed.

After breakfast she chivvied Brill into getting dressed again. In the Gruinmarkt her imported outfit, a tailored suit and blouse, had marked her out as a lady of the Clan, erecting an invisible barrier around her. Exotic dress was a common way in which minorities segregated themselves from a wider population. But here she looked like just another business traveller: she'd blend into the background just fine unless she opened her mouth. Miriam thought for a moment, then picked another jacket – this time a dressy one rather than one built for bad weather. She'd have to keep her pistol in her handbag, but she'd look less out of place traveling with Brill, and hopefully it would distract any killers hunting for a lone woman in her early thirties with thus-and-such features.

Miriam took the large suitcase when they left the room and

headed downstairs. Brill's eyes kept swiveling at everything from telephones to cigarette ads, but she kept her questions to herself as Miriam shepherded her into a nearby bank for ten minutes, then flagged down a taxi. 'What was that about?' Brill murmured after Miriam told the driver where to go.

'Needed to take care of some money business,' Miriam replied. 'Angbard gave me a line on some credit, but – ' she stopped, struggling. *I'm talking Martian again,* she realized.

'You'll have to tell me how this credit thing works some time,' Brill commented. 'I don't think I've actually seen a coin or tally since I came here. Do people use them?'

'Not much. Which makes some things easier – it's harder to steal larger amounts – and other things more difficult – like transferring large quantities of money to someone else without it being noticed.'

'Huh.' Brill stared out of the window at the passing traffic, the pedestrians in their dark winter colors, and the bright advertisements. 'It's so noisy! How do you get any thinking done?'

'Sometimes it's hard,' Miriam admitted.

She bought two tickets to Boston and shepherded Brill onto the express train without incident. They found a table a long way from anyone else, which turned out to be a good thing, because Brill was unable to control her surprise when the train began to move. 'It's so different!' she squeaked, taken aback.

'It's called a train.' Miriam pointed out of the window. 'Like that one, only faster and newer and built for carrying passengers. Where we're going is within a day's walk of Angbard's palace, but it'll only take us three and a half hours to get there.'

Brilliana stared at the passing freight train. 'I've seen movies,' she said quietly. 'You don't need to assume I'm stupid, ignorant. But it's not the same as *being* here.'

'I'm sorry.' Miriam shook her head, embarrassed. She looked at Brill appraisingly. She was doing a good job of bluffing, even though the surprises the world kept throwing at her must sometimes have been overwhelming. A bright kid, well-educated for her place in time, but out of her depth here – *How would I cope if someone gave me a ticket to the thirtieth century?* Miriam wondered. At a guess, there'd be an outburst of anger soon, triggered by something trivial – the realization that this wasn't fairyland but a real place, and she'd grown up among people who lived here and withheld everything in it from her. *I wonder which way she'll jump?*

Opposite her, Brilliana's face froze. 'What is it?' Miriam asked quietly.

'The . . . the second row of seats behind you – that's interesting. I've seen that man before. Black hair, dark suit.'

'Where?' Miriam whispered, tensing. Feeling for her shoulder bag, the small pistol buried at the bottom of it. *No, not on a train . . .*

'At court. He is a corporal of honor in service to Angbard. Called Edsger something. I've seen him a couple of times in escort to one or another of the duke's generals. I don't think he's recognized me. He is reading one of those intelligence papers the tinkers were selling at the palace of trains.'

'Hmm.' Miriam frowned. 'Did you see any luggage when he got onboard? Anything he carried? Describe him.'

'There is a trunk with a handle, like yours, only it looks like metal. He has it beside him and places one hand on it every short while.'

'Ah.' Miriam relaxed infinitesimally. 'Okay, is the case about the same size as mine?'

Brill nodded slowly, her eyes focused past Miriam's left shoulder.

'That means he's probably a courier,' Miriam said quietly. 'At a guess, Angbard has him carry documents daily between his palace and Manhattan. That explains why he spends so little time at court himself – he can keep his finger on the pulse far faster than the non-Clan courtiers realize. If I'm right, he'll be carrying a report about last night, among other things.' She raised a finger to her lips. 'Trouble is, if I'm right, he's armed and dangerous to approach. And if I'm wrong, he's not a courier. He's going to wait for the train to stop, then try to kill us.' Miriam closed her hand around the barrel of her pistol, then stopped. *No, that's the wrong way to solve this,* she thought.

Instead she pulled out her wallet and a piece of paper and began writing.

Brilliana leaned forward. 'He's doing it again,' she murmured. 'I think there's something in his jacket. Under his arm. He looks uncomfortable.'

'Right.' Miriam nodded, then shoved the piece of paper across the table at Brill. There was a pair of fifty-dollar bills and a train ticket concealed under it. 'Here is what we're going to do. In a minute, you're going to stand up while he isn't looking and walk to the other end of this carriage – behind you, over there, where the doors are. If – ' she swallowed – 'if things go wrong, don't try anything heroic. Just get off the train as soon as it stops, hide in the crowd, make damn sure he doesn't see you. There'll be another train through in an hour. Your ticket is valid for travel on it, and you want to get off at South Station. Go out of the station, tell a cab driver you want to go to this address, and pay with one of these notes, the way you saw me do it. He'll give you change. It's a small house; the number is on the front of the door. Go up to it and tell the woman who lives there that I sent you and I'm in trouble. Then give her this.' Miriam pushed another piece of paper across the table at her. 'After a day, tell Paulette to use the special number I gave her. That's all. Think you can do that?'

Brill nodded mutely. 'What are you going to do now?' she asked quietly.

Miriam took a deep breath. 'I'm going to do what we in the trade refer to as a hostile interview,' she said. 'What was his name, again?'

*

'Hello, Edsger. Don't move. This would not be a good place to get help for a sucking chest wound.'

He tensed and she smiled, bright and feral, like a mongoose confronting a sleepy cobra.

'What – '

'I said *don't move*. That includes your mouth. Not very good, is it, letting your mark turn on you?'

'I don't know what you're talking about!'

'I think you do. And I think it's slack of you, nodding off just because you're on the iron road and no world-walkers can sneak up from behind.' She smiled wider, seeing his unnerved expression. 'First, some ground rules. We are going to have a little conversation, then we will go our separate ways, and nobody needs to get hurt. But first, to make that possible, you will start by slowly bending forward and sliding that pistol of yours out into the shopping bag under the table.'

The courier leaned forward. Miriam leaned with him, keeping her pistol jammed up against his ribs through her jacket. 'Slowly,' she hissed.

'I'm slow.' He opened his jacket and slid a big Browning automatic out of the holster under his left armpit – two-fingered. Miriam tensed, but he followed through by dropping it into the open bag.

'And your cell phone,' she said. 'Now, kick it under the table. Gently.' He gave it a half-hearted shove with one foot.

'Put your hands between your knees and lean back slowly,' she ordered.

'Who are you?' he asked, complying.

'First, you're going to tell me who you're delivering that case to at the other end,' she said. 'Ordinary postal service – or Angbard himself?'

'I can't – '

She shoved the gun up against him, hard. 'You fucking *can*,' she snarled, slightly unhinged: 'Because if you don't tell me, you are going to read about the contents of that case on the front page of *The New York Times*, are you hearing me?'

'It goes to Matthias.'

'Angbard's secretary, right.' She felt him tense again. 'That was the correct answer,' she said quietly. 'Now, I want you to do something else for me. I've got a message for Angbard, for his ears only, do you understand? It's not for Matthias, it's not for Roland, it's not for any of the other lord-lieutenants he's got hanging around. Remember, I've got your number. If anyone other than Angbard gets this message, I will find out and I will tell him and he will kill you. What's going to happen next is: The train's stopping in a couple of minutes. You will stand up, take your case – not the bag with your phone – and get off the train, because I will be following you. You will then stand beside the train door where I can see you until it's ready to move off, and you will stay there while it moves off because if you don't stand that way I will shoot you. If you want to know why I'm so trigger-happy, you can ask Angbard yourself – after you've delivered his dispatches.'

'You must be – ' his eyes widened.

'Don't say my name.'

He nodded.

'You're going to be an hour late into Boston – an hour later than you would have been, anyway. Don't bother trying to organize a search for me because I won't be there. Instead, go to the Fort Lofstrom doppelgänger house, make your delivery to Matthias as usual, say you missed the train or something, then ask to see the old man and tell him about meeting me here.'

'What?' He looked puzzled. 'I thought you had a message.'

'*You* are the message.' She grinned humorlessly. 'And you've got to be alive to deliver it, so as long as you do what I say you get to live. We're slowing up: Do as I tell you and it'll all be over soon.'

He shook his head very slowly. 'He was right about you,' he said. But when she asked him who he meant, he just stared at her.

*

There was an old building on Central Avenue, with windows soundproofed against the roar of turbofans. Whenever the wind was from the southwest and inbound flights were diverted across the city, the airliners would rattle the panes. But perhaps there were other reasons for the soundproofing.

Two men sat in a second-floor office, Matthias leaning back behind a desk and Roland perched uncomfortably close to the edge of a sofa in front of it.

'Consignment F-12 is on schedule,' said Matthias. 'It says so right here on the manifest. Isn't that right?' He fixed Roland with a cold stare.

'I inspected it myself,' said Roland. Despite his stiff posture and the superficial appearance of unease, he sounded self-confident. 'Contractor Wolfe has the right attitude: businesslike attention to detail. They vet their workers thoroughly.'

'Well.' Matthias leaned across his desk. 'It's a pity the cargo is laid over in Svarlberg while a storm blows itself out, isn't it?'

'Damn.' Roland looked annoyed. 'That's recent, I take it?'

'Two days ago. I did a spot inspection myself. Impressed Vincenze to carry me across for the past week. I think you'd better warn Wolfe that F-12 is going to be at least four days late, possibly as much as seven.'

'Damn.' A nod. 'Okay, I'll do that. Usual disclaimers?'

'It's in the warranty fine print.' Neither of them cracked a smile. The Clan provided its own underwriting service – one that more than made up for the usurious transport charges it levied. The customer code-named Wolfe would damn well swallow the four- to seven-day delay and smile, because the cargo would arrive, one way or another, which was more than could be said for most of the Clan's competitors. If it didn't, the Clan would pay up in full, at face value, no question. 'We have a reputation to guard.'

'I'll get onto it.' Roland pulled out a small notebook and scribbled a cryptic entry in it. He caught Matthias staring. 'No names, no pack drill.' He tucked the notebook away carefully.

'It's good to know you can keep a secret.'

'Huh?'

'There's something else I wanted to talk to you about.' He didn't smile. 'Look at this.' Reaching into a desk drawer, Matthias pulled out a slim file binder and slid it across the desk. Roland rose and collected it, sat down, opened it, and tensed, frowning.

'Page one. Our prodigal dresses for dinner. Nice ass, by the way.'

A glare from the sofa. If looks could kill, Matthias would be ashes blowing on the wind.

'Turn over. That's her, leaving her room, shot from behind. Someone ought to tell her she oughtn't to leave security camera footage lying around like that, someone might steal it. Turn over.' Reluctantly, he turned over. 'That's her, in the passageway to a room in – ' Matthias coughed discreetly into his fist. 'And over, and oh dear, there seems to be a camera behind the bathroom mirror, doesn't there? I wonder how that got there. And now if you turn over, you'll see that – '

Roland slammed the folder shut with an inarticulate growl, then slapped it down on the desk. 'What's your point?' he demanded, shaking with anger. 'What the fuck do you want! Spying on me – '

'Sit down,' snapped Matthias.

Roland sat, shoulders hunched.

'You've put me on the spot, did you know that? I could show this to Angbard, you realize. In fact, I should show it to him. I've got a duty to show it to him. But I haven't – yet. I could show it to Lady Olga, too, but I think neither you nor she would care about that unless I embarrassed her publicly. Which would raise too many questions. What in Lightning Child's name were you thinking of, Roland?'

'Don't.' Roland hunched forward, eyes narrowed in pain.

'If Angbard sees this, he will rip you a new asshole. To be fair, he might rip her a new asshole too, but she's better positioned to survive the experience. You – ' he shook his head. 'I see a long future for you as Clan ambassador to a tribe of hairy-assed savages. For as long as any Clan ambassador lasts in one of those posts.'

'You haven't told him, though.' Roland stared at the floor in front of the desk, trying to hide his suspicions. Surely Matthias wouldn't be telling him this if he was just going to go straight to the duke?

'Well, no.' His interrogator fell silent for a while. 'I'm not a robot, you know. Loyal servant, yes – but I have my own ambitions.'

'Ambitions?' Roland looked up, his expression strained.

'The Clan doesn't offer an ideal career track for such as I.' He shrugged. 'I expect you to understand that better than most of them.'

Roland licked his lips. 'What do you want?' he asked quietly. 'What are you after?'

'I'm after the status quo ante.' He picked up the file and slid it into a desk drawer. 'Your little servant lass made waves where she shouldn't have. I want her out of the picture: I hasten to add, this doesn't mean dead, it just means invisible.'

'You want her to disappear.' For an instant, an expression of hope flickered across Roland's face.

'Possibly.' He nodded. 'I think you'd like that – if you went with her. Wouldn't you?'

'Damn you, three years was all I had . . . !'

'If you do as I say, then the folder and its contents – and all the

278

other copies – will vanish. And the Clan won't be able to touch you ever again. Either of you. What do you say?'

Roland licked his lips. 'I thought this was blackmail.'

'What makes you think it isn't?'

PART SIX

BUSINESS PLANS

LEARNED COUNSEL

The committee meeting was entering its third hour when the king sneezed, bringing matters to a head. His Excellency Sir Roderick was speaking at the time of the royal spasm. Standing at the far end of the table, before the red velvet curtains that sealed off the windows and the chill of the winter afternoon beyond, Sir Roderick leaned forward slightly, clutching his papers to his bony chest and wobbling back and forth as he recited. His colorless manners matched his startling lack of skin and hair pigmentation: He kept his eyes downcast as he regurgitated a seemingly endless stream of reports from the various heads of police, correspondents of intelligence, and freelance informers who kept his office abreast of news.

'I beg your pardon.' A valet flourished a clean linen handkerchief before the royal nose. John Frederick blinked, his expression pained. 'Ah-*choo!*' Although not yet in middle age, the king's florid complexion and burgeoning waistline were already giving rise to worries among his physiopaths and apothecaries.

Sir Roderick paused, awaiting the royal nod. The air in the room was heavy with the smell of beeswax furniture polish, and a faint oily overlay from the quietly fizzing gas lamps. 'Sire?'

'A moment.' John Frederick, by grace of God king-emperor of New Britain and ruler of the territories and dependencies thereof, took a fresh handkerchief and waved off his equerry while anxious faces watched him from all sides. He breathed deeply, clearly battling to control the itching in his sinuses. 'Ah. Where were we? Sir Roderick, you have held the floor long enough – take a seat, we will return to you shortly. Lord Douglass, this matter of indiscipline among the masses troubles me. If the effects of the poor grain harvest last year are not mitigated in the summer, as your honorable colleague forecasts' – a nod at Lord Scotia, minister for rural affairs – 'then there will be fertile soil for the ranters and ravers to till next autumn. Is there any risk of a *domestic* upset?'

Lord Douglass ran a wrinkled hand across his thinning hair as he considered his reply. 'As your majesty is doubtless aware – ' He paused. 'I had hoped to discuss this matter after hearing from Sir Roderick. If I may beg your indulgence?' At the royal nod, he leaned sideways. 'Sir Roderick, may I ask you to rapidly summarize the domestic situation?'

'By your leave, your majesty?' Sir Roderick cleared his throat, then addressed the room. 'Your majesty, my right honorable friends, the domestic condition is currently under control, but there are an increasing number of reports of nonconformist ranters in the provinces. In the past month alone the royal police have apprehended no less than two cells of Levelers, and uncovered three illicit printers – one in Massachusetts, one in your majesty's western New Provinces, and one in New London itself.' A whisper ran around the table: It was an open secret that the cellar press in the capital could print whatever they liked with only loose control, except for the most blatantly slanderous rumors and Leveler sedition. For there to be raids, the situation must be far worse than normal. 'This ignores the usual rumbling in the colonies and dominions. Finally, police operations uncovered a plot to blow up the Western Summer Palace at Monterey – I would prefer not to discuss this in open cabinet until we have resolved the situation. Someone or something is stirring up Leveler activists, and there have been rumors of French livres greasing the wheels of treason. Certainly it takes money to run subversive presses or buy explosives, and it must be coming from somewhere.'

Sir Roderick sat down, and Lord Douglass rose. 'Your majesty, I would say that if adventures are contemplated overseas, and if this should coincide with a rise in the price of bread, the introduction of new taxes and duties, *and* an outburst of Leveler ranting, I should not like to face the consequences without the continental reserves at Fort Victoria ready to entrain for either coast, not to mention securing the loyalty of the local regiments in each parliamentary district.'

'Well, then.' The king frowned, his forehead wrinkling as if to withstand another fit of sneezing: 'We shall have to see to such measures, shall we not?' He leaned forward in his chair. 'But I want to hear more on this matter of where the homegrown thorns in our crown are obtaining their finances. It seems to me that if we can snip this odious weed in the bud, as it were, and demonstrate to the satisfaction of our peers the meddling of the dauphin at work in our garden, then it will certainly serve our purposes. Lord Douglass?'

'By all means, your majesty.' The prime minister glanced at his minister for special affairs. 'Sir Roderick, if you please, can you see to it?'

'Of course, my lord.' The minister inclined his head toward his monarch. 'As soon as we have something more than rumor and suspicion, I will place it before your majesty.'

'Now if we may return to the agenda?' The prime minister suggested.

'Certainly.' The king nodded his assent, and Lord Douglass cleared his throat, to continue with the next point on an afternoon-long agenda. The meeting continued and in every way beside the sneezing fit it seemed a perfectly normal session of the Imperial Intelligence Oversight Committee, held before His Imperial Majesty John the Fourth, king of New Britain and dominions, in the Brunswick Palace on Manhattan Island in the early years of the twenty-first century. Time would show otherwise . . .

*

On the other side of a flipped coin's fall, in an office two hundred miles away in space and perhaps two thousand years away from the court of King John in terms of historical divergence, another meeting was taking place.

'A shoot-out.' The duke's tone of voice, normally icily deliberate, rose slightly as he abandoned his chair and began to pace the confines of his office. He paused beneath a pair of steel broadswords mounted on the wall above a battered circular shield. 'In the summer palace?' His tone hardened. 'I find it hard to believe that this was allowed to happen.' He looked up at the swords. 'Who was supposed to be in charge of her guard?'

The duke's secretary – his keeper of secrets – cleared his throat.

'Oliver, Baron Hjorth, is of course responsible for the well-being of all beneath his roof. In accordance with your orders I requested that he see to Lady Helge's security.' A moment's pause to let the implication sink in. 'Whether he complied with your orders bears investigation.'

The duke stopped pacing, standing in front of the broad picture windows that looked out across the valley below the castle. Heavily forested and seemingly empty of human habitation, the river valley ran all the way to the coast, marking the northern border of the sprawling kingdom of Gruinmarkt from the Nordmarkt neighbors to the north. 'And the Lady Olga?'

'She protests in the strongest terms, my lord.' The secretary shrugged slightly, his face expressionless. 'I sent Roland to attend to her personally, to ensure she is adequately protected. For what it's worth, there were no identifying marks on the bodies. No tattoos, no indications of who they were. Not Clan. But they had weapons and equipment from the other side and I am – startled – that Lady Olga, even with help from our runaway, survived the incident.'

'Our *runaway* is my niece, Matthias,' the duke reminded his secretary. 'A rather extraordinary woman.' His expression hardened. 'I want tissue samples, photographs, anything you can come up with. For the hit squad. Get them processed on the other side, run them across the FBI most-wanted database, pull whatever strings you can find, but I want to know who they were and who they thought they were working for. And how they got there. The palace was supposed to be securely doppelgängered. Why wasn't it?'

'Ah. I have already looked into that.' Matthias waited.

'Well then?' The duke clenched his hands.

'About three years ago, Baroness Hildegarde ordered our agents – via the usual shell company – to let out one side of the doppel-gänger facility to a secondary Clan-owned shipping company she was setting up. It was all above board and conducted in public at Beltaigne, approved in full committee, but the shipping company moved away a year later to more suitable purpose-built facilities, and they in turn sublet the premises. It was walled off from the original bonded store and converted into short-lease storage, leaving it wide open. Purely coincidentally, it covered the New Tower, and parts of the west wing of the palace were left undoppelgängered. Helge wouldn't have known enough to recognize this as unusual, but it left most of her suite wide open to attack by world-walkers.'

'And where was Oliver, Baron Hjorth, while this was going on?' the duke asked, deceptively mildly. A failure to doppelgänger the palace correctly – to ensure that it was physically collocated with secure territory in the other universe to which the world-walking and occasionally squabbling members of the Clan had access – was not a trivial oversight, not after the bloody civil war that had killed three out of every four members of the six families only a handful of decades ago.

'He was worrying about roofing costs, I imagine.' Matthias shrugged again, almost imperceptibly. 'If he even knew about it. After all, what does security matter if the building caves in?'

'If.' The duke frowned. 'That slime-weasel Oliver is in Baroness Hildegarde's pocket, you mark my words. An unfortunate coincidence that they can both deny responsibility for, and Helge is left facing assassins? It's almost insultingly convenient. She's getting slack – we shall have to teach her a lesson in manners.'

'What are your orders regarding your niece, my lord? Since she appears to have run away, like her mother before her, she could be found in breach of the compact – '

'No, no need for that just yet.' The duke walked slowly back to his desk, his expression showing little sign of the stiffness in his joints. 'Let her move freely for now.' He lowered himself into his chair and stared at Matthias. 'I expect to hear about her movements by and by. Has she made any attempt to get in touch?'

'With us? I've heard no messages, my lord.' Matthias raised one hand, scratched an itch alongside his nose. 'What do you think she'll do?'

'What do *I* think?' The duke opened his mouth, as if about to laugh. 'She's not a trained security professional, boy. She might do anything! But she is a trained investigative journalist, and if she's true to her instincts, she'll start digging.' He began to smile. 'I really want to see what she uncovers.'

*

Meanwhile, in a city called Boston in a country called the United States:

'You know something?' asked Paulette. 'When I told you to buy guns and drive fast I wasn't, like, expecting you to actually *do* that.' She put her coffee cup down, half-drained. There were dark hollows under her eyes, but apart from that she was as tidy as ever, not a hair out of place. Which, Miriam reflected, left her looking a bit like a legal secretary: short, dark, Italianate subtype.

Miriam shook her head. *I wish I could keep it together the way she does*, she thought. 'You said, and I quote from memory, "As your attorney I am advising you to buy guns and drive fast." Right?' She smiled tiredly at Paulette. Her own coffee cup was untouched. When she'd arrived at the other woman's house with Brilliana d'Ost in tow, the release of tension had her throwing up in the bathroom toilet. Paulette's wisecrack was in poor taste – Miriam had actually killed a man in self-defense less than twenty-four hours ago, and now things were starting to look *really* messy.

'What's an attorney?' asked Brill, sitting up on the sofa, prim and attentive: twentyish, blonde, and otherworldly in the terrifyingly literal way that only a Clan member could be.

'Not me, I'm a paralegal. Just in case you'd forgotten, Miriam. I'd have to study for another two years before I can sit for the bar exams.'

'You signed up for the course like I asked? That's good.'

'Yeah, well.' Paulette put her empty mug down. 'Do you want to go through it all again? Just so I know where I stand?'

'Not really, but . . .' Miriam glanced at Brill. 'Look, here's the high points. This young lady is Brilliana d'Ost. She's kind of an illegal immigrant, no papers, no birth certificate, no background. She needs somewhere to stay while we sort things out back where she comes from. She isn't self-sufficient here – she met her very first elevator yesterday evening, and her first train this morning.'

Paulette raised an eyebrow. 'R-i-i-ght,' she drawled. 'I think I can see how this might pose some difficulties.'

'I can read and write,' Brill volunteered. 'And I speak English. I've seen *Dynasty* and *Rob Roy*, too.' Brightly: 'And *The Godfather*, that was the duke's favorite! I've seen that one three times.'

'Hmm.' Paulette looked her up and down then glanced at Miriam. 'This is a kind of what you see is what you get proposition, isn't it?'

'Yes,' Miriam said. 'Oh, and her relatives will want her back. They might get violent if they find her, so she needs to be anonymous. All she's got are the clothes on her back. And then there's this.' She passed Paulette a piece of paper. Paulette glanced at it, then raised her other eyebrow and did a double take.

'This is valid?' She held up the check.

'No strings.' Miriam nodded. 'At least, as long as Duke Angbard doesn't cut off the line of credit he gave me. You've got the company paperwork together, ready to sign? Good. What we do is, we open a company bank account. I pay *this* into it and issue myself with shares to the tune of fifty grand. We write you up as an employee, you sign the contract, I issue you your first paycheck – eight thousand, covers your first month only – and a signing bonus of another ten thousand. You then write a check back to the company for that ten thousand, and I issue you the shares and make you company secretary. Got that?'

'You want me as a director?' Paulette watched her closely. 'Are you sure about that?'

'I trust you,' Miriam said simply. 'And I need someone on this side of the wall who's got signing authority and can run things while I'm away. I wasn't kidding when I told you to set this up, Paulie. It's going to be big.'

Paulette stared at the banker's draft for fifty thousand dollars dubiously. 'Blood money.'

'Blood is thicker than water,' Brill commented. 'Why don't you want to take it?'

Paulette sighed. 'Do I tell her?' she asked Miriam.

'Not yet.' Miriam looked thoughtful. 'But I promised myself a few days back that anything *I* start up will be clean. That good enough for you?'

'Yeah.' Paulette turned toward the kitchen doorway, then paused. 'Brilliana? Is it okay if I call you Brill?'

'Surely!' The younger woman beamed at her.

'Oh. Well, uh, this is the kitchen. I was going to make some fresh coffee, but I figure if you're staying here for a while I ought to start by showing you where things are and how not to – ' She glanced at Miriam. 'Do they have electricity?' she asked. Miriam shook her head minutely. 'Oh sweet Jesus! Okay, Brill, the first thing you need to learn about the kitchen is how not to kill yourself. See, everything works by electricity. That's kind of – '

Miriam picked up a bundle of official papers and a pen, and wandered out into the front hall. *It's going to be okay,* she told herself. *Paulie's going to mother-hen her. Two days and she'll know how to cross the road safely, use a flush toilet, and work the washing machine.* Two weeks, and if Paulie didn't kill her, she'd be coming home late from nightclubs with a hangover. *If* she didn't just decide that the twenty-first century was too much for her, and hide under the spare bed. Which, as she'd grown up in a world that hadn't got much past the late medieval, was a distinct possibility. *Wouldn't be a surprise; it's too much for* me *at times,* Miriam thought, contemplating the stack of forms for declaring the tax status of a limited liability company in Massachusetts with a sinking heart.

*

That evening, after Paulette and Miriam visited the bank to open a business account and deposit the checks, they holed up around Paulie's kitchen table. A couple of bottles of red wine and a chicken casserole went a long way toward putting Brill at her ease. She even managed to get over the jittery fear of electricity that Paulie had talked into her in the afternoon to the extent of flipping light switches and fiddling with the heat on the electric stove.

'It's marvelous!' she told Miriam. 'No need for coal, it stays just as hot as you want it, and it doesn't get dirty! What do all the servants do for a living? Do they just laze around all day?'

'Um,' said Paulette. One glance told Miriam that she was suffering a worse dose of culture shock than the young transportee – her shoulders were shaking like jelly. 'Like, that's the drawback, Brill. Where would *you* have the servants sleep, in a house like this?'

'Why, if there were several in the bedchamber you so kindly loaned – oh. I'm to drudge for my keep?'

'No,' Miriam interrupted before Paulette could wind her up any further. 'Brill, ordinary people don't have servants in their homes here.'

'Ordinary? But surely this isn't – ' Brill's eyes widened.

Paulette nodded at her. 'That's me, common as muck!' she said brightly. 'Listen, the way it works in this household is, if you make a mess, you tidy it up yourself. You saw the dishwasher?' Brill nodded, evidently enthralled. 'There are other gadgets. A house this big doesn't *need* servants. Tomorrow we'll go get you some more clothes – ' She glanced at Miriam for approval – 'then do next week's food shopping, and I'll show you where everything's kept. Uh, Miriam, this is gonna slow everything up – '

'Doesn't matter.' Miriam put her knife and fork down. She was, she decided, not only over-full but increasingly exhausted. 'Take it easy. Brill needs to know how to function over here because if it all comes together the way I hope, she's going to be over here regularly on business. She'll be working with you, I hope.' She picked up her wineglass. 'Tomorrow I'm going to go call on a relative. Then I think I've got a serious road trip ahead of me.'

'You're going away?' asked Brill, carefully putting her glass down.

'Probably. But not immediately. Look, what I said earlier holds – you can go home whenever you want to, if it's an emergency. All you have to do is catch a cab around to the nearest Clan safe house and hammer on the door. They'll have to take you back. If you tell them I abducted you, they'll probably believe it – I seem to be the subject of some wild rumors.' She smiled tiredly. 'I'll give you the address in the morning, all right?' The smile faded. 'One thing. Don't you *dare* bug out on Paulie without telling her first. They don't know about her and they might do something about her if they learn . . . mightn't they?'

Brill swallowed, then nodded. 'I understand,' she said.

'I'm sure you do.' Miriam realized Paulette was watching her through narrowed eyes. 'Brill has seen me nearly get my sorry ass shot to pieces. She knows the score.'

'Yeah, well. I was meaning to talk to you about that, too.' Paulette didn't look pleased. 'What the hell is happening over there?'

'It's a mess. First, Olga tried to kill me. Luckily she gave me a chance to talk my way out of it first – someone tried to set me up last time I visited you. Then the shit really hit the fan. Last night I figured out that my accommodation was insecure, the hard way, then parties unknown tried to rub out Olga and me, both. *Multiple parties.* There are at least two factions involved, and I don't have a clue who this new bunch are, which is why I'm here and brought Brill – she's seen too much.'

'A second gang? Jesus, Miriam, you're sucking them up like a Hoover! What's going on?'

'I wish I knew, believe me.' She drained her wineglass. 'Hmm. This glass is defective. Better fix it.' Before she could reach for the bottle, Paulette picked it up and began to pour, her hand shaking slightly. 'Had a devil of a time getting here, I can tell you. Nearly put my back out carrying Brill, then found some evil son of a bitch had booby-trapped the warehouse. Earlier I phoned Roland to come tidy up – someone had murdered the site watchman – but instead someone put a bomb in it.'

'I *told* you that smoothie would turn out to be a weasel,' said Paulette. 'It's him, isn't it?'

'I don't think so. Things are messy, very messy. We ran into one of Angbard's couriers on the train over, so I gave him a message that should shake things loose if it's anyone on his staff. And now . . . well.' She pulled out the two lockets from her left pocket. 'Spot the difference.'

Paulette's breath hissed out as she leaned forward to study them. 'Shit. That one on the left, the tarnished one – that's yours, isn't it? But the other – '

'Have a cigar. I took it off the first hired gun last night. He won't be needing it anymore.'

'Mind if I . . . ?' Paulette picked the two lockets up and sprang the catch. She frowned as she stared at the contents, then snapped them closed. 'The designs are different.'

'I guessed they would be.'

Brill stared at the two small silver disks as if they were diamonds or jewels of incalculable value. Finally she asked, timidly, 'How can they be different? All the Clan ones are the same, aren't they?'

'Who says it's a Clan one?' Miriam scooped them back into her pocket. 'Look, first I am going to get a good night's sleep. I suggest you guys do the same thing. In the morning, I'm going to hire a car. I'd like to be able to go home, just long enough to retrieve a disk, but – '

'No, don't do that,' said Paulette.

Miriam looked at her. 'I'm not stupid. I know they're probably watching the house in case I show up. It's just frustrating.' She shrugged.

'It's not that bad,' Paulette said. 'Either they got the disk the first time they black-bagged you – or they didn't, in which case you know precisely where it is. Why not leave it there?'

'I guess so,' Miriam replied. 'Yeah, you're right. It's safe where it is.' She glanced at Brill, who mimed incomprehension. Until she was forced to smile. 'Still. Tomorrow I'm going to spend some time in a museum. *Then* – ' She glanced at Paulette.

'Oh no, you're not going to do *that* again.'

'Oh yes, I am. It's the only way to crack the story wide open.' Her eyes went wide. 'Shit! I'd completely forgotten! I've got a feature to file with Steve for *The Herald*! The deadline's got to be real soon! If I miss it, there's no way I'll get the column – '

'Miriam.'

'Yes, Paulie?'

'Why are you still bothering about that?'

'I – ' Miriam froze for a moment. 'I guess I'm still thinking of going back to my old life,' she said slowly. 'It's something to hang onto.'

'Right.' Paulette nodded. 'Now tell me. How much money is there on that platinum card?'

Pause. 'About one point nine million dollars left.'

'Miriam?'

'Yes, Paulie?'

'As your legal advisor I am telling you to shut the fuck up and get a good night's sleep. You can sort out whether you're going to write the article tomorrow – but I'd advise you to drop it. Say you've got stomach flu or something. Then you can take an extra day over your preparations for the journey. Got it?'

'Yes, Paulie.'

'And another thing?'

'What's that?'

'Drink your wine and shut your mouth, kid, you look like a fish.'

*

The next day, Miriam pulled out her notebook computer – which was now acquiring a few scratches – and settled down to pound the keyboard while Paulette took Brill shopping. It wasn't hard work, and she already knew what she was going to write, and besides, it saved her having to think too hard about her future. The main headache was not having access to her Mac, or a broadband connection. Paulie, despite her brief foray into dot-com management, had never seen the point of spending money to receive spam at home. Finally she pulled out her cell and dialed *The Herald*'s front desk. 'Steve Blau, please,' she said, and waited.

'Steve. Who's this?'

'Steve? It's Miriam.' She took a deep breath. 'About that feature.'

'Deadline's this Thursday,' he rumbled. 'You needing an extension?'

She breathed out abruptly, nearly coughing into the phone. 'No, no, I'm ready to e-mail you a provisional draft, see if it fits what you were expecting. Uh, I've had a bit of an exciting life lately, got a new phone number for you.'

'Really?' She could almost hear his eyebrows rising.

'Yeah. Domestic incident, big time.' She extemporized hastily. 'I'm having to look after my mother. She's had an accident. Broken hip. You want my new details?'

'Sure. Hang on a moment. Okay, fire away.'

Miriam gave him her new e-mail and phone numbers. 'Listen, I'll mail in the copy in about an hour's time. Is there anything else you're looking for?'

'Not right now.' He sounded amused. 'They sprang a major reorg on us right after our last talk, followed by a guerilla page-plan redesign; looks like that slot for a new columnist I mentioned earlier is probably going to happen. Weekly, op-ed piece on medical/biotech investment and the VC scene, your sort of thing. Can I pencil you in for it?'

Miriam thought furiously. 'I'm busier than I was right after I left *The Weatherman*, but I figure I can fit it in. Only thing is, I'll need a month's notice to start delivering, and I'd like to keep a couple of generic op-ed pieces in the can in case I'm called away. I'm going to be doing a lot of head-down stuff in the next year or so. It won't stop me keeping up with the reading, but it may get in the way of my hitting deadlines once in a blue moon. Could you live with that?'

'I'll have to think about it,' he said. 'I'm willing to make allowances. But you're a pro. You'd give me some warning wherever possible, right?'

'Of course, Steve.'

'Okay. File that copy. Bye.'

She put the phone down for a moment, eyes misting over. *I've still got a real life,* she told herself. *This shit hasn't taken everything over.* She thought of Brill, trapped by family expectations and upbringing. *If I could unhook their claws, I could go back to being the real me. Really.* Then she thought about the rest of them. About the room at the Marriott, and what had happened in it. About Roland, and her. *Maybe.*

She picked the phone up again. It was easier than thinking.

Iris answered almost immediately. 'Miriam, dear? Where have you been?'

'Ma?' The full weight of her worries crashed down on her. 'You wouldn't believe me if I told you! Listen, I'm on to a story. It's – ' She struggled for a suitable metaphor. 'It's as big as Watergate. Bigger, maybe. But there's people involved who're watching me. I'd like to spend some time with you, but I don't know if it would be safe.'

'That's interesting.' She could hear her adoptive mother's mind crunching gears even on the end of a phone. 'So you can't come and visit me?'

'Remember what you told me about COINTELPRO, Ma?'

'Ah, those were the days! When I was a young firebrand, ah me.'

'Ma!'

'Stuffing envelopes with Jan Six, before Commune Two imploded, picketings and sit-ins – did I tell you about the time the FBI bugged our phones? How we got around it?'

'Mom.' Miriam sighed. 'Really! That student radical stuff is so *old*, you know?'

'Don't you *old* me, young lady!' Iris put a condescending, amused tone in her voice. 'Is your trouble federal, by any chance?'

'I wish it was.'

'Well then. I'll meet you at the playground after bridge, an hour before closing time.' *Click.*

She'd hung up, Miriam realized, staring at her phone. 'Oh sweet Jesus,' she murmured. *Never, ever, challenge a onetime SDS activist to throw a tail.* She giggled quietly to herself, overcome by a bizarre combination of mirth and guilt – mirth at the idea of a late-fifties Jewish grandmother with multiple sclerosis giving the Clan's surveillance agents the slip, and guilt, shocking guilt, at the thought of what she might have unintentionally involved Iris in. She almost picked up the phone to apologize, to tell Iris not to bother – but that would be waving a red rag at a bull. When Iris got it into her mind to do something, not even the FBI and the federal government stood much chance of stopping her.

The playground. That's what she'd called the museum, when she was small. 'Can we go to the playground?' she'd asked, a second-grader already eating into her parents' library cards, and Iris had smiled indulgently and taken her there, to run around the displays and generally annoy the old folks reading the signs under the exhibits until, energy exhausted, she'd flaked out in the dinosaur wing.

And *bridge.* Iris *never* played card games. That must mean . . . yes. The bridge over the Charles River. More confirmation that she meant the Science Museum, an hour before closing time. Right. Miriam grinned, remembering Iris's bedtime stories about the hairy years under FBI surveillance, the times she and Morris had been pulled in for questioning – but never actually charged with anything. When she was older, Miriam realized that they'd been too sensible, had dropped out to work in a radical bookstore and help with a homeless shelter before the hardcore idiots began cooking up bombs and declaring war on the System, a System that had ultimately gotten tired of their posturing and rolled over in its sleep, obliterating them.

Miriam whistled tunelessly between her teeth and plugged her cellular modem card back into the notebook, ready to send in her feature article. Maybe Iris could teach her some useful techniques. The way things were going, she needed every edge.

*

A landscape of concrete and steel, damp and gray beneath a sky stained dirty orange. The glare of streetlamps reflected from clouds heavy with the promise of sleet or rain tomorrow. Miriam swung the rental car around into the parking lot, lowered her window to accept a ticket, then drove on in search of a space. It was damply cold outside, the temperature dropping with nightfall, but eventually she found a free place and parked. The car, she noted, was the precise same shade of silver-gray as Iris's hair.

Miriam walked around the corner and down a couple of flights of stairs, then through the entrance to the museum.

Warm light flooded out onto the sidewalk, lifting her gloom. Paulette had brought Brill home earlier that afternoon, shaking slightly. The color- and pattern-enhanced marketing strategies of modern retail had finally driven Brill into the attack of culture shock Miriam had been expecting. They'd left Brill hunched up in front of the Cartoon Network on cable, so Paulette could give Miriam a lift to the nearest Avis rental lot. And now –

Miriam pushed through the doors and looked around. Front desk, security gates, a huge human-powered sailplane hanging from the ceiling over the turnstiles, staff busy at their desks – and a little old lady in a powered wheelchair, whirring toward her. Not so little, or so old. 'You're late! That's not like you,' Iris chided her. 'Where have you been?'

'That's new,' Miriam said, pointing to the chair.

'Yes, it is.' Iris grinned up at her, impishly. 'Did you know it can outrun a two-year-old Dodge Charger? *If* you know the footpaths through the park and don't give the bastards time to get out and follow you on foot.' She dropped the grin. 'Miriam, you're in *trouble*. What did I teach you about trouble?'

Miriam sighed. 'Don't get into it to begin with, especially don't bring it home with you,' she recited, 'never start a war on two fronts, and especially don't start a land war in Asia. Yes, I *know*. The problem is, trouble came looking for me. Say, isn't there a coffee shop in the food court, around the corner from the gift shop?'

'I think I could be persuaded – *if* you tell me what's going on.'

Miriam followed her mother's wheelchair along the echoing corridor, dodging the odd family group. It took them a few minutes, but finally Miriam got them both sorted out with drinks and a seat at a table well away from anyone else. 'It was the shoebox,' Miriam confessed. Iris had given her a shoebox full of items relating to her enigmatic birth-mother, found stabbed in a park nearly a third of a century ago. After all those years gathering dust in the attic the locket still worked, dumping Miriam into a world drastically unlike her own. 'If you hadn't given it to me, they wouldn't be staking out your house.'

'Who do you think *they* are?'

'They call themselves the Clan. There are six families in the Clan, and they're like this.' She knotted her fingers together, tugged experimentally. 'Turns out I'm, uh, well, how to put this? I'm not a *Jewish* princess. I'm a – '

'She was important,' Iris interrupted. 'Some kind of blue blood, right? Miriam, what does the Clan do that's so secret you can't talk but so important they need you alive?'

'They're – ' Miriam stopped. 'If I told you, they might kill you.'

Iris raised an eyebrow. 'I think you know better than that,' she said quietly.

'But – '

'Stop trying to overprotect me!' Iris waved her attempted justification away. 'You always hated it when I patronized you. So what is this, return-the-favor week? You're still alive, so you have something on them, if I know you. So it follows that you can look after your old mother, right? Doesn't it?'

'It's not that simple.' Miriam looked at her mother and sighed. 'If I knew you'd be safe . . .'

'Shut up and listen, girl.' Miriam shut up abruptly and stared at her. Iris was watching her with a peculiar intensity. 'You are, by damn, going to tell me *everything*. Especially who's after you, so that I know who to watch for. Because anyone who tries to get at you through me is going to get a very nasty surprise indeed.' For a moment, Iris's eyes were icy-cold, as harsh as the assassin in the orangery at midnight, two days before. Then they softened. 'You're all I've got left,' she said quietly. 'Humor your old ma, please? It's been a long time since anything interesting happened to me – interesting in the sense of the Chinese proverb, anyway.'

'You always told me not to gossip.'

'Gossip is as gossip does. Keep your powder dry and your allies briefed.'

'I'll – ' Miriam took a sip of her coffee. 'Okay,' she said, licking her dry lips. 'This is going to take a long time to tell, but basically what happened was, I took the shoebox home and didn't do anything with it until that evening. Which probably wasn't a good thing, because . . .'

She talked for a long time, and Iris listened, occasionally prompting her for more detail but mostly just staring at her face, intently, with an expression somewhere between longing and disgust.

Finally Miriam ran down. 'That's all, I guess,' she said. 'I left Brill with Paulie, who's looking after her. Tomorrow I'm going to take the second locket and, well, see if it works. Over here or over there.' She searched Iris's face. 'You believe me?' she asked, almost plaintively.

'Oh, I believe you, kid.' Iris reached out and covered her hand with her own: older, thinner, infinitely familiar. 'I – ' She paused. 'I haven't been entirely honest with you,' she admitted. 'I had an idea this was going to get weird before I gave you the box, but not like this. It seemed like a good time to pass it on when you began sniffing around their turf. Large-scale money laundering is exactly the sort of thing the, this Clan, would be mixed up in, and I suspected – Well, I expected you to come back and ask me about it sooner, rather than simply jumping in. Maybe I should have warned you.' She looked at Miriam, searchingly.

'It's okay, Ma.' Miriam covered Iris's hand with her other.

'No, it's *not* okay,' Iris insisted. 'What I did was wrong! I should have – '

'Ma, shut up.'

'If you insist.' Iris gave her a curious half-smile. 'This second knotwork design – I want to see that. Can you show me sometime?'

'Sure.' Miriam nodded. 'Didn't bring it with me, though.'

'What are you going to do next?'

'I'm – ' Miriam paused. 'I warned Angbard that if anybody touched a hair on your head, he was dead meat. But now there's a second bunch after me, and I don't have a hotline to their boss. I don't even know who their boss *is*.'

'Neither did Patricia,' murmured Iris.

'What did you say?'

'I'd have thought it was obvious,' Iris pointed out quickly. 'If she'd known, they wouldn't have gotten near her.' She shook her head. 'A really bad business, that.' For a moment she looked angry, and determined – the same expression Miriam had glimpsed in a mirror recently. 'And it hasn't gone away. Give me your secret phone number, girl.'

'My secret – what?'

'Okay, your dead-letter drop. So we can keep in touch when you go on your wanderings. You *do* want to keep your mom informed of what the enemies of freedom and civilization are up to, don't you?'

'Ma! Okay, here it is,' she said, scribbling her new, sanitized cell number down on a piece of paper and sliding it over to Iris.

'Good.' Iris tucked it away quickly. 'This locket you found – you think it goes somewhere else, don't you?'

'Yes. That's the only explanation I can come up with.'

'To another world, where everything will of course be completely different.' Iris shook her head. 'As if two worlds wasn't already one too many.'

'And mystery assassins. Don't forget the mystery assassins.'

'I'm not,' said her mother. 'From what you've been telling me . . .' She narrowed her eyes. 'Don't trust *any* of them. Not the Clan, not even the one you took to bed. They're all – they sound like – a bunch of vipers. They'll screw you as soon as you think you're safe.'

'Ma.' Miriam began to blush. 'Oh, I don't *trust* them. At least, not to do anything with my best interests at heart.'

'Then you're smarter than I was at your age.' Iris pulled on her gloves. 'Give an old lady a lift home? Or at least, back to the woods?

It's a cold and scary night. Mind you, I may have forgotten to bring your red cloak, but any wolves who try to lay hands on this old granny will come off worse.'

PAWNBROKER

'It's no good,' said Miriam, rubbing her forehead. 'All I get is crossed eyes, blurred vision, and a headache. It doesn't *work*.' She snapped the assassin's locket closed in frustration.

'Maybe it doesn't work here,' Brill suggested. 'If it's a different design?'

'Maybe. Or then again, it's a different design and it came through on the other side. How do I know where I'd end up if I *did* get it to work here?' She paused, then looked at the locket. 'Maybe it wasn't real clever of me to try that here,' she said slowly. 'I really ought to cross over before I try it again. If there's really a third world out there, how do we know there isn't a fourth? Or more? How do we know that using it twice in succession brings you back to the place you departed from – that travel using it is commutative? It raises more questions than it answers, doesn't it?'

'Yes – ' Brill fell silent.

'Do you know anything about this?' Miriam asked.

'No.' She shook her head slowly. 'I don't – they never spoke about the possibility. Why should they? It was as much as anyone could do to travel between this world and the other, without invoking phantoms. Would testing a new sigil not be dangerous? If it by some chance carried you to another world where wild animals or storms waited . . .'

'Someone must have tried it, mustn't they?'

'You would have to ask the elders. All I can tell is what I was told.'

'Well, anyway,' Miriam rubbed her forehead again, 'if it works, it'll be one hell of a lever to use with Angbard. I'll just have to take this one and cross over to the other side before I try to go wherever its original owner came from. Then try from there.'

'Can you do that?' Brill asked.

'Yes. But just one crossing gives me a cracking headache if I don't take my pills. I figure I can make two an hour apart. But if I run into something nasty on the far side – wherever this one takes me – I'll be in deep trouble if I need to get away from it in a hurry.'

Malignant hypertension wasn't a term she could use with Brill, but she'd seen what it could do to people. In particular she'd seen a middle-aged man who'd not bothered to take his antihypertensives. She'd been in the emergency room when the ambulance brought him in, eyes open and nobody home after the massive stroke. She'd been there when they turned the ventilator off and filled out the death certificate. She shook her head. 'It'll take careful planning.'

Miriam glanced at the window. Snow drifted down from a sky the color of shattered dreams. It was bitterly cold outside. 'What I *should* do is go across, hole up somewhere and catch some sleep, then try to cross over the next day so I can run away if anything goes wrong. Trouble is, it's going to be just as cold on the other side as it is here. And if I have to run away, I get to spend two nights camping in the woods, in winter, with a splitting headache. I don't think that's a really great idea. And I'm limited to what I can carry.'

When's Paulie due back? she wondered. *She'll be able to help.*

'What about a coaching house?' Brill asked, practical-minded as ever.

'A coaching – ' Miriam stopped dead. 'But I can't – '

'There's one about two miles down the road from Fort Lofstrom.' Brill looked thoughtful. 'We dress you as a, an oracle's wife, summoned to a village down the coast to join your husband in his new parish. Your trap broke a wheel and – ' She ran down. 'Oh. You don't speak Hoh'sprashe.'

'Yup.' Miriam nodded. 'Doesn't work well, does it?'

'No.' Brill wrinkled her nose. 'What a nuisance! We could go together,' she added tentatively.

'I think we'll have to do that,' said Miriam. 'Probably I play the deaf-mute mother and you play the daughter – I try to look older, you to look younger. Think it would work?'

From Brilliana's slow nod she realized that Brill did – and wasn't enthusiastic about it. 'It might.'

'It would also leave you stranded in the back of beyond up near, where was it, Hasleholm, if I don't come back, wouldn't it?' Miriam pointed out. 'On the other hand, you'd be in the right place. You could make your way to Fort Lofstrom and tell Angbard what happened. He'd take care of you,' she added. 'Just tell him I ordered you to come along with me. He'll swallow that.'

'I don't want to go back,' Brilliana said evenly. 'Not until I've seen more of this wonderful world.'

'Me too, kid. So we're not going to plan on me not coming back, are we? Instead, we're going to plan on us both going over, spending the night at a coaching house, and then walking down the road to the next one. They're only about twenty miles apart – it's a fair hike, but not impossible. Along the way, I disappear, and catch up with you later. We spend the night there, then we turn back – and cross back here. How does that sound?'

'Three days? And you'll bring me back here?'

'Of course.' Miriam brooded for a moment. 'I think I want some more tea,' she decided. 'Want some?'

'Oh yes!' Brilliana sat up eagerly. 'Is there any of Earl Grey's own blend?'

'I'll just check.' Miriam wandered into Paulette's kitchen, her mind spinning gears like a car in neutral. She filled the kettle, set it on the hob to boil, began searching for tea. *There's got to be a way to make this work better,* she thought. The real problem was mobility. If she could just arrange how to meet up with Brill fifteen miles down the road without having to walk the distance herself – 'Oh,' she said, as the kettle began to boil.

'What is it?' asked Brill, behind her.

'It's so obvious!' Miriam said as she picked the kettle up. 'I should have figured it out before.'

'Figured? What ails you?'

She poured boiling water into the teapot. 'A form of speech. I meant, I've worked out what I need to do.' She put the lid on the pot, moved it onto a tray, and carried it back into the living room. 'It's quite simple. I've been worrying about having to camp in the woods in winter, or make myself understood, or keep up appearances with you. That's wrong. What I should have been thinking about is how I can move *myself* about, over there, to somewhere where there's shelter, without involving anyone else. Right?'

'That makes sense. But how are you going to do that, unless you walk? You couldn't take a horse through. Come to think of it, I haven't seen any horses here – '

Miriam took a deep breath. 'Brill, when Paulie gets back I think we're going to go shopping. For an all-terrain bicycle, a pair of night-vision goggles, a sewing machine, and some fabric . . .'

*

The devil was in the details. In the end it took Miriam two days to buy her bicycle. She spent the first day holed up with cycle magazines, spokehead websites, and the TV blaring extreme sports at her. The second day consisted of being patronized in successive shops by men in skintight neon Lycra bodysuits, to Brill's quietly scandalized amusement. In the end, the vehicle of Miriam's desire turned out to be a Dahon folding mountain bike, built out of chromed aluminum tubes. It wasn't very light, but at thirty pounds – including carrying case and toolset – she could carry it across easily enough, and it wasn't a toy. It was a real mountain bike that folded down into something she could haul in a backpack and, more importantly, something that could carry herself and a full load over dirt trails as fast as a horse.

'What *is* that thing?' Brill asked, when she finished unfolding it on a spread of newspapers on Paulette's living room carpet. 'It looks like something you torture people with.'

'That's a fair assessment.' Miriam grimaced as she worked the alien keys on the saddle post, trying to get it locked at a comfortable height. 'I haven't ridden a bike in years. Hope I haven't forgotten how.'

'When you sit on that thing, you can't possibly be modest.'

'Well, no,' Miriam admitted. 'I plan to only use it out of sight of other people.' She finished on the saddle and began hunting for an attachment place for the toolkit. 'The Swiss army used to have a regiment of soldiers who rode these things, as mounted infantry – not cavalry. They could cover two hundred miles a day on roads, seventy a day in the mountains. I'm no soldier, but I figure this will get me around faster than my feet.'

'You'll still need clothing,' Brill pointed out. 'And so will I. What I came across in isn't suitable for stamping around in the forest in winter! And we couldn't possibly be seen wearing your camping gear if we expect to stay in a coaching inn.'

'Yup. Which is where this machine comes in.' Miriam pointed to the other big box, occupying a large chunk of the floor. 'I take it there's no chance that you already know how to use an overlocker?'

The overlocker took them most of the rest of the day to figure out, and it nearly drove Paulette to distraction when she came home from the errand she'd been running to find Miriam oiling a bicycle in the hall and Brill puzzling out the manual for an industrial sewing machine and a bunch of costume patterns Miriam had bought. 'You're turning my house into an asylum!' she accused Miriam, after kicking her shoes off.

'Yeah, I am. How's the office hunt going?'

'Badly,' snapped Paulette. Her voice changed: 'Offices, oy, have we got offices! You should see our offices, such wonderful offices you have never imagined! By the way, how long have you been in business? There'll be a deposit if it's less than two years.'

'Uh-huh.' Miriam nodded. 'How big a deposit?'

'Six months' rent. For two thousand square feet with a loading bay and a thousand feet of office above it, that comes to about thirty thousand bucks. Plus municipal tax, sewer, electric, and gas. And the broadband you want.'

'Hmm.' Miriam nodded to herself, then hit the quick-release bolts. The bike folded in on itself like an intricate origami sculpture and she locked it down in its most compact position, then eased the carrying case over it.

'Hey, that's real neat,' Paulette said admiringly. 'You turning into a fitness freak in your old age?'

'Don't change the subject.' Miriam grunted, then upended the case and zipped it shut. Folded, the bike was a beast. She could get the thing comfortably on her back but would be hard put to carry anything else. *Hmm.* 'Back in a minute.' She shouldered the bike pack and marched to the back door that opened on Paulette's yard. 'Here goes nothing,' she muttered, and pulled out her locket.

Half an hour later she was back without the bike, staggering slightly, shivering with cold, and rubbing her sore forehead. 'Oh, I really don't need to do that so fast,' she groaned.

'If you *will* do that with no preparation – '

'No, no. I took my pills, boss, honest. It's just *really* cold over there.'

'Where did you stash it?' Paulie asked practically.

'Where your back wall is, over on the other side, where there's nothing but forest. *Brrr.* Up against a tree, I cut a gash in the bark.' She brandished her knife. 'Won't be hard to find if we go over from here: Main thing will be walking to the road, the nearest one is about half a mile away. Better go in the morning.'

'Right,' Paulette said skeptically. 'About the rent.'

'Yeah. Look, give me fifteen minutes to recover and I'll get my coat. Then we can go look at the building, and if it's right we'll go straight to the bank and move another whack of cash so you can wave a deposit under their nose.' She straightened up. 'We'll take Brill. There's a theatrical costume shop we need to check out; it might speed things up a bit.' Her expression hardened. 'I'm tired of waiting, and the longer this drags on the harder it'll be to explain it to Angbard. If I don't get in touch soon, I figure he'll cut off my credit until I surface. So it's time to hit the road.'

*

Two days later, a frigid morning found Miriam dozing fitfully on a lumpy, misshapen mattress with a quietly snoring lump to her left. She opened her eyes. *Where am I?* she wondered for a moment, then memory rescued the day. *Oh.* A pile of canvas bags before her nose formed a hump up against the rough, unpainted planks of the wall. The snoring lump twitched, pushing her closer to the edge. The light streamed in through a small window, its triangular tiles of glass uneven and bubbled. She'd slept fully dressed except for her boots and cloak, and she felt filthy. To make matters worse, something had bitten her in the night, found her to its taste, and invited its family and friends along for Thanksgiving dinner.

'Aargh.' She sat up and swung her feet out, onto the floor. Even through her wool stockings the boards felt cold as ice. The thunder-mug under the bed was freezing cold too, she discovered as she squatted over it to piss. In fact, the air was so chilly it leached all the heat out of any part of her anatomy she exposed to it. She finished her business fast and shoved the pot back under the bed to freeze.

'Wake up,' she called softly to Brilliana. 'Rise and shine! We've got a good day ahead!'

'Oh, my head.' Brill surfaced bleary-eyed and disheveled from under the quilt. '*Your* hostelries aren't like this.'

'Well, this one won't stay like this for long if I get my way. My mouth tastes like something died in it. Let me get my boots on and warm my toes up a bit.'

'Hah.' Brilliana's expression was pessimistic. 'They let the fire run low, I'd say.' She found the chamber pot. Miriam nodded and looked away. *So much for en suite bathrooms,* she thought. 'You stand up, now,' Brill ordered after a minute.

'Okay. How do I look?' asked Miriam.

'Hmm. I think you will pass. Don't brush your hair until we are out of sight, though. It's too clean to be seen in daylight, from all those marvelous soaps everyone uses on the other side, and we don't want to attract attention. Humph. So what shall we do today, my lady?'

'Well, I think we'll start by eating breakfast and paying the nice man.' *Nice* was not an adjective Miriam would normally use on a hotelier like the one lurking downstairs – back home she'd be more inclined to call the police – but standards of personal service varied wildly in the Gruinmarkt. 'Let's hit the road to Hasleholm. As soon as we're out of sight, I'm going to vanish. You have your pistol?'

Brill nodded.

'Okay, then you're set up. It *should* just be a quiet day's walk for you. If you run into trouble, first try to get off the road, then shoot – I don't want you taking any chances, even if there isn't much of a bandit problem around these parts in winter. Luckily you're more heavily armed than anyone you could possibly meet except a Clan caravan.'

308

'Right.' Brill nodded uncertainly. 'You're sure that strange contraption will work?'

'Yes. Trust me.'

Breakfast below consisted of two chipped wooden bowls of oatmeal porridge, salted, eaten in the kitchen under the watchful (if squinting) eyes of the publican's wife – which made it harder for Miriam to palm her pills. She made a song and dance of reciting some kind of grace prayer over the bowls. Miriam waited patiently, moving her lips randomly – her mute and uncomprehending condition explained by Brill, in her capacity as long-suffering daughter.

Barely half an hour later, Miriam and Brill were on the road again, heading toward the coast, breath steaming in the frigid morning air. It was bitterly dry. A heavy frost had fallen overnight, but not much snow. Miriam hunched beneath a heavy canvas knapsack that held her bicycle and extra supplies. Brill, too, bore a heavy bag, for Miriam had made two trips through to cache essential supplies before they began this trip. Although they'd come only two miles from Paulette's house, they were centuries away in the most important way imaginable. Out here, even a minor injury such as a twisted ankle could be a disaster. But they had certain advantages that normally only the Clan and its constituent families would have – from their modern hiking boots to the hefty automatic pistol Brill carried in a holster concealed beneath her Thinsulate-lined cloak.

'This had better work.' Miriam's teeth chattered slightly as she spoke. 'I'm going to feel *really* stupid if it turns out that this locket doesn't work here, either.'

'My mother said you could tell if they're dead. Have you looked at it since we came through?'

'No.' Miriam fumbled in her pouch for it. It clicked open easily and she shut it at once. 'Ick. It'll work, all right, if I don't spill my guts. It feels *rougher* than the other one.'

Frozen leaf skeletons crunched beneath their boots. The post house was soon out of sight, the road empty and almost untraveled in winter. Bare trees thrust limbs out above them, bleak and barren in the harsh light of morning. 'Are we out of sight, yet?' asked Miriam.

'Yes.' Brill stopped. 'Might as well get an early start.'

Miriam paused beside her. She shuffled her feet. 'Don't wait long. If I don't return within about five minutes, assume it means everything's all right. Just keep walking and I'll join you at the post house. If you hear anyone coming on the road, hide. If I'm late, wait over for one day then buy a horse or mule, head for Fort Lofstrom, and ask to be taken to Angbard. Clear?'

'Clear.' For a moment Brill froze, then she leaned forward and embraced Miriam. 'Sky Father protect you,' she whispered.

'And you,' said Miriam, more surprised than anything else. She hugged Brill back. 'Take care.' Then she pulled away, pulled out the assassin's locket, and, standing in the middle of the road, stared into its writhing depths.

*

It was twelve o'clock, and all the church bells in Boston were chiming noon.

The strange woman received nothing more than covert glances as she walked along The Mall, eyes flickering to either side. True, she wore a heavy backpack – somewhat singular for a woman – and a most peculiar cap, and her dress was about as far from fashionable as it was possible to be without street urchins harassing her with accusations of vile popery; but she walked with an air of granite determination that boded ill for anyone who got in her way.

Traffic was light but fast, and she seemed self-conscious as she looked both ways repeatedly before crossing the street. An open Jolly-car rumbled past behind her, iron wheels striking sparks from the cobblestones. There was a burst of raucous laughter from the tars within, returning to the North Station for the journey back to the royal dockyards. She dodged nimbly, then reached the safety of the sidewalk.

The pedestrian traffic was thicker near the fish market and the chandlers and other merchant suppliers. The woman glanced at a winter chestnut seller, raised her nose as she sidestepped a senescent pure-collector mumbling over his sack of dogshit, then paused on the corner of The Mall and Jefferson Street, glancing briefly over one shoulder before muttering into her scarf.

'Memo: This is *not* Boston – at least, not the Boston I know. All the street names are wrong and the buildings are stone and brick, not wood or concrete. Traffic drives on the left and the automobiles – there aren't many – they've got chimneys, like steam locomotives. But the signs are in English and the roads are made of cobblestones or asphalt and it *feels* like Boston. Weird, really weird. It's more like home than Niejwein, anyway.'

She carried on down the street, mumbling into the tie-clip microphone pinned inside her scarf. A brisk wind wheezed down the street, threatening to raise it from her head: She tugged down briskly, holding it in place.

'I see both men and women in public – more men than women. Dress style is – hmm. Victorian doesn't describe it, exactly. Post-Victorian, maybe? Men wear cravats or scarves over high collars, with collarless double-breasted suits and big greatcoats. Hats all round, lots of hats, but I'm seeing suit jackets with yellow and blue stripes, or even louder schemes.' She strode on, past a baroque fire hydrant featuring cast-iron Chinese dragons poised ready to belch a stream of water. 'Women's costume is tightly tailored jackets and long skirts. Except lots of the younger ones are wearing trousers under knee-length skirts. Sort of Oriental in style.' A woman pedaled past her on a bicycle, primly upright. The bike was a black bone-shaker. 'Hm. For cycling, baggy trousers and something like a Pakistani tunic. Everyone wears a hat or scarf.' She glanced left. 'Shop prices marked in the windows. I just passed a cobbler's with a row of metal lasts and leather samples on display and – *Jesus Christ* – '

She paused and doubled back to stare into the small, grimy windows of the shop she'd nearly passed. A distant buzzing filled her ears. 'A mechanical adding machine – electric motor drive, with nixie tubes for a display. That's a divide key, what, nineteen-thirties tech? Punched cards? Forties? Wish I'd paid more attention in the museum. These guys are a *long* way ahead of the Gruinmarkt. Hey, that looks like an Edison phonograph, but there's no trumpet and those are tubes at the back. And a speaker.' She stared closer. The price . . . 'Price in pounds, *shillings,* and pennies,' she breathed into her microphone.

Miriam paused. A sense of awe stole over her. *This* isn't *Boston,* she realized. *This is something else again.* A whole new world, one that had vacuum tubes and adding machines and steam cars – a shadow fell across her. She glanced up and the breath caught in her throat. *And airships,* she thought. 'Airship!' she muttered. It was glorious, improbably streamlined, the color of old gold in the winter sunshine, engines rattling the window glass as it rumbled overhead, pointing into the wind. *I can really work here,* she realized, excitedly. She paused, looking in the window of a shipping agent: Greenbaum et Pty, 'Gateways to the world'.

''Scuse me, ma'am. Can I help you with anything?'

She looked down, hurriedly. A big, red-faced man with a bushy moustache and a uniform, flat-topped blue helmet – *Oops,* she thought. 'I hope so,' she said timidly. *Gulp. Try to fake a French accent?* 'I am newly arrived in, ah, town. Can you, kind sir, direct me to a decent and fair pawnbroker?'

'Newly arrived?' The cop looked her up and down dubiously, but made no move toward either his billy club or the brass whistle that hung on a chain around his neck. Something about her made up his mind for him. Maybe it was the lack of patching or dirt on her clothes, or the absence of obvious malnutrition. 'Well now, a pawnbroker – you'll not want to be destitute within city limits by nightfall, hear? The poorhouse is near to overflowing this season and you wouldn't want a run-in with the bench, now, would ye?'

Miriam bobbed her head. 'Thank you kindly, sir, but I'll be well looked after if I can just raise enough money to contact my sister. She and her husband sent for me to help with the children.'

'Well then.' He nodded. 'Go down Jefferson here, turn a left into Highgate. That'll bring you to Holmes Alley. *Don't* go down the Blackshaft by mistake, it's a rookery and you'll never find your way out. In Holmes Alley you can find the shop of Erasmus Burgeson, and he'll set you up nicely.'

'Oh *thank* you,' Miriam gushed, but the cop had already turned away – probably looking for a vagrant to harass.

She hurried along for a block then, remembering the cop's directions, followed them. More traffic passed on the road and overhead.

Tractors pulling four or even six short trailers blocked the street intermittently, and an incongruous yellow pony trap clattered past. Evidently yellow was the interuniverse color of cabs, although Miriam couldn't guess what Boston's environmentalists would have made of the coal burners. There were shops here, shops by the dozen, but no department stores, nor supermarkets, or gas-burning cars, or color photographs. The advertisements on the sides of the buildings were painted on, simple slogans like BUY EDISON'S ROSE PETAL SOAP FOR SKIN LIKE FLOWER BLOSSOM. And there was, now she knew what to look for, no sign of beggars.

A bell rang as Miriam pushed through the door of Erasmus Burgeson's shop, beneath the three gold spheres that denoted his trade. It was dark and dusty, shelves racked high with table settings, silverware, a cabinet full of pistols, other less identifiable stuff – in the other side of the shop, rack after rack of dusty clothing. The cash register, replete with cherubim and gold leaf, told its own story: And as she'd hoped, the counter beside it displayed a glass lid above a velvet cloth layered in jewelry. There didn't seem to be anybody in the shop. Miriam looked about uneasily, trying to take it all in. *This is what people here consider valuable,* she thought. *Better get a handle on it.*

A curtain at the back stirred as a gaunt figure pushed into the room. He shambled behind the counter and turned to stare at her. 'Haven't seen you in here before, have I?' he asked, quizzically.

'Uh, no.' Miriam shuffled. 'Are you Mr. Burgeson?' she asked.

'The same.' He didn't smile. Dressed entirely in black, his sleeves and trousers thin as pipe cleaners, all he'd need would be a black stovepipe hat to look like a revenant from the Civil War. 'And who would you be?'

'My name is Miriam, uh, Fletcher.' She pursed her lips. 'I was told you are a pawnbroker.'

'And what else would I be in a shop like this?' He cocked his head to one side, like a parrot, his huge dark eyes probing at her in the gloom.

'Well. I'm lately come to these shores.' She coughed. 'And I am short of money, if not in possessions that might be worth selling. I was hoping you might be able to set me up.'

'Possessions.' Burgeson sat down – perched – on a high, backless wooden stool that raised his knees almost to the level of the counter-top. 'It depends what type of possession you have in mind. I can't buy just any old tat now, can I?'

'Well. To start with, I have a couple of pieces of jewelry.' He nodded encouragingly, so Miriam continued. 'But then, I have in mind something more substantial. You see, where I come from I am of not inconsiderable means, and I have not entirely cut myself off from the old country.'

'And what country would that be?' asked Burgeson. 'I only ask because of the requirements of the Aliens and Sedition Act,' he added hastily.

'That would be – ' Miriam licked her lips. 'Scotland.'

'Scotland.' He stared at her. 'With an accent like that,' he said with heavy irony. 'Well, well, well. Scotland it is. Show me the jewelry.'

'One moment.' Miriam walked forward, peered down at the countertop. 'Hmm. These are a bit disappointing. Is this all you deal in?'

'Ma'am.' He hopped down from the stool. 'What do you take me for? This is the common stock on public display, where any mounte-bank might smash and grab. The better class I keep elsewhere.'

'Oh.' She reached into her pouch and fumbled for a moment, then pulled out what she'd been looking for. It was a small wooden box – purchased from a head shop in Cambridge, there being a pro-nounced shortage of cheap wooden jewelry boxes on the market – containing two pearl earrings. Real pearls. Big ones. 'For starters, I'd like you to put a value on these.'

'Hmm.' Burgeson picked the box up, chewing his lower lip. 'Excuse me.' He whipped out a magnifying lens and examined them minutely. 'I'll need to test them,' he murmured, 'but if these are real pearls, they're worth a pretty penny. Where did you get them?'

'That is for me to know and you to guess.' She tensed.

'Hah.' He grinned at her cadaverously. 'You'd better have a good story next time you try to sell them. I'm not sticking my neck in a noose for your mistress if she decides to send the thief-takers after you.'

'Hmm. What makes you think I'm a light-fingered servant?' she asked.

'Well.' He looked down his nose at her. 'Your clothes are not what a woman of fashion, or even of her own means, would wear – '

'Fresh off the boat,' Miriam observed.

'And earrings are among the most magnetic of baubles to those of a jackdaw disposition,' he added.

'And wanting a suit of clothes that does *not* mark me out as a stranger,' Miriam commented.

'Besides which,' he added with some severity, '*Scotland* has not existed for a hundred and seventy years. It's all part of Grande Bretaigne.'

'Oh.' Miriam covered her mouth. *Shit!* 'Well then.' She mustered up a sickly smile. 'How about this?'

The quarter-kilogram bar of solid gold was about an inch wide, two inches long, and half an inch thick. She set it down on the display case like an intrusion from another world, shimmering with the promise of wealth and power and riches.

'Well now,' breathed Burgeson, 'if *that* is what ladies of means pay their bills with in Scotland, maybe it's not such an unbelievable fiction after all.'

Miriam nodded. *It had better cover the bills,* she thought, *the damn thing set me back nearly three thousand dollars.* 'It all depends how honest you aren't,' she said briskly. 'There are more where this one comes from. I'm looking to buy several things, including but not limited to money. I need to fit in. I don't care if you're fiddling your taxes or lying to the government, all I care about is whether you're honest with your customers. You don't know me, and if you don't want to, you'll never see me again. On the other hand, if you say "yes" – ' she met his eyes – 'this need not be our last transaction. Not by a very long way.'

'Hmm.' Burgeson stared right back at her. 'Are you in French employ?' he asked.

'Huh?'

Miriam's fleeting look of puzzlement seemed to reassure him. 'Well *that's* good,' he said genially. 'Excuse me while I fetch the aqua regia: If this is pure I can advance you, oh, ten pounds immediately and another, ahum – ' he picked up the gold bar and placed it on the balance behind him – 'sixty-two and eight shillings by noon tomorrow.'

'I don't think so.' Miriam shook her head. 'I'll take ten today, and sixty tomorrow – plus five full pounds' credit in your shop, here and now, for goods you hold.' She'd been eyeing the price tags. The shilling, a twentieth of a pound, seemed to occupy the same role as the dollar back home, except that they went further. Pounds were *big* currency.

'Ridiculous.' He stared at her. 'Three pounds.'

'Four.'

'Done,' he said, unnervingly rapidly. Miriam had a feeling that she'd been had, somehow, but nodded. He strode over to the door and flipped the sign in the window pane to CLOSED. 'Let me test out this bar. I'll just take a sample with this scalpel, mind . . .' He hurried into the back room. A minute later he re-emerged, bearing a glass measuring cylinder full of water into which he dropped the gold bar. Scribbled measurements followed. Finally he nodded. 'Oh, most satisfying,' he muttered to himself before looking at her. 'Your sample is indeed of acceptable purity,' he said, looking almost surprised. Reaching into an inner pocket he produced a battered wallet, from which he plucked improbably large banknotes. 'Nine one-pound notes, milady, the balance in silver and a few coppers. I hope these are to your satisfaction; the bank across the street will happily exchange them, I assure you.' Next he produced a fountain pen and a ledger, and a wax brick and a candle and a metal die. 'I shall just make out this promissory note for sixty pounds to you. If you would like to select from my wares, I can work while you equip yourself.'

'Do you have a measuring tape?' she asked.

'Indeed.' He pulled one down from a hook behind the counter. 'If you need any alterations making, Missus Borisovitch across the way is a most excellent seamstress, works while you wait. And her daughter is a fine milliner, too.'

Over the next hour, Miriam ransacked the pawnbroker's shop. The range of clothing hanging in mothballs from rails all the way up to the ceiling, a dizzying twenty feet up, was huge and strange, but she knew what she wanted – anything that wouldn't look too alien while she realized her liquid assets and found a real dressmaker to equip her for the sort of business she intended to conduct. Which would almost certainly require formal business wear, as high finance and legal work usually did back home. For a miracle, Miriam discovered a matching jacket, blouse, and skirt that was in good condition and close enough to her size to fit. She changed in Burgeson's cramped, damp-smelling cellar while he reopened the shop. The outfit took some getting used to, but in his dusty mirror she saw someone not unlike the women she'd passed on her way into town.

'Ah.' Burgeson nodded to her. 'That is a good choice. It will, however, cost you one pound fourteen and sixpence.'

'Sure.' Miriam nodded. 'Next, I want a history book.'

'A history book.' He looked at her oddly. 'Any particular title?'

She smiled thinly. 'One covering the past three hundred years, in detail.'

'Hmm.' Burgeson ducked back into the back of the shop. While he was gone, Miriam located a pair of kidskin gloves and a good topcoat. The hats all looked grotesque to her eye, but in the end she settled on something broad-brimmed and floppy, with not too much fur. He returned and dumped a hardbound volume on the glass display case. 'You could do worse than start with this. *Alfred's Annals of the New British.*'

'I could.' She stared at it. 'Anything else?'

'Or.' He pulled another book up – bound in brown paper, utterly anonymous, thinner and lighter. 'This.' He turned it to face her, open at the fly-leaf.

'*The Hanoverian Exodus Reconsidered* – ' she bit her lip when she saw the author. 'Karl Marx. Hmm. Keep this on the bottom shelf, do you?'

'It's only prudent,' he said, apologetically closing it and sliding it under the first book. 'I'd strongly recommend it, though,' he added. 'Marx pulls no punches.'

'Right. How much for both of them?'

'Six shillings for the Alfred, a pound for the Marx – you *do* realize that simply being caught with a copy of it can land you a flogging, if not five years' exile in Canadia?'

'I didn't.' She suppressed a shudder. 'I'll take them both. And the hat, gloves, and coat.'

'It's been a pleasure doing business with you, madam,' he said fervently. 'When shall I see you again?'

'Hmm.' She narrowed her eyes. 'No need for the money tomorrow. I will not be back for at least five days. But if you want another of those pieces – '

'How many can you supply?' he asked, slipping the question in almost casually.

'As many as you can shift,' she replied. 'But on the next visit, no more than two.'

'Well then.' He chewed his lower lip. 'For two, assuming this one tests out correctly and the next do likewise, I will pay the sum of two hundred pounds.' He glanced over his shoulder. 'But not all at once. It's too dangerous.'

'Can you pay in services other than money?' she asked.

'It depends.' He raised an eyebrow. 'I don't deal in spying, sedition, or popery.'

'I'm not in any of those businesses,' she said, thinking *Popery*? 'But I'm really, truly, from a long way away. I need to establish a toehold here that allows me to set up an import/export business. That will mean . . . hmm. Do you need identity papers to move about? Passports? Or to open a bank account, create a company, hire a lawyer to represent me?'

He shook his head. 'From *too* far away,' he muttered. 'God help me, yes to all of those.'

'Well, then.' She looked at him. 'I'll need papers. *Good* papers, preferably real ones from real people who don't need them anymore – not killed, just the usual, a birth certificate from a babe who died before their first birthday,' she added hastily.

'You warm the cockles of my heart.' He stared at her thoughtfully. 'I'm glad to see you appear to have scruples. Are you sure you don't want to tell me where you come from?'

She raised a finger to her lips. 'Not yet. Maybe when I trust you.'

'Ah, well.' He bowed. 'Before you leave, may I offer you a glass of port? Just a little drink to our future business relationship.'

'Indeed you may.' She surreptitiously pushed back her glove to check her watch. 'I believe I have half an hour to spare before I must depart. My carriage turns back into a pumpkin at midnight.'

PART SEVEN

POINT OF
DIVERGENCE

HISTORY LESSON

'You are telling me that you *don't know* where she is?' The man standing by the glass display case radiated disbelief.

Normally the contents of the case – precious relics of the Clan, valuable beyond belief – would have fascinated him, but right now his attention was focused on the bearer of bad news.

'I told you she'd be difficult.' The duke's secretary was unapologetic. He didn't sneer, but his expression was one of thinly veiled impatience. 'You are dealing with a woman who was born and raised on the other side; she was clearly going to be a handful right from the start. I told you that the best way to deal with her would be to co-opt her and move her in a direction she was already going in, but you wouldn't listen. And after that business with the hired killer – '

'That *hired killer* was my own blood, I'll thank you to remember.' Esau's tone of voice was ominously low.

'I don't care whether he was the prince-magistrate of Xian-Ju province, it was dumb! Now you've told Angbard's men that someone outside the Clan is trying to kill her, and you've driven her underground, *and* you've ruined her usefulness to me. I had it all taken care of until you attacked her. And then, to go after her but kill the wrong woman by mistake when I had everything in hand . . . !'

'You didn't tell us she was traveling in company. Or hiding in the Lady Olga's rooms. Nor did we expect Olga's lady-in-waiting to get nosy and take someone else's bait. We're not the only ones to have problems. You said you had her as good as under control?' Esau turned to stare at Matthias. Today the secretary wore the riding-out garb of a minor nobleman of the barbarian east: brocade jacket over long woolen leggings, a hat with a plume of peacock feathers, and riding boots. 'You think forging the old man's will takes care of anything at all? Are you losing your grip?'

'No.' Matthias rested his hand lightly on his sword's hilt. 'Has it occurred to you that as Angbard's heir she would have been more open to suggestions, rather than less? Wealth doesn't necessarily translate into safety, you know, and she was clearly aware of her own isolation. I was trying to get her under control, or at least frightened into cooperating, by lining up the lesser families against her and positioning myself as her protector. You spooked her instead, before I could complete the groundwork. You exposed her to too much too soon, and the result is our shared loss. All the more so, since *someone* – whoever – tried to rub her out with Lady Olga.'

'And whose fault is it that she got away?' Esau demanded. 'Whose little tripwire failed?'

'Mine, I'll admit.' Matthias shrugged again. 'But I'm not the one who's blundering around in the dark around here. I really wanted to enlist her in our cause. Willingly or unwillingly, it doesn't matter. With a recognized heir in our pocket, we could have enough votes that when we get rid of Angbard . . . well. If that failed, we'd be no worse off with her dead, but it was hardly a desirable goal. It's a good thing for you that I've got some contingency plans in hand.'

'If the balance of power in the Clan tips too far toward the Lof-strom–Thorold–Hjorth axis, we risk losing what leverage we've got,' said Esau. 'Never mind the old bat's power play. What did she think she was up to, anyway? If the council suspected . . .' He shook his head. 'You have to get this back under control. Find her and neutral-ize her, or we likely lose all the ground we have made in the past two years.'

'I risk losing a lot more than that,' Matthias reminded him point-edly. 'Why did your people try to kill her? She was a natural dissident. More use to us alive than dead.'

'It's not for the likes of you to question our goals.'

Matthias tightened his grip on his sword and turned slowly aside, keeping his eyes on Esau the whole time. 'Retract that,' he said flatly.

'I – ' Esau caught his eye. A momentary nod. 'I apologize.'

'We are partners in this,' Matthias said quietly, 'to the extent that both our necks are forfeit if our venture comes to light. That being the case, it is essential that I know not only what your organization's intended actions are, but what goals you hope to achieve – so that I can avoid conflicts of interest. Do you understand?'

Esau nodded again. 'I told you there might be preexisting orders. There was indeed such an order,' he said reluctantly. 'It took time to come to light, that's all.'

'What? You mean the order for – gods below, you're still trying to kill the mother and her *infant*? After what, a third of a century?'

It was Esau's turn to shrug. 'Our sanctified elder never rescinded the command, and it is not for us to question his word. Once they learned of the child's continued existence, my cousins were honor-bound to attempt to carry out the orders.'

'That's as stupid as anything I've ever heard from the Clan council. Times change, you know.'

'I know! But where would we be without loyalty to our fore-fathers?' Esau looked frustrated for a moment. Then he pointed to the glass display case. 'Continuity. Without it, what would the Clan be? Or the hidden families?'

'Without – that?' Matthias squinted, as against a bright light. A leather belt with a curiously worked brass buckle, a knife, a suit of clothes, a leatherbound book. 'That's not the Clan, whatever you think. That's just where the Clan began.'

'My ancestor, too, you know.'

Matthias shook his head. 'It wasn't clever, meeting here.'

'We're safe enough.' Esau turned his back on the Founder's relics. 'The question is, what are we to do now?'

'If you can get your relatives to stop trying to kill her, we can try to pin the blame on someone else. A couple of candidates suggest themselves, mostly because they *have* been trying to kill her. If we do that then we can go back to plan A, which you'll agree is the most profitable outcome of this situation.'

'Not possible.' Esau drew a finger across his throat. 'The elders spoke, thirty-three years ago. I can't rescind that order. Only our cur-rent elder can do that, if he cares to do so. And he won't dishonor the ancestors' memories lightly.'

Matthias sighed. 'Well, if you insist, we can play it your way. But it's going to be a lot harder, now. I suppose if I can get my hands on her foster-mother that will probably serve as a lure, but it's going to cost you – '

'I believe I can arrange a gratuity if you'd take care of this loose end for us. Maybe not on the same scale as owning your own puppet countess, but sufficient recompense for your actions.'

'In that case I'll set the signs and alert my agents. At least here's something we can agree on.'

'Indeed.'

Matthias opened the door into the outer receiving room of the cramped old merchant's house. 'Come on.'

Esau followed Matthias out of the small storeroom and down a narrow staircase that led out into the courtyard. 'So what do you propose to do once she's dead?'

'Do?' Matthias stopped and stared at the messenger. 'I'm going to see if I can salvage the situation and go right on as I was before. What did you expect?'

'Do you really think you can take control of the Clan's security – even from your current position – without being an actual inner family member and Clan shareholder?'

'Watch me.'

*

Gathering twilight. Miriam hid from the road behind a deadfall half buried in snow while she stripped off her outer garments, her teeth chattering from cold as she pulled on a pair of painfully chilly jeans. She folded her outfit carefully into the upper half of her pack, then stacked the disguise she'd started out wearing in the morning on top. Then she unfolded and secured the bike. Finally she hooked the bulky night-vision goggles around her face – like wearing a telescope in front of each eye – zipped the seam in the backpack that turned it into a pair of panniers, slung them over the bike, and set off.

The track flew past beneath her tires, the crackle of gravel and occasional pop of a breaking twig loud in the forest gloom. The white coating that draped around her damped out all noise, and the clouds above were huge and dark, promising to drop a further layer of snow across the scene before morning.

Riding a bike wasn't exactly second nature, but the absence of other traffic made it easier to get to grips with. The sophisticated gears were a joy to use, making even the uphill stretches at least tolerable. *Seven-league boots,* she thought. The other town, whatever it was called, not-Boston, was built for legs and bicycles. She'd have to buy one of the local bikes next time she went there, whenever that was. Despite her toast to the prospects of future business with Burgeson, she had her reservations. Poor Laws, Sedition Acts, and a cop who obligingly gave directions to a clearly bent pawnbroker – it added up to a picture that made her acutely nervous. *It's so complex! What did he mean, there's no Scotland? Until I know what their laws and customs are like it's going to be too dangerous to go back.*

The miles spun by. After an hour and a half Miriam could feel them in her calf muscles, aching with every push on the pedals – but she was making good speed, and by the time darkness was complete the road dipped down toward the coast, paralleling the Charles River. Eventually she turned a corner, taking her into view of a hunched figure squatting by the roadside.

Miriam braked hard, jumped off the bike. 'Brill?' she asked.

'Miriam?' Brill's face was a bright green pool in the twilight displayed by her night goggles. 'Is that you?'

'Yes.' Miriam walked closer, then flicked her goggles up and pulled out a pocket flashlight. 'Are you okay?'

'Frozen half to death.' Brill smiled shakily. 'But otherwise unharmed.'

A vast wave of relief broke over Miriam. 'Well, if that's *all* . . .'

'This cloak lining is amazing,' Brill added. 'The post house is just past the next bend. I've only been waiting for an hour. Shall we go?'

'Sure.' Miriam glanced down. 'I'd better change, first.' It was the work of a few minutes to disassemble the bike, pull on her outfit over her trousers, and turn the bike and panniers into a backpack disguised by a canvas cover. 'Let's get some dinner,' said Miriam.

'Your magic goggles, and lantern.' Brill coughed discreetly.

'Oh. Of course.' Together they fumbled their way through the darkness toward the promise of food and a bed, be it ever so humble.

*

Almost exactly twenty-four hours later, Paulette's doorbell chimed. 'Who is it?' she called from behind the closed door.

'It's us! Let us in!' She opened the door. Brill stumbled in first, followed by Miriam. 'Trick or treat?'

'Trick.' Paulette stood back. 'Hey, witchy!'

'It is, isn't it.' Miriam closed the door. 'It itches, too. I don't know how to put this discreetly – have you got any flea spray?'

'Fleas! Away with you!' Paulette held her nose. 'How did it go?'

'I'll tell you in a few minutes. Over a coffee, once I've made it to the bathroom – oh shit.' Miriam stared up the staircase at Brilliana's vanishing feet. 'Well at least that's sorted.' She dropped her pack onto the carpet; it landed with a dull thump. ''Scuse me, but I am going to strip. It's an emergency.'

'Wait right there,' said Paulie, hurrying upstairs.

By the time she returned, bearing a T-shirt and a pair of sweats from the luggage, Miriam had her boots off and was down to outer garments. 'Damn, central heating,' she said wonderingly. 'There's nothing to make you appreciate it like three days in a Massachusetts winter without it. Well, two and a half.'

'Did you get where you wanted to go?' Paulie asked.

'Yeah.' Miriam cracked a wide, tired grin.

'Give me five, baby!'

High fives were all very well, but when Miriam winced Paulette got the message. 'Use the living room,' she said. 'Get the hell out of those rags and then go up to my bedroom, okay? I'll flea-bomb the carpet. You can use the bedroom shower.'

'You're a babe, babe.'

An hour later Miriam – infinitely warmer and cleaner – sat curled at one end of Paulette's living room sofa with a mug of strong tea. Brill, wrapped in a borrowed bathrobe, sat at the other end. 'So tell me, how was your walk in the woods?' Paulette asked Brill. 'Meet any bears?'

'Bears?' Brill looked puzzled. 'No, and a good thing – ' she caught Miriam's eye. 'Oh. No, it was uneventful.'

'Well then.' Paulie focused on Miriam. 'You had more luck, huh? *Not* just a walk in the woods?'

'Well, apart from Brill half freezing to death while I was trying not to get arrested, it was fine.'

'Getting. Arrested.' Paulette picked up the teapot and poured herself a mug. 'You're not getting away with that, Beckstein. Didn't they accept your press pass or something?'

'It's Boston, but not as we know it,' Miriam explained. 'About two miles southeast of here I found myself on the edge of town. They speak English and they drive automobiles, but that's about as far as the similarities go.' She pulled out her dictaphone and turned the volume up: *Zeppelin overhead, with a British flag on it! Uh, four propellers, sounds like diesel engines. There goes another steam car. They seem to make them big deliberately, I don't think I've seen anything smaller than a fifty-eight Caddy yet.'*

Paulette closed her mouth with a visible effort. 'Did you take photographs?' she asked.

'Uh-huh.' Miriam held up her wrist. 'You'll have them just as soon as I get my Casio secret agent watch plugged into the computer. I *knew* those Inspector Gadget toys would come in handy sooner or later.'

'Toys.' Paulette rolled her eyes.

'Well, now we've got a whole new world to not understand,' said Miriam. 'Any constructive suggestions?'

'Yep.' Paulette put her mug down. 'Before you go over again, girl, we work out what you're going to do. You need a lawyer or business manager over there, right? And you need money, and somewhere to live, and we need to find a place on the far side that's away from human habitation in Brill's world and we can rent on our own side. Right? And we need to understand what you're messing with before you get yourself arrested. So spill it all.'

Miriam reached into her bag and pulled out two books then dumped them on the table with a bump. 'History lesson time. Watch out for the one with the brown paper cover,' she warned. 'It bites.'

Paulette opened that one first, looked at the flyleaf, and sucked in her breath. 'Communist?' she asked.

'Nope, it's much weirder than that.' Miriam picked up the other book. 'I'll start with this one, you start with that one, then we'll swap.'

Paulette glanced at the window. 'It's nearly eleven, for Pete's sake! You want I should pull an overnighter?'

'No, that won't be necessary.' Miriam put her book down and looked at her. 'I've been meaning to raise this for a while. I've been staying here, and I didn't mean to. I really appreciate you putting Brill up, but two guests is two too many and – '

'Shut up. You're going to stay here till you've told me what you've seen and gotten your act together to move out properly! And hit the deadline,' she muttered under her breath.

'Deadline?' Miriam raised an eyebrow.

'The Clan summit,' Brill explained tonelessly. She yawned. 'I told Paulie about it.'

'You can't let them do it!' Paulette insisted.

'Do what?' Miriam blinked.

'Move to declare you incompetent and make you a permanent ward of whoever the Clan deems appropriate,' Brill explained. She looked puzzled. 'Didn't you know? That's what Olga said Baron Oliver was muttering about.'

*

Iris raised the cup of coffee to her lips with both hands. She looked a little shaky today, but Miriam knew better than to make a fuss. 'So what did you do next?' she asked.

'I went to bed.' Miriam leaned back, then glanced around. The level of background noise in the museum food court was high and all their neighbors seemed to be otherwise preoccupied. 'What else could I do? Beltaigne is nearly five months away, and I'm not going to let the bastards stampede me.'

'But the other place, this new one – ' Iris sounded distracted – 'doesn't it take you a whole day to go each way, even if you have somewhere to stay at the other end?'

'There's no point going off half-cocked, Ma.' Miriam idly opened a tube of sugar crystals and stirred them into her latte. 'Look, if Baron Hjorth wants to declare me incompetent, he's going to have to come up with some evidence. He might shove it through if I'm not there to defend myself, but I figure the strongest defense I can get is proof that there's a conspiracy out there – a conspiracy that murdered my birth-mother and is trying to murder me, too, not just the petty shit he and my – grandmother – are shoveling at me. A second-strongest defense is evidence that I may be erratic, but I've come up with something valuable. Now, the assassin's locket takes me to this other world – call it world three – and I've got to wonder. Does this mean they're not part of the Clan or families? They're working on the other side and in world three, while the Clan works on the other side and here, call *here* world two and Niejwein is part of world one. I'm, I guess, the first member of the Clan to actually become aware of world three and be able to get over there. That means that I can see about finding whoever's sending the killers – see defense one, above – or see about opening up a whole new trade opportunity – see defense two, above. I'm going to tie the whole story up with a bow and hand it to them. And mess up Baron Hjorth's game into the bargain.' She rolled up the empty sugar tube into a tight little wad and threw it at the back of the booth.

'That sounds like my daughter,' Iris said thoughtfully. 'Don't let the bastards realize you've got the drop on them until it's too late for them to dodge. Morris would be proud of you.'

'Um.' Miriam nodded, unable to trust her tongue. 'How have you been? How did you get away from them tonight?'

'Well, you know, I haven't had much trouble with being under surveillance lately.' Iris sipped her coffee. 'Funny how they don't seem to be able to tell one old woman in a motorized blue wheelchair from another, isn't it?'

'Ma, you shouldn't have!'

'What, give some of my friends an opportunity for a little adventure?' Iris snorted and pushed her bifocals up her nose. 'Just because my daughter thinks she can go haring off to other worlds, running away from her problems – '

'It's the source of my problems, not the solution,' Miriam interrupted.

'Well good, just as long as you understand that.' Iris met her eyes with a coolly unreadable expression that slowly moderated into one of affection. 'You're grown up now and there's not a lot I can teach you. Just as well really, one day I won't be around to do the teaching and it'd be kind of embarrassing if – '

'Mother!'

'Don't you "mother" me! Listen, I raised you to face facts and deal with the world as it really is, not to pretend that if you stick your head in the sand problems will go away. I'm in late middle age and I'm damned if I'm not going to inflict my hard-earned wisdom on my only daughter. Come to think of it, I wish someone had beaten it into me when I was a child. Pah. But anyway. You're playing with fire, and I would really hate it if you got burned. You're going to try and track down these assassins from another universe, aren't you? What do you think they are?'

'I think – ' Miriam paused. 'They're like the Clan and the families,' she said finally. 'Only they travel between world one and world three, while the Clan travel between world one and world two, our world. I figure they decided the Clan were a threat a long time ago and that's probably something to do with, with why they tried to nail my mother all those years ago. And they're smaller and weaker than the Clan, that much seems obvious, so I can maybe set up in world three, their stronghold, before they notice me. I think.'

'Ambitious.' Iris paused. 'What did I tell you when you were young, about not jumping to conclusions?'

'Um. You know better? Is there something you haven't been telling me?'

Iris nodded. 'Can you permit your mother to keep one or two things to herself?'

'Guess so. Can you give your daughter any hints?'

'Only this.' Iris met her gaze unflinchingly. 'Firstly, do you really think you'd have been hidden from the families for all these years without someone over there covering your trail?'

'Ma – '

'I can't tell you for sure,' she added, 'but I think someone may have been watching over you. Someone who didn't want you dragged into all this – at least not until you were good and ready to look out for yourself.'

Miriam shook her head. 'Is that all? You think I've got a fairy god-mother?'

'Not exactly.' Iris finished her coffee. 'But here's a "secondly" for you to think about. Shortly after you surfaced, the strangers, these assassins, started hunting for you. To say nothing of the second bunch who tried to wipe out this Olga person. Doesn't that suggest something? What about that civil war among the families that you told me about?'

'Are you trying to suggest it's part of some sixty-year-old feud? Or that it isn't over?'

'Not exactly. I'm wondering if the sixty-year-old feud wasn't part of *this* business, if you follow my drift. Like, started by outsiders meddling for their own purposes.'

'That's – ' Miriam paused for thought – 'Paranoid! I mean, *why* – '

'What better way to weaken a powerful enemy than to get it fighting itself?' Iris asked.

'Oh.' Miriam was silent for a while. 'You're saying that because of who I am – nothing more, just because of who my parents were – I'm the focus of a civil war?'

'Possibly. And you may just have reignited it by crawling out of the woodwork. I'm wishing I hadn't given you the shoebox now.' Iris looked thoughtful. 'Do you have any better suggestions? Are you involved in anything else that might explain what's going on?'

'Roland – ' Miriam stopped. Iris stared at her. 'You said not to trust any of them,' Miriam continued, 'but I think I can trust him. Up to a point.'

Iris met her eyes. 'People do the strangest things for money and love,' she said, a curious expression on her face. 'I should know.' She chuckled. 'Watch your back, dear. And . . . call me if you need me. I don't promise I'll be there to help – with my health that would be rash – but I'll do my best.'

*

The next morning Paulette arrived back at the house around noon, whistling jauntily. 'I did it!' she declared, startling Miriam out of the history book she was working up a headache over. 'We move in tomorrow!'

'We do?' Miriam shook her head as Brill came in behind Paulie and closed the door, carefully wiping the snow off her boots on the mat just inside.

'We do!' Paulette threw something at her; reaching out instinctively, Miriam grabbed a bunch of keys.

'Where to?'

'The office of your dreams, madam chief high corporate executive!'

'You found somewhere?' Miriam stood up.

'Not only have I *found* somewhere, I've rented it for six months up front.' Paulette threw down a bundle of papers on the living room table. 'Look. A thousand square feet of not-entirely-brilliant office space not far from Cambridgeport. The main thing in its favor is a downstairs entrance and a yard with a high wall around it, and access. The parking is on the street, which is a minus. But it was cheap – about as cheap as you can get anything near the waterfront for these days, anyway.' Paulie pulled a face. 'Used to belong to a small and not very successful architect's practice, then they moved out or retired or something and I grabbed a three-year lease.'

'Okay.' Miriam sighed. 'What's the damage?'

'Ten thousand bucks deposit up front, another ten thousand in rent. About eight hundred to get gas and power hooked up, and we're going to get a lovely bill from We the Peepul in a couple of months, bleeding us hard enough to give Dracula anemia. Anyway, we can move in tomorrow. It could really use a new carpet and a coat of paint inside, but it's open plan and there's a small kitchen area.'

'The backyard looked useful,' Brill said hesitantly.

'Paulie took you to see it?'

'Yeah.' Brill nodded. *Where'd she pick that up from?* Miriam wondered: Maybe she was beginning to adjust, after all.

'What did you think of it?' Miriam asked as Paulette hung her coat up and headed upstairs on some errand.

'That it's where ordinary people *work*? There's nowhere for livestock, not enough light for needlework or spinning or tapestry, not enough ventilation for dyeing or tanning, not enough water for brewing – ' She shrugged. 'But it looks very nice. I've slept in worse palaces.'

'Livestock, tanning, and fabric all take special types of building here,' Miriam said. 'This will be an office. Open plan. For people to work with papers. Hmm. The yard downstairs. What did you think of that?'

'Well. First we went in through a door and up a staircase like that one there, narrow – the royal estate agent, is that right? – took us up there. There's a room at the top with a window overlooking the stairs, and that is an office for a secretary. I thought it rather sparse, and there was nowhere for the secretary's guards to stand duty, but Paulie said it was good. Then there is a short passage past a tiny kitchen, to a big office at the back. The windows overlooking the yard have no shutters, but peculiar plastic slats hung inside. And it was dim. Although there were lights in the ceiling, like in the kitchen here.'

'Long lighting tubes.' Miriam nodded. 'And the back?'

'A back door opens off the corridor onto a metal fire escape. It goes down into the yard. We went there and the walls are nearly ten feet high. There is a big gate onto the back road, but it was locked. A door under the fire escape opens into a storage shed. I could not see into any other windows from inside the yard. Is that what you wanted to know?'

Miriam nodded. 'I think Paulie's done good. Probably.' *Hope there's something appropriate on the far side, in 'world three',* she thought. 'Okay, I'm going to start on a shopping list of things we need to move in there. If it works out, I'll start ferrying stuff over to the other side – then make a trip through to the far side, to see if we're in the right place. If this works, I will be very happy.' *And I won't have to fork out a second deposit for somewhere more useful,* she thought to herself.

'How was your reading?' Paulie asked, coming downstairs again.

'Confusing.' Miriam rubbed her forehead. 'This history book – ' she tapped the cover of the 'legal' one – 'is driving me nuts.'

'Nuts? What's wrong with it?'

'Everything!' Miriam raised her hands. 'Okay, look. I don't know much about English history, but it's got this civil war in the sixteen-forties, goes on and on about some dude called the Lord Protector, Oliver Cromwell. I looked him up in *Encarta* and yes, he's there, too. I didn't know the English had a civil war, and it gets better: They had a revolution in 1688, too! Did you know that? I sure didn't, and it's not in *Encarta* – but I didn't trust it, so I checked *Britannica* and it's there. Okay, so England has a lot of history, and it's all in the wrong order.'

She sat down on the sofa. 'Then I got to the seventeen-forties and everything went haywire.'

'Haywire. Like, someone discovered a time machine, went back, and killed their grandfather?'

'Might as well have. The Young Pretender – look, I'm not making these names up – sails over from France in 1745 and invades Scotland. And in *this* book, he got to crown himself king in Edinburgh.'

'Young pretender – what did he pretend to be?'

'King. Listen, in *our* world, he did the same – then he marched on London and got himself spanked, hard, by King George. That's the first King George, not the King George who lost the War of Independence. That was his grandson.'

'I think I need an aspirin,' said Paulette.

'What this means is that in the far side, England actually lost Scotland in 1745. They fought a war with the Scots in 1746, but the French joined in and whacked their fleet in the channel. So they whacked the French back in the Caribbean, and the Dutch joined in and whacked the Spanish – settling old scores – and then the Brits, while their back was turned. It's all a crazy mess. And somewhere in the middle of this mess things went wrong, wrong, *wrong*. According to *Britannica*, in *our* world, Great Britain got sucked into something called the Seven Years' War with France, and signed a peace treaty in 1763. The Brits got to keep Canada but gave back Guadeloupe and pissed off the Germans, uh, Prussians. Whatever the difference is. But according to this looking-glass history, every time the *English* – not the Brits, there's no such country – started getting somewhere, the king of Scotland tried to invade – there were three battles in as many years at some place called New Castle. And then somewhere in the middle of this, King George, the *second* King George, gets himself killed on a battlefield in Germany, and is succeeded by King Frederick, and I am totally lost now because there is *no* King Frederick in the *Encyclopedia Britannica*.'

Miriam stopped. Paulette was looking bright, fascinated – and a million miles away. 'That was when the French invaded,' she said.

'Huh?' Paulie shook her head. 'The French? Invaded where?'

'England. See, Frederick was the crown prince, right? He got sent over here, to the colonies as a royal governor or something – 'Prince of the Americas' – because his stepmother the queen really hated him. So when his father died he was over here in North America – and the French and Scottish simultaneously invaded England. Whose army, and previous king, had just been whacked. And they *succeeded*.'

'Um, does this mean anything?' Paulette looked puzzled.

'Don't you see?' demanded Miriam. 'Over on the far side, in world three, *there is no United States of America*: Instead there's this thing called New Britain, with a king-emperor! And they're at war with the French Empire – or cold war, or whatever. The French invaded and conquered the British Isles something like two hundred and fifty years ago, and have held it ever since, while the British royal family moved to North America! I'm still putting it all together. Like, where we had a constitutional congress and declared independence and fought a revolutionary war, *they* had something called the New Settlement and set up a continental parliament, with a king and a house of lords in charge.' She frowned. 'And that's as much as I understand.'

'Huh.' Paulette reached out and took the book away from her. 'I saw you look like that before, once,' she said. 'It was when Bill Gates first began spouting about digital nervous systems and the internet. Do you need to go lie down for a bit? Maybe it'll make less sense in the morning.'

'No, no. Look, I'm trying to figure out what *isn't* there. Like, they've had a couple of world wars – but fought with wooden sailing ships and airships. There's a passage at the end of the book about the "miracle of corpuscular transubstantiation" – I think they mean atomic power but I'm not sure. They've got the germ theory of disease and steam cars, but I didn't see any evidence of heavier-than-air flight or antibiotics or gasoline engines. The whole industrial revolution has been delayed – they're up to about the 1930s in electronics. And the social thing is weird. I saw an opium pipe in that pawnbroker's, and I passed a bar selling alcohol, but they're all wearing hats and keeping their legs covered. It's not like our 1920s, at least not more than skin-deep. And I can't get a handle on it,' she added. 'I'll just have to go over there again and try not to get myself arrested.'

'Hmm.' Paulette pulled up a carrier bag and dumped it on the table. 'I've been doing some thinking about that.'

'You have? What about?'

'Well,' Paulie began carefully, 'first thing is, nobody can arrest you and hold you if you've got one of these lockets, huh? Or the design inside it. Brill – '

'It's the design,' Brilliana said suddenly. 'It's the family pattern.' She glanced at Paulette. 'I didn't understand the history either,' she said plaintively. 'Some of the men . . .' she tailed off.

'What about them?' Asked Miriam.

'They had it tattooed on their arms,' she said shyly. 'They said so, anyway. So they could get away if someone caught them. I remember my uncle talking about it once. They even shaved their scalp and tattooed it there in reverse, then grew their hair back – so that if they were imprisoned they could shave in a mirror and use it to escape.'

Miriam stared at her in slack-jawed amazement. 'That's brilliant!' she said. 'Hang on – ' her hand instinctively went to her head. 'Hmm.'

'You won't have to shave,' said Paulie, 'I know exactly what to do. You know those henna temporary tattoos you can get? There's this dot-com that takes images you upload and turns them into tattoos, then sends them to you by mail order. They're supposed to last for a few days. I figure if you put one on the inside of each wrist, then wear something with sleeves that cover it – '

'Wow.' Miriam instinctively glanced at the inside of her left wrist, smooth and hairless, unblemished except for a small scar she'd acquired as a child. 'But you said you'd been thinking about something else.'

'Yup.' Paulette upended her shopping bag on the table. 'Behold: a pair of digital walkie-talkies, good for private conversations in a ten-mile radius! And lo, a hands-free kit.'

'This is going to work,' Miriam said, a curious smile creeping across her face. 'I can feel it in my bones.' She looked up. 'Okay. So tell me, Paulie, what do you know about the history of patent law?'

*

It took Miriam another day to work up the nerve to phone Roland. If she went outside she could phone him, either his voice mail or his own real-life ear, and dump all the unwanted complexities of her new life on a sympathetic shoulder. He'd understand: That was half the attraction that had sparked their whirlwind affair. He probably grasped the headaches she was facing better than anyone else, Brill included. Brill was still not much more than a teenager with a sheltered upbringing. But Roland knew just how nasty things could get. *If I trust him,* she thought. *Someone* had murdered the watchman and installed the bomb in the warehouse. She'd told Roland about the place, and then . . . *Correlation does not imply causation,* she reminded herself.

In the end she compromised, taking the T into town and finding a diner with a good range of exit options before switching on the phone and dialing. That way, even if someone had grabbed Roland and was actively tracing the call, they wouldn't find her before she hung up. It was raining, and she had a seat next to the window, watching the slug-trails of moisture run down the glass as her latte cooled and she tried to work up her nerve to call him.

When she dialed, the phone rang five times before he picked it up, a near-eternity in which she changed her mind about the wisdom of calling him several times. 'Hello?' he asked.

'Roland. It's me.'

'Hello, you.' Concern roughened his voice: 'I've been really worried about you. Where are – '

'Wait.' She realized she was breathing too fast, shallow breaths that didn't seem to be bringing in enough oxygen. 'You're on this side. Is anyone with you?'

'No, I'm taking a day off work. Even your uncle gives his troops leave sometimes. He's been asking about you, though. As if he knows I've got some kind of channel to you. When are you going to come in? What have you been doing? Olga had the craziest story – '

'If it's about the incident in her apartment, it's true.' Miriam stopped, glanced obliquely at the window to check for reflections. There was nobody near her, just a barrista cleaning the coffee machine on the counter at the other side of the room. 'Is Edsger around? He hasn't gone missing or anything?'

'Edsger?' Roland sounded uncertain. 'What do you know about – '

'Edsger. Courier on the Boston–New York run.' Quickly Miriam outlined her encounter with the courier. 'Did he arrive all right?'

'Yes. I think so.' Roland paused. 'So you're telling me somebody tried to kill you in the warehouse as well?' A note of anger crept into his voice. 'When I find out who – '

'You'll do nothing,' Miriam told him. 'And you're not going to tell me you can provide security. There's a mole in the organization, Roland, they'd work around you – and I've found out something more interesting. There's a whole bunch of world-walkers you don't know about, and they're coming in from yet another world, where everything's different. What we were talking about, the whole technology transfer thing, it can work there, too. In fact, that's what I'm doing now, with Brill. The politics – do you know anything about Baroness Hildegarde's interests? Olga said she's going to try to get the Clan committee to declare me incompetent. Before that happens I want to be able to make her look like an idiot. I'm working on the other side, Roland, in the third world, building a front company. So I'm going to stay out of touch for quite a bit longer.'

'Can I see you?' he asked. A pause. 'I really think we've got a lot to work out. I don't know about you.' Another pause. 'I was hoping we could . . .'

This was the hardest part. 'I don't think so,' Miriam heard herself saying. 'I'd love to spend some time with you, but I've got so much to do. And there isn't enough time to do it. I can't risk you being followed, or Angbard deciding to reel me in too soon. I want to, but – '

'I get it.' He sounded despondent.

'I'm not dumping you! It's just I, I need some time.' She was breathing too fast again. 'Later. Give me a week to sort things out, then we'll see.'

'Oh. A week?' The distant tone vanished. 'Okay, a week. I'll wait it out. You'll take care of yourself? You're sure you're safe where you are?'

'For now,' Miriam affirmed, crossing her fingers. 'And I'll have a lot more to tell you then, I'll need your advice.' *And everything else.* The urge to drop her resolve, grab any chance to see him, was so strong she had trouble resisting. *Keep it businesslike, for now.* 'I love you,' she said impulsively.

'Me too. I mean, I love you, too.' It came out in a tongue-tied rush, followed by a silence freighted with unspoken qualifications.

'I'd better go,' she said at last.

'Okay, then.'

'Bye.' She ended the call and stared bleakly at the rain outside the window. Her coffee was growing cold. *Now why did I really say that?* She wondered, puzzled: *Did I really mean it?* She'd said those words before, to her husband – now ex-husband – and she'd meant them at the time. Why did this feel different?

'Damn it, I'm a fool,' she told herself gloomily, muttering under her breath so that the waitress at the far end of the bar took pains to avoid looking at her. *I'm a fool for love, and if I don't handle this carefully, I could end up a* dead *fool. Damn it, why did I have to take that locket in the first place?*

The raindrops weren't answering, so she finished her latte and left.

*

She spent the next three days exercising her magic credit card discreetly.

Angbard hadn't put a stop on it. Evidently the message had gotten through: *Don't bug me, I'm busy staying alive.* A garden shed, a deluxe shooting hide, and enough gas-powered tools to outfit a small farm vanished into the trunk of Miriam's rental car in repeated runs between Home Depot and Costco and the new office near Cambridgeport. Miriam didn't much like the office – it had a residual smell of stale tobacco and some strange coffee-colored stains on the carpet that not even an industrial cleaner could get rid of – but she had to admit that it would do.

They moved a couple of sofa beds into the back room, and paid a locksmith to come around and beef up the door frame with deadbolts, and install an intruder alarm and closed-circuit TV cameras covering the yard and both entrances. A small fridge and microwave appeared in the kitchen, a television set and video in the front office.

Paulette and Miriam groaned at each other about their aches and pains, and even Brill hesitantly joined in the bitching and moaning after they unloaded the flat-pack garden shed. 'This had better be worth it,' Miriam said on day three as she swallowed a Tenolol tablet and a chaser of ibuprofen on the back of her lunchtime sub.

'You're going across this afternoon?' asked Paulie.

'I'm going in half an hour,' Miriam corrected her. 'First trip to see if it's okay. Then as many short ones as I can manage to ferry supplies over. I'll take Brill through to help get the shed up and covered, then come back to plot expedition one. You happy with the shopping list?'

'I think so.' Paulette sighed. 'This isn't what I was expecting when we got started.'

'I know. But I think this is going to work out. Listen, you've been going crazy with the both of us living on top of you for the past week, but once we're gone we'll be out of your hair for at least five days. Why don't you kick back and relax? Get in some of that partying you keep moaning about missing?'

'Because it won't be the same without you! I was planning on showing you some of the good life. Get you hitched up with a date, anyway.'

Miriam sobered. 'I don't need a date right now,' she said, looking worried – and wistful.

'You're – ' Paulette raised an eyebrow. 'You still hooked on him?'

'It hasn't gone away. We spoke yesterday. I keep wanting to see him.'

Paulette caught her arm. 'Take it from me: don't. I mean, really, *don't*. If he's for real, he'll be waiting for you. If he isn't, you'd be running such a huge risk – '

Miriam nodded, wordlessly.

'I figured that was what it was. You want him whether or not he's messed up with the shits who're trying to kill you or disinherit you, is that right?'

'I think he's probably got his reasons,' Miriam said reluctantly. 'For whatever he's doing. And I don't think he's working for them. But – '

'Listen, *no one* is worth what those fuckers want to do to you. Understand?'

'But if he *isn't* – ' it came out as more of a whine than Miriam intended.

'Then it will all sort itself out, won't it?' said Paulette. 'Eventually.'

'Maybe.'

They broke off as the noise of the door opening downstairs reached them. Two pairs of eyes went to the camera. It was Brill, coming in from the cold: She'd been out shopping on foot, increasingly sure-footed in the social basics of day-to-day life in the twenty-first century. 'I look at her, and I think she'll be like you when she's done some growing up,' Paulette commented.

'Maybe.' Miriam stood up. 'What've you got?' she called down the stairwell.

'Food for the trip. Do you have a spare gun?' she asked.

'Huh? Why?'

'There are wild animals in the hills near Hasleholm.'

'Oops.' Miriam frowned. 'Do you really think it's a problem?'

'Yes.' Brill nodded. 'But I can shoot. He is very conservative, my father, and insisted I learn the feminine virtues – deportment, dancing, embroidery, and marksmanship. If there are wolves, I'd like to have a long gun for dealing with them.'

'Well, in that case we'll have to look into getting you a hunting rifle as soon as possible. In the meantime, there's the pistol I took from the courier. Where did you stash it?'

'Back at Paulette's home. But I really could use something bigger in case of wolves or bears,' Brill said seriously. She shoved her hair back out of the way and sniffed. 'At least a pistol will protect me from human problems.'

'Try not to shoot any Clan couriers, huh?'

'I'm not stupid.'

'I know: I just don't want you taking any risks,' Miriam added. 'Okay, kids, it's time to move. And I'm *not* taking you through just yet, Brill.' She reached for her heavy hiking jacket, pulled it on, and patted the right pocket to check her own gun was in place. 'Wish me luck,' she said, as she walked toward the back door and the yard beyond.

CLEANING THE AIR

Miriam snapped into awareness teetering on the edge of an abyss. She flung herself sideways instinctively, grabbing for a tree branch – caught it, took two desperate strides as the ground under her feet crumbled, then felt her boots grip solid ground that didn't crumble under her feet.

'Damn!' She glanced to her left. A large patch of muddy soil lay exposed in the middle of the snowscape, exposed on the crest of a steep drop to a half-frozen streambed ten feet below and twenty feet beyond what would be the side of the yard. 'Damn.' She gasped for breath, icy terror forcing her to inhale the bitterly cold air. She looked down into the stream. *If we'd rented the next unit over, or if I'd carried Brill over* – a ducking in this sort of weather could prove fatal. *Or could I have come through at all?* She glanced up. She'd been lucky with the tree, a young elm that grew straight and tall for the first six feet. The forest hereabouts was thin. *I need to ask Brill what else she hasn't thought to tell me about world-walking,* she realized. Perhaps her mother was right about her being over-confident. A vague memory floated up from somewhere, something about much of Boston being built on landfill reclaimed from the bay. *What if I'd tried this somewhere out at sea?* she thought, and leaned against the tree for a minute or two to catch her breath. Suddenly, visions of coming through with her feet embedded in a wall or hovering ten feet above a lake didn't seem comical at all.

She closed her locket and carefully pocketed it, then looked around. 'It'll do,' she muttered to herself. 'As long as I avoid that drop.' She stared at it carefully. 'Hmm.' She'd gone through about a foot away from the left-hand wall of their yard: The drop-off was steepest under the wall. The yard was about twelve feet wide, which meant –

'Right here.' She took out her knife and carved a blaze on the tree around head height. Then she dropped her backpack and turned around, slowly, trying to take in the landscape.

The stream ran downhill toward the river a quarter of a mile away, but it was next to invisible through the woods, even with the barren winter branches blocking less of the view than the summer's profusion of green. In the other direction trees stretched away as far as she could see. 'I could walk for miles in this, going in circles,' Miriam told herself. 'Hmm.'

She carved another blaze on a tree, then began cautiously probing into the woods, marking trees as she went. After an hour she'd established that there was no sudden change in the landscape for a couple of hundred yards in two directions away from her little backyard. Sheer random chance had brought her through in nearly the worst possible place.

'Okay,' she said, squeezing her forehead as if she could cram the headache back inside the bones of her skull. 'Here goes.' And this time, she pulled down her left sleeve and looked at the chilly skin on the inside of her wrist – pale and almost blue with cold, save for the dark green-and-brown design stippled in dye below the pulse point.

It worked.

*

That night, Miriam didn't sleep well. She had a splitting headache and felt sick to her stomach, an unfamiliar nausea for one who didn't suffer migraines. But she'd managed a second trip after dark, only four hours after the first, and returned after barely an hour with aching back and arms (from lifting the heavy shooting hide and a basic toolkit) and a bad case of the shivers.

Brilliana fussed over her, feeding her moussaka and grilled octopus from a Greek take-out she'd discovered somewhere – Brill had taken to exploring strange cuisines with the glee of a suddenly liberated gourmet – and readied her next consignment. 'I feel like a goddamn mule,' Miriam complained. 'If only there were two of us!'

'I'd do it if I could,' Brill commented, stung. 'You know I would!'

'Yes, yes . . . I'm sorry. I didn't mean it that way. It's just – I can carry eighty pounds on my back, just. A hundred and twenty? I can't even pick it up. I wish I could take more. I should take up weight lifting . . .'

'That's what the couriers all do. Why don't you use a walking frame?' asked Brill.

'A walking – is this something the Clan does that I don't know about?'

Brill shook her head. 'I'm not sure,' she said, 'I never saw how they operate the post service. But surely – if we get a very heavy pack ready, and lift it so you can walk into it backwards, then just lock your knees, wouldn't that work?'

'It might.' Miriam pulled a face. 'I might also twist an ankle. Which would be bad, in the middle of nowhere.'

'What happens if you try to go through with something on the ground?' Brill asked.

'I don't.' Miriam refilled her glass. 'It was one of the first things I tried. If you jump on my back I can just about carry you for thirty seconds or so before I fall over – that's long enough. But I tried with a sofa a while ago. All that happened was, I got a splitting headache and threw up. I don't know how I managed it the first time, sitting in a swivel chair, except maybe it was something to do with its wheels – there wasn't much contact with the floor.'

'Oh, right.'

'Which says interesting things about the family trade,' Miriam added. 'They're limited by weight and volume in what they can ship. Two tons a day, normally. If we open up "world three" that'll go down, precipitously, although the three-way trade may be worth more. We've got to work out how to run an import/export business that doesn't run into the mercantilist zero-sum trap.'

'The what?' Brill looked blank.

Miriam sighed. 'Old, old theory. It's the idea that there are only a finite quantity of goods of fixed value, so if you ship them from one place to another, the source has to do without. People used to think all trade worked that way. What happens is, if you ship some commodity to a place where it's scarce, sooner or later the price drops – deflates – while you're buying up so much of the supply that the price rises at the source.'

'Isn't that the way things always work?' Brill asked.

'Nope.' Miriam took a sip of wine. 'I'm drinking too much of this stuff, too regularly. Hmm, where was I? This guy called Adam Smith worked it out about two centuries ago, in this world. Turns out you can create value by working with people to refine goods or provide services. Another guy called Marx worked on Smith's ideas a bit further a century later, and though lots of people dislike the prescription he came up with, his analysis of how capitalism works is quite good. Labor – what people do – enhances the value of raw materials. This table is worth more than the raw timber it's made out of, for example. We can create value, wealth, what-have-you, if we can just move materials to where the labor input on them enhances their value the most.' She drifted off, staring at the TV set, which was showing a talk show with the volume muted. (Brill said it made more sense that way.) 'The obvious thing to move is patents,' she murmured. 'Commercially valuable ideas.'

'You think you can use the talent to create wealth, instead of moving it around?' Brill looked puzzled.

'Yes, that's it exactly.' Miriam put her glass down. 'A large gold nugget is no use to a man who's dying of thirst in a desert. By the same token, a gold nugget may be worth a lot more to a jeweler, who can turn it into something valuable and salable, than it is to someone who just wants to melt it down and use it as coin. Jewelry usually sells for more than its own weight in raw materials, doesn't it? That's because of the labor invested in it. Or the scarcity of the end product, a unique work of art. The Clan seems to have gotten hung up on shipping raw materials around as a way of making money. I want to ship ideas around instead, ideas that people can use to create value locally – in each world – actually *create* wealth rather than just cream off a commission for transporting it.'

'And you want to eventually turn my world into this one,' Brilliana said calmly.

'Yes.' Miriam looked back at her. 'Is that a good thing or a bad thing, do you think?'

Brill gestured at the TV set. 'Put one of *those*, showing *that*, in every peasant's house? Are you kidding? I think it's the most

347

amazingly wonderful thing I've ever heard of! My mother would say that's typical of me, and my father would get angry and perhaps beat me for it. But I'm right, and they're wrong.'

'Ah, the self-confidence of youth.' Miriam picked up her glass again. 'Doesn't the idea of, like, completely wiping out the culture of your own people worry you? I mean, so much of what we've got here is such complete shit – ' She stopped. Brill's eyes were sparkling – with anger, not amusement.

'You really think so? Go live in a one-room hut for a couple of years, bearing illiterate brats half of whom will die before they're five! Without a fancy toilet, or even a thunder mug to piss in each morning. Go do that, where the only entertainment is once a week going to the temple where some fat stupid priest invokes the blessings of Sky Father and his court on your heads and prays that the harvest doesn't fail again like it did five years ago, when two of your children starved to death in front of your eyes. *Then* tell me that your culture's shit!'

Miriam tried to interrupt: 'Hey, what about – '

Brill steamed right on. 'Shut *up*. Even the children of the well-off – like me – grow up living four to a room and wearing hand-me-downs. We are married off to whoever our parents think will pay best bride-price. Because we're members of the outer families we don't die of childbed fever – not since the Clan so graciously gave us penicillin tablets and morphine for the pain – but we get to bear child after child because it's our duty to the Clan! Are you insane, my lady? Or merely blind? And it's better for us in the families than for ordinary women, better by far! Did you notice that within the Clan you had rights? Or that outside the Clan, in the ordinary aristocracy, you didn't? We have at least one ability that is as important, *more* important, than what's between our legs. But those ordinary peasants you feel such guilt for don't have any such thing. There's a better life awaiting me as a humble illegal immigrant in this world than there is as a lady-in-waiting to nobility in my own. Do you think I'd ever go back there for *any* reason except to help you change the world?'

Miriam was taken aback. 'I didn't realize all that stuff. No.' She picked up her wine glass again. 'It's post-colonial guilt, I guess,' she added by way of explanation. 'We've got a lot of history here, and it's

348

really ugly in parts. We've got a long tradition of conquering other people and messing them up. The idea of taking over and running people for their own good got a very bad name about sixty years ago – did anyone tell you about the Second World War – so a lot of us have this cringe reflex about the whole idea.'

'Don't. If you do what you're planning, you couldn't invade and conquer, anyway. How many people could you bring through? All you can do is persuade people to live their lives a better way – the one thing the families and the Clan have never bothered trying to do, because they're already swimming desperately against the stream, trying to hold their own lives together. It takes an outside view to realize that if they started building fabulous buildings and machines like these at home they wouldn't be dependent on imported luxuries from the world next door. And they never – ' her chest heaved – 'let us get far enough away to see that clearly. Because if we did, we might not come back.'

'You don't want to go back?' asked Miriam. 'Not even to visit, to see your family and friends?'

'Not really.' It was a statement of fact. 'This is *better*. I can find new friends here. If I go back there, and you fail – ' she caught Miriam's gaze. 'I might never be able to come back here.'

For a moment, looking at this young woman – young enough to be at college but with eyes prematurely aged by cynicism and the Clan's greedy poverty of riches – Miriam had second thoughts. The families' grip on their young was tenuous, always in danger of slipping. If they ever got the idea that they could just take their lockets or tattoos or scraps of paper and leave, the Clan would be gone within a generation. *Am I going to end up making this family tyranny stronger?* she wondered. *Because if so, shouldn't I just give up now . . .?* 'I won't fail you,' she promised. 'We'll fix them.'

Brill nodded. 'I know you will.' And Miriam nodded right back at her, her mind awash with all the other family children, her distant relatives – the siblings and cousins she'd never known, might never have known of, who would live and die in gilded poverty if she failed.

*

A woman dressed in black stepped out of the winter twilight.

She looked around curiously, one hand raised to cover her mouth. 'I'm in somebody's garden by the look of things. Hedge to my left, dilapidated shed in front of me – and a house behind. It looks a mess. The hedge is wildly overgrown and the windows are boarded up.'

She glanced around, but couldn't see into the neighboring gardens. 'Seems like an expensive place.' She furtively scratched an arrowhead on the side of the shed, pointing to the spot she'd arrived on, then winced. 'This light is hurting my head. *Ow* . . .' She hitched her coat out of the grayish snow then stumbled toward the house, crouching below the level of the windows.

She paused. 'It looks empty,' she muttered to the dictaphone. 'Forward.' She walked around to the front of the house, where the snow was banked in deep drifts before the doors and blank-eyed wooden window shutters. Nobody had been in or out for days, that much was clear. There was a short uphill driveway leading to a road, imposing iron gates chained in front. 'Damn. How do I get out?' She glanced round, saw a plaque on the front of the house – BLACK-STONES, 1923. There was a narrow wooden gate next to the pillar supporting one of the cast-iron gates: it was secured by a rusty bolt on the inside. Miriam waded toward it, shivering from the snow, levered the bolt back with her multitool, and glanced round one final time to look at the house.

It was *big*. Not a McMansion, but the real thing. And it was clearly mewed up, shutters nailed across those windows that weren't boarded, gates chained tight. She gritting her teeth against the cold. 'Right, you'll be mine.' Then she slipped through the wooden door and onto the sidewalk. The street here was partially swept. On the other side of it lay an open field in the middle of what was dense forest in world one and downtown Cambridge in world two. She could see other big town houses on the far side of the field, but that didn't matter. She turned left and began walking toward the crossroads she could see at the far corner of the quadrangle.

Her teeth were chattering by the time she reached the clock tower on the strange traffic circle at the crossroads. There was almost no traffic on this bitterly cold morning. A lone pony trap clattered past her, but the only vehicles she saw were strange two-deck streetcars, pantographs sparking occasionally as they whirred down the far side of the field and paused at a stand in the middle of the traffic circle. Miriam blinked back the instinctive urge to check her watch. *What day is it?* she wondered. A sign in heavy classical lettering at the empty tram stop answered her question: Sunday service only. *Oh.* Below it was a timetable as exact as anything she'd seen at an airport back home – evidently trams from this stop ran into the waterfront and over something called Deny Bridge once every half hour on Sundays, for a fare of 3d, whatever that meant. She shivered some more and stepped inside the wooden shelter, then fidgeted with the handful of copper change that she had left. Second thoughts began to occur to her. Was it normal for a single woman to catch a tram, unaccompanied, on a Sunday? What if Burgeson's shop was closed? What if –

A streetcar pulled up beside the shelter with a screech of abused steel wheels. Miriam plucked up her courage and climbed aboard. The driver nodded at her, then moved off without warning. Miriam stumbled, nearly losing her footing before she made it into the passenger cabin. The wooden bench was cold but there seemed to be a heater running somewhere. She surreptitiously examined her fellow passengers, using their reflections in the windows when she couldn't look at them directly without being obvious. They were an odd collection – a fat woman in a ridiculous bonnet who looked like a Salvation Army collector, a couple of thin men in oddly cut, baggy suits with hats pulled down over their ears, a twenty-something mother, bags under her eyes and two quietly bickering children by her side, and a man in what looked like a Civil War uniform coming toward her, a ticket machine hung in front of his chest. Miriam took a deep breath. *I'm going to manage this,* she realized.

'I'm going to Highgate, for Holmes Alley. How much is it, please, and what's the closest stand? And what's this stop called?'

'That'll be fourpence, miss, and I'll call you when it's your stop. This is Roundgate Interchange.' He looked at her slightly oddly as she handed him a sixpence, but wound off a strip of four penny tickets and some change, then turned away. 'Tickets, please!'

Miriam examined the tickets in her hand. *Is nothing simple?* she wondered. Even buying streetcar tickets was a minor ordeal of anticipation and surprise. *Brill did very well,* she began to realize. *Maybe too well.* A suspicious thought struck her. *That might explain why Angbard is letting me run . . .*

The tram trundled downhill at not much better than walking pace, the driver occasionally ringing an electric bell, then stopping next to a raised platform. The houses were much closer together here, lined up in rows that shared side walls for warmth, built out of cheap red brick stained black from smoke. There was an evil smell of half-burned coal in the air, and chimneys belched from every roofline. She hadn't noticed it in the nob hill neighborhood of Blackstones, but the whole town smelled of combustion, as if there'd been a house fire a block away. The air was acrid, a nasty sour taste undercutting the cold and coating her throat when she tried to breathe. Even the cloud above was yellowish. The tram turned into a main road, rattled around a broad circle with a snow-covered statue of a man on a horse in the middle, then turned along an alarmingly skeletal box-section bridge that jutted out over the river. Miriam, watching the waterfront through the gray-painted girders, felt a most unsettling wave of claustrophobia, as if she was being arrested for a crime she hadn't committed. She forced herself to shrug it off. *Everything will be all right,* she told herself.

The town center was almost empty compared to its state the last time she'd visited. It smelled strongly of smoke – chimneys on every side bespoke residents in the upstairs flats – but the shop windows were dark, their doors locked. A distant church bell clattered discordantly. Scrawny pigeons hopped around near the gutter, exploring a pile of horse dung. The conductor tapped Miriam on the shoulder, and she startled. 'You'll be wanting the next stop,' he explained.

'Thank you,' she replied with a wan smile. She stood up, waiting on the open platform as the stop swung into view, then pulled the bell string. She hopped off the platform, shook her coat out, hiked her bag up onto her shoulder, and stepped back from the tram as it moved off with a loud whirr and a gurgle of slush. Then she took stock of her surroundings.

Everything looked different in the chilly gloom of a Sunday morning. The shop fronts, comparatively busy last time she'd been here, looked like vacant eyes, and the peddlers hawking roast chestnuts and hand-warmers had disappeared. *Do they have Sunday trading laws here?* she wondered vaguely. That could be a nuisance –

Burgeson's shop was closed, too, a wooden shutter padlocked into place across the front window. But Miriam spotted something she hadn't noticed before, a solid wooden door next to the shop with a row of bell-pull handles set in a tarnished plaque beside it. She peered at them. E. BURGESON, ESQ. 'Aha,' she muttered, and pulled the handle.

Nothing happened. Miriam waited on the doorstep, her toes freezing and feeling increasingly damp, and cursed her stupidity. She put her hand on the knob and yanked again, and this time heard a distant tinkling reward. Then the door scraped inward on a bare-walled corridor. 'Yes?'

'Mr. Burgeson?' she smiled hopefully at him. 'I'm back.'

'Oh.' He was dressed as he had been in the shop, except for a pair of outrageous purple slippers worn over bare feet. 'You again.' A faint quirk tugged at the side of his upper lip. 'I suppose you'll be wanting me to open the shop.'

'If it's convenient.'

He sniffed. 'It isn't. And this is rather irregular – although something tells me you don't put much stock by regularity. Still, if you'd care to grace my humble abode with your presence and wait while I find my galoshes – '

'Certainly.'

She followed him up a tightly spiraling stone-flagged staircase that opened out onto a landing with four stout-looking doors. One of them stood open, and he went inside without waiting for her. Miriam began to follow, then paused on the threshold.

'Come on, come on,' he said irritably. 'Don't leave the door open, you'll let the cold in. Then I'll have to fetch more coal from the cellar. What's keeping you?'

'Oh, nothing,' she said, stepping forward and shutting the door behind her. The hall had probably once been wide enough for two people to stand abreast in, and it was at least ten feet high, but now it felt like a canyon. It was walled from floor to ceiling with bookcases, all crammed to bursting. Burgeson had disappeared into a kitchen – at least Miriam supposed it was a kitchen – in which a kettle was boiling atop a cast-iron stove that looked like something that belonged in a museum. The lights flickered as the door closed, and Miriam abruptly realized that they weren't electric. 'I see you've got more books up here than you have down in the shop.'

'That's work, this is pleasure,' he said. 'What did you come to disturb my Sunday worship for, this time?'

'Sunday worship? I don't see much sign of that around here,' Miriam let slip. She backed up hastily. 'I'm sorry. I hope I didn't cause you any trouble?'

'Trouble? No, no trouble, not unless you count having the King Street thief-taker himself asking pointed questions about my visitor of the other morning.' His back was turned to her, so Miriam couldn't see his expression, but she tightened her grip on her bag, as she suddenly found herself wishing that the pockets of her coat were deep enough to conceal her pistol.

'That wasn't my doing,' she said evenly.

'I know it wasn't.' He turned to face her, and she saw that he was holding a somewhat tarnished silver teapot. 'And you'd taken the Marx, so it wasn't as if it was lying around for him to trip over, was it? For which I believe I owe you thanks enough to cancel out any ill will resulting from his unwelcome visit.' He held up the pot. 'Can I offer you some refreshment, while you explain why you're here?'

'Sure.' She glanced in the opposite direction. 'In there?'

'The morning room, yes. I will be but a few moments.'

Miriam walked into Burgeson's morning room and got a surprise. The room was perfectly round. Even the window frames and the door were curved in line with the wall, and the plaster moldings around the ceiling described a perfect circle twelve feet in diameter. It was also extremely untidy. A huge chesterfield sofa of dubious provenance hulked at one side, half submerged beneath a flood of manuscripts and books. An odd-looking upright piano, its scratched lid supporting a small library, leaned drunkenly against the wall.

There was a fireplace, but the coals in it barely warmed the air immediately in front of it, and the room was icy cold. A plate with the remnants of a cold lunch sat next to the fireplace. Miriam sat gingerly on the edge of the sofa. The sofa was so cold that it seemed to suck the heat right out of her, despite her layers of heavy clothing.

'How do you take your tea?' Burgeson called. 'Milk, sugar?'

He was moving in the hall. She slipped a hand into her bag, pulled out her weapon and pointed its spine at him. 'Milk, no sugar,' she replied.

'Very good.' He advanced, bearing a tray, and laid it down in front of the fireplace. There were, she noticed, bags under his eyes. He looked tired, or possibly ill. 'What's that?' he asked, staring at her hand.

'One good history book deserves another,' she said evenly.

'Oh dear.' He chuckled hoarsely. 'You know I can't offer you anything for it. Not on a Sunday. If the police – '

'Take it, it's a gift,' she said impatiently.

'A *gift*?' From his expression Miriam deduced that the receipt of presents was not an experience with which Erasmus Burgeson was well acquainted – he made no move to take it. 'I'm touched, m'dear. Mind if I ask what prompted this unexpected generosity?' He was staring at her warily, as if he expected her to sprout bat wings and bite him.

'Sure. If you would pour the tea before it gets cold? Is it always this cold here in, uh, whatever this city is called?'

He froze for a moment, then knelt down and began pouring tea from the pot into two slightly chipped Delft cups. 'Boston.'

'Ah, Boston it is.' She nodded to herself. 'The cold?'

'Only when a smog notice is in effect.' Burgeson pointed at the fire. 'Damned smokeless fuel ration's been cut again. You can only burn so much during a smog, or you run out and then it's just too bad. Especially if the pipes burst. But when old father smog rolls down the Back Bay, you'd rather not have been born, lest pipes of a different kind should go pop.' He coughed for effect and patted his chest. 'You speak the King's English remarkably well for someone who doesn't know a blessed thing. Where are you from, really?'

She put the book down on the heap on the sofa. 'As far as I can tell, about ten miles and two hundred years away,' she said, feeling slightly light-headed at the idea of telling him even this much.

'Not France? Are you sure you don't work for the dauphin's department?' He cocked his head to one side, parrotlike.

'Not France. Where I come from they chopped his head off a long time ago.' She watched him carefully.

'Chopped his *head* off? Fascinating – ' He rose on one knee, and held out a cup to her.

'Thank you.' She accepted it.

'If this is madness, it's a most extraordinary delusion,' he said, nodding. 'Would you be so good as to tell me more?'

'In due course. I have a couple of questions for you, however.' She took a sip of the tea. 'Specifically, taking on trust the question of your belief in my story, you might want to contemplate some of the obstacles a traveler from, um, another world, might face in creating an identity for herself in this one. And especially in the process of buying a house and starting a business, when one is an unaccompanied female in a strange country. I don't know much about the legal status of women here other than that it differs quite significantly from where I come from. I think I'm probably going to need a lawyer, and possibly a proxy. Which is why I thought of you.'

'I see.' Burgeson was almost going cross-eyed in his attempts to avoid interrupting her. 'Pray tell, why me?'

'Because an officer of the law recommended you. I figure a fence who is also an informer is probably a safer bet than someone who's so incompetent that he hasn't reached a working accommodation with the cops.' There were other reasons too, reasons connected with Miriam's parents and upbringing, but she wasn't about to give him that kind of insight into her background. Trust only went so far, after all.

'A fence – ' He snorted. 'I'm not dishonest or unethical, ma'am.'

'You just sell books that the Lord Provost's Court wants burned,' she said. 'And the police recommend you. Do I need to draw a diagram?'

He sighed. 'Guilty as charged. If you aren't French, are you sure you aren't a Black Chamber agent playing a double game?'

'What's the Black Chamber?'

He looked gloomy. 'I suppose I should also have sold you an almanac.'

'That might have been a good idea,' she agreed.

'Well, now.' He brushed papers from the piano stool and sat on it, opposite her, his teacup balanced precariously on a bony knee. 'Supposing I avoid saying anything that might incriminate myself. And supposing we take as a matter of faith your outrageous claim to be a denizen of another, ah, world? Like this one, only different. No *le Roi Français*, indeed. What, then, could you be wanting with a humble dealer and broker in secondhand goods and wares like myself?'

'Connections. I need to establish a firm identity here, as a woman of good character. I have some funds to invest – you've seen the form they take – but mostly . . . hmm. In the place I come from, we do things differently. And while we undoubtedly do some things worse, everything I have seen so far convinces me that we are far, *far* better at certain technical fields. I intend to establish a type of company that as far as I can tell doesn't exist here, Mr. Burgeson. I am limited in the goods I can carry back and forth, physically, to roughly what I can carry on my back – but *ideas* are frequently more valuable than gold bricks.' She paused a moment. 'I said I'd need a lawyer, and perhaps a proxy to sign documents for my business. I forgot to mention that I will also want a patent clerk and a front man for purposes of licensing my inventions.'

'Inventions. Such as?' He sounded skeptical.

'Oh, many things. Mostly little things. A machine for binding documents together in an office that is cheap to run, compact, and efficient – so much so that where I come from they're almost as common as pens. A better design of brake mechanism for automobiles. A better type of wood screw, a better kind of electric cell. But one or two big things, too. A drug that can cure most fulminating infections rapidly and effectively, without side effects. A more efficient engine for aviation.'

Burgeson stared at her. 'Incredible,' he said sharply. 'You have some proof that you can come up with all these miracles?'

Miriam reached into her bag and pulled out her second weapon, one that had cost her nearly its own weight in gold, back home, a miniature battery-powered gadget with a four-inch color screen. 'When I leave, you can start by looking at that book. In the meantime, here's a toy we use for keeping children quiet on long journeys where I come from. How about some light Sunday entertainment?' And she hit the 'start' button on the portable DVD player.

*

Three hours and at least a pint of tea later, Miriam stepped down from a hackney carriage outside the imposing revolving doors of the Brighton Hotel. Behind her, the driver grunted as he heaved a small trunk down from the luggage rack – 'If you're going to try to pass in polite society you'll need one, no lady of quality would travel without at least a change of day wear and an evening dress,' Burgeson had told her as he gave her the trunk, 'and you need to be at least respectable enough to book a room.' Even if the trunk had been pawned by a penniless refugee and cluttered up his cellar for a couple of years, it looked like luggage.

'Thank you,' Miriam said as graciously as she could, and tipped the driver a sixpence. She turned back to the door to see a bellhop already lifting her trunk on his handcart. 'I say! You there.'

The concierge at the front desk didn't turn his nose up at a single woman traveling alone. The funereal outfit Burgeson had scared up for her seemed to forbid all questions, especially after she had added a severe black cap and a net veil in place of her previous hat. 'What does m'lady require?' he asked politely.

'I'd like to take one of your first-class suites. For myself. I travel with no servants, so room service will be required. I will be staying for at least a week, and possibly longer while I seek to buy a house and put the affairs of my late husband in order.' *I hope Erasmus wasn't stringing me along about getting hold of a new identity,* she thought.

'Absolutely. I believe room fourteen is available, m'lady. Perhaps you would like to view it? If it is to your satisfaction . . .'

'I'm sure it will be,' she said easily. 'And if it isn't you'll see to it, I'm sure, won't you? How much will it be?'

'A charge of two pounds and eleven shillings a night applies for room and board, ma'am,' he said severely.

'Hmm.' She sucked on her lower lip. 'And for a week? Or longer?'

'I believe we could come down from that a little,' he admitted. 'Especially if provision was made in advance.'

'Two a night.' Miriam palmed a huge, gorgeously colored ten-pound note onto the front desk and paused. 'Six shillings on top for the service.'

The concierge nodded at her. 'Then it will be an initial four nights?' he asked.

'I will pay in advance, if I choose to renew it,' she replied tone-lessly. *Bastard,* she thought angrily. Erasmus had primed her with the hotel's rates. Two pounds flat was the norm for a luxury suite: This man was trying to soak her. '*If* it's satisfactory,' she emphasized.

'I'll see to it myself.' He bowed, then stepped out from behind his desk. 'If I may show you up to your suite myself, m'lady?'

Once she was alone in the hotel suite, Miriam locked the door on the inside, then removed her coat and hung it up to dry in the niche by the door. 'I'm impressed,' she said aloud. 'It's huge.' She peeled off her gloves and slung them over a brass radiator that gurgled beneath the shuttered windows, then unbuttoned her jacket and knelt to unlace her ankle boots – her feet were beginning to feel as if they were molded to the inside of the damp, cold leather. *Chilblains as an occupational hazard for explorers of other worlds?* She stepped out of her shoes then carried them to the radiator, stockinged feet feeling almost naked against the thick pile of the woolen carpet.

Dry at last, she walked over to the sideboard and the huge silver samovar, steaming gently atop a gas flame plumbed into the wall. She poured a glass full of hot water and dunked a sachet of Earl Grey tea into it. Finally she plopped herself down in the overstuffed armchair opposite the bedroom door, pulled out her dictaphone, and began to compose a report to herself. 'Here I am, in room fourteen of the Brighton Hotel. The concierge tried to soak me. Getting a handle on the prices is hard – a pound seems to be equivalent to about, uh, two hundred dollars? Something like that. This is an *expensive* suite, and it shows; it's got central heating, electric lights – incandescent filaments, lots of them, dim enough you can look right at them – and silk curtains.' She glanced through the open bathroom door. 'The bathroom looks to be all brass and porcelain fittings and has a flushing toilet. Hmm. Must check to see what their power distribution system's like. Might be an opportunity to sell them electric showers.

'Tomorrow Erasmus will fix me up with a meeting with his attorney and start making inquiries about that house. He also said he'd look into a patent clerk and get me into the central reading library. Looks like their intellectual property framework is a bit primitive. I'll need to bring over some more fungibles soon. Gold is all very well, but I'm not sure it isn't cheaper here than it is back home. I wonder what their kitchens are short of,' she added.

'Damn. I wish there was someone to talk to.' She clicked off the little machine and put it down on the sideboard, frowning. Whether or not Erasmus Burgeson was trustworthy was an interesting question. Probably he was, up to a point – as long as he could sniff a way to put one over on the cops. But he was most clearly a bachelor, and there was something slightly strained about him when she was in his presence. *He's not used to dealing with women, other than customers in his shop,* she decided. *That's probably it.*

In any event, her head ached and she was feeling tired. *Think I'll leave the dining room for another day,* she decided. The bed seemed to beckon. Tomorrow would be a fresh start . . .

GOLD BUGS

The following morning Miriam awakened early. It was still semidark outside. She yawned at her reflection in the bathroom mirror as she brushed her hair. 'Hmm. They wear it long here, don't they?' It would have to do, she thought, as she dressed in yesterday's clothes once more. She sorted through her shoulder bag to make sure there was nothing too obtrusively alien in it, then pulled her boots on.

She paused at the foot of the main staircase, poised above the polished marble floor next to the front desk. 'Can I help you, ma'am?' a bellhop offered eagerly.

She smiled wanly. 'Breakfast. Where is it?' The realization that she'd missed both lunch and dinner crashed down on her. Abruptly she felt almost weak from hunger.

'This way, please!' He guided her toward two huge mahogany-and-glass doors set at one side of the foyer, then ushered her to a seat at a small table, topped in spotless linen. 'I shall just fetch the waiter.'

Miriam angled her chair around to take in the other diners as discreetly as possible. *It's like a historical movie!* she thought. One set in a really exclusive Victorian hotel, except the Victorians hadn't had a thing for vivid turquoise and purple wallpaper and the costumes were messed up beyond recognition. Men in Nehru suits with cutaway waists, women in long skirts or trousers and wing-collared shirts. Waiters with white aprons bearing plates of – fish? And bread rolls? The one familiar aspect was the newspaper. 'Can you fetch me a paper?' she asked the bellhop.

'Surely, ma'am!' he answered, and was off like a shot. He was back in a second and Miriam fumbled for a tip, before starting methodically on the front page.

The headlines in *The London Intelligencer* were bizarrely familiar, simultaneously tainted with the exotic. 'Speaker: House May Impeach

Crown for Adultery' – but no, there was no King Clinton in here, just unfamiliar names and a proposal to amend the Basic Law to add a collection of additional charges for which the Crown could be impeached – Adultery, Capitative Fraud, and Irreconsilience. *They can impeach the king?* Miriam shook her head, moved on to the next story, 'Morris and Stokes to Hang', about a pair of jewel thieves who had killed a shopkeeper. Farther down the page was more weirdness, a list of captains of merchantmen to whom had been granted letters of marque and reprise against 'the forces and agents of the continental enemy', and a list of etheric resonances assigned for experimentation by the Teloptic Wireless Company of New Britain.

A waiter appeared at her shoulder as she was about to turn the page. 'May I be of service, ma'am?'

'Sure. What's good, today?'

He smiled broadly. 'The kippers are most piquant, and if I may recommend Mrs. Wilson's strawberry jam for after? Does ma'am prefer tea or coffee?'

'Coffee. Strong, with milk.' She nodded. 'I'll take your recommendations, please. That'll be all.'

He scurried away, leaving her puzzling over the meaning of a story about taxation powers being granted by the King-in-Parliament to the Grand Estates, and enforcement of the powers of printing rights by the Royal Excise. Even the addition of a powerful dose of coffee and a plate of smoked fish – not her customary start to the day – didn't make it any clearer. *This place is so complex! Am I ever going to understand it?* she wondered.

She was almost to the bottom of her coffee when a different bell-hop arrived, bearing a silver platter. 'Message for the Widow Fletcher?' he asked, using the pseudonym Miriam had checked in under.

'That's me.' Miriam took the note atop the platter – a piece of card with strips of printed tape gummed to it. MEET ME AT 54 GRT MAURICE ST AT 10 SEE BATES STOP EB ENDS. 'Ah, good.' She glanced at the clock above the ornate entrance. 'Can you arrange a cab for me, please? To Great Maurice Street, in twenty minutes.'

Folding her paper she rose and returned to her room to retrieve her hat and topcoat. *The game's afoot,* she thought excitedly.

By the time the cab found its way to Great Maurice Street she'd cooled off a little, taking time to collect her thoughts and begin to work out what she needed to do and say. She also made sure her right glove was pulled down around her wrist, and the sleeve of her blouse was bunched up toward the elbow. Not that it was the ideal way to make an exit – indeed, it would wreck her plans completely if she had to escape by means of the temporary tattoo of a certain intricate knot – but she needed insurance in case Erasmus had decided to sell her out to the cops.

Great Maurice Street was a curving cobblestoned boulevard hemmed in on either side by expensive stone town houses. Little stone bridges leapt from sidewalk to broad front doors across a trench which held two levels of subterranean windows. The street and sidewalks had been swept free of snow, although huge piles stood at regular intervals in the road to await collection. Miriam stepped down from the cab, paid the driver, and marched along the sidewalk until she identified number 54. 'Charteris, Bates and Charteris,' she muttered to herself. 'Sounds legal.' She advanced on the door and pulled the bell rope.

A short, irritated-looking clerk opened the door. 'Who are you?' he demanded.

Miriam stared down her nose at him. 'I'm here to see Mr. Bates,' she said.

'Who did you say you were?' He raised a hand to cup his ear and Miriam realized he was half-deaf.

'Mrs. Fletcher, to see Mr. Bates,' she replied loudly.

'*Oh*. Come in, then, I'll tell someone you're here.'

Lawyers' offices didn't differ much between here and her own world, Miriam realized. There was a big, black, ancient-looking typewriter with a keyboard like a church organ that had shrunk in the wash, and there was an archaic telephone with a separate speaking horn, but otherwise the only differences were the clothes. Which, for a legal secretary in this place and time – male, thin, harried-looking – included a powdered wig, knee breeches, and a cutaway coat.

'Please be seated – ah, no,' said the secretary, looking bemused as a short, rotund fellow dressed entirely in black opened the door of an

363

inner office and waggled a finger at Miriam: 'This is His Honor Mr. Bates,' the secretary explained. 'You are . . . ?'

'I'm Mrs. Fletcher,' Miriam repeated patiently. 'I'm supposed to be seeing Mr. Bates. Is that right?'

'Ah, yes.' Bates nodded congenially at her. 'Please come this way?'

The differences from her own world became vanishingly small inside his office, perhaps because so many lawyers back home aimed for a traditional feel to their furnishings. Miriam glanced round. 'Burgeson isn't here yet,' she observed disapprovingly.

'He's been detained,' said Bates. 'If you'd care to take a seat?'

'Yes. How much has Erasmus told you?'

Bates picked up a pair of half-moon spectacles and balanced them on the bridge of his nose. His whiskers twitched, walruslike. 'He has told me enough, I think,' he intoned in a plummy voice. 'A woman fallen upon hard times, husband dead after years abroad, papers lost in an unfortunate pursuit – I believe he referred to the foundering of the *Greenbaum Lamplight*, a most unpleasant experience for you, I am sure – and therefore in need of the emollient reaffirmation of her identity, is that right? He vouched for you most plaintively. And he also mentioned something about a fortune overseas, held in trust, to which you have limited access.'

'Yes, that's all correct,' Miriam said fervently. 'I am indeed in need of new papers – and a few other services best rendered by a man of the law.'

'Well. I can see *at a glance* that you are no Frenchie,' he said, nodding at her. 'And so I can see nothing wrong with your party. It will take but an hour to draw up the correct deeds and post them with the inns of court, to declare your identity fair and square. Erasmus said you were born at Shreveport on, ah, if I may be so indelicate, the seventh of September, in the year of our lord nineteen hundred and sixty-nine. Is that correct?'

Miriam nodded. *Near enough*, she thought. 'Uh, yes.'

'Very well. If you would examine and sign this – ' he passed a large and imposing sheet of parchment to her – 'and this – ' he passed her another, 'we will set the wheels of justice in motion.'

Miriam examined the documents rapidly. One of them was a

declaration of some sort asserting her name, age, place of birth, and identity, and petitioning for a replacement birth certificate for the one lost at sea on behalf of the vacant authorities of – 'Why are the authorities of Shreveport not directly involved?' she asked.

Bates looked at her oddly. 'After what happened during the war there isn't enough left of Shreveport to *have* any authorities,' he muttered darkly.

'Oh.' She read on. The next paper petitioned for a passport in her name, with a peculiar status – competent adult. 'I see I am considered a competent adult here. Can you explain precisely what that entails?'

Bates leaned back in his chair, happily: *It's all billable hours*, Miriam realized. 'You are an adult, aged over thirty, and a widow; there is no man under whose mantle your rights and autonomy are exercised, and you are deemed old enough in law to be self-sufficient. So you may enter into contracts at your own peril, as an adult, until such time as you choose to remarry, and any such contracts as you make will then be binding upon your future husband.'

'Oh,' she said faintly, and signed in the space provided. *Better not marry anyone, then.* She put the papers back on his desk then cleared her throat. 'There are some other matters I will want you to see to,' she added.

'And what might those be?'

'Firstly,' she held up a finger, 'there is a house that takes my fancy; it is located at number 46, Bridge Park Lane, and it appears to be empty. Am I right in thinking you can make inquiries on my behalf about its availability? If it's open for lease or purchase I'd be extremely interested in acquiring it, and I'll want to move in as soon as possible.'

Bates sat up straight and nodded, almost enthusiastically. 'Of course, of course,' he said, scribbling in a crabbed hand on a yellow pad. 'And is there anything else?' he asked.

'Secondly, over the next month I will be wanting to create or purchase a limited liability company. It will need setting up. In addition, I will have a number of applications for patents that must be processed through the royal patent office – I need to locate and retain a patent agent on behalf of my company.'

'A company, and a patents agent.' He raised an eyebrow but kept writing. 'Is there anything else?'

'Indeed. Thirdly, I have a quantity, held overseas, I should add, of bullion. Can you advise me on the issues surrounding its legal sale here?'

'Oh, that's easy.' He put his pen down. 'I can't, because it's illegal for anyone but the Crown to own bullion.' He pointed at the signet ring he wore on his left hand. 'No rule against jewelry, of course, so long as it weighs less than a pound. But bullion?' He sniffed. 'You can perhaps approach the mint about an import license, and sell it to the Crown yourself – they'll give you a terrible rate, not worth your while, only ten pounds for an ounce. But that's the war for you. The mint is chronically short. If I were you, I'd sell it overseas and repatriate the proceeds as bearer bonds.'

'Thank you.' Miriam beamed at him ingratiatingly to cover up the sound of her teeth grinding together. *Ten pounds for an ounce? Erasmus, you and I are going to have strong words,* she thought. *Scratch finding an alternative, though.* 'How long will this take?' she asked.

'To file the papers? I'll have the boy run over with them right now. Your passport and birth certificate will be ready tomorrow if you send for them from my office. The company – ' he rubbed his chin. 'We would have to pay a parliamentarian to get the act of formation passed as a private member's bill, and I believe the going rate has been driven up by the demands of the military upon the legislature in the current session. It would be cheaper to buy an existing company with no debts. I can ask around, but I believe it will be difficult to find one for less than seventy pounds.'

'Ouch. There's no automatic process to go through to set one up?'

'Sadly, no. Like divorce, every company requires an Act of Parliament. Rubber-stamping them is bread and butter for most MPs, for they can easily charge fifty pounds or more to put forward an early-day motion for a five-minute bill in the Commons. Every so often someone proposes a registry of companies and a regulator to create them, but the backbenches won't ever approve that – it would take a large bite out of their living.'

'Humph.' Miriam nodded. 'All right, we'll do it your way. The patent agent?'

Bates nodded. 'Our junior clerk, Hinchliffe, is just the fellow for such a job. He has dealt with patents before, and will doubtless do so again. When will you need him?'

'Not until I have a company to employ him, a company that I will capitalize by entirely legal means that need not concern you.' The lawyer nodded again, his eyes twinkling. 'Then – let's just say, I have encountered some ingenious innovations overseas that I believe may best be exploited by patenting them, and farming out the rights to the patents to local factory owners. Do you follow?'

'Yes, I think I do.' Bates smiled like a crocodile. 'I look forward to your future custom, Mrs. Fletcher. It has been a pleasure to do business with such a perceptive member of the frail sex. Even if I don't believe a word of it.'

*

Miriam spent the rest of the morning shopping for clothes. It was a disorienting experience. There were no department or chain stores: Each type of garment came from a separate supplier, and the vast majority needed alterations to fit. Nor was she filled with enthusiasm by what she found. 'Why are fashion items invariably designed to make people look ugly or feel uncomfortable?' she muttered into her microphone, after experiencing a milliner's and a corsetière's in rapid succession. 'I'm going to stick to sports bras and briefs, even if I have to carry everything across myself,' she grumbled. Nevertheless, she managed to find a couple of presentable walking suits and an evening gown.

At six that evening, she walked through the gathering gloom to Burgeson's shop and slipped inside. The shop was open, but empty. She spent a good minute tapping her toes and whistling tunelessly before Erasmus emerged from the back.

'Oh, it's you,' he said distractedly. 'Here.' He held out an envelope.

Miriam took it and opened it – then stopped whistling. 'What brought this on?' she asked, holding it tightly.

His cheek twitched. 'I got a better price for the gold than I could be sure of,' he said. 'It seemed best to cut you in on the profits, in the hope of a prosperous future trade.'

'I see.' Miriam slid the envelope into a jacket pocket carefully. The five ten-pound notes in it were more than she'd hoped to browbeat out of him. 'Is your dealer able to take larger quantities of bullion?' she asked, abruptly updating her plans.

'I believe so.' His face was drawn and tired. 'I've had some thinking to do.'

'I can see that,' she said quietly. Fifty pounds here was equivalent to something between three and seven thousand dollars, back home. Gold was *expensive*, a sign of demand, and what did that tell her? Nothing good. 'What's the situation? Do you trust Bates?'

'About as far as I can throw him,' Erasmus admitted. 'He isn't a fellow traveler.'

'Fellow traveler.' She nodded to herself. 'You're a Marxist?'

'He was the greatest exponent of my faith, yes.' He said it quietly and fervently. 'I believe in natural rights, to which all men and women are born equal; in democracy; and in freedom. Freedom of action, freedom of commerce, freedom of faith, just like old Karl. For which they hanged him.'

'He came to somewhat different conclusions where I come from,' she said thoughtfully, 'although his starting conditions were dissimilar. Are you going to shut up shop and tell me what's troubling you?'

'Yes.' He strode over and turned the sign in the door, then shot the bolt. 'In the back, if you please.'

'After you.' Miriam followed him down a narrow corridor walled with pigeon holes. Parcels wrapped in brown paper gathered dust in them, each one sprouting a plaintive ticket against the date of its redemption – graveyard markers in the catacombs of usury. She kept her hand in her right pocket, tightening her grip on the small pistol, heart pounding halfway out of her chest with tension.

'You can't be a police provocateur,' he commented over his shoulder. 'For one thing, you didn't bargain hard enough over the bullion. For another, you slipped up in too many ways, all of them wrong. But I wasn't sure you weren't simply a madwoman until you showed me that intricate engine and left the book. He stepped sideways into a niche with a flight of wooden steps in it, leading down. 'It's far too incredible a story to be a flight-of-the mind concoction, and far too . . . *expensive*. Even the publisher's notes! The quality of the paper. And the typeface.' He stopped at the foot of the stairs and stared up at her owlishly, one hand clutching at a load-bearing beam for support. 'And the pocket kinetograph. I think either you're real or I'm going mad,' he said, his voice hollow.

'You're not mad.' Miriam took the steep flight of steps carefully. 'So?'

'So it behooves me to study this fascinating world you come from, and ask how it came to pass.' Erasmus was moving again. The cellar was walled from floor to ceiling in boxes and packing cases. 'It's fascinating. The principles of enlightenment that your republic was founded on – you realize they were smothered in the cradle, in the history I know of? Yes, the Parliamentary Settlement and the exile were great innovations for their time – but the idea of a *republic!* Separation of Church and State, a bill of rights, a universal franchise! After the second Leveler revolt, demands for such rights became something of a dead issue here, emphasis on the *dead* if you follow me . . . hmm.' He stopped in a cleared space between three walls of crates, a paraffin lamp dangling from a beam overhead.

'This is a rather big shop,' Miriam commented.

'So it should be.' He glanced at her, saw the hand in her pocket. 'Are you going to shoot me?'

'Why should I?' She tensed.

'I don't know.' He shrugged. 'You've obviously got some scheme in mind, one that means someone no good, whatever else you're doing here. And I might know too much.'

Miriam came to a decision and took her hand out of her pocket – empty.

'And I'm not an innocent either,' Erasmus added, gesturing at the crates. 'I'm glad you decided not to shoot. Niter of glycerol takes very badly to sudden shocks.'

Miriam paused, trying to get a grip on herself. She felt a sudden stab of apprehension: The stakes in his game were much higher than she'd realized. This was a police state, and Erasmus wasn't just a harmless dealer in illegal publications. 'Listen, I have *no* intention of shooting anyone if I can avoid it. And I don't care about you being a

Leveler quartermaster with a basement full of explosives – at least, as long as I don't live next door to you. It's none of my business, and whatever you think, I didn't come here to get involved in *your* politics. Even if it sounds better than, than what's out there right now. On the other hand, I have my own, uh, political problems.'

Erasmus raised an eyebrow. 'So who are your enemies?'

Miriam bit her lip. *Can I trust him this far?* She couldn't see any choices at this point but, even so, taking him into her confidence was a big step. 'I don't know,' she said reluctantly. 'They're probably well-off. Like me, they can travel between worlds – not to the one in the book I gave you, which is my own, but to a much poorer, medieval one. One in which Christianity never got established as the religion in Rome, the dark ages lasted longer. In that world the Norse migration reached and settled this coast, as far inland as the Appalachians, and the Chinese empire holds the west. These people will be involved in trading, from here to there – I'm not sure what, but I believe ownership of gold is something to investigate. They'll probably be a large and prosperous family, possibly ennobled in the past century or two, and they'll be rich and conservative. Not exactly fellow travelers.'

'And what is your problem with them?'

'They keep trying to kill me.' Now she'd said it, confiding in him felt easier. 'They come from over here. This is their power base, Erasmus. I believe they consider me a threat to them. I want to find them before they find me, and order things in a more satisfactory manner.'

'I think I see.' He made a steeple of his fingers. 'Do you want them to die?'

'Not necessarily. But I want to know who they are, and where they came here from, and to stop their agents trying to kill me. I've got a couple of suspicions about who they are that I need to confirm. If I'm correct I might be able to stop the killing.'

'I suggest you tell me your story then,' said Erasmus. 'And we'll see if there's anything we can do about it.' He raised his voice, causing her to start. 'Aubrey! You can cease your lurking. If you'd be so good as to fetch the open bottle of port and three glasses, you may count yourself in for a tall tale.' He smiled humorlessly. 'You've got our undivided attention, ma'am. I suggest you use it wisely . . .'

*

Back at the hotel a couple of hours later, Miriam changed into her evening dress and went downstairs, unaccompanied, for a late buffet supper. The waiter was unaccountably short with her, but found her a solitary small table in a dark corner of the dining room. The soup was passable, albeit slightly cool, and a cold roast with vegetables filled the empty corners of her stomach. She watched the well-dressed men and few women in the hotel from her isolated vantage point, and felt abruptly lonely. *Is it just ordinary homesickness,* she wondered, *or culture shock?* One or two hooded glances came her way, but she avoided eye contact and in any event nobody attempted to engage her in conversation. *It's as if I'm invisible,* she thought.

She didn't stay for dessert. Instead she retreated to her room and sought solace with a long bath and an early night.

The next morning she warned the concierge that she would be away for a few days and would not need her room, but would like her luggage stored. Then she took a cab to the lawyer's office. 'Your papers are here, ma'am,' said Bates's secretary.

'Is Mr. Bates free?' she asked. 'Just a minute of his time.'

'I'll just check.' A minute of finger twiddling passed. 'Yes, come in, please.'

'Ah, Mr. Bates?' She smiled. 'Have you made progress with your inquiries?'

He nodded. 'I am hoping to hear about the house tomorrow,' he said. 'Its occupant, a Mr. Soames, apparently passed away three months ago and it is lying vacant as part of his estate. As his son lives in El Dorado, I suspect an offer for it may be received with gratitude. As to the company – ' He shrugged. 'What business shall I put on it?'

Miriam thought for a moment. 'Call it a design bureau,' she said. 'Or an engineering company.'

'That will be fine.' Bates nodded. 'Is there anything else?'

'I'm going to be away for a week or so,' she said. 'Shall I leave a deposit behind for the house?'

'I'm sure your word would be sufficient,' he said graciously. 'Up to what level may I offer?'

'If it goes over a thousand pounds I'll have to make special arrangements to transfer the funds.'

'Very well.' He stood up. 'By your leave?'

Miriam's last port of call was the central library. She spent two hours there, quizzing a helpful librarian about books on patent law. In the end, she took three away with her, giving her room at the hotel as an address. Carefully putting them in her shoulder bag she walked to the nearest main road and waved down a cab. 'Roundgate Interchange,' she said. *I'm going home,* she thought. *At last!* A steam car puttered past them, overtaking on the right-hand side. *Back to clean air, fast cars, and electricity everywhere.*

She gazed out of the cab's window as the open field came into view through the haze of acrid fog that seemed to be everywhere today. *I wonder how Brill and Paulie have been?* she wondered.

*

It was dusk, and nobody seemed to have noticed the way that Miriam had damaged the side door of the estate. She slunk into the garden, paced past the hedge and the dilapidated greenhouse, then located the spot where she'd blazed a mark on the wall. A fine snow was falling as she pulled out the second locket and, with the aid of a pocket flashlight, fell headfirst into it.

She staggered slightly as the familiar headache returned with a vengeance, but a quick glance told her that nobody had come anywhere near this spot for days. A fresh snowfall had turned her hide into an anonymous hump in the gloom a couple of trees away. She waded toward it – then a dark shadow detached itself from a tree and pointed a pistol at her.

'Brill?' she asked, uncertainly.

'Miriam!' The barrel dropped as Brill lurched forward and embraced her. 'I've been so worried! How have you been?'

'Not so bad!' Miriam laughed, breathlessly. 'Let's get under cover and I'll tell you about it.'

Brill had been busy; the snow bank concealed not only the hunting hide, but a fully assembled hut, six feet by eight, somewhat insecurely pegged to the iron-hard ground beneath the snow. 'Come in, come in,' she said. Miriam stepped inside and she shut the door and bolted it. Two bunks occupied one wall, and a paraffin heater threw off enough warmth to keep the hut from freezing. 'It's been terribly cold by night, and I fear I've used up all the oil,' Brill told her. 'You really *must* buy a wood stove!'

'I believe I will,' Miriam said thoughtfully, thinking about the coal smoke and yellow sulfurous smog that had made the air feel as if she was breathing broken glass. 'It's been, hmm, three days. Have you had any trouble?'

'Boredom,' Brilliana said instantly. 'But sometimes boredom is a good thing. I have not been so alone in many years!' She looked slightly wistful. 'Would you like some cocoa? I'd love to hear what adventures you've been having!'

That night Miriam slept fitfully, awakening once to a distant howling noise that raised the hair on her neck. *Wolves?* she wondered, before rolling over and dozing off again. Although the paraffin heater kept the worst of the chill at bay, there was frost inside the walls by morning.

Miriam woke first, sat up and turned the heat up as high as it would go, then – still cocooned in the sleeping bag – hung her jeans and hiking jacket from a hook in the roof right over the heater. Then she dozed off again. When she awakened, she saw Brill sitting beside the heater reading a book. 'What is it?' she asked sleepily.

'Something Paulie lent me.' Brill looked slightly guilty. Miriam peered at the spine: *The Female Eunuch*. Sitting on a shelf next to the door she spotted a popular history book. Brill had been busy expanding her horizons.

'Hmm.' Miriam sat up and unzipped her bag, used the chamber pot, then hastily pulled on the now-defrosted jeans and a hiking sweater. Her boots were freezing cold so she moved them closer to the heater. 'You've been thinking a lot.'

'Yes.' Brilliana put the book down. 'I grew up with books; my father's library had five in Hoh'sprashe, and almost thirty in English. But this – the style is so strange! And what it says!'

Miriam shook her head. 'We'll have to go across soon,' she said, shelving the questions that sat at the tip of her tongue – poisonous questions, questions about trust and belief. Brill seemed to be going through a phase of questioning everything, and that was fine by her.

It meant she was less likely to obey if Angbard or whoever was behind her told her to point a gun at Miriam. Searching her bag Miriam came up with her tablets, dry-swallowed them, then glanced around. 'Anything to drink?'

'Surely.' Brill passed her a water bottle. It crackled slightly, but most of the contents were still liquid. 'I didn't realize a world could be so large and so empty,' Brill added quietly.

'I know how you feel,' Miriam said with feeling, running fingers through her hair – it needed a good wash and, now she thought about it, at least a trim – she'd spent the past four weeks so preoccupied in other things that it was growing wild and uncontrolled. 'The far side is pretty strange to me, too. I *think* I've got it under control, but – ' she shrugged. *Private ownership of gold is illegal so there's a black market in it, but opium and cocaine are sold openly in apothecary shops. Setting up a company takes an Act of Parliament, but they can impeach the king.* 'Let's just say, it isn't quite what I was expecting. Let's go home.'

'All right.'

They pulled their boots and coats on. Brill turned off the heater and folded the sleeping bags neatly, then went outside to empty the chamber pot. Miriam picked up her shoulder bag, and then went outside to join Brill on the spot she'd marked on her last trip. She took a deep breath, pulled out the locket with her left hand, took all of Brill's weight on her right hip for a wobbly, staggering moment that threatened to pull her over, and focused –

On a splitting headache and a concrete wall as her grip slipped and Brill skidded on the icy yard floor. 'Ow!' Brill stood up, rubbing her backside. 'That was most indelicately done.'

'Could be worse.' Miriam winced at the pain in her temples, glanced around, and shook her head to clear the black patches from the edge of her vision. There was no sign of any intrusion, but judging by the boxes stacked under the metal fire escape – covered with polythene sheeting against the weather – Paulette had been busy. 'Come on inside, let's fix some coffee and catch up on the news.'

The office door opened to Miriam's key and she hastily punched in the code to disable the burglar alarm. Then she felt the heat, a stifling warmth that wrapped itself around her like a hot bath towel. 'Wow,' she said, 'come get a load of this.'

'I'm coming! I'm coming!' Brill shut and locked the door behind her and looked around. 'Ooh, I haven't been this warm in *days*.' She hastily opened her jacket and untied her boots, the better to let the amazing warmth from the underfloor heating get closer to her skin.

'You'll want to use the shower next,' Miriam said, amused. 'I could do with it too, so don't be too long.' The shower in the office bathroom was cramped and cheap, but better than the antique plumbing arrangements on the far side. 'I'll make coffee.'

She found her cell phone in the front room. Its battery had run down while she'd been gone, so she plugged it in to recharge. She also found a bunch of useful items – Paulette had installed a brand-new desk telephone and modem line while she'd been away – and a bunch of paperwork from the city government.

She was drinking her coffee in the kitchen when the front door opened. She ducked out into the corridor, hand going to her empty jacket pocket before she realized what the reaction meant. 'Paulie!' she called.

'Miriam! Good to see you!' Paulette had nearly jumped right out of her skin when she saw Miriam, but now she smiled broadly. 'Oh wow. You look like you've spent a week on the wild side!'

'That's exactly what I've done. Coffee?'

'I'd love some, thanks.' There was someone behind her. 'In the front office, Mike, it needs to come through under the window,' she said over her shoulder. 'We're putting a DSL line in here. Hope you don't mind?'

'No, no, that's great.' She retreated back into the small kitchenette, mind blanking on what to do next. She'd been thinking about a debriefing session with Paulie and Brill, then a provisioning trip to the universe next door, then a good filling lunch – but not with a phone company installer drilling holes in the wall.

Paulette obviously had things well in hand here, and there was no way Miriam was going to get into the shower for a while. She stared at the coffee machine. *Maybe I should go and see Iris,* she wondered. *Or . . . hmm. Is it time to call Roland again?*

'Miriam, you're going to have to tell me how it's going.' Paulette waited in the kitchen doorway.

'In due course.' She managed a smile. 'Success, but not so total. How about at your end?'

'Running low on money – the burn rate on this operation is like a goddamn start-up,' Paulette complained. 'I'll need another hundred thousand to secure all the stuff you left on the shopping list.'

'And don't forget the paycheck.' Miriam nodded. 'Listen, I found one good thing out about the far side. Gold is about as legal there as heroin is here, and vice versa. I'm getting about two hundred pounds on the black market for a brick weighing sixteen troy ounces, worth about three thousand, three five, dollars here. A pound goes a *lot* further than a dollar, it's like, about two hundred bucks. So three and a half thousand here buys me the equivalent of forty thousand over there. Real estate prices are low, too. The place I need to buy on the far side is huge, but it should go for about a thousand pounds, call it equivalent to two hundred grand here. In our own Boston it'd be going for a couple of million, easily. But gold is worth so much that I can pay for it with five bars of the stuff – about eighteen thousand dollars on this side. I've found an, uh, black-market outlet who seems reasonably trustworthy at handling the gold – he's got an angle, but I know what it is. And it is *amazingly* easy to set up a new identity! Anyway, if I play this right I can build a front as a rich widow returning home from the empire with a fortune and then get the far side money pump running.'

'What are you going to carry the other way?' Paulette asked, sharply.

'Not sure yet.' Miriam rubbed her temples. 'It's weird. They sell cocaine and morphine in drugstores, over the counter, and they fly Zeppelins, and New Britain is at war with the French Empire, and their version of Karl Marx was executed for Ranting – preaching democracy and equal rights. With no industrial revolution he turned into a Leveler ideologue instead of a socialist economist. I'm just surprised he was born in the first place – most of the names in the history books are unfamiliar after about eighteen hundred. It's like a different branch in the same infinite tree of history; I wonder where

Niejwein fits in it . . . let's not go there now. I need to think of something we can import.' She brooded. 'I'll have to think fast. If the Clan realizes their drug-money pump could run this efficiently they'll flood the place with cheap gold and drop the price of crack in half as soon as they learn about it. There's got to be some *other* commodity that's valuable over here that we can use to repatriate our profits.'

'Old masters,' Paulette said promptly.

'Huh?'

'Old masters.' She put her mug down. 'Listen, they haven't had a world war, have they?'

'Nope, I'm afraid they have,' Miriam said, checking her watch to see if she could take another pain killer yet. 'In fact, they've had two. One in the eighteen-nineties that cost them India. The second in the nineteen-fifties that, well, basically New Britain got kicked out of Africa. Africa is a mess of French and Spanish colonies. But they got a strong alliance with Japan and the Netherlands, which also rule most of northwest Germany. And they rule South America and Australia and most of East Asia.'

'No tanks? No H-bombs? No strategic bombers?'

'I don't think so. Are you saying – '

'Museum catalogues!' Paulie said excitedly. 'I've been thinking about this a lot while you've been gone. What we do is, we look for works of art dating to before things went, uh, differently. In the other place. Works that were in museums in Europe that got bombed during World War Two, works that disappeared and have never been seen since. You get the picture? Just *one* lost sketch by Leonardo . . .'

'Won't they be able to tell the difference? I'd have thought the experts would – ' she trailed off.

'They'll be exactly the same age! They'd be the real thing, right? Not a hoax. What you do is, you go over with some art catalogues from here, and when you've got the money, you find a specialist buyer and you buy the paintings or marbles or whatever for your personal collection. Then bring them over here. It's about the only thing that weighs so little you can carry it, but is worth millions and is legal to own.'

'It'll be harder to sell,' Miriam pointed out. 'A *lot* harder to sell.'

'Yeah, but it's legal,' said Paulie. She hesitated momentarily. 'Unless you want to go into the Bolivian marching powder business like your long-lost relatives?'

'Um.' Miriam refilled her coffee mug. 'Okay, I'll look at it.' *Miriam Beckstein, dealer in fine arts,* she thought. *It has a peculiar ring to it, but it's better than Miriam Beckstein, drug smuggler.* 'Hmm. How's this for a cover story? I fly over to Europe next year, spend weeks trolling around out there in France and Germany and wherever the paintings went missing. Right? I act secretive and just tell people I'm investigating something. That covers my absence. What I'll really be doing is crossing to the far side then flying right back to New Britain by airship. Maybe I'll come home in the meantime, maybe I can work over there, whatever. Whichever I do, it builds up a record of me being out of the country, investigating lost art, and I use the travel time to read up on art history. When I go public over here, it's a career change. I've gone into unearthing lost works of art and auctioning them. Sort of a capitalist version of Indiana Jones, right?'

'Love it. Wait till I patent the business practice, "a method of making money by smuggling gold to another world and exchanging it for lost masterpieces"!'

'You *dare* – ' Miriam chuckled. 'Although I'm not sure we'll be able to extract anything like the full value of our profits that way. I'm not even sure we want to – having a world to live in where we're affluent and haven't spent the past few decades developing a reputation as organized criminals would be no bad thing. Anyway, back to business. How's the patent search going?'

'I've got about a dozen candidates for you,' Paulie said briskly. 'A couple of different types of electric motor that they may or may not have come up with. Flash boilers for steam cars, assuming they don't already have them. They didn't sound too sophisticated but you never know. The desk stapler – did you see any? Good. I looked into the proportional font stuff you asked for, but the Varityper mechanism is just amazingly complicated, it wouldn't simply hatch out of nowhere. And the alkaline battery will take a big factory and supplies of unusual metals to start making. The most promising option is still the disk brake and the asbestos/resin brake shoe. But I came up with another for you: the parachute.'

'Parachute – ' Miriam's eyes widened. 'I'll need to go check if they've invented them. I know Leonardo drew one, but it wouldn't have been stable. Okay!' She emptied the coffeepot into her and Paulette's mugs, stirred in some sugar. 'That's great. How long until the cable guy is done?'

'Oh, he's already gone,' Paulette said. 'I get to plug the box in myself, don't you know?'

'Excellent.' Miriam picked up her mug. 'Then I can check my voice mail in peace.'

She wandered into the front office as Brill was leaving the shower, wrapped in towels and steaming slightly. A raw new socket clung to the wall just under the window. Miriam dropped heavily into the chair behind the desk, noticing the aches of sleeping on a hard surface for the first time. She picked up her phone and punched in her code. Paulette intercepted Brill, asking her something as she led her into the large back office they'd begun converting into a living room.

'You have two messages,' said the phone.

'Yeah, yeah.' Miriam punched a couple more buttons.

'First message, received yesterday at eleven forty-two: Miriam? Oh, Sky Father! Listen, are you alright? Phone me, *please.'* It was Roland, and he didn't sound happy. 'It's urgent,' he added, before the click of the call ending.

'Second message, received yesterday at nine twelve: Miriam, dear? It's me.' *Ma,* she realized. There was a pause. 'I know I haven't been entirely candid with you, and I want you to know that I bitterly regret it.' Another, much longer pause and the sound of labored breathing. Miriam clutched the phone to her ear like a drowning woman. 'I've . . . something unexpected has come up. I've got to go on a long journey. Miriam, I want you to understand that I *am* going to be all right. I know exactly what I'm doing, and it's something I should have done years ago. But it's not fair to burden you with it. I'll try to call you or leave messages, but you are *not* to come around or try to follow me. I love you.' *Click.*

'Shit!' Miriam threw the cell phone across the room in blind panic. She burst out of her chair and ran for the back room, grabbed her jacket and was halfway into her shoes by the time Paulette stuck a curious head out of the day room door. 'What's going on?'

'Something's happened to Iris. I'm going to check on her.'

'You can't!' Paulette stood up, alarmed.

'Watch me.'

'But it's under – '

'Fuck the surveillance!' She fumbled in her bag for the revolver. 'If the Clan has decided to go after my mother I am going to kill someone.'

'Miriam – ' it was Brill – 'Paulie and I can't get away the way you can.'

'So you'd better be discreet about the murder business,' said Paulette. 'Can you wait two minutes? I'll drive.'

'I – yes.' Miriam forced herself to unclench her fists and take deep, steady breaths.

'Good. Because if it *is* the Clan, then rushing in is exactly what they'll expect you to do. And if it isn't, if it's the other guys, that's what they'll expect you to do, too.' She swallowed. 'Bombs and all. Which is why *I'm* going with you. Got it?'

'I – ' Miriam forced herself to think. 'Okay.' She stood up. 'Let's go.'

They went.

*

Paulette cruised down Iris's residential street twice, leaving a good five-minute interval before turning the rental car into the parking space at the side of her house. 'Nothing obvious,' she murmured. 'You see anything, kid?'

'Nothing,' said Miriam.

Brill shook her head. 'Autos all look alike to me,' she admitted.

'Great . . . Miriam, if you want to take the front door, I'm going to sit here with the engine running until you give the all-clear. Brill – '

'I'll be good.' She clutched a borrowed handbag to her chest, right hand buried in it, looking like a furtive sorority girl about to drop an unexpected present on a friend.

Miriam bailed out of the car and walked swiftly to Iris's front door, noticing nothing wrong. There was no damage around the lock, no broken windows, nothing at all out of the usual for the area. No lurking vans, either, when she glanced over her shoulder as she slipped the key into the front door and turned it left-handed, her other hand full.

The door bounced open and Miriam ducked inside rapidly, with Brill right behind her. The house was empty and cold – not freezing with the chill of a dead furnace, but as if the thermostat had been turned down. Miriam's feet scuffed on the carpet as she rapidly scanned each ground floor room through their open doors, finishing in Iris's living room –

No wheelchair. The side table neatly folded and put away. Dead flowers on the mantelpiece.

Back in the hall Miriam held up a finger, then dashed up the stairs, kicking open door after door – the master bedroom, spare bedroom, box room, and bathroom.

'*Nothing*,' she called, panting. In the spare bedroom she pulled down the hatch into the attic, yanked the ladder down – but there was no way Iris could have gotten up there under her own power. She scrambled up the ladder all the same, casting about desperately in the dusty twilight. 'She's *not here.*'

Down in the ground floor hallway she caught up with Paulette, looking grave. 'Brill said Iris is gone?'

Miriam nodded, unable to speak. It felt like an act of desecration, too monstrous to talk about. She leaned against the side of the staircase, taking shallow breaths. 'I've lost her.' She shut her eyes.

'Over here!' It was Brill, in the kitchen.

'What is it – '

They found Brill inspecting a patch of floor, just inside the back door. 'Look,' she said, pointing.

The floor was wooden, varnished and worn smooth in places. The stains, however, were new. Something dark had spilled across the back doorstep. Someone had mopped it up but they hadn't done a very good job, and the stain had worked into the grain of the wood.

'Outside. Check the garbage.' Miriam fumbled with the lock then got the door open. 'Come on!' She threw herself at the Dumpsters in the backyard, terrified of what she might find in them. The bins were huge, shared with the houses to either side, and probably not emptied since the last snowfall. The snow was almost a foot deep on top of the nearest Dumpster. It took her half a minute to clear enough away to lift the lid and look inside.

A dead man stared back at her, his face blue and his eyes frozen in an expression of surprise. She dropped the lid.

'What is it?' asked Paulette.

'Not Iris.' Miriam leaned against the wall, taking deep breaths, her head spinning. *Who can he be?* 'Check. The other bins.'

'Other bins, okay.' Paulette gingerly lifted the lids, one by one – but none of them contained anything worse than a pile of full garbage bags which, when torn, proved to contain kitchen refuse. 'She's not here, Miriam.'

'Oh god.'

'What now?' asked Paulie, head cocked as if listening for the sound of sirens.

'I take another look while you and Brill keep an eye open for strangers.' Steeling herself, Miriam lifted the lid on the bin's gruesome contents. She reached out and touched her hand to an ice-cold cheek. 'He's been dead for at least twelve hours, more likely over twenty-four.' A mass of icy black stuff in front of the body proved to be Iris's dish towels, bulked up by more frozen blood than Miriam could have imagined. She gingerly shoved them aside, until she saw where the blood had come from. 'There's massive trauma to the upper thorax, about six inches below the neck. Jesus, it looks like a shotgun wound. I saw a couple in the ER, way back when. Um . . . sawed-off, by the size of the entry wound, either that or he was shot from more than twenty yards away, which would have had to happen outdoors, meaning witnesses. His chest is really torn up, he'd have died instantly.' She dropped the wadding back in front of the body. He was, she noted distantly, wearing black overalls and a black ski mask pulled up over his scalp like a cap. Clean-shaven, about twenty years old, of military appearance. Like a cop or a soldier – or a Clan enforcer.

She turned around and looked at the back door. Something was wrong with it; it took almost a minute of staring before she realized –

'They replaced the door,' she said. 'They replaced the fucking door!'

'Let's go,' Paulette said nervously. 'Like right now? Anywhere, as long as it's away? This is giving me the creeps.'

'Just a minute.' Miriam dropped the Dumpster lid shut and went back inside the house. *Iris phoned me when the shit hit the fan,* she realized. *She was still alive and free, but she had to leave. To go underground, like in the sixties. When the FBI bugged her phone.* Miriam leaned over Iris's favorite chair, in the morning room. She swept her hand around the crack behind the cushion; nothing. 'No messages?' She looked up, scanning the room. The mantelpiece: dead flowers, some cards . . . birthday cards. One of them said 32 TODAY. She walked toward it slowly, then picked it up, unbelieving. Her eyes clouded with tears as she opened it. The inscription inside it was written in Iris's jagged, half-illiterate scrawl. *Thanks for the memories of treasure hunts, and the green party shoes,* it said.

'Green party shoes?'

Miriam dashed upstairs, into Iris's bedroom. Opening her mother's wardrobe she smelled mothballs, saw row upon row of clothes hanging over a vast mound of shoes – a pair of green high-heeled pumps near the front, pushed together. She picked them up, probed inside, and felt a wad of paper filling the toes of the right shoe.

She pulled it out, feeling it crackle – elderly paper, damaged by the passage of time. A tabloid newspaper page, folded tight. She ran downstairs to where Brill was waiting impatiently in the hall. 'I got it,' she called.

'Got what?' Brill asked, her voice incurious.

'I don't know.' Miriam frowned as she locked the door, then they were in the back of the car and Paulie was pulling away hastily, fish-tailing slightly on the icy road.

'When your mother phoned you,' Paulie said edgily, 'what did she say? Daughter, I've killed someone? Or, your wicked family has come to kidnap me, oh la! What is to become of me?'

'She said.' Miriam shut her eyes. 'She hadn't been entirely honest with me. Something had come up, and she had to go on a journey.'

'Someone died,' said Brill. 'Someone standing either just outside the back door or just inside it, in the doorway. Someone shot them with a blunderbuss.' She was making a singsong out of it, in a way that really got on Miriam's nerves. *Stress,* she thought. *Brill had never seen a murder before last week. Now she's seen a couple in one go, hasn't she?* 'So someone stuffed the victim in a barrel for Iris, went out and ordered a new door. Angbard's men will have been watching her departure. Probably followed her. Why don't you call him and ask about it?'

'I will. Once we've returned this car and rented a replacement from another hire shop.' She glanced at Brill. 'Keep a lookout and tell me if you see any cars that seem to be following us.'

Miriam unfolded the paper carefully. It was, she saw, about the same fateful day as the first Xeroxed news report in the green and pink shoebox. But this was genuine newsprint, not a copy, a snapshot from the time itself. Most of it was inconsequential, but there was a story buried halfway down page two that caught her attention, about a young mother and baby found in a city park, the mother suffering a stab wound in the lower back. She'd been wearing hippy-style clothes and was unable to explain her condition, apparently confused or intoxicated. The police escorted her to a hospital with the child, and the writer proceeded to editorialize on the evils of unconventional lifestyles and the effects of domestic violence in a positively Hogarthian manner. *No,* Miriam thought, *they must have gotten it wrong. She was murdered, Ma told me! Not taken into hospital with a stab wound!* She shook her head, bewildered. 'I'll do that. But first I need some stuff from my house,' she said. 'I'm not sure I dare go there.'

'What stuff?' asked Paulie. Miriam could see her fingers white against the rim of the steering wheel.

'Papers.' She paused, weighing up the relative merits of peace of mind and a shotgun wound to the chest. 'Damn it,' she said shortly. 'I need to go home. I need five minutes there. Paulie, take me home.'

'Is that really smart?' asked Paulette, knuckles tightening on the steering wheel.

'No. It's really *not* smart. But I need to grab some stuff, the disk with all your research on it. I'll be about thirty seconds. We can ditch the car immediately afterwards. You willing to wait?'

'Didn't you say they'd staked you out?'

'What does that mean?' Brill asked, confused. 'What are you talking about?'

Miriam sighed. 'My house. I haven't been back to it since my fun-loving uncle had me kidnapped. Roland said it was under surveillance so I figured it would be risky. Now – '

'It's even *more* risky,' Paulette said vehemently. 'In fact I think it's stupid.'

'Yes.' Miriam bared her teeth, worry and anger eating at her. 'But I *need* that disk, Paulie, it may be the best leverage I've got. We don't have time for me to make millions in world three.'

'Oh shit. You think it may come to that?'

'Yeah, "oh shit" indeed.'

'What kind of disk?' Brill asked plaintively.

'Don't worry. Just wait with the car.' Miriam focused on Paulette's driving. *The answer will be somewhere in the shoebox,* she thought, desperately. *And if Angbard had my ma snatched, I'll make him pay.*

Familiar scenery rolled past, and a couple of minutes later they turned into a residential street that Miriam knew well enough to navigate blindfolded. A miserable wave of homesickness managed to penetrate her anger and worry: This was where she belonged, and she should never have left. It was her home! And it slid past to the left as Paulette kept on driving.

'Paulie?' Miriam asked.

'Looking for suspicious-acting vehicles.'

'Oh.' Miriam glanced around. 'Ma said there was a truck full of guys watching her.'

'Uh-huh. Your mother spotted the truck. What did she miss?'

'Got you.' Miriam spared a sideways glance: Brill's head was swiveling like a ceiling fan, but her expression was more vacant than anything else. Almost as if she was bored. 'Want to drive round the block once more? When you get back to the house stop just long enough for me to get out, then carry on. Come back and pick me up in three minutes. Don't park.'

'You sure that you want to do this?'

'No, I'm not sure, I just know that I have to.'

Paulie turned the corner then pulled over. Miriam was out of the car a second before Paulette pulled away. There was nobody about – no parked occupied vans, no joggers. She crossed the road briskly, walked up to her front door, and remembered two things, in a single moment of icy clarity. Firstly, that she had no idea where her house keys might be, and secondly, that if there were no watchers that might be because –

Uh-oh, she thought, and backed away from the front step, watching where her feet were about to go with exaggerated caution. A cold sweat broke out in the small of her back, and she shuddered. But fear of trip wires didn't stop her carefully opening the yard gate, slipping around the side of the house, and up to the shed with the concealed key to the French windows at the back.

When she had the key, Miriam paused for almost a minute at the glass doors, trying to get her hammering heart under control. She peered through the curtains, thoughtfully. *They'll expect me to go in the front*, she realized. *But even so* . . . She unlocked the door and eased it open a finger's width. Then she reached as high as she could, and ran her index finger slowly down the opening, feeling for the faint tug of a lethal obstruction. Finding nothing, she opened the door farther, then repeated the exercise on the curtains. Again: nothing. And so, Miriam returned to her home.

Her study had been efficiently and brutally strip-searched. The iMac was gone, as were the boxes of CD-ROMs and the zip drive and disks from her desk. More obviously, every book in the bookcase had been taken down, the pages riffled, and dumped in a pile on the floor. It was a big pile. 'Bastards,' she said quietly. The pink and green shoebox was gone, of course. Fearing the worst she tiptoed into her own hallway like a timid burglar, her heart in her mouth.

It was much the same in the front hall. They'd even searched the phone books. A blizzard of loose papers lay everywhere, trampled underfoot. Drawers lay open, their contents strewn around. Furniture had been pulled out from the walls and shoved back haphazardly, and one of the hall bookcases leaned drunkenly against the opposite wall. At first sight she thought that the living room had gotten off lightly, but the damage turned out to be even more extensive – her entire music collection had been turned out onto the floor, disks piled in a loose stack.

'Fuck.' Her mouth tasted of ashes. The sense of violation was almost unbearable, but so was the fear that they'd taken her mother and found Paulie's research disk as well. The money-laundering leads were in the hands of whoever had done this to her. Whoever they were, they had to know about the Clan, which meant they'd know what the disk's contents meant. They were a smoking gun, one that was almost certainly pointing at the Clan's east coast operations. She knelt by the discarded CD cases and rummaged for a minute – found *The Beggar's Opera* empty, the CD-ROM purloined.

She went back into the front hall. Somehow she slithered past the fallen bookcase, just to confirm her worst fear. They'd strung the wire behind the front door, connecting one end of it to the handle. If she hadn't been in such a desperate hurry that she'd forgotten her keys, the green box taped crudely to the wall would have turned her into a messy stain on the sidewalk. *Assassin number two is the one who likes Claymore mines,* she reminded herself. Miriam couldn't take any more. She blundered out through the French windows at the back without pausing to lock them, round the side of the house, and onto the sidewalk to wait for Paulie.

Seconds later she was in the back of the car, hunched and shivering. 'I don't see any signs of anything going on,' Paulie said quietly. She seemed to have calmed down from her state at Iris's house. 'What do you want to do now? Why don't we find a Starbucks, get some coffee, then you tell us what you found?'

'I don't think so.' Miriam closed her eyes.

'Are you all right?' Brill asked, concern in her voice.

'No, I'm not all right,' Miriam said quietly. 'We've got to ditch the car, *now*. They trashed the place and left a tripwire surprise behind the front door. Paulie, the box of stuff my mother gave me was gone. And so was the disk.'

'Oh *shit*. What are we going to do?'

'I – ' Miriam stopped. 'I'm going to talk to Angbard. But not until I've had a few words with Roland.' She pulled an expression that someone who didn't know her might have mistaken for a smile. 'He's the one who told me about the surveillance. It's time to clear the air.'

PART EIGHT

CAPITALISM FOR BEGINNERS

INTERROGATIONS

The city of Irongate nestled in the foothills of the Appalachians, soot-stained and smoky by day, capped at night by a sky that reflected the red glow of the blast furnaces down by the shipping canal. From the center of town, the Great North-East Railway spur led off toward the coastline and the branches for Boston and New London. West of the yards and north of the banked ramparts of the Vauban-pattern fortress sloped a gentle rise populated by the houses of the gentry, while at the foot of the slope clustered tight rows of workers' estates.

Irongate had started as a transport nexus at the crossing of the canal and the railways, but it had grown into a sprawling industrial city. The canal and its attendant lock system brought cargos from as far as the Great Lakes – and, in another time, another world, it was the site of a trading post with the great Iroquois Nation, who dominated the untamed continental interior between the Gruinmarkt and the empire of the West.

There was a neighborhood down in the valley, rubbing shoulders with the slums of the poor and the business districts, that was uncomfortable with its own identity. Some people had money but no standing in polite society, no title or prospects for social advancement. They congregated here, Chinese merchants and Jewish brokers and wealthy owners of bawdy houses alike, and they took pains to be discreet, for while New Britain's laws applied equally to all men, the enforcers of those laws were only too human.

Esau walked slowly along Hanover Street, his cane tapping the cobblestones with every other stride. It was early evening and bitterly cold with it, but the street sweepers had been at work and the electric street lamps cast a warm glow across the pavement. Esau walked slowly, foregoing the easy convenience of a cab, because he wanted time to think. It was vital to prepare himself for the meeting that lay ahead, both emotionally and intellectually.

The street was almost empty, the few pedestrians hurrying with hands thrust deep in coat pockets and hats pulled down. Esau passed a pub, a blare of brassy noise and a stench of tobacco smoke drifting from the doorway as it opened to emit a couple of staggering drunks. 'Heya, slant-eye!' one of them bellowed after him. Esau kept on walking steadily, but he tightened his grasp on the butt of the small pistol in his pocket. *Don't react,* he told himself. *You can kill him if he attacks you. Not before.* Not that Esau looked particularly Oriental, but to the Orange louts of Irongate anyone who didn't look like themselves was an alien. And reports of a white man killed by a Chinee would inflame the popular mood, building on the back of a cold winter and word of defeats in the Kingdom of Siam. The last thing Esau's superiors needed right now was a pogrom on the doorstep of their East Coast headquarters.

The betting shops were closed and the pawnbrokers shut, but between two such shops Esau paused. The tenement door was utterly plain, but well painted and solidly fitted. A row of bell-pulls ran beside a set of brass plaques bearing the names of families who hadn't lived here in decades. Esau pulled the bottom-most bell-pull, then the second from the top, the next one down, and the first from the bottom, in practiced series. There was a click from the door frame and he pushed through, into the darkened vestibule within. He shut the door carefully behind him, then looked up at the ceiling.

'Esh'sh icht,' he said.

'Come on in,' a man's voice replied in accented English. The inner door opened on light and finery: a stairwell furnished with rich handwoven carpets, banisters of mahogany, illuminated by gilt-edged lamps in the shape of naked maidens. The guard stationed beside the staircase bowed stiffly as soon as he saw Esau's face. 'You are expected, lord,' he said.

Esau ignored him as he ascended. The tenement block above the two shops had been cunningly gutted and rebuilt as a palace. The rooms behind the front windows – visible from the street as ordinary bedrooms or kitchens – were Ames rooms barely three feet deep, their floors and walls and furniture slanted to preserve the semblance of depth when seen from outside. The family had learned the need for discretion long ago. Fabulous wealth was no social antidote for epicanthic folds and dark skins in New Britain, and if there was one thing the mob disliked more than Chinee-men, it was rich and secretive criminal families of Chinee-men.

Vermin, Esau thought of the two drunks who had harangued him outside the pub. *Never mind.* At the top of the staircase he bowed once to the left, to the lacquered cabinet containing the household shrine. Then he removed his topcoat, hat, and shoes, and placed them in front of the servant's door to the right of the stairs. Finally he approached the door before the staircase, and knocked once with the head of his cane.

The door swung open. 'Who calls?' asked the majordomo.

'It is I.' Esau marched forward as the majordomo bowed low, holding the door aside for him. Like the guard below, the majordomo was armed, a pistol at his hip. If the mob ever came, it was their job to buy the family time to escape with their lives. 'Where can I find the honorable Eldest?'

'He takes tea in the Yellow Room, lord,' said the majordomo, still facing the floor.

'Rise. Announce me.'

Esau followed the majordomo along a wood-floored passage, the walls hung with ancient paintings. Some of them were legacies of home, but others, in the European renaissance style, bore half-remembered names. The majordomo paused at a door just beyond a Caravaggio, then knocked. After a whispered conversation two guards emerged – guards in family uniform this time, not New British street clothes. In addition to their robes and twin swords (in the style this shadow-world called 'Japanese', after a nation that had never existed in Esau's family home), they bore boxy self-feeding carbines.

'His lordship,' said the majordomo. Both soldiers came to attention. 'Follow me.'

The majordomo and guards proceeded before Esau, gathering momentum and a hand's count of additional followers as befitted his rank: a scribe with his scrolls and ink, a master of ceremonies whose assistant clucked over Esau's suit, following him with an armful of robes, and a gaggle of messengers. By the time they arrived outside the Yellow Room, Esau's quiet entry had turned into a procession. At the door, they paused. Esau held out his arms for the servants to hang a robe over his suit while the majordomo rapped on the door with his ceremonial rod of office. 'Behold! His lordship James Lee, second of the line, comes to pay attendance before the elder of days!'

'Enter,' called a high, reedy voice from inside the room.

Esau entered the Yellow Room, and bowed deeply. Behind him, the servants went to their knees and prostrated themselves.

'Rise, great-nephew,' said the elder. 'Approach me.'

Esau – James Lee – approached his great-uncle. The elder sat cross-legged upon a cushioned platform, his wispy beard brushing his chest. He lacked the extravagant fingernails or long queue that popular mythology in this land imagined the mandarin class to have. Apart from his beard, his silk robes, and a certain angle to his cheekbones, he could pass for any beef-eating New Englishman. The family resemblance was pronounced. *This is how I will look in fifty years,* James Lee thought whenever he saw the elder. *If our enemies let me live that long.*

He paused in front of the dais and bowed deeply again, then once to the left and once to the right, where his great-uncle's companions sat in silence.

'See, a fine young man,' his great-uncle remarked to his left. 'A strong right hand for the family.'

'What use is a strong right hand, if the blade of the sword it holds is brittle?' snapped his neighbor. James held his breath, shocked at the impudence of the old man – his great-uncle's younger brother, Huan, controller of the eastern reaches for these past three decades. Such criticism might be acceptable in private, but in public it could only mean two things – outright questioning of the Eldest's authority, or the first warning that things had gone so badly awry that honor called for a scapegoat.

'You are alarming our young servant,' the Eldest said mildly. 'James, be seated, please. You may leave,' he added, past Esau's shoulder.

The servants bowed and backed out of the noble presence. James lowered himself carefully to sit on the floor in front of the elders. They waited impassively until the doors thumped shut behind his back. 'What are we to make of these accounts?' asked the Eldest.

'The accounts . . .?' Esau puzzled for a moment. This was all going far too fast for comfort. 'Do you refer to the reports from our agent of influence, or to the – '

'The agent.' The Eldest shuffled on his cushion. 'A cup of tea for my nephew,' he remarked over his shoulder. A servant Esau hadn't noticed before stepped forward and placed a small tray before him.

'The situation is confused,' Esau admitted. 'When he first notified me of the re-emergence of the western alliance's line I consulted with Uncle Stork, as you charged me. My uncle sent word that the orders of your illustrious father were not discharged satisfactorily and must therefore be carried out. Unfortunately, the woman's existence was known far and wide among the usurpers by this time, and her elder tricked us, mingling her party with other women of his line so that the servants I sent mistook the one for the other. Now she has gone missing, and our agent says he doesn't know where.'

'Ah,' said the ancient woman at the Eldest's right hand. The Eldest glanced at her, and she fell silent.

'Our agent believes that the elder Angbard is playing a game within the usurper clan,' Esau added. 'Our agent intended to manipulate her into a position of influence, but controlled by himself – his goal was to replace Angbard. This goal is no longer achievable, so he has consented to pursue our preferences.'

'Indeed,' echoed Great-Uncle Huan, 'that seems the wisest course of action at this time.'

'Stupid!' Esau jerked as the Eldest's fist landed on a priceless lacquered tray. 'Our father's zeal has bound us to expose ourselves to their attack, lost a valued younger son to their guards, and placed our fate in the hands of a mercenary – '

'Ah,' sighed the ancient woman. The Eldest subsided abruptly.

'Then what is to be done?' asked Uncle Huan.

'Another question,' said Esau's great-uncle, leaning forward. 'When you sent brothers Kim and Wu after the woman they both failed to return. What of their talismans?'

James Lee hung his head. 'I have no news, Eldest.' He closed his eyes, afraid to face the wrath he could feel boiling on the dais before him. 'The word I received from our agent Jacob is that no locket was found on either person. That the woman Miriam disappeared at the same time seems to suggest – ' His voice broke. 'Could she be of our line, as well?' he asked.

'It has never happened before,' quavered the ancient woman next to the Eldest.

He turned and stared at her. 'That is not the question, aunt,' he said, almost gently. 'Could this long-lost daughter of the western alliance have come here?' he asked Esau. 'None of them have ever done so before. Not since the abandonment.'

James Lee took a deep breath. 'I thought it was impossible,' he said. 'The family is divided by the abandonment. We come here, and they go . . . wherever it is that the source of their power is. They abandoned us, and that was the end of it, wasn't it? None of them ever came *here*.'

'Do we know if it's possible?' asked Huan, squinting at Esau. 'Our skill runs in the ever-thinning blood of the family. So does theirs. I see no way – '

'You are making unfounded assumptions,' the Eldest interrupted. He turned his eyes on Esau. 'The talisman is gone, and so is the woman. I find that highly suggestive. And worrying.' He ran his fingers through his beard, distractedly. 'Nephew, you must continue to seek the woman's demise. Seek it not because of my father's order, but because she may know our secrets. Seek her in the barbarian castles of Niejwein; also seek her here, in the coastal cities of the Northeast. You are looking for a mysterious woman of means, suddenly sprung from thin air, making a place for herself. You know what to do. You must *also* – ' he paused and took a sip of tea – 'obtain a talisman from the usurper clan by whatever means. When you have obtained one, compare it to your own. If they differ, then I charge you to attempt to use it, both here and in the world of our ancestors. See where it takes you, if anywhere! If it is to familiar territory, then we may rest easy. But if the talent lies in the pattern instead of the bearer, we are all in terrible danger.'

He glanced at the inner shrine, in its sealed cabinet on the left of the Yellow Room. 'Our ancestor, revered though he be, may have made a terrible error about the cause of the abandonment. Unthinkable though that is, we must question everything until we discern the truth. And then we must find a way to achieve victory.'

*

'Hello, Roland's voice mail. If it's still secure, meet me at the Marriott suite you rented, tonight at six p.m. Bye.' She stabbed the 'off' button on her phone then remarked to the air, 'Be there or be dead meat.'

Paulette was bent over the screen of her laptop, messing around with some fine arts websites, a browser window pointing to a large online bookstore: 'Are you sure you mean that?'

'I don't know.' Miriam frowned, arms crossed defensively. 'Give me the car keys, I'm going for a drive. Back late.'

Being behind the wheel of a car cleared Miriam's head marvelously. The simple routine of driving, merging with traffic and keeping the wheels on the icy road, distracted her from the worry gnawing away at her guts. At Home Depot she shoved a cart around with brutal energy, slowing only when a couple of five-gallon cans of kerosene turned it into a lumbering behemoth. Afterwards she left quickly and headed for the interstate.

She was almost a hundred and thirty miles south of Boston, driving fast, haunted by evil thoughts, when her phone rang. She held it to her ear as she drove.

'Yes?'

'Miriam?' Her breath caught.

'Roland? Where are you?'

'I'm in the hotel suite right now. Listen, I'm so sorry.'

You will be, if I find you're responsible, she thought. 'I'll be over in about an hour, hour and twenty,' she said. 'You're alone?'

'Yes. I haven't told anyone else about this room.'

'Good, neither have I.' They'd rented the room in New York for privacy. Now all she could think of was the man in her mother's Dumpster, eyes frozen and staring. 'Do you know if Angbard got my message?'

'What message?' He sounded puzzled. 'The courier – '

'The message about my mother.'

'I think so,' he said uncertainly. 'You sure you can't be here any faster?'

'I'm on the interstate.'

'Uh, okay. I can't stay too long – got to go back over. But if you can be here in an hour we'll have an hour together.'

'Maybe,' she said guardedly. 'I'll see you.'

She killed the phone and sped up.

It took her only an hour and ten minutes to make the last sixty miles, cross town, and find somewhere to park near the hotel. As she got out of the car she paused, first to pat her jacket pocket and then to do a double take. *This is crazy,* she thought, *I'm going everywhere with a gun!* And no license, much less a concealed-carry permit. *Better not get stopped, then.* Having to cross over in a hurry would be painful, not to say potentially dangerous; the temporary tattoos on her wrists seemed to itch as she pushed through the doors and into the lobby of the hotel.

The elevator took forever to crawl up to the twenty-fourth floor, then she was standing in the thickly carpeted silence of the hallway outside the room. She knocked, twice. The door opened to reveal Roland, looking worried. He looked great, better than great. She wanted to tear his clothes off and lick him all over – not an urge she had any intention of giving in to.

His face lit up when he saw her. 'Miriam! You're looking well.' He waved her into the room.

'I'm not looking good,' she said automatically, shoulders hunched. 'I'm a mess.' She glanced around. The room was anonymous as usual, untouched except for the big aluminum briefcase on the dressing table. She walked over to the row of big sealed windows overlooking the city. 'I've been living out of a suitcase for days on end. Why did you call me yesterday?' She steeled herself for the inevitable, ensuring that his next words came as a surprise.

'It's – ' He looked drawn. 'It's about Olga. She's been shot. She's stable, but – '

'What? Was it a shotgun?' Miriam floundered, her scripted confrontation utterly derailed.

'A shotgun? No, it was a pistol, at close range. After you disappeared, ran or whatever, she started acting very strangely. Refused to let anyone anywhere near her chambers then moved into your apartment at House Hjorth, deeply disconcerting Baron Oliver – she did it deliberately to snub him, I think.' He shook his head. 'Then someone shot her. The servants were in the antechamber to her room, heard a scuffle and shots – she defended herself. When they went in, there was blood, but no assassin to be seen.'

Miriam leaned against the wall, overcome by a sense that events were spinning out of control. 'After I ran, was there anything about a corpse in the orangery? Or a couple more in Olga's rooms? We sure left enough bullet holes in the walls – '

'What?' Roland stood up, agitated. 'I didn't hear anything about this! I got the message about you running, but not – '

'There were two assassination attempts.' Miriam tugged at the curtains, pulling them shut. *You can never be sure,* she thought, chilled: even though a high building was implicitly doppelgängered, inaccessible from the other worlds, a Clan sniper in a neighboring office block could shoot and then make a clean escape as soon as they reached ground level. 'The first guy tried to lure me into the garden. Unfortunately for their plans, Olga's chaperone Margit turned up instead. I went back to tell Olga and ran into two guys with machine pistols.'

'But – ' Roland shut his mouth, visibly biting his tongue, as Miriam stared at him.

'I don't think they were working together,' Miriam added after a brief pause. 'That's why I . . . left.'

'I ought to get you to a safe house right now,' said Roland. 'It's what Angbard will expect. We can't have random strangers trying to murder Clan heiresses. That they should have shot Olga is bad enough, but this goes far beyond anything I'd known about.' He stared at her. 'It's as if I'm being deliberately kept in the dark.'

'Tell me about Olga?' Miriam asked. *We know just how reliable Angbard thinks you are.* 'How is she being looked after? What sort of treatment is she receiving?'

'Whoa! Slowly. Baron Oliver couldn't afford to look as if he was ignoring an attack under his own roof – he personally got her across to an emergency room in New York, and notified the duke while they stabilized her. Angbard had her moved to Boston Medical Center by helicopter once she was ready: She's in a private room, under guard.' Roland looked mildly satisfied at her expression of surprise. 'She's got round-the-clock bodyguards and hot and cold running nurses. Angbard isn't taking any chances with her safety. We could provide bodyguards for you, too, if you want – '

'Not an issue. But I want to visit Olga.' Miriam put her shoulder bag down on the bed. 'Tonight.'

'You can't. She's stable, but that doesn't mean she's taking visitors. She's on a drip and pain killers with a hole in one arm and a head injury. Shock and blood loss – it took us nearly two hours to get her to the emergency room. Maybe in a couple of days, when she's feeling better, you can see her.'

'You said she had a head injury?'

'Yeah. The bad guy used a small-caliber popgun, that's why she's still alive.' He looked at her. 'You carry – '

Miriam pulled out her pistol. 'Like this?' she asked dryly. 'Fuck it, Roland, if I was going to kill Olga, I wouldn't mess around. You know damn well they were hoping to nail me instead.'

'I know, I know.' He looked glum. 'It wasn't you. Nobody with half a wit says it was you, and the fools that do don't have any pull at court. But your departure set more tongues flapping than anything else that's happened in years; a real scandal, say the idiots. Eloping with a lady-in-waiting, according to the more lurid imaginations. It doesn't look good to them, the shooting coming so soon after.'

'Well, I don't give a damn whether I look good or bad to the Clan.' Miriam stared at him through narrowed eyes. 'What about my mother?' she asked.

'Your mother? Isn't she all right? Is she – '

'I went over there this morning. She phoned last night while I was away. Something about going on a long journey. Today there is a new back door in her kitchen, and a dead man's body in the Dumpster behind her house, and not a sign of her to be found. I told Angbard that if anything happened to her, heads would roll, and I meant it.'

Roland sat down heavily in the room's armchair. 'Your mother?' His face was pale. 'This is the first I've heard of it.'

Miriam pursed her lips. 'Would Angbard tell you if he was going to order her abducted?'

'Abducted – But you said someone was shot on her doorstep?'

'You're catching on. Someone was shot with a sawed-off shotgun. And *she* sure as hell didn't stuff him into a Dumpster and repair the kitchen door before leaving, or mop up the blood stains. In case you didn't know, she's got multiple sclerosis. She's in a wheelchair right now, and even when the disease is in remission she walks with crutches.'

Miriam watched him go through the stages of surprise, denial, anger, and alarm. 'That doesn't make sense! Angbard put her under a protective watch! If someone had gotten through to her I would know about it!'

'Don't be so sure of yourself.'

'But it can't be!' He was vehement.

'Listen, I know a shotgun wound when I see one, Roland. I stuck my finger in it and waggled it about. You know something? It was sawed-off, either that or he was shot from at least fifty feet away, and I figure that would have attracted some attention. It makes a hell of a mess. Which ward is Olga in? I have *got* to go and see her. What the hell is Angbard playing at?'

'I don't know,' he said. 'He's not exactly been confiding in me lately.' His frown deepened.

Miriam took a deep breath. 'I went over to my house,' she said.

'Oh?' Roland looked slightly stunned, but it wasn't the expression of a would-be murderer confronted by a surprisingly animated victim: He looked much the way she felt.

'Someone searched it efficiently. They left a, uh, surprise. Behind the front door. I'm not sure what kind except that it's probably explosive and it's wired to the handle. Only reason I'm here is I forgot my keys and had to use the back way in.'

'Oh *shit* – ' He stood up, his hand going to his pocket instinctively. 'You're all right?'

'Not for want of somebody trying to kill me. Seems to me that we

401

have a pattern. First, someone tries to kill me or mess with Olga. They then try harder to kill me and succeed in killing Olga's chaperone. I shoot one killer and leave, taking Brill with me. Olga moves into my room at the palace and someone shoots her. Meanwhile, people who should know where I've gone don't, and my mother vanishes, and everywhere I'm likely to go on this side starts sprouting bombs. Can you tell me what kind of pattern I am seeing here, Roland? *Can* you?'

'Someone is out to get you,' he said through gritted teeth. 'More than one conspiracy, by the sound of it. And they're getting Olga by mistake. Repeatedly, for some reason. And they're lying to me, too. And Angbard is treating me as a potential security leak, keeping me in the dark and feeding me shit.'

'Right.' She nodded jerkily. 'So what are we going to do about it?' She watched him like a hawk.

'I think – ' He came to some decision, because he took a step toward her. 'I think you'd better come with me. I'm going to take you to Angbard in person and we'll sort this out face to face – he's over here now, taking personal control. We can accommodate you at Fort Lofstrom, a fully doppelgängered apartment, round-the-clock guards – '

She pushed his hand away. 'I don't think so.'

'What do you mean, you don't think so?'

'I can look after myself, thank you,' she said. 'I'm making arrangements. I'll get this sorted out by Beltaigne. One last question. Do you have any idea *who* might be trying to kill me?'

'Lots of suspects with motives, but no evidence.' Puzzlement and worry mingled in his expression. For a moment he looked as if he was about to say something more.

'Well then, that means I win because I *do* know roughly who's trying to kill me,' she said angrily. 'And I'm going to flush them from cover. Your clue is this: They're not part of the Clan, and a doppelgängered house on the other side is no defense – but they can't get at me while I'm here.'

'Miriam,' he rolled his eyes. 'You're being paranoid. I'll get your mother's house checked out immediately, but you'll be a lot safer if we put a dozen armed bodyguards around you – '

'Safer from what? Safe from some blood feud that was ancient before I was born? Or safe from the idiots who think they're going to inherit my mother's estate if I can be declared incompetent next May, in front of a Clan council? Get real, Roland, the Clan is nearly as big a threat to my freedom as the world-walking assholes who shot Olga and booby-trapped the warehouse!'

'Booby-trapped – ' his eyes widened.

'Yeah, a Claymore mine on a tripwire in the doorway. And nobody cleared up the night watchman's body. Do you begin to get it?' She began to back away toward the door. 'Someone set up the bomb, someone *inside* Angbard's security operation! And,' she continued in a low voice, 'you were in the right places at the right times.'

'Miriam, you can't mean that!' He paced across the room. 'Come on, look, let me sort everything out and it'll be okay, won't it? I'll vet your guards – '

'Roland.' She shook her head, angry with herself for wanting to give in and take him up on an offer that meant far more and went far further than words could express. 'I'm gone. If you know where I'm going, the bad guys will find out – if you aren't one of them.' She kept her hand in her pocket, just in case, but the idea of shooting him filled her with a sense of horror.

He looked appalled. 'Can't we just . . . ?'

'Just what? Kiss and make up? Jesus, Roland, don't be naive!'

'Shit.' He stared at her. 'You really mean it.'

'I am going to walk out the door in a minute,' she said, hating herself for her own determination, 'and we are not going to see each other again until next May, probably. At least, not in the next few days or weeks. We both need time out. I need to get my head together and see if I can flush the bastards who're trying to kill me. *You* need to think about who you are and who I am and where we're going before we take this any further – and you need to find whoever's wormed their way into Angbard's confidence and whoever shot Olga.'

'I don't *care* about Olga! I care about *you*!' he snapped.

'That is part of the problem I've got with you right now,' she said coldly, and headed for the door.

A thought occurred to her as she pulled the door open. 'Roland?'

'Yes?' He sounded coldly angry.

'Tomorrow I'm going to get lost again, probably until Beltaigne. Keep checking your voice mail – there's no need to hold this room any longer.'

'I wish you wouldn't do this,' he said quietly as she shut the door, her heart infinitely heavier than it had been when she arrived.

*

Ring, ring. There was a breeze blowing, and the park was bitterly cold: Miriam sat hunched at one end of a bench.

'Hello? Lofstrom Associates, how may I help you?'

'This is Miriam. I want to talk to Angbard.'

'I'm sorry, Mr. Lofstrom is unavailable right now – '

'I said I'm *Miriam.* If you don't know the name, check with someone who does. You have five minutes to get Angbard on the line before the shit hits the fan.'

'I'll see what I can do. Please hold – '

Beep, beep, beep . . .

'Hello?' A different voice, not Angbard's, came on the line.

'To whom am I speaking?' Miriam asked calmly.

'Matthias. And you are?'

'Miriam Beckstein. I want to talk to Angbard. Right now. This call has been logged by the front desk.'

'I'm sorry, but he's in a meeting. If – '

'If I don't get him on the line *right now* I'll make sure the *Boston Globe* receives a package that will blow your East Coast courier line wide open. You have sixty seconds.' Her fingers tensed on the handset.

'One moment.'

Click.

'Angbard here. What's this?'

'It's me,' said Miriam. 'Sorry I had to strong-arm my way past your mandarins, but it's urgent.'

'Urgent?' She could almost hear the eyebrows rising. 'I've never seen Matthias so disturbed since – well. Unpleasant events. What did you tell him?'

'Oh, nothing much.' Miriam leaned back, felt the cold bench bite through her coat, sat up straight again. 'Listen. I told you something about my mother. That if anything happened to her I would be really pissed off.'

'Yes?' Polite interest colored Angbard's voice.

'I'm really pissed off. Really, *really* pissed off.'

'What happened?'

'She's gone. There's a dead man in the Dumpster behind her house, killed with a shotgun. She had time to phone me to say she was going on a journey – I don't know if anyone was holding a gun to her head. Roland didn't know this. Apparently it happened at the same time that Olga was shot. And my house has been burgled and stuff taken, and somebody booby-trapped the front door.'

'Come here immediately. Or if you tell me where you are I'll send a carload of guards – '

'No, Angbard, that won't work. Listen. I am about to vanish more deeply than last time. Don't worry about Brilliana, she's safe. What I want you to do is . . . look for my foster-mother. Raise heaven and earth. I am going to visit Olga and I do *not* expect to be stopped. If I don't leave that meeting and reach a certain point, unhindered, later tomorrow, unpleasant letters will go in the mail. I am serious about this, I am pissed off, and I am establishing my own power base because I believe that civil war you told me about is not over and the faction who started it is trying to fire it up again, through me.'

'But Helge, that faction – they're your father's side of your family!'

'That's not the faction I'm thinking of. The people I have in mind never signed off on the cease-fire. Listen, I will be in touch ahead of the Beltaigne conference. I'm going to have some really big surprises for you all, including . . . well, anyone who tries to declare me incompetent is going to get a really nasty shock. I'm going to keep in touch through Roland, but he won't know where I'm hiding. So, if you find my mother tell Roland. More to the point, don't trust your staff. Someone is not telling you everything that happens in the field. I think you've got a mole.'

'Explain.' The terser he became the better Miriam felt.

She thought for a moment. *Tell him about Roland?* No, but . . . 'Ask Roland about the warehouse warning I phoned him. Find out why instead of cleaners calling, someone turned up and booby-trapped the place. Looks like the same style as whoever planted the bomb behind the front door of my house. You didn't know about that? Ask Matthias about the courier I intercepted on the train. Ask Olga about the previous assassination attempts. *Start asking questions.* By the way, if I think her life is in danger, I reserve the right to move Olga somewhere safer. Once she's out of immediate danger.'

'You're asking for a blank check,' he said. 'I've noticed the withdrawals. They're big.'

'I'm setting up an import/export business. I'll announce it to the Clan at Beltaigne. By then, I should have a return on investment that will, um, justify your confidence in me.' Another deep breath. 'I'd like another million dollars, though. That would make things run smoother.'

'Are you sure?' asked Angbard.

'A million here, a million there, pretty soon you're talking serious money. Yes, I'm sure. It's a new investment opportunity in the family tradition. Like I said, I'm not setting up in competition – think of it as proof of concept for a whole new business area the Clan can move into. And a way of making Baron Oliver Hjorth and his backers look really stupid, if that interests you.'

'Well, if you insist, I'll take your word for it.' He was using the indulgent paterfamilias voice again. 'It'll be in your account by the day after tomorrow. From central funds this time, not my own purse.' In a considerably icier tone: 'Please don't disappoint me in your investments. The Council has a very short way of dealing with embezzlement and even *your* rank would not protect you.'

'Understood. One other thing, uncle.'

'Yes?'

'Why didn't you tell me about the other branch of the Clan? The one that accidentally got mislaid a couple of hundred years ago and is now blundering around in the dark trying to kill people?'

'The – ' He paused. 'Who told you about them?'

'Sleep well,' she told him, and hit the 'off' button on her phone with a considerable sense of satisfaction. She looked at the sky, saw night was pulling in already. It was time to go pick up Brill and visit the hospital. She hoped Olga would be able to talk to visitors. All she needed was confirmation of one little point and she could be on her way back to the far side.

*

Boston Medical Center was much like any other big general hospital, a maze of corridors and departments signposted in blue. Uniformed porters, clerical officers, maintenance staff, and lots of bewildered relatives buzzed about like a swarm of bees. As they entered, Miriam murmured to Brill: 'Usual drill, do what I do. Okay?'

'Okay.' They walked up to reception and Miriam smiled.

'Hi there, I'm wondering if it's possible to visit a patient? An Olga, uh, Hjorth – '

The receptionist, bored, shoved hair up past her ear bug. 'I'll just check. Uh, what did you say your name was?'

'Miriam Beckstein. And a friend.'

'Yeah, they're expecting you, go right up. You'll find her on ward fourteen. Have a nice day!'

'This place smells strange,' Brill muttered as Miriam hunted for the elevators.

'It's a hospital. Full of sick people, they use disinfectant to keep diseases down.'

'An infirmary?' Brill looked skeptical. 'It doesn't look like one to me!'

Miriam tried to imagine what an infirmary might look like in the Gruinmarkt, and failed. *When were hospitals invented, anyway?* she wondered as the elevator doors slid open, and a bunch of people came out. 'Come on,' she said.

Ward 14 was on the third floor, a long walk away. Brill kept glancing from side to side as they passed open doors, a hematology lab here, the vestibule of another ward there. Finally they found the front desk. 'Hello?' said Miriam.

'Hello yourself.' The nurse at the desk glanced up. 'Visiting hours run until eight. You've got an hour. Who are you looking for?'

'Olga Hjorth. We're expected.'

'Hmm.' The nurse frowned and glanced down, then her frown

cleared. 'Oh, yeah, you're on the list. I'm sorry,' she looked apologetic. 'She's only taking a few visitors; we've got orders to keep strangers out. And she's on nil by mouth right now, so if you've brought any food or drink you'll have to leave it right here at the desk.'

'No, that's okay,' said Miriam. 'Uh, can you ask if she's willing to see my friend here? Brill?'

'That's me,' said Brill, mis-cueing off Miriam's request.

'Oh, well – you're on the clear list.' The nurse shrugged. 'It's just that somebody shot her. She's under guard. Spooks, if you follow my drift.'

Miriam gave her a sympathetic smile. 'I follow. They know us both.'

'That way.' The nurse pointed. 'Second door on the right. Knock before you open it.'

Miriam knocked. The door opened immediately. A very big guy in dark clothes and dark glasses filled it. 'Yes?' he demanded, in a vaguely central-European accent.

'Miriam Beckstein and Brill van Ost to see Olga. We're expected.'

'One moment.' The door closed, then opened again, this time unobstructed. 'She says to come in.'

It was a small anteroom and there were not one but three heavies in suspiciously bulky jackets and serious expressions hanging around. One of them was sitting down reading a copy of *Guns and Ammo*, but the other two were on their feet and they studied Miriam carefully before they opened the inner door. 'Olga!' cried Brill, rushing in. 'What have they done to you?'

'Careful,' warned Miriam, following her.

'Hello,' said Olga. She smiled slightly and shifted in the bed.

'Excuse *me*,' the young nurse said waspishly. 'I'll just be finishing here before you disturb her, if you don't mind?'

'Oh,' said Brill.

'I don't mind,' said Miriam, looking at Olga. 'How are you?' she asked anxiously.

'Bad.' Olga's greeting smile faded. 'Tired 'n' bruised. But alive.' Her eyes tracked toward the nurse, who was fiddling with the drip mounted on the side of the bed, and Miriam nodded minutely. The back of her bed was raised and there was a huge dressing over her right shoulder. Alarming-looking drain tubes emerged from it, and a bunch of wires from under the neck of her hospital gown fed into some kind of mobile monitor on a trolley. It chirped occasionally. 'Damn.' Half of her hair was missing, and there was another big dressing covering one side of her head, but no drain tubes – which, Miriam supposed, was a good sign. 'This feels most strange.'

'I'll bet it does,' Miriam said with some feeling. *Wow,* she thought, thinking about Brill's first reaction to New York, *she's handling it well.* 'Did they find whoever did it?'

'I'm told not.' Olga glanced at the nurse again, who glanced back sternly and straightened up.

'I'll just leave you to it,' she announced brightly. 'Remember, no food or drink! And don't tire her out. I'll be back in fifteen minutes; if you need me before then, use the buzzer.'

Miriam, Brill, and Olga watched her departure with relief. 'Strange fashions here,' Olga murmured. 'Strange buildings. Strange everything.'

'Yeah, well.' Miriam glanced at the drip, the monitoring gear, everything else. Cable TV, a private bathroom, and a vase with flowers in it. Compared to the care Olga would receive in the drafty palace on the other side, this was the very lap of luxury. 'What happened?'

'Ack.' Olga coughed. 'I was in your, your room. Asleep. He appeared out of nowhere and shot . . . well.' She shifted slightly. 'Why doesn't it hurt more?' she asked, sounding puzzled. 'He shot at me, but I am a light sleeper. I was already sitting up. And I sleep with my pistol under my pillow.'

Miriam shook her head. 'Did he get away?' she asked. 'If not, did you get his locket?'

'I wondered when you would ask.' Olga closed her eyes. 'Managed to grab it before they found me. It's in the drawer there.'

She didn't point at the small chest of drawers, but Miriam figured it out. Before she could blink, Brill had the top drawer open and lifted out a chain with a disk hanging from it. 'Give me,' said Miriam.

'Yes?' Brill raised an eyebrow, but passed it to her all the same.

'Hmm.' Miriam glanced at it, felt a familiar warning dizziness, and glanced away. Then she pulled back a cuff and looked at the inside of her right wrist. *The same.* 'Same as the bastard who killed Margit. *Exactly* the same. While the other bunch of heavies who tried to roll us over at the same time didn't have any lockets. At all.'

'Thought so,' murmured Olga.

'Listen, they're after us both,' said Miriam. 'Olga?'

'I'm listening,' she said sleepily. 'Don't worry.'

'They're after us both,' Miriam insisted. 'Olga, this is very important. You're probably going to be stuck here for two or three days, minimum, and it'll take weeks before you're well – but as soon as you're well enough to move, Angbard will want to take you back to his fortress on the other side. It is really important that you don't go there. I mean, it's *vital.* The killers can reach you on the other side, in Fort Lofstrom, even in a doppelgängered room. But they can't reach you here. Listen, I've got a friend here working for me. And Brill's here, too. You can stay with us, if you like. Or talk to Roland, get Roland to help. I'm pretty sure he's reliable – for you, at least. If you stay in Angbard's doppelgängered rooms on this side, the ones he uses to stop family members getting at him in the fort, you'll be safe from the lost family in world three, and from the other conspirators, but not from the mole. And if you go back to Niejwein, the conspirators will try to kill you.'

'Wait!' Olga struggled visibly to absorb everything. 'Lost family? World three? What's – '

'The assassin who killed Margit. It's a long story. I think they're after you, now, because of me.'

Olga shook her head. 'But why? I mean, what purpose could that serve?'

'Because it'll discredit me, or it'll restart the civil war, and I'm fairly certain that's what the bunch from world three, the long-lost relatives, want to achieve. If I die and it can be blamed on one half of the Clan, that starts it up again. If *you* die and it looks like I've schemed with Roland to get you out of the way so I can marry him, it starts up for a different reason. Do you see?'

'Vaguely.' Olga focused on Miriam. 'You'll have to explain it again later. Do you think they'll let me stay here?'

'Hmm.' Miriam thought for a moment. 'You can stay here to recover. I don't think even Angbard is stupid enough to move you while you're ill. You can lean on him to let you stay a bit longer to see what it's like, too. That might work. If he's got any sense he'll work it out from what I told him. But he isn't safe, Olga.'

Brill turned around. 'They abducted – or killed – Miriam's foster-mother, milady. Yesterday, at the same time they shot you.'

'Oh!' Olga looked pensive. 'So. What would you suggest?'

'I think you should stay here for now. When you're better, I want to – ' Miriam caught Brill's eye – 'introduce you to a friend of mine called Paulette. And then we'll see.' She licked her lips. 'I've got a business proposition in mind. One that will flush out the bastards who want us both dead, *and* make everybody involved wealthy beyond belief. Interested?'

AGREEMENTS

Almost exactly two weeks later, Miriam sat in front of a mirror in the Brighton Hotel, brushing her hair and pulling a face. It was definitely getting longer. *Damn that hairdresser!* She'd drawn the line at a wig, but even shoulder-length hair was considered eccentrically short by Boston polite society, and a reputation for eccentricity was something Miriam didn't want to cultivate – it would happen anyway, and could only get in her way. But she hadn't had hair even this long since she was a teenager. *Bloody nuisance,* she thought affectedly, then snorted with amusement. *This place is getting to me. Even the way they talk!*

The house purchase was going ahead, the conveyancing papers and legal to-ing and fro-ing well in hand. Erasmus had taken delivery of no less than ten pounds of twenty-three carat gold, an immense amount by any standard – back in Cambridge it would have paid Miriam's salary at *The Weatherman* for a year – and had warned his shadowy compatriots to expect much larger amounts to start flowing soon, 'from a sympathetic source'. His stock had risen. Meanwhile, Miriam had taken pains to quietly slip into at least two meetings of the Friendly Party to keep an eye on where the money was going. When she'd left money on the collecting tray, it had been with a sense that she was doing the right thing.

The Levelers, despite official persecution (and the imprisonment of many of their leading lights for sedition), had a political agenda she thought she understood, one not too alien from her own. High upon it was a bill of rights; the universal franchise (granting women the vote here for the first time); equal rights regardless of age, race, and sex; the abolition of slavery in the colonies; and separation of church from state. That the imperial government didn't take such things for granted gave Miriam one source of comfort; if she was going to get her start here by smuggling contraband gold to fund radicals, at least they were radical democrats. The ironies in the similarity between her activities and the Clan's own business model didn't leave her untouched. She consoled herself with two thoughts: Smuggling gold to undermine a despotic monarchy wasn't in the same moral league as being the main heroin connection for the East Coast, and she intended to switch to a different business model just as soon as she could.

Miriam checked her appearance in the mirror. With earrings and a pearl choker and the right haircut and dress she could just about pass, but she still felt she was walking a knife-edge in maintaining appearances. New Britain seemed to take class consciousness almost as seriously as the feudal nobility of the Gruinmarkt. It was depressing, and the need to dive into the detail work of setting up a business here left her no time to pursue casual friendships. When she had time to think about it, she was lonely. But at least she had the option of going home in a few more days. That was more than Brill had. Or Iris, wherever she was.

As she locked the jewel box, there was a knock at the door. A bellhop bobbed to her outside. 'Begging your pardon, ma'am, but you have a visitor.' He offered Miriam a card on a silver tray. Miriam nodded. 'Please show Sir Alfred Durant to my table in the dining room. I have been expecting him, and I will join him shortly. I'm also expecting a Mr. Humphrey Bates. If you'd care to see they are offered an aperitif first.'

Miriam left her room and headed downstairs, outwardly calm but inwardly tense. Paradoxically, some things were easier to do over here. The primitive state of business made it relatively easy to mount an all-out assault on the captains of industry, for which she was deeply grateful. (An SEC-approved due diligence background check such as she'd have faced at home would have smashed through her public identity as if it were made of wet cardboard.) But other things were harder to fake. People judged your trustworthiness by a whole slew of social indicators, your class background, and the way you spoke and dressed. The equivalent of a dark suit and a PowerPoint presentation would get you precisely nowhere unless you were a member of the right clubs or had been to the correct finishing school. If you were an outsider, you needed a special edge – and you needed to be at least twice as good.

She'd spent most of the day running scenarios for how this meeting could play, ranging from the irredeemably bad to the unexpectedly good. She'd gotten her story prepared, her answers ready, her lawyer in attendance, and just about everything – except her hair – straight. Now all that remained was to see if Sir Durant would bite . . . or whether he'd turn out to be an inveterate snob, or an overbred twit whose business was run for him by self-effacing middle-class technicians.

She'd reserved the Hanover Room off the back of the carvery downstairs. Most restaurants in this city were associated with clubs or hotels, and the Brighton's was a very expensive, very exclusive one. As she came through the door, two men rose. One of them was the lawyer, Bates, and the other – she smiled at him and dipped her head briefly. 'You must be Sir Alfred Durant?' she asked. 'I've been looking forward to meeting you.'

'A pleasure, ma'am,' he said, in a hoarse, slightly gravelly voice. Durant was thin and tall, imposing but with a hauteur that spoke more of a weary self-confidence than of arrogance. His eyes were soft, brown, and deceptively tired-looking. 'Please, you must call me Alfred. Mr. Bates has been pinning my ears back with stories about you.'

'Indeed.' Miriam's expression acquired a slightly fixed, glassy overtone as she nodded to her lawyer. 'Well, and have you arrived in good health? Has anyone offered you a drink? Waiter – '

The waiter hurried over. 'Yes, m'lady?'

Durant raised an eyebrow. 'Gin and tonic for me,' he said slowly – or was it melancholia? *He likes people to think he drives from the back seat,* Miriam noted. *Watch this one.*

'A sweet Martini for me,' Bates added. Next to Sir Durant he was short, plump, and somewhat overeager.

'Certainly.' Miriam relaxed slightly. 'A sherry, please,' she added. 'If you'd like to come in, I believe our table is waiting . . . ?'

The scandalous overtones of a single woman entertaining two

gentlemen to dinner in a closed room were mildly defused by her black dress and rumored widowhood. Bates had confirmed that there were no insalubrious rumors about Sir Durant's personal life – or at least none she need worry about. Miriam concentrated on being a perfect hostess while pumping Durant for information about himself, and keeping Bates from either drying up or running off at the mouth. Durant was not the most forthcoming of interview subjects, but after the soup she found a worthwhile button to press, and triggered a ten-minute monologue on the topic of car racing. 'It is without doubt the wooden track that makes it so exciting,' Durant droned over the salmon steak – expensively imported by airship from the north – 'for with the embankment of the course, and the addition of pneuma-tismic wheels, they get up to the most exhausting speeds. There was the time Timmy Watson's brakes failed on the inside straight toward the finish line at Yeovilton – '

After the best part of two hours, both Bates and Sir Durant were reclining in their chairs. Miriam felt bloated and silently cursed the etiquette that prevented her from leaving the table for a minute, but the last-minute addition of an excellent glass of vintage port seemed to have helped loosen Alfred up. Especially after Miriam had asked a couple of leading questions about brake shoe manufacture, which veered dangerously close to discussing business.

'You seem to me to be unusually interested in brakes,' Sir Durant said, cupping his glass in one hand and staring at her across the table with the expression of a well-fed and somewhat cynical vulture. 'If you'll pardon me for saying this, it's a somewhat singular interest in one of the fairer sex.'

'I like to think I have lots of singular interests.' Miriam smiled. *Patronizing old bastard.* 'I have spent much of my time traveling to far places and I'm afraid my education in the more feminine arts may be a little lacking. Business, however, is another matter.'

'Ah, business.' Bates nodded knowingly, and Miriam had to actively resist the temptation to kick him under the table.

'Business.' Durant, too, nodded. 'I noticed your purchase of a company – was it by any chance Dalkeith, Sidney and Fleming? – with interest. A fine engineering venture, once upon a time.'

Miriam nodded. 'I like to get my hands dirty. By proxy,' she added, glancing at Bates. 'It's something of a hobby. My father taught me never to take anything for granted, and I extended the lesson to the tools in his workshop.'

'I see.' Durant nodded. 'I found the, ah, *samples* you sent me most interesting.'

'Good.' When she smiled this widely, Miriam's cheeks dimpled: She hated to be reminded of it, but there was no escaping the huge gilt-framed mirror hanging above the sideboard opposite. 'That was the idea.'

'My men applied one of the samples to a test brake engine. The results were precisely as your letter promised.'

'Indeed.' Miriam put her glass down. 'I wouldn't waste your time, Sir Alfred. I don't like to mince words. I'm a woman in a hurry, and I wanted to get your attention.'

'Can you provide more samples?'

'Yes. It will take about a month to provide them in significant quantities, though. And the special assembly for applying them.' It had taken a week to get the chrysotile samples in the first place, and longer to set up the workshop, have them ground to powder, and set into the appropriate resin matrix. Epoxide resins were available here, but not widely used outside the furniture trade. Likewise, asbestos and rock wool – chrysotile – could be imported from Canada, but were only really used in insulating furnaces. The young industrial chemist Miriam had hired through Bates's offices, and the other three workers in her makeshift research laboratory, were initially startled by her proposal, but went along with it. The resulting grayish lumps didn't look very impressive, and could certainly do with much refinement, but the principle was sound. And she wouldn't be stopping with asbestos brakes – she intended to obsolesce it as rapidly as she'd introduced it, within a very few years, once she got her research and development department used to a steady drip feed of advanced materials from the other world. 'The patents are also progressing nicely, both on the brake material and on the refinements we intend to apply to its use.' She let her teeth show. 'The band brake and the wheel brake will be ancient history within two years.'

'I'd like to know how you propose to produce the material in sufficient volume to achieve that,' said Sir Durant. 'There's a big difference between a laboratory experiment and – '

'I'm not going to,' Miriam butted in. '*You* are.' She stopped smiling. 'That's what this meeting is about.'

'If I disagree?' He raised his glass. Miriam caught Bates shrinking back in his chair out of the corner of her eye.

'You're not the only fish in the lake.' Miriam leaned back and stifled a yawn. 'Excuse me, please, I find it rather hot in here.' She met Sir Durant's gaze. 'Sir Alfred, if man is to travel faster, he will have to learn to stop more efficiently first, lest he meet with an unfortunate accident. *You* made your fortune by selling pneumatismic wheels – if you pause to consider the matter, I'm sure you'll agree that cars that travel faster and stop harder will need more and better pneumatismics, too. I'm prepared to offer you a monopoly on the new brake material and a system that will use it more efficiently than wheel brakes or band brakes – in return for a share in the profits. I'm going to plow back those profits into research in ways to improve automotive transport. Here and *now* – ' she laid a fingertip on the table for emphasis – 'there is one car for every thirty-two people in New Britain. If we can make motoring more popular, to the point where there is one car for every two people – ' she broke off.

'Not very ambitious, are you?' Sir Durant asked lightly. At the other side of the table Bates was gaping at her, utterly at a loss for words.

Many thoughts collided in Miriam's mind at that moment, a multi-vehicle pileup of possible responses. But the one that found its way to her lips was, 'not hardly!' She picked up her glass, seeing that it was nearly empty, and raised it. 'I'd like to propose a toast to the future of the automobile: A car for every home!'

*

Miriam was able to rent premises for her company in a former engineering shop on the far side of town. She commuted to it by cab from the hotel while she waited for Bates to process the paperwork for her house purchase. She was acutely aware of how fast the luxury accommodation was gobbling her funds, but there didn't seem to be a sensible alternative – not if she wanted to keep up the front of being a rich widow, able to entertain possible investors and business partners in style. Eventually she'd have to buy a steam car – but not this year's model.

The next morning she hailed a cab outside without lingering for breakfast. The air was icy cold but thankfully clear of smog. As the cab clattered across tram rails and turned toward New Highgate, she closed her eyes, trying to get her thoughts in order.

'Two weeks,' she told herself. She'd been here for six nights already and it felt like an eternity. Living out of suitcases grew old fast and she'd shed any lingering ideas of the romance of travel back when she was covering trade shows and haunting the frequent flyer lounges. Now it was just wearying, and even an expensive hotel suite didn't help much. It lacked certain essential comforts – privacy, security, the sensation of not being in *public* the whole time. She was getting used to the odd clothing and weird manners but doubted she'd ever be comfortable with them. And besides, she was missing Roland, waking sometimes from vague sensual dreams to find herself alone in a foreign city. 'Seven more days and I can go home!' Home, to her own house, if she could just lean on Angbard a bit harder – failing that, to the office, where she could lock the door, turn on the TV, and at least understand everything she was seeing.

The cab arrived. Miriam paid the driver and stepped out. The door to the shop was already unlocked, so she went straight in and opened up the office. It was small but modern, furnished in wood and equipped with electric lamps, a telephone, and one of the weird chord-key typewriters balanced precariously on one of the high, slanted writing desks. It was also freezing cold until she lit the gas fire. Only when it was blazing did she go through the mail then head for the lab.

The lab was a former woodworking shop, and right now it was a mess. Roger had moved a row of benches up against one wall, balanced glass-fronted cabinets on top of them, and made enthusiastic use of her line of credit at an instrument maker's shop. The results included a small potter's kiln – converted into a makeshift furnace

– and a hole in the ceiling where tomorrow a carpenter would call to begin building a fume cupboard. Roger was already at work, digging into a wooden crate that he'd manhandled into the center of the floor. 'Good morning to you,' said Miriam. 'How's it going?'

'I'll tell you when I get into this,' Roger grunted. He was in his late twenties, untidy even in a formal suit, and blessed with none of the social graces that would have allowed him to hang onto his job when the Salisbury Works had shed a third of their staff three months earlier. Rudeness concealed shyness; he'd been completely nonplussed by Miriam at first, and was still uneasy in her presence.

'That'll be the chrysotile from Union Québécois,' she said. 'Isn't it?'

'It should be. If they haven't sent us rock salt by mistake again.' He laid down his crowbar and straightened up, panting, his breath steaming in the cold air.

'If they have, they'll pay for it. Go make yourself a pot of tea, I don't want you freezing to death on the job.'

'Um, yes, Ma'am.' Roger shuffled toward the other back room – the one Miriam intended to have converted into a kitchen and indoor toilet block for the work force – that currently held only a cast-iron wood stove, a stack of lumber, and a kettle. He gave her a wide berth, as if being female in the workplace might be contagious. Miriam watched his back disappear before she knelt to pick up the crowbar, and went around the lid of the crate levering out the retaining nails. *Men.* She laid the crowbar down and dusted herself off before he returned, bearing a chipped mug containing some liquid as dark as coffee.

'I think you'll find it easier to open now,' Miriam remarked, laying one hand on the lid. 'What have you got in mind for resin processing this week?'

'I was thinking about the vulcanization process,' Roger mumbled. 'I want to see how varying the sulfate concentration affects the stiffness of the finished mixture.'

'I was asking about resins,' Miriam pointed out. 'In particular, the epoxide sample I suggested you look into on Thursday. Have you done anything with it yet?'

'Um, I was getting to it.' Roger looked away bashfully.

'That's why I suggested a timetable,' said Miriam. 'You can estimate how long each batch will take to run; you already do that for yourself, don't you? Put the timetable on the blackboard and I won't have to keep asking you the same questions.'

'Oh, all right then.' He nodded.

'I wanted the epoxide sample running as soon as possible because we have a possible customer,' she added.

'A customer?' He brightened visibly.

'Yes, a customer. But we won't have them if we don't have a suitable product, will we? They're going to want an extensive range of samples in about four weeks' time, for their own materials-testing people. That's why I want you to get on to the epoxide-based samples right now. If you time the kiln runs right, you can probably put your sulfate experiments through at the same time. Just as long as they don't hold up the epoxide.'

'I'll do it that way, then,' he said, almost carelessly. And he would. She'd met Roger's type before, hammering keyboards into submission in dot-com start-ups. He'd work overnight if he had to, without even noticing, just to get the product ready to meet the deadline – as long as he had a target to aim for. All this thrashing about with rubber and vulcanization processes was just a distraction.

'I'm going to be in the office today,' she added. 'I've got an idea to work on. The carpenter will be in here tomorrow to work on the fume cupboard, and then the kitchen. Meanwhile, you wouldn't happen to know any model engineers looking for work? I have some mechanical assemblies to get started.'

'Mechanical – ' He almost went cross-eyed. 'Why?'

'A better way of applying this wonderful high-friction material to the task of stopping a moving vehicle. You think this high-friction compound will work well if you just clamp it to a pneumatismic? It'll work – right until the rubber wall of the pneumatismic wears through and it blows out. What we need is a hub-mounted disk bolted to the wheel with a block of brake material to either side, which can be clamped or released by hydraulic calipers, balanced to apply force evenly. With me so far?'

'Um, I think so.' He looked abstracted. 'I, I don't know any model artificers. I'm sorry. But I'm sure you'll find someone.'

'Oh I think I will, indeed I do.' She headed back to the office, leaving Roger wrestling a ten-kilogram lump of very high-grade rock wool onto his workbench.

The day passed in a blur. Miriam had rigged a travel transformer for her laptop, which she kept in a locked drawer in the office along with an inkjet printer and a small digitizer tablet. The CAD software was a pain to use with such a small screen, but far better than the huge draftsman's board and ink pens in the far corner of the room. Between calls she lost herself in an extruded 3D model of a brake assembly – one of her own invention, crude but recognizable as the ancestor of late-twentieth-century disk brakes. Another file awaited her attention – steel radial bands for reinforcing tires. The idea was sound, but she kept having to divert into her physics and engineering textbooks. Her calculus was rustier than she was willing to admit, and she was finding some of the work extremely hard.

But perfection didn't matter. *Getting there first* mattered. Get there first and just-good-enough and you could buy the specialists to polish the design to perfection later. This was the lesson Miriam had learned from watching over the shoulders of her Silicon Valley colleagues, and from watching a myriad of biotech companies rise and fall – and it was the lesson she intended to shove up New Britain's industrialists so hard it made them squeak.

One o'clock. Miriam blinked, suddenly dizzy. Her buttocks ached from the hard stool, she was hungry, and she needed the lavatory. She stood up and put the notebook PC away, then headed for the toilet – an outhouse in the backyard. Afterwards she slipped out the front door in search of lunch. Of such elements were a working day made.

In the public environment of the hotel, or the lab, she cut an eccentric, possibly scandalous figure. On the streets she was just another woman, better dressed than most, hurrying about her errands. Anonymity of a kind: *Treasure it while you can*, she told herself as she lined up at a street corner where a baker's boy had set up a stand to sell hot bacon rolls. *It won't last.*

She returned to the office and had been busy for an hour – phoning her lawyer, then calling a commercial agent at what passed for a recruiting house – when there was a peremptory knock on the side window. 'Who's there?' she demanded, standing up to open it.

'Police. Inspector Smith at your service.' A bushy moustache and a suspicious, beefy face shoved an imposing warrant card with a crown and heraldic beasts cavorting atop it at her through the open window. 'Homeland Defense Bureau. Are you Mrs. Fletcher?'

'Uh, yes.' Flustered, Miriam tried to pull herself together. 'How can I be of service?'

'I'd like a word with you if I may.'

'Come in, then.' Miriam hurried to open the door. *Shit, what did I do wrong?* She wondered. There was a deep hollow icy feeling in her stomach as she hauled the door open and smiled, ingratiatingly. 'What can I do for you, officer?' she asked, leaving the door and retreating behind the front desk.

'Ah, well.' He nodded, then remembered his manners and took his hat off.

Bizarre, thought Miriam. To her surprise she realized that she wasn't frightened for herself – only for her plans, which depended on continuity and legality for their success.

'Been in business long?' asked the Inspector.

'No,' she said. 'This is a new venture.'

'Ah *well.*'

He looked around slowly. Luckily she'd put the computer away before lunch, and everything was much as it should be in an office. He moved to shove the door closed. 'Don't do that,' Miriam said quickly.

'All right.' He found the one comfortable chair in the office – a wooden swivel chair too low to work at the writing desks – and looked her in the eyes. 'How long have you known Erasmus Burgeson?'

'Huh?' Miriam blinked. 'Not long. A few weeks?'

'I see.' Smith nodded portentously. 'How did you come to know him?'

'Is this an official investigation?'

'I'm asking the questions. How did you come to know him?'

'Oh.' Miriam considered her options. *Not official*, she decided. 'If this isn't an official investigation, why should I tell you?'

'Because.' He looked irritated. 'Little lady, if you don't want to cooperate while it's unofficial, I can go away and waste my time *making* it official. And then you'll have to cooperate, and it will be the worse for you because I won't have to knock on your door polite, like. Do I make myself clear?'

'Perfectly.' She didn't smile. 'I first met Erasmus Burgeson because one of your own officers directed me to him when I asked if he knew where I could find a pawnbroker. Is that what you wanted to know?'

'*Ah.* Well.' Smith looked even more annoyed now, but not in her direction. 'You wouldn't happen to know which officer this would be?'

'Hmm. He'd have been on duty in Highgate Close on, um, the afternoon of Saturday the sixteenth. I think he thought I might be lost. That might be enough for you to find his notebook?'

'Humph. So you asked for a pawnbroker and he gave you directions to Burgeson. Is that all? Why did you want a pawnbroker in the first place?'

The inspector's blunt manner was beginning to annoy Miriam. *But that's what he wants,* she realized suddenly: *He wants me to make a slip. Hmm.* 'I arrived on the India Line ship *Vespasian* that morning, after a crossing from Ceylon,' she told him, very deliberately keeping to her story – the *Vespasian* had indeed docked that day, with some passengers aboard, but was conveniently halfway across the Atlantic by now. 'I was so preoccupied with packing my possessions and getting ashore that I forgot to ask the purser to convert my scrip to honest currency. In addition, clothing suitable for the climate of Ceylon is inadequate here. So I thought a sensible first step would be to find a pawnshop and exchange an old pair of earrings and a small pearl necklace for a decent wool suit and the wherewithal to find a hotel room and cable my banker.'

All of which was, very remotely, true – and indeed Erasmus had arranged, for a fee and by way of a friend of a fellow traveler, for the purser of the *Vespasian* to find a passenger of her name in the ship's manifest should anyone ask – but it was only as Miriam spun it out in front of Smith's skeptical gaze that she realized how thin a tale it sounded. If she was in Smith's shoes she could dig holes in it with very little effort. But Smith simply nodded. 'I see,' he said. 'Your husband left you adequately provided for, didn't he?'

'Indeed.' *Keep it close. Make him dig.*

'And so you dabble in manufacturing.' It wasn't phrased as a question, so Miriam didn't answer. She just sat tight, wearing a politely interested expression, wishing for the phone to ring or something to disturb the silence that stretched out uncomfortably.

'I said, you dabble in manufacturing.'

'I do not "dabble" in anything, Mr. Smith,' Miriam finally stated in her iciest tone. 'You're a police officer. You can go ask the patent office questions – I'm sure Mr. Sagetree will be able to tell you whether there is any merit in the applications I filed last week. The first *three*, Inspector, of the many I have in mind.'

'Ah. I stand corrected.' Smith leaned back in his chair. 'Well then, may I rephrase? Do you have any opinion of Burgeson's business? Does he strike you as in any way at all being odd?'

Miriam shook her head and allowed an irritated expression to cross her face. 'He's a pawnbroker. He's a very *literate* pawnbroker with a good line in conversation, but I imagine sitting in the back of a shop gives him a lot of time to read, don't you?'

'A literate pawnbroker. So this would explain why you have visited his establishment on three occasions?'

Shit, shit, shit – 'The first time, as I've told you, I needed money and suitable attire. The second time – let me see, on my first visit I had noticed a hat that was not then out of hock. I went back to see if it was available, and also to redeem my earrings and necklace. On the *third* occasion – well, he'd shown me some of the antiquarian books various of his customers pawned when they fell upon hard times. I confess I was quite partial to a couple of them. Is that a crime?'

'No.' Inspector Smith stood, unfolding smoothly to a good six feet. He was a huge, imposing man, overweight but built like a football player, and now she noticed that his nose had been broken, although it had set well. 'But you should be careful who you associate with, Mrs. Fletcher. Some people question Mr. Burgeson's patriotism and devotion to the Crown. He keeps strange company, and you would not want to be taken for one among them.'

'Strange company?' She looked up at Smith.

'Strangers.' He wore a peculiar tight, smug expression. 'Frenchies, some of 'em. And papists. Uppity women suffragists, too.' Miriam glanced past his shoulder then looked away hastily. Roger was leaning in the laboratory doorway, one hand behind his back. *I don't need this*, she thought to herself.

'He hasn't done anything to hang himself yet,' Smith continued, 'but there's always a first time. I see *my* job as ensuring there isn't a second, if you catch my drift. And that the first 'appens as soon as possible.'

Miriam looked past him. 'Roger, go back to your workbench,' she called sharply.

Roger turned and shuffled away, bashfully. Inspector Smith shook himself, the spell broken, and glanced over his shoulder.

'Huh. Another bad 'un, I shouldn't be surprised.' Smith smirked at Miriam. 'Wouldn't want anything to 'appen to him, would you? I really don't know what the world's coming to, a single woman running a business full of strapping young men. Huh. So, let's see. The question is, are you a good citizen?'

'Of course I'm a good citizen,' said Miriam, crossing her arms. 'I really don't see what your point is.'

'If you're a good citizen, and you were to learn something about the personal habits of a certain pawnbroker – ' The inspector paused, brow wrinkled as if he'd just caught himself in an internal contradiction: 'casting no aspersions on your reputation, if you follow me, ma'am.' Another pause. 'But if you happened to know anything that would be of *interest*, I'm sure you'd share it with the police . . .'

'I've got a business to run, inspector,' Miriam pointed out coldly. 'This business pays taxes which ultimately go to pay your wages. You are getting in the way. I'm a law-abiding woman, and if I find out anything you need to know you will be the first to hear about it. Do I make myself understood?'

'Ah, well.' Smith cast her a sly little glance. 'You will, as well, won't you? Huh.' He paused in the doorway. 'If you don't you'll be bleeding *sorry*,' he hissed, and was gone like a bad smell.

'Oh shit,' Miriam whispered, and sat down heavily in the swivel chair he'd vacated. Now the immediate threat was past, she felt weary, drained beyond belief.

'Uh, ma'am?'

'Yes, Roger.' She nodded. 'Listen, I know you meant well, but, next time – if there is a next time – stay out of it. Leave the talking to me.'

'Uh, yes.' He ducked his head uncertainly. 'I meant to say – '

'And leave the *fucking* crowbar behind. Have you any *idea* what they'll do to you for attacking a police inspector?'

'Ma'am!' His eyes bulged – at her language, not the message.

She blinked. 'Roger, you're going to have to get used to hearing me curse like a soldier if you work for me for any length of time. At least, you'll hear it when the bastards are attacking.' She caught his eye. 'I'm not a lady. If I was, I wouldn't be here, would I?' she added. *And that's for sure, more than you'll ever know.*

'Ma'am.' He cleared his throat, then carefully pretended not to have heard a single word. 'It's about the furnace. I've got the first epoxide mixture curing right now, is that what you wanted?'

'Yes!' she exclaimed. 'That's what I wanted.' She began to calm down. A thought occurred to her. 'Roger, when you go home tonight, I'd like you to post a letter for me. Not through the pillar box outside, but actually into the letter box of the recipient. Will you do that?'

'Um.' He blinked. 'Would it be something to do with the King's man as called, just now?'

'It might be. Then again it might not. Will you?'

'Yes,' he said firmly. 'I don't like those folks. Not at all.'

After he retreated to his workbench Miriam sat down in front of the manual typewriter and threaded some paper into it – then paused. *They can identify typewriters by their typeface, can't they?* she remembered. *Sort of like a fingerprint. And they lift messages off used ribbons, too.* She pulled out the notebook computer and briefly tapped out a note, then printed it on the battery-powered inkjet printer she'd brought over with her. Let them try and identify that.

She took care to pull on her gloves before feeding the paper in, and before folding it and putting it in the envelope, leaving no fingerprints to incriminate. Then she addressed it and sealed it. If they were tailing Roger or had staked out Burgeson's shop it was just too bad – nothing she could do would help – but if they were still looking for information she doubted things would have gone that far. Besides which, Erasmus had agreed to make inquiries on her behalf: If the inspector nailed him for sedition, she'd lose her most fruitful line of inquiry after the hidden enemies who'd murdered her birth mother and tried to kill her.

It was only on her way home, having given the anonymous tip to Roger, that she realized she'd stepped over the line into active collusion with the Leveler quartermaster.

SNARK HUNTING

One week and two new employees later (not to mention a signed, formal offer for the house), Miriam practiced her breaking-and-entering skills on the vacant garden for the last time. After spending two uncomfortable hours in the hunting hide, she felt well enough to risk an early crossing.

Paulette was in the back office doing something with the fax machine when Miriam came in through the door. 'What on earth – ' She looked her up and down. 'Jesus, what's that you're wearing?'

'Everyday office outfit in Boston, on the other side.' Miriam dropped her shoulder bag, took her hat and topcoat off, then pulled a face. 'Any word on my mother?' she asked.

'Nothing I've heard,' said Paulie. 'I put out a wire search, like you said. Nothing's turned up.' She looked worried. 'She may be all right,' she said.

'Maybe.' Black depression clamped down on Miriam. She'd been able to keep it at bay while she was on the far side, with a whole different set of worries, but now she was home she couldn't hide it anymore. 'I'm going to the bathroom. I may be some time. Taking this stuff off is a major engineering undertaking.'

'Want me to make you some coffee?' Paulette called around the door.

'Yes! Thanks!'

'So you have to play dress-up all the time?' Paulie asked around the door.

'It's only dress-up if you can stop after a couple of hours,' Miriam said as she came back out, wearing her bathrobe. She accepted a coffee mug from Paulette. 'What you're wearing now would get you arrested for indecent exposure over there.' Paulette was in jeans and a plaid shirt unbuttoned over a black T-shirt.

'I think I get the picture. Sounds like a real bundle of laughs.' Paulette eyed her thoughtfully. 'Two thoughts strike me. One, you've got a hell of a dry cleaning bill coming up. Secondly, have you thought about putting artificial fibers on your to-do list?'

'Yeah.' Miriam nodded. 'Starting with rayon, that came first, I think. Then the overlocking sewing machine, nylon, and sneakers.' She yawned, winced at her headache, then stirred the coffee. 'So tell me, how have things been while I've been away?'

'Well.' Paulie perched on the desktop beside the fax. 'I've got the next gold shipment waiting for you. Brill is doing fine, and those, uh, feelers – ' She looked furtive. 'Let's just say she's going to be from Canada. Right?'

'Right,' Miriam echoed. 'What else has she been up to?'

'She's been visiting your friend Olga in the hospital. Once she spotted someone trying to tail her on the T, but she lost him quick. Olga is out of intensive and recovering nicely, but she's got a scar under her hairline and her arm's in a sling. The guards – ' Paulie shrugged. 'What is it with those guys?'

'What's what?'

'Last time she went, she said one of them said she ought to come home. Any idea what that's about?'

'Uh, yes, probably he was a relative of hers. You say she's visiting Olga now?'

'Why, sure. I've got an odd feeling about her. Great kid, but she's hiding something. I think.'

'If she wanted me out of the way she's had more than enough opportunities to do it quietly.'

'There is that,' Paulette agreed. 'I don't think she's out to get you. I think it's something else.'

'Me too. I just want to know for sure what she's hiding. The way she and Kara were planted on me by Angbard's office, she's probably just reporting back to him – but if she's working for someone else . . .' The fax machine bleeped and began to emit a page of curling paper. 'Hmm. Maybe I should check my voice mail.'

She didn't, not at first. Instead she went back into the bathroom and spent almost an hour standing in the cramped shower cubicle, at first washing and thoroughly cleaning her hair with detergents of a quality unimaginable in New Britain, even for the rich – then just standing there, staring at her feet beneath a rain the temperature of blood, wondering if she'd ever feel clean again. Thinking about the expression on Roger's face when he'd been ready to murder a secret policeman for her, and about Burgeson's kindly face, high ideals, and low friends. Friends who believed fervently in political ideals Miriam took for granted, and who were low subversives destined for the gallows if Smith and his friends ever caught up with them. Gallows where whoever had kidnapped or murdered Iris belonged – and that in turn led Miriam to think about her mother and how little time she'd spent with her in the past year, and how many questions she'd never asked. And more questions for Roland, and his face as he'd turned away, hurt by her rejection; a rejection he didn't understand because it wasn't anything personal, it was a rejection of the world he would unintentionally lock her into, rather than the person he was.

Miriam had lots of things to think of – all of them bleak.

She finished with the shower in much the same black mood she'd been in that fateful evening when she'd first opened the locket and unhitched a mind-gate leading to a world where things turned out to be paradoxically worse. *Why bother?* she wondered. *Why do I keep going?* True love would be a great answer if she believed in it. But she was too much the realist: While she'd love to find Roland in her bed and fuck him senseless – the need for him sometimes brought her awake from frustrated dreams in the still small hours – there wasn't a cozy little cottage for two at the end of that primrose path. Miriam had held her daughter in her arms, once, twelve years ago, kissed her on the head and given her up for adoption. Over the next few years she'd spent nights agonizing over the decision, trying to second-guess the future, to decide whether she'd done the right thing.

The idea of bringing another child, especially a daughter, into the claustrophobic scheming of the Clan filled her with horror. She was a big girl now, and the idea of expecting a man to protect her didn't strike her as cool. That wasn't what she'd gone through pre-med and college and divorce and most of med school and the postgraduate campus of hard knocks for. But facing all this on her own was so daunting that sometimes it made her lie awake wondering if there was any point.

She wandered through into the bedroom and sat on the futon beneath the platform bed in the corner. Her phone was still sitting on the floor next to it, plugged in to charge but switched off. She picked it up, switched it on, waited for it to log on, then hit her mailbox.

'You have messages. Message one . . .' A gravelly voice, calling from ten days ago. 'Miriam?' She sat up straight: It was Angbard! 'I have been thinking very deeply and I have concluded that you are right.'

Her jaw dropped. 'Holy shit,' she whispered.

'What you said about my security is correct. Olga is at evident risk. For the time being she remains in the hospital, but when you return, I release her into your care until Beltaigne, when I expect you *both* to appear before the Clan council to render an account of your persecution.'

Miriam found herself shaking. 'Is there anything else?'

'There's no news about your mother. I will continue to search until I find something positive to report to you. I am sorry I can't tell you anything more about her disappearance. Rest assured that no stone will go unturned in hunting for her assailants. You may call me at any time, but bear in mind that my switchboard might – if you are correct – be intercepted. Good-bye.'

Click. 'Message two – ' Miriam shook her head. 'Hello! This is a recorded greeting from Kleinmort Baintree Investments! Worried about your pension? You too – ' Miriam hit the delete button.

'Message three: Call me. Please?' It was Roland, plaintive. She hit 'delete' again, feeling sick to her stomach. *'Message four:* Miriam? You there? Steve, at *The Herald.* Call me. Got work for you.'

It was the last message. Miriam stared at her phone for a good few seconds before she moved her thumb to the delete key. It only traveled a millimeter, but it felt like miles. She hung up. 'Did I just hear myself do that?' she asked the empty room. 'Did I just decide to ignore a commission from *The Herald*?'

She shook her head, then began to rummage through the clothes in her burnished suitcase, looking for something to wear. They felt odd, and once dressed she felt as if she'd forgotten something.

'Weird,' she muttered and went back out into the corridor just as the front door banged open, admitting a freezing gust of cold air.

'Miriam!' Someone in a winter coat leapt forward and embraced her.

'Brill!' There was someone behind – 'Olga! What are you doing here?'

'What do you think?' Olga looked around curiously. 'What kind of house do you call this?'

'I don't. It's going to be a doppelgängered post office, though. Brill, let go, you're freezing!'

'Oh, I'm sorry,' she said earnestly. 'The duke, he sent a message to you with Lady Olga – '

'Yo! Coffee?' Paulie took one look at them and ducked back into the kitchenette.

'Come in. Sit down. Then tell me everything,' Miriam ordered.

They came in, stripping off outdoor coats: Olga had acquired a formal-looking suit from somewhere, which contrasted oddly with her arm in a sling. She shivered slightly. 'How strange,' she remarked, looking round. 'Charming, quaint! What's that?'

'A fax machine. Everything feeling strange?' Miriam looked at her sympathetically. 'I know that sensation – been having it a lot, lately.'

'No, it's how *familiar* it feels! I've been seeing it on after-dinner entertainments for so long, but it's not the same as being here.'

'Some of those tapes are quite old. Fashions change very fast over here.'

'Well.' Olga attempted a shrug, then winced. 'Oh, coffee.' She accepted the offered mug without thanks. Paulie cast her a black look.

'Uh, Olga.' Miriam caught her eye.

'What?'

'This is Paulette. She's my business manager and partner on this side.'

'Oh!' Olga stood up. 'Please, I'm so sorry! I thought you were – '

'There aren't any servants here,' Brill explained patiently.

'Oh, but I was so rude! I shouldn't have – '

'It's okay,' said Paulette. She glanced at Miriam. 'Is this going to happen every time? It could get old fast.'

'I hope not. Okay, Olga. What did Uncle A have to say for himself?'

'He came to visit me shortly after you left. I'd had time to think on your explanations, and they made uncommon sense. So much sense, in truth, that I passed them on to him in a most forthright manner.'

Brill cracked up.

'Care to share the joke?' Miriam asked carefully.

'Oh, it was mirthful!' Brill managed to catch her breath for a moment before the giggles came back. 'She told him, she told – '

Olga kept her face carefully neutral. 'I pointed out that my schooling was incomplete, and that I had been due to spend some time here in any case.'

'She *pointed* out – '

'Uh.' Miriam stared at Olga. 'Did she by any chance have something pointed to do the pointing out with?'

'There was no need, he took the message,' Olga explained calmly. 'He also said that desperate times required desperate measures, and your success was to be prayed for by want of avoiding – ' she glanced at Paulette – 'the resumption of factional disputes.'

'Civil war, you mean. Okay.' Miriam nodded. 'How long have you been out of the hospital?'

'But Miriam, this was *today*,' said Brilliana.

'Oh,' she said. 'I think I'm losing the plot.' She rubbed her forehead. 'Too many balls in the air, and some of them are on fire.' She looked around at her audience; Paulie was watching them in fascination. 'Olga, did you keep the locket you took from the gunman?'

'Yes.'

'Good. In that case, you may be able to help me earn more than the extra million dollars I borrowed from Angbard last month.' She pretended to ignore Paulette's sharp intake of breath. 'The locket doesn't work in this world,' she explained, 'but if you use it on the other side, it takes you to yet another place – more like this one than your home, but just as different in its own way.'

She took a mouthful of coffee. 'I'm setting up a business in, uh, world three,' she told Olga. 'It's going to set the Clan on its collective ear when they find out. It's also going to flush out our mystery assassins, who come from world three. Right out of wherever they're hiding. The problem is, it takes a whole day for me to world-walk across in each direction. Running a business there is taking all my time.'

'You want me to be a courier?' asked Olga.

'Yes.' Miriam watched her. 'In a week or two I'll own a house in world three that is in exactly the same place as this office. And we've already got the beginnings of a camp in world one, in the woods north of Niejwein, on the same spot. Once I've got the house established, it'll be possible to go from here to there without having to wander through a strange city or know much about local custom – '

'Are you trying to tell me I'm not fit to be allowed out over there?' Olga's eyes blazed.

'Er, no! No!' Miriam was taken aback until she noticed Brill stifling laughter. 'Er. That is, only if you want to. Have you seen enough of Cambridge yet? Don't you want to look around here, first, before going to yet another world?'

'Do I want – ' Olga looked as if she was going to explode: 'Yes! I want it all! Where do I sign? Do you want it in blood?'

*

Early evening, a discreet restaurant on the waterfront, glass windows overlooking the open water, darkness and distant lights. It was six-thirty precisely. Miriam nervously adjusted her clothing and shivered, then marched up to the front desk.

'Can I help you?' asked the concierge.

'Yes.' She smiled. 'I'm Miriam Beckstein. Party of two. I believe the person I'm expecting will already be here. Name of Lofstrom.'

'Ah, just a moment – yes, please go in. He's at a window table, if you'd just come this way – '

Miriam went inside the half-deserted restaurant, still filling up with an upmarket after-work crowd, and headed for the back. After weeks in New Britain she felt oddly exposed in a cocktail dress and tux jacket, but nobody here gave her a second glance. 'Roland?'

He'd been studying the menu, but now he rocketed to his feet, confusion in his face. 'Miriam – ' He remembered to put the menu down. 'Oh. You're just – '

'Sit down. I don't want you to offer me a seat or hold doors open when it's easier for me to do it myself.'

'Uh.' He sat, looking slightly flustered. She felt a sudden surge of desire. He was in evening dress, like the first time. Together they probably looked as if they were heading for a night at the opera. A couple.

'It's been how long?' she asked.

'Four weeks and three days,' he said promptly. 'Want the number of hours, too?'

'That would be – ' She stopped and looked at the waiter who'd just materialized at her elbow. 'Yes?'

'Would sir and madame care to view the wine list?' he asked.

'You go ahead,' she told Roland.

'Certainly. We'll have the Château Lafite '93, please,' he said. The waiter scurried away.

'Come here often?' she asked, amused despite her better judgment.

'A wise man said, when you're planning a campaign, preparation is everything.' He grinned wryly.

'Are we safe here?' she asked. 'Really?'

'Angbard sent a message. Your house appears to be clear, but it might be a bad idea to sleep over there. It's not doppelgängered, and even if it was, he couldn't vouch for its security. Apart from *that* – ' He looked at her significantly. 'I made sure nobody back at the office knows where I am tonight. And I wasn't tailed here.'

The wine arrived, as did the waiter. They spent a minute bickering good-naturedly over the relative merits of a warming chowder against the chef's way with garlic mushrooms. 'What has Angbard got you doing?'

'Well.' He looked ruefully out of the window. 'After our last meeting it was like you'd thrown a hornet's nest through his window. Everybody got to walk around downtown Cambridge in the snow, looking for a missing old lady in a powered wheelchair. I ended up spending a week spying on a private security firm we'd hired. Didn't find much except a few padded expense claims. Then Angbard quietly started shuffling people around – again, nothing turned up except a couple of guards on the take. So then he put me back on regular courier duty in the post room, with a guard assignment or two on the side, moved himself to a high-rise in New York – real estate above the thirtieth floor is going cheap these days – left Matthias running Fort Lofstrom and Angus in Karlshaven, and declared that the search for your foster-mother couldn't go on any longer. He figured we weren't going to find anything new after that much time – the trail was cold. Well.' He shrugged. 'I can't tell you any specifics about my current assignments, but his lordship told me that if you got in touch, I was to – ' He paused.

'I think I can guess,' she said.

'No, I promise! Angbard doesn't know about us. He thinks we're just friends.'

The appetizers arrived. Miriam took a sip of her chowder. The news about the hunt for Iris depressed her, but came as no real surprise. 'Angbard. Does not know. That we, uh, you know.' Somehow the thought made her feel free and sinful, harboring personal secrets – as well as strategic information about the third universe – that the all-powerful intelligence head didn't. She paused for a moment and studied the top of his head, trying to memorize every hair.

'I never told him,' Roland said, putting down his soup spoon. 'Did you think I would?'

'You can keep secrets when it suits you,' Miriam noted.

He looked up. 'I am an obedient servant to your best interests,' he said quietly. 'If Angbard finds out he'll kill us. If you want me to apologize for not giving him grounds to kill us, I apologize.'

She met his eyes. 'Apology noted.' Then she went back to her soup. It was deliciously fresh and lightly seasoned, and Miriam luxuriated in it. She stretched out her legs, and nearly spilled soup everywhere as she found his ankle rubbing against hers. Or was it the other way around? It didn't matter. Nearly two months of lonely nights was coming to the boil. 'What would you do for me?' she whispered to him over the remains of the appetizer.

'Anything.' He met her eyes. 'Almost anything.'

'Well, I'd like that. Tonight. On one condition.' The waiter removed their bowls, discreetly avoiding the line of sight between them – obviously couples behaving this way were a well-understood phenomenon in his line of work.

'What?'

'Don't, whatever you do, talk about tomorrow,' she said.

'Okay. I promise.' And it was that simple. He surrendered before the main course, a sirloin steak for him and a salmon cutlet for her, and Miriam felt something tight unwind inside her, a subliminal humming tension that had been building up for what felt like forever. She barely tasted the food or noticed as they finished the bottle of wine. He paid, but she paid no attention to that, either. 'Where to?' he asked.

'Do you still have an apartment here?' she replied.

'Yes.'

'Is it safe? You're sure nobody's, uh – '

'I sleep there. No booby traps. Do you want to – '

'Yes.' She knew it was a bad idea, but she didn't care about that – at least, not right now. What she cared about, as she pulled her jacket on and allowed him to take her arm, was the warmth at the base of her spine and the sure knowledge that she could count on tonight. All the tomorrows could take their chances.

He drove carefully, back to his apartment in a warehouse redevelopment not far from the restaurant. Miriam leaned back, watching him sidelong from the passenger seat of the Jaguar. 'This is it,' he said, pulling into the underground garage. 'Are you sure?' he asked, turning off the engine.

She leaned forward and bit his lower lip, gently.

'Ow – ' Their mouths met. 'Not here.'

'Okay. Upstairs.'

They worked their way into the elevator without getting too disheveled. It stopped on a neat landing with three doors. Roland freed up a hand to unlock one, and punched a code into a beeping alarm system. Then they were inside. He locked the door, put a chain across it, then bolted it – and she tackled him.

'Not here!'

'Where, then?'

'There!' He pointed through an open door into the living room, dimly lit by an old seventies lava lamp that shed moving patterns of orange and red light across a sofa facing the uncurtained window.

'That'll do.' She dragged him over, and they collapsed onto the sofa. He was ready for her, and it was all Miriam could do to force herself to unwrap a condom before she launched herself at him. There was no time to pull off his clothes. She straddled him, felt his hands working under her dress, and then she was –

– an hour later, sitting on the toilet, giggling madly as she watched him shower. Both of them frog-naked and sweaty. 'We've got to stop this happening to us!' she insisted.

'Come again?'

She threw the toilet roll at him.

'You're violent,' he complained: 'That isn't in *The Rules*!'

'You *read* that?'

'Olga's elder sister had a copy. I sneaked a peek.'

'Ugh!' Miriam finished with the toilet. 'Move over, you're not doing that right.'

'I've been showering myself for years – '

'Yes, that's what's wrong. Stand up.' She stepped into the bathtub with him and pulled the shower curtain across.

'Hey! This wasn't in *The Rules* either!'

'Where's the soap?'

'It does, doesn't – ow!'

Morning came late. Miriam stirred drowsily, feeling warm and secure and unaccountably bruised. There was something wrong with the pillow: It twitched. She tensed. *An arm! I didn't, did I . . . ?*

Memory returned with a rush. 'Your apartment is too big,' she said.

'It is?'

'Too many rooms.'

'What do you mean?'

She squirmed backwards slightly until she felt his crotch behind her. 'We managed the living room, the bathroom, and the bedroom. But you've got a kitchen, haven't you? And what about the back passage?'

'I, uh.' He yawned, loudly. She could feel him stiffening. 'Need the toilet,' he mumbled.

'And I was just getting my hopes up.' She rolled over and watched him stand up, fondly. *Aren't they funny in the morning?* she thought. *If only . . .* Then the numb misery was back. It was tomorrow, too soon.

Damn, she thought. *Can't keep it together for even a night! What's* wrong *with me?*

'Would you like some coffee?' he called through the open doorway.

'Yeah, please.' She yawned. Waking up in bed with him should feel momentous, like the first day of the rest of her life. But it didn't, it just filled her with angst – and a strong desire to spit in the faces of the anonymous killers who'd made it so. She *wanted* Roland. She wanted to wake up this way forever. She'd even think about the marriage thing, and children, if it was just about him. But it wasn't, and there was no way she'd sacrifice a child on the altar of the Clan's dynastic propositions. *Romeo and Juliet were just stupid dizzy teenagers,* she thought. *I know better. Don't I?*

She stood up and pulled her dress on. Then she padded into Roland's small kitchen. He smiled at her. 'Breakfast?' he asked.

'Yeah.' She smiled back at him, brain spinning furiously. *Okay, so why don't you give him a chance?* she asked herself. *If he is hiding something, let's see if he'll get it off his chest. Now.* She knew full well why she didn't want to ask, but not knowing scared her. Especially while Iris remained missing. On the other hand, a plausible bluff might make him tell her whatever it was, and if it was about Iris, that mattered. Didn't it? *So what can I use – oh.* It was obvious. 'Listen,' she said quietly. 'I know you're holding out on me. It doesn't take a genius to figure it out. You haven't told Angbard. So who knows about us?'

She wasn't sure what she'd been expecting: denial, maybe, or laughter; but his face crumpling up like a car wreck wasn't on the list. 'Damn,' he said quietly. 'Shit.'

Her mouth went dry. 'Who?' she asked.

Roland looked away from her. 'He showed me pictures,' he said quietly. 'Pictures of us. Can you believe it?'

'Who? Who are you talking about?' Miriam took a step back, suddenly feeling naked. *Ask and ye shall learn.*

Roland sat down heavily on a kitchen chair. 'Matthias.'

'Jesus, Roland, you could have told me!' Anger lent her words the force of bullets. He winced before them. 'What – '

'*Cameras*. All the cameras in Fort Lofstrom. Not just the ordinary security ones – he's got bugs in some of the rooms, hidden and wired into the surveillance net. You can't sweep for them, they don't show up, and they're not supposed to be there. He's a spider, Miriam. We were in his web.' Roland's face was turned toward her, white and tortured. 'If he tells the old man – '

'Damn.' Miriam shook her head – whether in disgust or denial, she was unsure. 'When?'

'After you disappeared. Miriam, he's blackmailing me. Not you, you might survive. Angbard'd kill me. He'd be honor-bound to, if it came out.'

Miriam glared. 'What. What did he ask. You to do?'

'*Nothing!*' Roland cried out. He was right on the edge. *I'm scaring him,* she realized, an echo of grim satisfaction cutting through the numbness around her. *Good.* 'At least, nothing yet. He says he wants you out of the picture. Not dead, just out of the Clan politics. Invisible. What you're doing now – he thinks I'm behind it.'

'Give me that coffee.'

'When you called about the body in the warehouse, I told Matthias because he's in charge of internal security,' Roland explained as he poured a mug from the filter machine. 'Then when you told me there was a bomb, I couldn't figure it out. Because if he wants to blackmail me he needs you to be alive, don't you see? So I can't see why he'd plant it, but at the same time – '

'Roland.'

'Yes?'

'Shut up. I'm trying to think.'

Matthias. Cameras everywhere. She remembered the servant's staircase. Roland's bedroom. *So Matthias wants us out of the way?* It was tempting. 'Two million dollars.'

'Huh?'

'We could go a long way on two million bucks,' she heard herself say. 'But not far enough to outrun the Clan.'

'You want to – '

'Shut up.' Roland had been holding out on her. For what sounded like good reasons, she admitted – but the thought made her blood run cold. Roland was no knight in shining armor. The Clan had broken him. Now all it took was Matthias pushing his buttons to make him do whatever they wanted. She wanted to hate him for it, but found that she couldn't. The idea of going up against an organization with billions of dollars and hundreds of pairs of hands was daunting. Roland had done it once already, and paid the price. *Okay, so he's not brave,* she thought. *Where does that leave me? Am I brave, or crazy?* 'Are you holding out anything else on me?' she asked.

Roland took a deep breath. 'No,' he said. 'Honest. The only person who's got anything on me is Matthias.' He chuckled bitterly. 'Nobody else. No other girlfriends. No boyfriends, either. Just you.'

'If Matthias has primed you for blackmail, he must want something you can do for him,' she pointed out. 'He knows he could get rid of both of us by just giving us a shitload of money and covering our trail. And if he was behind these attempts to kill me, I'd be dead, wouldn't I? So what does he want to do that involves me and needs you – and that he figures he needs a blackmail lever for?'

'I – I don't know.' Roland pulled himself together, visibly struggling to focus on the problem. 'I feel so stupid. I haven't been thinking rationally about this.'

'You'd better start, then.' Miriam took a mouthful of coffee and looked at him. 'What does Matthias want?'

'Advancement. Recognition. Power.' Roland answered immediately.

'Which he can't get, because . . . ?'

'He's outer family.'

'Right. Do you see a pattern here?' she asked.

'He can't get it, from the Clan. Not as long as it's run the way it is right now.'

'So.' Miriam stood up. 'We've been stupid, Roland. Shortsighted.'

'Huh?' He looked at her uncomprehendingly, lost in his private self-hatred.

'I'm not the target. You're not the target. *Angbard* is the target.'

He straightened up. 'You think Matthias wants to take over the whole Clan security service?'

'With whoever his mystery accomplices are. The faction who murdered my mother and kept the family feuds going with judicious assassinations over a thirty-year period. The faction from world three. Leave aside Oliver and that poisonous dowager granny and the others who'd like me dead, Matthias is in league with those assassins. And before he makes his move – '

'He'll tell Angbard about us, whatever we do. To get us out of the frame before he rolls the duke up. But we can't go to Angbard with it – we'd be openly admitting past disloyalty, hiding things from him. What are we going to *do*?'

PART NINE

STAKEOUT

TIP-OFF

It was a Friday morning late in January. The briefing room in the police fortress was already full as the inspector entered, and there was a rattle of chairs as a dozen constables came to their feet. Smith paused for a moment, savoring their attentive expressions. 'At ease, men,' he said, and continued to the front of the room. 'I see you're all bright and eager this morning. Sit down and rest your feet for a while. We've got a long day ahead, and I don't want you whining about blisters until every last one of our pigeons is in the pokey.'

A wave of approving nods and one or two coughs swept the room. Sergeant Stone stayed on his feet, off to one side, watching his men.

'You'll all be wondering what this is all about, then,' began Smith. 'Some of you'll 'ave heard rumors.' He glanced around the room, trying to see if anyone looked surprised. Rumors were a constable's stock in trade, after all. 'If any of 'em turns out to be true, I want to know about it, because if you've heard any rumors about what I'm telling you now, odds are the pigeons've heard it too. An' today we're going to smash a nest of rotten eggs.'

He scanned his audience for signs of unease: Here and there a head nodded soberly, but nobody was jumping up and down. 'The name of the game is smuggling,' he said. 'In case you was wondering why it's our game, and not the Excise's, it turns out that these smugglers have a second name, too: Godwinite scum. The illegal press we cracked last week was bankrolled from here, in *my* manor, by a Leveler quartermaster. We ain't sure where the gold's coming from, but my money is on a woman who's lately moved into town and who smells like a Frog agent to me. At least, if she ain't French she's got some serious explaining to do.'

Smith clapped his hands together briskly to warm them up.

'You men, your job is to help me give our little lady an incentive to sing like a bird. We are going to run this by shifts and you are going to stick to her like glue. Two tailing if she goes out, two on the manor, four hours on, four off, but the off team ready to go in if I says so. We are going to keep this up until she makes contact with a known seditionist or otherwise slips up, or until we get word that more gold is coming. Then we're going to get our hands on her and find out who her accomplices are. When that happens we are going to get them back here, make them talk, and cut out the disease that has infected Boston for the past few years. A lot of traitors to the Crown are going to go for a long walk to Hudson Bay, a bunch more are going to climb the nevergreen tree, and *you* are going to be the toast of the town. Now, Sergeant. If you'd like to run through the work details, we can get started . . .'

*

A few hours later, a woman stepped out from behind a hedge, kicked the snow from her boots, and glanced around a dilapidated kitchen garden.

'Hmm.' She looked at the slowly collapsing greenhouse, where holes in the white curtain revealed the glass panes that had fallen in. Then she saw the house, most of its windows dark and gloomy. 'Hah!'

She strode up the garden path boldly, a huge pack on her shoulders: When she came to the side door she banged on it with a confident fist. 'Anyone at home?' she called out.

'Just a minute there!' The door scraped ajar. 'Who be you, and what d'you want, barging into our garden – '

'That's enough, Jane, she's expected.' The door opened wide. 'Olga, come in!'

The maid retreated, looking suspiciously at the new arrival as she stepped inside and shut the door. Miriam called: 'Wait!'

'Yes'm?'

'Jane, this is Olga, my young cousin. She'll be staying here from time to time and you're to treat her as a guest. Even if she has an, uh, unusual way of announcing her arrival. Is that understood?'

'Yes'm.' The kitchen maid bobbed and cast a sullen glance at Olga.

'Come on in and get out of the cold,' Miriam told her, retreating through the scullery and kitchen into a short corridor that led to the huge wooden entrance hall. 'Did you have a good trip? Let's get that pack stowed away. Come on, I'll show you upstairs.' There was only one staircase in this house, with a huge window in front of it giving a panoramic view of the short drive and the front garden. Miriam climbed it confidently and gestured Olga toward a door beside the top step. 'Take the main guest bedroom. Sorry if it looks a bit under-furnished right now – I'm still getting myself moved in.'

The bedroom was huge, uncarpeted, and occupied by a single wardrobe and a high-canopied bed. It could have come straight out of House Hjorth, except for the gurgling brass radiators under the large-paned windows, and the dim electric candles glowing over-head. 'This is wonderful,' Olga said with feeling. She smiled at Miriam. 'You're looking good.'

'Huh. I'm taking a day out from the office, slobbing around here to catch up on the patent paperwork.' She was in trousers and a baggy sweater. 'I'm afraid I scandalized Jane the first time. Had to tell her I was into dress reform.'

'Well, what does the help's opinion matter? *I* say you look fine.' Olga slid out from under her pack and began to unbutton her over-coat. 'Do you have anything I can take for a headache?'

'Sure, in the bathroom. I'll show you. How would you like a guided tour of the town later?' she asked.

'I'd love it, when the headache is sorted.' Olga rubbed her fore-head. 'This cargo had better be worth it,' she said as Miriam knelt and began to work on the pack. 'I feel like a pack mule.'

'It's worth it, believe me.' Miriam worked the big, flattish box loose from the top of Olga's pack. 'A decent flat-panel monitor will make *all* the difference to running AutoCAD, believe me. And the medicine and clothes and, uh, other stuff.' *Other stuff* came in a velvet bag and was denser than lead, almost ten kilograms of gold in a block the size of a pint of milk. 'Once I've stored this safely and changed, we can go out. We'll need to buy you another set of clothes while you're over here.'

'It can wait.' Olga reached into her coat pocket and pulled out a pistol, offering it to Miriam. 'I brought this along, by the way. Lady Brilliana is waiting on the other side.'

'She is, is she? Good. Did she bring that cannon of hers?'

'Yes.' Olga nodded.

'You'd better put that away. People don't go armed here, except the police. You don't want to attract attention.'

'Yes. I noticed that in your world, as well.' Olga found an inner pocket in her coat and slid the gun into it carefully. 'Who's to defend you?'

'The thief-takers and constables, in theory. Ordinary thief-takers are mostly safe, but the police constabulary are somewhat different here – their official job is to defend the state against its own subjects. Unofficially some would say it's the same back home, but those people have never seen a *real* police state.' Miriam picked up the dense velvet bag with both hands and carried it to the doorway, glanced either way, then ducked through into the next room.

'This is your bedroom?' asked Olga.

'Yes. Here, help me move the bed.' There was a loose panel in the skirting board behind the bed. Miriam worried it free, to reveal a small safe which she unlocked. The bag of bullion was a tight fit because the safe was already nearly full, but she worked it closed eventually and put the wooden slat back before shoving the bed up against it. 'That's about ten thousand pounds,' Miriam commented – 'enough to buy this house nine times over.'

Olga whistled appreciatively. 'You're doing it in style.'

'Yeah, well, as soon as I can liquidate it, I'm going to invest it.' Miriam dusted herself down. 'You're sure Brill is all right?' she asked.

'Brilliana is fine. I don't believe you have anything to worry about on her part.'

'I don't believe she's a threat. A snoop planted by Angbard is another matter.'

Olga looked skeptical. 'I see.'

'Give me ten minutes? I need to get decent.'

'Certainly.' Olga retreated to the bathroom – opposite the guest-room – to play with the exotic fixtures. They weren't as efficient as those in Miriam's office or Fort Lofstrom, but they'd do.

Miriam met her on the landing, dressed for a walk in public, complete with a preposterous bonnet. 'Let's head to the tram stop,' she suggested. 'I'll take you by the office and introduce you to people. Then there's a friend I want you to meet.'

Miriam couldn't help but notice the way Olga kept turning her head like a yokel out in the big city for the first time. 'Not like Boston, is it?' she said, as the tram whined around the corner of Broad Street and narrowly avoided a costermonger's cart with a screech of brakes and an exchange of curses.

'It's – ' Olga took a deep breath: 'smellier,' she declared. She glanced around. 'Smaller. More people out and about. Colder. Everyone wears heavier clothing, like home, but well cut, tailored. Dark fabrics.'

'Yes,' Miriam agreed. 'Clothing here costs much more than in world two because the whole industrial mass production thing hasn't taken off. People wear hand-me-downs, insist on thicker, darker fabrics that wear harder, and fashion changes much more slowly. It used to be like that back home; in 1900 a pair of trousers would have cost me about four hundred bucks in 2000 money, but clothing factories were already changing that. One of the things on my to-do list is introducing new types of cloth-handling machines and new kinds of fabric. Once I've got a toehold chiseled out. But don't assume this place is wholly primitive – it isn't. I got some nasty surprises when I arrived.'

Something caught her eye. 'Look.' She pointed up into the air, where a distant lozenge shape bearing post from exotic Europe was maneuvering toward an airfield on the far side of town.

'Wow. That must be huge! Why don't your people have such things?'

'We tried them, long ago. They're slow and they don't carry much, but what really killed them was politics. Over here they've developed them properly – if you want to compare airships here with airships back home, they've got the U.S. beat hands-down. They sure look impressive, don't they?'

'Yes.'

Miriam stood up and pulled on the bell cord, and the tram slid to a halt. 'Come on,' she urged. They stepped off the platform into shallow slush outside a street of warehouses with a few people bustling back and forth. 'This way.'

Olga followed Miriam – who waited for her to catch up – toward an open doorway. Miriam entered, and promptly turned right into a second doorway. 'Behold, the office,' Miriam said. 'Declan? This is Miss Hjorth. Olga, meet Declan McHugh.'

'Pleased to meet you, ma'am.' Declan was a pale-faced draftsman somewhere in his late twenties, his face spotted badly by acne. He regarded Olga gravely from beside his board: Olga smiled prettily and batted her eyelashes, hamming it up. Behind Declan two other youths kept focused on their blueprints. 'Will you be in later, ma'am?' he asked Miriam. 'Had a call from O'Reilly's works regarding the wood cement.'

'I'll be in tomorrow. I'm showing Olga around today because she will be in and out over the next few months. She's carrying documents for me and talking to people I need to see on my behalf. Is that clear?'

'Er, yes.' Declan bobbed his head. 'You'll be wanting the shoe-grip blueprints tomorrow?'

'Yes. If you could run off two copies and see that one gets to Mr. Soames, that would be good. We'll need the first castings by Friday.'

'I will do that.' He turned back to his drawing board and Miriam withdrew.

'That,' she explained quietly, 'is the office. *There* is the lab, where Roger and Martin work: They're the chemistry team. Around that corner is going to be the metal shop. Soames and Oswald are putting it together right now, and the carpenter's busy on the kitchen. But it'll be a while before everything is in shape. The floor above us is still half derelict, and I'm going to convert a couple of rooms into paper storage and more drafting offices before we move the office work to new premises. Currently I've got eight men working here full-time. We'd better introduce you to all of them.'

She guided Olga into a variety of rooms, rooms full of furnaces, rows of glass jars, a lathe and drill press, gas burners. Men in suits, men in shirts and vests, red-faced or pale, whiskered or clean-shaven:

men who stood when she entered, men who deferred to Miriam as if she was royalty or management or something of both.

Olga shook her head as they came out of the building. 'I wouldn't have believed it. You've done it. All of them, followers, all doing your bidding respectfully. How did you manage it?'

Miriam's cheek twitched. 'Money. And being right, but mostly it was the money. As long as I can keep the money coming and seem to know what I'm talking about, they're mine. I say, cab! Cab!' She waved an arm up and down and a cabbie reined his nag in and pulled over.

'Greek Street, if you please,' Miriam said, settling into the cab beside Olga.

Olga glanced at her, amused. 'I remember the first time you met a carriage,' she said.

'So do I. These have a better suspension. And there are trains for long journeys, and steam cars if you can afford the expense and put up with the unreliability and noise.'

The cab dropped them off at Greek Street, busy with shoppers at this time of day. Miriam pulled her bonnet down on her head, hiding her hair. 'Come on, my dear,' she said, in a higher voice than normal, tucking Olga's hand under her arm. 'Oh, cab! Cab, I say!' A second cab swooped in and picked them up. 'To Holmes Alley, if you please.'

Miriam checked over her shoulder along the way. 'No sign of a tail,' she murmured as the cab pulled up. 'Let's go.' They were in the door of the pawn shop before Olga could blink, and Miriam whipped the bonnet off and shook her hair out. 'Erasmus?'

'Coming, coming – ' A burst of loud wet coughing punctuated his complaint. 'Excuse me, please. Ah, Miriam, my friend. How nice of you to visit. And who is this?'

'Olga, meet Erasmus Burgeson.' Miriam indicated the back curtain, which billowed slightly as Erasmus tried to stifle his coughing before entering. 'Erasmus, meet my friend Olga.'

'Charmed, I'm sure,' he said, and stepped out from behind the curtain. 'Yes, indeed I *am* charmed, I'm absolutely certain, my dear.' He bowed stiffly. 'To what do I owe the honor of this occasion?'

Miriam turned around and flipped the sign in the door to 'closed', then shot the bolt. She moved deeper into the shop. 'You got my letter?'

'It was most welcome.' Burgeson nodded. 'The fact of its exist-ence, if not its content, I should say. But thank you, anyway.'

'I don't think we were observed, but I think we'd better leave by the cellar.'

'You trust her?' Burgeson raised an eyebrow.

'Implicitly.' Miriam met his eyes. 'Olga is one of my business associates. And my bodyguard. Show him, Olga.'

Olga made her pistol appear. Burgeson's other eyebrow rose. She made it disappear again. 'Hmm,' said Burgeson. 'A fine pair of Amazon women! Nevertheless, I hope you don't need to use that. It's my experience that however many guns you bring to a fight, the Crown always brings more. The trick is to avoid needing them in the first place.'

'This is your agent?' Olga asked Miriam, with interest.

'Yes.' Miriam turned to Burgeson. 'I brought her here because I think it may be difficult for me to visit in person in the future. In par-ticular, I wanted to introduce her to you as an alternative contact against the time when we need to be publicly seen in different places at the same time. If you follow.'

'I see.' Burgeson nodded. 'Most prudent. Was there anything else?'

'Yes. The consignment we discussed has arrived. If you let us know where and how you want it, I'll see it gets to you.'

'It's rather, ah, large.' Burgeson looked grim. 'You know we have a lot of use for it, but it's hard to make the money flow so freely without being overseen.'

'That would be bad,' Miriam agreed. Olga looked away, then drifted toward the other side of the shop and began rooting through the hanging clothes, keeping one ear on the conversation. 'But I can give you a discount for bulk: say, another fifteen percent. Think of it as a contribution to the cause, if you want.'

'If I want.' Burgeson chuckled humorlessly: It tailed off in a hoarse croak. 'They hanged Oscar yesterday, did you hear?'

'Oscar?'

'The free librarian who fenced me the Marx you purchased. Two days before Inspector Smith searched my domicile.'

'Oh dear.' Miriam was silent for a moment. Olga pulled an outfit out to examine it more closely.

'It wouldn't be so bad if Russell hadn't shot Lord Dalgleish last year,' Burgeson mused. 'You wouldn't know about that. But the revolution, in that history book you gave me, the one in the Kingdom of Russ, the description all sounds exceedingly familiar, and most uncomfortably close to the bone. In particular, the minister named Stolypin, and the unfortunate end he came to.' He coughed damply.

Olga cleared her throat. 'Is there somewhere I can try this on?' she asked.

'In the back,' said Burgeson. 'Mind the stove on your way through.' He paused for breath as Olga squeezed past.

'Is she serious?' he asked Miriam quietly.

'Serious about me, and my faction. She's not politicized, if that's what you're asking about. Sheltered upbringing, too. But she's loyal to her friends and she has nothing to gain from the emergency here. And she knows how to shoot.'

'Good.' Erasmus nodded. 'I wouldn't want you to be placing your life in the hands of a dizzy child.'

'Placing my – *what*?'

'Two strangers. Not constabulary or plainclothes thief-takers, one of them looking like a Chinee-man. They've been drinking in the wrong establishments this past week, asking questions. Some idiots, the kind who work the wrong side of the law – not politicals – these idiots have taken their money. Someone has talked, I'm sure of it. A name, Blackstones, was mentioned, and something about tonight. I wrote to you but obviously it hasn't arrived. It's a very deep pond you're swimming in.'

'Erasmus, I am going to make this world fit to live in by every means at my disposal. Believe me, a couple of gangsters playing at cracksman won't stop me.'

The curtain rustled. Olga stepped out, wearing a green two-piece outfit. 'How do I look?' she asked, doing a twirl.

'All right,' said Miriam. 'I think. I'm not the right person to ask for fashion tips.'

'You look marvelous, my dear,' Erasmus volunteered gallantly.

'With just a little work, a seamstress will have the jacket fitting perfectly. And with some additional effort, the patching can be made invisible.'

'That's about what I thought.' Olga nodded. 'I'd rather not, though.' She grinned impishly. 'What do you say?'

'It's fine,' said Miriam. She turned back to Burgeson. 'Who leaked the news?' she asked.

'I want to find out.'

'Write to me, as I did to you, care of this man.' She wrote down Roger's address on a scrap of card. 'He works for me and he's trustworthy.'

'Good.' Erasmus stared at the card for a moment, lips working, then thrust it into the elderly cast-iron stove that struggled to heat the shop. 'Fifty pounds weight. That's an awful lot.'

'We can move it in chunks, if necessary.'

'It won't be,' he said absent-mindedly, as if considering other things.

'Miriam, dear, you really ought to try this on,' called Olga.

'Oh, really.' Miriam rolled her eyes. 'Can't you – '

'Did you ever play at avoiding your chaperone as a child?' Olga asked quietly. 'If not, do as I say. The same man has walked past the outside window three times while we've been inside. We have perhaps five minutes at the outside. Maybe less.'

She looked at Olga in surprise. 'Okay, give it to me.' She turned to Burgeson. 'I'm sorry, but I'm going to have to abuse your hospitality. I hope you don't have anything illegal on the premises?'

'No, not me. Not now.' He smiled a sallow smile. 'My lungs are giving me trouble again, that's why I locked up shop, yes? You'd better go into the back.'

Olga threw a heavy pinafore at Miriam. 'Quick, take off your jacket, put this on over your dress. That's right. Lose the bonnet.' She passed Miriam a straw hat, utterly unsuited to the weather and somewhat tattered. 'Come on, take this overcoat. You don't mind?' She appealed to Burgeson.

'My dear, it's an education to see two different women so suddenly.' He smiled grimly. 'You'd better put your old outfit in this.' He passed Miriam a Gladstone bag.

'But we haven't paid – '

'The devil will pay if you don't leave through the cellar as fast as you can,' Burgeson hissed urgently, then broke up in a fit of racking coughs. Miriam blinked. *He needs antibiotics,* she realized.

'Good-bye!' she said, then she led Olga – still stuffing her expensive jacket into the leather case – down the rickety steps into the cellar, just as the doorbell began to ring insistently.

'Come on,' she hissed. Glancing round she saw Olga shift the bag to her left hand. Shadows masked her right. 'Come *on*, this way.'

She led Olga along a narrow tunnel walled with mildewed books, past a row of pigeonholes, and then an upright piano that had seen better days. She stopped, gestured Olga behind her, then levered the piano away from the wall. A dank hole a yard in diameter gaped in the exposed brickwork behind it, dimly lit from the other side. 'Get in,' she ordered.

'But – '

'Do it!' She could already hear footsteps overhead.

Olga crawled into the hole. 'Keep going,' Miriam told her, then knelt down and hurried after her. She paused to drag the piano back into position, grunting with effort, then stood up.

'Where are we?' Olga whispered.

'Not safe yet. Come *on*.' The room was freezing cold, and smelled of damp and old coal. She led Olga up the steps at the end and out through the gaping door into a larger cellar, then immediately doubled back. Next to the doorway there was another one, this time closed. Another two stood opposite. Miriam opened her chosen door and beckoned Olga inside, then shut it.

'Where – '

'Follow me.' The room was dark until Miriam pulled out a compact electric flashlight. It was half full of lumber, but there was an empty patch in the wall opposite, leading back parallel to Burgeson's cellar. She ducked into it and found the next tunnel, set in the wall below the level of the stacked firewood. 'You see where we're going? Come on.'

The tunnel went on and on, twisting right at one point. Miriam held the flashlight in her mouth, proceeding on hands and knees and trying not to tear her clothes. She was going to look like a particularly grubby housemaid when she surfaced. She really hoped Olga was wrong about the visitor, but she had a nasty hunch that she wouldn't be seeing Burgeson again for some time.

The tunnel opened up into another cellar, hidden behind a decaying rocking horse, a broken wardrobe, and a burned bed frame with bare metal springs like skeletal ribs. Miriam stood up and dusted herself off as best she could, then made room for Olga. Olga pulled a face. 'Ugh! That was filthy. Are you all right?'

'Yes,' Miriam said quietly.

'It was the same man,' Olga added. 'About six and a half feet tall, a big bull with a bushy moustache. And two more behind him dressed identically in blue. King's men?'

'Probably. Sounds like Inspector Smith to me. Hmm. Hold this.' Miriam passed her the flashlight and continued to brush dirt and cobwebs out of the pinafore: It had started out white, and at best it would be gray by the time she surfaced. 'Right, I think we're just about ready to surface.'

'Where?'

'The next street over, in a backyard.' Miriam pulled the door open to reveal wooden steps leading up toward daylight. 'Come on. Put the flashlight away and for God's sake hide the gun.'

They surfaced between brick walls, a sky the color of a slate roof above them. Miriam unlatched the gate and they slipped out, two hard-faced women, one in a maid's uniform and the other in a green much-patched suit that had seen better days. They were a far cry from the dignified widow and her young companion who had called on Burgeson's emporium twenty minutes earlier.

'Quick.' Miriam guided Olga onto the first tram to pass. It would go sufficiently close to home to do. 'Two fourpenny tickets, please.' She paid the conductor and sat down, feeling faint. She glanced round the tram, but nobody was within earshot. 'That was too close for comfort,' she whispered.

'What was it?' Olga asked quietly, sitting next to her.

'We weren't there. They can't prove anything. There's no bullion on Erasmus's premises, and he's a sick man. Unless we were followed from the works to his shop . . .' Miriam stopped. 'He said some house-breakers were going to hit on us tonight,' she said slowly. 'This is *not* good news.'

'Housebreakers. Do you mean what I think you intend to say? Blackguards with knives?'

'Not necessarily. He said two men were asking around a drinking house for bravos who'd like to take their coin. One of them looked Oriental.'

Olga tensed. 'I see,' she said quietly.

'Indeed.' Miriam nodded. 'I think tonight we're going to see some questions answered. Oriental, huh? Time to play host for the long-lost relatives . . .'

*

The big stone house was set well back from the curving road, behind a thick hedge and a low stone wall. Its nearest neighbors were fifty yards away, also set back and sheltered behind stone walls and hedges. Smoke boiled from two chimneys, and the lights in the central hall burned bright in the darkness, but there were no servants. On arriving home Miriam had packed Jane and her husband Ronald the gardener off to a cheap hotel with a silver guinea in hand and the promise of a second to come against their silence. 'I want no questions asked or answered,' Miriam said firmly. 'D'you understand?'

'Yes'm,' said Jane, bobbing her head skeptically. It was clear that she harbored dark suspicions about Olga, and was wondering if her mistress was perhaps prone to unspeakable habits: a suspicion that Miriam was happy to encourage as a decoy from the truth.

'That'll do,' Miriam said quietly, watching from the landing as they trudged down the road toward the tram stop and the six-fifteen service into town. 'No servants, no witnesses. Right?'

'Right,' Olga echoed. 'Are you sure you want me to go through with this?'

'Yes, I want you to do it. But do it fast, I don't want to be alone longer than necessary. How are your temporary tattoos?'

'They're fine. Look, what you told me about Matthias. If Brill's working for – '

'She isn't,' Miriam said firmly. 'If she wanted me dead I'd be dead, okay? Get over it. If she's hiding anything, it's something else – that she's working for Angbard, probably. Bring her over here and if the bad guys don't show we'll just dig out a bottle of wine and have a late-morning lie-in tomorrow, all right?'

'Right,' Olga said doubtfully. Then she headed downstairs, for the kitchen door and the walk to the spot beside the greenhouse where Miriam had cleared the snow away.

Miriam watched her go, more apprehensive than she cared to admit. Alone in the house in winter, every creak and rustle seemed like a warning of a thief in the night. The heating gurgled ominously. Miriam retired to her bedroom and changed into an outfit she'd brought over on her last trip. The Velcro straps under her arms gave her some trouble, but the boots fitted well and she felt better for the bulletproof vest. With her ski mask in hand, revolver loaded and sitting on her hip, and night-vision goggles strapped to her forehead, she felt even more like an imposter than she did when she was dressed up to the nines to meet the nobility. *Just as long as they take me as seriously,* she thought tensely. Then she picked up her dicta-phone and checked the batteries and tape one last time – fully charged, ready for action. *I hope this works.*

The house felt dreadfully empty without either the servants or Olga about. *I've gotten used to having other people around,* Miriam realized. *When did* that *happen?*

She walked downstairs slowly, pausing on the landing to listen for signs of anything amiss. At the bottom she opened the door under the staircase and ducked inside. The silent alarm system was armed. Ronald the gardener had grumbled when she told him to bury the induction wire a foot underground, just inside the walls, but he'd done as she'd told him to when she reminded him who was paying. The control panel – utterly alien to this world – was concealed behind a false panel in the downstairs hall. She turned her walkie-talkie on, clipped the hands-free earphone into place, and continued her lonely patrol.

It all depended on Brill, of course. And on Roland, assuming Roland was on the level and wasn't one of *them* playing a fiendishly deep inside game against her. Whoever *they* were. She was reasonably sure he wasn't – if he was, he'd had several opportunities to dispose of her without getting caught, and hadn't taken any of them – but there was still a question mark hanging over Brill. But whatever game she was playing wasn't necessarily hostile, which was why Olga had gone back over to the hunting hide to fetch her. The idea of not being able to trust *Olga* just made Miriam's head hurt. *You have to start somewhere, haven't you?* she asked herself. If she assumed Olga was on her side and she was wrong, *nothing* she did would make any difference. And three of them would be a damn sight more use than two when the shit hit the fan, as it surely would, sometime in the small hours.

The big clock on the landing ticked the seconds away slowly. Miriam wandered into the kitchen, opened the door on the big cast-iron cooking range set against the interior wall, and shoveled coal into it. Then she turned the airflow up. It was going to be an extremely cold night, and even though she was warm inside her outdoor gear and flak jacket, Miriam felt the chill in her bones.

Two men, one of them Chinese-looking, in the wrong pubs. She shook her head, remembering a flowering of blood and a long, curved knife in the darkness. The feel of Roland's hands on her bare skin, making her go hot and cold simultaneously. Iris looking at her with a guarded, startled expression, as unmotherly as Angbard's supercilious crustiness. *These are some of my favorite things* – butter-pat sized lumps of soft metal glowing luminous in the twilight of a revolutionary quartermaster's shop – *Glock automatics and diamond rings . . .*

Miriam shook herself. 'Damn, if I wait here I'll doze off for sure.' She stood up, raised the insulating lid on the range, and pushed the kettle onto the hot plate. A cup of coffee would get her going. She picked up her dictaphone and rewound, listening to notes she'd recorded earlier in the day.

'The family founder had six sons. Five of them had families and the Clan is the result. The sixth – what happened to him? Angbard said he went west and vanished. Suppose – suppose he did. Reached the western empire, that is, but did so poor, destitute, out of luck. Along the way he lost his talisman, the locket with the knotwork. If he had to recreate it from memory, so he could world-walk, would he succeed? Would I? I know what happens when I look at the knot, but can I remember exactly what shape it is, well enough to draw it? Let's try.'

Whirr. Click. New memo. 'Nope. I just spent ten minutes and what I've drawn does nothing for me. Hmm. So we know that it's not that easy to recreate from memory, and I know that if you look at the other symbol you go here, not home. Hmm again.'

Whirr. Click. New memo. 'I just looked at both lockets. Should have done it earlier, but it's hard to see them without zoning out and crossing over to the other world. The knots – in the other one, there's an arc near the top left that threads over the outer loop, not under it, like in the one Iris gave me. So it looks like the assassin's one is, yeah, a corruption of the original design. So maybe the lost family hypothesis is correct.'

Whirr. Click. New memo. 'Why didn't they keep trying different knots until they found one that worked? One that let them make the rendezvous with the other families?'

Whirr. Click. New memo. 'It's a bloodline thing. If you know of only one other universe, and if you know the ability to go there runs in the family, would you necessarily think in terms of multiple worlds? Would you realize you'd misremembered the design of the talisman? Or would you just assume – the West Coast must have looked pretty much the same in both versions, this world and my own back then, more than two centuries ago – that you'd been abandoned by your elder brothers? Scumbags.'

Whirr. Click. New memo. 'Why me? Why Patricia? What was it about her ancestry that threatened them? As opposed to anyone else in the Clan? Did they just want to kill her to restart the blood feuds, or was there something else?'

Whirr. Click. New memo. 'What do they want? And can I use them as a lever to get the Clan to give me what *I* want?'

The door around the back of the scullery creaked as it opened.

Miriam was on her feet instantly, back to the wall beside the cooker, pistol in her right hand. She froze, breath still, listening.

'Miriam?' called a familiar voice, 'are you there?'

She lowered her gun. 'Yes!'

Olga shuffled inside, looking about a thousand years older than she had an hour before. 'Oh, my *head*,' she moaned. 'Give me drugs, give me strong medicine, give me a bone saw!' She drew a finger across her throat, then looked at Miriam. '*What* is that you're wearing?' she asked.

'Hello,' Brilliana piped up behind her. 'Can I come in?' She looked around dubiously. 'Are you *sure* this is another world?' she asked.

'Yes,' said Miriam. 'Here. Take two of these now. I'll give you the next two when it's time.' She passed the capsules to Olga, who dry-swallowed them and pulled a face. 'Get a glass of water.' Miriam looked at Brill. 'Did you bring – '

'This?' she asked, hefting a stubby-looking riot gun.

'Uh, yeah.' Miriam fixed Brill with a beady eye. 'You realize an explanation is a bit overdue?'

'An explan – oh.'

'It doesn't wash, Brill,' she said evenly. 'I know you're working for someone in Clan security. Or were you going to tell me you found that cannon in a cupboard somewhere?'

Olga had taken a step back. Miriam could see her right hand flexing. 'Why don't you go upstairs and get dressed for the party?' Miriam suggested.

'Ah, if you think so.' Olga looked at her oddly.

'I do.' Miriam kept her eyes on Brill, who stared back unwavering as Olga swept past toward the staircase. 'Well?'

'I got word to expect you two days before you arrived in Niejwein,' Brill admitted. 'You didn't really expect Angbard to hang you out to dry, did you? He said, and I quote, "Stick to her like glue, don't let her out of your sight on family territory, and especially don't give Baron Hjorth an opportunity to push her down a stairwell." So I did as he said,' she added, her self-satisfaction evident.

'Who else was in on it?' Miriam asked.

'Olga.' Brill shrugged. 'But not as explicitly. She's not an *agent*, but . . . you didn't think she was an accident, did you? The duke sent you down to Niejwein with her because he thought you'd be safer that way. And to add to the confusion. Conspirators and murderers tend to underestimate her because of the giggling airhead act.'

'So who do you report to?' said Miriam.

'Angbard. In person.'

'Not Roland?'

'Roland?' Brill snorted. 'Roland's useless – '

'So you world-walk? Why did you conceal it from me?'

'Because Angbard told me to. It wasn't hard: You don't know enough about the Clan structure to know who's likely to be outer family and who's going to have the talent.' She took a deep breath. 'I used to be a bit of a rebel. When I was eighteen I tried to join the U.S. Marine Corps.' She frowned. 'I didn't make the physical, though, and my mother had a screaming fit when she heard about it. She told Angbard to beat some sense into me and he paid for the bodyguard training and karate while I made up my mind what to do next. Back at court, my job – if we ever had to bring the hammer down on Alexis, I was tasked with that. Outside the Clan, nobody thinks a lady-in-waiting is a threat, did you know that? But outside the Clan, noble ladies aren't expected to be able to fight. Anyway, that's why Angbard stuck me on you as a nursemaid. If you ran into anything you couldn't handle . . .'

'Er.' The kettle began to hiss. Miriam turned to it, glad of the distraction, suffering from information overload. *My lady-in-waiting wanted to be a* marine? Presumably her bemusement with Boston had been an act, too. 'Want some coffee?'

'Yes please. Hey, did you know you look just like your Iris when you frown?'

Miriam stopped dead. 'You've seen her?' she demanded.

'Calm down!' Brilliana held up her hands in surrender. 'Yes, I've seen her in the past couple of days, and she's fine. She just needed to go underground for a bit. Same as you, do you understand? I met up with her when you left me in Boston with Paulie and nothing to do. After you shot your mouth off at Angbard, I figured he needed to know what had you so wound up. He takes a keen interest in her well-being, and not just because you threatened to kill him if he didn't. So *of course* I went over to see her. In fact, I visited every couple of days, to keep an eye on her. I was there when – ' Brill fell silent.

'It was you with the shotgun.'

'Actually, no.' Brill looked a little green. 'She kept it taped under her chair, the high-backed one in the living room. I just called the Clan cleaners for her afterwards. It was during your first trip over here when she, she had the incident. She phoned your office line, and I was in the office, so I picked up the phone. As you were over here I went around to sort everything out. I found – ' She shuddered. 'It took a *lot* of cleaning up. They were Clan security, from the New York office, you know. Outer family. She was so *calm* about it.'

'Let me get this straight.' Miriam poured the kettle's contents into a cafetière. Her hands were shaking, she noticed distantly. 'You're telling me that *my mother* gunned down a couple of intruders?'

'Huh?' Brill looked puzzled. 'Oh, *Iris*. That's right. Like "Miriam". "Listen," she said, "it gets to be a habit after the third assassination attempt. Like killing cockroaches."'

'Urk.' Miriam sat down hard and waited for the conceptual earthquake to stop. She fixed Brill with the stare she kept in reserve for skewering captains of industry she was getting ready to accuse of malfeasance or embezzlement. 'Okay, let me get this straight. You are telling me that my mother just *happens* to keep a sawn-off shotgun under her wheelchair for blowing away SWAT teams, a habit which she somehow concealed from me during my childhood and upbringing while she was a political activist and then the wife of a radical bookstore manager – '

'No!' Brill looked increasingly annoyed. 'Don't you get it? This was the first attempt on her life in over thirty years – '

Miriam's walkie-talkie bleeped at her urgently.

'We've got company.' Miriam eyed the walkie-talkie as if it might explode. *My mother is an alien,* she thought. *Must have been in the Weather Underground or something.* But there was no time to worry about that now. 'Is that thing loaded?'

'Yes.'

'Right. Then wait here. If anyone comes through the garden door, shoot them. If anyone comes through the other door, it'll be either me and Olga, or the bad guys. I'll knock first. Back in a second.'

Miriam dashed for the hall and took the stairs two at a time. '*Zone two breach,*' the burglar alarm chirped in her ear. Zone two was the east wall of the garden. 'Olga?' she called.

'Here.' Olga stepped out onto the landing. Her goggles made her look like a tall, angular insect – a mantis, perhaps.

'Come on. We've got visitors.'

'Where do you want to hold out?'

'In the scullery passage and kitchen – the only direct way in is via the front window, and there are fun surprises waiting for them in the morning room and dining room.'

'Right.' Olga hurried downstairs, cradling a loaded MP5.

'Brill,' Miriam called, 'we're coming in.' She remembered to knock.

Once in the kitchen she passed Brill a walkie-talkie with hands-free kit. 'Put this in a pocket and stick the headphone in. Good. Olga? You too.' She hit the transmit button. 'Can you both hear me?'

Two nods. 'Great. We've – '

'Attention. Zone four breach.'

' – That's the living room. *Wait* for it, dammit!'

'Attention. Zone five breach.'

'Dining room,' Miriam whispered. 'Right. Let's go.'

'Let's – what?'

She switched her set to a different channel and pressed the transmit button.

'Attention. Zone four smoke release. Attention. Zone five smoke release. Attention. Zone six smoke release.'

'What – '

'Smoke bombs. Come on, the doors are locked on the hall side and I had the frames reinforced. We've got them bottled up, unless they've got demolition charges. Here.' Miriam passed Brill a pair of handcuffs. 'Let's go. Remember, we want to get the ringleader alive – but I don't want either of you to take any risks.'

Miriam led them into the octagonal hallway. There was a muffled thump from the day room door, and a sound of coughing. She waved Olga to one side, then prepared to open the door. 'Switch your goggles on,' she said, and killed the lights.

Through the goggles the room was a dark and confusing jumble of shapes. Miriam saw two luminous green shadows moving around her – Brill and Olga. One of them gave her a thumbs-up, while the other raised something gun-shaped. 'On my mark. I'm going to open the door. Three, two, one, *mark*.' Miriam unlocked the door and shoved it open. Smoke billowed out, and a coughing figure stumbled into the darkened hall. Olga's arm rose and fell, resulting in a groan and a crash. 'I'm in.' Miriam stepped over the prone figure and into the smoke-filled room. It was chilly inside, and her feet crackled on broken glass. *Bastards,* she thought angrily. Something vague and greenish glowed in the smoke at the far corner, caught between the grand piano and the curtains. 'Drop your gun and lie down!' Miriam shouted, then ducked.

Bang-bang: The thud of bullets hitting masonry behind her was unmistakable. Miriam spat, then knelt and aimed deliberately at the shooter. *Can I do this*? Rage filled her. *You tried to kill my mother!* She pulled the trigger. There was a cry, and the green patch stretched up then collapsed. She froze, about to shoot again, then straightened up.

'Stop! Police!' Whistles shrilled in the garden. '*Attention. Zone three breach.*'

'That's the south wall! What the fuck?' Miriam whispered. She keyed her walkie-talkie. 'Status!'

'One down.' Brill, panting heavily. 'Olga's got the guy in the hall on the floor. They tried to shoot me.'

'Listen.' Whistles loud in the garden, flashlight beams just visible through the smoke. 'Into the hall! Brill, can you drag the fucker? Get him upright? You take him and I'll carry Olga.'

The sound of breaking glass came from the kitchen. Miriam darted back through the doorway and nearly ran straight into Olga.

'Quick!' Olga cried. 'I can't do it, my head's still splitting. You'd better – '

'Shut up.' Miriam pushed her goggles up, grabbed Olga around the waist, and mashed a hand against the light switch. She fumbled with her left sleeve, saw the blurry outline clearly for a moment, tried to focus on it, and tightened her grip on Olga painfully. 'Brill?'

'Do it!' Brill's voice was edgy with tension and fear. More police whistles then a cry and more gunshots, muffled by the wall.

Miriam tensed and lifted, felt Olga grab her shoulders, and stared at her wrist. Her knees began to buckle under the weight: *Can't keep this up for long,* she thought desperately. There was a splintering sound behind her, and the endless knotwork snake that ate its own tail coiling in the darkness as it reached out to bite her between the eyes. She fell forward into snow and darkness, Olga a dead weight in her arms.

FACING THE MUSIC

Miriam was freezing. She had vague impressions of ice, snow, and a wind coming in off the bay that would chill a furnace in seconds. She stumbled to her feet and whimpered as pain spiked through her fore-head. 'Ow.' Olga sat up. 'Miriam, are you all right?' Miriam blinked back afterimages of green shapes moving at the far end of the room. She remembered her hot determination, followed by a cry of pain. She doubled over abruptly and vomited into the snow, moaning.

'Where's the hut?' Olga demanded in a panicky voice. 'Where's the – '

'Goggles,' Miriam gasped. Another spasm grabbed her stomach. *This cold could kill us,* she thought through the hot and cold shud-ders of a really bad world-walk. 'Use your goggles.'

'Oh.' Olga pulled them down across her eyes. 'I see it!'

'Miriam?' Brill's voice came from behind a tree. 'Help!'

'Aaarh, aarh – '

Miriam stumbled over, twigs tearing at her face. It was snowing heavily, huge flakes the size of fingernails twisting in front of her face and stinging when they touched her skin. Brill was kneeling on top of something that thrashed around. 'Help me!' she called.

'Right.' Miriam crashed to her knees in front of Brill, her stomach still protesting, and fumbled at her belt for another set of restraints. Brill had handcuffed the prisoner but he'd begun kicking and she was sitting on his legs, which was not a good position for either of them. 'Here.'

'Lay *still*, damn you – '

'We're going to have to make him walk. It's that or we carry him,' said Olga. 'How big is he?'

'Just a kid. Just a goddamn kid.'

'Watch *out*, he may have friends out here!'

Miriam stood up and pulled her night-vision goggles back down. Brill and the prisoner showed up as brilliant green flames, Olga a hunched figure a few feet away. 'Come on. To the cabin.' Together with Brill she lifted the prisoner to his feet – still moaning incoherently in what sounded like blind panic – and half-dragged him toward the hunting blind, which was still emitting a dingy green glow. The heat from the kerosene heater was enough to show it up like a street light against the frigid background.

It took almost ten minutes to get there, during which time the snow began to fall heavily, settling over their tracks. The prisoner, apparently realizing that the alternative was freezing to death slowly, shut up and began to move his feet. Miriam's head felt as if someone was whacking on it with a hammer, and her stomach was still rebelling from its earlier mistreatment. Olga crept forward and hunted around in the dark, looking for signs of disturbance, but as far as Miriam could see they were alone in the night and darkness.

The hut was empty but warm as Brill and Miriam lifted the youth through the door. With one last effort they heaved him onto a sleeping mat and pulled the door shut behind them to keep the warmth in. 'Right,' said Miriam, her voice shaking with exhaustion, 'let's see what we've got here.' She stood up and switched on the battery-powered lantern hanging from the roof beam.

'Please don't – ' He lay there shaking and shivering, trying to burrow away into the corner between the wall and the mattress.

'It speaks,' Brill observed.

'It does indeed,' said Miriam. He was shorter than she was, lightly built with straight dark hair and a fold to his eyes that made him look slightly Asian. And he didn't look more than eighteen years of age.

'Check him for an amulet,' said Miriam.

'Right, you – got it!' A moment of struggle and Brill straightened up, holding out a fist from which dangled a chain. 'Which version is it?'

Miriam glanced in it, then looked away. 'The second variation. For world three.' She stuffed it into a pocket along with the other. 'You.' She looked down at the prisoner. 'What's your name?'

'Lin – Lin.'

'Uh-huh. Do you have any friends out in this storm, Mr. Lin Lin?' Miriam glanced at the door. 'Before you answer that, you might want to think about what they'll do to you if they find us here. Probably shoot first and ask questions later.'

'No.' He lay back. 'It's Lee.'

'Lin, or Lee?'

'I'm Lin. I'm a Lee.'

'Good start,' said Brill. 'What were you doing breaking into our house?'

Lin stared back at her without saying anything.

'Allow me,' Miriam murmured. Her headache was beginning to recede. She fumbled in her jacket, pulled out a worryingly depleted strip of tablets, punched one of them out, and swallowed it dry. It stuck in her throat, bitter and unwanted.

'Listen, Lin. You invaded my house. That wasn't very clever, and it got at least one of your friends shot. Now, I have some relatives who'd like to ask you some questions, and they won't be as nice about it as I am. In about an hour we're going to walk to another world, and we're going to take you with us. It's a world your family can't get to, because they don't even know it exists. Once you're there, you are going to be *stuck*. My relatives there will take you to pieces to get the answers they want, and they will probably kill you afterwards, because they're like that.'

Miriam stood up. 'You have an hour to make up your mind whether you're going to talk to me, or whether you're going to talk to the Clan's interrogators. If you talk to me, I won't need to hurt you. I may even be able to keep you alive. The choice is yours.'

She looked at Brill. 'Keep an eye on him. I'm going to check on Olga.'

As she opened the door she heard the prisoner begin to weep quietly. She closed it hastily.

Miriam keyed her walkie-talkie. 'Anyone out there? Over.'

'Just me,' replied Olga. 'Hey, this wireless talkie thing is great, isn't it?'

'See anyone?'

'Not a thing. I'm circling about fifty yards out. I can see you on the doorstep.'

'Right.' Miriam waved. 'I just read our little housebreaker the riot act.'

'Want me to help hang him?'

'No.' Miriam could still feel the hot wash of rage at the intruder in her sights, and the sense of release as she pulled the trigger. Now that the anger had cooled, it made her feel queasy. The first time she'd shot someone, the killer in the orangery, she'd barely felt it. It had just been something she had to do, like stepping out of the path of an onrushing juggernaut: He'd killed Margit and was coming at her with a knife. But this, the lying in wait and the hot rush of righteous anger, left her with a growing sense of appalled guilt. *It was avoidable*, wasn't it? 'Our little housebreaker is just a chick. He's crying for momma already. I think he's going to sing like a bird as soon as we get him to the other side.'

'How are you doing?' asked Olga. 'You came through badly.'

'Tell me about it.' Miriam shuddered. 'The cold seems to be helping my head. I'll be ready to go again in about an hour. Yourself?'

'I wish.' Olga hummed to herself. 'I never had that headache pill.'

'Come over here, then,' said Miriam. 'I've got the stuff.'

'Right.'

They converged on a tree about five yards from the hut. Miriam stripped off a glove and fumbled in her pocket for the strip of beta-blockers and the bottle of ibuprofen. 'Here. One of each. Wash it down with something, huh?'

'Surely.' Miriam waited in companionable silence while Olga swallowed, then pulled out a small hip flask and took a shot.

'What's that?'

'Spiced hunter's vodka. Fights the cold. Want some?'

'Better not, thanks.' Miriam glanced over her shoulder at the hut. 'I'm giving him an hour. The poor bastard thinks I'm going to give him to Angbard to torture to death if he doesn't tell me everything I want to know immediately.'

'You aren't going to do that?' Olga's expression was unreadable.

'Depends how angry he makes me. There's been too much killing already, and it's been going on for far too long. We're going to have to stop sooner or later, or we'll run out of relatives.'

'What do you mean, relatives? He's the enemy – '

'Don't you get it yet?' Miriam asked impatiently. 'These guys, the strangers who pop out of nowhere and kill – they've got to be blood relatives somewhere down the line. They're world-walkers too, and the only reason they go between this world and New Britain, instead of this world and the USA, is because that's the pattern they use. I'm thinking they're descended from that missing branch of the first family, the brother who went west and disappeared, right after the founder died.'

Olga looked puzzled. 'You think they're the sixth family?'

'I'm not sure, and I don't yet know why they're trying to start up the civil war again. But don't you think we owe it to ourselves to find out what's going on before we hand him over to the thief-takers for hanging?'

Olga rubbed her head. 'This is going to be the most *fascinating* Clan council in living memory,' she said.

'Come on.' Miriam waved at the hut. 'Let's get moving. I think it's time we dragged Roland into this.'

*

One o'clock in the morning. *Ring, ring . . .* 'Hello?' Roland's voice was furred with sleep.

'Roland? It's me.'

'Miriam, you do pick your times – '

'Not now. Got a family emergency.'

'Emergency? What kind?' She could hear him waking up by the second.

'Get a couple of soldiers who you trust, and a safe house. *Not* Fort Lofstrom or its doppelgänger, it needs to be somewhere anonymous but secure on this side. It *must* be on this side. We've got a prisoner to debrief.'

'A prisoner? What kind – '

'One of the assassins. He's alive, terrified, and spilling his guts to Olga right this moment.' Olga was in the back office with Lin and Miriam's dictaphone, playing Good Cop. Lin was chattering, positively manic, desperate to tell her everything she wanted. Lin wasn't even eighteen. Miriam felt ashamed of herself until she thought about what he'd been involved in. Boy soldiers, bright-eyed and bushy-tailed, recruited to defend their family's honor against the children of the hostile elder brothers – elder brothers who had stolen their birthright many generations ago, abandoning them to the nonexistent mercy of the western empire.

'He needs to be kept alive, and that means keeping him away from the security leak in Angbard's operation. And, uh, your little friend, assuming they're not one and the same person. Someone there is working with this guy's people. And here's another thing: I want a full DQ Alpha typing run on a blood sample, and I want it compared to as many members of the Clan – full members – as you can get. I want to know if he's related, and if so, how far back it goes.'

And I want him out of here before Paulette shows up in the morning, Miriam thought. Paulie was a good friend and true, but some things weren't appropriate for her to be involved in. Like kidnapping.

'Okay, I'll sort it. Where do I go?'

'You come here.' Miriam rattled off directions, mentally crossing her fingers. 'I've got a new amulet for you, one that takes you from the other side to world three, my hideaway. Watch out, it is *very* different, as different from this world as you can imagine.'

'Okay – but you'd better be able to explain why if the duke starts asking questions. I'll roust Xavier and Mort out of bed and be round in an hour. They'll keep their mouths shut. Is there anything else you need?'

'Yeah. Is Angbard over here?'

'I think so.'

'I've got to call him right away. Then I'm probably going to be gone before you get here. Got to go back to the far side to clean up the mess when the little prick broke into my house.'

'He broke in – hey! Are you all right?'

'I'm alive. Olga and Brill can fill you in. Got to go. Stay safe.' She rang off before she could break down and tell him how much she wanted to see him. *Cruel fate* . . . the next number was preprogrammed as well.

'Hello?' A politely curious voice.

'This is Helge Lofstrom-Hjorth. Get me Angbard. This is an emergency.'

'Please hold.' No messing around this time, Miriam noted. Someone was awake at the switchboard.

'Angbard here.' He sounded amused rather than tired. 'What is it, Miriam? Having trouble sleeping?'

'Perhaps. Listen, the Clan summit on Beltaigne is three months away. Is there a procedure for bringing it forward, calling an extraordinary general meeting?'

'There is, but it's most unusual – nobody has done it in forty years. Are you sure you want me to do this for you? Without a good reason, there are people who would take it as a perfect opportunity to accuse you of anything they can think of.'

'Yes.' Miriam took a deep breath. 'Listen. I know you've got my mother.' Dead silence on the phone. She continued: 'I don't know why you're holding her, but I'm going to give you the benefit of the doubt – for now. But I need that meeting, and she needs to be there. If she isn't, you're going to be in deep shit. I'm going to be there, too, and it has to be *now*, in a couple of days' time, not in two months, because we've got a prisoner and if you've not found your leak yet the prisoner will probably be dead before Beltaigne.'

'A prisoner – '

'You told me about a child of the founder who went west,' Miriam said. 'I've found his descendants. They're the ones who tried to kill Patricia and who've been after Olga and me. And I figure they may be mixed up with the mole in your security staff. You want to call this emergency meeting, Angbard, you *really* want to do this.'

'I believe you,' he said after a momentary pause, in a tone that said he wished he didn't. 'How extraordinary.'

'When is it going to be ready?'

A pause. 'Count on it in four days' time, at the Palace Hjorth. Any sooner is out of the question. I'll have to clear down all nonessential mail to get the announcement out in time – this will cost us a lot of goodwill and money. Can you guarantee you'll be there? If not, then I can't speak for what resolutions will be put forward and voted through by the assembled partners. You have enemies.'

'I will be there.' She hesitated for a moment. 'If I don't make it, it means I'm dead or incapacitated.'

'But you're not, now.'

'Thank Brilliana and Olga,' she said. 'They were good choices.'

'My Valkyries.' He sounded amused.

'I'll see you in four days' time,' Miriam said tensely. 'If you need to know more, ask Olga, she knows what I'm doing.'

Then she hung up on him.

*

Two days later, Miriam looked up from her office ledger and a stack of official forms in response to a knock on the office window. 'Carry on,' she told Declan, who looked up inquiringly from his drafting board. 'Who is it?' she demanded.

'Police, ma'am.'

Miriam stood up to open the door. 'You'd better come in.' She paused. 'Ah, Inspector Smith of the Homeland Defense Bureau. Come to tell me my burglars are a matter of national security?' She smiled brightly at him.

'Ah, well.' Smith squeezed into the room and stood with his back to the cupboard beside the door where she kept the spare stationery. The constable behind him waited in the hall outside. 'It was a most peculiar burglary, wasn't it?'

'Did you *catch* any of the thieves?' she asked sharply.

'You were in New London all along,' he said, accusingly. 'Staying in the *Grange Mouth Hotel*. Into which you checked in at *four o'clock* in the morning the day after the incident.'

'Yes, well, as I told the thief-taker's sergeant, I dined in town then caught the last train, and my carriage threw a wheel on its way from the railway station. And I stayed with it because cabs are thin on the ground at two o'clock.'

'Humph.' Smith looked disappointed, to her delight. *Gotcha!* she thought. She'd set off from her office in Cambridge at midnight, floored the accelerator all the way down the near-empty interstate, and somehow managed not to pick up any speeding tickets. There were no red-eye flights in New Britain, nor highways you could drive along at a hundred miles an hour with one hand on the wheel and the other clutching an insulated mug of coffee. In fact, the fastest form of land travel was the train – and as she'd be happy to point out to the inspector, the last train she could have caught from Boston to arrive in New London before 4 a.m. had left at eight o'clock the night before.

It had been a rush. She'd parked illegally in New York – her New York, not the New London the inspector knew – and changed into her rich widow's weeds in the cramped confines of the car. Then she'd crossed over and banged on a hotel door in the predawn light. She'd been able to establish a watertight alibi by the skin of her teeth, but only by breaking the New Britain land speed record on a type of highway that didn't exist in King John the Fourth's empire . . .

'We haven't identified the Chinee-man who was asking after you,' Smith agreed. 'Nor the unknown assailant who fled – who we are investigating with an eye for murder,' he added with relish.

Miriam sagged slightly. 'Horrible, horrible,' she said quietly. 'Why me?'

'If you turn up in town flashing money around, you must expect to pick up unsavory customers,' Smith said sarcastically. 'Especially if you willingly mix with lowlifes and Levelers.'

'Levelers? Who do you have in mind?'

'I couldn't possibly say.' Smith looked smug. 'But we'll get them all in the end, you'll see. I'll be going now, but first I'd like to introduce you to Officer Fitch from the thief-taker's office. I believe he has some more questions to ask about your burglar.'

Fitch's questions were tiresome, but not as tiresome as those of the city's press – two of whose representatives had already called. Miriam pointedly referred them to her law firm, then refused to say anything until Declan and Roger had escorted them from the premises with dire threats about the law of trespass. 'We will call you if we arrest anyone,' Fitch said pompously, 'or if we recover any stolen property.' He closed his notebook with a snap. 'Good day to you, Ma'am.' And with that he clumped out of her office.

Miriam turned to Declan and rolled her eyes. 'I can live without these interruptions. How's the self-tightening mechanism coming along?'

Declan looked a trifle startled, but pointed to a sketch on his drafting board. 'I'm working on it . . .'

Miriam left the office in the late afternoon, earlier than usual but still hours after she'd ceased being productive. She caught a cab home, feeling most peculiar about the whole business – indignant and angry, and sick to her stomach at what she'd done – but not guilty. The morning room was a freezing mess, the glaziers still busily working on the shattered window frames. The elderly one tugged his forelock at her as she politely looked over his shoulder and tut-tutted, trying to project the image of a house-proud lady bearing up under one of life's little indignities.

She found Jane in the kitchen. 'Is the dining room going to be ready by this evening?' she asked.

'No, ma'am. They broke two chairs and scratched the dining table!'

'Well, at least nobody was hurt. Piece of luck, sending you away, wasn't it?' Miriam shook her head. She'd forgotten about the dining room. The windows were boarded up, but the furniture – 'I think I'm going to have to hire a butler, Jane.'

'Oh *good*,' Jane said, startling Miriam.

'Well, indeed.' Miriam left the kitchen and was about to climb the staircase when a bell began to jangle from the hall. It was the household telephone. She stalked over and picked up the earpiece, then leaned close to the condenser and said, 'Hello?'

'Fletcher residence?' The switchboard operator's voice was tinny but audible. 'Call from 87492, do you want to accept?'

'Yes,' said Miriam. *Who can it be?* she wondered.

'Hello?' asked a laid-back, slightly jovial man's voice. 'Is Mrs. Fletcher available?'

'Speaking.'

'Oh I'm sorry, I wasn't expecting you so soon. Durant here. Are you well, I hope? I read about your little unpleasantness.'

'I'm quite all right,' Miriam managed through gritted teeth. Suddenly her heart was right up at the base of her throat, threatening to fly away. 'The burglars damaged some furniture, then they appear to have fallen out among themselves. It is all most extraordinarily distressing, and a very good thing for me that I was visiting my sister up in New London at the weekend. But I'm bearing up.'

'Oh, good for you. I trust the thief-takers are offering you all possible assistance? If you have any trouble at all I can put in a word with the magistrate-in-chief – '

'I don't think that'll be necessary, but I'm very grateful,' Miriam said warmly. 'But can we talk about something else, please?'

'Certainly, certainly. I was telephoning to say – ah, this is such a spontaneous, erratic medium! – that I've been reviewing your proposal carefully. And I'd like to proceed.'

Miriam blinked, then carefully sat down on the stool next to the telephone. Her head was swimming.

'You want to go ahead?' she said.

'Yes, yes. That's what I said. My chaps have been looking at the brake assembly you sent them and they say it's quite remarkable. When the other three are available we'll fit them to a Mark IV carriage for testing, but they say they're in no doubt that it's a vast step forward. However did you come up with it, may I ask?'

'Feminine intuition,' Miriam stonewalled. *Oh wow*, she thought. *So close to success* . . . 'How do you want to proceed?'

'Well,' said Durant, and paused.

'Royalty basis or outright purchase of rights? Exclusive or nonexclusive?'

He whistled quietly past the condenser. 'I believe a royalty basis would be acceptable,' he said. 'I'll want exclusive rights for the first few years. But I'll tell you what else. I should like to invest in your business if you're open to the idea. What do you say to that?'

'I say – ' she bit the tip of her tongue carefully, considering: 'I think we ought to discuss this later. I will not say yes, definitely, but in principle I am receptive to the idea. How large an investment were you thinking of?'

'Oh, a hundred thousand pounds or so,' Sir Durant said airily. Miriam did the conversion in her head, came up with a figure, double-checked it in disbelief. *That's thirty million dollars in real money!*

'I want to retain control of my company,' she said.

'That can be arranged.' He sounded amused. 'May I invite you to dine with me at, let's say, the Brighton's Hanover Room, a week on Friday? We can exchange letters of interest in the meantime.'

'That would be perfect,' Miriam said with feeling.

They made small talk for a minute, then Durant politely excused himself. Miriam sat on the telephone stool for several minutes in stunned surprise, before she managed to get a grip on herself. 'He's really going to buy it!' Back home, in another life, this was the kind of story she'd have covered for *The Weatherman*. Bright new three-month-old start-up gets multimillion-dollar cash injection, signs rights deal with major corporation. *I'm not covering the news anymore, I'm* making *it*. She stood up and slowly climbed the stairs to her bedroom. *Two more days to go*, she remembered. *I wonder how Olga and Brill are doing?*

*

The next morning Miriam telephoned her lawyer. 'I'm going to be away for a week from tomorrow,' she warned Bates. 'In the meantime, I need someone to handle the payroll and necessary expenditures. Can you recommend a clerk who I can leave things with?'

'Certainly. I can have my man Williams sit in for you if you want. Will that do?'

'Yes, as long as he's reliable.' They haggled over a price, then agreed that Williams would show up on that afternoon for her to hand him the reins.

Later in the morning, a post boy knocked on the door. 'Parcel for Fletcher?' he piped to Jane, who accepted it and carried it to Miriam, then waited for her to open the thing.

'Curiosity,' Miriam said pointedly, 'is not what I pay you for.' Jane left, and Miriam stared at her retreating back before she reached for a paper knife from her desk and slit the string. *If I've got to have servants around, I need ones who can keep their mouths shut*, she thought gloomily. *It wasn't like this with Brill and Kara*. The parcel opened up before her to reveal a leatherbound and clearly very old book. Miriam opened the flyleaf. *A True and Accurate History of the Settlement of New Britain*, it said, by some author whose name didn't

478

ring any bells. A card was slipped into the pages. She pulled it out and saw the name on it, blinked back sudden tears of relief. 'You're all right,' she mumbled. 'They couldn't pin anything on you.' Suddenly it was immensely important to her to know that Burgeson was safe and out of the claws of the political police. A sense of warm relief filled her. For a moment, all was right with the world.

The doorbell rang yet again at lunchtime. 'Oh, ma'am, it'll be a salesman,' said Jane, hurrying from the kitchen to pass Miriam, who sat alone in the dining room, toying with a bowl of soup and reading the book Erasmus had sent, her thoughts miles away. 'I'll send him – '

Footsteps. 'Miriam?'

Miriam dropped her spoon in the soup and stood up. 'Olga?'

It was indeed Olga, wearing the green outfit she'd bought from Burgeson by way of disguise. She smiled broadly as she entered the dining room and Miriam met her halfway in a hug. 'Are you all right?' Olga asked.

'Yes. Have you eaten?'

'No.' Olga rubbed her forehead.

'Jane, another place setting for my cousin! How good of you to call.' As Jane hurried to the kitchen, Miriam added, 'We can talk upstairs while she's washing up.' Louder, 'I was just preparing for my trip to New London tomorrow. Are you tied down here, or do you fancy the ride?'

'That's why I came,' said Olga, sitting down and leaning back as the harried maid planted a place setting before her. 'You didn't think I'd let you go there all on your own, did you, cuz?' Jane rushed out, and Olga winked at Miriam. 'You're not getting out of it so easily! What did you say to put the Iron Duke in such a mood?'

'It's going to be such a party tomorrow night!' Miriam said enthusiastically, then waited for Jane to place a bowl before Olga and withdraw to the scullery. Quietly, 'I told him his little shell game was up. Why didn't you tell me?'

'Tell you what?' Olga paused, blowing on a spoonful of hot broth.

'That Angbard had planted you on me. As a bodyguard.'

'A what?' Olga shook her head. 'This is intelligence of a rare and fantastic nature. Not me, Helge, not me.' She grinned. 'Who's been spinning you these tales?'

'Angbard,' said Miriam. Are you *certain* you don't work for him?'

'Certain?' Olga frowned. 'About as certain as I am that the sun rises in the east. Unless – ' she looked annoyed ' – you are telling me that he has been *using* me?'

'I couldn't possibly comment,' Miriam said, then changed the subject as fast as possible. *Let's just say Angbard's definition of someone who works for him doesn't necessarily match up to the definition of an employee in federal employment law.* 'I suppose you know about the extraordinary meeting?'

'I know he's called one.' Olga looked at Miriam suspiciously. 'Is it your fault?'

'Yup. Did you bring the dictaphone?'

'The what? Oh, your recording angel? Yes, it is in my bag. Paulie gave it to me, along with these battery things that it eats. Such a sweet child he is,' she added. 'A shame we'll have to hang him.'

'We – ' Miriam caught herself. 'Who, the Clan? Lin, or Lee, or whatever he's called? I don't think that's a good idea.'

'He knows too much about us,' Olga pointed out. 'Like the fact that we're operating here. Even if he's from the lost family, that's not enough to save his life. They've been trying to kill you, Miriam, they've been picking away at us for decades. They *did* kill Margit, and I have not forgiven them for that.'

'Lin isn't guilty of that. He's a kid who was drafted into his family's politics at too early an age, and did what they told him to. The one who killed Margit is dead, and if anyone else deserves to get it in the neck it's the old men who sent a boy to do a man's job. If you think the Clan should execute him, then by the same yardstick his family had a perfect right to try to murder you. True?'

'Hunh.' Miriam watched a momentary expression of uncertainty cross Olga's face. 'This merciful mood ill becomes you. Where does it come from?'

'I told you the other day, there's been too much killing. Family A kills a member of Family B, so Family B kills a Family A member straight back. The last killing is a justification for the next, and so it goes on, round and about. It's got to stop somewhere, or it'll stop with the extinction of all the families. Hasn't it occurred to anyone that the utility of world-walking, if you want to gain wealth and power, is proportional to the square of the number of people who can do it? Network externalities – '

Olga looked at her blankly. 'What are you talking about?'

Miriam sighed. 'The cell phones everyone carries in Cambridge. You've seen me using one, haven't you?'

'Oh yes! Anything that can get Angbard out of bed in the middle of the night – '

'Imagine I have a cell phone with me right now, here on the table.' She pointed to the salt shaker. 'How useful is it?'

'Why, you could call – oh.' She looked crestfallen. 'It doesn't work here?'

'You can only call someone else who has a phone,' Miriam told her. 'If you have the only phone in the world, it might as well be a salt shaker. If I have a phone and you have a phone we can talk to each other, but nobody else. Now, if *everyone* has a phone, all sorts of things are possible. You can't do business without one, you can't even live without one. Lock yourself out of your home? You call a locksmith round to let you in. Want to go to a restaurant? Call your friends and tell them where to meet you. And so on. The usefulness of a phone relates not to how many people have got them, but to how many lines you can draw between those people. And the Clan's one real talent is – ' she shrugged – 'forget cargo, we can't shift as much in a day as a single ox-drawn wagon. The *real* edge the Clan has got is its ability to transmit messages.'

'Like phones . . . ?'

Miriam could almost see the light bulb switch on over her head. 'Yes. If we can just break out of this loop of killing, even if it costs us, if we can just start trading . . . think about it. No more messing around with the two of us running errands. No more worries about the amount we can carry. And nobody trying to kill us, which I'd call a not-insignificant benefit – wouldn't you?'

'Nice idea,' said Olga. 'It's surely a shame the other side will kill you rather than listen.'

'Isn't that a rather defeatist attitude?'

'They've been trying to keep the civil war going,' Olga pointed out. 'Are you sure they did not intrigue it in the first place? A lie here and a cut throat there, and their fearsome rivals – we families – will kill each other happily. Isn't that how it started?'

'It probably did,' Miriam agreed. 'So? What's your point? The people who did that are long since dead. How long are you going to keep slaughtering their descendants?'

'But – ' Olga stopped. 'You really *do* want him alive,' she said slowly.

'Not exactly. What I *don't* want is him dead, adding to the bad blood between the families. As a corpse he's no use to anyone. Alive, he could be a go-between, or an information source, or a hostage, or something.'

Miriam finished with her soup. 'Listen, I have to go to the office, but tomorrow evening I need to be in Niejwein. At the Castle Hjorth. Lin, whoever he is, was from out of town. Chances are we can get there from here without being noticed by anyone in this world, at least anyone but Inspector Smith. This afternoon I'm going to the office. I suggest that tomorrow morning we catch the train to New London. That's New York in my world. When we get there – how well do you know Niejwein? Outside of the palaces and houses?'

'Not so well,' Olga admitted. 'But it's nothing like as large as these huge metropoli.'

'Fine. We'll go to the railway terminal, cross over, and walk in bold as brass. There are two of us and we can look after each other. Right?'

Olga nodded. 'We'll be back in my apartment by afternoon. It will be a small adventure.' She put her spoon down. 'The council will meet on the morrow, won't it? I'm not sure whether that's good or bad.'

'It'll have to be good. It can't be anything else.'

EXTRAORDINARY MEETING

Two women sat alone in a first-class compartment as the morning train steamed through the wintry New England countryside. Puffs of smoke coughed past from the engine, stained dirty orange by the sun that hung low over icy woods and snow-capped farmland. The older woman kept her nose buried in the business pages of *The London Intelligencer*, immune to the rattle of track joints passing underneath the carriage. The younger woman in contrast started at every strange noise and stared out at the landscape with eyes eager to squeeze every detail from each passing town and village. Church steeples in particular seemed to fascinate her. 'There are so many people!' Olga exclaimed quietly. 'The countryside, it's so packed!'

'Like home.' Miriam stifled a yawn as she read about the outrageous attempts of a consortium of robber barons from Carolingia to extract a royal monopoly on bituminous path-making, and the trial of a whaler's captain accused of barratry. 'Like home, ninety years ago.' She unbuttoned her jacket; the heating in the carriage was efficient but difficult to control.

'But this place is so rich!'

Miriam folded her paper. 'Gruinmarkt will be this rich too, and within our lifetimes, if I have my way.'

'But how does it *happen*? How do you make wealth? Nobody here knows how the other world got so rich. Where does it come from?'

Miriam muttered to herself, 'Teach a mercantilist dog new tricks . . .' She put the paper aside and sat up to face Olga. 'Look. It's a truism that in any land there is so much gold, and so much iron, and so much timber, and so many farmers, isn't it? So that if you trade with a country, anything you take away isn't there anymore. Your gain is their loss. Right?'

'Yes.' Olga nodded thoughtfully.

'Well, that's just plain wrong,' said Miriam. 'That idea used to be called mercantilism. Discarding it was one of the key steps that distinguishes my world from yours. The essential insight is that human beings *create* value. A lump of iron ore isn't as valuable as a handful of nails, because it takes human labor to turn it into nails and nails are more useful. Now, if you have iron ore but no labor, and I have labor but no iron ore, *both* of us can profit by trade, can't we? I can take your iron ore, make nails, give you some of them in payment, and we're both better off, because before we had no nails at all. Isn't that right?'

'I think I see.' Olga wrinkled her brow. 'You're telling me that we don't trade? That the Clan has the wrong idea about how to make money – '

'Yes, but that's only part of it. The Clan doesn't add value, it simply moves it around. But another important factor is that a peasant farmer is less good at creating value than, say, a farmer who knows about crop rotation and soil maintenance and how to fertilize his fields effectively. And a man who can sit down all day and make nails is less productive than an engineer who can make a machine that takes in wire feedstock at one end and spits out nails at the other. It's more productive to make a machine to make nails, and then run it, than to make the nails yourself. Educated people can think of ways to make such machines or provide valuable services – but to get to the wealth, you've got to have an educated population. Do you see that?'

'What you're doing, you're taking ideas where they're needed, and teaching people with iron ore to make nails and, and do other things, aren't you?'

'Yes. And while I can't easily take the fruits of that trade home with me, I can make myself rich over here. Which in turn should serve to give me some leverage with the Clan, shouldn't it? And there's another thing.' She looked pensive. 'If the goal is to modernize the Gruinmarkt, the land where the Clan holds so much power, it's going to be necessary to import technologies and ideas from a world that isn't as far ahead as the United States. There's less of a gap to jump between New Britain and the eastern kingdoms. What I want to do is to develop riches in this realm, and use them to finance seed investments in the kingdoms. If the Clan won't let me live away from them, at least I can try to make my life more comfortable. No more drafty medieval castles!'

'Castles. You'd build a house like your own near Niejwein? Bandits, the southern kingdoms – '

'No bandits,' said Miriam, firmly. 'First, we need to improve the efficiency of farming. What I saw looked – no offense – like the way things were done five or six hundred years ago in Europe. Strip cultivation, communal grazing, no reaping or sowing machines. By making farming more efficient, we can free up hands for industry. By providing jobs, we can begin to produce more goods – fabric, fuel, housing, ships – and see to the policing of the roads and waterways along which trade flows. By making trade safer we make it cheaper, and increase the profits, and by increasing the profits we can free up money to invest in education and production.'

Olga shook her head. 'I'm dizzy! I'm dizzy!'

'That's how it happened in England around the industrial revolution,' Miriam emphasized. 'That's how it happened here, from 1890 onwards, a century later than in my world. The interesting thing is that it *didn't* happen in the Gruinmarkt, or in Europe, over there. I've got this nagging feeling that knowing why it failed is important . . . still. Given half a chance we'll make it happen.' She leaned toward Olga. 'Roland tried to run away and they dragged him back. If they're going to try to drag me away from civilization, I'm going to try to bring civilization with me, middle-class morality and all. And then they'll be sorry.'

The train began to slow its headlong charge between rows of red-brick houses.

'If you go down this path, you'll make enemies,' Olga predicted. 'Some of them close to home, but others . . . Do you really think the outer families will accept an erosion of their relative status? Or the king? Or the court? Or the council of lords? *Someone* will think they can only lose by it, and they'll fight you for it.'

'They'll accept it if it makes them rich,' Miriam said. She glanced at the window, sniffed, and buttoned her jacket up. 'Damn, it's cold out there.' A thought struck her. 'Will we be all right on the other side?'

'We're always at risk,' Olga remarked. She paused for a moment. 'But, on second thoughts, I think we are at no more risk than usual.' She nudged the bag at her feet. 'As long as we don't linger.'

The train sneaked along a suburban platform and stopped with a hissing of steam; doors slammed and people shouted, distant whistles shrilling counterpoint. 'Next stop?' Miriam suggested. She pulled out a strip of tablets, took one, and offered another to Olga.

'Thanking you – yes.'

The train pulled away into a deep cutting, its whistle hooting. Buildings on either side cast deep shadows across the windows, then Miriam found herself watching the darkness of a tunnel. 'I'm worried about the congress,' she admitted.

'Leave that to the duke. Do you think he would have called for it if he didn't trust you?'

'If anything goes wrong, if we don't get there, if Brill was lying about my mother being safe – '

The train began to slow again. 'Our stop!' Olga stood up and reached for her coat.

They waited at one end of the platform while the huge black and green behemoth rumbled away from the station. A handful of tired travelers swirled around them, making for the footbridge that led over the tracks to the main concourse. Miriam nodded at a door. 'Into the waiting room.' Olga followed her. The room was empty and cold. 'Are you ready?' Miriam asked. 'I'll go across first. If I run into trouble, I'll come right back. If I'm not back inside five minutes, you come over too.'

Olga discreetly checked her gun. 'I've got a better idea. You're too important to risk first.' She pulled out her locket and picked up her bag: 'See you shortly!'

'Wait – ' It was too late. Miriam squinted at the fading outline. *Funny,* she thought, irritated, *I've never seen someone else do that.* 'Damn,' she said quietly, pulling out her own locket and opening it up so that she could join Olga. 'You'd better not have run into anything you can't handle – '

Ouch. Miriam took a step back and a branch whacked her on the back of the head.

'Are you all right?' Olga asked anxiously.

'*Ouch*. And again, ouch. How about you?'

'I'm fine, except for my head.' Olga looked none the worse for wear. 'Where are we?'

'I should say we're still some way outside the city limits.' Miriam put her bag down and concentrated on breathing, trying to get the throbbing in her head under control. 'Are you ready for a nice bracing morning constitutional?'

'Ugh. Mornings should be abolished!'

'You will hear no arguments from this quarter.' Miriam bent down, opened her bag, and removed a cloak from it to cover her alien clothes. 'That looks like clear ground over there. How about we try to pick up a road?'

'Lead on,' said Olga.

*

They'd come out in deciduous woodland, snow lying thick on the ground between the stark, skeletal trees; it took them the best part of an hour to find their way to a road, and even that was mostly dumb luck. But, once they'd found it, Niejwein was already in sight. And what a sight it was.

Miriam hadn't appreciated before just how crude, small, and just plain smelly the city was. It stood on a low bluff overlooking what might, in a few hundred years, mutate into the Port Authority. Stone walls twenty feet high followed the contours of the ground for miles, bascules sprouting ominously every hundred yards. Long before they reached the walls, she found herself walking beside Olga in a cloud of smelly dust, passing rows of windowless tumbledown shacks. Scores of poor-looking countryfolk – many in clothes little better than lay-ered rags – drove heavily laden donkeys or small herds of sheep toward the city gates. Miriam noticed that they were picking up a few odd looks, especially from the ragged mothers of the barefoot urchins who cast stones across the icy cobbles, but she avoided eye contact and nobody seemed interested in approaching two women who knew where they were going. Especially after Olga pointedly allowed the barrel of her gun to slip from under her cloak, in response to an importuning rascal who attempted to get too close. 'Hmm, I see why you always travel by – ' Miriam stopped and squinted at the gate-house. 'Tell me that's not what I think it is, nailed to the wall,' she said.

'Not what – oh, that.' Olga looked at her oddly. 'What else would you have them do with bandits after they quarter them?'

'Um.' Miriam swallowed. 'Not that.' The city gates were wide open and nobody seemed to be guarding them. 'Is there meant to be anyone on watch?'

'Invasion comes from the sea, most often.'

'Um.' *I've got to stop saying that,* Miriam told herself. Her feet were beginning to hurt with all the walking, she was picking up dust and dirt, and she was profoundly regretting not making use of the dining carriage for breakfast. Or crossing all the way over, phoning for Paulie to pick them up, and driving the rest of the way in the back of an air-conditioned car. 'Which way to the castle?'

'Oh, that's a way yet.' Olga beamed as a wagon laden with bales of hay clattered past. 'Isn't it grand? The largest city in the Gruinmarkt!'

'Yes, I suppose it is,' Miriam said hollowly. She'd seen something like this before, she realized. Some of the museum reconstructions of medieval life back home were quite accurate, but nothing quite captured the reek – no, the overwhelming stench – of open sewers, of people who bathed twice a year and wore a single set of clothes all the time, of houses where the owners bedded down with their live-stock to share warmth. *Did I really say I was going to modernize this?* she asked herself, aghast at her own hubris. *Why yes, I think I did. Talk about jumping in with both feet . . .*

Olga steered her into a wide boulevard without warning. 'Look,' she said. Huge stone buildings fronted the road at intervals, all the way up to an imposing hill at the far end, upon which squatted a massive stone carbuncle, turreted and brooding. 'You see? There is civilization in Niejwein after all!'

'That's the palace, isn't it?'

'It is indeed. And we'll be much better off once we are inside its walls.' A hundred yards more and Olga waved Miriam into what at first she mistook for an alleyway – before she worked out that it was the drive leading to the Hjorth Palace.

'I didn't realize this – ' Miriam stopped, coming to a halt behind Olga. Two men at arms were walking toward them, hands close to their sword hilts.

'Chein bet hen! Gehen'sh veg!'

'Ver she mishtanken shind?' said Olga, drawing herself up and glaring at them icily.

'Ish interesher'ish nish, when sheshint the Herzogin von Praha – ' said one, sneering contemptuously.

'Stop right there,' Miriam said evenly, pulling her right hand inside her cloak. 'Is Duke Lofstrom in residence?'

The sneering one stopped and gaped at her. 'You . . . say, the duke?' he said slowly in broken English. 'I'll *teach* you – '

His colleague laid a hand on his arm and muttered something urgent in his ear.

'Fetch the duke, or one of his aides,' Miriam snapped. 'I will wait here.'

Olga glanced at her sidelong, then turned her cloak back to reveal her gun and her costume. What she wore would be considered respectable in New London: Over here it was as exotic as the American outfits the Clan members wore in private.

'I take you inside,' said the more prudent guard, trying to look inoffensive. 'Gregor, gefen she jemand shnaill'len, als iffoor leifens-dauer abhngtfon ihm,' he told his companion.

Olga grinned humorlessly. 'It does,' she said.

A carriage rattled up the drive behind them; meanwhile, booted feet hurried across the hall. A man, vaguely familiar from Angbard's retinue, glanced curiously at Miriam. 'Oh great Sky Father, it's *her*,' he muttered in a despairing tone. 'Please, come in, come in! You came to see the duke?'

'Yes, but I think we should freshen up first,' said Miriam. 'Please send him my compliments, tell these two idiots to let us in, and we will be with him in half an hour.'

'Certainly, certainly – '

Olga took Miriam's hand and led her up the steps while the duke's man was still warming up on the hapless guards. A couple more guards, these ones far more alert-looking, fell in behind them. 'Your apartment,' said Olga. 'I took the liberty of moving some of my stuff in. I hope you don't mind?'

'Not at all.' Miriam winced. 'I'll need more than half an hour to freshen up.'

'Well, you'll have to do it fast.' Olga rapped on the huge double doors by the top of the main stairs. 'The duke detests being kept waiting.'

'Indeed – Kara! – oof!'

'My lady!'

Miriam pushed her back to arm's length. 'You've been all right?' she asked anxiously. 'No murderers lurking in your bedroom?'

'None, milady!' Kara flushed and let go of her. 'Milady! What *is* that you're wearing? It's so frumpy! And you, lady Olga? Is this some horrid new fashion from Paris that we'll all be wearing in a month? Has somebody been biting your neck, that you've got to hide it?'

'I hope not,' Miriam said dryly. 'Listen.' She towed Kara into the empty outer audience chamber. 'We're going to see Angbard in half an hour. *Half* an hour. Get something for me to wear. And warn Olga's maids. We've been on the road half a day.'

'I shall!' She bounced away toward the bedchamber.

Miriam rubbed her forehead. 'Youth and enthusiasm.' She made a wry curse of it.

Her bedroom was as she'd left it four months ago – Olga had taken the Queen's Room, for there were four royal rooms in this apartment – and for once Miriam didn't drive Kara out. 'Help me undress,' she ordered. 'Aah, that's better. Um. Fetch the pot. Then would you mind getting me a basin of hot water? I need to scrub my face.'

Kara, for a wonder, left Miriam alone to wash herself – then doubled the miracle by laying out one of Miriam's trouser suits and retiring to the outer chamber. 'She's learning,' Miriam noted. It felt strange to be dressing for an ordinary day in the office world, doubly strange to be doing so with medieval squalor held at bay outside by guards with swords. 'What the hell.' She looked at herself in the mirror. Her hair was past shoulder length, there were worry lines around her eyes that hadn't been there six months ago, and her jacket was loose at the waist. 'Not bad.' Then she spotted a couple of white hairs. 'Damn. Bad.' She combed it back hard, held it in place with a couple of pins, and turned her back on the mirror. 'Hostile takeover time, kid. Go kill 'em.'

*

There were no simple chambers for the duke. He'd taken over the royal apartment in the west wing, occupying half of the top floor, and his guards had staked out the entire floor below as a security measure. Nor was it possible for Miriam to pay him a quiet visit. Not without first picking up a retinue of a palace majordomo, a bunch of guards led by a nervous young officer, and an overexcited teenager. Kara fussed around behind Miriam as she climbed the stairs. 'Isn't it exciting?' she squealed.

'Hush.' Miriam cast her eye over the guards with a jaundiced eye. Their camouflage jackets and submachine guns sounded a jarring note. Strip them from the scene and this might merely be some old English stately home, taken over for the duration of a rich multi-national's general meeting. 'Am I always supposed to travel with this much protection?'

'I wouldn't know,' Kara said artlessly.

'Make a point of finding out, then,' Miriam said sharply as she climbed the last few steps toward the separate guard detachment outside Angbard's residence.

Two soldiers came to attention on either side of the door to the royal apartment. Their sergeant strode forward. 'Introduce me,' Miriam hissed at the majordomo.

'Ahem! May I present my lady, Her Excellency the Countess Helge Thorold-Hjorth, niece of the Duke Angbard of that family, who comes to pay her attendance on the duke?' The man ended on a strangled squeak.

The sergeant checked his clipboard. 'Everything is as expected.' He saluted, and Miriam nodded acknowledgment at him. 'Ma'am. If you'd like to come this way.' His eyes lingered on Kara. 'Your lady-in-waiting may attend. The guards – '

'Very well,' said Miriam. She glanced over her shoulder: 'Wait here, I'm not expecting my uncle to try to kill me,' she told her retinue. *Yet,* she added silently. The doors swung open and she stepped through into a nearly empty audience chamber. The doors slammed shut behind her with a solid thud of latches, and she would have paused to look around but for the sergeant, who was already halfway across the huge expanse of hand-woven carpet.

He paused at the inner door and knocked twice: 'Visitor six-two,' he muttered to a peephole, then stood aside. The inner door opened just wide enough to admit Miriam and Kara. 'If you please, ma'am.'

'Hmm.' Miriam entered the room, then stopped dead. 'Mother!'

'Miriam!' Iris smiled at her from her wheelchair, which stood beside the pair of thrones mounted at one end of the audience room. A pair of crutches leaned against one of them.

Miriam crossed the room quickly and leaned down to hug her mother. 'I've missed you,' she said quietly. 'I was so worried – '

'There, there.' Iris kissed her lightly on the cheek. 'I'm all right, as you can see.' Miriam straightened up. 'You look as if you're keeping well!' Then she noticed Kara's head in the doorway, jaw agape. 'Oh dear, another one come to stare at me,' she sighed. 'I suppose it can't be helped. It'll all be over by this time tomorrow, anyway, isn't that the case, Angbard?'

'I would not make any assumptions,' said the duke, turning away from the window. His expression was distant. 'Helge, Miriam.'

'So, it *is* true,' said Miriam. She glanced at Iris. 'He brought you here?' She rounded on Angbard: 'You should be ashamed of yourself!'

'Nonsense.' He looked offended.

'Don't blame him, Miriam.' Her mother looked at her strangely. 'Drag up a seat, dear. It's a long story.'

Miriam sat down beside her. 'Why?' she asked, her thoughts whirling so that she couldn't make her mind up what word to put next. 'What is she doing here then, if you didn't kidnap her?' she asked, looking at Angbard. 'I thought it was against all your policies to take people from – '

'Policies?' Angbard asked, raising his nose. He shrugged dismissively then looked at Iris. 'Tell her.'

'Nobody kidnapped me,' said Iris. 'But after a party or parties unknown tried to kill me, I phoned Angbard and asked for help.'

'Um. You *phoned* him?'

'Yes.' Iris nodded encouragingly. 'Isn't that how you normally get in touch with someone?'

'Well yes, but, but . . .' Miriam paused. 'You had his number,' she said slowly. 'How?'

Iris glanced at the duke, as if asking for moral support. He raised his eyebrows slightly, and half-turned away from Miriam.

'Um.' Iris froze up, looking embarrassed.

Miriam stared at her mother. 'Oh no. Tell me it isn't true.'

Iris coughed. 'I expected you to look at the papers, use the locket or not, then do the sensible thing and ask me to tell you all about it. I figured you'd be fairly safe, your house being in the middle of open woodland on this side, and it would make explaining everything a lot easier once you'd had a chance to see for yourself. Otherwise – ' She shrugged. 'If I'd broken it to you cold you'd have thought I was crazy. I didn't expect you to go running off and getting yourself shot at! I was so worried!'

'Ma.' She had difficulty swallowing. 'You're telling me you knew about. The Clan. All along.'

A patient sigh from the window bay. 'She appears to be having some difficulty. If you would allow me – '

'No!' Iris snapped, then stopped.

'If you can't, I will,' the duke said firmly. He turned back to face Miriam. 'Your mother has had my number all along,' he explained, scrutinizing her face. 'The Clan has maintained emergency telephone numbers – a nine-eleven service, if you like – for the past fifty years. She only saw fit to call me when you went missing.'

'Ma – ' Miriam stopped. Glanced at Angbard again. 'My *mother*,' she said thoughtfully. 'Not, um, foster-mother, is it?'

Angbard shook his head slightly, studying her beneath half-hooded eyes.

Miriam stared at Iris. 'Why all the lies, then?' she demanded.

Iris shuffled deeper into her chair. 'It seemed like a good idea at the time, is all I can say.' A pause. 'Miriam?'

'Yeah?'

'I know I brought you up not to tell lies. All I can say is, I wish I could have lived up to that myself. I'm sorry.'

Angbard took a step forward, then moved to stand behind Iris's wheelchair.

'Don't be too hard on her,' he said warningly. 'You have no idea what she's been through – ' He shook his head. 'No idea.'

'So explain,' said Miriam. Her gaze slid past Iris to focus on Kara, who was doing her best imitation of a sheet of wallpaper – wallpaper with a fascinated expression. 'Whoa. Kara, please wait outside. Now.'

Kara skidded across the floor as if her feet were on fire: 'I'm going, I'm going!' she squeaked.

Miriam stared at Iris. 'So why did you do it?'

Iris sighed. 'They'd shot Alfredo, you know.'

She fell silent for a moment.

'Alfredo?'

'Your father.'

'Shot him, you said.'

'Yes. And Joan, my maid, they killed her too. I got across but they'd done a good job on me, too – I nearly bled to death before the ambulance got me to a hospital. And then, and then . . .' She trailed off. 'I was in Cambridge, unidentified, in a hospital, with no chaperone and no guards. Can you understand the temptation?'

Miriam looked sideways: Angbard was watching Iris like a hawk, something like admiration in his eyes. Or maybe it was the bitterness of the dutiful brother who stuck to his post? It was hard to tell.

'How did you meet Morris?' she asked her mother, after a momentary pause.

'He was a hospital visitor. Actually he was writing for an underground newspaper at the time and came to see if I'd been beaten up by the pigs. Later he sorted out our birth certificates – mine and yours, that is, including my fake backstory leading out of the country, and the false adoption papers – when we moved around. Me being a naturalized foreigner was useful cover. There was a whole underground railroad going on in those days, left over from when the SDS and the Weather Underground turned bad, and it served our purpose to use it. Especially as the FBI wasn't actually looking for us.'

'So I – I – ' Miriam stopped. 'I'm not adopted.'

'Does it make any difference to you?' Iris asked, sounding

slightly puzzled. 'You always said it didn't. That's what you told me.'

'I'm confused,' Miriam admitted. 'You were rich and powerful. You gave it all up – brought your daughter up to think she was adopted, went underground, lived like a political radical – just to get away from the in-laws?'

Angbard spoke. 'It's her grandmother's fault,' he said. 'You met the dowager duchess, I believe. She has always taken a, ah, utilitarian view of her offspring. She played Patty like a card in a game of poker, for the highest stakes. The treaty process, re-establishing the braid between the warring factions. I think she did so partially out of spite, to get your mother out of the way, but she is not a simple woman. Nothing she does serves only a single purpose.' His expression was stony. 'She is untouchable. Unlike whoever tried to ruin her hand by murdering my half-sister and her husband.'

Iris shifted around, trying to make herself more comfortable. 'Don't trouble yourself on my account. If you ever find Alfredo's body, you'd best not tell me where it's buried – I'd have a terrible time getting back into my wheelchair after I pissed on it.'

'Patricia,' his smile was razor-thin, 'I usually find that death settles all scores to my complete satisfaction. Just as long as they stay dead.'

'Well, I don't agree. And you weren't married to Alfredo.'

'Mother!' Miriam stared at both of them in shock: Just as she was certain Angbard was serious, she was more than half afraid that her mother was, too.

'Don't you "mother" me!' Iris chided her. 'I was mooning at the national guard before you were out of diapers. I'm just not very mobile these days.' She frowned and turned to Angbard. 'We were speaking of *mother*,' she reminded him.

'I can't keep her out forever,' said Angbard, his frightening smile vanishing as rapidly as it had appeared. 'You two clearly need more time together, but I have an audience with his majesty in an hour. Miriam, can you fill me in quickly?'

Miriam took a deep breath. 'First, I need to know where Roland is.'

'Roland – ' Angbard looked at his watch, his face intent. Then back at Miriam. 'He's been looking after Patty for the past month,' he said, his tone neutral. 'Right now he's in Boston, minding the shop. You don't need to worry about his reliability.'

For a moment Miriam felt so dizzy that she had to shut her eyes. She opened them again when she heard her mother's voice. 'Such a suitable young man.' She glared at Iris, who smiled lazily at her. 'Don't let them get together, Angbard, or they'll be over the horizon before you have time to blink.'

'It's not. That.' Miriam was having difficulty breathing. 'There's a hole in your security,' she said as calmly as she could. 'It's at a very high level. I told Roland to do something about a corpse in an inconvenient place and instead a bunch of high explosives showed up. It turns out that Matthias has been blackmailing him.' She felt dizzy with the significance of the moment.

'Roland? Are you sure?' Angbard leaned forward. His face was expressionless.

'Yes. He told me everything.' She felt as if she were floating. 'Listen, it was on the specific understanding that I would intercede with you to clear it up. Your secretary has been running his own little game and seems to have decided that getting a handle on Roland would help him cover his traces.'

'That was a mistake,' Angbard said, his voice deceptively casual. His expression was immobile, except for his scarred left cheek, which twitched slightly. 'How did you find out?'

'It happened in the warehouse my chamber is doppelgängered onto here. Most of this pile is collocated with a bonded warehouse, but one wing sticks out into a real hole-in-the-wall shipping operation.' She swallowed, then forced herself to speak. 'There was a night watchman. Emphasis on the *was*.' She explained what had happened when she'd first carried Brill through to New York.

'Roland, you say,' said Angbard. 'He's been blackmailed?'

'I want your word,' Miriam insisted. 'No consequences.'

A sharp intake of breath. 'Well – ' Angbard started to pace. 'Did he betray any secrets?'

Miriam stood up. 'Not as far as I know.'

'And did anyone die as a result of his actions?'

Miriam paused for a moment before answering: 'Again, not as far as I know. Certainly not directly. And certainly not as a result of anything he knew he was doing.'

'Well. Maybe I will not have to kill him.' Angbard stopped again, behind Iris's chair. 'What do you think I should do?' he asked, visibly tense.

'I think – ' Miriam chewed her lower lip. 'Matthias has tapes. I think you should hand the tapes over to me, unwatched. I'll burn them. In front of you both, if you want.' She paused. 'You'll want to remove all his responsibilities for security operations, I guess.'

'This blackmail material,' Iris prodded. 'These tapes – is it something personal? Or has he been abusing his position in any way?'

'It's absolutely personal. I can swear to it. Matthias just got the drop on Roland's private life. Nothing illegal; just, uh, sensitive.'

Iris – Patricia, the long-lost countess – stared at her for a long moment, then turned to look at her half-brother. 'Do as she says,' she said.

Angbard nodded, then cast her a sharp look. 'We'll see,' he said.

'No, we won't!' Iris snapped. She continued quietly but with emphasis: 'If your secretary has been building up private dossiers on nobles, you're in big trouble. You need all the friends you can get, bro. Starting by pardoning anyone who isn't an active enemy will clear the field. And make damn sure you burn those tapes *without* watching them, because for all you know some of them are fabrications that Matthias concocted just in case you ever stumbled across them. It's untrustworthy evidence, all of it.' She turned to Miriam. 'What else have you dug up?' she demanded.

'Well.' Miriam leaned against a priceless lacquered wooden cabinet and managed to muster up a tired smile to conceal her sense of relief. 'I'm pretty sure Matthias is in league with whoever was running the prisoner.'

'The prisoner,' Angbard echoed distantly. By his expression, he was already wrapped up in calculating the requirements of the coming purge.

'What prisoner?' asked Iris.

'Something your daughter's friends dragged in a couple of days ago,' Angbard dropped offhandedly. To Miriam he added, 'He's downstairs.'

'Have you worked out who he is, yet?' Miriam interrupted.

'What, that he's a long-lost cousin? And so are the rest of his family, stranded with a corrupt icon that takes them to this new world you have opened up for our trade? Of course. Your suggestion that we do DNA fingerprinting made it abundantly clear.'

'Cousins? New world?' Iris asked. 'Would one of you please back up a bit and explain, before I have to beat it out of you with my crutches?'

Angbard stood up. 'No, I don't think so. You kept Miriam in the dark for nearly a third of a century, I think it's only fair that we keep you in suspense for a third of a day.'

'So nobody else knows?' Miriam asked Angbard.

'That's correct. And I'm going to keep it that way, for now.'

'I want to talk to the prisoner,' Miriam said hastily.

'You do?' Angbard turned the full force of his icy stare on her. 'Whatever for?'

'Because – ' Miriam struggled for words – 'I don't have old grudges. I mean, his relatives tried to *kill* me, but . . . I have an idea I want to test. I need to see if he'll talk to me. May I?'

Angbard looked thoughtful. 'You'll have to be quick, if you want to collect your pound of flesh before we execute him.'

Miriam swallowed bile. 'That's not what I have in mind.'

'Oh, really?'

'Give me a chance?' she asked. 'Please?'

'If you insist. But don't lose the plot.' He stared at her, and for a moment Miriam felt her bones turn to water. 'Remember not all your relatives are as liberal-minded as I am, or believe that death heals all wounds.'

'I won't,' Miriam said automatically. Then she looked at Iris again, a long, appraising inspection. Her mother met her gaze head-on, without blinking. 'It's all right,' she said. 'I'm not going to stop being your daughter. Just as long as you don't stop being my ma. Deal?'

'Deal.' Iris dropped her gaze. 'I don't deserve you, kid.'

'Yes, you do.' Angbard looked Miriam up and down. 'Like mother, like daughter, don't you know what kind of combination that makes?'

He chuckled humorlessly. 'Now, if you will excuse me, Helge, you have made much work for this old man to attend to . . .'

*

I should have realized all castles had dungeons, thought Miriam. If not for keeping prisoners, then for supplies, ammunition, food, wine cellars – even ice. It was freezing cold below ground, and even the crude coal-gas pipes nailed to the brickwork and the lamps hissing and fizzing at irregular intervals couldn't dispel the chill. Miriam followed the guard down a surprisingly wide staircase into a cellar, then up to a barred iron door behind which a guard waited patiently. Finally he led her into a well-lit room containing nothing but a table and two chairs.

'What is this?' she asked.

'I'll bring the prisoner to you, ma'am,' the sergeant said patiently. 'With another guard. The gate at the front won't be unlocked again until he's back in his cell.'

'Oh.' Miriam sat down, feeling stupid, and waited nervously as the guard disappeared into the basement tunnels beneath the castle. *The dungeon. I put him here,* she thought. *What must he be thinking?*

A clattering outside brought her back to herself, and she turned around to watch the door as it opened. The sergeant came in, followed by another soldier, and a hunched, thin figure with his arms behind his back and a hood over his head. *He's manacled,* Miriam realized.

'One moment.' The guards positioned the prisoner against the wall opposite Miriam's table. The guard knelt, and Miriam heard something click into place – padlocks. 'That's it,' said the sergeant. He pulled off the prisoner's hood, then he and the other guard withdrew to stand beside the door.

'Hello, Lin,' Miriam said as evenly as she could. 'Recognize me?'

He flinched, clearly terrified, and was brought up short by his chains. A sense of horror stole over Miriam as she peered at him in the dim light. 'They've been beating you,' she said quietly. *The things on the gatehouse walls* – no, she didn't want to be involved in this. It was all a horrible mistake. *Multiple contusions, some bleeding and inflammation around the left eye.* He stared past her left shoulder, shivering fearfully, but didn't say anything. Miriam resisted the urge to turn around and yell at the guards. She had a hopeless feeling that all it would do was earn the kid another beating when she was safely out of the way.

Her medical training wouldn't let her look away. Up until this moment she'd have sworn she was angry with him: But she hadn't expected them to treat him like this. Breaking into her house on the orders of someone placed in authority over him – sure, she was angry. But the real guilty parties were a long way away, and if she didn't do something fast, this half-starved kid was going to join the grisly chunks of meat on the gatehouse wall, for the crime of following orders. And where was the justice in that?

'I'm not going to hit you,' she said.

He didn't reply. His posture said he didn't believe her.

'Listen.' She pulled one of the chairs out from the table, turned it around, and sat down on it, her arms folded across the back. 'I just want some answers. That's all. Lin of, what did you call yourself?'

'Lin. Lin Lee. My family is called Lee.' He kept glancing past her, as if trying to conceal his fear: *I'm not going to hit you, but my guards –*

'That's good. How old are you?'

'Fifteen.' *Fifteen! They're running the children's crusade!* A thought struck her. 'Have they been feeding you? Giving you water? Somewhere to sleep?'

He managed a brief, painful croak: Maybe it was meant to be laughter.

Miriam looked around. 'Well? Have you been feeding him?'

The sergeant shook himself. 'Ma'am?'

'What food, drink, and medical attention has this child had?'

He shook his head. 'I really couldn't say, ma'am.'

'I see.' Miriam's hands tensed on the back of the chair. She turned back to Lin. 'I didn't order this,' she said. 'Will you tell me who sent you to my house?'

She saw him swallow. 'If I do that you'll kill me,' he said.

'No, that's not what I've got in mind.'

'Yes you will.' He looked at her with bitter certainty in his eyes. 'They'll do it.'

'Like you were going to kill me?' she asked quietly.

He didn't say anything.

'You were supposed to find out if I was from the Clan,' she said. 'Weren't you? A strange new woman showing up in town and making waves. Is that it? And if I was from the Clan, you were supposed to kill me. What was it to be? A bomb in my bedroom? Or a knife in the dark?'

'Not me,' he whispered. 'One of the warriors.'

'So why were you there? To spy on me? Are they that short-handed?'

He looked down at the table, but not before she saw shame in his eyes.

'Ah.' She glanced away for a moment, trying desperately to think of a way out of the impasse. She was hopelessly aware of the guards standing behind her, waiting patiently for her to finish with the prisoner. *If I leave him here, the Clan* will *kill him,* she realized, with a kind of hollow dread she hadn't expected to be able to summon up for a housebreaker. Housebreaker? What his actions said about his family, *that* was something she could get angry about. 'Hell.' She made up her mind.

'Lin, you're probably right about the Clan. Most of them would see you dead as soon as look at you. There've been too many years of their parents and grandparents cutting each other's throats. They're suspicious of anything they don't understand, and you're going to be high on any list of mysteries. But I'll tell you something else.' She stood up. 'You know how to world-walk, don't you?'

Silence.

'I said – ' She stopped. 'You ought to know when you can stop holding it in,' she said tiredly. Thinking back to Angbard, and how she'd managed to face him down over Roland: *Don't look too deep. Everything on the surface.* The families all worked that way, didn't they? 'Nothing you say to me can make your position worse. It might make it better, though.'

Silence.

'World-walking,' she said. 'We *know* you can do it, we got the locket you carried. So why lie?'

Silence.

'The Clan can world-walk too, you know,' she said quietly. 'It isn't a coincidence. Your family are relatives, aren't they? Lost for a long time, and this murder – the killing, the feuding, the attempts to reopen old wounds – isn't in anyone's interests.'

Silence.

'Why do they want me dead?' she asked. 'Why are you people killing your own blood relatives?'

Maybe it was something in her expression – frank curiosity, perhaps – but the youth looked away at last. The silence stretched out for a long moment, lengthened toward a minute, punctuated only by the sound of one of the guards shifting position.

'You betrayed us,' he whispered.

'Uh?' Miriam shook her head. 'I don't understand.'

'In the time of the loyal sons,' said Lin. 'All the others. They abandoned my ancestor. The promise of a meeting in the world of the Americans. Reduced to poverty, he took years to gain his freedom, then he spent his entire life searching for them. But they never came.'

'This is all news to me,' Miriam said quietly. 'He was reduced to poverty?'

Lin nodded convulsively. 'This is the tale of our family,' he said, in sing-song tones. 'That of the brothers, it was agreed that Lee would go west, to set up a trading post. And he did, but the way was hard and he was reduced to penury, his caravan scattered, his goods stolen by savages, abandoned by his servants. For ten years he labored as a bond servant, before buying his freedom: He lost everything, from his wife to the first talisman of the family. Finally he forged a new talisman, working from memory, earned his price, and bought himself liberty. He was a very determined man. But when he walked to the place assigned for meeting, nobody was there to wait for him. Every year, at the appointed day and hour, he would go there; and never did anyone come. His brothers had abandoned him, and over the years his descendants learned much of the eastern Clan. The betrayers, who profited from his estate.'

Oops, a betrayal-for-a-legacy myth. So he accidentally mangled the knotwork and ended up going to New Britain instead of – she blinked.

'You've seen my world,' she said. 'Do you know, that's where the Clan have been going all along? Where you go when you world-walk, it's all set up by the, uh, talisman. Your illustrious ancestor recreated it wrong. Sending himself over to, to, New Britain. For all you know, the other brothers thought that your ancestor had abandoned *them*.'

Lin shrugged. 'When are you going to kill me?' he asked.

'In about ten seconds if you don't shut up about it!' She glared at him. 'Don't you see? Your family's reasons for feuding with the Clan are bogus. They've been bogus all along!'

'So?' He made a movement that might have been a shrug if he hadn't been wearing fetters. 'Our elders, now dead, laid these duties upon our shoulders. We must obey, or dishonor their memory. Only our eldest can change our course. Do you expect me to betray my family and plead for mercy?'

'No.' Miriam stood up. 'But you may not need to beg, Lin. There is a Clan meeting coming up tomorrow. Some – most – of them will want your head. But I think it might be possible to convince them to let you go free, if you agree to do something.'

'No!'

She rolled her eyes. 'Really? You don't *want* to go home and deliver a letter to this elder of yours? I knew you were young and silly, but this is ridiculous.'

'What kind of letter?' he asked hesitantly.

'An offer of terms. It seems to me that you need it more than we do, I hasten to add. Now we can get into *your* world – ' he flinched – 'and there are many more of us, *and* there's the other world you saw, the one the Clan's power is based in. Did you see much of America?' His eyes went wide: He'd seen enough. 'From now on, in any struggle, we can win. There is no "maybe" in that statement. If the eldest orders your family to fight it out, they can only lose. But I happen to have a use for your family – I want to keep them alive. And you. I'm willing to settle this thing between us, the generations of blood and murder, if your eldest is willing to accept that declaring war on the Clan was wrong, that his ancestor was not deliberately abandoned, and that ending the war is necessary. So I'm going to do everything I can to convince the committee to send you home with a cease-fire proposal.'

He stared at her as if she'd sprouted a second head.

'Will you carry that message?' she asked.

He nodded, slowly, watching her with wide eyes.

'Don't get your hopes up,' she warned. She turned to the door. 'Take this one back to his cell,' she said. 'I want you to make sure he's given food and water. And take good care of him.' She leaned toward the sergeant. 'There is a chance that he is going to run an errand for us. I do *not* want him damaged. Do you understand?'

Something in her eyes made the soldier tense. 'Yes, ma'am,' he grunted warily. 'Food and water.' His companion pulled the door open, staring at the wall behind her, trying to avoid her gaze.

'See that you do.'

She came out of the cellars shivering into the evening twilight, and headed upstairs as fast as she could, to get back to a warm fireplace and good company. But it was going to take more than that to get the chill of the dungeon out of her bones, and out of her dreams.

PART TEN

MELTDOWN

ESCAPE PLANS

'He's done *what*?' demanded Matthias, in a tone of rising disbelief.

During Angbard's lengthy absence the duke's outer office in Fort Lofstrom served as a headquarters from which the Clan's operations in Massachusetts were coordinated. One of a chain of nine such castles up and down the eastern seaboard (in the Gruinmarkt, but also in the free kingdoms to the north and south), it coordinated the transshipment of Clan cargo along the entire eastern continental coast. Half a dozen junior Clan members were stationed there at any time, each shuttling back and forth at eight-hour intervals. Every three hours a message packet would arrive from Cambridge, and Matthias would be the first to open it and read any confidential dispatches.

This packet had contained a couple of letters, and a terse coded message. It was the latter that had whetted Matthias's curiosity, then raised his ire.

The youth standing in front of his desk looked very frightened, but held his ground. 'It came over the wireless just now, sir, an order to shut down. A blanket order, for the duration of the extraordinary general meeting, sir.' He cleared his throat. 'Isn't that unusual?'

'Hmm.' Matthias looked at him hard. 'Well, Poul.' The lad was barely out of his teens, still afflicted by acne and a bad case of deference to authority – especially the kind of deadly, self-confident authority that Matthias exuded – but for all that he was brave. 'We'll just have to shut down the postal service, won't we?' He allowed his expression to relax infinitesimally, determined not to give the youth any hint of his anger and apprehension.

'Are those your orders, sir?' Poul asked eagerly.

'No.' Matthias cocked his head. A Clan extraordinary meeting, held without warning . . . it didn't smell good. In fact, it smelled extraordinarily bad to him. Ever since Esau's asshole relatives had started trying to rub out the long-lost countess and another bunch of interlopers had joined in, things had looked distinctly unstable. 'It sounds to me as if there's something very big going on,' Matthias said slowly. 'On that basis, I don't think suspending the post is sufficient. We have assets on the other side who may not have got the warning. I'll need you to make one more crossing to deliver a message, as soon as possible. *Then* we shut down. Meanwhile, it will be necessary to secure the fort.'

'Secure the – sir? Do you know what's going on?'

Matthias fixed the young man with a grim stare. 'I have a notion that it's no good. The civil war, lad, that's what this is about. Pigeons are coming home to roost and promises made thirty years ago are about to be delivered on.' He snorted. 'Idiots,' he muttered bitterly. 'Wait here. I have to go and get the special dispatches out of the duke's office. Then I'll go over what you have to do to deliver them.'

Matthias rose and let himself through the door into the duke's inner study. Everything was as it had been when Angbard departed, a week ago. Matthias closed the door, then leaned his head against the wall and cursed silently. *So close, so damned close!* But he couldn't just sit here. Not with that bitch about to spill her guts at the meeting. Esau's confession – that the eldest had authorized repeated attempts on Helge's life – had shaken him. He'd had Helge, Miriam, in his sights: She was a natural fellow traveler for his plans. He'd been getting positioned to bring her into his orbit until the idiot fanatics started trying to kill her, making her suspicious of everyone and everything. With no friends but Roland, she'd been easy meat before. But now –

He read through his illicit decrypt one more time. The original message wasn't addressed to him, but that had never stopped Matthias in the past; as Angbard's secretary he was used to reading the duke's correspondence – and also mail for other people on station that passed through the post room. People such as Sir Huw Thoms, lieutenant of the guard, who right now was over on the other side, making a delivery run. And he had access to the code books, too.

ACTION THIS DAY STOP ARREST MATTHIAS VAN HJORTH
ANY MEANS NECESSARY STOP CHARGES OF TREASON TO
FOLLOW STOP

Matthias crumpled the letter in his fist, his face a tight mask of anger. *Bitch*, he thought. Either his hold on Roland wasn't as strong as he'd believed, or she was more ruthless than he'd imagined. But the old man has made a mistake. Poul, the callow messenger, was in the next room. That gave him an edge, if he could only work out how to use it.

He went back out to his own office, and opened another desk drawer. He smiled to himself at the thought of Angbard's reaction should he discover what Matthias kept in it, the use to which Matthias had put his access to the duke's personal files. But there was no time now for self-indulgent daydreams. What Matthias needed was a smokescreen to cover his own disappearance, and smokescreens didn't come any thicker than this one.

First, Matthias removed the most recent addition from the safe: an anonymous CD, the enigmatic phrase 'deep throat' scrawled on it in a feminine hand. Obtaining it had taken him a lot of detective work; only the hints turned up by the duke's background checks on Miriam had kept him searching until it came to light, buried in her music collection. Next, he removed three stamped, addressed envelopes, each containing a covering letter and another item. When he left his office a minute later, the drawer was locked and empty of incriminating evidence. And the letters were on the first stage of their journey to Cambridge, Massachusetts, by Clan courier. Letters addressed to local FBI and DEA offices.

*

The huge ballroom at the back of the Clan's palace could, when the situation demanded it, be converted into a field hospital – or a boardroom large enough to hold all the voting members of an ancient and prolific business partnership. It was only when she saw it filled that Miriam began to grasp the scale of the power the Clan wielded in the Gruinmarkt.

The room was dominated by a table at one end, behind which sat a row of eight chairs: three for administrative officers of the committee, and one for each head of one of the families. Rows of green leather-topped benches had been installed facing the table, the ones farther back raised to give their occupants a view of the front. The huge glass doors that in summer would open onto the garden were closed, barricaded outside by heavy oak shutters.

The main entrance to the room was guarded by soldiers in black helmets and body armor, armed with automatic rifles. They stood impassively by as Miriam entered, Kara trailing her. 'Ooh, look! It's your uncle!' Kara whispered.

'Tell me something new. Like, where do I sit?' Angbard occupied one of the three raised chairs at the middle of table, a black robe drawn over his suit. His expression was as grim as a hanging judge's. The room was already beginning to fill, men and women in business attire seeking out their benches and quietly conversing. The only anomalous touch was their attendants, decked out in archaic finery.

'Excuse me, where should milady sit?' Kara asked a uniformed functionary who, now that Miriam was getting her bearings, seemed to be one of many who were unobtrusively directing delegates and partners to one side or another.

'Thorold-Hjorth – that would be there. Left bench, second row if she is to be called.'

Miriam drifted toward the indicated position. *Like a company's annual general meeting*, she noted. It was oddly familiar, but in no way comforting. She looked up at the front table and saw that three of the high seats had already been filled – one of them by Oliver Hjorth, who caught her watching and glared at her. The other two held dusty nonentities, elderly men who looked half-asleep already as they leaned heads together to talk. *I wish Roland were here*, she thought. *Or – no, I just wish I wasn't facing this alone. Roland would be supportive, but he wouldn't be much use, would he?*

'May I join you?' someone asked. Miriam glanced up.

'Olga? Yeah, sure! Did you have a good night?'

Olga sat down next to her. 'No intruders,' she said smugly. 'A pity. I was rather hoping.'

'Hoping?'

'To test my new M4 Super 90. Ah well. Oh, look, it's Baron Gruinard.' She indicated one of the dried sticks at the board table.

'Is that good or bad?'

'Depends if he's sitting for the Royal Assizes and you're brought up in front of him. At most other times he's rather harmless, but one hears the most frightful things when his court is in session.'

'Um.' Miriam noticed another familiar figure, an elderly dowager in a blue twinset and pearls. Her stomach twisted. 'I spy a grandmother.'

'Don't make a habit of it.' Olga beamed in the direction of the elderly duchess, who spotted Miriam and frowned, horribly. 'Isn't she impressive?'

'Is that meant to be a compliment?'

The duchess cast Olga a hideous glare and then diverted her attention elsewhere, to a balding middle-aged man in a suit who fawned and led her toward the far side of the room.

'Where's – '

'Hush,' said Olga. Angbard had produced a gavel from somewhere. He rapped it on the edge of the table peremptorily.

'We are gathered today for an extraordinary meeting,' Angbard announced conversationally. He frowned and tapped the elderly looking microphone. 'We are gathered . . . state of emergency.' The sound system cut in properly and Miriam found that she no longer had to make an effort to hear him. 'Thirty-two years ago, Patricia Thorold-Hjorth and Alfredo Wu were attacked on their way to this court. The bodies of Alfredo and his guards were found, but that of Patricia remained lost. Until very recently it was believed that she and her infant daughter had perished.'

A quiet ripple of conversation swept the hall. Angbard continued after a brief pause. 'Four months ago an unknown woman appeared in the wilds of Nether Paarland. She was apprehended, and a variety of evidence – backed up by genetic fingerprinting, which my advisors tell me is infallible for this purpose – indicated that she was the long-lost infant, Helge Thorold-Hjorth, grown to majority in the United States.'

The conversational ripple became a cascade. Angbard brought his gavel down again and again. 'Silence, I say silence! I will have silence.'

Finally the room was quiet enough for him to continue. 'A decision was taken to bring Helge into the Clan. I personally took responsibility for this. Her, ah, induction, was not an immediate success. Upon her arrival here a number of unexpected events transpired. In particular, it appears that someone wanted her dead – someone who couldn't tell the difference between a thirty-two-year-old countess and a twenty-three-year-old chatelaine, traveling together. In the interests of clarity I must add that *nobody* in this room is presently under suspicion.'

Miriam's scalp prickled. Glancing aside she realized that half the eyes in the room were pointed at her. She sat up and looked back at Angbard.

'I believe we now have evidence enough to confirm the identity of the parties behind the attacks on Patricia and Alfredo, *and* on Patricia's daughter, Helge. These same parties are accused of fomenting the civil war that split this Clan into opposing factions fifty-seven years ago – ' Uproar. Angbard sat back and waited for almost a minute, then brought his gavel down again – 'Silence, please! I intend to present the witnesses that Clan Security has uncovered before you in due course. The floor will then be opened for motions bearing on the matter at hand.' He turned to his neighbor, an elderly gentleman who until this point appeared to have been half asleep on his throne. 'Julius, if you please . . .'

'Aha!' The old scarecrow bolted upright, raised a wobbling hand, and declaimed: 'Calling the first witness – ' he peered at a paper that Angbard slid before him, and muttered: 'Can't call her, she's dead, dammit!'

'No, she isn't,' retorted Angbard.

'Oh, all right then. Think I'm senile, do you?' Julius stood up. 'Calling Patricia Thorold-Hjorth.'

Half the room were on their feet shouting as the side door behind the table opened. Miriam had to stand, too, to see over heads to where Brilliana was entering the room, pushing a wheelchair containing her mother. Who looked bemused and rather nervous at being the focus of such uproarious attention.

'Did they take her motorized chair away to stop her running?' Miriam asked Olga.

'Order! Order or I shall have the guards – order I say!'

Slowly order was restored. 'That's odd,' quavered Julius, 'I was sure she was dead.' A ripple of laughter spread.

'So was I,' Iris – Patricia – called from her chair. Brill steered her over to one side of the table.

'Why did you run away?' asked Oliver Hjorth, leaning sideways so he could see her, an unpleasant expression of impatience on his face.

'What, uns gefen mine mudder en geleg 'hat Gelegenheit, mish'su 'em annudern frau-clapper weg tu heiraten?' Iris asked dryly. There was a shocked titter from somewhere in the audience. 'Obviously not. And if you have to ask that question I also doubt very much that you've ever had a gang of assassins trying to murder you. A pity, that. You could benefit from the experience.'

'What's she saying?' Miriam nudged Olga. *I really must try to learn the language,* she thought despairingly.

'Your mother is convincingly rude,' Olga replied, *sotto voce.*

'This is an imposter!' someone called from the floor. Miriam craned her neck; it might be the dowager duchess, but she couldn't be certain. 'I demand to see – '

'Order!' Angbard whacked his hammer down again. 'You will be polite, madam, or I will have you escorted out of this room.'

'I apologize to the chair,' Iris responded. 'However, I assure you I'm no imposter. Mother dearest, by way of proof of my identity, would you like me to repeat what I overheard you telling Erich Wu in the maze at the summer palace gardens at Kvaern when I was six?'

'You – you!' The old dowager stumbled to her feet, shaking with rage.

'I believe I can prove my case adequately, with or without blood tests,' Iris said dryly, addressing the gallery. 'As any of you who have consulted the register of proxies must be aware, my mother has a strong motive for refusing to acknowledge me. Unfortunately, as in so many other circumstances, I must disobey her wishes.'

'Nonsense!' blurted the duchess, an expression of profound horror settling on her face. She sat down quickly.

'As her half-brother I can attest that she is no imposter,' said Angbard. 'If anyone requests independent verification, that can be arranged. Does any party to this meeting so desire?' He glanced around the room, but no hands went up. 'Very well.' He rapped on the table again with his gavel. 'I intend to bring up the issue of Lady Thorold-Hjorth's absence again, but not at this session. Suffice to say, *I* am convinced of her authenticity. As you have just seen, her mother appears to be convinced, too.' Spluttering from the vicinity of the dowager failed to break his poise. 'Now, we have more urgent matters to consider. My reason for reintroducing Lady Patricia to this body was to, ah, make it clear where the next matter is coming from.'

'Clear as mud,' the elderly Julius remarked to nobody in particular.

'I'd like to call the next witness before the committee,' Angbard continued, unperturbed. 'Lady Olga Thorold has been the subject of outrageous attempts upon her person, and has had her lady-in-waiting murdered, very recently – while traveling in the company of Lady Helge. All of this has occurred in the past six months. Please approach the table.'

Olga rose and walked to the front of the table. The room was silent.

'In your own words, would you please tell us about the series of attacks on your person, when and where they began, and why they were unsuccessful?'

Olga cleared her throat. 'Last December I was summoned to spend time with Duke Lofstrom at his castle. I had for a year before then been petitioning him for an active role, in the hope that he could find a use for me in the trade. He asked me to escort Helge Thorold-Hjorth, newly arrived and ignorant of our ways, both to educate her and to ensure that no harm came to her. I do not believe he anticipated subsequent events when we arrived at this house – ' She continued to enumerate intrusion after intrusion, outrage by outrage, pausing only when interrupted from the floor by a burst of voices demanding further explanation.

Miriam watched in near-astonishment. 'Is everyone here something to do with Clan Security?' she asked Kara quietiy.

'Not me, milady!' Kara's eyes were wide.

Olga finished by recounting how Miriam had brought her to a new world, and how they had been assaulted there, too, by strangers. A voice from the floor called out. 'Wait! How do you know it was another world? Can't it possibly have been another region of 'Merica?'

'No, it can't,' Olga said dismissively. 'I've seen America, and I've seen this other place, and the differences are glaringly obvious. They both sprang from the same roots, but clearly they have diverged – in America, the monarchy is not hereditary, is it?' She frowned for a moment. 'Did I say something wrong?'

More uproar. 'What's all this nonsense about?' demanded Baron Hjorth, red-faced. 'It's clear as day that this can't be true! If it was, there might be a whole new world out there!'

'I believe there is,' Olga replied calmly.

The gavel rose and fell on the resulting babble. 'Silence! I now call Helge Thorold-Hjorth, alias Miriam Beckstein. Please approach the table.'

Miriam swallowed as she stood up and walked over.

'Please describe for the Clan how you come to be here. From the day you first learned of your heritage.'

'We'll be here all day – '

'Nevertheless, if you please.'

'Certainly.' Miriam took a deep breath. 'It started the day I lost my job with a business magazine in Cambridge. I went to visit my mother – ' a nod to Iris ' – who asked me to fetch down a box from her attic. The box was full of old papers . . .'

She kept going until she reached her patent filing in New Britain, the enterprise she was setting up, and Olga's shooting. Her throat was dry and the room was silent. She shook her head. 'Can I have a glass of water, please?' she asked. A tumbler appeared next to her.

'Thank you. By this time I had some ideas. The people who kept trying to murder Iris – sorry, Patricia – and who kept going after me, or getting at Olga by mistake – they had to be relatives. But apart from the one attempt, there was never any sign of them on the other side, in America that is. I remembered being told about a long-lost brother who headed west in the earliest days of the Clan. You know – we learned – that they, too, use a pattern to let them world-walk, however they can travel only from here to New Britain, to the place I've just been telling you about.

'What I've pieced together is that a very long time ago one of the brothers headed west. He fell on hard times and lost his amulet. In fact, he ended up as an indentured slave and took nearly ten years to save the cash to buy his freedom. Once free, he had to reconstruct the knot design from memory. Either that, or his was deliberately sabotaged by a sibling. Whichever, the knot he painted was *different*. I can't emphasize that strongly enough; where you go when you world-walk depends on the design you use as a key. We now know of two keys, but there's another fact – the other one, this lost brother's knot, doesn't work in America. Our America. The one we go to.

'Anyway, he crossed over repeatedly, because it had been arranged that at regular intervals he should check for his brothers. They evidently intended to send a trade caravan to meet him, somewhere in Northern California perhaps. But he never found his business partners waiting for him, because they were elsewhere, traveling to another world where, presumably, they interpreted his absence as a sign that he'd died. He was cut off completely, and put it down to betrayal.'

'Preposterous!' Someone in the front row snorted, prompting Angbard to bring down the gavel again. Miriam took the opportunity to help herself to a glass of water.

'This brother, Lee, had a family. His family was less numerous, less able to provide for themselves, than the Clan. Just as the ability was lost to your ancestors for a generation or two, so it was with his descendants – and it took longer before some first cousins or cousins married and had an infant with renewed ability. They prospered much as you have, but more slowly. The New British don't have a lot of time for Chinese merchants, and as a smaller family they had far fewer active world-walkers to rely on.

'Now, the Lees only found the Clan again when the family Wu moved west, less than a century ago. The Lees reacted – well, I think it was out of fear, but they basically conducted the campaign of assassinations that kicked off the feud. Everyone in the Clan knew that the murders could only have been carried out by world-walkers, so the attacks on the western families were blamed – understandably – on their cousins back east.'

She paused. The level of conversation breaking out in the benches made continuing futile. Angbard raised his gavel but she held up a hand. 'Any questions?' she asked.

'Yes! What's this business – '

' – How did you travel – '

' – We going to put up with these lies?'

Bang! Miriam jumped as Angbard brought down the gavel. 'One at a time,' he snapped. 'Helge, if you please. You have the floor.'

'The new world, where the other family – the Lees – go, is like the one I grew up in, but less well developed. There are a number of reasons for this, but essentially it boils down to the apparent fact that it diverged historically from the world of the United States about two hundred and fifty years ago. If you want evidence of its existence I have witnesses, Lady Olga and Brilliana d'Ost, and video recordings. I can even take you over there, if you are willing to accept my directions – remember, it is a very different country from the United States, and if you don't bear that in mind you can get into trouble very quickly. But let me emphasize this. I believe *anyone* who is sitting in this room now can go there quite easily, by simply using a Lee family talisman instead of a Clan one. You can verify this for yourselves. I repeat: It appears that if you have the ability to world-walk, you can go to different worlds simply by using a different kind of talisman.

'New Britain only had an industrial revolution a century ago. I've established a toehold over there, by setting up an identity and filing some basic engineering patents on the automobile. They'll be big in about five to ten years. My business plan was to leverage inventions from the USA that haven't been developed over there, rather than trading in physical commodities or providing transportation. But by doing this, I attracted the Lee family's attention. They worked out soon enough that I'd acquired one of their lockets and was setting up on their territory. As Olga told you, they attempted to black-bag my house, and we were waiting for them.' She glanced at Angbard for approval. He nodded to her, so she went on. 'We took a prisoner, alive. He was in possession of an amulet and he's indisputably a world-walker, but he's not of the Clan. I asked for some medical tests. Ah, my lord?'

The duke cleared his throat. 'Blood tests confirm that the prisoner is a very distant relative. And a world-walker. It appears that there are six families, after all.'

Now he resorted to his hammer again, in earnest – but to no avail. After five minutes, when things began to quieten down, Angbard signaled for the sergeant at arms to bring order to the hall. *'Order!'* he shouted. 'We will recess for one hour, to take refreshments. Then the meeting will resume.' He rose, scowling ominously at the assembled Clan shareholders. 'What you've heard so far is the background. There is more to come.'

*

Morning on the day shift in Boston. The office phones were already ringing as Mike Fleming swiped his badge and walked in past security.

'Hi, Mike!' Pete Garfinkle, his office mate, waved on his way back from the coffee machine.

''Lo.' Mike was never at his best, early in the morning. Winter blues, one of his ex-girlfriends had called it in a forgiving moment. Blues so deep they were ultraviolet, the same girlfriend had said as she was moving out – blues so deep she'd gotten radiation burns. 'Anything in?'

'What? On the – ' Pete waved a finger.

'Office. Okay, give me five minutes.'

Mike wandered along to the vending machine, passing a couple of suits from the public liaison office, and collected a mug of coffee. Traffic was bad this morning, really bad. And he hadn't shaved properly either. It was only nine but he already had a five o'clock shadow, adding to his bearish appearance. *Don't mess with me.*

Pete was already nose-deep in paperwork that had come in the morning mail when Mike finally made it to his desk. Pete was a morning guy, always frazzled by six o'clock – when Mike was just hitting his stride. 'Tell me the news,' Mike grunted. 'Anything happening?'

'On the Hernandez case? Judge Judy has it on her docket.' Pete grinned humorlessly.

'Judge Judy couldn't find his ass with a submarine's periscope and a map.' Mike pulled a face, put his mug of coffee down, and rubbed his eyes. The urge to yawn was nearly irresistible. 'Judge Judy is about the *least* likely to sign a no-knock – '

'Yeah, yeah, I know all about your pissing match with hizzonner Stephen Jude. Can it, Mike, he works for Justice, it's his *job* to gum up the works. No point taking it personal.'

'Huh. That fucker Julio needs to go down, though. I mean, the goddamn Pope knows what he's at! What the hell else do we need to convince the DA he's got a case?'

'Fifty keys of crack and a blow job from the voters.' Pete leaned his chair perilously far back – the office was so cramped that a sideswipe would risk demolishing piles of banker's boxes – and snorted. 'Relax, dude. We'll get him.'

'Huh. Give me that.' Mike held out a huge hand and Pete dumped a pile of mail into it. 'Ack.' Mike carefully put it down on his desk, then picked up his coffee and took a sip. 'Bilge water.'

'One of these days you'd better try and kick the habit,' Pete said mildly. 'It can't be doing your kidneys any good.'

'Listen, I *run* on coffee,' Mike insisted. 'Lessee – '

He thumbed rapidly through the internal mail, sorting administrative memos from formal letters – some branches still ran on paper, their intranets unconnected to the outside world – and a couple of real, honest, postal envelopes. He stacked them in three neat piles and switched on his PC. While he waited for it to boot he opened the two letters from outside. One of them was junk, random spam sent to him by name and offering cheap loans. The other –

'Holy *shit*!'

Pete started, nearly going over backwards in his chair. 'You want to keep a lid – '

'*Holy* shit!'

Pete turned around. Mike was on his feet, a letter clutched in both hands and an expression of awe on his face. 'What?' Pete asked mildly.

'Got to get this to forensics,' Mike muttered, carefully putting the letter down on his desk, then carefully peering inside the envelope. A little plastic baggie with something brown in it –

'Evidence?' asked Pete, interestedly: 'Hey, I thought that was external?'

'You're not kidding!' Mike put it down as delicately as if it was made of fine glass. 'Anonymous Tip-Offs "R" Us!'

'Explain.'

'This letter.' Mike pointed. 'It says it's fingering the Phantom.'

'You're sure about that?' Pete looked disbelieving. Mike nodded. 'Jesus, Mike, you need to learn some extra-special new swear words for that one. Show me that thing – '

'Whoa!' Mike carefully lifted the envelope. 'Witness. You and me, we're going down to the lab to see what's in this baggie. If it's what the letter says, and it checks out, it's a sample from that batch of H that hit New York four months ago. You know? The really big one that co-incided with that OD spike, pushed the price down so low they were buying it by the ounce? From the Phantom network?'

'So? Somebody held onto a sample.'

'*Somebody* just sent us a fucking tip-off that there's an address in Belmont that's the local end of the distribution chain. Wholesale, Pete. Name, rank, and serial number. Dates – we need to check the goddamn dates. Pete, this is an *inside* job. Someone on the inside of the Phantom wants to come in from the cold and they're establishing their bona fides.'

'We've had falsies before. Anonymous bastards.'

'Yeah, but this one's got a sample, and a bunch of supplementaries. From memory, I think it checks out – at least, there's not anything obviously wrong with it at first glance. I want it dusted for fingerprints and DNA samples before we go any further. What do you think?'

Pete whistled. 'If it checks out, and the dates match, I figure we can get the boss to come along with us and go lean on Judge Judy. A break on the Phantom would be just too cool.'

'My thoughts exactly. How well do you think we can resource this one?'

'If it's the Phantom? Blank check time. Jesus, Mike, if this is the Phantom, I think we've just had the biggest break in this office in about the last twenty years. It's going to be all over *Time* magazine if this goes down!'

*

In the hallway outside the boardroom, the palace staff had busied themselves setting up a huge buffet. Cold cuts from a dozen game animals formed intricate sculptures of meat depicting their animate origins. Jellied larks vied with sugar-pickled fruit from the far reaches of the West Coast, and exotic delicacies imported at vast expense formed pyramids atop a row of silver platters the size of small dining tables. Handmade Belgian truffles competed for the attention of the aristocracy with caviar-topped crackers and brightly colored packets of M&Ms.

Despite the huge expanse of food, most of the Clan shareholders had other things in mind. Though waiters with trays laden with wine glasses circulated freely – and with jugs of imported coffee and tea – the main appetite they exhibited seemed to be for speech. And speech with one or two people in particular.

'Just keep them away from me, please,' Miriam asked plaintively, leaning close to Olga. 'They'll be all over me.'

'You can't avoid them!' Olga took her arm and steered her toward the open doors onto the reception area. 'Do you want them to think you're afraid?' she hissed in Miriam's ear. 'They're like rats that eat their own young if they smell weakness in the litter.'

'It's not that – I've got to go.' Miriam pulled back and steered Olga in turn, toward the door at the back of the boardroom where she'd seen Angbard pushing her mother's wheelchair, ahead of the crush. Kara, her eyes wide, stuck close behind Miriam.

'Where are you going?' asked Olga.

'Follow.' Miriam pushed on.

'Eh, I say! Young woman!'

A man Miriam didn't recognize, bulky and gray-haired, was blocking her way. Evidently he wanted to buttonhole her. She smiled blandly. 'If you don't mind, sir, there'll be time to talk later. But I urgently need to have words with – ' She gestured as she slid past him, leaving Kara to soothe ruffled feathers, and shoved the door open.

'Ma!'

It was a small side room, sparsely furnished by Clan standards. Iris looked around as she heard Miriam. Angbard looked round, too, as did a cadaverous-looking fellow with long white hair who had been hunched slightly, on the receiving end of some admonition.

'Helge,' Angbard began, in a warning tone of voice.

'Mother!' Miriam glared at Iris, momentarily oblivious.

'Hiya, kid.' Iris looked tired. 'Allow me to introduce you to another of your relatives. Henryk? I'd like to present my daughter.' Iris looked at Angbard: 'Cut her a little slack, all right?'

The man who'd been listening to Angbard tilted his head on one shoulder. 'Charmed,' he said politely.

The duke coughed into a handkerchief and cast Miriam a grim look. 'You should be circulating,' he grumbled.

'Henryk was always my favorite uncle,' Iris said, glancing at the duke. 'I mean, there had to be one of them, didn't there?'

Miriam hung back uncomfortably, unwilling to meet Angbard's gaze. Meanwhile, Henryk looked her up and down. 'I see,' she said after a moment. 'Well, that's all right then, isn't it?'

'Helge.' Angbard refused to be ignored. 'You should be out front. Mixing with the guests. You know how much stock they put in appearances.' *Harrumph.* 'This is their first sight of you. Do you want them to think you're a puppet? Conspiring with the bench?'

'I *am* conspiring with you,' she pointed out. 'And anyway, they'd eat me alive. You obviously haven't done enough press conferences. You don't throw the bait in the water if you want to pull it out intact later, do you? You've got to keep these things under control.'

Angbard's frown intensified. 'This isn't a press conference; this is a beauty show. If you do not go out there and make the right moves they will assume that you cannot. And if you can't, what are you good for? I arranged this session at your request. The least you can do is not make a mess of it.'

'There's going to be a vote later on,' Iris cut in. 'Miriam, if they think you're avoiding them it'll give the reactionary bastards a chance to convince the others that you're a fraud, and that won't go in your favor, will it?'

Miriam sighed. 'That's what I like about you, Ma, family solidarity.'

'She's right, you know,' Henryk spoke up. 'Motions will go forward. They may accept your claim of title, but not your business proposals. Not if names they know and understand oppose it, and you are not seen to confront them.'

'But they'll – ' Miriam began.

'I have a better idea!' Olga announced brightly. 'Why don't you both go forth to charm the turbulent beast?' She beamed at them both. 'That way they won't know who to confront! Like the ass that starved between two overflowing mangers.'

Iris glanced sidelong at Miriam. Was it worry? Miriam couldn't decide. 'That would never do,' she said apologetically. 'I couldn't – '

'Oh yes you can, Patricia,' Angbard said with a cold gleam in his eye.

'But if I go out there Mother will make a scene! And then – '

Miriam stared at Iris in exasperation, sensing an echo of a deeper family history she'd grown up shielded from. 'The dowager will make a scene, will she?' Miriam asked, a dangerous note in her voice: 'Why shouldn't she? She hasn't seen you for decades. Thought you were dead, probably. You didn't get along with her when you were young, but so what? Maybe you'll both find the anger doesn't matter anymore. Why not try it?' She caught Angbard's eye. Her uncle, normally stony-faced, looked positively anesthetized, as if to stifle an image-destroying outburst of laughter.

'You don't know the old bat,' Iris warned.

'She hasn't changed,' Angbard commented. 'If anything, she's become even worse.' *Harrumph.* He hid his face in his handkerchief again.

'She's been getting worse ever since she adopted that young whipper-snapper Oliver as her confidant,' Henryk mumbled vaguely. 'Give me Alfredo any day, we'd have straightened him out in time – ' He didn't seem to notice Iris's face tightening.

'Ma,' Miriam warned.

'All right! That's enough.' Iris pushed herself upright in her wheelchair, an expression of grim determination on her face. 'Miriam, purely for the sake of family solidarity, you push. You, young lady, what's your name – '

'Olga,' Miriam offered. ·

' – I know that, dammit! Olga, open the doors and keep the idiots from pushing me over and letting my darling daughter sneak away? Angbard – '

'I'll start the session again in half an hour,' he said, shaking his head. 'Just remember.' He turned a cool eye on Miriam, all trace of levity gone: 'It cost me a lot to set this up for you. Don't make a mess of it.'

GOING POSTAL

Down in the post office in the basement of Fort Lofstrom, two men waited nervously for their superior to arrive. Both of them were young – one was barely out of his teens. They dressed like law firm clerks or trainee accountants. 'Is this for real?' the younger one kept asking, nervously. 'I mean, has it really happened? Why does nobody tell us anything? Shit, this sucks!'

'Shut up and wait,' said the elder, leaning against a wall furnished with industrial shelving racks, holding a range of brightly colored plastic boxes labeled by destination. 'Haven't you learned anything?'

'But the meeting! I mean, what's going on? Have the old guys finally decided to stop us going over – '

'I said, shut the fuck up.' The older courier glared at the kid with all the world-weary cynicism of his twenty-six years. Spots, tufts of straggly beard hair – *Sky Father, why do I get to nurse the babies?* 'Listen, nothing is going to go wrong.'

He nudged the briefcase at his feet. Inside its very expensive aluminum shell was a layer of plastic foam, inside which nestled an HK MP5 submachine gun. The kid didn't need to know that, though. 'When the boss man gets here, we do a straight delivery run then lock down the house. *You* stay with the boss and do what he says. *I* get the fun job of telling the postmen to drop everything and yelling at the holiday heads to execute their cover plans. Then we arrest anyone who tries to drop by. Get it? The whole thing will be over in forty-eight hours, it's just a routine security lockdown.'

'Yes, Martijn.' The kid shook his head, puzzled. 'But there hasn't been an extraordinary meeting in my lifetime! And this is an emergency lockdown, isn't it? Shutting down everything, telling all our people on the other side to go hide, that sucks. What's going on?'

The courier looked away. *Hurry up and get the nonsense out of your system*, he thought. 'What do you think they're doing?' he asked.

'It's obvious: They envy us, don't they? The old dudes. Staying over, fitting in. You know I'm going back to college in a couple of weeks, did I tell you about the shit my uncle Stani's been handing out about that? I've got a girlfriend and a Miata and a place of my own and he's giving me shit because he never had that stuff. "What do you need to learn reading for if you've got scribes?" he told me. And you know what? Some of them, if they could stop us going back – '

The door opened, stemming his tirade in full flood. The older courier straightened up; the young one just flushed, his mouth running down in a frightened stammer. 'Uh, yessir, uh, going back, uh – '

'Shut up,' Matthias said coldly.

One more squeak and the kid fell silent. Matthias nodded at Martijn, the older one. 'You ready?' he asked.

'Yes, my lord.'

'Very well.' Matthias didn't smile, but some of the tension went out of his shoulders. He wore a leather flying jacket and jeans, with gloves on his hands and a day pack slung over one arm. 'Kid. You are going to carry me across. Ready?'

'Uh.' *Gulp*. 'Yessir. Yes. Sir.'

'Go on, then.' He advanced on the youth. 'I'm heavier than any load you're used to. You will need to have your key ready in one hand. When you are ready, speak, and I'll climb on your back. Try not to break.'

'Yessir!'

A minute later they were in another post room. This one was slightly smaller, its shelves less full, and a row of wheeled suitcases were parked on the opposite wall inside an area painted with yellow stripes. The kid collapsed to his knees, gasping for breath while Matthias looked around for the older courier. 'Martijn, you have your orders?'

'Yes, my lord.'

'Execute them.'

Matthias removed a briefcase from the rack on one wall then walked toward the exit from the room. He unlocked it then waved Martijn and the younger courier through. Once they were in the elevator to the upper floors, Matthias shut the door – then turned on his heel and headed for the emergency stairs to the garage.

The silver-blue BMW convertible was waiting for him, just as he'd ordered. Finally, Matthias cracked a smile, thin-lipped and humorless. There was barely room for the briefcase in the trunk, and his day pack went on the passenger seat. He fired up the engine as he hit the 'door open' button on the dash, accelerating up the ramp and into the daylight beyond.

'Fifteen minutes,' he whispered to himself as he merged with the traffic on the turnpike. 'Give me fifteen minutes!'

The time passed rapidly. Waiting at an intersection, Matthias pulled out a cheap anonymous cell phone and speed-dialed a number. It rang three times before the person at the other end answered.

'Who is this?' they asked.

'This is Judas. Listen, I will say this once. The address you want is . . .' he rattled through the details of the location he'd just left. 'Got that?'

'Yes. Who are you and – '

Matthias casually flipped the phone out of the half-open window then accelerated away. Moments later, an eighteen-wheeler reduced it to plastic shrapnel.

'Fuck *you* very much,' he muttered. 'You can't fire me: I quit!'

It wasn't until he was nearly at the airport with his wallet full of bearer bonds and a briefcase full of Clan secrets that he began to prepare for the next step.

*

A ghastly silence fell across the grand hall as Miriam stepped out of the doorway. She took a deep breath and smiled as brightly as she could. 'Don't mind me!' she said.

'That's right,' Iris whispered, 'mind *me,* you back-stabbing faux-aristocratic bastards!'

'Mother!' she hissed, keeping a straight face with considerable effort.

'Oligarchic parasites. Hah.' Louder: 'Steer *left,* if you please, can't

527

you tell left from right? That's better. Now, who do I have to bribe to get a glass of Pinot Noir around here?'

Iris's chatter seemed to break an invisible curtain of suspense. Conversations started up again around the room, and a pair of anxious liveried servants hurried forward, bearing trays with glasses.

Iris hooked a glass of red wine with a slightly wobbly hand and took a suspicious sniff. 'It'll pass,' she declared. 'Help yourself while you're at it,' she told Miriam. 'Don't just stand there like a rabbit in the headlights.'

'Um. Are you sure it's wise to drink?'

'I've always had difficulty coping with my relatives sober. But yes, I take your point.' Iris took a moderate sip. 'I won't let the side down.'

'Okay, Ma.' Miriam took a glass. She looked up just in time to see Kara across the room, looking frightened, standing beside an unfamiliar man in late middle age. 'Hmm. Looks like the rats are deserting or something. Olga?'

Beside her and following her gaze, Olga had tensed. 'That's Peffer Hjorth. What's she doing talking to *him*, the minx?'

'Peffer Hjorth?'

'The baron's uncle. Outer family, not a member.'

Iris whistled tunelessly. 'Well, well, well. One of yours?' she asked Miriam.

'I thought so.' Miriam took a sip of wine. Her mouth felt bitter, ashy.

'Lady Helge, what a story! Fascinating! And your mother – why, Patricia? It's been such a long time!'

She looked around, found Iris craning her neck, too. 'Turn me, please, Miriam – ' Iris was looking up and down: 'Mors Hjalmar! Long time indeed. How are you doing?'

The plumpish man with a neatly trimmed beard and hair just covering his collar – like a middle-aged hippy uncomfortably squeezed into a dark suit for a funeral or court appearance – looked happy enough. 'I'm doing well, Patricia, well!' His expression sank slightly. 'I was doing better before this blew up, I think. They mostly ignore me.' He rubbed his left cheek thoughtfully. 'Which is no bad thing.' He looked at Olga, askance. 'And who do I have the pleasure of meeting?'

'This is Lady Olga Thorold,' Iris offered.

'And you are of the same party as these, ah, elusive Thorold-Hjorths?'

'Indeed I am!' Olga said tightly.

'Oh. Well, then.' He shrugged. 'I mean no offense, but it's sometimes hard to tell who's helping who, don't you know?'

'Lady Olga has only our best interests at heart,' Miriam replied. 'You knew my mother?'

Iris had been looking up at Mors all this time, her mouth open slightly, as if surprised to see him. Now she shook her head. 'Thirty years,' she muttered darkly. 'And they haven't murdered you yet?' Suddenly she smiled. 'Maybe there's hope for me after all.'

'Do *you* know what she means?' Miriam asked Olga, puzzled.

'I, ahem, led an eccentric life many years ago,' said Mors.

Iris shook her head. 'Mors was the first of our generation to actually demand – and get – a proper education. Yale Law School, but they made him sign away his right of seniority, if I remember rightly. Wasn't that so?' she asked.

'Approximately.' Mors smiled slightly. 'It took them a few years to realize that the Clan badly needed its own attorney on the other side.' His smile broadened.

'*What?*' Iris looked almost appalled. 'No, I can't see it.'

'So don't. Is it true?' His eyes were fixed on Iris.

'If she says it's true, it's true,' Iris insisted, jerking her head slightly in Miriam's direction. 'A credit to the family. Not that that's what I wanted, but – '

' – We don't always get what we want,' Mors finished for her, nodding. 'I think I see.' He sounded thoughtful. Then he looked at Miriam. 'If you need any legal advice, here's my card,' he said.

'Thank you,' said Miriam, pocketing it. 'But I think I may need a different kind of help right now.' *All too damned true,* she thought, seeing what was bearing down on them. Nemesis had two heads and four arms, and both heads wore haughty expressions of utmost disdain, carefully tempered for maximum intransigence.

'Well, if it isn't the runaway,' snorted head number one, Baron Hjorth, with a negligent glance in Miriam's direction.

'Imposter, you mean,' croaked head number two, glaring at her like a Valkyrie fingering her knife and wondering who to feed to the ravens next.

'Hello, mother.' Iris *smiled*, a peculiar expression that Miriam had seen only once or twice before and which filled her with an urgent desire to duck and cover. 'Been keeping well, I see?'

'I'll just be off,' Mors started nervously – then stopped as Iris grabbed his wrist. In any case, the gathering cloud of onlookers made a discreet escape impossible. There was only one conversation worth eavesdropping in this reception, and this was it.

'I was just catching up on old times with Mors,' Iris cooed sweetly, her eyes never leaving the dowager's face. 'He was telling me all about your retirement.'

Nasty. Miriam forced herself to smile, glanced sideways, and saw Olga glaring at head number one. The baron somehow failed to turn to stone, but his hauteur seemed to melt slightly. 'Hello, Oliver,' said Miriam. 'I'm glad to see you're willing to talk to me instead of sneaking into my boudoir when I'm not about.'

'I have never – ' he began pompously.

'Stow it!' snapped Iris. 'And *you*, mother – ' she waved a finger at her mother, who was gathering herself up like a serpent readying to strike – 'I gather you've been encouraging this odious worm. Is it true?'

'Who I encourage or not is none of your business!' Hildegarde hissed. 'You're a disgrace to family and Clan, you whore. I should have turned you out the day I gave birth to you. As for your bastard – '

'I believe I understand, now.' Miriam nodded, outwardly cordially, at Baron Hjorth. Startled, he pretended to ignore her words: 'Your little plan to get back the Clan shares ceded to trust when my mother vanished – I got in the way, didn't I? But not to worry. An insecure apartment, a fortune-seeking commoner turned rapist, and an unlocked door on the roof would see to that, wouldn't it?' *If not a couple of goons with automatic weapons*, she added mentally. *Just by way of insurance.*

The duchess gasped. 'I don't know what you're talking about!'

'Quite possibly you don't,' Miriam agreed. She jabbed a finger: '*He* does, don't you?'

Baron Oliver had turned beet-red with her first accusation. Now he began to shake. 'I have *never* conspired to blemish the virtue of a Clan lady!' he insisted. The duchess stared at him. 'And if you allege otherwise – '

'Put up or shut up, I'd say,' Iris said flatly. 'Mors, wouldn't you say that any accusations along those lines would require an indictment? Before the committee, perhaps?'

'Mmm, possibly.' Mors struck a thoughtful pose, seeming to forget his earlier enthusiasm to be elsewhere. 'Were there witnesses? Unimpeachable ones?'

'I don't think any charges against the baron could be made to stick,' Miriam said slowly, watching him. He watched her right back, unblinking. 'And you will note that I made no allegation of involvement in a conspiracy to commit rape on your part,' she added to Hjorth. *Or to send gunmen round to Olga's rooms.* 'Although I might change my mind if you supplied sufficient cause.'

'You bitch,' he snarled.

'Just remember where I got it from.' She nodded at her grandmother, who, speechless with rage, hung on Hjorth's arm like an overripe apple, ruddy-faced and swollen with wasps. 'We really must get together for a family reunion one of these days,' she added. 'I'm sure you've got a lot of poison recipes to share with me.'

'I'd stop, if I were you,' Iris observed with clinical interest. 'If you push her any further the only reunion you'll get is over her coffin.'

'You treacherous little minx!' Hildegarde was shaking with fury.

'So it's treachery now, is it? Because I had higher standards than you and didn't want to marry my way to the top of the dung heap?' Iris threw back at her.

'Children,' Miriam sighed. She caught Olga's eye.

'I didn't notice you making an effort to find any suitable alternatives!' the duchess snapped. 'And it got the Wu and Hjorth factions to stop murdering each other. Would you rather the feuding had continued? We'd both be dead a dozen times over by now!' She was breathing deeply. 'You've got no sense of duty,' she said bitterly.

'The feuding, in case you've been asleep, was caused by forces outside our control,' Iris retorted. 'You gained precisely nothing, except for a wife-beating son-in-law. Your *granddaughter*, now, has actually done something useful for the first time in living memory in this Clan of parasites. She's actually uncovered some of the reasons *why* we've been messed up for so long. The least you could do is apologize to her!'

'There's nothing to apologize for,' Hildegarde said stiffly. But Miriam saw her grip on Hjorth's arm tighten.

'Don't worry, my dear,' Oliver Hjorth muttered in her ear: 'You're quite right about them.' He cast a poisonous stare at Miriam. 'Especially *that* one.'

'You – ' Miriam was brought up short by Olga's hand on her shoulder.

'Don't,' Olga said quietly. 'He wants you to react.'

For the first time, Hjorth smiled. 'She's right, you know,' he said. 'On that note, I shall bid you adieu, ladies. If I may conduct you back to civilized conversation, madam?' he added to the dowager.

Iris stared bleakly at the receding back of her mother. 'I swear she'll outlive us all,' Iris muttered. Then she glanced at Miriam. 'There's no justice in this world, is there?'

'What was she talking about?' Miriam asked slowly. 'The treachery thing.'

'An old disagreement,' said Iris. She sounded old and tired. 'A bit like picking at scabs. Most families have got the odd skeleton in the closet. We've got a whole damn graveyard in every wardrobe, practicing their line dancing. Don't sweat it.'

'But – ' Miriam stopped. She remembered her wine glass and took a mouthful. Her hand was shaking so badly that she nearly spilled it.

'You won,' Olga said thoughtfully.

'Huh?'

'She's right. You went eyeball to eyeball with the baron, and he blinked. They'll know you've got balls now. That counts for everything here. And I – ' Iris stopped.

'You got your mother on the defensive,' said Miriam. 'Didn't you?'

'I'm not sure,' Iris said uncertainly. 'Old iron-face must be rusting. Either that, or there's a deep game I don't know about. She never used to concede *anything*.'

'Iron-face?'

'What we called her. Me and your aunt Elsa.'

'I have an aunt, too?'

'Had. She died. Olga, if you don't mind taking over my chair? Miriam seems to be having trouble.'

'Died – '

'You didn't think I had it in for the old bat just because of how she treated *me*, did you?'

'Oh.' Miriam bolted back the rest of her wine glass, sensing the depths she was treading water over. 'I think I need another glass now.'

'Better drink it quick, then. Things are about to get interesting again.'

*

There was a low bed with a futon mattress on it. It occupied most of a compact bedroom on the third floor of an inconspicuous building in downtown Boston. The bed was occupied, even though it was late morning; Roland had been awake for most of the night, working on the next month's courier schedule, worrying and reassigning bodies from a discontinued security operation. In fact, he'd deliberately worked an eighteen-hour shift just to tire himself out so that he could sleep. The worries wouldn't go away. *What if they find her incompetent?* was one of them. Another was, *What if the old man finds out about us?* In the end he'd slugged back a glass of bourbon and a five-milligram tab of Valium, stripped, and climbed into bed to wait for the pharmaceutical knockout.

Which was why, when the raid began, Roland was unconscious: dead to the world, sleeping the sleep of the truly exhausted, twitching slightly beneath the thin cotton sheet.

A faint bang shuddered through the walls and floor. Roland grunted and rolled over slowly, still half-asleep. Outside his door, a shrill alarm went off. 'Huh?' He sat up slowly, rubbing at his eyes to clear the fog of night, and slapped vaguely at the bedside light switch.

The phone began to shrill. 'Uh.' He picked up the handset, fumbling it slightly: 'Roland here. What is it?'

'We're under attack! Some guys just tried to smash in the front door and the rooftop – '

The lights flickered and the phone died. Somewhere in the building the emergency generator cut in, too slowly to keep the telephone switch powered. Roland put the handset down and hastily dragged on trousers and sweater. He pulled his pistol out of the bedside drawer, glanced at the drawn curtains, decided not to risk moving them, and opened the door.

A young Clan member was waiting for him, frantic with worry. 'Wh-what are we going to do, boss?' he demanded, jumping up and down.

'Slow down.' Roland looked around. 'Who else is here?'

'Just me!'

'On site, I mean,' he corrected. He shook his head again, trying to clear the haze. At least he could world-walk away, he realized. He never removed his locket, even in the shower. 'Is the door holding?'

'The door, the door – ' The kid stopped shaking. 'Yessir. Yessir. The door?'

'Okay, I tell you what I want you to do.' Roland put a hand on the kid's shoulder, trying to calm him. He was vibrating like an over-revved engine. 'Calm down. Don't panic. That's first. You have a tattoo, yes?'

'Y-yessir.'

'Okay. We are going to go below then, and – when did you last walk?'

'Uh, uh, hour ago! We brought the lord secretary over – '

'The secretary?' Roland stopped dead. 'Shit. Tell me you didn't.' The kid's expression was all the confirmation Roland needed.

'Wh-what's wrong?'

'Maybe nothing,' Roland said absently. *Shit, shit,* he thought. *Matthias.* It was a gut-deep certainty, icy cold, that Matthias was behind this. Whatever was going on. 'Follow me. Quickly!' Roland grabbed his jacket on the way out and rummaged in one pocket for a strip of pills. With his hair uncombed and two days' growth of beard, he probably looked a mess, but he didn't have time to fix that now. He dry-swallowed, pulling a face. 'Go down the stairs all the way to the bottom, fast. When you get to the parcel room, pick up all the consignments in bin eleven that you can grab and cross over immediately. If men with guns get the drop on you, either cross immediately or surrender and let them take you, then cross as soon as you can, blind. Don't try to resist; you're not trained.'

'You, sir?' The kid's eyes were wide.

'Me neither.' Roland shrugged, tried to muster up a grin, gave up. 'C'mon. We need to get word out.'

He clattered down the concrete emergency stairwell taking the steps two at a time, stopping at the ground floor. He motioned the kid on down. 'Send word as soon as you get through,' he called. Then he stopped, his heart hammering.

'Sir?' He looked up. It was Sullivan, one of the outer family guards who lived on the premises.

'What's going on?' he demanded. 'Tell me!'

A hollow boom rattled through the corridor and Sullivan winced. 'We're on skeleton strength,' he said. 'They're trying to batter down the door!' The front door was armored like a bank vault, and the walls were reinforced. A normal ram wouldn't work, it would take explosives or cutting tools to get through it.

'Who?' Roland demanded.

'Cops.'

'How many we got here?'

'Nine.'

'I just sent the kid away. Walkers?'

Sullivan just looked at him.

'Shit.' Roland shook his head, dumbfounded. 'There's *nobody*?'

'Martijn and young Poul came in with the lord secretary this morning. They're the only walkers who've come over since Marissa and Ivar finished their shift last night. And I can't find Martijn or his lordship's proxy.'

'Oh.' Everything became clear to Roland. 'How long can we hold out?'

'Against the feds?' Sullivan shrugged. 'We're buttoned up tight; it'll take them time to bring in explosives and cutting gear, and shields. At least, it will if we risk shooting back.'

'The escape tunnel – '

'Someone sealed it at the other end. I don't think it would help, anyway.'

'Let's hit the control room.' Roland started walking again. 'Have I got this straight? We're under siege and I'm the only walker who knows. The lord secretary came over, but he went missing before the siege began. So did his number-one sidekick. The outer rooms are shuttered and locked down and we've got supplies, power, and ammo, but no way out because somebody's blown the escape tunnel. Is that it?'

'Pretty much so,' Sullivan agreed. He stared at Roland. 'What are you going to do?'

'What am I going to do?' Roland paused in the office doorway. 'What *can* I do?' He opened the door and went in. The control room had desks with computer monitors around the wall. CCTV screens showed every approach to the building. Everything looked normal, except for the lack of vehicular traffic and the parked vans on every corner. And the van parked right up against the front door. Obviously the ram crew had used it for cover.

'We have half a ton of post in transit at any one time. There's about fifty kilos of confidential memos, documents, stuff like that – enough to flame out the entire East Coast circuit.' There was a knock on the door. Sullivan waved in the man outside, one of the colorless back-office auditors the Clan employed to keep an eye on things. 'We've got another quarter of a ton of produce in transship-ment. It was due out of here next week. That's enough to bankroll our ops for a year, too.'

Sullivan looked pissed. 'Is that your priority?' he demanded.

'No. My priorities are: number one, getting all of us out of here; and number two, not letting that fucker Matthias take down our entire operation. It's going to take eighteen walks to pull everyone out – more than I could do in a week. And about the same to pull out the goods.' Roland pulled out a chair and sat. 'We can't drive away or use the tunnel. How long for them to get in? Six hours? Twelve?'

'I think it'll be more like three, unless we start shooting,' Sullivan opined.

'Shooting – ' Roland froze. 'You want me to authorize you to shoot at FBI or DEA agents. Other than in self-defense.'

'It's the only way,' said the auditor, looking a little green.

'Huh. I'll table it.' Roland, unfrozen, drummed his fingers on the nearest desk. 'I *really* don't like that option, it's too much like sticking your dick in a hornet's nest. They can always point more guns at us than we can point back at them. Has anyone phoned the scram number?'

'Huh?' Sullivan looked puzzled. 'Bill?'

'Tried it five minutes ago, sir,' the auditor said with gloomy satisfaction. 'Got a number-unavailable tone.'

'I am beginning to get the picture. Have you tried your cell phone?'

'They've got a jammer. And snipers on the rooftops.'

'Fuck.' *I am going to have to make a decision,* Roland thought. *And it had better be one I can live with,* he realized sickly.

'Someone needs to walk over and yell like hell,' Roland said slowly. Sullivan tensed. 'But, I'm working on the assumption that this is deliberate. That bastard Matthias, I've been watching him.' It was easy to say this, now. 'I sent the kid, what's his name?'

'Poul,' Bill offered.

'I sent him over alone.' Roland's eyes went wide. 'Shit.'

'What are you thinking?' Sullivan leaned forward.

'My working assumption right now is that Matthias has betrayed the Clan. This is all preplanned. He rigged this raid to cover his escape. So he isn't going to want a random courier walking into Fort Lofstrom and raising the alarm, is he?'

Sullivan's eyes narrowed as Roland stood up. 'You and I,' he announced, trying to keep his voice from shaking, 'are going to cross over together. I know what you've been thinking. Listen, Matthias will have left some kind of surprise. It's going to be a mess. Your job is to keep me alive long enough to get out of the fort. Then there's a, a back route. One I can use to get word to the Clan, later today. It'll take me about six or seven hours to get from Fort Lofstrom to Niejwein, and the same again to come back with a bunch of help – every damn courier I can round up. I'm assuming Matthias sent everyone away from the fort before pulling this stunt. Can you hold out for twenty-four hours? Go into the subbasement storm shelter with all the merchandise and blow the supports, bring the building down on top of you?' He addressed the last question to Bill, the auditor.

'I think so,' Bill said dubiously.

'Right. Then you're going to have to do that.' Roland met his eyes. 'We can't afford for the feds to lay hands on you. And whatever you may think I'm thinking, I figure you're too valuable to write off. *Any* family member, inner or outer, is not expendable in my book. Sully, think you can handle that?'

Sullivan grinned humorlessly at him. 'I'll do my best.' He nodded at the auditor: 'He'll be back. Trust me on this.'

*

The extraordinary meeting resumed with an argument. 'The floor is open for motions,' quavered the ancient Julius. 'Do I hear – '

'I have a motion!' Miriam raised her hand.

'Objection!' snapped Baron Hjorth.

'I think you'll find she already has the floor,' Angbard spat out. 'Let her speak first, then have your say.'

'Firstly, I'd like to move that my venture into New Britain be recognized as a Clan subsidiary,' Miriam said, carefully trying to keep a still face. It was bitterly disappointing to risk ceding control, but as Olga had pointed out, the Clan took a very dim view of members striking out on their own. 'As part of this motion I'd like to resolve that the issue of this sixth family be dealt with by participants in this subsidiary, because clearly they're the members most directly affected by the situation.'

'Objection!' Shouted someone at the back of the hall. 'Clan feud takes precedence!'

'Are you saying the Clan can afford to lose more people?' asked Miriam.

'Damn the blood! What about our dead? This calls for revenge!' Ayes backed him up: Miriam forced herself to think fast, knowing that if she let the heckling gather pace she could very easily lose control of the meeting.

'It seems to me that the lost family is sorely depleted,' she began. 'They had to send a child to supervise an adult's job. You know, as I know, that the efficiency of a postal service like the one responsible for the Clan's wealth is not just a function of how many world-walkers we have. It's also a function of the number of routes we can send packages over. They're small, and isolated, and they're not as numerous as we are. However, rooting them out in the name of a feud will uncover old wounds and risk depleting our numbers for no gain. I'm going to stick my neck out and assert that the next few years are going to be far more dangerous for the Clan than most of you yet realize.'

'Point of order!' It was Baron Hjorth again. 'This is rubbish. She's trying to frighten us. Won't you – '

'Shut *up*,' grated Angbard. 'Let her finish a sentence.'

Miriam waited a moment. 'Thank you,' she said. 'Factors to think about. Firstly, a new world. This is going to be important because it opens up new opportunities for trade and development, as I've already demonstrated. Secondly, the state of the Clan's current business. I don't know how to approach this subtly so I won't: You're in *big* trouble.

'Your current business model is obsolescent. You can keep it running for another two to five years, but then it'll go into a nosedive. In ten years, it'll be dead. And I'm not just talking about heroin and cocaine shipments. I mean *everything*.

'You'll have noticed how hard it has become to launder the proceeds of narcotics traffic on the other side in the past few years. With the current antiterrorist clampdown and the beefing up of police powers, life isn't going to get any easier. Things are changing very fast indeed.

'The Clan used to be involved in different types of commerce: gold smuggling, gemstones, anything valuable and lightweight. But those businesses rely on anonymity, and like I said, the anti-terrorist clampdown is making anonymity much harder to sustain. Let me emphasize this, the traditional business models *don't work anymore* because they all rely on the same underlying assumption – that you can be anonymous.

'Many of you probably aren't aware of the importance of electronic commerce. I've been working with specialists covering the development of the field. What you need to know is that goods and services are going to be sold, increasingly, online. This isn't an attempt to sell you shares in some fly-by-night dot-com; it's just a statement of fact – communications speed is more important than geographical location, and selling online lets small specialist outfits sell to anyone on the planet. But with the shift to online selling, you can expect cash money to become obsolete. High-denomination euro banknotes already come with a chip, to allow transactions to be traced. How long do you think it'll be before the greenbacks you rely on stop being anonymous?

'The fat times will be over – and if you've spent all your resources pursuing a blood feud, you're going to be screwed. No money on the other side means no imports. No imports mean no toys, antibiotics, digital watches, whatever, to buy the compliance of the landowners. No guns to shoot them with, either. If you try to ignore reality you will be screwed by factors outside your control.

'But this isn't inevitable. If you act now, you can open up new lines of revenue and new subsidiaries. Take ancient patents from my world, the world you're used to using as a toy chest, and set up companies around them in the new world, in New Britain. Take the money you raise in New Britain and import books and tools *here*. Set up universities and schools. Build, using your power and your money to establish factories and towns and laboratories over here. In a couple of generations, you can pull Gruinmarkt out of the mire and start an industrial revolution that will make you a true world power, whether or not you depend on the family talent.

'You can change the world – if you choose to start now, by changing the way you think about your business.'

There was total silence in the hall. A puzzled silence, admittedly, but silence – and one or two nodding heads. *Just let them keep listening,* Miriam thought desperately. Then voices began to pipe up.

'I never heard such a – '

' – What would you have us put our money into?'

' – Hear, hear!'

' – Gather that educating the peasants is common over – '

'Silence,' Angbard demanded testily. 'The chair has a question.'

'I'm ready.' Feeling tensely nervous, Miriam crossed her fingers behind her back.

'Describe the business you established in the new world. What did you take with you to start it? And what is it worth?'

Miriam forced herself to keep a straight face, although the wave of relief she felt at Angbard's leading question nearly made her go weak at the knees. 'Exchange rate irregularities – or rather, the lack of them – make it hard to establish a true currency conversion rate, and I'm still looking for a means of repatriating value from the new world to the United States, but I'd have to say that expenditure to date is on the order of six hundred thousand dollars. The business in New Britain is still working toward its first contract, but that contract should be worth on the order of fifty thousand pounds. Uh, near as I can pin it down, one pound is equivalent to roughly two to three hundred dollars. So we're looking at a return on investment of three hundred percent in six months, and that's from a cold start.'

A buzz of conversation rippled through the hall, and Angbard made no move to quell it. The figures Miriam had come up with sounded like venture capitalist nirvana – especially with a recession raging in the other world, and NASDAQ in the dumps. 'That's by selling a product that's been obsolete for thirty years in the US,' Miriam added. 'I've got another five up my sleeve, waiting for this first deal to provide seedcorn capital for reinvestment. In the absence of major disruptive factors – ' *like a war with the hidden family,* she added mentally ' – I figure we can be turning over ten to a hundred million pounds within ten to fifteen years. That would make us the equivalent of IBM or General Motors, simply by recycling ideas that haven't been invented yet over there.'

The buzz of conversation grew louder. 'I've done some more spreadsheet work,' Miriam added, now more confident. 'If we do this, we'll push the New British economic growth rate up by one or two percent per annum over its long-term average. We could do the same, though, importing intermediate technologies from there to here. There's no point trying to train nuclear engineers or build airports in the Gruinmarkt, not with a medieval level of infrastructure, and a lot of the technologies up for sale in the US are simply too far ahead to use here. Those of you who've wired up your estates will know what I'm talking about. But we can import tools and ideas and even teachers from New Britain, and deliver a real push to the economy over here. Within thirty years you could be traveling to your estates by railway, your farmers could be producing three times as much food, and your ships could dominate the Atlantic trade routes.'

Angbard rapped his gavel on the wooden block in front of him for attention. 'The chair thanks Countess Helge,' he said formally. 'Are there any more questions from the floor?'

A new speaker stood up: a smooth-looking managerial type who smiled at Miriam in a friendly manner from the bench behind her grandmother. 'I'd like to congratulate my cousin on her successful start-up,' he began. 'It's a remarkable achievement to come into a new world and set up a business, from scratch, with no background.' *Who is this guy, and when's he going to drop the hammer?* Miriam thought uneasily. 'And I agree completely with everything she says. But clearly, her efforts could be aided by an infusion of support and experience. If we accept her motion to transfer the new business to the Clan as a subsidiary enterprise, it can clearly benefit from sound management – '

'Which it already has,' Miriam snapped, finally getting his drift. 'If you would like to discuss employment opportunities – ' *and a pound of flesh in return for keeping out of my way, you carpetbagger* ' – that's all very well – but this is not the time and place for it. We have an immediate problem, which is relations with the sixth family. I'll repeat my proposal; that the new business venture be recognized as a Clan business, that membership in it be open to the Clan, and that handling the lost family be considered the responsibility of this business. Can we put this to a vote?'

Oliver Hjorth made to interrupt, but Angbard caught his hand and whispered something in his ear. His eyes narrowed and he shut up.

'I don't see why we can't settle it now,' muttered Julius. 'Show of hands! Ayes! Count them, damn your eyes. Nays!' He brought his own hammer down briskly. 'The Ayes have it,' he announced. He turned to Miriam. 'It's yours.'

Is that it? Miriam wondered dumbly, feeling as if something vast and elusive had passed her by in an eyeblink while her attention was elsewhere.

'Next motion,' said Angbard. 'Some of you have been misinformed that I announced that I was designating Helge as my heir. I wish to clarify the issue: I did not do so. However, I *do* intend to change my designated successor – to Patricia Thorold-Hjorth, my half-sister. Can anyone dispute my right to do so?' He looked around the room furiously. 'No?' He nudged Julius. 'See it minuted so.'

Miriam felt as if a great weight had lifted from her shoulders – but not for long. 'A new motion,' said Oliver Hjorth. He frowned at Miriam. 'The behavior of this long-lost niece gives me some cause for concern,' he began. 'I am aware that she has been raised in strange and barbarous lands, and allowances must be made; but I fear she may do herself an injury if allowed to wander around at random. As her recent history of narrow scrapes shows, she's clearly accident-prone and erratic. I therefore move that she be declared incompetent to sit as a member of the Clan, and that a suitable guardian be appointed – Baroness Hildegarde – '

'Objection!' Miriam turned to see Olga standing up. 'Baron Hjorth, through negligence, failed to see to the subject's security during her residence here, notionally under his protection. He is not fit to make determinations bearing on her safety.'

Oliver rounded on her in fury. 'You little minx! I'll have you thrown out on the street for – '

Bang! The gavel again. 'Objection sustained,' Julius quavered.

Oliver glared at him. 'Your time will come,' he growled, and subsided into grim silence.

'I am an adult,' Miriam said quietly. 'I am divorced, I have created and managed a Clan subsidiary, and I am not prepared to surrender responsibility for my own security.' She looked around the hall. 'If you try to railroad me out of the New London operation, you'll find some nasty surprises in the title deeds.' She stared at Oliver: 'Or you can sit back and wait for the profits to roll in. It's your choice.'

'I withdraw my motion,' Oliver growled quietly. Only his eyes told

Miriam that he resented every word of it. There'd be a reckoning, they seemed to say.

*

'Check your gun.'

'I don't need to.'

'I said, check it. Listen, I told Poul to go for help. Think he'll have made it?'

'I don't see why not.' Sullivan looked dubious, but he ejected the magazine and worked the slide on his gun, then reloaded and safed it.

'Matthias believes in belt and braces. I think he'll have left a surprise or two for us.'

'So?' Sullivan nodded. 'You ready?'

'Ready?' Roland winced, then flipped his locket open. 'Yes. Come on. On my back – Sky Father, you're heavy! Now – '

Roland's vision dimmed and his head hammered like a drum. His knees began to give way and he fell forward, feet slipping on the damp floor. Sullivan rolled off him with a shout of dismay. 'What's – '

Roland fell flat, whimpering slightly as one knee cracked hard on the concrete. Red, everything seemed to be *red* with bits of white embedded in it, like an explosion in an abattoir. He rolled over, sliding slightly, smelling something revolting and sweet as the noise of Sullivan being violently sick reached his ears.

The pounding headache subsided. Roland sat up, dismayed, staring at the wall behind him. It was chipped and battered, stained as if someone had thrown a tin of blackish paint at it. *The smell.* Roland leaned forward and squeezed his eyes shut. The blackness stayed with him, behind his eyelids. 'Belt and braces.'

Sullivan stopped heaving. The stench refused to clear. Roland opened his eyes again. The post room in the basement of Fort Lofstrom had been painted with blood and bits of flesh and bone, as if a live pig or sheep had been fed through a wood chipper. There were small gobbets of stuff everywhere. On his hands, sticking to his trousers where he'd fallen down. He pulled a hunk of something red with hairs sprouting from it off the back of his hand. The furniture was shredded, and the door hung from its hinges as if an angry bull had kicked it.

'Belt and braces,' Roland repeated hoarsely. 'Shit.'

Sullivan straightened up. 'You sent Poul into this,' he said flatly. He wiped his mouth with the back of one hand.

'Oh no.' Roland shook his head. A pair of legs, still wearing trousers, still attached at the hips, had rolled under the big oak table in the middle of the room. A horrified sense of realization settled over him. 'Why hasn't someone – '

'Because they are all fucking *dead*,' Sullivan hissed, moving to the side of the door and bringing his gun up. 'Shut up!'

Silence. The stink of blocked sewers and slaughterhouse blood and recent vomit filled Roland's nostrils. His skull pounded, bright diamond-flashes of light flickering in his left eye as the edges of his visual field threatened to collapse. He'd walked too soon after taking the beta-blocker, and now he was going to pay the price. 'Matthias planted a Claymore mine on a wire at least once before,' he said quietly. 'Well, someone did – and my guess is Matthias. Sloppy work, using the same trick over. Think there'll be another one, or will he have used something else?'

'Shut *up*.' Sullivan darted around the corner and stopped, his back visible: Roland cringed, but there was no explosion. 'Yeah. Looks like it was an M18A1, we keep about a dozen in the armory. Here's the clacker. Bastard.'

'See any more?' Roland shuffled forward slowly, still woozy and in pain from the too-hasty transfer.

'No, but – wait.' Sullivan came back into the devastated post room and looked around twitchily, ignoring Roland.

'What are you after?'

'Some kind of pole. Lightweight. And a flashlight.'

'Let me.' Roland shambled over to the curtain-covered sigil and yanked hard on the curtain. The curtain rail bent and he grabbed it, pulled it away from the wall. 'Will this do?' he asked, carefully not looking at the knotwork design on the wall behind it.

'Yeah.' Sullivan took the rod and went back out into the corridor, advancing like an arthritic sloth. 'Fuck me, that was bad.'

A thought struck Roland. 'Are there any explosives in the armory, apart from the mines? And detonators?'

'Are you kidding?' Sullivan barked something that in better times might have been a laugh. 'About a hundred kilos of C4, for starters! And gunpowder. Shitloads of it. Some of his farms, they've been, well, productive. Matthias took a serious interest in blowing things up, you know?'

'Gunpowder.' Roland digested the unpleasant possibilities this news opened up. 'The fort should be locked down. Where *is* everybody?'

'Like I said, dead or gone.' Sullivan looked around at him. 'What are you going to – '

Roland pushed past him. 'Follow me.'

'Hey wait! There might be mines – '

'There won't be.' Roland dashed down the corridor. There was a servant's staircase at the end. He took the steps two at a time, until he was gasping for breath. 'He dismissed the help. Good of him.' The staircase surfaced in the scullery, and the door was shut. 'If I'm right, he's put the whole damn fort on a time fuse. It could blow any minute.'

'A bomb? There could be more than one, couldn't there?'

Roland opened the door half an inch, running a finger up and down the crack to make sure there were no wires. 'It's clear.'

'If you do that too fast – '

'Come on!' Through the scullery and up another short flight of steps, round a corner, then into the main ground-floor hallway. The fort was eerily empty, cold and desolate. Roland didn't bother with the main door, but instead opened an arched window beside it and scrambled through. 'Stables!'

Matthias might have sent the servants away, but he sure as hell hadn't thought about the livestock. Sullivan and Roland saddled up a pair of mares, and the guard worked one of the big gates open while Roland waited, clutching a blanket around his shoulders. 'You go get help,' Sullivan panted up at Roland. 'I'll go see if the armory is wired. I might be able to stop it.'

'But you'll – '

'Shut the fuck up and listen for once! If you get help, you'll need a safe post room to walk through, won't you? I'm not doing this for you, I'm doing it for the others. Go get the gods-damned Clan and get back here as fast as you can. I'll see it's safe for you.'

Roland paused for a moment. 'Take my keys,' he said, and tossed them to the guard. 'They're a master set – only place they won't get you into is the old man's office.'

Sullivan took the keys, then watched until Roland disappeared around the first bend in the road before he turned and headed back into the compound thoughtfully. He hadn't expected it to be this easy: He hadn't even had to hint about the place being booby-trapped. Now all he needed was time to complete the boss's business, and a lift home, then he could claim his reward.

*

The meeting was winding down in a haze of fatigue, recriminatory posturing, and motions to hear trivial complaints. Miriam slumped back in her seat tiredly. *Please, let this be over,* she thought, watching Iris from the other side of the room. If she was aching and bored, her mother must be feeling ten times worse.

Baron Horst of Lorsburg had the floor, and was using it for all it was worth. 'While the provisions of article eighteen of the constitution are still valid, I'd like to raise a concern about paragraph six,' he droned, in the emollient tones of a lay preacher trying to get across the good message without boring his flock into catatonia in the process. 'The issue of voting partners failing to attend to bills of – '

He was interrupted by a tremendous banging on the outer door. 'What's that?' demanded Julius the ancient. 'Sergeant! Have silence outside the room!'

The sergeant-at-arms marched over to the door, yanked it open, prepared to berate whoever was outside – but instead took a step back.

Roland lurched into the room. He was dressed for the road in a battered gray coat and a hat pulled down over his face: His expression was deadly. Miriam had another surprise coming: Brill was right behind him. 'Permission to approach the Dean of Security?' he rasped.

'Approach,' Angbard called. 'And explain yourself. Assuming the news is fit for public hearing.'

Roland glanced round the room. 'Don't see why not.' He passed Miriam without any indication that he'd seen her. 'Big problem,' he announced tersely, and Miriam swallowed her anger as she realized he was exhausted and out of breath, walking painfully, as if his clothes chafed.

'We've been betrayed. Fort Lofstrom is cut off, here *and* on the other side. What's worse is, they've got the February shipment from Panama sitting in Boston along with the post, and someone has told the Feds – there's a DEA stakeout in progress.' He nodded at Angbard. 'Looks like our traitor has identified himself. Bad news is, he got away and he's decided to take down the entire Massachusetts end. I only just got out by the skin of my teeth. We've got nine outer family members trapped on the other side with a SWAT team on their doorstep. To make matters worse, there are booby traps in Fort Lofstrom – at least one bomb. We lost Poul, Poul of Hjalmar. He walked into a Claymore mine.'

'Order! Order!' Angbard leaned down and stared at Roland. 'Let's get this straight. Fort Lofstrom on this side has been barred to us. On the other side, its doppelgänger is under siege. There is a huge consignment sitting over there, and family members who lack the talent to extricate themselves. Is that broadly correct?'

'Yes.' Roland slumped against the table. 'I world-walked into the fort. Blood all over the walls of the post room. Sullivan got me a horse and, and I rode over to a place Miriam told me about. Used the spare locket she gave me, the one she took from the enemy.' The room was in uproar, half the Clan on their feet. 'Lady Brilliana got me on a train in the new world, from Boston to New London. That's how I got here so fast. The shit hit the fan yesterday. By now, we're either looking at a pile of rubble on the other side with our people trapped under it and the FBI digging toward them, or something worse.' He rubbed his head carefully, as if unsure whether it was still there. 'I had to make three crossings in the past twelve hours.'

'Security summit, clear the room!' called the sergeant-at-arms. 'By your leave, sir,' he told Julius apologetically.

'Can we get in from the far side? From New Britain?' asked Miriam.

Angbard stared at her. 'You know more about that than we would, I think,' he said. 'Your opinion?'

Miriam thought for a moment. 'You're sure it was Matthias?' she asked Roland.

Roland nodded wordlessly. 'Sir?' He looked up at Angbard, tiredly.

'Yes,' Angbard said darkly. 'I've been keeping an eye on him. I've had my suspicions for a while now.' He paused, looking as if he'd tasted something unpleasant. 'Obviously I haven't been watching him closely enough. That's not a mistake I'm going to repeat.' He looked at Miriam. 'Do you have anything to add?' he demanded.

'I don't know, but I don't believe in coincidences, and the way the hidden family kept going after me – ' she glanced at Baron Hjorth, who stared back at her for a moment, then looked away. 'I think it's clear who he was in the pay of.' She shrugged. 'It doesn't change my position. I think you should release Lin, send the kid home with a message offering a cease-fire. If they accept, it means your Keeper of the Secrets is cut off with no retreat and no friends. If they refuse, we're no worse off. It might make them think we're weak, but that can only be an advantage right now.'

'I'll think about it,' Angbard said coolly. 'But right now it's not a priority. What would you suggest doing about Boston? If you have any ideas, that is.'

'Um.' She paused. 'Two or three crossings a day: If we do more we'll be in no condition for anything, and this needs to be fixed quick. I think we'll have to cross over to New London, won't we? If Olga and I and a bunch of others go, it'll take us a bit longer to get to Boston by steam train, but from there it's one hop into Fort Lofstrom by the back door. Faster than going by stagecoach, anyway. We'll have to carry some extras, who'll need to go over into the basement under siege and pull in our people before the FBI and DEA dig through to them. Would that work?'

'I think it's our only chance.' Roland looked worried. He was certainly avoiding eye contact with her.

'Do it,' said Iris, unexpectedly. 'It's your future.' She met Miriam's gaze. 'I'll be all right.'

'I know *you* will.' Miriam walked toward her. 'Please be here when I get back,' she said. 'We've got a lot of talking to do.'

Brill cleared her throat. 'I'm coming,' she said calmly.

'You can't – oh.' Miriam turned back to Angbard. 'She can come.'

'She'll have to. How many copies of the lost family's sign have you got?'

'More than you thought, bro,' Iris butted in. She reached into a pocket and pulled out a battered-looking locket. 'I took this off the one who killed my husband and maid and tried to cut your throat,' she told Miriam. She grinned, humorlessly. 'It never occurred to me to look inside it until you tipped me off. Not that I'm in any condition to use it.'

'Ah. Then we've got – ' Miriam did a quick stock-take. Hers, Brill's, Olga's, the one she'd given Roland, now this one. Plus the smudged and fading temporary tattoos she and Olga wore. 'Only five reliable ones. Any more?'

Iris snorted. 'Here.' She pulled out a bunch of glossy photographs. 'What the hell did you think Polaroid cameras were invented for?' Miriam gaped. 'Close your mouth, kid, you'll catch a fly.'

'Get some muscle,' Miriam told Roland. 'Ones who can world-walk with us. We'll need guns and medicine. And clothing that can pass at a distance in New London or on the train – ' She paused. 'And a plan of the Fort Lofstrom doppelgänger, and a compass and map of the area. We can pick one up in New London and find where its doppelgänger location is, and then someone to get us in – ' Another pause. 'Why are you all looking at me like that?' she asked.

*

Another day, another first-class compartment – this one crammed with seven bodies, plus another seven in the compartment behind them – with the window open to let the heat out. 'How conspicuous are we going to be?' asked the guy with the toothbrush moustache.

'Just as long as you don't stop, Morgan,' said Miriam. 'Your suit's all wrong, your coat isn't a fashion item, and – hell, your hat isn't right either. They'll probably take you for a foreigner.' The train clattered over points as it began to slow. 'Which would be very bad.'

'She's not kidding,' said Brill. 'It's not like our Boston at all, under the surface.'

'Be over soon,' said Roland, staring out the window at the passing countryside. 'It all looks like something out of a history book – '

'May you live in interesting times,' muttered Olga, raising a startled glance from Brill.

'Miriam's been corrupting you.'

'You say that like it's a bad thing.'

'Ladies, ladies!' They turned and glared as one at Roland. 'Is this our stop?' he asked plaintively. He looked decidedly off-color. Miriam decided to forgive him – her own headache wasn't getting any better, and four trips in thirty-six hours was more than anyone should ever have to make, even with beta-blockers and pain killers.

'Not yet.' Miriam refolded the map she'd bought at the station near where Niejwein would be in this world.

'Let me see that.' Ivor, short and squat, leaned over. 'Ah.' A stubby finger followed the line into town. 'This is Cambridgeport, in Cambridge. The fort was built on a bluff overlooking the river almost exactly here. That's – '

'Blackshaft. A rookery,' said Miriam. 'Next to Holmes Alley.' She bit her knuckle. 'What happens if you try to world-walk somewhere where you'd come out underground?'

'It doesn't work and you get a headache.' Roland looked at her curiously. 'Why?'

'Nothing,' she said, watching him sidelong.

Brill caught her eye. 'Nothing.' She snorted. 'It's that revolutionary friend of yours, isn't it?'

'Well.' Miriam sighed. 'I suppose so.'

'What's this?' asked Ivor.

'Miriam's got dodgy friends,' said Olga. 'Why is it that we only seem to do business with criminals?'

'I don't think he's a criminal; the law disagrees with me, but the law is an ass,' said Miriam. 'Anyway, he's got access to cellars. Lots of cellars and backyards running into the rookery. I think we can go down there, then try to cross over. If we can't, we can't. If we succeed we'll be somewhere in the basement levels. How'd that work out?'

'Angbard gave me some of his keys.' Roland patted his pocket. 'We can give it a try. The only thing worrying me is the time it's taking.'

Liar, thought Miriam, watching him in side-profile. *You and me, when this is over, we're going to need to clear the air between us.* She focused on the line of his jaw and for some reason her heart tried to skip a beat. *See if we can catch some quality time together with nobody trying to kill me or blackmail you.* For a moment she felt a deep stab of longing. *We've got a lot to talk about, haven't we?* But not right now, in the middle of a compartment full of Clan couriers, serious-faced and wound up for action.

The train slowed, slid into a suburban station, and paused. Then it was off again, for its final destination – the royal station, five minutes down the line. 'Go tell the others, we want the next stop,' said Miriam. 'Remember, follow my lead and try not to say anything. It's not far, but we look like a mob, and a weird one at that. If we hang around we'll pick up unwanted attention.'

Olga raised an eyebrow. 'If you say so.'

'I do.' The train hissed and shuddered as it lurched toward the platform. 'Hats on and spirits up. This shouldn't take long.'

The walk to the pawnbroker's shop seemed to take forever, a frightening eternity of hanging on Roland's arm – steering discreetly and trying to look carefree, while keeping an eye open for the others – but Miriam made it, somehow.

'This is it?' he asked dubiously.

'Yeah. Remember he's a friend.' Miriam opened the shop door, shoved him gently between the shoulder blades, turned to catch Morgan and Brill's eyes, then went inside.

'Hello? Can I help – '

'I'm sure you can.' Miriam smiled sweetly at the man behind the counter – a stranger she'd never seen before in her life. 'Is Inspector Smith here?'

'No.' He straightened up. 'But I can get him if you want.'

'That won't be necessary.' Miriam drew her pistol. 'Lie down. Hands behind your back.' She stepped forward. 'Come on, tie him!' she snapped at Roland.

'If you say so.' The doorbell jangled and he glanced up at her as Olga and the two other guards entered the shop, followed rapidly by

Brill and Ivor, and then the rest of the group. With fourteen youngish Clan members inside, it was uncomfortably packed. 'What are you going to do with him?' asked Olga.

'Take him with us, stash him in Fort Lofstrom. Got a better idea?'

'You're making a big mistake,' the man on the floor said quietly.

'You're a constable,' said Miriam. 'Aren't you? Where's Burgeson?' He didn't say anything. 'Right,' she said grimly, lifting the counter and walking behind it. *I hope he's all right,* she thought distantly. *Another spell in His Majesty's concentration camps will kill him, for sure.* 'You two, carry this guy along. The rest of you, follow me.'

They trooped down the steep wooden steps in the back of the shop, along an alley hemmed in with pigeonholes filled with sad relics, individually tagged and dated with their owners' hopes and fears. Miriam looked round. 'This will do,' she said. 'I'm going to try the crossing. If I succeed and there's trouble, I'll come right back. If I'm not back in five minutes, the rest of you come over. Roland, carry Brill. You, carry Olga. Brill, Olga, you carry us over to the far side, to world two: I don't want anybody making two successive crossings without a rest between. Be ready for trouble.'

She took her coat off. Beneath it she wore her hiking gear and a bulky bulletproof vest from the Clan's Niejwein armory. It looked out of place here, but might be a lifesaver on the other side. She barely noticed the captive policeman's eyes go wide as he watched the cellar full of strangers strip down to combat fatigues and body armor.

'Are you sure about this?' asked Roland as she picked up her shoulder bag again.

'I'm sure.' Miriam grimaced. 'Time to go.'

'You'll never get away with this,' the secret policeman mumbled as she pulled out her locket and, taking a deep breath, focused on it.

Everything went black and a spike of pain seemed to split her skull. *Buried alive!* she thought, appalled – then reached out a hand in front of her. *No, just in the dark.* She took another breath, smelling mildew, and swallowed back bile that threatened to climb her throat. Her heart pounded. *The flashlight* –

She fumbled for a moment over the compact LED flashlight, then managed to get enough light to see by. She was in a cellar all right, a dusty and ancient wine store with bottle racks to either side. 'Phew,' she said aloud. She took a second or two to let her racing heart slow down toward normal, then marched toward the door at the end of the tunnel.

The light switches worked, and the cellar flooded with illumination – bright after a minute of flashlight. 'Do I wait?' she asked herself. 'Like hell. We've got people to rescue.' She turned the handle and cautiously entered the passage that led to the servants' stairs.

Her head ached furiously. It had been aching for days now, it seemed, and she felt worse than sick. If she stood up fast, or moved suddenly, her vision went dark. *I can't do this again,* she thought to herself, leaning against the corridor wall. *It'll kill me.*

Two hops in a day – one from Niejwein to New London, then another into Fort Lofstrom's dingy cellars. If she made a return trip to Boston now, she was sure she'd pop an artery. *Cerebral hemorrhage, what a way to go.* Half of the others were piggybacking, staying fresh as long as possible.

For her sins she'd carried Brill through on the first trip. Now she was paying the price in aching muscles and a borderline migraine.

'Matthias,' she said aloud, with a flash of rage. *Bastard thought he could use me, did he?* Well, she'd see about that. Once the crisis was under control, and once she'd repossessed Paulie's stolen CD-ROM. She was certain Matthias had it, and there were only two things to do with it that made sense. Send it to the FBI, or leave it on Angbard's desk, along with the photos of her and Roland – a potentially lethal embarrassment if Angbard interpreted it as a plot by the lovers to elope and blackmail the Clan into silence. Miriam's money was on the latter. Once the immediate business was sorted, she fully intended to give Paulie a discreet request and a bunch of cash: enough to hire some private detectives. There were ways and means of finding people who didn't want to be found, when your resources and patience were unlimited, and she was willing to bet that a spider like Matthias wouldn't be able to camouflage himself as well as he thought once he left the center of his web. She'd spend whatever it took to find him.

After a couple of minutes she sighed, then pushed herself upright. She dry-swallowed a painkiller, which stuck uncomfortably in her throat. She was light-headed, but not too light-headed to find her way up to the basement level. Passing the scullery, she ducked inside to grab a glass of water to help the pill go down. Something caught her eye: The door to the cold store lay ajar. She looked inside.

'Oh shit. Oh shit.' She breathed fast as she leaned over the top of the pile – three, maybe four corpses sprawling and stiff, not yet livid – and saw the cruel edges of bullet wounds. 'Shit.' She pushed herself upright and looked to the entrance. 'Cameras – '

Matthias has a little helper, she realized. *How many people did he kill?* A great house like this, you couldn't send all of the servants away – but murdering the skeleton staff bespoke a degree of extreme ruthlessness. Angbard hadn't been suspicious enough of his own deputy: He'd let Matthias pick and choose staff assignments. Now it looked like she was going to be stuck paying the price.

'Matthias always has a backup plan,' she muttered to herself. 'If I was a sick spider sitting at the center of a web, waiting to sting my employer, what would I do?'

She opened the door cautiously. 'Roland was afraid of bombs – ' She stopped. *Where?* 'The armory is where you store explosives. It's built to contain a blast. But if Matthias had an *accomplice* the explosive might be human – '

She panted, taking in shallow breaths. *Stop that. Matthias blackmailed people. How many? And what could he make them do – wait for the Clan rescue expedition to show up, then bring the house down on them?*

The pantry was empty, a door standing ajar on the kitchen and servants' stairwell at the end of the hall. Miriam hit the stairwell. It corkscrewed upstairs dizzyingly, halls branching off it toward each wing of the family accommodation. She climbed it carefully, revolver in hand, cautiously scanning the steps ahead for signs of a tripwire. Hoping that the dead servants meant that there'd be no eyes left to watch the video screens. *Second floor, east wing, through the security doors on the left,* she repeated to herself, hoping that the surveillance, if it existed at all, would prove to be habit-blind.

The east wing corridor was as silent as a crypt, as empty as the passages of a high-class hotel in the small hours of the morning while the guests sleep. Any guests here were liable to be dead in their beds. Miriam came out of the servants' stairwell and darted down the side of the corridor, crouching instinctively. She paused at the solid wooden doors at one side of the passage and swiped the card-key she'd borrowed from Roland through the scanner at one side. When she heard the latch click, she pushed one door open with a toe and stepped through. *This is the security zone?* It looked like more rooms, opening off a short corridor – offices, maybe, and Angbard's outer office door right ahead.

She paused before the door. Her heart was pounding. She looked at it. Someone was behind it. Whoever killed the servants. A ticking human bomb. Growing anger made her feel dizzy. She carefully moved to one side and raised her gun.

'I really wouldn't do that,' said a sad voice right behind her left ear. 'Put the gun down and turn around *slowly*.'

She froze, then dropped the pistol and turned around. 'Why?' she asked.

A nondescript man leaned against the wall behind her. He was unshaven, and although he was wearing a suit – standard for a courier – his tie was loose. He looked tired, but also pleased with himself. 'It's about time,' he said.

His gun, Miriam realized. It was pointed at her stomach. She couldn't identify it. Bizarrely complex, it sprouted handles and magazines and telescopic sights seemingly at random. It looked like a movie prop, but something in his manner said he had complete confidence in it. The sights glowed red, a dot tracking across her chest.

'It's about time,' she echoed. 'What the hell is that supposed to mean?'

The gunman grinned humorlessly. 'The boss told me a lot about you. You're the new countess, aren't you? He's got tapes, you know. *And* a disk.'

She moved toward him, froze as the gun came up to point at her head. 'You were responsible for what's in the cellar – '

'No, actually.' He shook his head. 'Not me. He's . . . Matthias likes to hunt. He stalks wild animals. Stalks his enemies, too, looking for a weak point to bring them down.' He grinned. 'He showed me the tapes he took of you, looking for a weak spot.'

Her vision hazed over for a moment, turning black with a mixture of rage and the worst headache she'd ever experienced. 'What do you fucking *want*?' she demanded.

'Simple. I'm the rear guard. Your arrival means the Clan rescue party is on its way, doesn't it?' She said nothing, but his grin widened just the same. 'Knew it. You're my ride out of here, y'know? Little pony, we'll just be leaving by the back steps, then blow the house down. And I'll ride out on you. There's a meeting spot, ready and surveyed and waiting for me. *Nice* pony.'

'Listen,' she said, trying to focus through her blinding headache, 'have you actually *done* anything for Matthias? Killed anyone? Planted any bombs?'

The gunman stopped smiling. 'Shut the fuck up. *Now*,' he snarled. *'Kneel! Move!'*

Miriam knelt slowly. Everything seemed to be happening in slow motion. Her head pounded and her stomach, even though it was empty, seemed about to make a bid for freedom through her mouth. 'Whatever he paid you – ' she began.

''S'not money. Fucking Clan bitch. It's who we *are*. Got it, yet?'

'You and Matthias?'

'That's right.' He kicked the gun away. 'Keep your hands on the floor. Lean forward. *Slowly* put your wrists together in front. I'll kill you if you fuck up.' He carefully kept the gun on her as he pulled a looped cable tie out of a back pocket. '*Nice* pony, we're going to go riding together. Over to Boston, and then maybe out west to the ranch to see some of my friends. You won't like it there, though.'

'Shoot me and you won't get away alive,' she heard someone say in the distance, through a throbbing cloud bank of darkness.

'What the fuck.' He yanked the cable tie tight around her wrists. 'You think I give a shit about that, you bitch? Live fast, die young.' He grabbed her hair and pulled, and she screamed. 'Leave a pretty corpse.'

Miriam tried to stand: Her legs had turned to jelly somewhere along the line. *This is crazy,* she thought vaguely. *I can't let him blow up the fort with everyone under it, or on the other side –* She leaned drunkenly, almost falling over.

'Stand, bitch!' Someone was slapping someone else's face. Suddenly there was a hand under her armpit. 'Fuck, what's wrong with you?'

'Three jumps, two hours,' she slurred drunkenly.

'Crap.' A door opened and he shoved her forwards. 'Fucking get over it or I'll start on your fingernails. You think your head hurts, you don't know shit.'

'What do you *want*?' she mumbled.

'Freedom.' He pushed her toward the low leather-topped sofa opposite Matthias's desk. 'Freedom to travel. Freedom to live away from this fucking pesthole. A million bucks and the wind in my hair. The boss looks after his own. Drop the fort and deliver you and I've got it made. Loads of money.'

He pushed her down onto the sofa. 'Now you and me are going to sit tight until your friends are over on the other side.' He waved at the CCTV monitor on Matthias's workstation. 'Then I set a timer and we leave by the back door.' He cleared his throat. 'Meantime, there's something I've been wondering. Do you give good head?' he inquired, leaning over her.

Something flickered at the edge of Miriam's vision. She focused past his shoulder, saw the door open and Roland standing there with a leveled pistol. The gunman turned, and something made a noise like a sewing machine, awfully loudly. Hot metal rain, cartridge cases falling. A scream. Miriam kicked out, catching him on one leg. Then the back of his head vanished in a red mist, and he collapsed on top of her.

'Oh Miriam, you really are no good at this!' trilled Olga, 'but thank you for drawing his attention! That creep, he makes me *so* angry . . .' Then her voice changed: 'Dear Lightning Child! What's happened to Roland?'

'I – ' Miriam tried to sit up, but something was pinning her down. Everything was gray. 'Where is he?'

'Oh dear.' Olga knelt in the doorway, beside something. Someone. 'Are you wounded?' she asked urgently, standing up and coming toward Miriam. 'It was his idea to follow you – '

Miriam finally sat up, shoving the deadweight aside. Strangely, her stomach wasn't rebelling. 'Get. Others. Go across and finish off. I'll look after him.' Somehow she found herself on the other side of the room, cradling Roland. 'He'll be all right.'

'But he's – '

She blinked, and forced herself to focus as Olga leaned over her, face white. 'He'll be all right in a minute,' Miriam heard herself explain. 'Scalp wounds are always bloody, aren't they?' Somewhere a door opened and she heard Olga explaining something to someone in urgent tones, something about shock. 'Aren't they?' she asked, still confused but frightened by Olga's tone. She tried to rub her sore eyes, rendered clumsy by her tied hands, but they were covered in blood. Then Brill rolled up her sleeve and slid a needle into her arm.

'What a mess,' Brill told someone else, before the blessed darkness stifled her screams.

EPILOGUE

'Fourteen of them, you say?' said Inspector Smith, raising an eyebrow.

'Yessir. Nine coves and five queans all went into the shop mob-handed, like.'

'Fourteen.' The other eyebrow rose to join it. 'Jobson never reported back.'

'There's no sign of blood, sir, or even a struggle,' the inspector's visitor said apologetically. 'And they wasn't in the premises when me and my squad went in, ten minutes later. Weren't in the basement, neither. Nor any of the tunnels we've explored.'

'*Fourteen,*' Smith said with a tone of increasing disbelief.

'Sir, we took fingerprints.' The visitor sounded annoyed. 'None of them except the Fletcher woman are in our files, and her prints were old. But we had a spook watching as they went in. The count is reliable: fourteen in and none of them came out again! It's a very rum do, I'll agree, but unless you have reason to suspect that a crime has been committed – '

'I have, dammit! Where's Jobson?' Smith stood up, visibly annoyed. 'Are you telling me that one of my agents has disappeared and the people responsible aren't to be found? Because if so, that sounds like a pretty bad sign to me, too.'

'I'll stand by it, sir.' The regular thief-taker stood firm. 'We took the entire block apart, brick by brick. *You* had the pawnbroker in custody at the time, need I remind you? And his lawyer muttering about habeas corpus all the while. There is, I repeat, no evidence of anything – except fourteen disappearing persons unknown, and a constable of the Defense Bureau who's nowhere to be seen. Which is not entirely unprecedented, I hope you'll concede.'

'Bah!' The inspector snorted. 'Did you take the cellar walls apart?'

His eye gleamed, as if he expected to hear word of an anarchist cell crouched beneath every block.

'We used Mr. Moore's new sound-echo apparatus.' The thief-taker stood up. 'There are no hollow chambers, sir. You can have my hat and my badge if you uncover any, as I stand by my word.'

'Bah. *Get out.*' Smith glared at the superintendent of thief-takers. 'I have a call to make.' He waited for the door to bang shut behind the other man before he added, 'Sir Roderick is going to be very annoyed. But I'll make sure that damned woman gets her comeuppance soon enough . . .'

*

Weeks passed: days of pain, days of loss, days of mourning. Finally, an evening clear of snow beneath the winter skies over New London found Miriam standing in the foyer of the Brighton Hotel, dressed to the nines in black, smiling at the guests with a sweet solicitude she hardly felt. '*Hello*, Lord Macy! And *hello* to you too, Lady Macy! How have you been? Well, I trust?' The line seemed to stretch around the block, although the red carpet stopped at the curb – many of the visitors were making a point of showing up in new Otto cars, the ones the Durant Motor Company was fitting with the new safety brakes.

'Hello, my dear lady! You're looking fine.'

Her smile relaxed a bit, losing its grim determination. 'I think I am, indeed,' she admitted. 'And yourself? Is this to your satisfaction?'

'I think – ' Sir Durant raised one eyebrow – 'it will do, yes.' He grinned, faintly amused. 'It's your party: Best enjoy it as much as you can. Or are you going to stand by your widowhood forever and a day?'

He tipped his hat to her and ambled inside, to the dining room that Miriam's money had taken over for a night of glittering celebration, and she managed to keep on smiling, holding the line against desolation and guilt. The party was indeed glittering, packed with the high and the mighty of the New London motor trade, and their wives and sons and daughters, and half the board of trade to boot.

Miriam sighed quietly as the carpet emptied and the doors stopped revolving for a moment. 'Busy, isn't it?' Brill remarked cheerfully behind her.

'I'll say.' Miriam turned to face her. 'You're looking beautiful tonight,' she mimicked, and pulled a face. 'Anyone would think I was selling them pinup calendars, not brake shoes.'

Brill grinned at her cheekily. 'Oh, I don't know,' she began. 'If you put out a calendar with yourself on it, that might improve sales – ' She held out a full glass of something sparkling.

'Here, give me that. It's not suitable for young ladies!' Miriam took it and raised it. 'To . . . something or other.' Her daringly bare shoulders slumped tiredly. 'Success.'

Brill raised the other glass: 'Success. Hey, this isn't bad.' She took a big mouthful, then wiped her lips with the back of one glove. 'Do you think they're enjoying it?'

'They will.' Miriam looked at the dining room doors, then back at the front: It was almost time for the meal to begin. 'Or else,' she added bitterly.

'You haven't seen Lady Olga yet?' asked Brill.

'No – ' Miriam caught her eye. 'Why?'

'Oh, nothing. It was meant to be her surprise, that's all. I shan't give it away.' Brill did her best impression of an innocent at large, nose in the air and glass in hand. 'Success,' she muttered. '*Most* women would be after true love or a rich husband, but this one wants to own skyscrapers.'

'True love and a helmet will stop bullets,' Miriam said bitterly.

'You weren't to know.' Brill looked at her askance. 'Was it *really* true love?'

'How the fuck should I know?' Miriam drained her glass in one gulp, so that she wouldn't have to explain. *Was it?* she wondered, confused, still numb. *Damn it, he should be here, now. We had so much to talk about.*

'Owning skyscrapers makes the need for a rich husband irrelevant,' Brill pointed out. 'And anyway, you're still young. True love is bound to – ' She stopped. Another car was pulling up outside, and a small crowd of partygoers was climbing out.

'Here, take this,' Miriam said, passing her an empty glass. 'Got to be the hostess again.'

'That's all right, don't mind me.' Brill took a step back as Miriam straightened her back and tried to bend her face into a welcoming mask once more. *Only another five minutes.*

The door opened. 'Olga!' she exclaimed.

'My dear!' Olga swept forward and insisted on planting a kiss on her cheek. 'I brought you a present!'

'Huh?' Miriam looked past her. The door was still revolving – slowly, for the occupant seemed to be having some trouble. Finally he shuffled out and slowly advanced. 'Uncle, you aren't supposed to be out – '

'Miriam.' He stopped in front of her, looking faintly amused. His costume was, as ever, impeccable, even though he must have found it passing strange. 'I thought I should come and see the new business that the prodigal has built for us.' His smile slipped. 'And to apologize for nursing that viper. I understand he cost you more than money can ever repay.'

'Oh hell.' She frowned at him. *Easy for you to be gracious, now Roland's dead and you don't have to worry about your precious braids anymore* – But somehow the harsh thoughts didn't have any fire behind them. She crossed the six feet between them. 'Uncle.' He did his best to return the hug, although he winced somewhat. She leaned her chin on his shoulder. 'I'm pleased to see you. I think.'

'It was all her idea,' he said, jerking his chin over his shoulder.

'Her? Why – mother!'

The revolving door ejected another late guest who seemed to be walking with a slight limp. Bundled in a voluminous gown and leaning heavily on a cane, she glowered truculently about the hall for a moment, then spotted Miriam and beamed.

'Hello, dear! You're looking every inch the princess tonight.'

'Hah.' Miriam walked forward and kissed her mother on the forehead. 'Wait till you meet my disreputable friends.'

'I wouldn't miss it for the world, dear. We've got a family tradition to uphold, haven't we?'

'Indeed.' A thought struck Miriam. 'Where are you staying tonight? I've got a suite here. Olga, if you don't mind – '

'I *do* mind,' said Olga. 'If you want me to give up the guest room, I demand the imperial suite here!'

'But you know that's booked – ' Miriam began, then the doors revolved again and her eyes widened. 'What are *you* doing here?'

'Is that any way to greet a friend?' Paulette grinned widely as she looked around. 'Hey, plush! I thought this was going to be all horse manure and steam engines!'

'This is Brill's fault,' Olga confided. 'When she heard about the party, she began plotting – '

'Yeah!' Paulie agreed enthusiastically. 'We couldn't let you keep the limelight all to yourself. Say, is that really a gaslight chandelier? Isn't that amazing?'

'Children, you'll be late for dinner!' Brill interrupted. 'Take it up some other time, huh? I don't want to miss Sir Brakepad's speech. Isn't he cute?'

She gently moved them in the direction of the dining room, steering Angbard discreetly. Miriam followed behind, arm in arm with her mother, and for the first time in months she dared to hope that the worst was behind her.

Charles Stross was born in Leeds, England, in 1964. He has worked as a pharmacist, software engineer and freelance journalist, but now writes full-time. To date, Stross has won two Hugo Awards and been nominated twelve times. He has also won the Locus Award for Best Novel, the Locus Award for Best Novella and has been short-listed for the Arthur C. Clarke and Nebula awards. In addition, his fiction has been translated into around a dozen languages.

Stross lives in Edinburgh, Scotland, with his wife Feòrag, a couple of cats, several thousand books, and an ever-changing herd of obsolescent computers.